MAXIM JAKUBOWSKI is a London-based novelist and editor. He was born in the UK and educated in France. Following a career in book publishing, he opened the world-famous Murder One bookshop in 1988 and has since combined running it with his writing and editing career. He has edited a series of 12 bestselling erotic anthologies and two books of erotic photography, as well as many acclaimed crime collections. His novels include *It's You That I Want To Kiss, Because She Thought She Loved Me* and *On Tenderness Express*, all three recently collected and reprinted in the USA as *Skin In Darkness*. Other books include *Life In The World Of Women, The State Of Montana, Kiss Me Sadly* and *Confessions Of A Romantic Pornographer*. In 2006 he will be publishing a major erotic novel which he directed and on which 15 of the top erotic writers in the world have collaborated on, *America Casanova* and his collected erotic short stories as *Fools For Lust*. He is a winner of the Anthony and the Karel Awards, a frequent TV and radio broadcaster, crime columnist for the *Guardian* newspaper and Literary Director of London's Crime Scene Festival.

The Mammoth Book of

INTERNATIONAL EROTICA

Edited by
Maxim Jakubowski

CARROLL & GRAF PUBLISHERS
New York

Carroll & Graf Publishers
An imprint of Avalon Publishing Group, Inc.
245 W. 17th Street
11th Floor
New York NY 10011–5300
www.carrollandgraf.com

AVALON
publishing group incorporated

First published in the UK by Robinson,
an imprint of Constable & Robinson Ltd 1996

This revised Carroll & Graf edition 2006

Collection copyright © Maxim Jakubowski 1996, 2006

ISBN–13: 978-0-78761-728-6
ISBN–10: 0-7867-1728-9

Printed and bound in the EU

CONTENTS

ACKNOWLEDGMENTS

MRS FOX by Michael Crawley, © 1996 by Michael Crawley. Reproduced by permission of the author and his agent Tal Literary Agency.

TRUCK STOP RAINBOWS by Iva Pekarkova, © 1993 by Iva Pekarkova. First appeared in YAZZYK. Reproduced by permission of Farrar, Straus & Giroux Inc.

ROSES by Evelyn Lau, © 1993 by Evelyn Lau. First appeared in FRESH GIRLS. Reproduced by permission of the author's agent Denise Bukowski and Hyperion Publishing.

WHITE NIGHT by Françoise Rey, © 1994 by Françoise Rey. First appeared in NUITS D'ENCRE. Reproduced by permission of Franck Spengler.

THREE FOR THE MONEY by Marilyn Jaye Lewis, © 2004 by Marilyn Jaye-Lewis. First appeared in THREE-WAY, edited by Alison Tyler. Reproduced by permission of the author.

FOURTH DATE, FIRST FUCK by Dion Farquhar, © 1996 by Dion Farquhar. Reproduced by permission of the author.

LUST by Elfriede Jelinek, © 1989 by Elfriede Jelinek. First appeared in LUST. Reproduced by permission of Serpent's Tail.

UNTITLED by Paul Mayersberg, © 1996 by Paul Mayersberg. Reproduced by permission of the author.

BEAUTY'S RELEASE by Anne Rice writing as A. N. Roquelaure, © 1985 by Anne Rice. First appeared in BEAUTY'S RELEASE. Reproduced by permission of Dutton Signet, a division of Penguin Books USA Inc. and Little, Brown, UK.

RUSSIAN DRESSING by Svetlana Boym, © 1993 by Svetlana Boym. First appeared as "Romances of the Era of Stagnation" in CHEGO KHOCHET ZHENSHCHINA. Reproduced by permission of the author.

THE OPERA by Sonia Rykiel, © 1998 by Sonia Rykiel. First appeared in PLAISIRS DE FEMMES. Reproduced by permission of Editions Blanche.

CUCKOO by Brian Fawcett, © 1994 by Brian Fawcett. First appeared in GENDER WARS. Reproduced by permission of the author.

LIES by Geraldine Zwang, © 2005 by Geraldine Zwang. First appeared in FEMMES AMOUREUSES. Reproduced by permission of Editions Blanche.

THE NAUGHTY YARD by Michael Hemmingson, © 1994 by Michael Hemmingson. Reproduced by permission of Permeable Press.

LILING'S CURE by Delilah De Silva, © 2005 by Delilah De Silva. First appeared in THE INTERNATIONAL JOURNAL OF EROTICA. Reproduced by permission of the author.

SWEATING PROFUSELY IN MÉRIDA: A MEMOIR by Carol Queen, © 1994 by Carol Queen. First appeared in a different form in LOCOMOTIVE. Reproduced by permission of the author and Down There Press.

ALMOST TRANSPARENT BLUE by Ryu Murakami, © 1976 by Ryu Murakami. Reproduced by permission of Kodansha International.

WHERE THE WILD ROSES GROW by Mark Timlin, © 1996 by Mark Timlin. Reproduced by permission of the author.

NICOLE by William T. Vollman, © 1991 by William T. Vollman. First appeared in WHORES FOR GLORIA. Reproduced by permission of the author.

THE NEW FIANCÉE by N. T. Morley, © 2004 by N. T. Morley. First appeared in THREE-WAY, edited by Alison Tyler. Reproduced by permission of the author.

THE PLEASURE CHATEAU by Jeremy Reed, © 1994 by Jeremy Reed. Reproduced by permission of Creation Books.

JOU PU TUAN by Li-Yü, first appeared in English in 1963, translated from the German version by Richard Martin. Translation by permission of Grove Press. Public domain.

WATCHING by J. P. Kansas, © 1996 by J. P. Kansas. Reproduced by permission of the author.

HER FIRST BRA by Cris Mazza, © 1996 by Cris Mazza. Reproduced by permission of the author.

EMILIA COMES IN MY DREAMS by Jindrich Styrsky, © 1933 by Jindrich Styrsky. First appeared in YAZZYK. Reproduced by permission of YAZZYK.

A MAP OF THE PAIN by Maxim Jakubowski, © 1996 by Maxim Jakubowski. First appeared in LIFE IN THE WORLD OF WOMEN. Reproduced by permission of the author.

GINCH by Michael Perkins, © 1977 by Michael Perkins. First appeared in PRUDE. Reproduced by permission of the author.

BLACK LILY by Thomas S. Roche, © 1996 by Thomas S. Roche. Reproduced by permission of the author.

LEONE by Régine Deforges, © 1988–1993 by Régine Deforges. First appeared in LOLA ET QUELQUES AUTRES. Reproduced by permission of Franck Spengler.

THE GIFT by Stella Duffy, © 1996 by Stella Duffy. Reproduced by permission of the author.

HOT NAZIS, DABBLING IN S&M, LOWER HAIGHT, TAHOE and HIGHWAY 1 by Bana Witt, © 1992 by Bana Witt. First appeared in MOBIUS STRIPPER. Reproduced by permission of Manic D Press.

A CASTLE IN MILTON KEYNES by Sonia Florens, © 1996 by Sonia Florens. First appeared in. Reproduced by permission of the Dolorès Rotenberg Literary Agency.

THE SEX LIVES OF CHAMELEONS by Cristiana Formetta, © 2005 by Cristiana Formetta. Reproduced by permission of the author.

MEMORIES THAT LINGER ON by Carlos Benito Camacho, © 2003 by Carlos Benito Camacho. First appeared in THE INTERNATIONAL JOURNAL OF EROTICA. Reproduced by permission of the author.

THE CASTLE OF COMMUNION by Bernard Noël, © 1990 by Bernard Noël. Reproduced by permission of Paul Buck.

LILLY'S LOULOU by Michéle Larue, © 2000 by Michèle Larue. First appeared in EROTIC TRAVEL TALES, edited by Mitzi Széreto. Reproduced by permission of the author.

ALL EYES ON HER by M. Christian, © 1996 by M. Christian. Reproduced by permission of the author.

KISMET by Michael Crawley, © 1996 by Michael Crawley. Reproduced by permission of the author and his agent Tal Literary Agency.

TAROT by Florence Dugas, © 1998 by Florence Dugas. First appeared in PLAISIRS DE FEMMES. Reprinted by permission of Editions Blanche.

CRASH by J. G. Ballard, © 1973 by J. G. Ballard. Reproduced by permission of the author, the author's agent Margaret Hanbury and Farrar, Straus & Giroux Inc.

PRENUPTIALS by Lucy Taylor, © 1996 by Lucy Taylor. Reproduced by permission of the author.

INTRODUCTION

Ever since the collapse of the Tower of Babel, sex has been the common language uniting men and women (as well as other fascinating combinations all reflected by the all-inclusive and indulgent field of erotic writing) throughout the world, so following the success of *The Mammoth Book of Erotica*, we put together an International version in 1996, of which this is now a reissue, with a couple of handfuls of the original stories consigned to the depths of the past and replaced by another ten previously uncollected tales to refresh the volume.

Initially, it was my intention to demonstrate how wide the spectrum of writing on sex, love and sensuality could be. And how the art of the erotic tale actually thrived in contemporary writing. Little did I know that over ten years later, the series would reach over 15 volumes which have since included Historical Erotica, Short Erotic Novels, five annual best of the year volumes, Gay, Lesbian and Erotic Poetry as well as two volumes I am very proud of, displaying the best of the world's erotic photography (an ironic state of affairs as I am known to have taken a somewhat limited number of photographs in my whole life, much preferring the art of voyeurism to the act of photography . . .).

So, mission accomplished and, today, the bookstore shelves are now crowded by a plethora of competing, thematic and otherwise anthologies from colleagues in the UK and America, and I would hazard a higher standard of sensuous, provocative writing than was the case when this series began.

Another fact that brings a satisfied smile to my face is the fact that since the initial volume of *The Mammoth Book of International Erotica*, two of the authors who willingly accepted to be part of the project have been rewarded most gratifyingly: Elfriede Jelinek of course has won the Nobel Prize for Literature and Stella Duffy made the shortlist for the Orange Prize for fiction. A random demonstration that not all occasional erotic scribes are just hacks . . .

And there has been resounding acclaim for a whole slew of novels and books from foreign shores singing the flesh and the erotic: viz the commercial success of books in translation by Alina Reyes, Almudena Grandes, Régine Deforges, Vanessa Duriès, Cathy Millet, Marthe Blau, Tobsha Learner, Florence Dugas, Melissa P. and countless others.

So, erotic prose is not just an Anglo-Saxon phenomenon but a universal one and this revised edition of this influential volume still only skims the surface of what is being written in France and Italy for instance, both countries so fertile right now that they could provide their own bumper Mammoth volumes of erotica and still neglect dozens of worthy writers such is the depth of talent currently active there. And I deplore my own lack of fluency in other languages like Spanish and German where, browsing through publishers' catalogues reveals possible treasures . . .

But I am confident there is enough here to satisfy your curiosity and tease your senses most delightfully.

So I will end by repeating what I said in the introduction to the first edition: welcome again to a realm of bizarre and fascinating beauty as imaginations run galore in an empire of the senses that literally spans the globe. By ready for everything as anything literally goes, leave your clothes and your blinkers at the door, allow your emotions to control you, sit yourselves down and relax and follow the words of all these true artists of the flesh, the erotic writers who can blend emotion and sex into a dizzy, seductive maelstrom that will often have you catching your breath in sheer excitement.

Let the great worldwide carnival begin!

Maxim Jakubowski

MRS FOX

Michael Crawley

ELEVEN DAYS AFTER I broke up with Angie I ran into Jeff, sitting in a booth at Sombrero Jack's. He was with a woman, so I tried to make it "Hi and Bye", but he insisted I join them.

"Paul, this is Mrs Fox – Cynthia Fox. Cynthia – Paul. We worked at Blackstock's together, years ago."

I half-stood and reached across to squeeze limp fingers.

"Call me 'Cyn'." Did her fingertips drag on my palm for a fraction of a second? I wasn't sure.

I knew straight away why Jeff wanted me there long enough to get a good look at her. He'd always been joking-jealous of me. I was bigger, and had all my hair. Some of the women in the old office had hung around my desk during coffee breaks, playing at flirting. It hadn't meant anything, but they hadn't done the same at his desk. He'd resented that.

Now he was with this woman – an older woman who was quite lovely – and I was alone. He wanted to make the most of it. I could live with that.

He said, "Cynthia and I live together."

I said, "You're a lucky man," and meant it. Her age showed in the laugh-lines around her big dark eyes, but her black hair was crisp and short and her body looked lithe, with hard high breasts, half exposed by the shawl neckline of a sweater in clinging black jersey. She wasn't wearing a bra. She didn't need one.

Jeff ordered a round and poked the gold card he'd left on the table from side to side, to make sure I saw it. I resolved that when the time came for me to pay my shot I'd use cash. It'd spoil it for him if I used *my* gold card.

Jeff did the talking. It was impressive stuff – big deals with Chile and so on. He was selling prefabricated buildings or something. Maybe he *was* working hard. He had dark bags under bloodshot eyes. I half-listened and kept my eyes on "Cyn", which was what he wanted me to do.

When she excused herself to go the ladies' room I watched her hips slink away into crowded darkness.

"What do you think of her?" he asked.

"Very nice. A sexy lady." I couldn't comment on her personality because she'd hardly said a word.

"You don't know the half of it."

I was supposed to ask for details. I didn't. I'm no prude, but some things should be kept private.

Cyn seemed jittery when she came back. Her arm stretched halfway across the table to fiddle with the little glass ball that held the candle, to adjust the condiments, to take a napkin from the holder and shred it. She had nice hands – longish fingernails – very pointed – painted deep pink. Her fingers were slender. Tiny blue veins showed inside her wrists. Higher on her pale arms I noticed some bruising and broken skin, as if a bracelet had caught in something and yanked off, or like a rope-burn maybe.

It was none of my business.

Her collar seemed to gape more now, or perhaps it was just her leaning towards me. There was a purplish mark above her collarbone and another mark, the size of a thumb-print, on the slope of her right breast.

It was still none of my business.

It wasn't any of my business when Jeff's hand dropped out of sight and she winced, still looking straight into my eyes.

They stood to leave, with Jeff leering, "Bed time, Cynthia."

She took my hand in a proper shake, not that "fingertip" thing. Something pressed into my palm.

I gave them five minutes before I looked. It was a note, written on that tan paper they use for towels in washrooms, and a key. The note read, "I must see you. I need your help. Midnight."

There was an address and a lipstick kiss. The paper was damp. Tears, or moist palms?

They were supposed to live together, but maybe Jeff had lied about that, or perhaps he was flying to Peru to do another of his multi-million dollar deals.

I thought for a while, but it had been eleven days since Angie, and I've always been a sucker for a "damsel in distress", even when I'm not horny.

I knocked on her apartment door, but too lightly for anyone inside to hear unless they were listening for it. I still could have turned around, but I didn't.

I used the key.

The hallway was dark. I said, "Cynthia? Mrs Fox? Cyn?"

There was a line of light under a door at the end. Something swished and cracked. A soft voice yelped. I strode on the balls of my feet and cracked the door. The bedroom was lit by candles. Cyn was on the bed, on her face, spread-eagled and naked. Her wrists and ankles were tied to the four corners of a scrolled brass frame. Jeff was stripped to his waist, his belt doubled in his hand, raised high. It came down hard, across her bottom.

When I see abuse something cold takes over. I did things to his wrist and his face and then he was whimpering on the floor. I prodded his thigh with the toe of my shoe and told him, "You have five minutes to get your things and go."

It took him three, with me watching him. Cyn needed me but I wasn't going to turn my back on him.

As soon as the front door closed I bent to the cords around Cyn's ankle.

"Please? There's some salve in the bathroom?"

It seemed obscene to leave her tied like that, but she knew what she needed first better than I did.

"It's awkward for me," she said. "Would you mind very much if you did it for me?"

I was as gentle as I could be. Thank goodness I'd got there on time, for there were only four weals, one high across the backs of her slender thighs, one crossing her bottom at an angle, and two, close together and parallel, blooming into darkness across her cheeks where they were fullest. There were other welts, faded to just pink lines under the translucent pallor of her skin. I smoothed ointment over those as well, though it was too late for it to do much good.

"Could you rub it in?" she asked. "It'll sting, but it does more good if it's worked in."

So I smeared the stuff all over and massaged.

She said, "Harder, please. Harder than that. Don't be afraid to hurt me."

I felt muscles twitch and writhe under my hands. It should have been very sexy, rubbing the naked bottom of a beautiful woman, but my concern for her pain blocked any erotic response on my part.

I wiped my hands and untied her. She rolled over and sat up but she didn't grab the bedclothes to cover herself so I found a satin robe hanging behind the door and draped it over her.

"Don't leave me," she said. "He might come back." Her fingers found my hand and drew it between her breasts. "I need to have you around, for tonight."

"I'll sleep on your couch."

"If that's what you want."

It wasn't. Now she was untied and partly covered, my body was reacting to her body, but if I'd made a move on her I'd have been exploiting the situation, and how do you embrace a woman whose rear is so tender?

She woke me with coffee, naked under that satin robe. "Do you have to go somewhere?"

"My office, sorry."

"Could you do my bottom again before you go?"

She lay flat on her tummy and tucked the robe up to her waist. The marks had faded to a pattern of bruises. In the daylight I could see that her skin wasn't broken, thank goodness. The salve must have been cool and soothing on her burning flesh, because when she squirmed under my hands it wasn't from wincing, but from pleasure. She purred once, when my fingers accidentally trailed into the crease between her buttocks.

"You'll come back?" she asked.

"After work. About six."

"Not for lunch?"

"I can't. Sorry."

When I got back she had a place set for one and a t-bone with a baked potato and mushrooms waiting. There was red wine and

two full glasses. She was still naked under her robe, but dewy, as
if fresh from a bath. Eartha Kitt was on the stereo, husking
something about needing someone to bind her.

"Aren't you eating?" I asked.

"I ate earlier. I'll just watch you."

I ate and she looked at me. "You saved me, you know."

"It was nothing."

"You know what the Chinese say about when you save someone?"

"What?"

"You're responsible for them. You *own* them, but you have to
take care of them."

I said, "We aren't Chinese," but her words stirred me. The
idea of "owning" her appealed to something in my libido.

"You are my knight in shining armour," she said.

I shrugged.

"I *owe* you."

"No – not really."

"I owe you *this*, at least."

She came round and wriggled onto my lap. I just had time to
swallow before her head tilted up and the prickle of her nails on
the back of my neck urged my mouth down to hers.

It was a nice kiss, but not a "normal" one, if any kiss can be
normal. She held her face away from mine by half an inch and
slavered her wine-wet tongue across my lips, from corner to
corner. I went to bend lower, but she held my head in place. Her
tongue lapped backwards and forwards, as if my steak had left
grease on my lips and that was what she was after. With me still
held in position, her tongue centred and slithered between my
lips. It withdrew, and slithered in once more, making slow
sensuous love to my mouth.

As her tongue soft-raped my lips, she writhed on my lap,
pressing down hard. It was as if her mouth was under perfect
control but her bottom was passionate. I was concerned about her
soreness but my cock wasn't. It was enjoying every urgent squirm.

She turned away at last, and took a mouthful of wine. Her lips
covered mine. Wine flowed from her mouth to mine, sweet and
warm with her saliva.

"Give *me* some wine," she said. "Squirt it into my mouth."

Her mouth opened like a hungry chick, giving me no choice but to jet wine in a long stream, straight onto her tongue. The more wine she swallowed, the more frantically her bottom twisted on my lap.

"Aren't you sore?" I asked.

She jumped up. With her back to me, looking back over her shoulder, she shot a hip and pulled the skirts of her robe to one side. "See? Almost better? All it needs is . . ."

"Is?"

"A 'kiss-better'."

What could I do? I planted a peck on one cheek, but she flexed it at me, so I licked from the crease where her thigh met her bottom to the small of her back.

"Oh yes! Being a bit tender makes me so much more sensitive. More, please?"

I'd known a number of women, and no two are alike, but this was the strangest seduction I'd ever experienced. I'd licked a few women's bums before, but never before I'd even touched their breasts, or made love to them in a more conventional fashion. The weirdness of it – the out-of-order of it – made it incredibly exciting.

I nibbled at the base of her spine.

She bent forward, hands on knees. "That's nice. Touch me, please?"

Where? Wherever I liked, I guessed. After you've kissed a woman's bottom, what caress is forbidden?

I reached around her and pulled her sash loose. My left hand smoothed up over her ribcage, enjoying the ridged smoothness, to cup her pendant breast. My right hand did spider-fingers up the inside of her thigh, touched springy hairs, fumbled, and found moist heat. I rotated three fingers on her, pressing gently. My teeth nipped at the pad of muscle just above her bottom's cleft. My left hand spread into a fan and strummed across the tip of a springy nipple.

Cyn said, "I could get off on what you're doing, Paul. You won't be shocked, will you? When I blow, I blow very wet."

I wasn't sure which of my caresses was getting to her, so I continued with all three. My left hand flickered faster. Two fingers of my right folded up into slick softness while a third found the head of her clit, and rubbed over it. My tongue traced an inch lower, to her tailbone – her coccyx.

She said, "Harder."

She hadn't been specific, so I plucked at her nipple, pinching its tip, substituted my thumb for the fingers that were inside her pussy so that I could use them to manipulate her clit, and rubbed the flat of my tongue in tight circles.

In a totally calm voice, she said, "I'm going to blow now. Don't worry. I can do it again, and again, for a long time."

She juddered on my palm, and hot-flooded into it. She'd been right. She did "blow wet". She soaked me to the wrist. Her spending smelled like fresh-baked bread.

"Now like this." Her two hands took my one and slapped it up against the soft saturated lips of her sex. "Do it hard," she said. "I'll keep blowing."

It made splashy sounds. I bit into her left buttock, forgetting how sore it had to be, and kept slapping up at her until she groaned and toppled forwards onto her hands and knees.

She rolled onto her back, looked at me from under hooded lids, and said, "I blew three times. Now it's your turn."

"I can wait a while."

"No – I'm on the boil. Keep me boiling. I'm hot for you, Paul. Hot, hot, hot."

I stood and tossed my jacket aside.

"No time for that," she said. "Get it out and get it in me. Is it big? Is it a nice big one?"

How do you answer that? I didn't try. I didn't have to. She was up on her feet, the dishes pushed aside, and bent over the table, legs spread. That was something I knew how to respond to. Her squishy-wet pussy was poking back at me between her thighs. Its lips were spread, stuck by their own juice. I unzipped, pulled myself out, and entered her.

I didn't have to do much more. She went crazy from her hips down, rotating, bucking, flicking her bum from side to side, jerking back at me as if it was a battle. I just held on, pressing against her hard enough not to be twisted out.

I'm not usually quick, but I was then. My cock was like a water pistol with a blocked muzzle. Her gyrations pumped the trigger until the blockage had to burst, and then I gushed and gushed until my come was squirting back at me between her sex's lips and my shaft.

I took a step back, plopping out. "I'm sorry . . ."

"It's always quick the first time, isn't it? With someone new? Have some more wine. I'll be right back."

I made myself decent and sprawled in her recliner armchair. When she came back the tightly curled hairs of her pubes were glistening but the rest of her was dry. I assumed she'd used a douche or something.

She asked me, "How do you feel about oral sex?"

"I'm for it. Did you want me to . . . While I recover my strength?"

"No. Sit up."

She undressed me. All I had to do was lift up at the right times. It was sexy, being taken care of by a naked woman. My cock thickened along my thigh, but it didn't lift. It was too soon after a really spectacular orgasm.

She knelt, took me in a cool palm, and addressed the head of my cock. "We'll soon have you up again," she told it.

"Give it a few more minutes," I said.

Cyn glared at me. "When I say you'll have an erection," she spat, "you'll have an erection. I'll be gentle this time."

It sounded like a threat.

Cyn squatted, naked, between my bare feet. The light was behind her. Her delta was black shadow. I had a silhouette to look at – a long shallow curve under one thigh, an outline like the cleft blunt end of an egg, bulging down, and then the swoop of another long curve. The cleft wasn't regular. One side had a slightly out-turned lip. There was a spiked fuzziness on the other side of the egg-shape, as if water had matted her pubic hair.

I'd been *inside* that fleshy egg. My *cock* had split it, and beyond, deep beyond, past the hot mushiness into the throttling slick channel.

The thought brought a pulse.

Cyn lifted the base of the recliner, tilting me back and lifting my feet to the level of her breasts. She took hold of my right foot and her left breast. Her nipple dragged up over the sole of my foot, from the hardness of my heel to beneath where my toes curled over. It's sensitive in there, at the bases of your toes. I could feel the tantalizing spike there as well as with my fingertips. She folded my toes down with her palm, gripping her nipple with my toes, and writhed, prodding rigid flesh between my big toe and the next one.

"You're growing," she said. She was right. My cock was thickening and lifting.

Cyn plucked her nipple from my toes. Her head bent, mouth wide. She engulfed three toes, wet and hot. Her tongue squirmed over, and between, and under. She put her nipple back and flickered it from side to side, frotting its tip on my soaking toes.

My cock lifted higher.

"Keep perfectly still!" Cyn ordered.

She stood and bridged me, her arms straight and her hands on the chair's arms. My fingers wanted me to reach out to her dangling breasts but she'd said I had to keep still. I didn't want to spoil whatever she had planned.

My cock was straight up by then, not fully erect, but close.

Her arms bent, lowering her face towards my cock. Cyn's mouth stretched. She paused, my naked glans an inch from her gaping lips, pointed directly into her mouth.

She swooped. My cock passed between her lips, past her teeth, over her tongue, all without touching, and butted the back of her throat. With her mouth still open too wide to make contact, she made a deep gargling sound, *and pushed*.

Little bubbles from her throat burst against the glossy-tight skin of my glans. There was vibration, vibration so *intimate* that it seemed my cock's head had to be pressed against her larynx.

She nodded, once, twice, three times, and then withdrew slowly, closing her mouth on me as she dragged it off my stem. By the time my cock flipped out from between her lips it was hard enough to burst.

Cyn scrambled up the chair. Brief slithers of fevered skin electrified me as she climbed over me. Her knees bracketed my waist. She reached down between us, took my cock in one hand and her pussy in her other, and slammed her hips down.

I froze, letting her impale herself. She looked down at me, wild, almost hating. "Don't move! Don't you dare move! I'm going to have a big one. I can feel it building. Keep still!"

Her hips juddered. She glared into my eyes. Her lips twisted. Her face contorted. Her sex was slapping at me, mashing down. She wasn't focused on the feel of my cock inside her, just on rubbing her clit's head against my pubic bone. She wasn't making love to me. She was *using* me to masturbate with.

There was froth on her lips. Her eyes were insane. She reared up, made two tiny fists, and punched down. I flinched, but she didn't hit me. She pounded the chair's back to either side of my head.

"Drag me down harder. Pull down on my shoulders!"

I got a grip and pressed down through her entire body, to where we were united. She bore down with all of her might, trying to squirm her way through me, not riding my cock, just frictioning her squishy pubes and stiff clit, grinding and grinding.

Cyn screamed and toppled sideways, over the chair's arm, to plop to the floor, sprawling, limp, lifeless.

I hadn't come. It'd been an incredible experience. I'd never known a woman so totally *consumed* by her passion, but I hadn't come. She looked to be absolutely sated, but I hadn't come and my cock was nagging at me. I gave myself a stroke.

Cyn sat up. "Don't you *dare*! That's *mine*."

"I thought . . ."

"I *told* you I was multi-orgasmic. Be patient, damn you!"

She crawled around in front of the chair again, put both hands flat on the foot-piece, and pushed it down. I was lifted up. She leaned over my thighs, dragging the points of her nipples over their hairiness and took me into her mouth again. Her two hands lifted the edge, pulling me back, drawing me almost out of her mouth and then pushed down, driving me back into the steamy soft cavern. Up and down. In and out. I just lay there, letting her rock me towards . . .

My cock's head exploded inside her mouth. She sucked and sucked until I was dry.

"I didn't spill a single drop," she said.

"No – you didn't."

"I never will. If I do, you must punish me."

That was the first time she'd mentioned my punishing her. I didn't take much notice. It was just a figure of speech, wasn't it?

It was down before she let me rest. That was okay. It was Saturday morning. I could sleep in.

I woke at noon to the smell of bacon and eggs. After breakfast she suggested I might like to go get some wine and vodka because we'd drunk the last of her booze. When I got back she was made-up and wearing that jersey sweater and nothing else but a pair of metallic black stay-up hose.

I'd been contemplating maybe another session that evening, not at two in the afternoon, but my cock took one look at that tiny triangle of curls, black on white and framed by black jersey above and black nylon below, and made my decision for me. I took her in my arms for a long kiss with my hands checking out how well the weals on her bottom were healing.

They were doing well, but still tender. Whenever my fingertip grazed a ridge she shivered and gasped into my mouth. Her pubes bumped at me as well, which didn't discourage me.

"I wasn't nice to you, when you were on the recliner," she said. "I plan to make that up to you."

"You were fine – more than fine – fantastic," I said.

"No – I forgot your pleasure. I feel guilty. Let me do it right, please?"

It'd been a while since a woman had asked me to let her screw me, "please". I let her undress me and sit me back on the chair. She poured two half-tumblers of straight vodka over ice, set them on a side table, and climbed up astride me.

"I'm not ready," I apologised.

"You will be."

She did that shared-drink thing again, with vodka. That, and the heat that was radiating down from her pussy onto my cock, started to take effect. She chewed at my bottom lip for a while, tickle-touching my ribs and chest, brushing her fingertips across my nipples, and then she swooped down and bit one, quite hard.

"Ouch!"

She grinned at me. "Did that hurt?"

I rubbed my chest. "Some."

She tugged her sweater up into a roll above her breasts and said, "So – take your revenge."

I nipped.

"I bit you harder than that."

"Harder."

I clamped my teeth as hard as I could short of drawing blood. Cyn sucked air, arched at me, and clawed one hand down my chest.

I jerked back. *She'd* drawn blood. There were four parallel furrows with little curls of skin at the ends.

Cyn said, "Kiss better."

Her tongue-tip traced them, one at a time. When all four had been tingled she sat back and said, "And antiseptic." She poured icy vodka over my chest. It stung the scratches but then she put her tongue to work again, lapping and sucking it out of my wounds.

"More?"

I nodded.

"Watch closely. Don't be chicken."

I watched. She rested the heel of her hand on my sternum. Her fingers curled. Four nail-points prickled. I stared down as they made tiny dents.

"Say when."

The tension was unbearable, so I said, "When."

I reared from the searing, but it was *good*. Her nails had cut deeper this time, but that just left wider wounds to be tongue-lapped and vodka-stung. She was still licking at me when her hand groped to wrap around my shaft and she lowered herself onto it and I sunk right up into her sponginess.

Then she went berserk. By the time I came my face was soaked with the sweat she'd flicked with her flailing hair and my shoulders were sore from the gouges, but it was worth the pain. It was worth every delirious moment of it.

Then we had to have a shower together. I was sure I wasn't up to any more but she turned away from me and had me soap her long back and her round bottom and all the time she was reaching behind and slithering her soapy palm up and down on my cock, rubbing its head over her firm smooth slippery buttock, and I found that I *could* get another erection, and have another orgasm. I came thick and foamy, dribbling obscenely down the back of her glossy thigh.

When you come *on* a woman, instead of *in* her, it's like you mark her as your territory. It defiles her the way a brand defiles the haunch of a cow, making her more precious because she's *yours*.

We called out for fried chicken and she licked my fingers for me and then finger-painted her own breasts with chicken-grease, so it was early in the morning before we slept again.

Sunday was the same, from noon till four in the morning. I was glad to go to my office on Monday.

She phoned at three. "What time do I expect you, and what would you like for supper?"

"Six. Whatever. Should I bring something in?"

"Lamb chops. What are you going to do to me tonight, Paul?"

"Do to you?"

"In bed, on the chair, on the floor?"

"Make long passionate love to you, Cyn."

"Give me the details. I want to be thinking about it till you get here."

"I'll call you back."

When I'd thought, and I called her, all she said was, "Is that all? You can do better than that, darling. Leave it to me tonight then."

I came home and found her on the bed, naked except for one stocking. The other was wrapped around her wrists and tied to the bedrail.

She said, "You bastard! You've got me in your power now, haven't you. I'm helpless and you can do anything you like to me."

I can play games. I sat on the bed beside her and rested my palm on her pubes. Leering, I said, "Do anything I like to *this*," and gave her a squeeze.

Her thighs spread wide under my hand. "I bet you plan to oil your hand," she nodded sideways towards the bottle of baby oil that stood ready open, "and work it right up into me, no matter what I say."

I took off my jacket and rolled my shirt sleeve up. The oil was cool in my palm. I smoothed it over her pubes and her pussy's pulpy lips.

"I might scream," she said. "I might beg you to stop, but you'll be merciless, won't you."

"Merciless," I agreed. I folded three fingers together and worked them into her.

"I thought you were going to be cruel."

I straightened my hand into a blade and forced all four fingers and half of my palm between her lips.

"You were going to use your whole hand."

I added my thumb and wriggled, pushing as hard as I dared. Cyn set her feet flat on the bed and lifted her hips at me.

"Deeper. I can take it."

Women have babies, don't they? And don't necessarily split? I pushed harder, against slippery convoluted resistance. My hand sank in, deeper, to the heel of my palm. She was incredibly strong in there. Her vaginal muscles clamped. I struggled against the pressure. I pushed. Her constriction folded my hand into a fist. It was like my hand was in a hot wet rubber sack that was shrinking, slowly crushing my fingers.

"I have to take it out," I told her. "I'm getting a cramp."

"No! Revolve it first. Twist your fist in me."

I turned it left and then right and then started to withdraw, slowly, gingerly, unfolding my fingers as soon as I was able, and finally I was free.

"I'll be loose for about an hour," she said. "Better turn me over."

It took me a moment to understand, but then I did, and flipped her, and shucked my clothes. She was kneeling rump-up, ready. I oiled my cock and poured more oil over her sphincter. Two thumbs pressed her open. I got my cock's head in place and then pushed down on it with the ball of one thumb. It slowly sank into her, and disappeared.

"Am I tight, back there?" she asked.

"Damned tight. Wonderfully tight."

"Cocks like 'tight', don't they?"

"Yes."

"You know how I'd be tighter?"

"How?"

"If there were two of you, one buggering me while the other one screwed me."

I stopped in mid-thrust. "I'm not into that – sharing."

She twisted her hips, plucking herself off me. "How *dare* you! I'm a one-man woman. You should know that. I was just thinking of something special to make you happy. Now you've spoiled it."

I apologized, but it was no good. She didn't speak to me for the rest of the night. I felt bad, but at least I got some sleep.

We made up the next morning. I moved in on the weekend. On the Monday I found she'd thrown out my robe and bought me a new one. I understood. Women always do that when a man moves in. They think they can smell the previous woman on it.

"It was a horrible disgusting thing. I don't know how you could have worn it."

That wasn't necessary. Perhaps my anger at her rudeness showed, because she instantly begged my forgiveness and suggested I might feel better if I punished her.

In the brief interludes between sex, she sometimes talked about her past. She'd been raped by a friend of the family when she was thirteen. She'd been raped again when she was twenty and working as a model. A guy she'd lived with, Bill something, had brought three friends home once and gang-banged her.

If I'd kept track right, she'd been raped on a total of seven different occasions and abused in other ways by every man she'd ever known.

We watched tv once in a while. I counted five celebrities that she told me she'd either had affairs with or fought off, including two women.

I found out what she'd been getting at when she'd suggested she'd be tighter if there were two men. She liked it if there was a vibrator deep her rectum when I took her vaginally, and in her pussy when I buggered her. When I couldn't get it up, two vibrators were fine. It was best for her if I tied her up before going to work with the twin dildos, then "she couldn't stop me, no matter what I did to her".

Once she told me, "I wouldn't need this if you were as big as Jeff was."

Later she apologized again – and suggested I punish her again. That time I did. She complained that I didn't spank like I meant it and my hand was too soft. Mr Fox had done a lot of woodwork so his palms were hard. When *he* spanked a woman she knew she'd been spanked by a *real* man.

One night when I was seeing to her pleasure she made a pencil mark on a pad. When I asked why, she told me I'd given her eleven orgasms so far that night and she wanted to keep score. I really worked that night. By morning the score-pad read "twenty-seven". I remarked, hopefully, that it had to be some kind of record. "Not by a long way. Bill got me up to fifty, once."

We didn't go out much. When we did, she flirted with the waiter or someone at the next table and we ended up fighting.

I took her swimming in the pool in her building. That was fun until a couple of young guys came in. Somehow or another she lost the top of her bikini and that made her squeal loud enough to turn the lads' heads. I left her chatting to them, clutching her bra-top to her breasts.

When she finally came up she woke me to tell me I'd misunderstood her natural friendliness.

"I suppose you expect another spanking," I said.

"With your soft hands? Anyway, you aren't man enough, you hear me? You're a wimp, Paul, with a puny little cock. Those boys down in the pool, though, they were real men. You should have seen the size of the erections they got from looking at me."

I grabbed her and got her over my lap but even mad as I was I had to take care not to break her arms so she managed to wriggle off me. I pushed her down flat on the bed. The cords were there, tied to the four corners, ready for "play". I used them.

I slapped her bum four times, almost hard.

She said, "Wimp."

I grabbed my belt off the chair, lifted it high . . . and tossed it aside.

She twisted her face towards me as I pulled my underpants up. "What are you doing?"

"I'm going. This is where I came in."

TRUCK STOP RAINBOWS

Iva Pekarkova

Translated by David Powelstock

I LAY NEXT to the road – and only the sensations I desired had permission to approach me. But a hostile, disturbing sound invaded my pleasant and harmonious space, and began to come nearer along the highway feeder road. At first it sounded like the buzzing of a bumblebee somewhere in the distance, but then this bumblebee began growing and getting closer, until its buzz became the unmistakable sound of a motor.

The sound did not go whizzing by me – the car stopped, and I lazily prepared to open at least one eye: it was probably some kindhearted guy who wanted to give me a ride and would ask me envious questions about my vacation; I'd have to explain that I was sunbathing at the moment and wasn't interested.

I raised an eyelid.

Two cops stood next to the ditch. Each one had the sun in his hair and one flat shoe half imbedded in the clay; they looked at me with a suspicious expression that struck me as kind of cute. I smiled, at both of them.

(The main thing is not to resist. Don't be insolent, just pretend you're an adorable, ditzy, idiot, Fialinka . . .) One of them said, "What are you doing here? Where are you from? Were you headed somewhere for vacation? Alone? Let's have a look at your Citizen's Identification Booklet; yes, a routine check . . ."

He said it diffidently, abstractly – it really was kind of cute the way the practiced, subtly threatening tone that saturated the voice of every law officer was shrouded by his charming Brno accent . . . Let's have look – he said it as if there were syllables in L written at least a fourth part higher on the scale: *Let's have a look* . . . Oh, Brno.

(Be careful, Fialinka, blush; most important, don't be a wise-ass, for God's sake, don't be a wise ass.)

"Comrades" – but just slipped out – "I just *adore* the way you Brnians talk. Say something else for me. Let's have a a look at my ID . . . *Let's have a look* . . . It's so refreshing, comrades, I just can't get over that Brno accent, I just can't . . . Let's a have a l – "

They released me from the police station in the center of town about three hours later. It was recommended that I head straight home and not even think of hitchhiking on the highway – the comrades would be keeping an eye on me. I was told that my behavior was extremely suspicious and that the comrades in Prague would be checking up on my studies. So I shouldn't be surprised when they called . . . Do you understand, comrade *student*?

I took the tram (without buying a ticket, of course) that ran most directly out to the Southern Road. A tight-lipped, severe, not very pretty smile of determination was ripening on my lips. A sneer.

My mind was made up. I was on my way to look for that wheelchair for Patrik.

The sun had been at its zenith a long time already when my tram finally jolted up to the end of the line. I worked my way over to the prohibited highway through the honeycombed mire of dried and cracked puddles. I ran down from the overgrown embankment and took a look around. No cops in sight. And as soon as the promisingly Western silhouette of an Intertruck appeared on the horizon, I thrust out my chest and stuck out my arm. Not the usual supplicant gesture of humble, honorable hitchhikers everywhere, I stretched it out seductively and imperiously, like a girl who had the price of admission.

The rig began to slow down almost immediately, and the screech of brakes in that cloud of swirling dust on the shoulder added to my self-confidence. I didn't sprint the few meters to the cab as usual. I picked my pack up out of the ditch deliberately and approached with the slow step of a queen of the highway. I caught sight of a face reflected in the side mirror. The driver backed up right to my feet, jumped out, and ran around to open the door for me.

And since I'd noticed a little D next to the truck's license plate, I cleared my throat and said: *"Fahrst du nach Pressburg?"*

I didn't add *bitte* or anything like that – I chose the informal *du* over *Sie* without even being at all sure how old he was.

It made no difference anyway.

He smiled (pleased I spoke German), nodded, and, when I added a regal *danke* after he lifted my pack up into the cab, he observed cheerfully, *"Aber du sprichst Deutsch sehr gut!"*

And that was the beginning of the long period, maybe too long, when I decided to become what almost every cop already assumed I was.

I had decided to get Patrik that wheelchair.

After twenty kilometers of small talk I was pleasantly surprised at my long-untested German. I smoked Marlboros (somehow convinced that without a cigarette clasped between my delicately outstretched fingers – even though they were still smeared with dirt – the impression wouldn't be complete) and, with a few successfully composed complex sentences, brought the conversation around to the difficulty of life in a socialist state. Kurt (we'd long ago exchanged names) steered with the barest touch of his left hand and, with his face turned toward me, nodded attentively. He was taking the bait. I don't know if he was listening, probably not, but he still kept saying how much he admired my German: God knows how few of these highway girls knew anything more than *bunsen*, the German word for fuck. He doesn't look unsympathetic, and I could do worse for my first time, I thought to myself. I babbled on cheerfully – and contemplated what would probably happen. This was not like an adventure that comes to you. This was not the work of my old friend Serendipity. I still wasn't used to my role – and I knew that I was going to have to take matters into my own hands.

Kurt asked, "Are you hungry? Do you want to eat with me? *Willst du essen?*"

"Sure," I said. "*Warum nicht? Ich will fressen,*" I added, replacing the verb "to eat" with the verb "to feed" (like an animal).

Kurt burst out laughing and leaned over to clap me on the shoulder. His hand slipped down by my breast.

"*Aber du sprichst Deutsch sehr sehr gut. Wo hast du alles gelernt?*"

"Right here," I lied, and pointed over my shoulder to the well-appointed little Intertruck sleeper. "*Hier . . . hier habe ich alles gelernt.*"

Kurt was already sitting almost next to me on the seat and weighing my tits on his palm. "*Du bist so fantastisch! Ist das möglich?*"

Everything is *möglich*, I thought for a second, everything is possible, you horny, half-assed imperialist bastard. But right now you're going to have to wait, old boy, because first we're going to discuss the terms.

I rolled that word "terms" around on my tongue and suddenly felt myself endowed with a power and strength I'd never known before. I was a girl who had the price of admission.

At a rest area Kurt got out and went around to the food pantry he had on the side of his cab. He returned with bread, a hunk of cheese, and a big salami such as I'd never seen in my life: like Hungarian salamis, only more tender . . . and the smell, God, how good it smelled! My stomach started rumbling.

Then Kurt showed me how to lift my seat and haul out from under it a huge storage chest of drinks in cans; I almost went blind gazing at all the different brands and types of juices, colas, beers, and soft drinks. I reached for one completely at random and opened it, careful not to aim it at myself. When it popped and a couple of drops sprinkled on the floor, Kurt gave me a congratulatory smile, almost like the one you give a good doggy when he offers you his paw. Oh God, how gifted I am! I can even open a soda can!

"I'd like to take you somewhere for lunch," he said apologetically, "but I don't know of any decent restaurant around here. And besides . . . in Czechoslovakia, actually anywhere in your

Eastern Europe . . . well, I really don't like to eat at any of the places, I like to bring everything with me . . . Otherwise, I get sick, and I can't afford that, you see?"

He said it as if apologizing, but at the same time it didn't occur to him that he was speaking with someone who practically never saw anything but the local food . . . It never made me sick, I was used to it . . . It suddenly hit me that he saw Czechoslovakia as something like a pigsty – even though I, poor little piglet, was cute enough, he wasn't about to stick his snout into the slop that sustained me from day to day. It could make him sick.

The Southern Road, by the way, unlike the Northern Road, was definitely not lined with homey, warm and smoky, cozily bespattered taverns. On the Northern Road you could have a plate of gristly goulash for a fiver or soup for two crowns – and that's what we ate up there. The Southern Road, on the other hand, was lined with a bunch of so-called first-class restaurants, where trying to eat for less than fifty crowns was considered to be in bad taste, and the waiters, all spoiled by hard-currency tips, would give the cold shoulder from on high to any piddling Czech who happened to stray in there. In short, the places on the Southern Road were specially designed for the filthy-rich drivers of Western semis.

Kurt unwrapped the enticing yellowish-brown loaf of imperialist bread and a packet of margarine. He sliced the salami and cheese on a paper tablecloth stretched out across the space between us – and meanwhile I spread margarine on some slices of bread. Perfect teamwork . . . I didn't hesitate for a second that day: I was hungry – And good manners? Ha! Why pretend, girl? After all, is this guy really worth being proper? Is anybody really worth all those contrived social lies?

I started stuffing myself with salami and cheese. I was dimly aware that this was the best salami and cheese I'd tasted in my life – and the bread with margarine was substantially better than if it had been smeared with socialist "Fresh Butter of the Highest Sort". I was pigging out without mercy, and Kurt, taking only an occasional bite, looked at me agreeably and hospitably, as if he were feeding his favorite dog. He injected, *"Gut?"*

I nodded with my mouth full and bit off another piece of bread. I suddenly found myself in the middle of a dream. Or – if I had any inclination toward acting – I would say I found myself in the middle of a theater piece. I'd plunged headlong into one of the leading roles, without a clue as to how the whole drama (or was it a comedy?) began or ended. I hadn't learned my lines, I wasn't thinking in advance about what to say the next second, and there was no time to recall what I'd said a minute ago. I was standing in the middle of an unfamiliar stage – and yet it was as if sometime long ago I'd played this role a hundred times before. I didn't know what I was supposed to say, what would happen or what the male lead would say to me. But a prompter (not the one who poked her head out occasionally from a booth below the stage, but one that was fixed somewhere in my head and was speaking to me directly), an unfamiliar prompter always assigned me just the right line or gesture at just the right moment to fit my part. I could see everything from the inside and the outside at the same time, evaluating my dramatic performances as I went and finding it satisfactory. As for the rest, the director and the audience were irrelevant. The main thing was that I was completely satisfied with my role, that I was comfortable in it; it seemed to me that it had been tailored especially for my body, that the author of the play had written it for me and nobody else but me, for this second Fialinka, for a worse and more cynical I. I knew that I would never have wanted this to be my everyday existence – but I had always known that such a person lived somewhere within me, and it was intoxicating to be able to act out my second I . . .

Who am I now and who had I really been before? I had *always* been playing a part, I, the notorious seeker of truth. I had lied. I had deceived with my body . . . Was I deceiving any more than I had before? I adapted to Kurt, my fellow player, I made myself the way he wanted me to be: supple, just the slightest bit unlike the others, not stupid, but not overly clever either, with a superficial, suggestive wit . . . a promising girl, who's easy to get to know.

I stuffed myself with bread and margarine, greedily sucked at my fingers, still stained with Brno clay (my entire back and the back of my pants were caked with clay, but that made no difference at all at the time) – and the precise, perfect prompter in my head kept telling me what to do next. The prompter determined what I was to say, how to act, what faces to make, how to move my hands, my body. She decided what I was to think about. *How* I was to think.

(You're a shitty actress, Fial, Patrik used to say to me. You don't know how to transform yourself, and if someone ticks you off, you insult him right to his face. If only you could just pretend a little for the pigs. Just the tiniest bit . . .)

And now I could feel within myself dozens, hundreds, maybe thousands of potentially possible lives, from which I'd chosen just one at some point long ago (and God only knows if it had even been I who'd chosen it). It was embarrassing: at some point I had developed into a compete personality, fully balanced according to all the psychiatric norms. But those ten thousand voices were arguing, fighting, and voicing their opinions inside my skull, and it was making my head spin. And those hundreds of complete, plausible, legitimate lives – each of which wanted to be lived – were locked in a battle for their rights. I was feeding on West German bread and perfect, moist salami, more delicately seasoned than any I'd ever tasted – and I allowed one of those other lives to grow and dominate. I gave it permission to be lived.

No, this was no longer just a prompter. A little sadly, I closed my eyes (from the outside it looked like a blissful fluttering of the eyelids from tasting the salami) and plunged headfirst into metamorphosis.

After a good lunch, one needs a rest, observed Kurt. He drew the curtains closed, and the atmosphere in the cab, heated by the summer sun, suddenly became erotically sultry. The curtains were red and turned my little German's cheeks pink. The remains of lunch had long been carefully cleared away. After rolling them up in the paper tablecloth, this great lover of order had chucked the whole mess out the window and instructed me to do the same with the juice and beer cans. (A guy who had until then been sitting idly nearby in his little Skoda MB had immediately shot out to scoop up this rare prize.) A few last crumbs that had slipped out of the paper were now itching me under my back as this person pulled me over next to him and started sounding the depths with his hot, impatient hands. Actually, he wasn't doing much sounding. He was quite sure of himself.

I let him fondle my breasts a little – just through my T-shirt – and then I pulled away and got right to the point: "*Ich brauche Geld.*"

(This time the prompter in my head seemed to have made a

small mistake – even though Kurt had probably heard those words a million times, my tone didn't quite fit the image of the average highway hooker. I said it too significantly with too much urgency: I was going to have to make a lot of money – as much as possible in hard currency – in order to get Patrik that wheelchair.)

Kurt was a little taken aback. Just the tiniest bit. Then he reached into the glove compartment. He opened it a crack, just enough to stick his hand in (I wasn't supposed to see everything he had in there, I realized), and groped around. He pulled out a large bottle of shampoo. *"Willst du das? Willst du?"* He turned the fine container around in his hands, like a shopkeeper displaying his merchandise. Look, little girl, how shiny! Now, how 'bout a feel of those titties? The shampoo really did glimmer beautifully; it was tempting stuff: even from where I was sitting I could smell its sweet apple scent. "You have such beautiful, wonderful hair, Via . . . This will be a little something just for you . . . Just a sort of small gift. Out of friendship. Would you like it?"

I shook my head – and I suddenly felt pretty awkward. I couldn't explain my desire to him at all, why I needed cash. There was no time to go through the whole story about Patrik. He wouldn't have listened – and if he had, he still wouldn't have believed it. Any long-distance trucker could tell you that every single Czechoslovakian girl had, as a rule, all kinds of relatives and at least two dozen best friends, all on their deathbeds with terminal diseases.

I didn't feel like going into that whole story. He simply wasn't worth it.

(Oh yes, if we had met under different circumstances, I would have run up to your truck . . . refused your cigarettes . . . I would have used the formal *Sie* with you, at least at the beginning . . . and we might even have talked for real. Actually communicated. But I had already decided that my words were not going to communicate anything; I would use them only to weave a web, in which I had to catch at least a few West German marks. Perhaps we could even have gotten along, Kurt, you don't look stupid. But you have been chosen, selected for this beginning, and you can't change a thing about it now. Neither of us can. It's impossible.)

"Ich Brauche Geld," I said. With shocking offhandedness

(shocking to me), I pulled a Marlboro out of his pack – and without making even the slightest move to light it for myself, I waited for him to lean toward me with the lighter flame.

"Do you understand?" I said through the cloud of smoke. "I don't need your damn shampoo. If you want it . . . if you really want it . . . then I need cash."

With no less shocking offhandedness, I undid the button of my jeans and the fly unzipped by itself. (The majority of zippers of Czechoslovakian manufacture immediately leaped at such opportunities to unzip themselves – Patrik always claimed that this was one of the methods by which Czechoslovakian manufacturing enterprises contributed to the campaign to encourage population growth.) I undid the jeans sort of casually. They peeled away from my hips a little.

"*Wieviel?*" he whispered. He was getting to the point.

(It occurred to me later that this must have been monotonous for him, to say the same words to various girls. *Veefeel?* – this much some of them must have understood. *Veefeel? Veefeel?*)

He didn't look as if he wanted to pay very much, even though at the moment, by all appearances, he was longing to make love to me. Christ, why put it so delicately – I mean, he wanted to fuck, it was clear from certain physical signs. Impressively obvious physical signs, I couldn't help thinking, and the not-for-profit part of my physical instinct had already begun looking forward to it, more or less. The commercial part asked, "How much can you give me?" and it repeated, "I really need cash, get it, I need cash."

This was a sport, a game, I was gradually realizing. Kurt was definitely not poor, and even though he probably picked up some girl on every trip he made through Czechoslovakia and had to pay for it, I was sure he could afford to hand me a couple of hundred marks. It was a sport: pick up as many girls as possible in the East and then outdo all the other drivers bragging about who nailed what girl for how little. Supposedly, the consensus among Western Intertruckers was that "Czech whores are good whores, the cheapest whores on earth" – and except for a few insignificant cases, the truckers tried not to spoil them . . . it was a sport. I remember this one Dutchman, a pretty nice guy, who once gave me a lift on the same route I was riding that day, but under different circumstances: he gave Fialinka Number One a lift, while today a newborn second Fialinka rode that highway. He told me how he and his friend once made a bet on who could score a Czech highway girl for the lowest price. I had one for five marks, the Dutchman said modestly. I couldn't get breakfast for that in the Netherlands. But my friend, he outdid me. He bargained this one girl down to one mark, *one mark*, can you imagine, howled the Dutchman, and she wasn't all that bad. True, she gave him the clap . . .

I'd always laughed at those prices, determined more by location and nationality than by the quality and appearance of the girl. And sometimes I was ashamed for my countrymen – still, it'd simply never occurred to me just how damn personally those highway prices could affect me. "*Verstehst du mich?*" I repeated. "*Ich brauche Geld.*"

And poor, dear Kurt (in different circumstances I certainly could have gotten along with him and, God knows, maybe even have made love to him on an entirely different philosophical basis), this Kurt stared at the strip of tummy below my T-shirt, sighed, and said, "*Funfzig Marks? Ist das okay?*"

I thought it over, then nodded.

The red curtains were made for lovemaking (that is, if this particular act didn't call for a change of terminology); the conditions were almost brothel-like. The sun, already substantially lower in the sky, shone straight into the cabin and illuminated it perfectly. Redly. Shamefully. Maybe red actually is the only color for this, I said to myself, and I noticed the shadow of the fabric pattern on that other face; maybe only red light will do, because suddenly there was not a trace of shame in that cab.

I'd never done anything like that in the cab of a truck during the day before; not that I needed darkness for such acts, quite the contrary; but that clear summer day outside somehow didn't seem right. Actually, I just didn't feel like it – even the other one, the buyer, didn't show any special enthusiasm. Any real desire. He was simply buying himself a whore and he'd just closed the deal with her . . .

He quickly kissed me: tongue thrashing in my mouth, a kiss supposedly passionate but in reality commercial and lukewarm. I guess he figured it was his duty.

He hurriedly checked the swaying folds of the curtains, to make sure no prying eye could look in. "*Gut*," he said, satisfied.
Then he pulled down his shorts.

The prompter in my head, that precise, intrusive internal voice, never let go of my hand. I knew exactly what to do, even though I'd never slept with anyone under these circumstances before: it had always started with my consciousness becoming pleasantly, mistily bedewed by someone I liked, so that the pleasurable feelings were always clear and unambiguous. But today I didn't even know whether I liked Kurt or not – and it made no difference at all. I had always wanted to be warmly intoxicated with perfectly mellowed (though perhaps only transient) desire; I would let myself dissolve into pleasant reverie – and the truckers who caught on were then allowed to come after me. Come into me. Pay a tender, longed-for, intimate visit. Always for a limited time.
But now – now I saw everything with perfect and loathsome sobriety. Without ardor. Without desire. I examined the shameful lighting in our little cab without shame: everything had perfectly clear, absolutely sharp outlines; gone was that undulating, dewy translucence I needed so badly during my Nights of Distances, my Nights of Instants. I was stone sober and wide awake: I was an actor on the stage of my own private theater, and the role was translated by my lips and movements with perfect precision. It became the way I could seductively (like a typical easy woman) slip out of even that clay-caked T-shirt. It became the bowing of the head I used to inconspicuously avoid direct eye contact; the precise and realistic movements of body, hands, lips. I knew exactly what to do, although I had never behaved this way before. And he didn't get it. How could he have guessed I had a prompter directing me from inside my defenseless-looking head? He surrendered himself to my hands and lips without the least sign of surprise. I did exactly what he anticipated. I did exactly what he expected and wanted, and if anything especially turned him on, it was that he didn't have to ask for anything. He was not so experienced that I couldn't surprise him. I was functioning. I didn't try to assess him, to figure out whether I liked him at all. I paid attention only to myself – concertedly, critically. I did everything I could think of doing – and although I'd never

studied what was most pleasing to (average) men, my intuition
helped me. I kissed him deeply, a kiss no less clinging than the
one he had given me before – and I let him sigh blissfully. Or
semi-blissfully. It was an experienced and wet kiss, well calculated – but still just a sort of half-kiss. Everything was halves and
semis . . . Our semi-rapport. Our semi-commercial exchange.
The half-light. Semi-desire. And we were half-human. We were
marionettes, waving our hands, moving, living according to the
puppet master's nimble fingers . . . And when that large, actually
very large, and hard piece of flesh (*Fleisch*, it occurred to me,
Fleisch) plunged into me, I realized that even this time I would
feel pleasure. Semi-pleasure. I was making my acting debut on
the stage of the Southern Road – and the sun had shifted slightly
in the sky, so that the shameful lighting colored my rival's face.
(Yes, he was my rival, though not my enemy.) Perhaps all my old
sins and loves returned to me and aroused me as I conscien-
tiously, attentively (and no doubt artfully), rode him like a
hobbyhorse, rocking and plunging. Men like it when they don't
have to exert themselves too much, reasoned the prompter in my
head. And I was willing to provide good service for good money.
I rocked and plunged, more vigorously and deeper, to the point
where it hurt – and through the filter of perfectly sober thought I
felt my eyes becoming moist and saw the same voluptuous
moisture in my rival's eyes and my thighs quivering with the
first tendrils of pleasure that were beginning to spread from my
crotch, after all . . . After all . . . ? No, there was no after all about
it, this was the approach of a powerful, compact, nearly painful
orgasm, its potent, absolutely unfeigned spasms gripping my
rival like a velvet vice. I bit his shoulder and neck to stifle the
moans and the scream that struggled to leave my throat. We
weren't the only ones parked at that rest area. I gripped him again
and again in the velvet vise and looked with my misty but
perfectly sober eyes directly into his; I observed how his face
twisted, how he cried out and groaned and pulled me toward him,
his nails digging into my buttocks, one hand on each, spreading
them. He pulled me toward him and his face twisted with the
animal grimace of genuine ecstasy: the quivering spread to my
thighs and groin and down my legs . . . I knew the convulsion
would come soon – and it would be a painful one – but payment
had been made. I held on, and when I felt the hot liquid

streaming into me like a firehose into a burning house, I calmly realized how perfectly my prompter had everything planned: these were my safest days of the month . . . Soon the convulsions stopped in my thighs, replaced only by a trembling exhaustion, and my rival, or sexual partner, was still quivering too. He was overcome. And lying next to him afterward, tired, trembling, my prompter did not forget to speak up and show me precisely how to place my hand on his heaving shaggy chest so that it would seem intimate without applying too much pressure – though, of course, this meant nothing at all. I was still trying to catch my breath in the sultry atmosphere of the shamefully lit cab. That was good, solid lovemaking, it occurred to me.

A good fuck.

ROSES

Evelyn Lau

THE PSYCHIATRIST CAME into my life one month after my eighteenth birthday. He came into my life wearing a silk tie, his dark eyes half-obscured by lines and wrinkles. He brought with him a pronounced upper-class accent, a futile sense of humor, books to educate me. *Lolita. The Story of O.* His lips were thin, but when I took them between my own they plumped out and filled my mouth with sweet foreign tastes.

He worshipped me at first because he could not touch me. And then he worshipped me because he could only touch me if he paid to do so. I understood that without the autumn leaves, the browns of the hundreds and the fiery scarlets of the fifties, the marble pedestal beneath me would begin to erode.

The first two weeks were tender. He said he adored my childlike body, my unpainted face, my long straight hair. He promised to take care of me, love me unconditionally. He would be my father, friend, lover – and if one was ever absent, the other two were large enough on their own to fill up the space that was left behind.

He brought into my doorway the slippery clean smell of rain, and he possessed the necessary implements – samples of pills tiny as seeds, a gold shovel. My body yielded to the scrapings of his hands.

He gave me drugs because, he said, he loved me. He brought

the tablets from his office, rattling in plastic bottles stuffed to the brim with cotton. I placed them under my tongue and sucked up their saccharine sweetness, learning that only the strong ones tasted like candy, the rest were chalky or bitter. He loved me beyond morality.

The plants that he brought each time he came to visit – baby's breath, dieffenbachia, jade – began to die as soon as they crossed the threshold of my home. After twenty-four hours the leaves would crinkle into tight dark snarls stooping towards the soil. They could not be pried open, though I watered his plants, exposed them to sunlight, trimmed them. It was as if by contact with him or with my environment, they had been poisoned. Watching them die, I was reminded of how he told me that when he first came to Canada he worked for two years in one of our worst mental institutions. I walked by the building once at night, creeping as far as I dared up the grassy slopes and between the evergreens. It was a sturdy beige structure, it didn't look so bad from the outside. In my mind, though, I saw it as something else. In my mind it was a series of black-and-white film stills; a face staring out from behind a barred window. The face belonged to a woman with tangled hair, wearing a nightgown. I covered my ears from her screams. When he told me about this place I imagined him in the film, the woman clawing at him where the corridors were gray, and there was the clanking sound of tin and metal. I used to lie awake as a child on the nights my father visited my bed and imagine scenes in which he was terrorized, in pain, made helpless. This was the same. I could smell the bloodstains the janitors had not yet scrubbed from the floors. I could smell the human discharges and see the hands that groped at him as he walked past each cell, each room. The hands flapped disembodied in the air, white and supplicating and at the same time evil.

He told me that when he was married to his first wife, she had gone shopping one day and he had had to take their baby with him on his hospital rounds, "I didn't know where to put him when I arrived," he said. "So I put him in the wastepaper basket." When he returned the child had upended the basket and crawled out, crying, glaring at his father. "I had no other choice," he said, and he reached into his trenchcoat and gave me a bottle of pills. "I love you," he said, "that's why I'm doing this."

I believed that only someone with a limitless love would put his baby in a trash can, its face squinched and its mouth pursing open in a squawk of dismay. Only someone like that could leave it swaddled in crumpled scraps of paper so he could go and take care of his patients. I could not imagine the breadth of the love that lay behind his eyes, those eyes that became as clear as glass at the moment of orgasm.

He bought a mask yesterday from a Japanese import store. It had tangled human hair that he washed with an anti-dandruff shampoo, carefully brushing it afterwards so the strands would not snap off. It had no pupils; the corneas were circles of bone. He took it home with him and stared at it for half an hour during a thunderstorm, paralysed with fear. It stared back at him. It was supposed to scare off his rage, he said.

After two weeks his tenderness went the way of his plants – crisp, shriveled, closed. He stopped touching me in bed but grew as gluttonous as dry soil. I started to keep my eyes open when we kissed and to squeeze them shut all the other times, the many times he pulled my hand or my head down between his legs.

He continued to bring me magazines and books, but they were eclipsed by the part of him he expected me to touch. Some days, I found I could not. I thought it was enough that I listened to his stories. I fantasized about being his psychoanalyst and not letting him see my face, having that kind of control over him. I would lay him down on my couch and shine light into his eyes while I remained in shadow where he could not touch me.

His latest gift, a snake plant, looks like a cluster of green knives or spears. The soil is so parched that I keep watering it, but the water runs smartly through the pot without, it seems, having left anything of itself behind. The water runs all over the table and into my hands.

Tonight I did not think I could touch him. I asked him to hit me instead, thinking his slim white body would recoil from the thought. Instead he rubbed himself against my thigh, excited. I told him pain did not arouse me, but it was too late. I pulled the blankets around my naked body and tried to close up inside the way a flower wraps itself in the safety of its petals when night falls.

At first he stretched me across his knees and began to spank me. I wiggled obediently and raised my bottom high into the air, the way my father used to like to see me do. Then he moved up to rain blows upon my back. One of them was so painful that I saw colors even with my eyes open; it showered through my body like fireworks. It was like watching a sunset and feeling a pain in your chest at its wrenching beauty, the kind of pain that makes you gasp.

How loud the slaps grew in the small space of my apartment – like the sound of thunder. I wondered if my face looked, in that moment, like his Japanese mask.

The pain cleansed my mind until it breathed like the streets of a city after a good and bright rain. It washed away the dirt inside me. I could see the gutters open up to swallow the candy wrappers, newspaper pages, cigarette butts borne along on its massive tide. I saw as I had not seen before every bump and indentation on the wall beside my bed.

And then he wanted more and I fought him, dimly surprised that he wasn't stronger. I saw as though through the eye of a camera this tangle of white thighs and arms and the crook of a shoulder, the slope of a back. I scraped his skin with my finger-nails. I felt no conscious fear because I was the girl behind the camera, zooming in for a close-up, a tight shot, an interesting angle. Limbs like marble on the tousled bed. His face contorted with strain. He was breathing heavily, but I, I was not breathing at all. I knew that if I touched his hair my hand would come away wet, not with the pleasant sweat of sexual exertion, but with something different. Something that would smell like a hospital, a hospital with disinfectant to mask the smells underneath.

And when he pushed my face against his thigh, it was oddly comforting, though it was the same thigh that belonged to the body that was reaching out to hit me. I breathed in the soft, soapy smell of his skin as his hand stung my back – the same hand that comforted crying patients, that wrote notes on their therapeutic progress, that had shaken with shyness when it first touched me. The sound of the slaps was amplified in the candlelit room. Nothing had ever sounded so loud, so singular in its purpose. I had never felt so far away from myself, not even with his pills.

I am far away and his thigh is sandy as a beach against my cheek. The sounds melt like gold, like slow Sunday afternoons. I think of cats and the baby grand piano in the foyer of my father's house. I think of the rain that gushes down the drainpipes outside my father's bathroom late at night when things begin to happen. I think of the queerly elegant black notes on sheets of piano music. The light is flooding generously through the windows and I am a little girl with a pink ribbon in my hair and a ruffled dress.

I seat myself on the piano bench and begin to play, my fingertips softening to the long ivory, the shorter ebony keys. I look down at my feet and see them bound in pink ballerina slippers, pressing intermittently on the pedals. Always Daddy's girl, I perform according to his instruction.

When it was over he stroked the fear that bathed my hands in cold sweat. He said that when we fought my face had filled with hatred and a dead coldness. He said that he had cured himself of his obsession with me during the beating, he had stripped me of my mystery. Slapped me human. He said my fear had turned him on. He was thirsty for the sweat that dampened my palms and willing to do anything to elicit more of that moisture so he could lick it and quench his tongue's thirst.

I understood that when I did not bleed at the first blow, his love turned into hatred. I saw that if I was indeed precious and fragile I would have broken, I would have burst open like a thin shell and discharged the rich sweet stain of roses.

Before he left he pressed his lips to mine. His eyes were open when he said that if I told anyone, he would have no other choice but to kill me.

Now that he is gone, I look between my breasts and see another flower growing: a rash of raspberry dots, like seeds. I wonder if this is how fear discharges itself when we leave our bodies in moments of pain.

The psychiatrist, when he first came, promised me a rose garden and in the mirror tomorrow morning I will see the results for the first time on my own body. I will tend his bouquets before he comes again, his eyes misty with fear and lust. Then I will listen to the liquid notes that are pleasing in the sunlit foyer and smile because somewhere, off in the distance, my father is clapping.

WHITE NIGHT

Françoise Rey

Translated by Maxim Jakubowski

WE'D BEEN DRIVING for some time already. The night was cold and icy. Thin snow was falling. Suddenly, we moved straight into a blizzard. The flakes rushed towards us through the daze of the headlights, waltzing wildly, blinding our sight of the road. You slowed down.

"I'm married," you suddenly said. This did not offend me, interrupting as it did a lengthy silence I had neither sought nor wanted.

"I know," I answered. You looked down at your left hand and examined, as if it had never been there before, the ring, smiled as if confronted by undeniable evidence and my admission that I already knew. Which implied some form of idle curiosity on my part at least. Then you looked round at my own hands.

I think I wore five or six rings, but in the semi-darkness you had no time to count them as the road was becoming increasingly treacherous and invisible. You peered up through the wind-screen, changed the wipers' speed, looked round at me again quizzically. I answered your silent question with a faint laugh and, still smiling, you accepted both my silence, and my wish to say nothing . . .

It was warm in the lorry's cab, I was feeling good. Then you said: "My wife is at a ski resort, with the small ones." I answered:

"We're also in the snow." You put your hand on my knee and I closed my eyes.

Our meeting had been a bit of a miracle. Because of the time of year . . . It was the evening of December 24th . . .

My luggage in hand, I had crossed the road a bit too fast. There were a lot of people, many of them laden with parcels. A bike had shuffled against me, awkwardly squeezing me against the hood of a parked car, against which my case noisily brushed.

You were on the other side of the street, about to climb into your lorry. A big lorry which had probably just delivered oysters to the covered market which stood nearby. The company's name was painted in large letters on the side of the vehicle, together with its address: "Rue B. Patoiseau – MARENNES."

You halted in mid-ascent, then climbed down again to come to my rescue. I was a trifle shaken, no more.

"Are you OK?" you asked. "You're not hurt?"

You picked up my case. You were much taller than me, film star-size. With a cheerful, sly glint in your winter sea green eyes, which reminded me – why not? – of clear, fresh oysters.

"You were leaving on holiday?"

"Yes," I answered. "I was going to spend Christmas with my family in La Rochelle. But I'm worried that my train might be full and I forgot to make a reservation . . ."

You looked me straight in the eyes, pondered just half a second, turned toward your lorry.

"Say, I've thought of something . . ."

And there we are . . .

Just enough time for you to go to some office to complete the paperwork and for me to make a phone call, and we were on our way, on a long, unexpected, delicious Christmas Eve journey.

We had reached a hill. You slowed down, had to change gear, your hand left my knee for a moment, then swiftly returned. "The truth is," you said to me, "I'm very shy." And I was so enjoying this strange conversation where words seemed to be possessed of different meanings. The charming way you said "the truth is", so pregnant with possibilities.

"Really?" Did I doubt you?

"Not usually," you added.

"But tonight?" I sought confirmation.

"A bit."

"Because of me?"

"Thanks to you."

"And does it feel good?"

"It's delectable!"

I thought that for a lorry driver your vocabulary was quite charming. And I loved the way you thought.

"How funny . . ." I said.

"Yes, for a lorry driver, eh?" you answered, and smiled once again. I looked back at you and drowned my gaze in your deeply lined brow. I had always known vile seducers had wrinkles just like yours. And I allowed myself to be seduced . . .

I put my hand on yours. It was warm, strong. Wise. I pulled my skirt up and encouraged your large hand to shed its innocence and explore further.

"You're really funny!" you said. "You don't really look like . . ."

"But I'm not . . ."

"What, only tonight?"

"Yes."

"Why?"

"It's Christmas!"

The disappointment on your face was almost comic.

"I thought it was because of me . . ."

"Thanks to you!" I corrected you.

And we sealed our complicity with an exchange of meaningful looks and smiles.

"Keep your eyes on the road. Our hands are old enough to look after themselves. Especially yours."

"It's not always an advantage to have such large hands," you said, as your fingers approached the edge of my knickers.

I did not answer but pulled my buttocks up, and pulled off the piece of underwear obstructing you. And wedged myself deep into the seat, opened my thighs and again closed my eyes.

Your hand sported intelligence. At first, it made no demands. Wandered quietly over my fur, knuckles slowly skimming over its surface, a pleasing caress. The hum of the lorry's engine and the bumps in the road echoed all the way through to my sex, where I could feel a whole network of nerve terminals vibrating in unison. It was like a sort of telephone switchboard in my lower stomach, impatiently awaiting calls and demands.

"Tell me . . ." you asked.

I did not misunderstand your request. All you wanted to hear from me was how I felt right then.

"I know it's called a pussy," I said. "I feel as if it's about to miaow!"

"I love animals," you answered.

"They always return your affection," I whispered back, my voice suddenly quite hoarse as one of your errant fingers penetrated me.

You found it amusing to enter and withdraw from me in a slow, gentle rhythm. I slipped my hand under the palm of your hand, still warming my mons, found my bud and delicately landed on it, careful not to rush anything, to make this holy moment last as long as possible, this very instant when imagination moves residence and settles in highly secret places.

My dreams were at sea, balanced on the waves. My cunt was the sea, waves crashing against each other, ebb and flow, ebb and flow . . .

I was in the depths, dark, salty, wetter than wet and my stomach was initiating a new, steady pulse, ever increasing in strength: hold back, hold on, hold back, hold on . . . I was becoming an underwater cave, a dizzy abyss. Soon I would require something stronger, something to war against, to fight back, to digest. I beckoned the myths of the great sea serpent, the indefatigable swimmer, the steel-membered Argonaut. I begged to be taken . . .

You were still driving, your eyes on the road, a foreigner to all that was happening between my thighs. You kindly offered me another finger. It was welcome, but the angle of penetration slowed its movements, causing pain in the midst of pleasure.

"You're wet!" you said.

"You're the one who's making me wet. I'm like a jetty covered in kelp, you know, after the wave has subsided . . . A jetty after the storm . . ."

I thought of mooring bitts. I placed my left hand on your flies.

You raised yourself slightly to allow me to unbutton your top button, as it was too tight. The rest came easy. I quickly found you.

It's damn crazy to jerk off like that, a thick cock in hand, and dreaming of being elsewhere. Can drive you mad.

I don't really know you, but there's a place for you inside of me.

Several places, even. This was the moment when I realized how perfectly we complemented each other. This cock I held in my hand, I wanted to take it everywhere into me, wherever it might fit. I also felt like devouring it, an imperious desire, a ferocious appetite, a pressing need to be one with it, to commune in agony. But if I bent towards you, you would have had to let go of me, and I did not want that. The explosion was approaching, I could no longer control it. I looked around at you, disturbed.

"I think I'm . . ."

"Yes, of course. Yes!" you gently said. As you would put a friend at ease. The kindness of this permission reassured me and banished all the mental storm clouds away.

But, please, don't let it make you stop!

And you understood so well both the situation and the urgency clearly, and your fingers pursued their passionate, dizzy journey inside me, this hesitant waltz strong enough to melt all resistance, travails worthy of Sisyphus and the ocean and handfuls of planets. Forward, further, much further, gently, back a bit, almost pulling out, ever so slowly, forward, much further, back a bit gently . . . I keep company with you, with all my soul, with all my guts and I'm chased by a giant wave riding behind me, biting at my heels, catching me . . . Lo, here it comes . . .

I held your cock tight in the grip of my hand, froze, winced, riding the crest of the giant tidal wave lifting me up, sitting on the throne of an eruption of sheer undiluted pleasure, cushioning all its aftershocks . . .

You parked smoothly on the side of the road, switched off the engine. I turned towards you, short of breath, still boiling. You explained: "It was either that, or move into second gear . . ." I acquiesced. Yes, yes, you were quite right to do so! If you'd switched gears, the let-down would have been awful, a true low in my career . . . The teacher in me smiled at the analogy, but offered him no explanation . . . Anyway, all my energy had quite dissipated . . .

"It was good!" I said, with a lack of conviction that saw you roar with laughter.

"I'm absolutely delighted," you declared theatrically, waving your hands upwards, and for just one second, I saw the sheen of my lust shine on your fingers.

Wait, just you wait and see how I can please you too!

I bend toward you. Your cock had a heady smell. Reminiscent of the corduroy fabric of your trousers. But also the smell of man. Wild. Lingering . . .

The joy in my stomach, which still hadn't subsided, rose sharply again. I laid my tongue on the tip of your cock. It was slippery. A thin, appetizing, salty stream pearled out of the thin hole and I spread it all over the pink, round, bare, stirring glans. Men's cocks are custom-made to be devoured. There's nothing more eatable in a man. It's firm, elastic, spongy, so soft you feel your tongue should dance on tiptoe over it, like a cheeky skater on a bed of ice.

Your cock is so thick I don't think I could suck on all of it . . . At any rate, not in my present position . . . Under my skirt, the echo continues. My cunt is still quivering.

"Give it to me . . ."

"Ask, come on, you can ask better . . ."

"Please, please, please. I want it badly . . ."

"You can do better!"

"Come to me, please . . . I am so hot inside. Touch me, touch, I'm on fire, I'm so wet, put it inside, I'll go crazy. I'll suck you off so good. Come!"

"Ask! Ask again!"

"Damn it! Come . . . Look, how it needs me too: it can't even stand still, it's ready to burst if you don't put it in, put it inside me, fuck me, please? Come. I'm hungry, hungry for you, hungry for it. Look, it will slide in so easily, it's ready . . . You can't keep it, this big dumb thing, all to yourself? Look, look, I'm opening up for it, see. See how I gape wide open, hurry, hurry, or I'll come without you, just the thought of you screwing me . . . We will lose it all . . ."

The threats had the desired effect. You laid me down onto the seat, down on your knees on the other seat you pulled me across, pushed your trousers down . . . Lust stabbed through my heart. And I still hadn't even seen your balls!

You move into me like butter. I can almost feel your taste. It's a famished beast I have between my thighs. Eat, feast yourself, my little animal! It's Christmas, I'm your midnight supper!

I swallow you whole with torrid pleasure. Your cock is hard, I can feel it butt against my walls, at the back, and the soft blows reverberate all the way through to my arse. It's exhilarating . . .

I've a finger on my clit, doing God knows only what, and it feels good, like a mandolin player. And with my left hand, I held your balls, heavy, thick, gorgeous. My imagination is on fire thinking of them, swollen and creamy. Eat, kiddo, eat! Soon it will be time for dessert . . . This guy is soon about to spurt all the way into you, the way you like it! My brain grows more excited as it pictures visions of eruptions surging upwards at the speed of light. I naively press hard against your balls, as if to empty them.

"Come, come . . ."

"No, not before you do. Come quickly."

"I can't. I just can't, yet."

How could I explain that my lust was dependent on yours?

"You first, you first . . . you keep on saying," and I realize that you are going to wait as long as it takes while I'm almost suffocating here, suspended above the abyss.

"Tell me what you want me to do? Tell me . . . You're so good to me."

"Take me everywhere. Behind, also."

You are obedience personified. My desires are orders. You stab my arsehole with your thick, aggressive, fiery thumb. It scares me and fills me with joy at the same time.

"Do you feel me, there? [Hard not to. I feel only you.] Are you ready to come, now? Ready?"

"If you keep on stretching me open so, everywhere, yes, yes, it'll soon come . . . Listen, listen, it's coming, it's coming, it's almost here, it's . . . now, right now, give, give it to me, you too . . ."

You fell upon me. You're much heavier than I thought you would be. And so much more gentle, too.

When I opened my eyes, the snow had stopped falling. You caught your breath back, readjusted your clothing, settled again behind the steering wheel. My chest is still resonating, my ears too, full of the roar of the giant wave that has washed me away. With sharp burns everywhere, their scars gradually declining and being replaced by a wholesome feeling of lassitude.

"You can sleep, if you want to."

You indicate the cot, behind the front seats. No, I don't wish to leave you on your own. I will not sleep.

And the journey continues, quietly, slowly. We're in a sleigh smoothly sliding through a white and sleepy landscape.

From time to time, you stop. People wish you a merry Christ-

mas. We go again. There are bells in my head, champagne
flowing through my body, and my heart. Small bubbles sparkle
and tickle me everywhere. You're nice, you're funny. I don't
regret anything.

In the morning, you lightly brush against my drowsiness.

"We're arriving in La Rochelle. Where do you want me to drop
you?"

I open my eyes, see a dead town amidst a still black dawn.

"At the railway station."

"What?"

"Yes, I have to tell you. You know, when we met, I wasn't
leaving Lyon. I'd just arrived. I was going to spend Christmas
there. I didn't feel like it . . ."

"You'd just come from La Rochelle?"

"No, from Grenoble."

"But . . .? Why did you tell me of La Rochelle?"

"I saw you. I saw your lorry, the sign 'Marennes'. I thought,
'That's where that guy is going back to, tonight.' And I reckoned
'Why not?'"

Your eyes flickered with laughter.

"It's funny."

"Why?"

"Because, when you saw me, I was about to hand over the lorry
to a mate. I wasn't supposed to bring it back. I was scheduled to
sleep in Lyon. I'd already been driving all day."

"That's why you had to go to the office?"

"Yes, that's where I was meant to meet up with him. I told
Dupré, 'I'm replacing you.' He didn't mind."

"Is it legal?"

"No, not really, but it can be done . . . He'd found this chick in
Lyon. Gave him the chance to spend Christmas Eve with her. He
was pleased."

"Weren't you supposed to spend Christmas with your family?"

"No, I was going to wait for the next lorry to do the journey."

"So, now, what are you going to do?"

"First, sleep a bit. Then return to Lyon."

"When?"

"Tomorrow morning, maybe."

"So . . .?"

"Yes, why not?"

THREE FOR THE MONEY

Marilyn Jaye Lewis

Yesterday, I went to a funeral uptown. When I left my apartment in the morning, it had been the proverbial spring day, birds chirping, daffodils blooming in the park – the works. Naturally, by the time I came up from the subway station an hour and a half later, it had begun to rain. Funerals are a bit like rain dances in that way; people gather together in mourning, and the earth itself cries.

The dead guy, Marten Santos, had been notoriously rich and depraved while he was alive. He had never tried to pass as righteous, though, never pretended to be perfect. We all knew about his peculiar tastes and erratic passions, and loved him for that. Nevertheless, he'd been raised a strict Roman Catholic and so the funeral was a stuffy, conservative affair, held at Our Lady of Divine Sorrows. After the funeral, as the teary-eyed pall-bearers removed the casket from the church and solemnly loaded it into the back of the hearse, Our Lady's bell tolled mournfully, sounding all the more poignant in the gray drizzle of rain. He was a man who was going to be missed by a lot of good people.

In life, Mr Santos had been one of my favorite tricks. When he died suddenly of a heart attack three days ago, the newspaper said that he was pushing seventy. During the year when he'd been one of my regulars, he claimed to be fifty-five. It says a lot that after all these years I was moved enough by a sense of loss to attend his funeral. But then, he hadn't always been a trick. With Mr Santos, I'd done the unthinkable and allowed a favorite john to become a lover, or nearly so. The shame of that slip-up on my part, and a difficult scene he put me through in a cheap hotel room, had caused us to part on uncomfortable terms. Still, it made me no less fond of him.

I don't turn tricks anymore, I haven't for years. I'm almost forty now. I work in a respectable office and I earn a respectable living. I present a very hard-assed, successful-bitch version of myself to the world and it's helped me to succeed and keep my past where it should be, in the past. The frantic, frenetic survival skills acquired by all New Yorkers makes the town a forgiving place. As long as you don't wind up at the heart of a sordid public scandal in a court of law, where New Yorkers show their ugly sides and revel in seeing your past mistakes slung at you like so much mud, you can do just about anything to get ahead in this town and not have to worry too much that it'll come back to haunt you.

Mr Santos and I first met in an upscale espresso shop on the Upper East Side. This was back in the 80s, when a whole lot of people had money to burn. Mr Santos was friends with the owner, Hajid, who was one of my regulars, too. Hajid liked getting blow jobs behind the desk in his office. His office was in the basement of the coffee house. It was decidedly downscale in that dark, damp, vermin-infested cellar. However, a simple blow job, as long as I was willing to have my pants around my knees and keep my naked ass out for his viewing pleasure, lasted only about ten minutes and garnered me two hundred tax-free dollars, so I found ways to make even that *ratskeller* seem erotic.

The evening I met Mr Santos, I was actually just having coffee. I wasn't engaged in business. Hajid and I were on friendly terms. He introduced me to Mr Santos, with a nod and a wink, and Mr Santos pulled up a chair. He got right down to the business of getting to know me better. He ended the meeting by paying my modest tab and then asking me for my phone number, which of course I gave him since it was obvious he was loaded – even more so than Hajid.

Our trysts started out simple and straightforward. Mr Santos would always arrange for me to meet him in other rich people's high-class apartments. The people he knew went on extended vacations, traveled on business to faraway places, or had primary homes in other countries. Mr Santos was married back then, and apparently he and his other married male friends formed a cozy circle of infidels, each leaving the rest of the crew a key to his empty apartment for extramarital liaisons in his absence. I don't think the wives ever had a clue what was taking place in the sanctity of their homes while they were off on holiday.

I was never to touch anything, never allowed to get too comfortable in the jaw-dropping luxury of our trysting places. Mr Santos liked anal and that was pretty much the sole basis of our get-togethers, at first. Without fanfare, he would unzip his trousers; let them fall unceremoniously to his ankles, along with his boxers. He'd slip on a rubber; slather it with the lube that he carried in his pocket in handy individual foil packets. Then I'd bend over anything steady and he'd slide his cock up my ass.

He fucked me like a man who had important meetings to get to, so he usually came pretty quickly. I didn't have to say anything weird, or dress in anything unusual. I simply had to show up with an absolutely clean asshole, bend over and let him ream me; that was all he required. For that, I got five hundred dollars cash; five crisp, one-hundred-dollar bills, folded in the middle, which he'd place under my nose while I was still bending over – before he'd even pulled his cock out of me, I'd get paid.

There was something about the way he paid me that tended to make me feel a little humiliated, but he didn't seem to think twice about it. By the time I'd turn around, he'd have the used condom off, his trousers pulled up, and would be heading to the toilet to flush the condom down. He never said anything like. "Here's your money you whore," or "Take that, bitch." He just had a funny habit of leaving it parked under my nose while my ass was still stuffed with him.

I remember when we had our first real conversation. It was a day when he seemed to be at leisure. He wasn't pressed for time, wasn't hurrying. It was a day when he wandered around the spacious apartment we were using, looking for the perfect place to bend me over, making small talk, making jokes. "Bend over that chair there, let me see the view. Pull up your skirt. No, we can find something better."

When he finally decided on the perfect spot – an ergonomically correct artist's stool – he lifted my skirt himself, pulled my panties down (an intimate gesture he'd never once done before) and then said, "You know what this reminds me of?"

My naked ass in the air, my thighs spread in anticipation, my head hanging down, I said, "No, what?"

"Church. This reminds me of church."

He didn't elaborate and I had no idea what he was talking about. But the thought of church seemed to make him feel even more jovial. He sank to his knees and rimmed me, his hot, wet tongue expertly stroking my puckered hole. It felt sensational. I actually moaned and felt like touching myself.

Having his nose in my ass seemed to arouse his passion, for that day he fucked my ass especially vigorously, nearly knocking me off the stool several times. The mounting pressure of his thickening hard-on sucking in and out of my ass made me cry out. When he came, he pulled his cock out a little aggressively, gave me a resounding smack on my upturned ass, and said, "Here you go. Thanks, kiddo." And the money was once again placed in front of my face – on this occasion, I'd been staring at a parquet floor.

His breezy pre-sex conversing, combined with his sudden rugged manner with me during sex, made me see Mr Santos in a different light. He was a handsome man, I decided, as I watched him zip up his trousers and go off in search of the toilet. I still had my panties around my knees when he came back into the room. I was lingering in my little swoon.

"What's with you?" he asked.

Snapping out of it and feeling embarrassed, I moved to pull up my panties.

"No, wait." He stopped me. "Not yet. You feel like making a little extra money today?"

I was caught off guard. He fished out his wallet and surveyed its contents. "Well, I have ten whole dollars." He found this amusing. "What do you feel like doing for ten dollars?"

"What did you have in mind?"

"I want to try something and see if I can make you come."

I never, under any circumstances, came with a trick. But Mr Santos intrigued me. "You think you can make me come for ten dollars?"

"Ten bucks, and a nice dinner. What do you say to that? My wife's out of town and I've got all the time in the world. I'll make it up to you next time about the money. You know I'm good for it."

I was feeling game. I liked Mr Santos. I wasn't worried about the money.

He told me to step out of my panties completely, then to squat down on the parquet floor. He told me that under no circumstances should I touch myself; he wanted to do all the work. He lubed two of his fingers, squatted down next to me, held me around my shoulders to sort of brace me, and then he stuck the two lubed fingers up my ass. He wiggled them vigorously in there, pushing hard against my perineum, rubbing the wall of muscle with all his strength.

"*Oh god*," I squealed in sheer ecstasy, clutching him tight, a stream of piss suddenly squirting out of me and forming a puddle on the nice wood floor.

"Go for it, baby. Let everything go. We can clean this up later. Bear down on me."

I did as he suggested, pushing my asshole down around his hardworking fingers, never dreaming that I could be launched into orgasm like a rocket without direct pressure applied to my clit. But it happened. My thighs shook as I squatted and bore down, more fluids gushing out of my open pisshole. My body was overwhelmed by waves of pleasure as his fingers rubbed more vigorously against the pressure of my now frantically contracting sphincter.

When I was through hyperventilating and convulsing like a lunatic, Mr Santos was still holding me, smiling. "Did you come?" he asked, very pleased with himself.

I didn't take the extra ten dollars that day, but I took him up on his offer to buy me dinner and that was the beginning of a new chapter in our "business relationship."

He continued to pay me whenever we got together, but we talked more, he took more time with me, he felt challenged to give me orgasms in unexpected ways. Soon, he was paying for rooms in five-star hotels, where we'd disappear for entire days together, relying on room service for sustenance. He introduced blindfolds, light bondage, and spanking to the list of things we were now doing with each other regularly in a lavish king-sized bed.

"Do you ever eat pussy?" he asked me one afternoon. "I mean, do you ever get asked to do that when you're out on a calls?"

I looked at him uneasily, not at all pleased that the world of my other tricks was even remotely entering into our time together.

"Do you even know *how* to eat pussy?"

"Of course I do."

"You get paid to do that?"

"Sometimes." I didn't feel much like discussing it.

"I'd like to see you eat pussy, you know that?"

You and every other trick on earth, I told myself. The last thing I wanted was to bring another girl into our scene, a girl who might prove to be more novel than me, a girl who might walk off with his number in her purse and then I would lose my favorite trick. Mr Santos was now the man I fantasized about when I was home alone in bed. I didn't think he would leave his wife for me, or anything like that, but I naively considered us lovers. I'd begun to hate the fact that he still paid me.

"What's that face for?" he said. "You aren't into pussy?"

"Girls are all right."

"I was thinking more along the lines of a woman – not a girl."

He immediately piqued my interest. "You mean you have someone in mind?"

"To be honest, there's a woman I've been seeing off and on for years, since before I was married. Occasinally, we get together when our spouses are otherwise detained and we have sex. I told her about you. How much fun you are. How amenable you can be."

And whose idea was it to make it a threesome, I wondered suspiciously, hers, or his?

"She'll pay you the same amount I do; you'll get double your usual fee. It wouldn't be a question of taking advantage. I would really like to see you eat her pussy. And I think she has an idea of a scene of her own. She's very willing to pay you," he repeated. "I don't think she's ever paid anyone to do a scene with her. Or to have *any* kind of sex with her, for that matter. She's just a regular married woman, but a good friend of mine."

She sounded harmless enough. But you'd think after my years of turning tricks. I would have known beyond a doubt that people who sound harmless can be the most difficult customers when it's all said and done.

Still, I agreed to do the three-way. We made an appointment for an afternoon the following week. For some reason, we were meeting in a tacky hotel in midtown – gone was the luxury of the king-sized bed, the crisp white sheets and room service. Everything about the hotel they'd chosen was dingy, seedy, and low class.

Mr Santos had asked me to bring along an outfit that would be suitable for a naughty little girl routine. Even though I'd never gone to Catholic school myself, I had a vintage Catholic school-girl uniform that fit me perfectly. I figured Mr Santos would get off on the religion thing so that's what I packed for my change of clothes.

I'd been getting steadily more into the idea of the three-way as the day approached. Anything that involved the unpredictability of Mr Santos's lusty libido aroused my own sexual appetites. He was nothing like an average trick. So when I knocked on the hotel room door that afternoon, I was already horny, already sopping wet between my legs. Until Mr Santos let me into the room and introduced me to his woman friend.

Oh my god, I realized in sick horror, *it's Mrs Hamilton*.

She'd been my tenth grade sociology teacher. A woman who'd made my life a living hell for an entire year. I was certain it was her. To this day, I don't know if she recognized me, too. If she did, she never once let on. But I *knew* it was her. She was simply using a fake name, like a lot of tricks do.

"Call me either 'Daddy' or 'Sir' today," Mr Santos was instructing me. "And this is your new stepmother, Louise."

Louise? They couldn't come up with anything less corny than Louise?

I had that feeling of panic in my gut that I used to get in my early days of hustling; I wanted to bolt. But then I focused on the money: one thousand dollars cash for a single afternoon's work. It would be worth it. But I saw immediately that it was going to be just that – work.

Mrs Hamilton had never been an unattractive woman; it was just that she'd always been a mean bitch of a teacher. In my years since high school, she'd managed to stay attractive; she'd taken good care of herself. I figured that if she knew Mr Santos, she must have money, too, and that always helps women stay good-looking. Yet it made me wonder why she'd chosen to teach at all. Perhaps for the sick thrill of tormenting teenagers?

"Louise wants to help you change clothes," Mr Santos told me. "It'll give you two a chance to get comfortable with each other. I'm going to run across the street to the liquor store. This trashy hotel doesn't even supply booze."

Shit. He was leaving me alone with her. The dreaded moment was starting to look even worse. Not only would I have to get naked for Mrs Hamilton, I would have to be completely alone with her while it happened. No horny Mr Santos around to use as a buffer zone.

When he was gone, she went right into "efficient teacher" mode. "Come here," she said flatly. "Let's get you out of those clothes and into something more appropriate."

She didn't act like it made her at all nervous to be around a prostitute, to be doing a scene. I wondered if she was anybody's horny lesbo stepmother in real life. The implications of that thought creeped me out. I had to force myself to keep my mind a blank.

Mrs Hamilton was going through my bag, pulling out my change of clothes. She seemed to recognize the uniform for what it was – something *real* girls wore in *real* high schools. "Are you Catholic?" she asked. "Not that it's any of my business."

"Yes," I said. "But I went to *public* schools." The sudden rudeness in my tone surprised even me.

She eyed me coolly, taking in that last remark. "Come over here," she said.

Shit. She was actually making me nervous. But I went over to her. Without hesitating, she began undressing me. "Let me tell you something," she explained carefully, unbuttoning my shirt with manicured fingers. "While we're in the confines of this room, while we're on the clock, so to speak, I have no qualms whatsoever about making it very clear which one of us is on top." The sound of her words alone felt like a slap. She had my shirt off. She was moving to unfasten my bra then, her fingers were touching the skin on my back, her face was close to mine. I didn't like it. "If you want to keep talking to me in that rude tone," she continued, "go right ahead. But consider yourself warned. I'm not afraid of girls like you. I deal with your kind every day."

My bra was off. My tits were right there in front of her, my nipples shivering to stiff points from the sudden change in temperature. How many times had I bared my tits for strange clients? But this took the cake for strangeness. I felt exposed.

She didn't touch me, though. She barely even paused to look at my nakedness. She was already on to my tight jeans, unzipping them, tugging them down to my ankles.

I was in that state of half-undressed nervousness when Mr Santos came back to the room, carrying a fifth of gin and a large carton of Tropicana OJ.

Jesus, I wondered, *how trashy are we going to get?* Where was the top-shelf bourbon, or at the very least, some cheap champagne?

"Well," he said, regarding us with satisfaction, "we're certainly progressing here. Anyone want a drink?"

We all did. Mr Santos played bartender while keeping a keen eye on us.

Mrs Hamilton had me completely undressed, except for my panties. Those she seemed to want to take more time with. She lowered them slowly, anticipating the unveiling of my neatly trimmed snatch. She was actually squatting down in front of me, apparently wanting an up close and personal view. It made me even more uncomfortable – not so much that Mrs Hamilton was squatting down in front of me, so obviously aroused by the imminent sight of another woman's pussy, but the fact that I was getting off on it, too. I was suddenly wet again.

"*Good lord*," she said quickly under her breath. She'd peeled my panties past my mound, rolled them partially down my thighs and seen the strand of gooey wetness connecting my soaking hole to the cotton crotch of my underwear. She looked up at Mr Santos, who was now standing next to us, offers of drinks in his hands. "She's so wet," Mrs Hamilton explained in quiet earnestness, as if the sight of a twat swollen in arousal pained her deliciously.

I took my drink from Mr Santos and gulped it down. I needed fortification. Mrs Hamilton was fucking *hot*. And now she was licking me, her mouth was actually on me down there, and I was getting off on it.

Jesus, I wondered; what was going to happen here? Alone, unsupervised with two horny tricks who could get me this worked up; two people apparently intent on doing a pseudo-incest scene, with me playing the part of the helpless bottom, two tops wanting to have their way with me, and all of us downing cheap gin?

I was light-headed. I parted my legs as much as I could for Mrs Hamilton, but it wasn't easy with my panties around my thighs.

She held tight to my ass cheeks, her mouth flush with my mound. She moaned as her hot tongue slid eagerly around in the folds of my pussy lips, occasionally landing directly on the tip of my clit. I was soon so aroused by the lusty sounds she made, that I actually held on to her head to keep myself steady. I had a handful of Mrs Hamilton's hair in one hand, and a plastic cup of gin and OJ in the other. It all seemed so decadently tawdry. The cheap thrill of it made me press Mrs Hamilton's face even closer to my snatch, rubbing her face in the slippery folds of it. The horny bitch moaned even more.

Mr Santos lit a cigarette. He stood close to us, watching it all unfold, feeling up my titties while he watched – taking firm handfuls of titty flesh and squeezing, kneading, then tugging roughly on my stiff, aching nipples. He took a drag off his cigarette and then put his mouth on mine, forcing exhaled smoke into my open mouth along with his tongue.

The feel of his tongue filling my mouth, and Mrs Hamilton's tongue deep between my sopping lips, while Mr Santos kept up his avid mauling of my breasts – I thought I'd come right on the spot.

But Mr Santos had his thoughts elsewhere. He pulled away from me the second before I had a chance to come. "This is going to be good," he announced.

The sound of his voice seemed to bring Mrs Hamilton back to earth. She got up from between my legs abruptly, her mouth a slick mess. She went straight for the drink awaiting her on the dresser. I could see her mentally pulling herself together; reminding *herself* which one of us girls was on top.

Within moments, she was in stepmother mode. "I want you to go into the bathroom and put on your clothes. Your father and I want to be alone. We'll tell you when to come out."

I did as I was told, stopping first to refresh my drink. I closed myself up in the small, ugly bathroom and got into my uniform. Outside, I could hear the lusty sounds of them going at each other. I didn't know in what way. Had they managed to strip out of their clothes in record time and begin fucking? Were they only partially undressed and sucking each other, or – just what were they doing? I was not only keenly curious, I was also jealous. I didn't want Mr Santos to enjoy Mrs Hamilton *that* much; after all, he was *my* lover.

Of course, I'd been instructed to stay put in the bathroom until I was given permission to come out. But that was all part of the scene. Naughty girls went wide-eyed into every opportunity to misbehave. Otherwise, you'd deprive your scene-mates of the chance to spank you bare-assed – or worse, depending on the infraction.

I quietly cracked open the bathroom door and peeked out at them.

I'll be damned, I thought.

They were fucking, all right. But they were, for the most part, still dressed. Mrs Hamilton was bent over the foot of the bed with her pants tugged down to her knees, while Mr Santos, cock out of his unzipped trousers, rode her hard from behind.

I was transfixed – they were in such a frenzy of lust. Plus the cheap booze had gone to my head. I couldn't believe I was watching Mrs Hamilton get nailed, and in such an unflattering posture. Her white ass looked huge, sticking out like that.

I worked my hand up under my skirt and inside my white panties. I wiggled my clit furiously as I watched them fuck like dogs.

As if on cue, Mrs Hamilton glanced over at the bathroom door and caught me spying on them. It seemed to make her ass jut out even more, if that was possible. But she got a queer look on her face, too, like she couldn't wait to get down and nasty on my own ass. I quickly closed the bathroom door and tried to mind my own business.

Naturally it was too late, and the incest-punishment scene was in full swing. There was soon a knock on the bathroom door. When I opened it, it was "Daddy." He said, "Your stepmother wishes to speak to you."

I came out of the bathroom to find my "stepmother" stark naked, sitting on the bed. She looked good naked, but she looked angry. "Come over here," she said.

I expected to get thoroughly spanked by her and I wasn't sure whether or not I would get off on it; she was still Mrs Hamilton after all, a woman I had once despised. As I went to her, there was a fear in my belly reminiscent of what I had once felt facing actual punishment as a child. Of course, this wasn't a scene remotely close to anything that would have gone on in my own house. I hadn't lost sight of the fact that we were all here for sex.

Daddy, still fully clothed, only his cock jutting out from his pants, sat down on the bed next to the naked "Louise." He had a stern expression on his face that made him look even more handsome. I was hoping he would force me to make it up to him somehow – all his disappointment in how I had misbehaved. But for now, the emphasis was on Louise. This was decidedly her scene, the part she was paying for.

"Come closer," she said.

I stood directly in front of her, cowering in my schoolgirl uniform.

"What were you doing in there?" she demanded.

"Nothing."

"It was more than nothing, young lady. You were spying on us, weren't you?"

"Yes," I meekly confessed.

"Weren't you told to stay in there until someone came for you?"

"Yes."

"And why did you disobey me?"

"I don't know."

"I'll tell you why, because you're a dirty little girl, aren't you? What do you suppose happens to a dirty little girl who disobeys and sticks her nose where it doesn't belong?"

I gave it some serious thought. The look in Mrs Hamilton's eyes was dark and unpleasant. Mr Santos, however, was in the throes of lust. He was watching it all while avidly stroking himself.

"I asked you a question," my stepmother went on. "What do you suppose happens to a dirty little girl who disobeys?"

"I don't know," I replied.

"I think you do."

I said nothing.

"Answer me."

"I guess I need to get spanked!" I finally blurted.

I was playing my part to the hilt now and Mrs Hamilton had succumbed completely to the erotic pull of her role. She was so obviously entranced by the power of her anger. "That's right. You need a good spanking to teach you a lesson. Get over here, right over my knee, young lady."

She grabbed me and pulled me over her knee, positioning me

across her lap in such a way that everything between my legs would be facing Mr Santos. She lifted my skirt. "I'll teach you to be a dirty little girl," she said, lowering my panties with deliberate patience, slowly revealing the round, white globes of my ass, then tugging the panties down my thighs.

She held my wrists tight and then gave my ass a resounding spank. "Why do you dirty girls always have to learn the hardest way how to behave?" She gave me another well-placed, stinging spank.

"I want you to tell Daddy exactly what you did; tell him why I'm so angry with you." Another severe smack heated my cheeks, making me jump.

"Because I was watching," I cried out.

"Watching what?" The smacks were coming more quickly now, stinging, landing relentlessly on the same spot. My ass burned. I tried to wriggle away from the aim of her blows, but it was to no avail. "Answer me; you were watching what?"

"I was watching Daddy fuck you."

"And what else were you doing?"

She pulled gently but firmly on my hair, forcing me to look up into her face. "And what else were you doing?" she asked again, her eyes nearly glowing with lust.

"I was touching myself," I said.

"Don't tell me, tell Daddy."

Daddy had gotten off the bed and come around in front of me. He was slowly jerking himself off in my face. I looked up at him, now, too. God, he looked hot. I confessed to him in my tiniest voice, "I was touching myself while I watched you fuck her."

Daddy seemed to be in a swoon. He stuck the head of his cock between my lips. Arching my head back uncomfortably with one hand, he worked his thick tool in and out of my mouth.

Louise worked two fingers up my hole then, giving me a thorough finger-fucking while Daddy worked on my eager mouth. Within moments, Daddy had pulled a condom from his pocket.

"It's Daddy's turn to punish you now," he explained. "I want you to kneel on the edge of the bed and lick Louise's pussy." He slathered some gooey lube on his sheathed dick. "You're to lick her until she comes, you understand me? No fingers, just lick her. Lick her while Daddy punishes you."

I understood. Louise was laying flat across the bed now and I knelt between her spread legs. I began licking her swollen pussy with gusto, centering on her tiny, erect clit.

But Daddy's idea of punishment was sublime. As I knelt between Louise's legs, my smarting red ass at the edge of the bed, my panties around my knees and my schoolgirl uniform shoved up around my waist, Daddy reamed my ass. He went at my hole aggressively, going in deep and pulling out slow, thoroughly opening the hole, giving me the fucking of my life.

It was my turn to moan into Louise's snatch while she writhed around on my tongue. She kept my face pressed close to her mound while my tongue licked furiously at her clit, wiggled it and swirled it. It didn't take much, really, to make her come. Daddy was grunting, seriously riding my ass in the depths of his own orgasm when Louise came in my mouth. I came just moments after she did, feeling positively delirious.

But the downside of it all was that shortly after this little explosion of mutual climaxes, they paid me my fee and told me I was free to go, even though it was obvious that they were in no hurry to leave. That's when Mr Santos's idea of what our relationship consisted of became brutally clear to me. I was still just a hooker to him, just one that he had an unusual amount of fun with.

It had been a rude awakening for me, one that made me less inclined to arrange many trysts with him afterward. I never let on to him that Mrs Hamilton had once been my high school teacher, or that it had been an unnerving liaison for me in a number of ways. I kept my thoughts to myself and went through the motions of earning my five hundred bucks. Eventually, I stopped seeing him altogether.

But yesterday, watching his casket disappear into the back of the hearse as I stood in the chill of the drizzling rain, I wished I'd spent just a little more time fucking him. I was going to miss that guy. I felt lucky I'd known him at all.

FOURTH DATE, FIRST FUCK

Dion Farquhar

BACK WHEN THEY were dating, before they were sure of each other, before they'd lived together for years and done just about every kind of fucking – positions, places, toys – and before they'd worried about money together, before they'd fought about who-should-have-done-what in the division-of-labor, back in their prehistory, there had been a first time.

Lying in bed alone and half awake, hand cupping her cunt, she enjoyed an orderly remembering of the extraordinary week that just ended. She was in love – again. Resilience has been her forte, and this time, like every other, she hoped she'd gotten it right and chosen a grown-up who could be a full-time partner and not just a weekend lover.

Things so often go slower these days, she thought, given AIDS and the age, not to mention their age. With an inadvertent smile, she tried to account for their not jumping into bed on the first or even the second date. Sex on the fourth date was something of a rarity in her experience as opposed to the more common variety – the slam-you-up-against-the-wall, I-could-fuck-you-right-here first date kind. With Josh, it was four dates before they got to bed. A week later, now that she was spending every night with him, it seemed both fast and slow. But what mattered, was that they got there at their own pace, and that was so right, she thought, feeling a ripple of desire course through her stomach.

Although an astute observer would have pointed to the awkwardness of their leave-takings, to the close timing of their dates,
to their eagerness to be together and laugh and talk until workers
shooed them out of closing cafés, and other indicators of mutual
desire, she had only known for sure that he was interested in sex
with her because of where he sat on his couch. The body always
gives it away. On their third date, the first time she had been in
his house, they had sat at opposite ends of his couch. They'd had
a great time, and laughed and talked until she said, sensing sex
was too much to take on that night, "Well, it's getting late, I'd
better get home."

But on the fourth date, they'd watched a video of the incredibly
sexy Carlos Saura film *Carmen*. During the awkward transition
from the video to who-knew-what's-next, she reached over to the
coffee table for the half-smoked joint and relit it. When he
returned to the couch after refilling their seltzers, she noticed
he was sitting much closer to her this time, only inches away from
her corner perch. Unable to stop herself from smiling at him, she
held out the joint to him, and her reached for it, his fingers
grazing hers, returning her smile. This was fun, she thought. He
inhaled deeply, and they looked at each other, smiles breaking out
across their faces.

Feeling more relaxed by the minute, she took her shoes off and
swung a cushion around for her back so she could sit perpendicular towards him. "That was quite a movie," she said, smiling.
"Yah, it's pretty intense," he replied. They smiled at each other,
allowing themselves to show their delight in each other's company and savor their effervescing desire.

Although quite relaxed from a combination of the grass and the
late hour, her head was racing. This was powerful stuff. As she
shifted her position on the couch slightly, she realized that she
was wet, a little surprised at the effect that the film and their
unacknowledged desire for each other was having on her. Her
body ahead of her, telling her she wanted him, even though the
movie was just plain hot. This was more than mood. Regarding
him, she remembered what good sex was like. Not having had any
in months since her breakup with a French Department –
Romance Studies they called it at his university – Don Juan
who needed his space when he wasn't telling her he'd never been
more up for it.

But here she was – falling-in-love-again – in California, a continent and three time zones away from home, on this new man's couch, turned on and happy.

She knew what she liked – both for herself and in her men. Hungry, sensitive, passionate. And she knew what she wanted. A man who wanted sex and intensity to go on. Not just the weekend/party model. She wanted a man who, like her, refused to trade off the domestic for passion. A future, a history. Now on their fourth date (ancient history, for Christ's sake), she sat on the same side of his couch but perpendicular to him as he sat in the middle, only inches away from her. But this time, she noted, he sat closer to her, in roughly the middle of the couch. This feels completely different, she thought. Better. In every way. Emboldened, she ventured to tuck her toes under the side of his butt. She watched his face register the contact. Instantly, with no hesitation, he gently reached one hand over to touch and then caress and squeeze her feet. She acknowledged his gesture by wriggling her toes, as she snuggled closer and less tentatively. His hand felt so good rubbing her feet. They were saying hello.

One thing led to another. Her eyes closed as she pressed against him, feeling how good their fit was. This is great, she thought. I can't believe it. What a good kisser he is, she mused, as they moved from the discrete footrub to kissing and rolling around the couch. Mouths and tongues eager for each other. A lot of kissing, touching, hugging. "Do you think we might be more comfortable on a bed?" she ventured after a while, feeling the limits of the couch's design. "Absolutely," he said, "let's go." Another awkward move, and then the digression of the bathroom stop, each waiting for the other on the bed, still dressed and not knowing what to do, how to wait. "Would a candle be good?" he asked her, standing in the bedroom doorway, an erection visible through his jeans. "Yah, very," she heard herself say, liking his attention to detail. This man had a life, a place, even a kitchen with food in it. While she was thinking about the ways in which Josh's attention to detail and self-sufficiency augured well, he came back in carrying a round blue candle on a plate. She watched him place it on the dresser across the room from the bed and light it. They both "ahhed" at the light it cast.

Then he joined her on the bed. They reached out to hold each other and reestablish their very recently found pleasure in their bodies together. They lay together, alternately hugging and kissing and watching the candle flicker, enjoying looking at each other in the candlelight. Although they would go on to fuck in every gradation of light and in no light, the light of one or two candles always remained one of their preferences, one associated with particularly luscious sex.

"You feel so good," she told him, backing away just enough to see his face. His eyes opened to meet hers and he looked at her with so much love and desire she thought she'd melt. "*You* feel so good," Josh told her. Thank you, Ilene, she thought, of their mutual friend who introduced them. A sentiment they would echo often over the next several years. Though neither knew it then. This was only their fourth date.

They began to hug and kiss and wrap themselves around each other again, only briefly derailed by the move to the bedroom. Then came the undressing. She wanted to feel him skin to skin, but her desire mixed with hesitation – evoking feelings of need and loss and mistrust. Noticing her deep inhalation that was almost a sigh, she had a stoned flash of literally taking a plunge, into his arms. First-time sex is like walking off a cliff, she thought. What was she waiting for? she thought, as she felt their tongues probing each other's mouths, relaxing into his body and into the feeling that their pressed-together groins generated. A source of heat and desire. First times are good to get over, she thought, as they pulled each other's tee shirts off. She liked what came after first times even better.

Their chests together made her dizzy with desire. She loved the feel of his chest and its hair and texture, especially the way it made her breasts feel. He moaned as she rubbed her breasts over his chest. "Oh, I love your beautiful breasts," he whispered, reaching up to take them in his hands, gently rubbing them in circles. They eventually moved on to unzipping each other's resistant jeans and coaxing them off hips and legs.

At last, they snuggled under the covers and luxuriated in the feel of flesh upon flesh, the contrast of hairy and hairless legs, and hard cocks and wet spots moving around each other. Smooth against rough. Hipbones and smells of sex. They took turns running a leg up and down the other's leg and butt. Rolling over and sliding along each other's body, exploring all that heat and cool, breasts and penis and cunt. Ear and breast sucking, nibbling, biting. Fingers inside her, around her. Sighs of "umm" into the night. Fingers inside him. Far inside. His writhing with pleasure. Moaning. And breaks for more seltzer refills to combat drymouth. They finally brought the two-liter bottle in from the kitchen.

At one point during their kissing and sucking and touching, she heard herself say, in a low voice, "I want to fuck you soon." "How about right now?" he replied, reaching down by the bed to get a condom. He extracted it from its package and began to put it on his erect cock. She leaned toward him and put her hand over his half-condomed cock to help him roll it on. Her hands stroking his sides. "Oh, God," he said, as she ran her hand over his cock. She climbed up on him, and slowly, very slowly lowered her cunt over his cock. She reached down and with her hand, she guided him in. First the tip, then a little further, then taking the entire long shaft inside her, she pressed her weight down over him. What a nice big hard cock, she thought. Not too big, but substantial, and just right. She couldn't believe how good he felt inside her.

She watched his head burrow back into the pillow, moaning with pleasure, at the same time that his hands gripped her hips, moving her slightly back and forth over him. After a while, she leaned down over him until her breasts touched and then pressed into his chest. He pulled her head over his and their tongues sought each other out, in and out and around their mouths. Their fucking went on until she couldn't tell whose cock and whose cunt was whose. At the same time, he seemed to grow even larger inside of her, or she grew tighter around him. The result was an intensification of feeling right there in that indistinguishable cunt-cock place. Oh God, she thought, this guy can fuck. This is wonderful. Their thrusts intensified and eventually he came in a paroxysm of feeling that echoed throughout her body with an intensity that both satisfied and stimulated her.

Good fucking. Hours of it. Urgent. Him above, across, around, her. A prepositional orgy.

She awoke with a start, unsure of where she was, what day it was, gripped with the fear that she'd missed an important appointment. As she fought to remember where she was, she surveyed the large pastel bedroom pooled around her double bed adrift on a buttery plush carpet. The peach and pumpkin and

beige duvets were not hers. Immediately, she remembered that
she was subletting a house near the university that hosted her
summer program. From a faculty member in Modern Languages.
The linen closet had post-ums labelling the sheets "double",
"queen". The holes in window screens are patched with small
rectangles of mesh. Must be a German teacher, she thought, the
house is too neat and clean for a French or Italian professor. They
all had two-car garages, that in reality were one-car garages
because of all the stuff people store in them. If you want to
get two cars in, you have to get a three-car garage. She, a carless
Manhattanite, pondered the diversity of national custom and life
style. California was fieldwork in anthropology for her.

Every summer, lucky grant recipients scattered from their
homes, fanning out across the country to major research institutions hosting seminars and institutes on a variety of scholarly
topics. A kind of Fresh Air Fund for junior faculty, the hordes of
unsung and underpublished wannabees, she thought, distancing
herself from her fellow participants. A jobless part-timer, she
thought, but at least I'm not stuck in Oklahoma or Tennessee.
She laughed, as she padded across the carpet lining the floor from
her bedroom in the summer rental all the way to the kitchen, at
such behavior patterns in adult humans. Twenty-five competi-
tively chosen participants (they'd had to write pages justifying
their interest and experience in the topic at hand, fill out forms,
garner letters of recommendation, enough to derange even a well-
ordered life) had left their homes and loved ones, if they had any,
and converged on this California university resort town for two
months of lectures and comraderie.

When she wasn't with her lover, during the first two weeks of
the seminar, she ate dinner, a sacred social ritual in her home city,
with strangers, she thought, as she put water up to boil on the
glacially slow surface of the electric range in the rented house.
Her new manicured suburban neighbourhood, nestled at the foot
of the university hills, was plunked down in what had been two
decades ago cattle grazing fields and bulb farms. The university,
looking more like a state park, was donated by a logging company.
Good move. Each term, more years of forest growth was consumed by the book orders of ambitious professors than the havoc
the multis could wreck in a decade.

After graduate school was military training. Each recruit stuck in his own isolated warren, alone with a series of confrontations of programmed obstacles, monsters, masters, hazards he must confront and survive. Only the all-seeing administration knows/sees the behavior of each recruit from its privileged altitude. By the time the recruit has survived his trials, he believes that he merits the condescending praise dished out by his superiors. He learns to copy the masters until one day, he finds not only that he can do it, but that mastery was a bit pumped up and overinvested to begin with.

The town had beach, seals, sunlight, redwoods, cliffs, sand, and surfers, but no city. No graffiti, no garbage, no crowds. Social homogeneity instead of diversity of people. Nature in the country. Culture in the city. Here the house and its boundaries and connections to the outside were manipulable, relational categories. The two pages of instructions on "Lawn and Garden" included reference to "blue hibiscus", "camellias", Japanese maple, bougainvillea, rhododendrons, large fuchsia. When she sat out in the back yard, the scent of the lemon tree ever present, the sound of printers sputtered like chain saws.

After the third day of the seminar, she knew there was no one there to fuck. Twenty men out of twenty-five people, and only one interested her. But he had a live-in girlfriend in tow, so she called her girlfriend in San Francisco, who wanted to introduce her to a man. "Tell me again about your friend, the man you want me to meet," she said, "there's no one here." "He's single, heterosexual, and interested in a lot of the same things you are, the same age, divorced," her friend said. "What's his phone number?" She called, they made a date, and here she was, a week and a half later.

Twenty-four hours after they'd gotten almost to sleep, she slept alone the next night. Now fully awake the next morning, she let the recent time with Josh flood her memory as she poured herself a cup of tea, watching the steam rise as she stirred her tea with a spoon. What she had particularly loved about sex with Josh was that it wasn't over when he had come. No more than, many times later, it was over when she had come first. After a pause, they always started in again until each had come enough. Although she didn't know it yet, one of the things that made their sex so good was that it gave him as much pleasure to make her come as it gave her to make him come. She looked beyond the patio doors to the flowering trees in the backyard, enjoying her recollection of that first night, a little more than a day ago.

His hand lightly tracing circles over her cunt brought her back. They lay together enjoying the feeling of having fucked their hearts out. She felt the cool of the wet spot on the sheets made by the mix of their fluids, and shifted her body a fraction to a drier spot. He moved with her, never breaking their contact. "You have to show me what you like," he said, running a finger gently over her cunt lips, then veering toward her clit. She shuddered with pleasure, sensing the arch of her neck thrown back, the muscles of his hips and thighs. Lying there having her clit stroked and rubbed evoked a flood of images. Multiple screens flashed images of femmes fatales, discus throwers poised and bent to throw. She became a high-heeled, bejeweled, slinky-dressed femme, and he a tango-leading, tall and black-booted stud.

He moved his leg over hers, feeling her tense against him. "There, like that," she managed. He touched her lightly at first, in teasing motions, making her move toward him, show him with the motion of her pelvis toward or away from his hand exactly what she wanted. "Harder," she said, and he continued, rhythmically and more firmly. She moved under his touch onto plateaus of more and more pure pleasure until she couldn't bear it any more, coming with an arch of her back and a moan that surprised her. "Oh, my God," she said, pressing herself onto his hand, still coming. "Oh, baby, come," he said, smiling over at her as she opened her eyes. "Oh, God, that was wonderful," she said, kissing him on the lips. "Next time, I'll bring my vibrator," she said. "Fine, I'd like to meet it," he said.

They lay together, quietly, kissing lightly, his hand cupping her cunt. What a beginning, she thought. I like him. Josh spooned her with his body, "Good night, baby," he said. "Good night, love." Unbeknownst to them, this was only the beginning.

LUST

Elfriede Jelinek

Translated by Michael Hulse

IN ALL SERIOUSNESS I call upon you: air and lust for one and all!

The woman will be with you in a moment, can you hold? First she has to collect herself: for a kiss it'd be best to be collected, all five senses, collect the set. The student is well developed, a perfect picture of a man, no need for touching up, so she lets him touch her up. He places his arm between her thighs. With his eye on the way ahead and the main chance, he rummages under her clothes, which consist chiefly of a plain dressing-gown, which won't be in the way for long. Many have to take terrible buses and regret it terribly when they remain on the wrong genitals for too long. The owner, or rather the passenger of his three-in-one wishes, grows too used to us and won't let us out of his ground-level hospitable apartment. Let me explain that three-in-one: woman is a trinity of pleasures, to be grabbed up top, down below, or in the middle! Till at length they can move on to various amiable kinds of sport, possessing each other without understanding. Bawling and bawling. The woman is eager for the driver to drive her around a little, step on it.

It can't simply be because the toilet's in the corridor that we feel impelled to go out at night and, in front of the door, look slyly around to see if anyone's watching as we stand there with our hands on our sex, as if we might be due to lose it before we can place it in its hand-painted chipboard box.

Of the many kinds of accommodation he might choose, the young man opts for this one alone. But the closet won't keep still, no, it's even hurrying off ahead in the dark and the cold! This Gerti beats him to the enclosure. Many a one has talked of kissing here. Spread their torchlight wide. And cast great shadows on the walls, so that for one other person they will be greater than just anyone, just anyone on a ski lift. As if sheer carnal desire could make them greater, bigger! As if they could draw themselves up so erect that they'd slam the ball straight in the basket! Players can be mighty fine specimens, tall and erect, and there they stand before their partners, fully equipped, with all the necessary tackle. So many requirements, all of them pressing, pressed into the service of hygiene and filth alike, simply to possess each other. As the phrase inaptly goes. This dusty junk shop's where we end up. Two household objects. Of simple geometrical design. Wanting to fit together and be good as new again! Now! Suddenly there's a woman in combinations in the corridor, a jug of water in her hand; has she been casting spells, calling forth a storm, or is she only going to make some tea? In no time at all a woman can make a home of the plainest, barest, most spartan of places. That is to say, even the plainest of women can make a man feel at home by baring all, in no time he places his spar. This young man who has entered her life might be the great intellectual? Now everything will be different from how it was planned. We'll make a new plan on the spot. Our heads will swell good and proper. Oh, your boy plays the violin as well? But not at this very moment, surely, since no one's punching his start button.

Come on, she yells to Michael. As if she were demanding money of a shopkeeper who hates us customers. And yet he can't get by without us. He has to tempt us into his store or go penniless. Now the woman wants a pleasure that lasts at last. First of all, one! two! (you can do it too, sitting in your car, your speed as limited as your mental horizons) we lunge at each other's mouths, then we plunge into all the other orifices; in thy orifices may I be remembered. And all of a sudden our partner means everything to us. Presently, in a minute or two, Michael will penetrate Gerti, whom he hardly knows and has barely taken a look at. Just as a sleeping car attendant always knocks first with a hard object. He lifts the woman's dressing-gown over her head and with his mouth, in an excitement of his own creation, prompts her who was without form and void to make a frightful commotion in the queue. The queue at the cash desk where we're all waiting, money clenched and balled behind our flies. We are our own worst enemies in matters of taste. People all like different things, isn't that so? But what if we want to be liked? What will we do, in our infinite indolence: call upon sex to do the work for us?

Michael yanks the woman's legs about him like the legs of high-tension masts. In his exploratory zeal he gives intermittent attention to her undouched cleft, a gnarled version of what every other woman has on her person in a discreet shade of lavender or lilac. He pulls back and takes a good look at the place where he is repeatedly disappearing, only to reappear, a huge great thing, fun for one and all. A funster, this fellow. But flawed. Sport being one of his flaws, and hardly the least. The woman is calling him. What's got into him? Why hasn't it got into her? Since Gerti didn't have an opportunity to wash, her hole looks murky, as if it were plastic-coated. Who can resist jamming a finger in (you can use peas, lentils, safety pins or marbles if you like), try it and see what an enthusiastic response you'll get from your lesser half. Woman's unyielding sex looks as if it were unplanned. And what is it used for? So that Man can tussle with Nature, and the children and grandchildren have somewhere to come trailing their clouds of glory from. Michael scrutinizes Gerti's complicated architecture and yells like a stuck pig. As if he were dissecting a corpse, he seizes her hairy cunt, stinking of secret dissatisfaction and dissatisfied secretions, and buries his face in it. You tell a horse's age by the teeth. This woman isn't so young any more either, but nonetheless this wrathful bird of prey is flapping at her door.

Michael laughs: he's terrific. Will we ever learn from these transactions? Will the one ever be able to cross the gap to the other, to talk and be understood and understand? Women's genitals, so outrageously located in a hillside, tend to be quite distinct, claims the expert. Just as no two people are entirely alike. They can wear quite different headgear, for instance. And the ladies are particularly prone to difference. No two of them are entirely alike. Not that a lover cares, when they lie prone: what he sees is what he's used to seeing on other women. In the mirror he sees himself reflected, his own deity. In the waters' depths. Fishing, plenty of fish in the sea, just hang out your dripping rod and wait for a catch, another woman to toss off your godhead in and then toss back. Ah, the privy parts and privy arts of mankind! All that's required of womankind is that she reck his rod (not wreck his rod), rock his godhead, toss his rocks off.

Let observation with extended view survey mankind . . . and what you'll see is the gaping gawp of somebody's integrated, semi-conducted craving for ecstasy. Go ahead. Try for something of real value! Feeling, perhaps, that guide who takes the tour party into terrain he's unfamiliar with, burgeoning through your skull? We don't have to watch him grow. We can choose another pupil to waken and give us pleasure. Yet the ingredients are stirred as we are. Our dough rises, puffed up with the sheer force of air, the atomic cloud mushrooming over the mountaintop. A door slams shut. And we're on our own again. Gerti's jolly husband, who is forever dangling his hose with a nonchalant air, as if his waters sprang from some precious source, isn't here right now to reach out his hand to his wife or torment his offspring on the rack of music. The woman laughs out loud at the thought. The young man is ramming his piston forcefully home, every stroke an attempt to get a little locomotion going, stoke her engine, can't you hear that whistle blow? He is taking a lively interest at present. Well aware of the changes even the least likely of women can undergo at the hands of a red-hot fresh and scented wad of male sex. Sex is the downtown of our lives, shopping precinct and leisure centre and red light district all in one, but it isn't where we live. We prefer a little elbow room, a bigger living room, with appliances we can turn on and off. Within her, this woman has already done an about-turn and is heading straight back for her own familiar allotment where she can pick the fruits of sensuality from her private plot herself and do the job with her own hands. Even alcohol becomes volatile at a certain point. But still, almost blubbing with joy at the changes he has wished upon himself, the young man is rummaging about the cosy taxi. He even looks under the seat. He opens Gerti, and then snaps her shut again. Nothing there!

Of course we can don hygienic caps if we like, to avoid the risk of disease. Otherwise, we have everything we need. And though the lordsandmasters cock their legs and slash their waters into their women, they can't remain but must hurry on, restless, to the next tree, where they waggle their genital worms till someone takes an interest. Pain flashes like lightning into women, but it does no permanent damage, no need to cry over charred furniture or molten appliances. And out it dribbles once again. Your partner will be willing to forgo anything but your feelings. After all, she likes to cook up feelings too. Poor people's food. I'd even say she's specialized in economy cooking, she's out to have men's hearts in a preserve jar at last. The poor prefer to turn away without being shoo'd about by tour guides. Their pricks even lay them down to rest before they do. And the source from which their waters spring is the heart. They leave the sheet unstained, and off we go.

At any rate, there are glasses that contain nothing of any greater sense than the wine. The Direktor likes looking into the glass: when it's raised to his lips he can see the bottom, and similarly he wants to drain his own immense tank, right into Gerti. The moment he sees her he exposes himself. His rain comes pouring from the cloudburst before she has a chance to run for shelter. His member is big and heavy and would fill the pan if you added his eggs. In the old days he used to invite many a woman to breakfast, they gobbled him up, slipped down a treat, but now he no longer calls in the hungry folk to eat at his table. Deformed by the opulence of leisure, humanity reclines in its deckchairs, resting its sex, or else strolls the gravel paths, sex in its pockets, hands in its pockets. Work restores humankind and all its attributes to the savage animal condition that was its original intended state. Thanks to one of Nature's whims, men's members are usually too small by the time they've got the knack of handling them. And there they go, leafing through the catalogues of exotic women, high-performance models that are more economical to run and need less fuel. The dipsticks plunge their dipsticks in the sump they know best, which happens to be their wives. Whom they wouldn't trust as far as they could throw them. So they stay home to keep a watch on them. Then their gaze pans across to the factory in the mist. Though, if they applied themselves a little more patiently, they could take a holiday as far afield as the Adriatic. Where they could dip their sticks in other waters. Their gangling danglers, carefully packed in their elasticated bathing trunks. Their wives wear sawn-off swimsuits. Their breasts are close friends, but they also like making new acquaintances, how do you do, a firm grip, perhaps too firm, uncouthly dragging them from the recliners where they were lounging, lazy and tender, tearing them out, crumpling them in careless fingers and tossing them into the nearest wastepaper basket.

There are signposts along the roads, pointing the way to the towns. Only this woman has to go messing about where children are trying to get their first bearings in life. Calm down and carry on! Hereabouts it is distinctly frosty and foresty. There's a smell of hay. Of straw. Strewn for us, for the animal within. The dog in the manger. How often we've taken the mangy creature walkies! How many before us – who would gladly have buried their wives if they could harvest a goodly crop of women from the place – have splashed and sprayed here! Like winning a motor race! Or like giving it all away: someone, for instance, has thrown a condom away before turning homeward once again. Most men have no idea what you can perform on that keyboard, the clitoris. But they've all read the magazines that prove there's more to women than anyone ever imagined. A millimetre or so more, to be exact.

The student crushes the woman to him. The hissing that escapes from his pent valve can be stopped by the merest touch, he can do it himself. He doesn't want to squirt off yet, nor does he want the wait to have been in vain. As she reclines there in his upholstered crate, he clumsily paws and pinches the most unseemly parts of the woman's anatomy, so that she has to spread her legs further apart. He rummages in her slumbering sex, squeezes it into a pout and smacks it abruptly apart again. Oughtn't he to excuse himself, given that he's treating her worse than the furniture? He slaps her derrière and heaves her onto her back once more.

He'll sleep well tonight, that's for sure, like anyone who's done an honest day's work and then taken his innocent rest and recreation.

His hands clawed tight in her hair, the student quickly fucks the woman shitless, it messes the car seats but what the fuck. As he services her, he does not look out at the world, where only the beautiful come in for care and maintenance, a major service every few thousand miles. He looks at her, trying to read something in that face which has been rendered indecipherable by her husband. Men are capable of detaching themselves from the world for as long as they want. Only to take a tighter grip on their own tour group afterwards. They have the option. Everyone who has any idea about men knows who we mean: that male world, a couple of thousand people involved in sport, politics, the economy, the arts. Where the rest come a cropper. And who will love them all, that crop of puffed-up flatulent bigmouths? What does the student see, beyond his own body's unctions and functions? The woman's mouth, a source from which streams well up, and the floor, from where her image laughs at him. They don't bother with any rubber protection. The man half turns away in order to watch his rigid member entering and exiting. The woman's socket gapes wide. The piggy bank squeaks, it's designed for paying in, only to pay everything promptly out again. Both transactions are of equal importance in this business, but you try telling that to any modern businessman, he'll raise his eyebrows in alarm, he'll raise the alarm, he'll lift his kids up so high so that they don't step in their inferiors' anger.

Gradually the spasms the man has set going in the woman calm and subside. She's had hers and perhaps she'll even get a second helping. Quiet! Now only the senses are doing the talking. But we don't understand what they're saying, because under the seat they've changed into something incomprehensible.

The student spills his packetful into the animals' cratch, fills his packet into the animal's snatch. Now it is deepest night. Clad in deepest black. Elsewhere, people are turning over, thinking of other more finely built specimens they've seen in magazines before they dock their bodies alongside for love. When Michael unbuckled his skis, he didn't pause to consider that sport, that eternal constant of our world, which hath its dwelling place in the TV set, doesn't simply stop when you've shot down your slope. The whole of life is sport. Sports dress enlivens our existence. All our relatives under the age of eighty wear tracksuits and T-shirts. Tomorrow's eggs are on sale today so you can count your chickens before they're hatched. There are others who are better-looking or cleverer than we are, for it is written. But what will become of those of whom no mention at all is made? And their inactive unattractive penises: where shall they channel their little rivers? Where is the bed for them to flow and lay their heads to rest? On this earth they are forever worrying about their wretched little organs, but where oh where shall they spray the antifreeze to afford protection in the winter to come, so their engines don't refuse to start? Will they negotiate union, or negotiate with a union? What ridges and ranges of perfumed flesh strew the path of dalliance, all the way till the stock feel the knife on the throat and the family feel the ramrod and lash? For those who are attractive, and who generally tend to be the most active too, are not mere décor in our lives. They want to plug their members into other people's sockets, and will do. Always bear in mind that, in their attempt to get what they want, people will hide away far inside each other, inseparable. So the atom doesn't split them.

Even before the minute hand of happiness can stroke the two of them, Michael has emitted a fluid, and that's it. But, in the woman, nuclear energy is powering her higher. These are the headwaters of which she has secretly dreamt for decades. Ah, the faithful old work-horse, pulling the man's body at the woman's whiplash behest! These forces are felt in even the tiniest remotest ramifications of the female. They spread like wildfire. The woman hugs the man tight as if he had become a part of her. She cries out. Presently, her head turned by what she feels, she'll be going on her way, dripping the seeds of discord in the petty principality of her household, and wherever the seed touches the earth mandrakes and other creatures will shoot up and grow, for her sake. This woman belongs to love. Now, for sure, she has to make certain she revisits this wonderful leisure centre. Again and again. Because this young man has hauled out his tool (now next to useless) and waved it about, see you again, Gerti suddenly sees his face with the pimple at the top right in a totally new and meaningful light. It is a face she'll have to see again, of course. Her future will depend on this go-getter's talent for gun-running, the secret arms trade hidden in his trousers. From now on, his one and only joy shall be to dwell inside Gerti. But here come the windy gusts. The breezy gusto. Bang on time. For holidays over the hills and far away are ruffling and dishevelling and tousling the desire of girls and women, so that they want a good hard regular brushing. In town, where you can go dancing in the cafés, the women on holiday congregate in deadened leaden droves. Ready to fall when night falls. Michael, who is interested in shooting off the lead in his pencil, will have to invest in rubber. And make his choice of the women dressed in their *après ski* best. All of them are natural beauties with natural tastes in natural sex, naturally, that's what he likes best. Make-up painted over pimples would blow him clean away.

Long before opening time, poor Gerti is sure to be at the telephone tomorrow, pestering it. This Michael, if the signals he's sending us and has himself received from various magazines can be relied on, is a blond creature off the cinema screen. Looking as if he'd been out in the sun for some time, with gel in his hair. Prompting us to finger our own sex, he's giving us the finger, he won't give us the finger for real. He is and always will be far away from us. Remote even when he's close. He enjoys nightlife. Keeping the night alive, lively. Not a man who cares for restraint. It's not easy to account for lightning, either: but in middle age we women are herded together in an enclosure of weekend assignations, and the bolt will strike one of us, that's for sure, before we have to leave.

Mind how you go. You may have something about your person that men like that would find a use for!

The animals are falling asleep, and desire has drawn Gerti out of herself, has struck a spark from her little pocket lighter, but where's this draught come from that's made the flame burn higher? From this heart-shaped peep-hole? From some other loving heart? In winter they go skiing, in summer they are the children of light, playing tennis or swimming or finding other reasons to undress, other smouldering fires to stamp out. When once a woman's senses are bespoke you can be sure she'll make other slips of the tongue. This woman hates her sex. Which once she was the finest flower of.

The simpler folk hidden away behind their front gardens will soon be silent. But the woman is crying out loud for her idol Michael, long promised her in photographs that look like him. He's just been for a fast drive in the Alps, now she roars and turns the vehicle of her body in every direction. It's a steep downhill stretch. But even as she lies there whining and pining the clever housewife is planning the next rendezvous with her hero, who will provide shade on hot days and warm her on cold. When will they be able to meet without the lugubrious shadow of Gerti's husband falling across them? You know how it is with the ladies: the immortal image of their pleasures means more to them than the mortal original, which sooner or later they will have to expose to life. To competition. When, fevering, chained to their bodies, they show up at a café in a new dress, to be seen in public with somebody new. They want to look at the picture of their loved one, that wonderful vision, in the peace and quiet of the marital bedroom, snuggled up side by side with the one who sometimes idly juggles his balls and pokes his poker in. Every one of these images is better accommodated in memory than life itself. On our own, we pick the memories from between our toes: how good it was to have properly unlocked oneself for once! Gerti can even bake herself anew and serve up her fresh rolls to the Man in the breadroom. And the children sing the praises of their Baker.

All of us earn the utmost we can carry.

The meadows are frozen entirely over. The senseless are beginning to think of going to bed, to lose themselves altogether. Gerti clings to Michael; let her climb every mountain, she still won't find another like him. In the school of life, this young man has often been a beacon of light to his fellows, who are already taking their bearings from his appearance and his nose, which can always sniff out the genuine article from among the column inches of untruth. Most of the houses hereabouts hang aslant the slope, the sheds and byres clinging on to the walls with the last of their strength. They have heard of love, true. But they never got round to the purchasing of property that goes with it. So now they're ashamed to be seen by their own TV screen. Where someone is just losing the memory game, the memory he wanted to leave with the viewers, the bill-and-cooers at home in their love-seats, hot-seats, forget-me-not-seats. Still, they have the power to preserve the image in their memories or reject it. Love it or shove it. Over the cliff. I can't figure it out: is this the trigger on the eye's rifle, this eyeful, is this the outrigger on the ship of courting senses, this sensitive courtship? Or am I completely wrong?

Michael and Gerti can't get enough of touching. Necking. Checking to see if they're still there. Clawing and pawing each other's genitalia, done up in festive regalia as if for a première. Gerti speaks of her feelings and how far she'd like to follow them. Michael gapes as he realizes what he's landed. Time to get out the rod and go fishing again. He hauls the woman round by the hair till she's flapping above him like a great bird. The woman, awoken from the sedation of sex, is about to use her gob for uninhibited talking, but while it's open Michael can think of better things to do with it and shoves his corncob in, amazing. The woman's dragged by the hair against Michael's firm belly, then skewered face-first on Michael's shish-kebab. This continues for a while. Scarcely conceivable, that thousands of other insensate beings are wallowing in their misery at this very moment, forced by a terrible God to be parted from their loved ones all week long, in his illuminated factory. I hope your fate can be loosened a notch or two, so you can fit more in!

These two want to wonder and wander and squander each other, they have plenty of themselves in store and all the latest catalogues of erotica at home. Just think of those who don't need the expensive extras, who hold each other dear without the sundries! Their special offers are themselves. They flood their banks and dykes, they won't be dammed or damned, they go with the flow of experience, the tide takes them where it will. Suddenly Gerti has an irresistible urge to piss, which she does, first hesitantly, then full force. The vapour fills the confined space. She wraps the dressing-gown about her thighs and it gets wet. Michael playfully cups his hands and catches some of the audible jet, laughing he washes his face and body, then thumps Gerti onto her back and chews at her dripping labia, sucking and wringing out the rags. Then he drags Gerti into her own puddle and splashes her in it. She rolls her eyes upward but there's no lightbulb up there, just the darkness inside her grinning skull. This is a feast. We're on our own, talking to our sex: our dearest of guests, though one who is forever wanting the choicest titbits. The dressing-gown, which the woman has pulled back on again, is torn off her once more, and she beds down deep in the hay. On the floorboards there's a wet patch. As if some superior being no one saw coming had made it. The only light is moonlight. Illuminating the present. Expecting a present in return.

The pallid bags of her breasts sag on her ribcage. Only one man and one child have ever made use of them. The Man back home ever bakes his impetuous daily bread anew. If your breasts hang right down on the table at dinner you can get an operation. They were made for the child and for the Man and for the child in the Man. Their owner is still writhing in her excreted fluid. Her bones and hinges are rattling with cold. Michael, racing down the slope, chomps at her privates and clutches and tugs at her dugs. Any moment now his God-given sap will rise in his stem, his cup will overflow. Hurry up, stuff that prick in its designated slot, no loitering. You can hear her shrieks, you can see the whites of her eyes, what are you waiting for?

The young man is suddenly alarmed at the totality with which he can spend himself without being spent. Again and again he reappears from within the woman, only to bury his little bird in the box again. He's now licked Gerti from top to toe. His tongue's still tart with the taste of her piss. Next her face. The woman snaps at him and bites. It hurts, but it's a language animals understand. He grabs her head, still by the hair, pulls it up off the floor and slams it back where he first found it. Gerti splays her mouth wide open and Michael's penis gives it a thorough go. Her eyes are shut. He jabs his knees in, forcing the woman to spread her thighs again. The novelty of this has worn off, unfortunately, since he did it the same way last time. So there you are, all skin and flick, and your desire is always the same old film! An endless chain of repetitions, less appealing every time because the electronic media and melodies have accustomed us to having something new home-delivered every day. Michael spreads Gerti wide as if he wanted to nail her to a cross and were not presently going to hang her in the wardrobe with the other clothes he rarely wears, which is what he'd actually intended. He stares at her cleft. This is familiar territory now. When she looks away, because she cannot bear his scrutiny and the groping, pinching hands that examine her, he hits her. He wants to see and do everything. He has a right to. There are details you can't see, and, in the event of there being a next time, a flashlight would come in handy. Before going in out of the night to the bodywork repairs shop. This woman had best learn to take the lordand-master's examination of her sex. And not hang her feelings on his peg. For thereby hangs a tale.

Hay cascades over her, warming her slightly. The master is finished. The woman's wound is throbbing and swollen. Retracting his instrument abruptly, Michael signals that he wants to retire to the tidy quarters of his own body. Already he has become a platform for this woman, from which she will speak on the subject of her longing and his long thing. Thus, without so much as being photographed in underwear and framed, one can become the centre-piece of a well-appointed room. This young man created the white and awe-inspiring mountains of flesh before him. Like the evening sun, he has touched that face with red. He has taken a lease on the woman, and as far as she's concerned he can now grope under her dress whenever he likes.

Gerti covers Michael with soft and downy kisses. Soon she will return to her house and her lord and master, who has qualities of his own. For we always wish to return to the place of our old wounds and tear open the gift wrapping in which we have disguised the old as the new, to conceal it. And our declining star teaches us nothing at all.

UNTITLED

Paul Mayersberg

GREG AWOKE TO the fact that he was going nowhere. He didn't think of himself as an imprecise man, but by his thirty-fifth birthday he was still without a defined career in the movies. He had had a long sequence of odd jobs: as a floor runner, assistant location manager, unit driver. He had no flat to call his own. He stayed with friends, rented when he could afford it, house sat, squatted.

His relationship with women had proved equally short-lived and imprecise. Greg had not found what he wanted in a woman. When he examined the long sequence of girls he had had he could not find a common denominator. Not in age or appearance or lifestyle. With women, like work, he took what he could get. Nothing lasted. There was no pattern to any of it. Sexually he was without direction.

Greg was naturally an optimistic man but now he gave in to depression. He found himself in a flat without a television and where the phone had been cut off. His dole cheque had stopped since he had been out of work for six months. For cash work, he went from door to door in good neighborhoods, knocking on doors, offering to wash cars parked in the street. His only evening solace was masturbation.

Looking for stimulation he rummaged through the two-room flat for books with sexy passages, old fashion magazines, women's clothes catalogues. Underwear, swimwear, skin beauty products. The place, left empty for the summer by an acquaintance of an acquaintance, had obviously been occupied by one or two women. Among the magazines, books, junk mail and bills Greg found a typed manuscript, a screenplay.

The front page read UNTITLED. There was no author's name but there was a date. The work was four years old. Greg started to read. It brought him back to his imagined career in films. "Untitled" was an erotic story in the style popular a few years back.

Two working girls, sharing a flat with one bedroom, took it in turns to bring their boyfriends home for the night. One night, one of the boyfriends came out of the bedroom at three in the morning and climbed into the sofa bed in the sitting room to set about seducing the other girl, while her friend was asleep.

To begin with it looked like a story of betrayal, but then it turned out that the girls had pre-arranged it. They had embarked on a programme of sharing their men. But without telling them. The next day the girls compared notes on the sexual performance of the boyfriends.

Greg read the script right through at a sitting. It was clear to him that one or other or both the girls had written it as an account of their own experience in this flat. The sofa he was now sitting on as he read it was the sofa-bed referred to on page 18 where Rick first put his hand inside Annie's pajama top. Annie had protested to begin with but not too vehemently. She enjoyed his attentions. She let him take off her pajama trousers. She allowed him to touch and kiss any part of her. But wouldn't let him enter her. That, she told him, would be too much. After all, he was Kate's boyfriend and Kate was her friend.

Reading this, Greg found himself sharing Rick's frustration. He put the script aside and relieved himself of the tension.

On page 27, four days later in the story, Annie allowed Rick to come between her breasts. On page 29 Kate laughed when Annie told her at breakfast, after Rick had gone, how she insisted that he lick the sperm from her skin. Otherwise, she said, she would never let him touch her again. Rick had not enjoyed the experience. It made him feel sick. Greg was with Rick on this. It made him feel queasy.

On page 31 Kate encouraged Rick to come in her mouth.

Which he did. Then she kissed him open-mouthed and pushed his come back into his own mouth. She asked him to swallow it. After all, she had on several occasions. Greg's throat contracted. He felt himself gag.

Greg's sex life, his lovemaking, had been very conventional. He had read of these games but had never played them himself. The effect of reading and re-reading "Untitled" was to make him recognize that he had been as imprecise about his sexual life as he had been about his film career. In both he had taken more or less what was on offer. He had not sought more. Like Rick, he had a low expectancy of himself. Perhaps low self-esteem was the reason for his non-career.

Greg read the script countless times. He came to know it by heart. He never for one moment considered whether it was good or bad as art or craft. It was enough that it stimulated him. He lived the scenes from "Untitled" in the flat where they happened. He lay in the bed where Annie's boyfriend, Alec, had covered his full condom with KY jelly and entered her anus. Greg had never found a girl who wanted him to attempt this. But so real was the scene to him that he bought some KY jelly with his food money in order to re-create the event exactly. It did not seem strange to him, masturbating inside a condom, when he could have done it without, without the expense of buying the thing. The point was, for those few minutes he, Greg, became Alec.

For three weeks Greg's fantasies did not depart from the script as written. He muttered the dialogue as he re-created the scenes. It wasn't masturbation as he had known it. He was shooting and re-shooting the script. One time he was Alec. Another, he was Rick.

Then, whether out of boredom through repetition, or through a half-conscious desire to go further, he transferred his sensuality to the girls, to what they were feeling. Until now Kate and Annie had been undefined, unspecific girls. He had imagined their limbs, their breasts, their movements, but not their faces. The script itself had not been specific about their appearance. They were in their twenties. They had hair. They did things. They talked. But it was all very general.

For the first time, it dawned on Greg that "Untitled" was not a very good screenplay. It needed crafting if he were to continue getting satisfaction from the material. He would have to re-write it, at least in his head. He sharpened his mental pencil.

What did the girls look like? He made Kate a blonde with short hair, like an old girlfriend whose name he couldn't remember. He made Annie dark with long hair. She was based on a fashion picture from *Marie-Claire* in the bathroom. He gave them blue eyes and dark eyes respectively. Their breasts posed questions. If he made Kate blonde she ought to have full breasts with large pale pink nipples. Oughtn't she?

And Annie, as a brunette, should have small tits with small dark nipples. It seemed right. Didn't it? He designed her narrow hips with pronounced jutting bones. He could hold on to them. The pubic hair posed a problem. The familiar dark bush, or something more interesting? What about long straight strands? He could comb and part the hair. It could be something of a game, if not a ritual. Then, while he was doing that she could be painting her toenails. It would make a nice complexity of angled limbs, her hands and his hands, all reaching forward. Greg was no more a painter than a writer. But his erotic impulses moved him in the direction of art.

Kate came out quite lush-looking. Five or seven pounds overweight. So pale was her skin he could see the tracery of veins in her heavy breasts. Her pubic hair would be curly blonde, glistening, so her slit was quite clearly visible. A great contrast with Annie. Now he had the basis of conflict within himself. He might have to choose between them one day.

Greg was less clear about their faces. He kept changing his mind with regard to their mouths. When they spoke it was with the same husky voice. He discovered, to his surprise, that the voice was more important than the flesh. He started to give the girls things to say. Dialogue came into the equation. He was no writer so they talked, not just with the same voice, but like him. His thoughts, their voice, one mouth. Greg was alone in the flat. His expression was a monologue. But that too became repetitious, unsatisfactory. He needed conversation, guidance, surprise. Greg couldn't surprise himself. He became bored and went back to simple voyeurism.

He would watch Annie and Kate, dressing, undressing, alone, together, in bed, in the bath. It worked well for a time. He was back on track, keeping within his limitations. Then, without his wishing it, the boyfriends appeared.

Rick's presence in the flat irritated Greg. The man was in the way. How could he play with Kate in the bathroom with Rick there? What should Rick do? Stay in the sitting room reading a magazine? Of course not. He'd come into the bathroom to see what was going on. He'd get angry at Greg screwing his girl-friend. Then in another scene Rick sat on the lavatory watching them together. That didn't appeal to Greg one bit. It inhibited him. Rick wanted to join in. A threesome. Greg wasn't up for that, having Rick fuck Kate from behind while he was getting a blow job. No. Rick had to go.

Greg decided to write him out. What were the options? Rick could be called away on business. Or he could meet with an accident. But who *was* Rick? While Greg had spent days working on the appearance of the girls, Rick and Alec were faceless guys without lives of their own, or jobs. Rick became a salesman. Greg hated salesmen.

So Rick was called away to another town. Fine. Now Greg got on with his plan to take Kate and Annie to bed together. Now there was a threesome he felt comfortable with. To begin with he had the girls kneel facing each other. They moved close to each other so their nipples touched. They liked that. Then they kissed. Greg enjoyed that. But when he put his hands between them neither Kate nor Annie responded to him. They rolled over and got on with loving each other.

When Annie spread Kate's legs and put her tongue to Kate's vulva Greg's hard frustration turned to resentment. They were supposed to be there for him, not for each other. Greg was furious when Kate trembled to a climax. He pushed Annie aside and straddled Kate's thighs. He slipped in and out of her and came quickly. But it wasn't properly satisfying. He hadn't made her come.

Greg identified a difficulty here. In fact, it had been present all along. His characters were starting to behave the way *they* wanted. They were no longer under his control. Greg didn't realize that this was the beginning of what every author longs for, characters who develop a life of their own, outside the manip-ulation of their creator. In his ignorance he reined them back. He urged them to conform to his desire. Specifically Greg wanted Kate and Annie to come simultaneously under his hands.

Technically this proved impossible. He would need two penises to do the job properly. So he had to content himself with sucking Annie while penetrating Kate. While each girl appeared to climax within seconds of the other, Greg couldn't get rid of the thought that one, or both, was faking it just to please him. That writer's problem again. Manipulation might be formally satisfying at the time of writing, but there was a residue of doubt when you read the passage back the next day. It seemed forced. The frustration remained.

If the purpose of writing was to shape random events and disparate characters into a pattern, Greg was perplexed that describing sex, creating erotic scenes for his own pleasure, left him dissatisfied. Why wasn't there a proper climax in the words, the sentences, the paragraphs, as there was in the act of fucking? Why wasn't writing, where you were free to invent anything you wanted, why wasn't it orgasmic? It was exciting, yes, gave you a hard on, but it didn't make you come.

So what was it for? The untitled screenplay, however he rewrote it, in his head or in notes, had become an indictment of his solitary life. Its intention remained vague. Being alone had metamorphosed into loneliness. The trouble was, he couldn't think of a title for the damned screenplay. If only he could do that he'd be halfway to where he was going.

It was evening when Greg got back from washing cars. He switched on the light by the door and immediately sensed he was not alone in the flat. There was a faint smell, food or coffee, he wasn't sure. He ought to have been afraid, but he wasn't. He needed another human being. Curiosity and hope drew him to the kitchen.

Alec was there, naked, stirring himself a cup of instant coffee. Before he turned to Greg he said: "Is that you, Annie?"

"No, it fucking isn't," Greg replied.

"Come here."

What did he mean, come here? How could Alec mistake Greg for a girl? Was he crazy?

"Come and hold this." Alec lifted his cock in one hand. He really thought Greg was Annie. Enough.

A cheese-smeared bread knife on the green plastic-topped table invited Greg to pick it up. He advanced on Alec, gripping the knife. Alec's penis rose to meet it. Action. And later, the plunge, the nightmare.

Greg was still asleep when the phone rang. He jumped. Was he still dreaming? No, the phone was ringing beside the bed. Someone must have re-connected it. Nervously, he lifted the receiver. A woman's voice.

"Is Annie there?"

"Who?"

"That is 352 0251, isn't it?"

"I don't know." Greg looked down at the phone. There was no identifying number on it. Panic set in. "Who are you?"

"Who are *you*?" The woman's husky tone became impatient. Greg didn't answer. Should he hang up?

"Look, where's Annie?" Demanding now.

Annie? Should he tell the voice that Annie was in Greg's head? And in the pages of a screenplay.

"This is Kate. Whoever you are, I want to talk to Annie."

Kate! No. Impossible. Greg panicked and hung up. His hands were trembling.

Almost immediately the phone rang again. He left it. It rang a hundred times, it seemed. When it finally stopped Greg took the receiver off. But it was no solution. Greg felt unsafe. He put a pillow over the receiver to muffle the high-pitched buzz. But he couldn't suppress his mind. That dialogue. It had come by phone this time. Last time Alec had spoken in the kitchen. But Alec wasn't real!

Annie and Kate were *his* characters. They were real to him. Greg forgot they had been drawn from an untitled screenplay. He concluded that he must now be hallucinating. He hadn't heard or talked to anyone for days, weeks. Apart, of course, from himself. The phone had unnerved him. He left the pillow on it.

Greg had been in the bath for an hour. The water was tepid. He turned the hot tap on. Behind the splashing sound Greg heard another noise. A door closing. He turned off the flow and listened. Footsteps. He sat up. The water slipped over the side of the tub.

He stared at the woman in the doorway. It was Annie. *His* Annie. She was dressed in a raincoat, but her face . . . Annie.

Greg must have said the name out loud because she said, "Yes." Then: "Who are you?" She had the husky voice.

"Greg."

"Well, Greg, what the fuck are you doing in my bathroom?"

The mouth was perfect, an exact version of the mouth he had given her.

"I'm . . . staying here."

"No, you're not. Get out."

She waited. Greg couldn't tell whether she was angry or just insistent. Did she mean get out of the bath, or get out of the flat?

"Come on."

Annie reached down for the fallen bathrobe. She held it up. Greg was now more embarrassed than fearful. He eased himself up. Annie watched him. There was no point trying to cover himself. He climbed out of the bath. He slipped. Annie caught his arm. He felt stupid.

"When you're dressed you can tell me what you're doing here."

Greg pulled the robe round him. Annie left the bathroom. Greg started to dry himself. Keep calm, he told himself. There's nothing to be afraid of. He had imagined a woman and now she had come to life. Now he had a different role, always provided that he stayed on in the flat. Would there be room for him? Or would he go the way of Rick and Alec?

Annie came out of the bathroom and got into bed beside Kate. They yawned simultaneously and laughed together. Greg loved the way their breasts wobbled when they laughed. It was strange that he hadn't seen or heard Kate come back to the flat. She was just there. Ah well, he would sleep on the sofa. He had nowhere else to go.

"He's asleep."

"What are we going to do with him?"

"We'll have to give him a name."

"Who's going to talk to him?"

Kate took a coin and spun it.

"Tails," called Annie.

It was heads.

"That's appropriate," said Kate.

She went into the dark sitting room. Greg was asleep on the sofa wearing Annie's bathrobe. He snored faintly. Kate knelt down. She parted the robe without untying it. She smiled. Greg was semi-erect. The tip glistened.

"Halfway house," Kate whispered. "Unformed, but you've got the makings of an interesting character." She licked him with the tongue of a cat.

Greg awoke.

BEAUTY'S RELEASE

Anne Rice

1 Through the City and into the Palace

BEAUTY OPENED HER eyes. She had not been sleeping, and she knew without having to see through a window that it was morning. The air in the cabin was unusually warm.

An hour ago she had heard Tristan and Laurent whispering in the dark, and she had known the ship was at anchor. And she had been only slightly afraid.

After that, she had slipped in and out of thin erotic dreams, her body wakening all over like a landscape under the rising sun. She was impatient to be ashore, impatient to know the full extent of what was to happen to her, to be threatened in ways that she could understand.

Now, when she saw the lean, comely little attendants flooding into the room, she knew for certain that they had come to the Sultanate. All would be realized soon enough.

The precious little boys – they could be no more than fourteen or fifteen, despite their height – had always been richly dressed, but this morning they wore embroidered silk robes, and their tight waist sashes were made of rich striped cloth, and their black hair gleamed with oil, and their innocent faces were dark with an unusual air of anxiety.

At once, the other royal captives were roused, and each

slave was taken from the cage and led to the proper grooming table.

Beauty stretched herself out on the silk, enjoying her sudden freedom from confinement, the muscles in her legs tingling. She glanced at Tristan and then at Laurent. Tristan was suffering too much still. Laurent, as always, looked faintly amused. But there was not even time now to say farewell. She prayed they would not be separated, that whatever happened they would come to know it together, and that somehow their new captivity would yield moments when they might be able to talk.

At once the attendants rubbed the gold pigmented oil into Beauty's skin, strong fingers working it well into her thighs and buttocks. Her long hair was lifted and brushed with gold dust, and then she was turned on her back gently.

Skilled fingers opened her mouth. Her teeth were polished with a soft cloth. Waxen gold was applied to her lips. And then gold paint was brushed onto her eyelashes and eyebrows.

Not since the first day of the journey had she or any of the slaves been so thoroughly decorated. And her body steamed with familiar sensations.

She thought hazily of her divinely crude Captain of the Guard, of the elegant but distantly remembered tormentors of the Queen's Court, and she felt desperate to belong to someone again, to be punished for someone, to be possessed as well as chastised.

It was worth any humiliation, that, to be possessed by another. In retrospect, it seemed she had only been a flower in a full bloom when she was thoroughly violated by the will of another, that in suffering for the will of another she had discovered her true self.

But she had a new and slowly deepening dream, one that had begun to flame in her mind during the time at sea, and that she had confided only to Laurent: the dream that she might somehow find in this strange land what she had not found before; someone whom she might truly love.

In the village, she told Tristan that she did not want this, that it was harshness and severity alone she craved. But the truth was that Tristan's love for his Master had deeply affected her. His words had swayed her, even as she had spoken her contradictions.

And then had come these lonely nights at sea of unfulfilled yearning, of pondering too much all the twists of fate and fortune.

And she had felt strangely fragile thinking of love, of giving her secret soul to a Master or Mistress, more than ever off balance.

The groom combed gold paint into her pubic hair, tugging each curl to make it spring. Beauty could hardly keep her hips still. Then she saw a handful of fine pearls held out for her inspection. And into her pubic hair these went, to be affixed to the skin with powerful adhesive. Such lovely decorations. She smiled.

She closed her eyes for a second, her sex aching in its emptiness. Then she glanced at Laurent to see that his face had taken on an Oriental cast with the gold paint, his nipples beautifully erect like his thick cock. And his body was being ornamented, as befitted its size and power, with rather large emeralds instead of pearls.

Laurent was smiling at the little boy who did the work, as if in his mind he was peeling away the boy's fancy clothes. But then he turned to Beauty, and, lifting his hand languidly to his lips, he blew her a little kiss, unnoticed by the others.

He winked and Beauty felt the desire in her burning hotter. He was so beautiful, Laurent.

"O, please don't let us be separated," she prayed. Not because she ever thought she would possess Laurent – that would be too interesting – but because she would be lost without the others, lost . . .

And then it hit her with full force: she had no idea what would happen to her in the Sultanate, and absolutely no control over it. Going into the village, she had known. She had been told. Even coming into the castle, she had known. The Crown Prince had prepared her. But this was beyond her imagining, this place. And beneath her concealing gold paint she grew pale.

The grooms were gesturing for their charges to rise. There were the usual exaggerated and urgent signs for them to be silent, still, obedient, as they stood in a circle facing each other.

And Beauty felt her hands lifted and clasped behind her back as if she were a senseless little being who could not even do that much herself. Her groom touched the back of her neck and then kissed her cheek softly as she compliantly bowed her head.

Still, she could see the others clearly. Tristan's genitals had also been decorated with pearls, and he gleamed from head to toe, his blond locks even more golden than his burnished skin.

And, glancing at Dmitri and Rosalynd, she saw that they had both been decorated with red rubies. Their black hair was in magnificent contrast to their polished skin. Rosalynd's enormous blue eyes looked drowsy under their fringe of painted lashes. Dmitri's broad chest was tightened like that of a statue, though his strongly muscled thighs quivered uncontrollably.

Beauty suddenly winced as her groom added a bit more gold paint to each of her nipples. She couldn't take her eyes off his small brown fingers, enthralled by the care with which he worked, and the way that her nipples hardened unbearably. She could feel each of the pearls clinging to her skin. Every hour of starvation at sea sharpened her silent craving.

But the captives had another little treat in store for them. She watched furtively, her head still bowed, as the grooms drew out of their deep, hidden pockets new and frightening little toys – pairs of gold clamps with long chains of delicate but sturdy links attached to them.

The clamps Beauty knew and dreaded, of course. But the chains – they really agitated her. They were like leashes and they had small leather handles.

Her groom touched her lips for quiet and then quickly stroked her right nipple, gathering a nice pinch of breast into the small gold scallop-shell clamp before he snapped it shut. The clamp was lined with a bit of white fur, yet the pressure was firm. And all of Beauty's skin seemed to feel the sudden nagging torment. When the other clamp was just as tightly in place, the groom gathered the handles of the long chains in his hands and gave them a tug. This was what Beauty had feared most. She was brought forward sharply, gasping.

At once the groom scowled, quite displeased with the open-mouthed sound, and spanked her lips with his fingers firmly. She bowed her head lower, marveling at these two flimsy little chains, at their hold upon these unaccountably tender parts of her. They seemed to control her utterly.

She watched with her heart contracting, as the groom's hand tightened again and the chains were jerked, and she was pulled forward once more by her nipples. She moaned this time but she did not dare to open her lips, and for this she received his approving kiss, the desire surging painfully inside her.

"O, but we cannot be led ashore like this," she thought. She could see Laurent, opposite, clamped the same as she was, and blushing furiously as his groom tugged the hated little chains and made him step forward. Laurent looked more helpless than he had in the village on the Punishment Cross.

For a moment, all the delightful crudity of village punishments came back to her. And she felt more keenly this delicate restraint, the new quality of servitude.

She saw Laurent's little groom kiss his cheek approvingly. Laurent had not gasped or cried out. But Laurent's cock was bobbing uncontrollably. Tristan was in the same transparently miserable state, yet he looked, as ever, quietly majestic.

Beauty's nipples throbbed as if they were being whipped. The desire cascaded through her limbs, made her dance just a little without moving her feet, her head suddenly light with dreams of new and particular love again.

But the business of the grooms distracted her. They were taking down from the walls their long, stiff leather thongs; and these, like all other objects in this realm, were heavily studded with jewels, which made them heavy instruments of punishment, though, like strips of sapling wood, they were quite flexible.

She felt the light sting on the back of her calves, and the little double leash was pulled. She must move up behind Tristan, who had been turned towards the door. The others were probably lined up behind her.

And quite suddenly, for the first time in a fortnight, they were to leave the hold of the ship. The doors were opened, Tristan's groom leading him up the stairs, the thong playing on Tristan's calves to make him march, and the sunlight pouring down from the deck was momentarily blinding. There came with it a great deal of noise – the sound of crowds, of distant shouts, of untold numbers of people.

Beauty hurried up the wooden stairs, the wood warm under her feet, the tugging of her nipples making her moan again. What precious genius, it seemed, to be led so easily by such refined instruments. How well these creatures understood their captives.

She could scarcely bear the sight of Tristan's tight, strong buttocks in front of her. It seemed she heard Laurent moan behind. She felt afraid for Elena and Dmitri and Rosalynd.

But she had emerged on the deck and could see on either side the crowd of men in their long robes and turbans. And beyond the open sky, and high mud-brick buildings of a city. They were in the middle of a busy port, in fact, and everywhere to right and left were the masts of other ships. The noise, like the light itself, was numbing.

"O, not to be led ashore like this," she thought again. But she was rushed behind Tristan across the deck and down an easy, sloping gangplank. The salt air of the sea was suddenly clouded with heat and dust, the smell of animals and dung and hemp rope, and the sand of the desert.

The sand, in fact, covered the stones upon which she suddenly found herself standing. And she could not help but raise her head to see the great crowds being held back by turbaned men from the ship, hundreds and hundreds of dark faces scrutinizing her and the other captives. There were camels and donkeys piled high with wares, men of all ages in linen robes, most with their heads either turbaned or veiled in longer, flowing desert headdresses.

For a moment Beauty's courage failed her utterly. It was not the Queen's village, this. No, it was something far more real, even as it was foreign.

And yet her soul expanded as the little clamps were tugged again, as she saw gaudily dressed men appear in groups of four, each group bearing on its shoulders the long gilded rods of an open, cushioned litter.

Immediately, one of these cushions was lowered before her. And her nipples were pulled again by the mean little leashes as the thong snapped at her knees. She understood. She knelt down on the cushion, its rich red and gold design dazzling her slightly. And she felt herself pushed back on her heels, her legs opened wide, her head bowed again by a warm hand placed firmly on her neck.

"This is unbearable," she thought, moaning as softly as she could, "that we will be carried through the city itself. Why were we not taken secretly to His Highness the Sultan? Are we not royal slaves?"

But she knew the answer. She saw it in the dark faces that pressed in on all sides.

"We are only slaves here. No royalty accompanies us now. We are merely expensive and fine, like the other merchandise brought from the hold of the ships. How could the Queen let this happen to us?"

But her fragile sense of outrage was at once dissolved as if in the heat of her own naked flesh. Her groom pushed her knees even wider apart, and spread her buttocks upon her heels as she struggled to remain utterly pliant.

"Yes," she thought, her heart palpitating, her skin breathing in the awe of the crowd, "a very good position. They can see my sex. They can see every secret part of me." Yet she struggled with another little flair of alarm. And the gold leashes were quickly wound around a golden hook at the front of the cushion, which made them quite taut, holding her nipples in a state of bittersweet tension.

Her heart beat too fast. Her little groom further frightened her with all his desperate gestures that she be silent, that she be good. He was being fussy as he touched her arms. No, she must not move them. She knew that. Had she ever tried so hard to remain motionless? When her sex convulsed like a mouth gasping for air, could the crowd see it?

The litter was lifted carefully to the shoulders of the turbaned bearers. She grew almost dizzy with an awareness of her exposure. But it comforted her just a little to see Tristan kneeling on his cushion just ahead, to be reminded that she was not alone here.

The noisy crowd made way. The little procession moved through the huge open place that spread out from the harbor.

Overcome with a sense of decorum, she dared not move a muscle. Yet she could see all around her the great bazaar – merchants with their bright ceramic wares spread out upon multicolored rugs; rolls of silk and linen in stacks; leather goods and brass goods and ornaments of silver and gold; cages of fluttering, clucking birds; and food cooking in smoking pots under dusty canopies.

Yet the whole market had turned its chattering attention to the captives who were being carried past. Some stood mute beside their camels, just staring. And some – the young bareheaded boys, it seemed – ran along beside Beauty, glancing up at her and pointing and talking rapidly.

Her groom was at her left, and with his long leather thong he made some small adjustment of her long hair, and now and then fiercely admonished the crowd, driving it backwards.

Beauty tried not to see anything but the high mudbrick buildings coming closer and closer.

She was being carried up an incline, but her bearers held the litter level. And she struggled to keep her perfect form, though her chest heaved and pulled at the mean little clamps, the long gold chains that held her nipples shivering in the sunlight.

They were in a steep street, and on either side of her windows opened, people pointed and stared, and the crowd streamed along the walls, their cries growing suddenly louder as they echoed off the stones. The grooms drove them back with even stricter commands.

"Ah, what do they feel as they look at us?" Beauty thought. Her naked sex pulsed between her legs. It seemed to feel itself so disgracefully opened. "We are as beasts, are we not? And these wretched people do not for a moment imagine that such a fate could befall them, poor as they might be. They wish only that they might possess us."

The gold paint tightened on her skin, tightened particularly on her clamped nipples.

And try as she might, she could not keep her hips entirely still. Her sex seemed to churn with desire and move her entire body with it. The glances of the crowd touched her, teased her, made her ache in her emptiness.

But they had come to the end of the street. The crowd streamed out into an open place where thousands more stood watching. The noise of voices came in waves. Beauty could not even see the end of this crowd, as hundreds jostled to get a closer look at the procession. She felt her heart pound even harder as she saw the great golden domes of a palace rising before her.

The sun blinded her. It flashed on white marble walls, Moorish arches, giant doors covered in gold leaf, soaring towers so delicate that they made the dark, crude, stone castles of Europe seem somehow clumsy and vulgar.

The procession turned to the left sharply. And, for an instant, Beauty glimpsed Laurent behind her, then Elena, her long brown hair swaying in the breeze, and the dark, motionless figures of Dmitri and Rosalynd. All obedient, all still upon their cushioned litters.

The young boys in the crowd seemed to be more frenzied. They cheered and ran up and down, as though the proximity of the palace somehow heightened their excitement.

Beauty saw that the procession had come to a side entrance, and turbaned guards with great scimitars hanging from their girdles drove the crowd back as a pair of heavy doors were opened.

"O, blessed silence," Beauty thought. She saw Tristan carried beneath the arch, and immediately she followed.

They had not entered a courtyard as she had expected. Rather they were in a large corridor, its walls covered in intricate mosaics. Even the ceiling above was a stone tapestry of flowers and spirals. The bearers suddenly came to a halt. The doors far behind were closed. And they were all plunged into shadow.

Only now did Beauty see the torches on the walls, the lamps in their little niches. A huge crowd of young dark-faced boys, dressed exactly like the grooms from the ship, surveyed the new slaves silently.

Beauty's cushion was lowered. At once, her groom clasped the leashes and pulled her forward onto her knees on the marble. The bearers and the cushions quickly disappeared through doors that Beauty hardly glimpsed. And she was pushed down onto her hands, her groom's foot firm on the back of her neck as he forced her forehead right to the marble flooring.

Beauty shivered. She sensed a different manner in her groom. And, as the foot pressed harder, almost angrily, against her neck, she quickly kissed the cold floor, overcome with misery that she couldn't know what was wanted.

But this seemed to appease the little boy. She felt his approving pat on her buttocks.

Now her head was lifted. And she saw that Tristan was kneeling on all fours in front of her, the sight of his well-shaped backside further teasing her.

But as she watched in stunned silence, the little gold-link chains from her clamped nipples were passed through Tristan's legs and under his belly.

"Why?" she wondered, even as the clamps pinched her with renewed tightness.

But immediately she was to know the answer. She felt a pair of chains being passed between her own thighs, teasing her lips. And now a firm hand clasped her chin and opened her mouth, and the leather handles were fed to her like a bit that she must hold in her teeth with the usual firmness.

She realized this was Laurent's leash, and she was now to pull him along by the damnable little chains just as she herself was to be pulled by Tristan. And if her head moved in the slightest involuntary way, she would add to Laurent's torment just as Tristan added to hers as he pulled the chains given him.

But it was the spectacle of it that truly shamed her.

"We are tethered to one another like little animals led to market," she thought. And she was further confused by the chains stroking her thighs and the outside of her pubic lips, by their grazing her taught belly.

"You little fiends!" she thought, glancing at the silk robes of her groom. He was fussing with her hair, forcing her back into a more convex position so that her rear was higher. She felt the teeth of a comb stroking the delicate hair around her anus, and her face flooded with a hot stinging blush.

And Tristan, did he have to move his head, making her nipples throb so?

She heard one of the grooms clap his hands. The leather thong came down to lick at Tristan's calves and the soles of his naked feet. He started forward, and she immediately hurried after him.

When she raised her head just a little to see the walls and ceiling, the thong smacked the back of her neck. Then it whipped the undersides of her feet just as Tristan's were being whipped. The leashes pulled at her nipples as if they had life of their own.

And yet the thongs smacked faster and louder, urging all the slaves to hurry. A slipper pushed at her buttocks. Yes, they must run. And, as Tristan picked up speed, so did she, remembering in a daze how she had once run upon the Queen's Bridle Path.

"Yes, hurry," she thought. "And keep your head properly lowered. And how could you think you would enter the Sultan's Palace in any other manner?"

The crowds outside might gape at the slaves, as they probably did at the most debased of prisoners. But this was the only proper position for sex slaves in such a magnificent palace.

With every inch of floor she covered, she felt more abject, her chest growing warm as she ran out of breath, her heart, as ever, beating too fast, too loudly.

The hall seemed to grow wider, higher. The drove of grooms flanked them. Yet still she could see arched doorways to the left and right and cavernous rooms tiled in the same beautifully colored marbles.

The grandeur and the solidity of the place worked their inevitable influence upon her. Tears stung her eyes. She felt small, utterly insignificant.

And yet there was something absolutely marvelous in the feeling. She was but a little thing in this vast world yet she seemed to have her proper place, more surely than she had had in the castle or even in the village.

Her nipples throbbed steadily in the fur-lined grip of the clamps, and occasional flashes of sunlight distracted her.

She felt a tightness in her throat, an overall weakness. The smell of incense, of cedar wood, of Eastern perfumes, suddenly enveloped her. And she realized that all was quiet in this world of richness and splendor; and the only sound was that of the slaves scurrying along and the thongs that licked them. Even the grooms made no sound, unless the singing of their silk robes was a sound. The silence seemed an extension of the palace, an extension of the dramatic power that was devouring them.

But as they progressed deeper and deeper into the labyrinth, as the escort of grooms dropped back a bit, leaving only the one little tormentor with his busy thong, and the procession went round corners and down even wider halls, Beauty began to see out of the corner of her eye some strange species of sculpture set in niches to adorn the corridor.

And, suddenly, she realized that these were not statues. They were living slaves fitted into the niches.

At last, she had to take a good look, and struggling not to lose her pace, she stared from right to left at these poor creatures.

Yes, men and women in alternation on both sides of the hall, standing mute in the niches. And each figure had been wrapped tightly from neck to toe in gold-tinted linen, except for the head held upright by a high ornamented brace and the naked organs left exposed in gilded glory.

Beauty looked down, trying to catch her breath. But she couldn't help looking up again immediately. And the spectacle became even clearer. The men had been bound with legs together, genitals thrust forward, and the women had been bound with legs apart, each leg completely wrapped and the sex left open.

All stood motionless, their long, shapely, gold neck braces fixed to the wall in back by a rod that appeared to hold them securely. And some appeared to sleep with eyes closed, while others peered down at the floor, despite their slightly lifted faces.

Many were dark-skinned, as the grooms were – and showed the luxuriant black eyelashes of the desert peoples. Almost none were as Tristan and Beauty were. All had been gilded.

And in a silent panic, Beauty remembered the words of the Queen's emissary, who had spoken to them on the ship before they left their sovereign's land: "Though the Sultan has many slaves from his own land, you captive Princes and Princesses are a special delicacy of sorts, and a great curiosity."

"Then surely we can't be bound and placed in niches such as these," Beauty thought, "lost among dozens and dozens of others, merely to decorate a corridor."

But she could see the real truth. This Sultan possessed such a vast number of slaves that absolutely anything might befall Beauty and her fellow captives.

As she hurried along, her knees and hands getting a little sore from the marble, she continued to study these figures.

She could make out that the arms had been folded behind the back of each one, and that the gilded nipples too were exposed and sometimes clamped, and that each figure had his or her hair combed back to expose the ears which wore jeweled ornaments.

How tender the ears looked, how much like organs!

A wave of terror passed over Beauty. And she shuddered to think of what Tristan was feeling – Tristan, who so needed to love one Master. And what about Laurent? How would this look to him after the singular spectacle of the village Punishment Cross?

There came the sharp pull of the chains again. Her nipples itched. And the thong suddenly dallied between her legs, stroking her anus and the lips of her vagina.

"You little devil," she thought. Yet as the warm tingling sensations passed all through her, she arched her back, forcing her buttocks up, and crawled with even more sprightly movements.

They were coming to a pair of doors. And with a shock, she saw that a male slave was fixed to one door and a female slave to the other. And these two were not wrapped, but rather completely naked. Gold bands around the foreheads, the legs, waist, neck, ankles, and wrists held each flat to the door with knees wide apart, the soles of the feet pressed together. The arms were fixed straight up over the head, palms outward. And the faces were still, eyes cast down, and the mouths held artfully arranged bunches of grapes and leaves that were gilded like the flesh so that the creatures looked very much like sculptures.

But the doors were opened. The slaves passed these two silent sentinels in a flash.

And the pace slowed as Beauty found herself in an immense courtyard, full of potted palm trees and flower beds bordered in variegated marble.

Sunlight dappled the tiles in front of her. The perfume of flowers suddenly refreshed her. She glimpsed blossoms of all hues, and for one paralyzing instant she saw that the vast garden was filled with gilded and caged slaves as well as other beautiful creatures fixed in dramatic positions atop marble pedestals.

Beauty was made to stop. The leashes were taken from her mouth. And she saw her groom gather up her own leashes as he stood beside her. The thong played between her thighs, tickling her, forcing her legs a little apart. Then a hand smoothed her hair tenderly. She saw Tristan to her left and Laurent to her right, and she realized that the slaves had been positioned in a loose circle.

But all at once the great crowd of grooms began to laugh and talk as though released from some enforced silence. They closed in on the slaves, hands pointing, gesturing.

The slipper was on Beauty's neck again, and it forced her head down until her lips touched the marble. She could see out of the corner of her eye that Laurent and the others were bent in the same lowly posture.

In a wash of rainbow colors the silk robes of the grooms surrounded them. The din of conservation was worse than the noise of the crowd in the streets. Beauty knelt shuddering as she felt hands on her back and on her hair, the thong pushing her legs even wider. Silk-robed grooms stood between her and Tristan, between her and Laurent.

But suddenly a silence fell that utterly shattered the last of Beauty's fragile composure.

The grooms withdrew as if swept aside. And there was no sound except the chattering of birds, and the tinkling of wind chimes.

Then Beauty heard the soft sound of slippered feet approaching.

2 Examination in the Garden

It was not one man who entered the garden, but a group of three. Yet two stood back in deference to one who advanced alone and slowly.

In the tense silence, Beauty saw his feet and the hem of his robe as he moved about the circle. Richer fabric, and velvet slippers with high upturned curling toes, each decorated by a dangling ruby. He moved with slow steps, as if he was surveying carefully.

Beauty held her breath as he approached her. She squinted slightly as the toe of the wine-colored slipper touched her cheek, and then rested upon the back of her neck, then followed the line of her spine to its tip.

She shivered, unable to help herself, her moan sounding loud and impertinent to her own ears. But there was no reprimand.

She thought she heard a little laugh. And then a sentence spoken gently made the tears spring to her eyes again. How soothing was the voice, how unusually musical. Maybe the unintelligible language made it seem more lyrical. Yet she longed to understand the words spoken.

Of course, she had not been addressed. The words had been spoken to one of the other two men, yet the voice stirred her, almost seduced her.

Quite suddenly she felt the chains pulled hard. Her nipples stiffened with a tingling that sent its tentacles down into her groin instantly.

She knelt up, unsure, frightened, and then was pulled to her feet, nipples burning, her face flaming.

For one moment the immensity of the garden impressed her. The bound slaves, the lavish blooms, the blue sky above shockingly clear, the large assemblage of the grooms watching her. And then the man standing before her.

What must she do with her hands? She put them behind her neck, and stood staring at the tiled floor, with only the vaguest picture of the Master who faced her.

He was much taller than the little boys – in fact, he was a slender giant of a man, elegantly proportioned, and he seemed older by virtue of his air of command. And it was he who had pulled the chains himself and still held the handles.

Quite suddenly he passed them from his right hand to his left. And with the right hand, he slapped the undersides of Beauty's breasts, startling her. She bit down on her cry. But the warm yielding of her body surprised her. She throbbed with the desire to be touched, slapped again, for an even more annihilating violence.

And in the moment of trying to collect her wits, she had glimpsed the man's dark wavy hair, not quite shoulder length, and his eyes, so black they seemed drawn in ink, with large shining beads of jet for the irises.

"How gorgeous these desert people can be," she thought. And

her dreams in the hold of the ship suddenly rose to mock her. Love him? Love this one who is but a servant like the others?

Yet the face burnt through her fear and agitation. It seemed an impossible face suddenly. It was almost innocent.

The ringing slaps came again, and she stepped back before she could stop herself. Her breasts were flooded with warmth. At once, her little groom thrashed her disobedient legs with the thong. She steadied herself, sorry for the failure.

The voice spoke again and it was as light as before, as melodious and almost caressing. But it sent the little grooms into a flurry of activity.

She felt soft, silken fingers on her ankles and on her wrists, and before she realized what was happening, she was lifted, her legs raised at right angles to her body and spread wide by the grooms who held her, her arms forced straight up in the air, her back and head supported firmly. She shivered spasmodically, her thighs aching, her sex brutally exposed. And then she felt another pair of hands lift her head, and she peered right into the eyes of the mysterious giant of a Master, who smiled at her radiantly.

O, too handsome he was. Instantly, she looked away, her lids fluttering. His eyes were tilted upwards at the outsides, which gave him a slightly devilish look, and his mouth was large and extremely kissable. But, for all the innocence of the expression, a ferocious spirit seemed to emanate from him. She sensed menace in him. She could feel it in his touch. And, with her legs held wide apart as they were, she passed into a silent panic.

As if to confirm his power, the Master quickly slapped her face, causing her to whimper before she could stop herself. The hand rose again, this time slapping her right cheek, and then the left again, until she was suddenly crying audibly.

"But what have I done?" she thought. And through a mist of tears she saw only curiosity in his face. He was studying her. It wasn't innocence. She had judged wrongly. It was merely fascination with what he was doing that flamed in him.

"So it's a test," she tried to tell herself. "But how do I pass or fail?" And shuddering, she saw the hands rising again.

He tilted her head back and opened her mouth, touching her tongue and her teeth. Chills passed over her. She felt her whole body convulse in the hands of the grooms. The probing fingers touched her eyelids, her eyebrows. They wiped at her tears, which were spilling down her face as she stared at the blue sky above her.

And then she felt the hands at her exposed sex. The thumbs went into her vagina, and she was pulled impossibly wide as her hips rocked forward, shaming her.

It seemed she would burst with orgasm, that she couldn't contain it. But was this forbidden? And how would she be punished? She tossed her head from side to side, struggling to command herself. But the fingers were so gentle, so soft, yet firm as they opened her. If they touched her clitoris, she would be lost, incapable of restraint.

But mercifully, they let her go, tugging at her pubic hair, and only pinching her lips together quickly.

In a daze, she bowed her head, the sight of her nakedness thoroughly unnerving her. She saw the new Master turn and snap his fingers. And through the tangle of her hair she saw Elena hoisted instantly by the grooms just as she had been.

Elena struggled for composure, her pink sex wet and gaping through its wreath of brown hair, the long delicate muscles of her thighs twitching. Beauty watched in terror as the Master proceeded with the same examination.

Elena's high, sharply angled breasts heaved as the Master played with her mouth, her teeth. But when the slaps came Elena was utterly silent. And the look on the Master's face further confused Beauty.

How passionately interested he seemed, how intent upon what he was doing. Not even the cruel Master of Postulants at the castle had seemed so dedicated as this one. And his charm was considerable. The rich velvet robe was well tailored to his straight back and shoulders. His hands had a beguiling grace of movement as he spread Elena's red pubic mouth and the poor Princess pumped her hips disgracefully.

At the sight of Elena's sex growing full and wet and obviously hungry, Beauty's long starvation at sea made her feel desperate. And when the Master smiled and smoothed Elena's long hair back from her forehead, examining her eyes, Beauty felt raging jealousy.

"No, it would be ghastly to love any of them," she thought. She couldn't give her heart. She tried not to look anymore. Her own legs throbbed, the grooms holding them back as firmly as ever. And her own sex swelled unbearably.

But there were more spectacles for her. The Master came back to Tristan. And now he was lifted into the air, and his legs spread wide in the same manner. Out of the corner of her eye, Beauty saw that the little grooms struggled under Tristan's weight, and Tristan's beautiful face was crimson with humiliation as his hard and thrusting organ was examined closely by the Master.

The Master's fingers played with the foreskin, played with the shiny tip, squeezing out of it a single drop of glistening moisture. Beauty could feel the tension in Tristan's limbs. But she dared not look up to see his face again as the Master reached to examine it.

In a blur she saw the Master's face, saw the enormous ink-black eyes, and the hair swept back over the ear to reveal a tiny gold ring stabbing the ear lobe.

She heard him slapping Tristan, and she closed her eyes tight as Tristan finally moaned, the slaps seeming to resound through the garden.

When she opened her eyes again it was because the Master had laughed softly to himself as he passed in front of her. And she saw his hand rise almost absently to squeeze her left breast lightly. The tears sprang to her eyes, her mind struggling to understand the outcome of his examinations, to push away the fact that he drew her more than any being who had hitherto claimed her.

Now, to her right and slightly in front of her, it was Laurent who must be raised up for the Master's scrutiny. And, as the enormous Prince was lifted, she heard the Master make some quick verbal outburst which brought laughter from all the other grooms immediately. No one needed to translate it for her. Laurent was too powerfully built, his organ was too splendid.

And she could see now that it was fully erect, well trained as it was, and the sight of the heavily muscled thighs spread wide apart brought back to her delirious memories of the Punishment Cross. She tried not to look at the enormous scrotum, but she could not help herself.

And it seemed that the Master had been moved by these superior endowments to a new excitement. He smacked Laurent hard with the back of his hand several times in amazingly rapid succession. The enormous torso writhed, the grooms struggling to keep it still.

And then the Master removed the clamps, letting them drop to the ground and pressed both of Laurent's nipples as Laurent moaned loudly.

But something else was happening. Beauty saw it. Laurent had looked at the Master directly. He had done it more than once. Their eyes had met. And now as his nipples were squeezed again, very hard it seemed, the Prince stared right at the Master.

"No, Laurent," she thought desperately. "Don't tempt them. It won't be the glory of the Punishment Cross here. It will be those corridors and miserable oblivion." Yet it absolutely fascinated her that Laurent was so bold.

The Master went round him and the grooms who held him, and now took the leather thong from one of the others and spanked Laurent's nipples over and over again. Laurent couldn't keep quiet, though he had turned his head away. His neck was corded with tension, his limbs trembling.

And the Master seemed as curious, as fastened upon his test as ever. He made a gesture to one of the others. And, as Beauty watched, a long gilded leather glove was brought to the Master.

It was beautifully worked with intricate designs all the way down the leather length of the arm to the large cuff, the whole gleaming as if it had been covered in a salve or unguent.

As the Master drew the glove over his hand and down his arm to the elbow, Beauty felt herself flooded with heat and excitement. The Master's eyes were almost childlike in their studiousness, the mouth irresistible as it smiled, the grace of the body as he approached Laurent now entrancing.

He moved his left hand to the back of Lauren's head, cradling it, his fingers curled in Laurent's hair as the Prince stared straight upward. And with the gloved hand, the right hand, he pushed upward slowly between Laurent's open legs, two fingers entering his body first, as Beauty stared unabashedly.

Laurent's breathing grew hoarse, rapid. His face darkened. The fingers had disappeared inside his anus, and now it seemed the whole hand worked its way into him.

The grooms moved in a little on all sides. And Beauty could see that Tristan and Elena watched with equal attention.

The Master, meanwhile, seemed to see nothing but Laurent. He was staring right at Laurent's face, and Laurent's face was twisted in pleasure and pain as the hand moved its way deeper and deeper into his body. It was in beyond the wrist, and

Laurent's limbs were no longer shuddering. They were frozen. A long, whistling sigh passed through his teeth.

The Master lifted Laurent's chin with the thumb of his left hand. He bent over until his face was very close to Laurent's. And in a long, tense silence the arm moved ever upward into Laurent as the Prince seemed to swoon, his cock stiff and still, the clear moisture leaking from it in the tiniest droplets.

Beauty's whole body tightened, relaxed, and again she felt herself on the verge of orgasm. As she tried to drive it back, she felt herself grow limp and weak, and all the hands holding her were in fact making love to her, caressing her.

The Master brought his right arm forward without withdrawing it from Laurent. And in so doing, he tilted the Prince's pelvis upward, further revealing the enormous balls, and the glistening gold leather as it widened the pink ring of the anus impossibly.

A sudden cry came out of Laurent. A hoarse gasp that seemed a cry for mercy. And the Master held him motionless, their lips nearly touching. The Master's left hand released Laurent's head and moved over his face, parting his lips with one finger. And then the tears spilled from Laurent's eyes.

And very quickly, the Master withdrew his arm and peeled off the glove, casting it aside, as Laurent hung in the grasp of the grooms, his head down, his face reddened.

The Master made some little remark, and again the grooms laughed agreeably. One of the grooms replaced the nipple clamps, and Laurent grimaced. The Master immediately gestured for Laurent to be placed on the floor, and the chains of Laurent's leashes were suddenly fixed to a gold ring on the back of the Master's slipper.

"O, no, this beast can't take him away from us!" Beauty thought. But that was the mere surface of her thoughts. She was terrified that it was Laurent and Laurent alone who had been chosen by the Master.

But they were all being put down. And suddenly Beauty was on hands and knees, neck pressed low by the soft velvety sole of the slipper, and she realized that Tristan and Elena were beside her and all three of them were being pulled forward by their nipple chains and whipped by the thongs as they moved out of the garden.

She saw the hem of the Master's robe to her right, and behind him the figure of Laurent struggling to keep up with the Master's strides, the chains from his nipples anchoring him to the Master's foot, his brown hair veiling his face mercifully.

Where were Dmitri and Rosalynd? Why had they been discarded? Would one of the other men who had come in with the Master take them?

She couldn't know. And the corridor seemed endless.

But she didn't really care about Dmitri and Rosalynd. All she cared about truly was that she and Tristan and Laurent and Elena were together. And, of course, the fact that he, this mysterious Master, this tall and impossibly elegant creature, was moving right alongside of her.

His embroidered robe brushed her shoulder as he moved ahead, Laurent struggling to keep pace with him.

The thongs licked at her backside, licked at her pubis, as she rushed after them.

At last, they came to another pair of doors, and the thongs drove them through into a large lamp-lighted chamber. She was bid to stop by the firm pressure of a slipper on her neck once more, and then she realized that all the grooms had withdrawn and the door had been shut behind them.

The only sound was the anxious breathing of the Princes and Princesses. The Master moved past Beauty to the door. A bolt was thrown, a key turned. Silence.

Then she heard the melodious voice again, soft and low, and this time it was speaking, in charmingly accented syllables, her own language:

"Well, my darlings, you may all come forward and kneel up before me. I have much to say to you."

3 Mysterious Master

A tumultuous shock to be spoken to.

At once the group of slaves obeyed, coming round to kneel up in front of the Master, the golden leashes trailing on the floor. Even Laurent was freed now from the Master's slipper and took his place with the others.

As soon as they were all still, kneeling with their hands clasped to the backs of their necks, the Master said:

"Look at me."

Beauty did not hesitate. She looked up into his face and found it as appealing and baffling now as it had been in the garden. It was a better-proportioned face than she had realized, the full and agreeable mouth finely shaped, the nose long and delicate, the eyes well spaced and radiantly dominant. But, again, it was the spirit that magnetized her.

As he looked from one to another of the captives, Beauty could feel the excitement coursing through the little group, feel her own sudden elation.

"O, yes, a splendid creature," she thought. And memories of the Crown Prince who had brought Beauty to the Queen's land and of her crude Captain of the Guard in the village were suddenly threatened with complete dissolution.

"Precious slaves," he said, eyes fixing on her for a brief, electric moment. "You know where you are and why you are here. The soldiers have brought you by force to serve your Lord and Master." So mellifluous the voice, the face so immediately warm. "And you know that you will serve always in silence. Dumb little creatures you are to the grooms who attend you. But I, the Sultan's steward, cherish no such illusions that sensuality obliterates high treason."

"Of course not," Beauty thought. But she didn't dare to voice her thoughts. Her interest in the man was deepening rapidly and dangerously.

"Those few slaves I pick," he said, his eyes traveling again, "those I choose to perfect and offer to the Sultan's Court are always apprised of my aims, and my demands, and the dangers of my temper. But only in the secrecy of this chamber. In this chamber I want my methods to be understood. My expectations to be fully clarified."

He drew closer, towering over Beauty, and his hand reached for her breast, squeezing it as he had done before, just a little too hard, the hot shiver passing down into her sex immediately. With the other hand he stroked the side of Laurent's face, thumb grazing the lip as Beauty turned to watch, utterly forgetting herself.

"That you will not do, Princess," he said, and at once he slapped her hard and she bowed her head, her face stinging. "You will continue to look at me until I tell you otherwise."

Beauty's tears rose at once. How could she have been so foolish?

But there was no anger in his voice, only a soft indulgence. Tenderly, he lifted her chin. She stared at him through her tears.

"Do you know what I want of you, Beauty? Answer me."

"No, Master," she said quickly. Her voice alien to her.

"That you be perfect, for me!" he said gently, the voice seeming so full of reason, of logic. "This I want of all of you. That you be nonpareils in this vast wilderness of slaves in which you could be lost like a handful of diamonds in the ocean. That you shine by virtue not merely of your compliance but by virtue of your intense and particular passion. You will lift yourself up from the masses of slaves who surround you. You will seduce your Masters and Mistresses by a lustre that throws others into eclipse! Do you understand me!"

Beauty struggled not to sob in her anxiousness, her eyes on his, as if she could not look away even if she wanted to. But never had she felt such an overwhelming desire to obey. The urgency of his voice was wholly different from the tone of those who had educated her at the castle or chastised her in the village. She felt as if she was losing the very form of her personality. She was slowly melting.

"And this you will do for me," he said, his voice growing even more soft, more persuasive, more resonant. "You will do it as much for me as for your royal Lords. Because I desire it of you." He closed his hand around Beauty's throat. "Let me hear you speak again, little one. In my chambers, you will speak to me to tell me that you wish to please me."

"Yes, Master," she said. And her voice once again seemed strange to her, full of feelings she hadn't truly known before. The warm fingers caressed her throat, seemed to caress the words she spoke, coax them out of her and shape the tone of them.

"You see, there are hundreds of grooms," he said, narrowing his eyes as he looked away from her to the others, the hand still clasping her. "Hundreds charged with preparing succulent little partridges for Our Lord the Sultan, or fine muscular young bucks and stags for him to play with. But I, Lexius, am the only Chief Steward of the Grooms. And I *must* choose and perfect the finest of all playthings."

Even this was not said with anger or urgency.

But as he looked again at Beauty, his eyes widened with intensity. The semblance of anger terrified her. But the gentle fingers massaged the back of her neck, the thumb stroking her throat in front.

"Yes, Master," she whispered suddenly.

"Yes, absolutely, my little love," he said, crooning to her. But then he became grave, and his voice became small, as if to command greater respect by speaking its words simply.

"It is absolutely out of the question that you do not distinguish yourselves, that after one glimpse of you the great luminaries of this house do not reach out to pluck you like ripe fruit, that they do not compliment me upon your loveliness, your heat, your silent, ravening passion."

Beauty's tears flowed again down her cheeks.

He withdrew his hand slowly. She felt suddenly cold, abandoned. A little sob caught in her throat, but he had heard it.

Lovingly, almost sadly, he smiled at her. His face was shadowed and strangely vulnerable.

"Divine little Princess," he whispered. "We are lost, you see, unless they notice us."

"Yes, Master," she whispered. She would have done anything to have him touch her again, hold her.

And the rich undertone of sadness in him startled her, enchanted her. O, if only she could kiss his feet.

And, in a sudden impulse she did. She went down on the marble and touched her lips to his slipper. She did it over and over. And she wondered that the word "lost" had so delighted her.

As she rose again, clasping her hands behind her neck, she lowered her eyes in resignation. She should be slapped for what she had done. The room – its white marble, its gilded doors – was like so many facets of light. Why did this man produce this effect in her? Why . . .

"Lost." The word set up its musical echo in her soul.

The Master's long, dark fingers came out and touched her lips. And she saw him smiling.

"You will find me hard, you will find me impossibly hard," he said gently. "But now you know why. You understand now. You belong to Lexius, the Chief Steward. You mustn't fail him. Speak. All of you."

He was answered by a chorus of "Yes, Master." Beauty heard even the voice of Laurent, the runaway, answering just as promptly.

"And now I shall tell you another truth, little ones," he said. "You may belong to the most High Lord, to the Sultana, to the Beautiful and Virtuous Royal Wives of the Harem . . ." He paused, as if to let his words sink in. "But you belong just as truly to me!" he said, "as to anyone! And I revel in every punishment I inflict. I do. It is my nature, as it is yours to serve – my nature, when it comes to slaves, to eat from the very same dish as my Masters. Tell me that you understand me."

"Yes, Master!"

The words came out of Beauty like an explosion of breath. She was dazed with all he had said to her.

She watched him intently as he turned now to Elena, and her soul shrank, though she did not turn her head a fraction of an inch or move her steady gaze from him. Yet still, she could see that he was kneading Elena's fine breasts. How Beauty envied those high, jutting breasts! Nipples the color of apricot. And it hurt her further that Elena moaned so bewitchingly.

"Yes, yes, exactly," said the Master, the voice as intimate as it had been with Beauty. "You will writhe at my touch. You will writhe at the touch of all your Masters and Mistresses. You will give up your soul to those who so much as glance at you. You will burn like lights in the dark!"

Again a chorus of "Yes, Master."

"Did you see the multitude of slaves who make up the ornaments of this house?"

"Yes, Master," from all of them.

"Will you distinguish yourselves from the gilded herd by passion, by obedience, by putting into your silent compliance a deafening thunder of feeling!"

"Yes, Master."

"But now, we shall begin. You will be properly purified. And then to work immediately. The Court knows that new slaves have come. You are awaited. And your lips are once again sealed. Not under the sternest punishment are you to make a sound with them parted. Unless otherwise commanded you crawl on hands and knees, buttocks up and forehead near to the very ground, almost touching it."

He walked down the silent row. He stroked and examined each slave again, lingering for a long time on Laurent. Then with an abrupt gesture, he ordered Laurent to the door. Laurent crawled as he had been told to do, his forehead grazing the marble. The Master touched the bolt with the thong. Laurent at once slid it back.

The Master pulled the nearby bell cord.

4 The Rites of Purification

At once the young grooms appeared and silently took the slaves in hand, quickly forcing them on hands and knees through another doorway into a large, warm bathing place.

Amid delicate tropical flowering plants and lazing palms, Beauty saw steam rising from the shallow pools in the marble floor and smelled the fragrance of the herbs and spiced perfumes.

But she was spirited past all of this into a tiny private chamber. And there was made to kneel with legs wide apart over a deep, rounded basin in the floor through which water ran fast from hidden founts and down the drain continuously.

Her forehead was once again lowered to the floor, her hands clasped upon the back of her neck. The air was warm and moist around her. And immediately the warm water and soft scrub brushes went to work upon her.

It was all done with much greater speed than at the bath in the castle. And within moments, she was perfumed and oiled and her sex was pumping with expectation as soft towels caressed her.

But she was not told to get up. On the contrary, she was bid to be still by a firm pat of the hand on her head, and she heard strange sounds above her.

Then she felt a metal nozzle entering her vagina. Immediately her juices flowed at the long-awaited sensation of being entered, no matter how awkwardly. But she knew this was merely for cleansing – it had been done other times to her – and she welcomed the steady fount of water that suddenly gushed into her with delicious pressure.

But what startled her was the unfamiliar touch of fingers on her anus. She was being oiled there, and her body tensed, even as the craving in her was doubled. Hands quickly took hold of the soles of her feet to keep her firmly in place. She heard the grooms laughing softly and commenting to one another.

Then something small and hard entered her anus and forced its way in deep as she gave a little gasp, pressing her lips tightly together. Her muscles contracted to fight the little invasion, but this only sent new ripples of pleasure through her. The flush of water into her vagina had stopped. And what happened now was unmistakable: A stream of warm water was being pumped into her rectum. And it did not wash back out of her as did the douching fluids. It filled her with ever-increasing force, and a strong hand pressed her buttocks together as if bidding her not to release the water.

It seemed a whole new region of her body came to life, a part of her that had never been punished or even really examined. The force of the flow grew stronger and stronger. Her mind protested that she could not be invaded in this final way, that she could not be rendered so helpless.

She felt she would burst if she did not let go. She wanted to expel the little nozzle, the water. But she dared not, she could not. This must happen to her now and she accepted it. It was part of this realm of more refined pleasures and manners. And how dare she protest? She began to whimper softly, caught between a new pleasure and a new sense of violation.

But the most enervating and taxing part was yet to come, and she dreaded it. Just when she thought she could bear no more, that she was full to overflowing, she was lifted upright by her arms, and her legs were pulled even wider apart, the little nozzle in her anus plugging her and tormenting her.

The grooms smiled down at her as they held her arms. And she looked up fearfully, shyly, afraid of the utter shame of the sudden release that was inevitable. Then the nozzle was slipped out, and her buttocks were spread apart, and her bowels quickly emptied.

She squeezed her eyes shut. She felt warm water poured over her private parts, front and back, heard the loud full rush in the basin. She was overcome with something like shame. But it wasn't shame. All privacy and choice had been taken from her. Not even this act was to be hers alone anymore, she understood. And the chills passing through her body with every spasm of release locked her into a delirious sense of helplessness. She gave herself over to those who commanded her, her body limp and unprotesting. She flexed her muscles to help with the emptying, to complete it.

"Yes, to be purified," she thought. And she experienced a great undeniable relief, the awareness of her body cleansing itself becoming exquisite as she shuddered.

The water continued to flow over her, over her buttocks, her belly, down into the basin, washing away all the waste. And she was dissolving into an overall ecstasy that seemed a form of climax in itself. But it wasn't. It was just beyond her reach, the climax. And as she felt her mouth open in a low gasp, she rocked back and forth on the brink, her body pleading silently and vainly with those who held her. All the invisible knots were gone from her spirit. She was without the slightest strength, and utterly dependent upon the grooms to support her.

They stroked her hair back from her forehead. The warm water washed her again and again.

And then she saw, as she dared to open her eyes, that the Master himself was there. He was standing in the doorway of the room and he was smiling at her. He came forward and lifted her up out of this moment of indescribable weakness.

She stared at him, stunned that it was he who held her as the others covered her in towels again.

She felt as defenseless as she had ever been, and it seemed an impossible reward that he led her out of the little chamber. If she could only embrace him, only find the cock under his robes, only . . . The elation of being near him escalated immediately into pain.

"O, please, we have been starved and starved," she wanted to say. But she only looked down demurely, feeling his fingers on her arm. That was the old Beauty speaking the words in her head, wasn't it? The new Beauty wanted to say only the word "Master".

And to think that only moments ago she had been considering love for him. Why, she loved him already. She could breathe the fragrance of his skin, almost hear his heart beat as he turned her and directed her forward. His fingers clasped her neck as tightly as they had before.

Where was he taking her?

The others were gone. She was set on one of the tables. She shivered in happiness and disbelief as he himself began to rub more perfumed oil into her. But this time there was to be no covering of gold paint. Her bare flesh would shine under the oil. And he pinched her cheeks with both hands to give them color as she rested back on her heels, her eyes wet from the steam and from her tears, watching him dreamily.

He seemed deeply absorbed in his work, his dark eyebrows knit, his mouth half open. And, when he applied gold leash clamps to her nipples, he pressed them tight for an instant with a little tightening of his lips that made her feel the gesture all the more deeply. She arched her back and breathed deeply. And he kissed her forehead, letting his lips linger, letting his hair brush her cheek.

"Lexius," she thought. It was a beautiful name.

When he brushed her hair it was almost with angry, fierce strokes, and chills consumed her. He brushed it up and wound it on top of her head. And she glimpsed the pearl pins that he used to fasten it. Her neck was naked now, like the rest of her.

As he put the pearls through her ear lobes, she studied the smooth dark skin of his face, the rise and fall of his dark lashes. He was like a finely polished thing, his fingernails buffed to look like glass, his teeth perfect. And how deftly yet gently he handled her.

It was over too fast, and yet not fast enough. How long could she writhe, dreaming of orgasm? She cried because there had to be some release, and when he put her on the floor her body ached as never before, it seemed.

Gently, he pulled the leashes. She bent down, forehead to the ground, as she crept forward, and it seemed to her that she had never been more completely the slave.

If she had any ability left to think, as she followed him out of the bath, she thought that she could no longer remember a time when she had worn clothes, walked and talked with those who did, commanded others. Her nakedness and helplessness were natural to her, more natural here in these spacious marble halls than anywhere else, and she knew without a doubt that she would love this Master utterly.

She could have said it was an act of will, that after talking with Tristan she had simply decided. But there was too much that was unique about the man, even in the delicate way that he himself had groomed her. And the place itself, it was like magic to her. And she had thought she loved the harshness of the village!

Why must he give her away now? Take her to others? But it was wrong to question . . .

As they moved along the corridor together, she heard for the first time the soft breathing and sighs of the slaves who decorated the niches on either side of them. It seemed a muted chorus of perfect devotion.

And a confusion of all sense of time and place overcame her.

RUSSIAN DRESSING

Svetlana Boym

"YOU'RE FRIGID," he told her as they passed the Gorky statue on Kirov Avenue. She was hurt that he no longer had his hand on her shoulder under the thick wool coat, but was walking aloof, chewing pink Finnish gum. Frigid – *frigidna* . . . Frigida – Fetida, Femida – probably a Roman goddess, with small classical breasts and pupilless eyes of cool marble. It might have been her in that picture in the history book, standing near the handsome Apollo with broken masculine arms. Right before the Barbarian invasion . . . or was it after? She caught her embarrassed reflection in the window of the Porcelain Shop. It felt uncomfortably damp and raw. She wanted so much to replay the whole scene, to put his hand back under her wool coat, to experience the meaningful weight of his warm fingers, to press her cheek against his frosted mustache in that split second before they reached the faded neon "P" of the Porcelain Shop. But it was too late now; he wouldn't give her another chance, another touch. They had already crossed the tram routes and were parting by the park fence where there was the poster for Leningrad Dixieland. Season: 1975.

"Excuse me, miss, are you the last in line?"
    "Yes."
    "Well, not anymore. I'm after you . . . And what's the line for? Grilled chickens or 'Addresses and Inquiries'?"

"Addresses and Inquiries, I hope."

"Good . . . good . . . let's hope together. That's the only thing
we can do these days – hope. Right? I see you're not from around
here . . ."

"Oh, yes, I am . . ."

"Oh yeah? You sure don't look like it . . . Forgive my curiosity,
miss, if you're from round here, why are you waiting at the
Information Kiosk?"

"I'm just looking up my school friends . . ."

"Oh, okay. One has to do that from time to time . . . I thought
you were some kind of foreigner or something . . ."

Anya realized she had forgotten how to make small talk in
Russian. She had lost that invisible something that makes you
an insider, whether it's a tone of voice, a gesture of habitual
indifference, or half-words half said but fully understood. Anya
left the Soviet Union fifteen years ago; then she had been told
that it would be forever, that there would be no way back; it was
like life and death. But now she was able to visit Leningrad again.
The city had changed its name, and so had she. She came back as
an American tourist, and stayed in the overpriced hotel where
you could drink chilled orange juice, that item of bourgeois
charm. Like other idle Westerners she began to collect communist antiques, little Octubrist star-pins showing baby Lenin with
gilded curls, red banners with embroidered gold inscriptions "To
the Best Pig Farmer for Achievement in Labor" or "To the
Brigade with a High Level of Culture". She wanted to pass for a
native, but her unwarranted smiles were giving her away and the
Petersburgians frowned at her suspiciously in passing.

Anya was born on the Ninth Soviet Street in Leningrad and
now she lived on the Tenth West Street, New York. Could she
make small talk in New-Yorkese? Yes, of course. During these
years she had learned how to be an insider-foreigner, a New-
Yorker-foreigner, along with other resident and non-resident
aliens, legal and illegal city dwellers. Anya was among the lucky
green-card-carrying New Yorkers and could show her picture
with the properly exposed right ear and the finger print. New
York felt like home. It struck her now that she was much more
comfortable in a place *like* home than she was at home. She was a
regular at *Lox Around the Clock*, and could spell her name fast

over the phone. R-o-s-en-b-l-u-m A-n-y-a no, it's not Annie, it's N-Y, like in 'New-York' – Thank you – You too.''

Surely, she had an accent, but it was "so very charming", a delicious little extra, like the dressing on a salad that comes free with an order of Manhattan chowder – "What dressing would you like on your salad, dear?" the waiter would ask her. "Italian, French, Russian, or blue cheese?" "Russian, please," she would say, "with lots of fresh pepper . . ."

She worked free-lance doing voice-overs for commercials, whenever they needed someone with an accent. The last one she had done was "La Larta. European youglette. Passion. Fat-free – I can't believe it's not yogurt." Female voice: "Remember your first taste of Larta? Was it in Lisboa? Sofia? Odessa? (A mountain landscape, Caucasian peaks and a sparkling sea – a woman with Isabella Rossellini's lips, her face radiant with Lancôme) Remember La Larta – natural and fresh like first love."

"Oh," said the director, "you have to pronounce each sound distinctly. L is soft and French, the back of your tongue touches the palate – let me show you . . . look here, softly but firmly, and then breathe out on the A, open your lips, yes, yes as if for a kiss . . . Then tease me, yes, tease me with your Rrr – roll it deep in your throat – yes – rr stands for mystique, and then – suddenly – you let your tongue tickle your teeth – playful and light Ta-ta-ta-Larrta-ta ta-ta – the audience wants to taste it now, yes, yes, yes. 'La Larta. Passion. Fat-free.' "

And then Anya had done several AT&T commercials, she did a voice over the video of falling Berlin Wall. But that happened a few years ago, when it was still news. In any case, these were only temporary jobs. Eastern European accents went in and out of fashion. Anya had been an understudy for the new line of soft drinks: "A Revolution is brewing in the Orient. A Revolution in Cola," but the role was given to a Romanian. She must have had better connections.

"Are you in line for information?"

"Yes . . ."

"And where is the line for addresses?"

"It's here too."

"Well, what I really need is a phone number . . . And it would

be great to get a home address too, but I know they're not listed
. . . It's dangerous now . . . I don't blame them. What you need
nowadays is an iron door . . . Don't look at me like that . . . You
think I'm joking . . . I know you're young, miss, you probably
think – an iron door, well that's a bit much . . . but let me tell you,
I know a really honest guy, who was an engineer in the good old
days . . . he makes excellent iron doors. Real quality iron. You
can call him, tell him I gave you his number . . . "

"Thanks, I'll think about it . . ."

"Well, don't think too long or it'll be too late . . . Sorry, you
should spit when you say it, that or touch wood – we don't wish
anything bad to happen . . . Maybe we'll have law and order here
some day . . . or at least order . . ."

"Hm . . ."

"Come to think of it, maybe they don't list the phone numbers
either . . . Have you got a pen, miss? Oh this is a great one! 'Ai luf
Niu Iork!' Did you get it in Gostiny Dvor or in the House of
Friendship?"

Anya began to fill out her "inquiry cards" to avoid any
further discussion of iron doors. She wanted to find her
teenage loves, Sasha and Misha with whom she had had
her first failed perfect moments. Both relationships had been
interrupted. In the case of Sasha, they had split up after he
told her she was frigid; with Misha, they had parted after
sealing the secret erotic pact of Napoleonic proportions. She
wanted to write an end to their love stories, to recover a few
missing links, to fill in the blanks. They were complete
antipodes, Sasha and Misha. Sasha was blond, Misha dark,
Sasha was her official boyfriend, Misha was a secret one.
Sasha was beautiful, Misha intellectual. Sasha had known
too many girls, Misha had read too much Nietzsche at a
young age. It was almost twenty years ago and the popular
song of the day had been "First Love". "Oh, first love, it
comes and goes with the tide," sang the Yugoslav pop star, the
beautiful Radmila Karaklaic, as she blew kisses out to the
sparkling sea somewhere near the recently bombed town of
Dubrovnik . . .

In his white coat with blood-red lining . . . Sasha was beautiful, he wore a long black scarf and the aura of a black market

professional. He sang the popular song by Salvatore Adamo about falling snow: "The snow was falling. You wouldn't come this evening. The snow was falling. Everything was white with despair . . ." *Tombait la neige. Tu ne viendras pas ce soir.* His masculine voice caressed her with the foreign warmth. French snow was falling over and over again, slowly and softly, slowly and softly . . . Was it possible for her not to come that evening, how was it possible that she wouldn't come that evening? Oh, she would have to come . . . and she just couldn't resist. She recalled the shape of his lips, soft, full and cracked, but she couldn't remember at all what they had talked about. Oh, yes, she had been a bit taken aback when she found out he had never read Pasternak. On the other hand, he was a real man and sang beautiful songs. He had put his hand under her sweater. Touched her. Tried to unfasten her bra. But those silly little hooks in the back wouldn't come undone. "Oh, it doesn't matter, let me help . . ." But he felt that a man should be a man, that there were things a man should do himself. Just at that moment a noise in the corridor had interrupted them. It was Sasha's father, a former sea captain, coming home after work. So, once again, they had nowhere else to go; there were no drive-ins, no cars, no back seats, no contraception, and only cheap Bulgarian wine. Like all Leningrad teenagers they went to walk on the roofs of the Peter and Paul Fortress. They walked under the sign that said: "No dogs allowed. Walking on the roofs is strictly prohibited . . ." It would get all icy there and one could easily slip down, distracted by the gorgeous panorama of the Neva embankment. But it was quite spectacular: the imperial palace, dissolving in the mist, the dark grey ripples on the river, a poem or two . . . Wait, do you remember how it goes . . .? "Life is a lie, but with a charming sorrow . . ." Yes, she would say, "yes . . .".

They had parted that day at the park entrance. On the way there she had worried that her nose was getting too frozen and red and that she didn't look good any more. She was too embarrassed to look at him and could only catch glimpses of his blond curls, his scarf and the dark birth mark on his cheek. Then there were some clumsy gestures and an unexpected wetness on her lips. Did she kiss him or not? She tried to concentrate because this was supposed to be her perfect moment.

"You're frigid," he said very seriously.

Frigid . . . frigid . . . a blushing goddess. So, that's what it was
called? This clumsiness, arousal, alienation, excitement, tongue-
tiedness, humidity, humility, humiliation.

"Are you waiting for apricot juice?"
"No . . ."
"You mean, it's gone? I don't believe it . . . this is really
incredible . . . All they have is the Scottish Whisky" . . .
"Miss, where are you from?"

This time Anya did not protest. She began to fill out the card for
Misha – all in red ink. Misha didn't know any French songs and
he didn't care much about Salvatore Adamo. They spoke only
about Nietzsche, orgasms and will to power. "Orgasms: they
have to be simultaneous, or nothing at all. They're beyond good
and evil . . . For protection women can simply insert a little
piece of lemon inside them. It's the most natural method,
favoured by poets of the Silver Age . . ." If her relationship
with Sasha had been a conventional romance with indispensable
walks on the roofs of the fortress, then her relationship with
Misha was an example of teenage non-conformism. They had
dated mostly on the phone and had seen each other only about
three times during their two-year-long erotic conversation. She
could still hear his voice which had already lost its boyish pitch
and acquired a deep guttural masculinity, resounding in her
right ear.

When she thought of Misha, she saw herself sitting on an
uncomfortable chair near the "communal" telephone, counting
the black squares on the tiled floor. The telephone was in the hall
and was shared by everyone in the apartment. While talking to
Misha she had had to lower her voice, because Valentina Petrovna, the voracious gossip, would conspicuously walk back and
forth between her room and the kitchen, slowing down as she
neared the phone. The rest of the time she was probably standing
behind the door to her room, busily filling in the gaps in Anya's
and Misha's fragmented conversation. With Misha Anya had
been very intimate but theirs was a safe intimacy, and distance
had protected them from self-censorship. They knew they were
part of a larger system of official public communication. The
invisible presence of the others, the flutter of slippers in the hall

had only stimulated them, provoked confessions about the things that had never happened in real life.

Anya met Misha on the "Devil's Wheel" – a special ride in the Kirov Park of Culture and Leisure. Misha fell victim to the calumnia of Anya's girlfriend – Ira – who observed his immediate fondness for Anya. "He's handsome," Ira said, "but he has smooth rosy cheeks – like a girl. You know what I mean . . ."

"He has smooth rosy cheeks like a girl . . ." – this strange sentence haunted Anya the whole day, that beautiful spring day when they were riding on the "Devil's Wheel", trying to touch each other in the air in an instant of ephemeral intimacy, and then pushing each other away, as they swung on the chains. The song went like this:

> Just remember long ago in spring
> We were riding in the park on the "Devil's Wheel"
> Devil's wheel, Devil's wheel
> and your face is flying, close to me
>
> But I'm swinging on the chains,
> I'm flying – OH!

"Ahh . . ."

"Oh?"

"Ahh – 'I'm swinging on the chains, I'm flying Ahh . . .' " "I thought you were humming the old song 'Devil's Wheel'. It hasn't been on the radio for ages . . . It must be ten years old . . ."

"Yeah . . . I don't know why it stuck with me."

"It's a nice song. I remember that great Muslim Magomaev used to sing it on TV on New Year's Eve. It was when I was still married to my ex-wife and our son was in the Army . . . She would be making her New Year potato salad in the kitchen with my mother-in-law and I would be watching that TV show called 'Little Blue Light'. And there would be a clock and the voice of comrade Brezhnev – first it was comrade Brezhnev himself, then it was his voice, and in the last years the voice of an anchorman reading Brezhnev's speech . . . poor guy had a tic . . . but the speech always sounded so warm and familiar and it went so well with a little glass of vodka and herring: 'Dear Soviet citizens . . . I wish you good health, happiness in your personal life and success

in your labor.' And then Muslim Magomaev would sing –
'Devil's Wheel'. Just remember long ago in the spring . . . We
were riding in the park on 'Devil's Wheel, Devil's Wheel, Devil's
Wheel . . .' I know you're not supposed to remember things like
that these days . . . Now it's called 'the era of stagnation . . .'."

"But it was such a good song . . ."

Anya was afraid to lose Misha's face forever at the next swing.
"Devil's Wheel, Devil's Wheel and your face is flying close to
me". The words of this popular song shaped their romance. But
in this whirlpool of excitement, in the chains of the Devil's
Wheel, in the cool air of the Russian spring Misha's cheeks were
getting rosier and rosier. Ira's words froze on the tip of her
tongue. He blushed like a girl. They were doomed . . .

They would have made a strange couple anyway – he with his
girlish rosy cheeks and his deep masculine voice, and she with her
boyish clumsiness and long red nails painted with an imported
Polish nail-polish. They didn't know what to do with their
excessively erotic and intellectual selves. After the encounter
on the Devil's Wheel came months of phone calls. They would
carefully plan their next meeting and then always postpone it.
Finally they decided, that it was now or never, they would
conduct a secret ritual, to penetrate deep mysteries of the soul.

She left her house and walked away from the city center. She
passed the larger-than-life portrait of Lenin made of red fishnet
in the 1960s. Behind the statue of the Russian inventor of the
radio was an urban no-man's land, with the old botanical gardens,
the ruined greeneries and endless fences made of wood and iron.
This was the border zone – exactly the place that Misha wanted to
perform their secret ritual. "This can be done only once in a life
time," he said seriously. "Napoleon did it to Josephine."

She had to stand against the iron fence with her hands behind
her back and her eyes open wide. He touched her eye with his
tongue. He touched it deeply, trying to penetrate the darkness of
her pupil. He lingered for a second, and then he licked the white
around her eyelids, as if drawing the contours of her vision from
inside her. Her gaze reacquired a kind of primordial warmth and
humidity. They paused for a moment. Her eyes overflowing with
desire.

They never deigned to kiss or hold each other; or saying
romantic "I love yous" on the roof of the fortress. They despised

such conventional games. They committed a single Napoleonic transgression, a dazzling eye-contact, a mysterious pact of intimacy signed with neither ink nor blood.

"Miss, you'll have to rewrite this . . . We don't accept red ink. And try to be neat . . ."

"Forgive me, I have terrible handwriting . . ."

"That's your problem, not mine. And hurry please, we close in an hour . . ."

"But we've been waiting an hour and a half."

"Well, yesterday, they were waiting for three hours and in drizzling rain. Be grateful that you're in line for information, and not bread . . ."

"Oh, by the way, miss, speaking of bread, you should see what they sell in the cooperative bakery around the corner. Their heart-shaped sweet bread now cost five hundred rubles . . . I mean this is ridiculous . . . They used to be twenty kopecks – max."

"What are you talking about? We didn't have heart-shaped breads before . . . If it were up to people like you, we'd still be living in the era of stagnation or even worse, in the time of the great purges . . . You can't take any change . . ."

"Hey, Comrades, Ladies and Gentlemen, whatever . . . Stop yelling while you are in line. These working conditions are impossible! I can't give out any information with all this shouting!"

And in New York there were a hundred kinds of bread – Anya suddenly felt ashamed – bread with and without calories, with and without fat, bread which is not really bread at all but only looks like it. Bread that never gets stale, that is non-perishable, eternally fresh and barely edible. Sometimes you have to rush to an expensive store, miles away to get foreign bread that lasts only a day, that's fattening and crusty and doesn't fit into the toaster. So Anya did not express her views on the heart-shaped bread. She tried hard to remain neutral and friendly with all the strangers in line and concentrated on filling out her inquiry cards. But those two intimate episodes were her main clues for tracking down Sasha and Misha. The rest was the hearsay of well-meaning friends, rumors, that were mostly fifteen years old.

Sasha, rumor had it, was married and was drinking. Or rather, at first, he did everything right – he flirted with the black market in his early youth, but then he cut off all his blond curls and ties with foreigners and entered the Naval Academy. He married his high school sweetheart, whom he had begun to date in the resort town of Z just about the time of their romance, and who had waited for him heroically throughout the years. Naturally, they had had a very proper wedding in the Palace of Weddings on the Neva embankment and they had placed the crown of flowers in the Revolutionary Cemetery and taken lots of pictures with her white lacy veil and his black tuxedo. Sasha wanted to be a gentleman officer, like his father, a youngish-looking, well-built man who often played tennis with Sasha at the courts of the town of Z. Sasha was made of the "right stuff". But then something unforeseen happened. Some time in the early 80s he started developing strange symptoms, losing hair and getting dark rashes on his arms . . . Nobody was sure what it was . . . During his service somewhere in the Arctic Circle, Sasha might have received an excessive dose of radiation. But those were the things one didn't talk about, you know what I mean . . . He quit the service, left the city and underwent special medical treatment somewhere far away. He came back completely cured. Anya's distant cousin, Sasha's occasional tennis partner, said that he was in Leningrad, but that he had moved from his old apartment, and no longer spent summers in the town of Z. Another common friend had spotted him down in the subway, but Sasha hadn't said hello . . . Then again, the crowds had been moving fast, the light was dim, and, who knows, it might have been someone else . . .

As for Misha, he was considered lucky . . . Like Sasha, he hadn't kept in touch with the old friends, but everyone knows that those old friends did not keep in touch with each other either, gathering only occasionally for someone's birthday or for a farewell party. Misha started out as unconventionally as one would have expected. In the late 70s he had managed to get into the Philosophy Department, which was almost impossible to do without connections. So he had settled for the Evening Division, which meant that he had to serve time in the Army. What might have seemed like a tragedy turned out to have a "happy ending". Misha spent two years in the Far East, in the most dangerous area near the Chinese border. He told her during one of their last long conversations after returning from the Army that he was the only person with a high-school education in his detachment. While intellectuals were generally despised and abused, he wasn't. His will to power won. He made the soldiers polish his boots; they squatted in front of him brushing away methodically every bit of dust. He had liked it. He said that of all the things in the world, he loved power the most. Anya assumed he was still into Nietzsche. By the age of 21 he was chosen to enter the Communist Party on a special basis, that is two years before the official age of eligibility which was 23. During the 1980 Russian Olympic Games – the last epic event of the Brezhnev era – Misha was elected to the Leningrad Olympics Committee. He had called her then, appearing very friendly and promising to get her some Ceylon tea which had long since vanished from the stores and could only be acquired by the privileged few.

She couldn't forgive him that tea for a long time. Maybe it wasn't the tea itself but his tone of voice . . . That year she had become something like an internal refugee and had to leave the university, "voluntarily expelled". She applied to emigrate and soon after that friends stopped visiting her. Occasionally they would call from the public phones and speak in strange voices, and then when something squeaked in the receiver, they would say goodbye: "Forgive me, I'm out of change. I'll call you later." Anya ran endless errands, as a therapy against fear, collecting inquiry cards and papers – *spravki* – to and from various departments of Internal Affairs. . . . And yes, good tea was hard to get in those days, especially the sweet and aromatically prestigious Ceylon tea. She often imagined meeting Misha somewhere in the noisy subway, in the middle of a crowd. He would be proudly wearing his fashionable brand-new T-shirt with the winking Olympic Bear, made in Finland "I've been transferred to Moscow, you know," – he would shout at her. "I've been very busy lately." "Me too," Anya would shout back. "I'm emigrating, you know . . ." She knew she would be compromising him at that moment, that she would be saying something one didn't say in public, something one could whisper in private only and never over the phone. A few strangers would conspicuously turn around to look at them, as if to photograph Misha's face and hers with their suspicious eyes. And then Misha would blush, in his unique girlish fashion, his cheeks turning embarrassingly rosy, like in those teenage years, and he would vanish into the crowd.

But all of this was many years ago, and Anya no longer had any problems with tea. Those fragments of intimacy with Misha and Sasha, those tactile embarrassments and unfulfilled desires were the few things that remained vivid in her mind from the "era of stagnation". Those incomplete narratives and failed perfect moments were like fragile wooden logs, unreliable safeguards on the swamp of her Leningradian memory which otherwise consisted of inarticulate fluttering and stutters, smells and blurs.

Anya had already performed some of the obligatory homecoming rituals but they had been too literal and therefore disappointing. She had walked by the aging but still cheerful Gorky on the now renamed Kirov Avenue approaching the windows of the Porcelain store that now sold everything from grilled chickens to "Scottish Whisky" and Wrangler jeans. Across the street from the square with the monument to the Russian inventor of radio (whose invention, along the others, is now questioned) she searched in vain for the shadow of Lenin made of red fishnet. The house where she used to live was under repair and on the broken glass-door of the front entrance she found a poster advertising a popular Mexican soap opera "The Rich Cry Too". Otherwise the facade looked exactly like it had in the old days, but it was more like an impostor of her old house, a stage set that was a clumsy imitation of the original. Anya climbed up to their communal apartment through piles of trash. The place looked uncanny. The old communal partitions, including the secret retreats of Valentina Petrovna who had borne witness to her teenage romances, had been taken apart and the whole narrative of communal interaction was destroyed. On the floor she found telephone wires, worn-out slippers and the broken pieces of a French record. She looked through the window: black bottomless balconies were still precariously attached to the building, inhabited only by a few rootless plants. A lonely drunk was melancholically urinating near the skeleton of the old staircase.

"Comrades, Ladies and Gentlemen. Remember who's the last in line and don't let in anyone else. Can I trust you?"

"But, of course . . . We're all family here, miss. We know who's in line and who's out, who's with us and who's against us . . ."

"Hurry up, comrades. Fill out your inquiry cards neatly. Be sure to include name and patronymic, place of birth, nationality, permanent address . . . We're short of time here . . ."

Indeed we're short of time, thought Anya. We are all only a phone call away from each other. Misha, Sasha, let's all get together . . . Let bygones be bygones – God, we used to learn so many proverbs in our English classes and then never had the occasion to use them . . . Let's chat, remember the golden seventies, have a drink or two. What do you think? There are a lot of blank spaces in our life stories, and we don't have to fill them all, it's OK. We'll just have fun. Let's meet in some beautiful spot with a view, definitely with a view. We don't need broad panoramas, no. And I don't think the Church of our Savior on the Blood is such a good place either – (I heard they took the scaffolding down and you can actually see it now, it's been restored after so many years . . .) Let's meet on a little bridge with golden-winged lions. "Let's tell each other compliments, in love's special moments" – I didn't make up this song; it really existed.

Relax, Sasha . . . I know what happened. I've heard . . . I don't have much to say about it, only that it could have been worse . . . Listen, you looked really gorgeous in that white coat with red lining and I was totally and completely seduced by that silly song about the falling snow . . . I must have had a real crush on you. I even forgave you for not reading Pasternak. It's just that we took ourselves so seriously in those days, you and me . . . But tell me how did you come up with that cruel Latin word "frigid"? In America, you know, women are rarely frigid, but the weather frequently is . . .

Hey, Misha, I've really forgotten about that Ceylon tea of yours . . . it doesn't matter any more, I've brought you some Earl Grey . . . Remember our telephonic orgasms in the communal hall? God, I wish someone had taped those . . . Should we try to continue with that in a more sedate, grown-up fashion and shock the long-distance operator? I remember something about you, from those earlier days. The taste of your tongue in my eyes . . . There was spring dirt on your boots then, they were still unpolished . . . Where are you now? Way up or low down? As usual, beyond good and evil? I'm joking, of course, you might have forgotten your high school Nietzsche . . .

Me, I'm fine really. I love New York, as they say. Like New Yorkers, I love it and hate it. It feels like home and I feel a bit home-sick now, for that little studio of mine on Tenth West Street, bright but rather messy, without any pretense of coziness. Sometimes I go traveling to the end of the world, or at least to the southernmost point in the United States, Key West. Last time I nearly slipped on the wet rocks. You see, I need that, to get perspective, to estrange myself. It's risky to get attached to one place, don't you think?

And, yes, naturally I must be having great sex. For that's what we do "in the West" and it couldn't be otherwise. It's actually almost true and not a big deal. I have a Canadian boyfriend, we work out a lot . . . Sometimes he says he hasn't found himself yet (found whom? – you would ask . . .) I know it might sound funny here. Some people try to lose themselves and others try to find themselves. Oh well, let's have a cup of coffee . . .

Where shall we go? You're local, you must know some place. Yesterday we tried to have a drink with my old girlfriend and couldn't find a place to sit down. It was raining out. So we ended up going to the movie theater "The Barricade" on Nevsky. They have a nice coffee shop there. We even bought tickets to the movies, just in case. They were showing *Crocodile Dundee* – The cleaning woman tried to get us to go see it. "Hey, kids, it's such a funny movie," she said, "You just can't stop laughing . . . Our movies are never funny like that."

"No," I said, "we bought tickets but really we just want to sit in the coffee shop since it's open till the next show."

"But you can't do that –" she said, "the coffee shop is for moviegoers only and what kind of moviegoers are you?"

"I already saw *Crocodile Dundee*," I protested.

"It's impossible . . . Don't try to fool me. This is the opening night . . ."

"I saw it in a drive-in theater in New London," I insisted . . .

"Look, miss, leave the coffee shop this very minute. I tell you that in plain Russian, loud and clear. Coffee is for moviegoers only."

Maybe we'll see a movie, Misha, something slow, with long,

long takes. Wait, Misha, don't rush . . . I'm sure we'll find a place nearby . . . I could invite you for a bagel, but it's far away . . . We could talk about Napoleon. He's sort of out of fashion now . . . I bet the waitress would take us for ageing foreign students . . .

"The Information Kiosk closes in fifteen minutes."

"But we've waited for so long . . ."

"This is a public abuse. I demand the *Book of Complaints and Suggestions* . . ."

"I'm sorry, comrade, we don't have one here. You would have to go to the Central Information Bureau on Nevsky. But they close at two today, so you're too late. And tomorrow is their day off."

"That's the whole problem . . . Whatever the reason, Russian people love to complain . . . I would have prohibited those *Books of Complaints and Suggestions* . . . What we need is *The Book of Constructive Proposals*."

"And who are you, mister? Are you a People's Deputy, or what?"

"No, I am not."

"Well, we're very glad that you're not a People's Deputy. People have a right to information. If they can't get the information, they can complain . . . We've been silenced for too long . . ."

"So what? Before we didn't have any information and now it's all over the place . . . But who needs it when we can't afford toothpaste! We don't have toothpaste, but we've got glasnost to freshen our breaths . . . Information . . . If you want my opinion, there's too much information these days, too much talk and no change . . ."

"Excuse me," said Anya very politely. "It says here clearly: 'The Information Kiosk is open from 11 a.m. to 5 p.m. Monday through Thursday'. Today is Thursday and it's quarter to four now, therefore the Kiosk should be open for another hour and fifteen minutes."

"Hey, lady . . . who do you think I am? Do you think I can't read or something? You try working here for a fucking hundred rubles an hour. I would be making twice as much in the cooperative bakery . . . But I stay here anyway . . . I feel sorry for folks like you, having to fill out those fucking inquiry cards in the cold . . . Someone has to give people the information they need . . ."

"Excuse me, miss . . . Where are you from?"

THE OPERA

Sonia Rykiel

translated by Maxim Jakubowski

Goose bumps.

Skin bumps
moving
singing
and moving again.
Legs held up high.
Embroidered material slashed open,
Opened skirt,
unhooked, wanton.
Above him.
Brilliant gems.
Exquisite surroundings
Beautiful
Start again, and again.
On the ground for a long time,
Terrific.
Invention, insolence
Touched front and rear, everywhere
Moving again
touched behind.

At the Opera, two salons bordered with mirrors, a thousand mirrors. Warm mirrors, mirrors like the sun, cold mirrors, mirrors like the moon.

Endlessly watching myself listening to the music from *Tosca*, *La Traviata*, or *La Bohème*.

Was I right?

Making love to Mimi's tune, pulling her skirt up, holding on to her legs, her arms, her heart, her cunt.

Straightening her back, holding her tight.

She is held aloft, he is under her.

Crying, screaming.

Your sex is inside me.

Unveiled.

Even filled, I will not cry.

I am hollow, flat.

But still I keep on lying.

Don't put the phone down.

Where is chance, where is beauty? I slide, I leave, I move on.

You turn round. Look at me. I feel a need to see you in those thousand mirrors.

"Raise your face, raise your cunt. Where are your eyes?"

I can no longer see you.

The most exquisite pain takes hold of me, a moist exquisite languor. Where is my dress, where are my stockings, my shoes, my hands? Where is he, him?

I seek ecstasy.

"Get up, come here."

Waiting to be picked up, labelled, manipulated, passed around like a bottle.

I sigh, almost drunk.

The liquid is melting me inside.

Have I fallen, am I obscene, deranged?

Like a newspaper from hell.

Made up, painted, my lips so red, my eyes so dark my skin so white, my hips so curvy, my arse so voluptuous.

No, not voluptuous, exciting, lustful, on offer.

And my pear-shaped breasts, and my thin waist.

I gifted him with all of me that evening at the Opera, in the "Moon" boudoir, in the "Sun" room.

Whose existence no one else is aware.

Beauty.

Lost.

Enigma.

There is no more beautiful sight than those two rooms connected by a long, ornate walkway.

The atmosphere is electric. In five minutes, it will be *Pelleas et Melisande*.

I was dressed in pink, with orange seams.

But stark naked in the golden salon.

Spread like a saint, arms laid out like a cross, legs wide open, scarlet toed feet.

Outrageously on offer.

All that is missing is a cushion under my head.

"Here, take this scarf."

"To cover myself?"

"No, for your head."

The man is standing, shameless, his cock at attention, handing me the scarf.

His eyes are sharp, moving from my face to the upper area of my thighs. He bends over, moves closer to me, takes my head into his hands, squeezes me, approaches, bites my lips, caresses my face, pulls my hair back, holds me still, observing me.

The curtain rises. Debussy?

Mortal passion.

He holds my body high, makes me swirl, pulls me back beneath him, enters me, slips my shoe back on.

He's killing me.

Despite it all, I feel relaxed, my face now obscured by the scarf I have replaced over me.

Then he picks me up again, pulling at my arm, drags me across the floor, ploughs me, hammers me, ties me with the scarf. He shouts.

"What about Debussy?"

I am dizzy.

He nails me to the ground.

I had earlier noticed the patterns on the floor, wooden squares mottled with red, black and brown washes.

I'm crushed by the weight of his body, I sway from one side to the other.

Have I been drinking, smoking?

Complicit.

I swivel over, find my own rhythm again, lose my soul, close my eyes.

He holds me tight.

Assault, tenderness, scandal.

To be doing "this" at the opera.

Like Melisande, I am lost.

Do not touch me or I will throw myself into the water.

He looks at me.

"Who hurt you?"

Does he think he is Golaud?

"I can't say."

And do I believe I'm Melisande?

I let myself go, I want to listen to the orchestra serenading me; I want to abandon myself to the seductive voices, the sound of the violins. I want to implode.

Obsessed, he turns my lips to fire, discards the scarf concealing my face, dislocates me, pulls me to his right and then his left, rises and places his foot on my breast.

His eyes are blue, ever so blue.

Half naked on the cold floor, I slip and he catches me.

There are shadows on the walls,

Maybe I could float if only I could hear him clearly, if I could gift myself to him fully, my hair falling wildly across my face.

I pull my knees together in an attempt to get my breath back.

"I like the way you move, I like your breasts."

I am confused, I am on display.

He draws back.

"Get up on your feet."

"Naked in front of the mirrors?"

Naked a thousand times, reflected, reshaped, wrong.

He approaches, touches me, feels me, takes my hand, lowers it to his cock.

It's a part, I'm an actress, the camera is rolling, I am obeying the film director.

"Caress me."

I stroke him.

Scandal.

I love "this".

Bodies in lust.

Pleasure at its peak, sharp and true.
I am without reason, torn, asunder.
My pearl is dripping onto the wooden floor, I am gasping.
A gust of wind.
"Don't fret."
I'm trying not to rush, not to interrupt the flow.
"Stop."
Like flowers . . .

CUCKOO

Brian Fawcett

FERRIS CAN'T QUITE decide why the first sight of the ferry dock makes him shiver. Is it fear or expectation, or is it simply the bracing spring air? With one hand, he grips the bouquet of yellow tulips he's carrying a little tighter, pulls his jacket closer to his neck with the other, and the shivers pass.

He doesn't expect the island to be the same after ten years. Islands change, people change, nothing remains the same. If it has taught him nothing else, travelling across four continents has driven home the ubiquitousness of change, although too often the specific message received is twisted between "Yankee Go Home" and "Everything changes – into a mall".

Yet from a distance, the island is at least similar, and it isn't until the ferry closes in on the dock that the changes become visible. Vince is waiting for him at the terminal, as expected. But he's standing beside a nearly new Volkswagen Jetta, not slouched down comfortably in the seat of a battered GMC panel. From this distance, Vince could be mistaken for an ordinary middle-aged man, his face obscured by a beard that is more grey than black. To Ferris, he's dead easy to recognize, and anything but ordinary. Vince is Ferris's secret life – together with Ava.

Looking at him, Ferris shivers once again. That's the most familiar feeling of all, and it doesn't have anything to do with the weather conditions. Ferris has seen him waiting like this fifty, a hundred times, in every conceivable kind of weather, and the shiver has always been part of it. There is uneasiness and curiosity in it, and a tingling, *what now?* expectancy. But ten years have changed the shiver, too. The intensities have shifted. This morning, curiosity leads.

The ferry taps the dock, recoils a little, and the ramp mechanisms drop the heavy steel plates onto the decks. Ferris hangs back as the other passengers tramp across the plates and onto the wooden dock, an anonymous surge of eager human flesh that has debarked here the same way, in the same colourful chaos ten times a day since he was last here. How many crowds is that? Ferris tries to do the calculation in his head and settles at somewhere near forty thousand.

He leans against the ferry rail and makes an inventory. The mossy cedars and firs of the bay are more sparse than he remembers, and there are fewer of them. He glimpses several plush new buildings half-hidden among them, expensive homes defined by the unmistakable ostentation of wealthy people who want solitude, comfort, and convenience at the same time. The road leading down to the ferry slip looks more congested with cars and passengers than it used to be, but the sewery-salt odour of the marina is the same, and when he peers down through its murky iridescence, he can see neither improvement nor the bottom.

Ferris knows that the changes here, whatever they turn out to be, probably won't be for the better. Everything gets uglier and more vulgar. This island and its contents more than most places, probably. Less nature, more people, more toxins and shit. The crabs and shellfish all up the coast, he recalls, were declared unfit for eating several years ago, a combination of pulp mill dioxins and too much sewage washing through to the beaches from the new developments.

He steps onto the ramp, continuing his gloomy inventory. In the marina behind the ferry slip, the boats are bigger than they once were, more of them Fiberglas. And there are houseboats. He wonders how *that* happened. The islanders had once been willing to form their own navy to keep them out. Somebody has paid a lot of money for the privilege of having their living room roll around like a toy boat in a bathtub every ninety minutes when the ferries come in.

Vince catches sight of him as he reaches the end of the ramp and booms out a greeting. "Hey, hey! Cuckoo! Over here!"

Ferris almost flinches. He hasn't heard that nickname in a long time, not since the last time Vince used it. Trust him to bring it up before anything. He looks over and sees that Vince has a wide grin on his face – and that he's waiting for Ferris to come to him. Some things don't change.

They shake hands and then embrace, awkwardly. Vince glances at the tulips, but doesn't acknowledge them. "You don't change much," he says.

Ferris shrugs. "I've got a few creaks."

"No," Vince says, as if reading his thoughts. "You look young. Your face. And this," he pokes at Ferris's gut, "pretty good."

"Well, it isn't like I've had to work at it," Ferris answers. "Good genetics, I guess."

Vince's face hardens momentarily. "Oh, yeah, sure. But you haven't led a hard life. All you do is travel to glamorous places and sit on your ass. Hop in." He gestures toward the passenger side of the Jetta.

Ferris leans through the open window and looks inside. The car is immaculate. "Nice car," he says. "What happened to your junk heap?"

At one time Vince had four mid-fifties GMC pickup trucks in his backyard to rob for parts to keep the panel he drove running. It wasn't that he liked working on cars, or that he was saving money. It was a gesture to his father, a master mechanic who could make or repair anything.

Vince doesn't answer for a moment, as if he can't quite remember. "Oh, shit," he says, finally, "that was a long time ago. Someone hauled them all to the dump when we sold the house."

Ferris opens the car door, tosses the bouquet into the back seat, and climbs in. When he closes the car door, it comes to with a satisfyingly soft thump. Vince clambers in, reads Ferris's mind once again.

"The old man's dead, you know."

Ferris doesn't know, but he isn't surprised. Vince's father had been in poor health for years, and he didn't much like doctors or hospitals.

Ferris had been fond of Vince's father and had got along better with him than Vince did. Ferris would have loved the old man, but that wasn't permitted. After Ferris's parents died, the old man had taken Ferris under his wing and offered him everything that familial love confers. He was about the only male role model Ferris ever accepted. He'd given Ferris his nickname – Cuckoo – joking that Ferris was trying to push Vince out of the nest.

"When'd he go?" Ferris asks, breaking his reverie. "How long?"

"A couple of years ago," Vince answers after a pause. "His heart blew up on him while he was pulling the transmission on a truck. Never knew what hit him."

"I liked your old man a lot," Ferris says, then revises. "I loved him. I'm sorry he's gone."

"Yeah, me too," Vince answers, as if it were the least important thing on his mind. "I miss him sometimes. And," he pauses again, "sometimes I don't. Sometimes I'm glad he's gone. He could be a miserable old bastard when he wanted to."

"We should have grown up to be men like him," Ferris says.

"We didn't." Vince stares through the windshield for a moment, as if considering what kind of men he and Ferris *had* become. "That's for sure."

He starts the car, and they drive off the ferry slip past the line of cars waiting to load.

"How's Ava doing?" Ferris asks.

"You know how it goes," Vince answers, noncommittally. "Up and down. You'll see."

Ferris wants to ask him if Ava is still beautiful, but it occurs to him that Vince might not understand what he's asking. There had always been a strange lack of interiority in the way Vince viewed Ava. He seemed to know that she was an attractive woman, and he admired her sexual athletics and her unpredictability – but Ferris didn't think he ever thought of her in terms of beauty. Not the way he did. And does.

They reach the turnoff to the northerly part of the island. Vince yanks hard on the steering wheel – too hard – and the Jetta sloughs around the corner. Ferris can't think of anything to say, so he looks out the window. The island has, to use the misleading euphemism of real estate agents, developed. New homes sear the roadside, replacing the dense thickets of alder and fir that had been there since the glaciation.

The changes are so many that Ferris doesn't recognize Vince and Ava's old house when they pass it. Vince has to point it out. An addition has been built on, the yard backfilled, fresh paint. It looks

like most of the other houses around it – an upmarket bungalow.
When Vince and Ava lived there, it looked like what it was: a prefab
starter home in a swampy yard filled with wrecked pickup trucks.

"When did you sell it?" Ferris asks.

"Four years ago, when Bobby moved out. I built the addition,
and then we didn't need it . . ." Vince trails off into silence.

That sounds about right to Ferris. Vince was always good at
starting projects, not so great at figuring out the correct scale, and
lousy at finishing them. Twelve years ago, Ferris helped him put
in a fancy new septic system, an experimental one that didn't
work as advertised. Whenever it rained, the already swampy
backyard turned into a private sewage lagoon, replete with
floating turds and streamers of toilet paper. At least part of
the cause was that Vince decided to route the eavestroughs into
it, for reasons Vince couldn't quite explain and which Ferris
never got his mind around.

They talk briefly about what they've been doing in the last few
years – or rather, Ferris questions Vince about what he's been
doing – teaching retarded teenagers – now challenged pre-adults
– for some government program. Vince asks no questions and
seems to have no curiosity about Ferris's doings. Several miles
pass. The density of development drops off and the island begins
again to resemble the island Ferris knew.

"What's the new place like?" he asks.

"Very different. You'll see in a minute. Here's the turnoff."

Vince makes a right turn off the main road and bumps down a
steep gravel hill toward the water. They've moved closer to the
ocean, at least, Ferris thinks. For a moment it looks as if they're right
on the beach, but at the last minute Vince turns left into a deep draw
sheltered by huge fir trees. It's like a park, protected from both the
main road above and the ocean winds. Vince pulls into a tiny
driveway that backs onto a shed-like structure, cuts the ignition.

"Here we are," he announces.

Ferris can't see any house, and Ava isn't to be seen either.
Ferris retrieves the flowers from the rear seat and follows Vince
along a treed path around the shed. Down a short but steep
incline he can see a tiny cottage. It's covered in varnished shiplap,
with deep eaves, and a roof of shingled cedar. Smoke drifts up
from the chimneys at each end. Beyond it is another building,
unfinished, but about the same size.

"This is a change," Ferris says, still wondering why Ava hasn't appeared. In the old days, she always came out to greet him, a habit he attributed to her Yugoslav ethnic background – it was not then necessary to know if that meant Serbian, Slovenian, Croatian, or Muslim. It was, as far as he could see, her only ethnic tic. Otherwise she was as disenculturated as any WASP.

Vince waves his arm forward in reply, and Ferris skids down the mossy slope after him, and in his wake, tramps his way to the cottagey wooden back door. There is a small bell over it, on a string, and Vince tugs the string before entering. Ferris isn't sure whether to expect Ava, or Goldilocks and the Three Bears. Vince pushes the door open.

Over his shoulder Ferris can see a sign that says "NO SHOES". Vince bends over to remove his, and there is Ava. Her dark hair is peppered with grey, but God, she's still beautiful. Ferris drinks her in, transfixed by a sense of relief. Without being conscious of it, he's been imagining all kinds of horrible transformations – weight gain, accident scars, the coarsening of the features that women sometimes get under extended stress. For ten years he's seen and heard nothing of or from her except a single telephone call he made five years ago. It wasn't a long call. Ava cut him off in the middle of the opening pleasantries, saying that she and Vince were having problems; no, there was nothing Ferris could do, please stay clear.

"Ferris," she says. "You're here. It's been a long time."

Before Ferris can hand her the bouquet, Vince straightens up, completely blocking his view with his bulk. "Take off your shoes, Cuckoo," he orders, curtly. "Things have changed."

The last time Ferris saw Ava, he had anal intercourse with her while Vince had vaginal intercourse with her. As Ferris waits for Vince to move out of the doorway so he can remove his shoes and continue the conversation with Ava, he recognizes that something about that night was disturbing enough that he's completely blocked it out. He can't, for instance, remember the physical configuration of it. And that in itself is strange. In the past few days, a thousand other details of those years have flooded his memory, but not that one. It has vanished, including any memory of pleasure.

When he first met Ava, more than twenty-some years ago, he thought she was the prettiest – no, the most beautiful – woman he'd ever seen. And movie-star beautiful rather than model-beautiful. She was tall, dark-haired, and darker eyed, with full breasts and hips, statuesque. Her breasts were too large for modelling, and she carried and cared for herself indifferently – without any sense of glamour. She rarely wore make-up and Ferris couldn't recall seeing her in high heels. Here, he can't even remember seeing her dressed up except the day she and Vince got married. That was the day Ferris met her.

It took a while, but when he got to know Ava, he liked her. She seemed bright enough even though she didn't talk much. Ferris put that down to the fact that no one talked much around Vince. He dominated most conversations, and when he talked, you listened.

He never asked them when they got into group screwing, which of them initiated it, or exactly why they were doing it, but it had started before he entered their orbit. A few years after they got married, Vince began to talk about it – proudly, as if it were a badge of their openness and modernity. At first Ferris thought he was bullshitting. Talk is cheap, and Vince was a talker. And even if he was telling the truth, well, so what? It was the aftermath of the 1960s, when everybody thought they had the duty – and maybe even a basic right – to grope anyone they found attractive in whatever configuration appealed to them at the moment. The more bizarre the better.

Oh, Ferris had his fantasies about such things, but in strictly democratic terms, as a foursome, in which he and whatever partner he was with would sleep with others. Like most men (and maybe women) in those days, he was as interested as the next person in sleeping with new partners, but giving up bodily possession of his own in the deal was just too threatening. He'd occasionally entertained fantasies of a threesome involving two women, but not with much enthusiasm. He assumed that such a configuration would be centred on the male, and he had enough doubts about his stamina and gifts as a lover that he didn't indulge the fantasies very far. Two men and a woman hadn't occurred to him.

The first time Vince asked Ferris to join them, he said no. Thankfully, Vince didn't persist beyond calling him a reactionary. Ferris didn't say so, but he was quite willing to be reactionary. It was easier just to screw around, thanks. He preferred to have his adventures one-on-one, where the social politics were a little easier to sort out.

*   *   *

Ferris dutifully removes his shoes and tries to evaluate what he's seen so far – Vince's relative silence on the drive over, the look on Ava's face as she greeted him. He's asked for the visit, so he can't fault them if they don't want to be hospitable. It occurs to him that he'd asked Vince, and that Vince has never denied him anything. Judging from Ava, she has misgivings about him being there.

Well, what should I expect, Ferris muses as he parks his shoes beside Vince's larger ones and picks up the bouquet. He's already frustrated by the palpable barrier between them, but he doesn't know what to do about it. Lord only knows why it's really there – it's been ten years, they've had a rough time domestically, and he still knows nothing definite about why.

He has a theory, if you can call it that, based on what Vince told him on the phone. Eight years ago they adopted a foster child about a year younger than Bobby, an eleven-year-old girl with learning disabilities. It was Vince's way of bringing his work home, and Ferris's guess is that it went badly. How or why, he doesn't have a clue. It occurs to him now that the one time he talked to Ava, also on the phone, they were probably in the midst of that mess.

There is another possibility, a simpler one. Maybe they're just wary of him and of what he might want. That makes a certain sense, except that wariness isn't something he's seen in either of them before. When you've been in every nook and cranny of another person's body, and that person has shown no hint of reluctance or displeasure, you don't expect them to respond to you with suspicion, not even after ten years. Or at least Ferris doesn't.

He's a bit simple-minded about certain things, our Ferris. He thinks, for instance, that intimacies are permanent even though he will tell you that nothing lasts forever. Some tangled circuit in his brain insists, against logic and common sense, that anyone who has cared for him once always will. He understands that the world and human beings aren't perfect, but he retains a perfect ego anyway. Is this familiar to anyone out there? Is there another name for this? Stupidity?

Ferris follows Vince into the tiny kitchen. Vince, Ferris notes, brushes past Ava without touching her. Ferris stops in front of her and presents her with the bouquet. He most definitely does want to touch her, to look at her, to see for himself. For a moment he just looks at her, and she stares back without taking the flowers out of his hand, a slight smile on her lips that doesn't touch her eyes. He brushes back a stray lock of her hair and leans in to kiss her cheek.

"Well," she says, taking a step backward but not quite flinching, "do come in and sit down. Would you like some tea or coffee?"

The three of them negotiate a pot of herbal tea, and while Ava finds a vase for the bouquet, Ferris looks around. Despite the hominess of the cottage, it is Spartan. There are no paintings or prints on the walls, and no personal mementos to be seen. Vince and Ava, Bobby, the foster daughter, and everyone else – parents and friends alike – have been disappeared.

Ferris ambles over to the couch, sits down, and surveys the cottage. The orderliness of it is startling. The Vince he knows isn't like this, not in any way. He's always been a bouncer – a project here, an idea there – the projects never quite complete, the ideas never entirely coherent. Ava lived amidst his chaos without any evident discomfort, or, now that he considers it, deep interest. She wasn't a compulsive housekeeper or much of a cook. She seemed to be in her own private universe, even as a parent – not that he saw much parenting or much of Bobby – the boy was always visiting "elsewhere" when Ferris visited. Ferris suspected that Ava was competent but slightly indifferent as mothers go. But if she didn't exert much control in the household, in the bedroom she was definitely in charge – and the bedroom had very elastic proportions.

There was the time she greeted him on arrival with a blowjob: no formalities permitted, not a word of explanation. Ferris stood in the doorway with his back to the road, his arms braced against the doorjambs and watched her slip his cock in and out of her throat with an exquisitely firm touch grasping and sucking on the in-stroke, and vibrating her tongue across his glans on the out.

Anyone driving by would have recognized exactly what she was up to, but it didn't take very long, and the road remained empty. When she was finished, she stood up, kissed him, and slipped his own come into his mouth. Then, grinning, she told him it was an experiment – she wanted to see how fast she could make him come.

★   ★   ★

Watching Vince and Ava dither in the kitchen, Ferris has another moment of doubt. Why *did* he come here? With some fatuous hope that nothing changes? Aside from a salting of grey hair, Ava seems to be the same woman – physically. But she is wary, chastened, closed, and now it comes to him, unerotic. Why?

Ferris is suddenly assailed by a flood of erotic memories. The way it started, for instance: Vince invites him for dinner. Ferris is between relationships, so he comes alone, dressed in bluejeans and shirt and tie, bringing a bottle of wine and flowers – they were chrysanthemums, so it would have been autumn. Ferris always keeps his seasons straight that way.

He's expecting a family dinner, to yap with the kid, and leave early. When he arrives there are only the two of them. Bobby is staying with an aunt.

At the dinner table the conversation rolls around to sex. Vince is doing the talking. Ferris isn't saying much, and Ava is impersonating the Mona Lisa, watching them both with an amused expression on her beautiful face. The flashpoint is sexual jealousy which Ferris uncomfortably admits to feeling. Who doesn't?

"I don't," Vince claims. "I've never felt a twinge of it."

"I don't believe you," Ferris says.

Vince grins. "That's just your threatened sexuality talking," he answers. "Ava can fuck with whoever she wants. So long as she experiences pleasure, I do too."

"I suppose you sit on your hands and watch."

"Sometimes." Vince answers as if it were a completely mundane matter of fact. "But usually not for long."

Ferris eyes Ava, imagining her moaning and bucking in a stranger's embrace while Vince calmly watches. It's an arousing image, but one that makes his spine contract. It's Ferris's ex-girlfriend making it with her new man, and Ferris is being forced to watch – or is it Vince watching him and his ex?

Across the table, Ava unbuttons her blouse. She's not wearing a brassiere. She begins to fondle her nipples. They're inverted, and as Ferris stares, they grow erect beneath her fingers. Vince is watching her too, saying something Ferris doesn't follow. He sounds like a television game show host. With an effort, Ferris focuses on what he's saying.

"Well," Ferris hears Vince saying, "why don't you show Ferris what I'm talking about?"

Ava murmurs an "Uh*hmm*" that is neither concurrence nor question, and stands up, sloughing off her blouse as she does so. She walks around the table, slips to her knees in front of Ferris, and begins to unzip his fly, nuzzling his crotch as she does it. Woodenly, Ferris helps her, undoing his belt and freeing his erect penis from his jeans. She inhales it expertly. Within seconds he's on the verge of coming, and she senses it. She pulls back, holding the head between two fingers, and looks up at him.

"Oh, no you don't," she says.

She leads him to the couch, where she slips off her skirt and sinks back against the material. She's not wearing panties. Ferris crouches between her thighs and lifts her legs over his shoulders. He tried to give her head, but she isn't very interested. She grabs his hair and looks into his eyes, the same amused look on her face.

"I want you inside me," she said. It's an order.

It's like a pornographic movie to Ferris, and he has to remind himself that this is really happening. He looks over at Vince, who is still sitting at the dinner table with an I-told-you-so smirk on his face. Ferris tries to slow down, to think of other things as he strips off his clothes, but it's impossible. His sense of irony has deserted him, and for the first time he can remember, there is no part of him standing aside, watching and analyzing. Vince is the watcher, here.

For a while, anyway. Ferris glimpses Vince removing his clothes, and as he kneels in front of Ava again, Vince moves past him to sit on the arm of the couch, his erection bobbing against her face. She slurps it hungrily as Ferris penetrates her.

Ferris comes in a few strokes, and in a state that is about equal parts tumescence and culture shock he watches his first live blowjob. At a distance of less than two feet, it goes on too long and it looks awkward. Eventually Vince pulls away, and as if Ferris isn't there, he pulls Ava off the couch onto the rug and mounts her.

Ferris does not quite know what to do, so he covers his confusion with a feigned empiricism. He lies on the rug beside them, watching Ava's face as they fuck. It's easier to watch her than him, somehow, or *it*. She remains composed and conscious, taking his hand and pulling it in to fondle her nipples as Vince pumps away, lost in his own groaning, grunting ecstasy. He takes what seems like forever to have an orgasm, and through most of it Ava's eyes are locked on Ferris, beads of sweat rolling off her forehead and neck, her hand rhythmically gripping his wrist as Vince's thrusts pound into her. When Vince finally does come it sounds and looks like he's dying. Ferris is half convinced that he and Vince are from a different species. But he doesn't get to think that one through. Ava reaches over, grabs his hair and pulls him to her. He kisses her lips, licks the sweat from her face. Behind him he feels Vince running his tongue along his spine. He closes his eyes.

Ava comes out of the kitchen with a teapot and three mugs on a tray. Vince follows with small cream and sugar jugs in matching ceramics, and some spoons. She slides the tray onto the coffee table, and Ferris realizes that she's left the vase back in the kitchen.

"That's milk there," she says, motioning at the cream jug. "I trust that will be fine."

The way she says it lets Ferris know she's not interested in the answer.

"Milk's fine," he says.

Vince eases his big body into the chair across from the couch, and Ava pulls one of the wooden chairs from the table and sits down opposite him, beside Vince.

"What do you think?" Vince asks, leaning over to pour the tea.

Ferris isn't sure what he's referring to, then realizes that he's being asked his opinion about the cottage.

"It looks pretty good," he says. "But very different, no? The old place was . . ."

"Bigger," Ava intervenes. "There's just the two of us, you know. And we live very quietly."

"I'll show you the workshop later," Vince adds. "You'll like it."

"You did all this yourself?"

"We did it," Ava says, emphasizing the "we".

Ferris can't quite stifle a smile. The Vince he knew would have cut off both thumbs before a quarter of this got completed. "You mean, you did it."

"I took a carpentry course, actually," Ava answers, a dry smile crossing her face momentarily.

Vince hands Ferris a mug of tea, with milk and sugar already in it. Not the kind of detail he'd have expected Vince to remember, but he does. And Ferris doesn't point it out. Instead, he recognizes that this is the most formal the three of them have ever been with one another, and the tension is exquisite. On the tail of that thought rides another: We want this to be over, all three of us. In our different ways.

Ferris doesn't know where to begin. Nothing new in that, Ferris muses. Well, there were always interminable awkwardnesses to this. How can you have casual conversation with a married couple immediately after you've had sex with them? You can't talk about the weather, because there isn't any. The world disappears, replaced by one's own overdrawn senses. You place your fingers in front of your nostrils and there is her scent, yours, and a third. There is a drop of come on your leg. Whose is it?

Then there were the other, trickier questions that Ferris couldn't quite ask: What is this for? Why Ferris and not someone else? Where is this supposed to lead?

If Vince had answers to those questions, he didn't offer them. He travelled in Ava's erotic wake, revelling in the foam of her mysterious agenda like a dolphin in the backwash of a ship. For Ava, there didn't seem to be any questions. She was inside, and of, the events, and one event simply led to the next.

Not Ferris. The minute the event was done, he wanted to know where, and why, and what. And the only answers he got were what came next.

There were *explanations* to be had, of course. The first was predictable, and it brooked no further inquiry: *Why not?* That was the battle cry of their generation, but in this case Ferris couldn't quite separate the question and its answer from *Why me and not others?*

That got explained indirectly. There *were* others. A woman, whose name he was given along with explicit descriptions of what had gone on. She was Ava's choice, Ferris gathered, although no one said so. Ferris wanted to know whose choice he'd been, but he didn't ask.

The other explanations made his head spin. They'd wanted him for years. They loved him, in fact. Both of them, yes. Love, and friendship. Why not?

This revelation muddied things further. In theory he too loved his friends, Vince included. Maybe particularly. But neither love nor friendship would have occasioned him to invite Vince to sleep with his women, alone or with Ferris watching or participating. What did Vince get out of this? Was it just for the erotic kick he got?

"All those things are part of sex, Cuckoo," Vince explained one night when Ferris pushed the subject. "Ava wanted you. I did too."

"We didn't pick you out of a police line-up," Ava added. "Don't make this too complicated or it'll screw you up."

"It is complicated," Ferris said.

"Well," Ava said, "you know what they say."

"What do they say?"

"They say that when a married woman wants to sleep with another man it means there's something wrong with her marriage."

"What do they say about men doing the same thing?"

She laughed. "They say it just means he has testicles."

"Yeah, well, who the hell are *they*, anyway?" Ferris said, getting irritable.

"They're the part of you that wants to believe what they say."

That didn't quite answer the question Ferris couldn't bring himself to ask either of them: Why does Ava *love* me?

The question, after ten years, is still there. In fact, it has grown. Now he wants to know *how* Ava loved him, not just why. And his perfect ego, stupid as always, wants to know if she still does.

Both Ava and Vince are gazing at him impatiently.

"Well," Ferris says, pausing to sip the tea. "I guess we should get on with it."

"I'm not sure what we're supposed to get on with," Ava answers, irony distributed about equally through the sentence. It coats each word with ice.

"I guess," Ferris says, hesitantly, "I want to know what's become of you. And I still don't quite understand *us*."

Another hesitation. Ava arches her eyebrows, Vince looks out the window. Ferris knows he sounds like a fifteen-year-old explaining why he's come home late with the family car.

"What happened, like."

Ava rolls her tongue around across her top lip. Ferris recognizes the gesture, but it means something quite new.

"*You* disappeared," she says. "That's what happened. Not a word, no goodbye, no nothing. Why do you want to know what happened? You were there. And you weren't. Were we supposed to come looking for you?"

Ferris shivers again, involuntarily. Was it really that open? A free choice, openly offered despite the nature of their arrangement and its strange discretions? Maybe.

He senses that it was, and then again it wasn't. It explains how easily he walked away from it, and it explains why they didn't come looking for him. But it doesn't explain either what they did together. And it leaves out the intervening years, and it says nothing about the obvious truth that a ménage-à-trois isn't exactly a configuration built for stability, emotional or any other kind. It was asymmetrical, unbalanced. With them – or maybe it was only with Ferris – the imbalances shifted constantly, creating new ground that was always somehow weirder. He'd get his head around one part of it, and the norm would move beyond, out there.

Vince doesn't say anything. He looks over at Ava and smiles, wearily. She smiles back, wryly, as if she's explaining something obvious to an obtuse child. "Maybe it's time you told us what was happening, Ferris."

Ferris puzzles over the solidarity he senses between Vince and Ava. It doesn't have anything to do with sex. Its basis is an almost monastic separateness, a formality that precludes sexuality rather than preludes it.

If he's reading it right, it's a dramatic change for Ava. The one certainty about her was her readiness for sex, anytime, any place, the weirder the better. She simply liked to have cocks around her or inside her, preferably more than one. Well, "simply" isn't the right word. She seemed to take her greatest pleasures from controlling him and Vince – from making them lose control, to be exact, and in being able to dictate where, when, and how they got off. She liked to see them come – liked to see the imminent orgasms, the helpless heedlessness of them, in their eyes. Sometimes Ferris thought he detected a kind of contempt for their immense, brainless neediness.

He's pretty sure she didn't have orgasms herself. And God knows he tried to make her have them. For nearly a year he became obsessed by it, going down on her literally for hours, licking and stroking every fold of flesh he could get his tongue on, keeping himself glued to her clitoris while Vince fucked her, whatever he could think of to get her over.

It never quite happened. She'd reach a plateau of pleasure, cruise it for a brief time, and then subside back to her zone of control. Vince seemed oblivious to all this, and Ferris didn't ever ask either of them about it. It was, after all, her show, and if not, then their show.

After an arduous session one night, Vince went off for a shower, leaving him to cuddle Ava. She suddenly sat up on the bed with her back to him.

"I'm in love with you, Ferris," she said, very slowly and carefully, as if she were pronouncing some sort of curse. He felt his heart constrict. Vince had already established that she loved him, but this was different. The situation was already crazy, and this zoomed it a lot crazier. Here was a woman, someone else's wife, a woman he'd been intimate with in almost every way except the conventional ones, and now she seemed to be saying she wanted to have an affair with him, and maybe a lot more than that.

"You know how I feel about you," Ferris answered after a tense silence. It was a careful answer, as careful as he could make it. Ferris wasn't sure what he felt for her, and he didn't want to use the word "love". Love is something people settle into, a comfortable, conventional intimacy. This wasn't comfortable, and it sure as hell wasn't conventional. He'd tried to convince himself that it was just sex, something they did without needing to talk about it. He knew that this wasn't quite accurate, but it made it easier to cope with.

"I don't know," she said, still not looking at him. "I don't know what you feel at all, Ferris, and I don't know what you think. You come here and we do all this, we make love, we fuck, but what does it count for?"

"A lot."

That was true. It did count for a lot, but what "a lot" meant, he couldn't have said. And here was a problem. It was great sex, great. No other word sufficed. And it satisfied his hunger for transgression, his need to affront convention. But how important was that out in the world? Not very, if he could walk away from it for weeks and months at a stretch. And what did it say about how he felt toward either of them? Not much.

"A lot?" she repeated. "You leave here in the morning like you're escaping. Where do you go? I don't know anything about your life. Do you ever think about me – about us – when you don't have your face buried between my legs?"

It was a deadly question – and he didn't have to answer it. Vince came out of the bathroom, still wet from the shower, with a towel around his head and shoulders. "So," he asked, "what are you two talking about?"

Before Ferris could dodge, Vince told him what he thought the conversation was about. "Ava wants to have a child with you. I think it's a good idea."

This wasn't what he and Ava were talking about, was it? He glanced at Ava and could read nothing, either way, from her expression. Maybe this is how she explained it to Vince, or maybe it was how Vince explained it to himself, made it into a practical reality. Vince's version was the more frightening, but either way, it scared the shit out of Ferris.

"You already have a child," Ferris said, tentatively. "If you want another, why don't you just go ahead and have one?"

"We didn't think about it until a little while ago," Vince said. "I had a vasectomy last year. Didn't think we'd want more kids. But Ava really loves you, Ferris. So do I. And why not?"

Ferris's head was spinning. On this one, he could think of several dozen reasons why not, the best of them practical. Whose child would it be? Who would raise it? He was number three in this relationship in every way, and so far that had been fine. But what would happen if they were to throw a child out into the mix? Would the child have two fathers?

Oh no, Ferris could see that this was altogether too crazy.

"This is a pretty amazing proposition," he said, trying to compose himself. "I need some time to think about it."

"Oh, sure," Vince said, very serious now. "Think about it."

Ferris takes a sip of tea. "I'm thinking about that time you asked me if I wanted to father a child with you," he says. "I never understood that."

Vince shrugs. "What's to understand? At the time, it was a serious offer. But you would have had to make a commitment, and you didn't. So it passed. That's when I began to realize just how screwed up you were, actually."

Ferris looks to Ava for confirmation. She looks out the window, and then back at him. "It was a bad idea," she says, slowly. "We had a lot of those, if you recall."

Oh yes, indeed. The worst one was Ferris's, kicked off from that incident. He decided that he wanted Ava for himself. Or at least, he wanted to see what it would be like between just the two of them. An affair, or whatever it might be called in the circumstances. The nomenclature would need to be peculiar, but then his feelings for her were peculiar. Until that moment putting a name to them hadn't seemed relevant, or rather, it hadn't seemed possible.

Ava went along with it, for as far as it went. They met several times in anonymous hotels. Ferris was all over her, and she was either bored or diffident – Ferris couldn't decide which it was. He did everything he could to make her lose control of her reserve, to orgasm, but even though he licked and sucked and fucked her until she was raw he couldn't get her half as close as Vince and he did together. She let him do whatever he wanted, affectionate and slightly impatient at the same time, as if she were humouring a child. Whatever he thought he was doing, it was wide of the mark, and Ava gave him no hint of any alternative. Maybe she felt guilty because Vince wasn't there. After a while, Ferris did.

Alone, he and Ava discovered they had little to talk about. By unspoken agreement, they didn't talk about Vince or about the ménage-à-trois. They didn't talk about being in love, or about having a child, although Ferris imagined that he might be getting her pregnant. They didn't discuss how either of them got to the hotel, or how she would get back to the island afterward, they didn't discuss work or children, and they barely talked about the weather. They were left with a present that had to subsist within the walls of the hotel room, and a future that they might be risking by being there.

They met in the hotel lobby, rushed to the room, made love, and lay in the darkness without speaking. If this was the real thing, it wasn't nearly as exciting as the unrealities they were cheating on. Ava didn't get pregnant, and they stopped meeting without having to admit they were going to. Ferris was disappointed and relieved at the same time.

Now, here, he has a sudden instinct that Vince had known about it all along, and that if not, he certainly knew now. "I had some dumb ideas in those days," Ferris says, looking at Vince and feeling guilty.

"You mean like trying to take Ava away from me?" he says. "Yeah, I knew you were trying. I wasn't worried. I thought you'd figure it out for yourself soon enough."

"How did you find out?"

"Ava told me she was seeing you. I told you we trusted each other completely. You didn't believe it like you didn't believe a lot of the rest of what I said. More tea?"

Ferris decided to leave "the rest of it" alone. "Another cup is fine. Why didn't you stop it?"

"Why should I? Ava was crazy about you . . . and I thought you might see what we were offering you."

Ava fills Ferris's cup, tops up her own and Vince's, and goes off to the kitchen to make more. Watching her do this simple thing, Ferris tries to fathom how she sorted out complexities like the ones he'd created for her. Did she sort them out at all? He could hardly fault her if she didn't. He hadn't, not really.

From the beginning of it, Ferris had difficulty living with the idea that he was sexually involved with a married couple. How many times had he sat on the ferry on the trip back and told himself it was too weird, that he couldn't handle it any longer?

Yes, but it was also the ferry rides, together with the isolation of the island, that protected it, and him. No one knew he had this other life. To his friends, Ferris was someone who sometimes disappeared for a few days, that's all. Not generally available on weekends. If a friend asked where he was, he mentioned business. If business associates asked, he used his friends as an excuse.

After the "affair" ended, it got harder, and he didn't return to the island at one point for almost eight months. He found several new lovers, tried hard to stay interested in them, but couldn't. When he started coming back to the island regularly, there were no recriminations, no oblique punishments, no reluctances. But there was a subtle erotic escalation, so subtle that he didn't notice it at first.

Ferris was conducting his own subtle escalation. He was competing with Vince, holding off his orgasms until after Vince had his, or breaking off to watch them fuck, nestling close to Ava, cuddling her, kissing her breasts or face or neck, holding her eyes with his while Vince came. Then he'd have her to himself, and he put on performances that were as much for Vince as for Ava.

They weren't always comfortable performances, because Vince had some unsubtle ways of watching. He'd lie with his face next to Ava's vagina, slipping Ferris's cock out of her and into his mouth for a few strokes. Or while Ferris was fucking with Ava, Vince would play with his balls, or lick his asshole. Several times Vince insisted on joining in on fellatio – at least once, due to last-second manoeuvres, Ferris came in Vince's mouth. Vince seemed to enjoy all of this, and Ferris, well, didn't.

Meanwhile, the configurations and combinations were escalating, getting wilder and weirder. Each round of love-making seemed to require a new configuration. Some of them were simply contortions – easy enough to adapt to. Then came vibrators and dildos, an uncomplicated fourth partner. There was a decipherable symmetry to the escalations. Each time, Ferris was offered the more extreme posture. At the next session, Vince began there. Oils appeared, anal intercourse was introduced. At that, Ferris at first balked.

"Don't be a prude," Vince said. "It isn't painful if it's done right. You lubricate properly, and come into her from the front, just like conventional fucking. You'll like it. She does."

Ava, lying between them on the bed, arched her back and licked her lips.

Then Ava wanted them both in her vagina at the same time. It was a difficult, contorted manoeuvre, and Ferris was convinced that it was painful for her. A few days afterward, he phoned and asked her point-blank.

"It was pleasant," she said, her voice cool. "Should we be talking about this on the phone?"

"It didn't look like it was pleasant," he said. "It looked painful. And it felt painful."

"It hurt you?" she answered, her tone still cool.

"No, damn it. It hurt you. I hurt you."

"Ferris, sweetie," she said as if instructing a child. "Sometimes it's hard to tell the difference between pleasure and pain. In any case, if I'd wanted you to stop, I would have said so."

"You would have."

"Yes. Don't you understand that?"

He told her he did.

Ferris realizes that he's staring at Ava, remembering being in those strange and stranger embraces with her, helplessly recalling her scent and taste and the myriad erotic postures in which he's seen her exquisite body. He knows more about her, been more intimate with her than any woman he's been with. At the same time, he knows nothing about her, nothing comfortably human. Doesn't intimacy leave indelible traces? Where are they, here?

"Don't, Ferris," Ava says. "I don't want to be looked at like that. Not by you, or Vince, or anyone else."

"I'm sorry," he says. He *is* sorry. "That certainly isn't why I'm here."

"So why are you here, exactly?"

Tough question. Mentally he goes over the list: curiosity about the events of the last ten years, an old friend's and lover's distant concern, some personal curiosity about how a beautiful woman has aged. All acceptable motives. But there's a surprise item on the list, and it isn't acceptable: Ferris isn't sure he wouldn't tumble into the sack with them right now if they proposed it.

He frowns, tries to rid himself of the thought. "Tell me what happened with the child you adopted."

Ava looks at the floor, and Vince sinks back in his chair with a sigh.

"There's not much to tell," he says. "She had learning disabilities, you knew that. She didn't improve, and by the time she was fifteen, we had a major behaviour problem on our hands. All sorts of incidents, one thing after another. Eventually she was caught breaking into the house of one of our neighbours, and she got sent to a juvenile home. We sprung her, but after that, it was worse. She'd be here for a few days, and then she'd disappear for weeks on end. Then she stopped coming. We don't even know where she is, now. In jail, I think."

"I'm sorry," Ferris says. "What about Bobby?"

"What about him?" Vince replies. "He's around. He has his own place in town, works, goes to school part-time. He just outgrew the island, that's all. This isn't much of a place for young people."

"Are you two happy?"

Ava answers. "Sometimes. Yes." There's a long hesitation. "We've been in therapy for three years. That's helped a lot."

"What for?" Ferris asks, without thinking.

"It got out of hand," Vince answers for her. "There was nothing in our lives but sex. It was an addiction."

Their distance makes it feel more like there's a continent between them and him rather than a few feet. The distance was there when he arrived, but now it is tangible. And it is growing, solidifying.

"We didn't understand that, not really. Nobody does, anymore.

We thought the pleasure we wanted, or whatever it is life is about, was somewhere else, something else, some*one* else. That's what you were all about, what that whole thing was about. It felt like a big mountain we were climbing, but we were only climbing out of ourselves. We discovered that what matters is the village at the base of the mountain. Now we get up in the morning and work on things. One day at a time."

Ferris can feel disappointment straining against his discretion. Vince has just given him a cliché-ridden Alcoholics Anonymous speech. It's evidently a sincere one, and the small smile on Ava's face as he speaks confirms her agreement.

"But you know, Ferris," Vince says after an awkward silence Ferris doesn't break, "we're okay, now. It started to come around when we realized that life isn't supposed to be easy. None of what we did was a total waste of time. We had to go through it and come out on the other side. I think that's what you're doing, too, in your own way. It's too bad you have to do it alone."

Ferris shrugs. Maybe, just maybe, it is that simple. The way they lived, the dangers must have kept growing, while the payoffs got smaller, or at least harder to find. Eventually, the accumulated discretions and indiscretions must have toppled over on them in some terrible way. Maybe in the real world, maybe just in their minds. But maybe they just got tired of the complications, and stopped. So maybe the unfinished business he came here to settle isn't unfinished, and there are no revelations forthcoming.

Well, not quite. Ever since he got on the ferry this morning, he's been wrestling, somewhere in his subconscious, with the puzzle of how Vince and he performed simultaneous anal and vaginal intercourse with Ava. He's certain it took place, because he can distinctly remember the sensation of his and Vince's penises touching through the thin membrane between them. What's bothering him – what's been bothering him for a long time – is the configuration.

It was part of an obscure fidelity Ferris kept, and he'd been subtle enough with it that he was certain that neither Vince nor Ava were aware of it. But throughout everything they did, Ferris had not once entered Ava unless they were face to face. Now, suddenly, he realizes the configuration he wants isn't physically possible. He's been deluding himself. Vince had been on his back, she kneeling forward on his chest, and Ferris was squatting behind her. In the crudest possible sense, Ferris had fucked her up the ass, impersonally, like a dog would. And for ten years, he'd been blocking the memory of it.

"What's wrong, Ferris?" he hears Ava asking. His consternation must have shown in his face. "Were you expecting more?"

Ferris looks at the ceiling. "No," he says. "I just thought of something. It's obscure stuff. Nothing to do with you."

He wants to tell Ava he's sorry, but what he's sorry about is so oblique there's no way he can make her understand – even if she wanted to. It's the truth, but sex delivers an almost infinite number of truths, all equal. It's also true that he didn't return after that because he was frightened to. Beyond unrestricted pleasure he'd glimpsed its opposites: violence and pain. And in Ferris's mind, they had crossed the boundary.

Or maybe that's what *I'm* seeing and saying, and Ferris is nothing but a sexual cuckoo that vacated the nest when it got too hot inside. I'd like Ferris to see it, but what's the point of inflicting my erotic insights on him – or on Vince and Ava? I could do all sorts of comforting things here. I could make Ferris grovel for forgiveness, join their chapter of Sexaholics Anonymous – or form his own. I could force him to admit that he'd started a primary relationship soon after he left, and when that failed, another, ad nauseam. Or less comforting, I could make him confess a secret he's kept even from himself: that sex was never so good as it was with them, not before, nor after.

But there's nothing discreet for him to say, nothing he needs to know or say about this. By a different route, he's come to the same conclusions they have. It's time to go.

"I should catch the next ferry back," Ferris says. "But you're right. Life isn't supposed to be easy: I just wish I'd known that twenty years ago."

Ava smiles. It's a real one this time, and as Ferris gets up to leave, she reaches over and grasps his hand. "So do we," she says. "But we didn't."

It's too early to leave for the ferry, so Ferris and Vince wander out to the workshop, where Vince shows him an array of power tools and a birdhouse he's planning to elevate next to the living-room window. It's a mess, big enough to house a raven, but Ferris doesn't say so.

On the ferry back from the island, Ferris writes this in his notebook:

What if our erotic lives are not written on water; but are a kind of graffiti scribbled on the planetary and cosmic slate, an inscription of meaningless insights and temporary states of emotions and prejudice by which we are nonetheless going to be mercilessly judged, not by a divine being but by the volume of darkness and misery we generate with them.

"Well then," he says aloud. "I will generate no more darkness."

The man sitting next to him looks up from the book he's been dozing over. "What did you say? Were you talking to me?"

Ferris laughs. "No," he says. "Not directly. Thinking out loud, I guess."

He pulls his bag onto his shoulder. The ferry is nearing the mainland terminal, but he's got time for a pee before it docks. After that, he has distant places to go, faraway people to meet and write lies about.

Over the urinal is scribbled the following barely literate message:

I just had fuck a chery Nazi asshole

I guess the confusion is universal, Ferris thinks to himself as he tries to come up with an answer to the graffito. Trouble is, it exists in specific conditions. Some of them lead easily to violence, others get resolved by small bursts of insight, and some simply remain unanswered and unrelieved.

He feels the gentle bump of the ferry meeting the slip, hears the rumble of the motors as they reverse. He leaves the graffito unanswered, and seconds later he's back in the crowd of travellers hurrying to the next destination.

LIES

Geraldine Zwang

translated by Maxim Jakubowski

It was past four in the morning when I opened the door to my flat, hesitant like a thief. I felt dirty, exhausted by what I had just come through. In the hallway's mirror I quickly noticed the darkness surrounding my eyes, as well as a look of exaltation I had never glimpsed before. In the penumbra of the hallway, the mirror was showing me the very image of a loose woman, so far from the conservative and restrained bourgeois fifty year old image I tried to adhere to.

I silently made my way to the bathroom when I heard my husband's voice from the corridor.

"Do you know what time it is?"

Unknowingly, he was saying the exact same words my father would throw at me whenever as a teenager I returned from parties at my friends. A wave of fear coursed through me, a fear which quickly changed into anger. Anger towards the proprietary male, the accountant in our couple. I'm anything but a submissive woman, far from it, but there has always been a kernel in me that makes any woman of my age her husband's woman.

As a soothing April dawn neared, I knew I no longer wanted this relationship and that from now onwards I would lead a new life according to my own will.

"I've just been fucked," I said, enunciating the words carefully, with an assurance that surprised me.

Sometimes silences can feel endless, but this one lasted an eternity.

"Is that your idea of a joke?" my husband asked disbelievingly.

I knew for a fact that his voice was not that of someone who had just woken up. He had been waiting for me. I wasn't surprised when he appeared at the door fully dressed. His eyes moved between wrath, incredulity and consternation. The ironic tone of his earlier question disappeared as soon as he looked at my face. I really did look like a woman who had been fucked. Eyes tired but grateful, lips ever so swollen by kisses and bites and an over-indulged body that had lost its social remoteness.

The "where have you been?" triggered an avalanche of questions: who had I been with? what had I done?

The more he spoke, the more he was overtaken by fear. Without even providing him with any answer I was already assuming a dominant position, watching him shrink with every passing moment. I was no longer afraid and could observe this man who was my husband with detachment, even with curiosity. How could I ever have been physically content with this man for so many years? I was now resentful for the cold years when physical desire had faded to just being a memory. So, in a spirit of vengeance, to test him also, I decided to tell him everything, with nothing left out and invited him into the salon and ordered him to sit, facing me, behind his desk.

I confessed that I had had an adventure with two men I had met at an art gallery opening.

My husband's face froze and I was unable to read any of his feelings right then. It was as if he was discovering a new woman he had never truly known. All of a sudden, all his certainties were falling apart. His voice all muted, he continued his interrogation.

"But what actually happened, you didn't go with them together, surely?"

"I did, one in my cunt and the other in . . . my mouth then . . . in my bum."

My honesty and poise affected him even more than if he had witnessed the act. I saw him tighten his fists but, visibly excited, he still wanted to learn more. I knew from that very moment that power had shifted from him to me.

"Did you know when you followed them, what they were expecting of you?" he stuttered.

"Of course. Each one as they rubbed against me whispered into my ear what they would do to me. I was both embarrassed and flattered by their lust."

"What did they say?"

"The first man was just about thirty years old. He was short but well proportioned. He hadn't said a single word before he moved against me. I could clearly feel the tip of his cock against my leg. I'd noticed him a few times already moving around the art gallery and had found him handsome. I don't know what came about me but I pressed hard against him to confirm I could feel his cock and didn't mind him rubbing against me."

"But what did he say to you?"

My husband couldn't contain his excitement.

"He said: 'I'd love to split your luscious middle-class arse open while you're sucking my friend off.' His lips barely moved next to my ear, but the faint breath that came from him was already making me wet with desire. He rubbed himself against me even harder. 'Once you've expertly lubricated him, he'll slide underneath you to fuck you.' There was a smoothness and a lack of aggression to his vulgarity. Without even thinking, I asked him: 'Where is your friend? I'd like to feel his cock against me too.'"

My husband's patience exploded.

"Sophie, how could you ever say something like that?"

"I wanted that man, so why not his friend too if he was pleasant enough? Why be a hypocrite and wait for another day to gift myself to the other man?"

"It's disgusting."

"Why should it be disgusting to provide pleasure to two nice young men and get some in return? Would you consider it healthier to masturbate while watching your porn tapes?"

Once again I'd defeated him, and he would rather suffer and know more than order me to be silent. I continued:

"Jean-Marc introduced me to his friend Yvan. He was a very young boy, not quite twenty. He was quite beautiful and his youthful features were fascinating. I could have been his mother. I was proud of the fact they desired me. I felt young and was entertained by the envious looks of the other women surrounding us. Yvan moved towards me, his two arms outstretched as if he was about to lead me onto a dance floor.

"She looks really hot; we're going to have great fun. You warm her up a bit more and then come and join me at the bar," Jean-Marc said.

Yvan took me in his arms as if he had always known me. I didn't even try and avoid the hard bump of his cock as it brushed against me. I could feel he was hard. As much in defiance as in provocation, I swivelled shamelessly against his young cock. His voice was very soft, still tinged with echoes of childhood, but his erotic vocabulary was way beyond his age.

"So what was he telling you?" my husband interrupted me.

"Do you really think I should let you know? You're already so agitated."

Sitting behind his desk, I could guess my husband was touching himself, but I pretended to ignore the fact.

"Yes, Sophie, tell me everything."

"OK," I sighed, "but you asked for it. Both Yvan and Jean-Marc were whispering sheer filth in my ear, like 'You'll chew on my balls to get me hard again after I've discharged into your clammy hole.' These salacious words they had probably said to hundreds of women before no doubt were making me crazy. For the first time in my life, I felt like a slut and I kept on pressing my parts against his cock. Yvan said that if I continued he might even come right there and then, and as a precaution moved slightly away from me. We joined Jean-Marc at the buffet table.

"Once we had reached the table, he took my hand in his and positioned it against his cock and said quietly in my ear: 'Look how hard you've made me, it's full of come, all for you. We're going to feed you well, you pretty slut. You're going to love it.'

"His impudence was electrifying me and I daringly moved the envelope one step further.

"'I'll have you spitting into all three of my holes, you pretty things. You'll throw up a white flag once my tongue gets working on you.'

"Yvan smiled in admiration and caressed my arse. I did not stand back when he moved one of his fingers into my arse hole, pushing the material of my skirt into it. I groaned, still holding on for dear life to Jean-Marc's cock, indifferent to all the people around us in the room who meant nothing more to me any longer.

"Jean-Marc indicated it was time for us to go and we were soon in his car. Yvan sat me in the back. As soon as we drove off, he kissed me eagerly and took hold of my breasts in both his hands. My own hands liberated his cock and I began steadily jerking it off while playing with his youthful balls. Jean-Marc loudly encouraged me.

" 'Milk that dong, you fat cow, suck his cunt juice out.'

"His driving was erratic, he was in a hurry for us to get back to his place. I could no longer hold back; I had already swallowed Yvan's cock to the hilt a few times while fingering myself. I felt like a young girl again, all excited, with her very first lover, my lust flying in all directions.

"In the elevator taking us up to Jean-Marc's flat, I caught a brief glimpse of myself in the mirror and I decidedly looked beautiful, young and flushed. They roughly placed me between them and took turns rubbing their cocks against me. I moaned wordless sounds, begging for them to take me. We exited the elevator, the men pulling me out each with a finger stuck inside me.

"Once inside the apartment, I rushed towards Yvan, whose cock was sticking out of his trousers. I crouched on all fours so that my arse was well exposed and sucked him with savage glee. Jean-Marc brutally pulled up my skirt and viciously pulled the elastic of my garter belt aside and let it slam back against my thighs; it wasn't that painful but the sharp sound it made was exciting. I heard him undress behind me. I craved for him to take me with no warning, just to feel his hard sex penetrate me before I could even feel the approach of his body. Yvan pulled his cock out of my mouth, about to come. He left the room, leaving me there on all fours. Jean-Marc forbade me to look back and ordered me to 'polish your cunt to warm yourself up'."

Having reached this part of the story, Sophie was increasingly overcome by excitement; she couldn't help rubbing her legs against each other in search of further pleasure. She was intensely living the evening all over again and had banished me from her world. I had already come in my trousers. Feverishly awakened by my ejaculation and my wife's violent story, my own cock refused to lie down as I listened to her with fascination.

"He handed me a bottle of rosé wine, a long and cold bottle, and I was summoned to fuck myself with it. The initial contact with the icy neck of the bottle saw my flesh contract and only served to increase my frenzy. Yvan was back and was verbally encouraging me: 'Yes, fill that pretty pussy, cool it down for me.' I had only introduced a few centimetres of the bottle into me, when Jean-Marc sharply pushed it in even deeper. I felt as if I had been split open, gaping in a way I had never been before. I screamed with pleasure, with shame and joy blending exquisitely in my mind and body. I felt Jean-Marc spitting against my arse hole and spreading his saliva across the pucker of my hole. I was scared; I hadn't experienced anal sex often. He entered me with one single push forward, despite the bottle still filling my vagina. I was in heaven; my body had come to life thanks to the cock now ploughing my innards. Yvan was masturbating himself in front of me and I held my head high to eat him, milk him. All I could see was that dark column of flesh that I couldn't reach and I begged him to let me have it. He found it amusing to tease me, to move his cock to the tip of my lips before withdrawing it again out of reach on a few occasions. I was going crazy and was impaling myself further down onto the bottle, spreading myself open even more. With a thrust of his cock, Jean-Marc pushed me toward Yvan's member. Yvan had now sat himself down in front of me. He delicately pulled the bottle out and positioned me onto his friend's cock. They must have done this before, as the manoeuvre was rapid and expertly done. I came at the very moment that Yvan's glans pushed its way past my outer lips and again when he reached the pit of my cunt. Each thrust from the two men inside me had me screaming. As I felt Jean-Marc's sperm flooding my arse, I shouted to Ivan: 'Come in my cunt, come, come . . .'

"And he did.

"The three of us collapsed in a pile and it took some time for our energy to return.

"I needed to pee and asked where the toilet was. The two men accompanied me and asked me to pee in the bath tub with them present. Like a madwoman, I did so. Initially embarrassed, I soon let myself go and spread my thighs wide so that they might enjoy the view. Once I had finished urinating, their cocks had become hard again and I felt like sucking them. First I sucked Yvan off while Jean-Marc caressed my breasts.

" 'Now I feel like peeing,' said Yvan, 'but I'd like to pee on your pretty whorish face.'

"He had barely said the words when a warm and bitter jet invaded my mouth. I gagged but nonetheless continued to guide the stream of pee towards my face as if I were taking a shower. I had never felt so wet, inside and outside, my slit was dripping and I managed to insert four fingers into my cunt while Yvan shook his last drops against my tongue and I swallowed them.

"Jean-Marc joined me inside the bathtub and mounted me doggie style. He parked himself deep inside my pussy and began peeing inside me. I roared as the hot liquid conjured up a whole new feeling.

"Later, they both sodomized me slowly until each came deep inside my arse.

"The three of us took a shower together, still fondling each other wildly, and then they escorted me to a taxi rank.

"There you are, I've told you all."

As soon as I'd finished my story, my husband leaped on me, his cock harder than I'd seen it for a very long time. Without a word, he threw me onto the settee and forced my lips apart with his girth. His lust was pleasing; my husband wanted me again. His erection was a gift for me and I sucked him off as if my very life depended on it, forcing him to spit out a torrent of come that I swallowed like a divine offering. His pleasure roared.

I gazed at my man with love, as if I was discovering him anew: "Oh, the sort of things you have me imagining, my love."

"Thank, you, *mon amour.*"

THE NAUGHTY YARD

Michael Hemmingson

YES, YES, OKAY now, it is time, you've been waiting long enough, it is indeed time, so gather around now, gather close, don't be afraid to sit close to one another, maybe not *too* close, but close enough, all of us, around this fire, because it is story time now, it's time for a story, a story set in the past, basically, you could even categorize this as *an historical romance* if you will, set in a time when there wasn't so much fear about getting close, fear about sex&death, that horrid thing called AIDS was just around the corner like some foolish kid on his bike, going too fast and not looking where he's destined – although right now (the time of this parable) it was rather remote and not widespread; you see, it is when this yarn begins, and people were happily careless when it came to (sex), careless because there was not that (fear of death), and you may not believe it now (but history proves this), as this tale (which is history) will prove it, and we will begin with the opening scene, as such: inside one of the bedrooms of a two bedroom apartment in Southern California, where we find a petite young lady of twenty-three, dark-haired, modestly tanned, in bed with myself, and her name happens to be, for the sake of this text, Kathy, she is in bed with me and we are making love, we are fucking, call it what you will, because this girl – Kathy – this girl and I don't even know each other that well – I mean, we *know* each other, we're friends as such, we have been friends for quite a while, were lovers for some time, until she called it off, called it off for a few months – that is, until this night in question here, where we have connected again, we are fucking again: at her proposal – you see, we were at this bar, drinking, talking, drinking&drinking (she loves beer) and we came back here, to her place, and we went into her bedroom and started to take off our clothes and then, well, you get the gist of the scenario; NEVERTHELESS, so here we are, so there we were, Kathy&-myself, myself&Kathy, on her bed (which happens to be a noisy bed) the springs going *eeeech eeeech* with each thrust of myself into Kathy's self, *eeeech eeeech* goes the bed, and she's moaning. I'm moaning, we are, in fact, enjoying the moment, and – and I feel myself coming, yes yes yes, you understand this feeling (both you men and women listening to this), the intensity, you know it, the *joy joy joy*, this sudden moment where the world is ready to come apart like a badly stitched garment, where the Universe itself is on the verge of imminent collapse, as this bed is on the margin of destruction, and I come, I scream, I empty my balls into Kathy's warm cunt (making it warmer), and in that brief moment I frightfully think of the moon, and Beth, my darling Beth now gone from me, but I push these baneful head things away for this is neither the time nor place, I should concentrate on Kathy, and Kathy grabs at me, legs in the air, going *yes yes yes*, come, and I am: and when I am done, I fall on her, she doesn't mind, she rubs her hands up my back, into my hair, and I roll off her, light a cigarette, and she watches me as I smoke (she doesn't smoke), my come starting to leak out of her, her pussy red and still open, and she watches me and she says I'm spent and she says (head propped up on pillow as Jackie Collins always puts it in her books) she says I feel good you know I'm glad you decided to come over.

I say that I am glad she invited me over.

She says well you know there we were, sitting in that bar again, that same bar we used to always go to, having the same drinks we always used to drink, and you know we were talking about all this&that, bric&brac, but you know I wasn't really *listening* to what you were gabbing about.

I say you weren't listening to me?

She says I wasn't listening to *us*. She says I just kept saying to myself in my head *I really want to fuck him tonight*.

I tell her I had the same thoughts.

She says I was just thinking you know like we used to do.

I say it was nice the just-like-we-used-to-do – and then it stopped and there was no more just-like-we-used-to-do.

Kathy says maybe I was dumb to stop our just-like-we-used-to-dos.

I say yes you were yes you were.

There are two bottles of wine on the floor. One empty, one full. I pick up the full one, which isn't all that full, and take a drink.

Kathy says well you aren't supposed to say that, that's *not* what you're supposed to say. What you're *supposed* to say is: *no, Kathy my dear Kathy, you weren't being dumb you were just confused so there's a difference.*

I say I was angry.

She says you didn't show it.

No?

Maybe I wasn't watching.

Watching?

She says you acted – I dunno. You didn't seem all that angry; or hurt; I wasn't sure if you cared or not.

I say no I guess I didn't show it; I never do; I should have; I think I could have; if I had set my mind on it.

She says I didn't know you were mad at me.

I say well not real mad.

Good.

I didn't understand, that's all.

She says there's nothing really to understand.

I drink.

She says maybe I was afraid.

Afraid?

She says you used to make me nervous.

I say I don't know what *nervous* is.

She says I think you still do.

What?

Make me nervous.

What?

She laughs and takes the wine bottle from me and says just kidding.

I hope so.

Don't look at me like you're hurt.

Maybe I am.

She drinks some wine and says are you?

Sure.

She says well oh well a lot of men make me nervous you know what I mean?

A lot of men?

Men in general.

General men?

She says you don't make me nervous anymore.

No?

Nope. Awww contrary . . . she smiles and drinks wine and I light another cig and she looks around her room and she says to me I don't know why I feel that way; I mean about men. Most of my friends have been men. Are men. Boys, men, guys, you know. The opposite sex and stuff. I've never really had any girlfriends, any close women friends. Female bonding! I don't think I have ever been able to identify with women. Other ladies. Girls. They're all strangers to me. Don't have anything to do with them, except for a few obvious parts.

She adds to this by saying I'll never make it as a feminist, Mike.

I say to her but you were telling me about your roommate.

She says Cynthia, yes, we met at work.

I say I thought you said school.

She says school, work – the job I had on campus; the campus work.

I nod.

She says we are pretty good friends. Much more than just roommates. We talk; we even talk about men.

I say well there you go: female bonding.

She says I was telling you about that bar Cynthia and I went to last week? was I saying that? was I telling you that?

I think so.

She says the same bar we went to six months ago.

I say well we've been to a lot of bars.

She says it was that 50s revival bar; all the guys in there looked like James Dean.

Yeah; okay.

She gives me back the bottle and says I went there last week but it has changed style, has changed clientele; it's turned into a gay bar. Not discriminatory: men *and* women. We didn't know this at first;

we just went in. I wondered what happened to all the James Deans. Anyway, Cynthia and me were sitting and drinking some beers and we started to play some pool, just minding our own beeswax, when this drunk woman, in her late forties or so, comes up to us and she starts talking to us and her hair's really dirty and she kinda stinks, she has on this funky dress and ratty old coat, and she smells like vodka or something, and she just stands there watching us and she says real loud-like *I'm a dyke and I'm proud of it!* I wanted her to go away. Cynthia gives me a funny look and this lady says *wanna go have some reeeeealll fun, honey?* So I tell her well I'm not your type and she says not my type and I go no and she goes don't you lie to me I know a bitch dyke when I see one and I can tell that your sweet mouth has been muff-diving aplenty.

I say you're messing with me. I say that didn't really happen did it?

She says it did! Kathy says to me this is what she said I swear to you! I told her to please just go away please and leave us be we're trying to play some pool here and this lesbian old drunk says to me *I know what you do with your friend here; I know what you do with her in secret behind closed doors!* I told her to die and go to hell and she just laughs at me and goes *you think it's all a dream but one day you're gonna wake up, sweetie.* That's what she said, honest Injun.

I say weird.

She says I'm never going back to that bar again.

I hold out the bottle to her and ask if she wants more.

She says I think I've had enough to drink tonight.

I say so well that lez made a move on you – it's just like that one time –

What time? Oh, at the club?

Yeah.

Kathy says I remember that now. We were dancing. It was late but we'd been doing coke. I was feeling very very good, this I do recall. Cocaine always makes me feel good. You went into the bathroom. This girl came up to me. She was wearing a polka-dotted dress. She comes up to me and says hi my friends and I were wondering and she points to the corner of the club where there's these two other girls, looking over at us, and they were also wearing dresses with polka dots, and she says to me, she says we were wondering: are you gay or bi? and when I told her I was straight, quite straight, she just laughed like she didn't believe me or something. Now that was weird too.

I say it is.

She says why do some people think I'm gay? I don't understand this. I don't *look* like a lesbian, do I?

I say I dunno.

She says I'm not.

I sit up from the bed.

She says I know I am not.

I am naked and standing up.

She says I'm *not*.

I say are you sure?

I should know!

I say have you ever had an experience? with another female?

She says have you ever had that kind of experience?

I walk about her room and I talk, I say to her look, here is your bedroom window; this is your window; you look out your window and you see things; you see outside; you see things outside; the things you see: you can hear them but they cannot hear you; you strain for certain thoughts; these thoughts elude you, these thoughts you thought you thought; your notions ask *do you know me?* And here is your desk, your small desk, the desk you have had since you were a child. A desk of memories. Who can say what used to be in these desk drawers, other than what is in them now; past things used to inhabit: objects of girlhood. And what do you have here now – old magazines, notes for college classes. Here is your word processor, an old model but still trustworthy. It gets the job done; floppy disks: slow&sloppy. A printer that prints dot-matrix. It prints the things you write. And what do you write, little girl, hmmmn? Poems? Stories? Belles lettres? What are you writing now, what is here on the screen, these paragraphs&words, these words&sentences, what could it be, eh? Not a poem or story, no, that is not you; that is not what you do; it's – lemme look – it's a research paper on marine biology. You are on page five. So here, Kathy, here we have a college term paper, one of them anyway. How long have you been working on it?[1] Is it important?[2] Is all the time and effort worth it?[3] How much actual

---

[1] She was working on it for about a week.
[2] It counted for 2/3 of her grade.
[3] Later, she would confide in me that she often pondered on this.

research did you do?[4] Do you have your footnotes straight,[5] your bibliography,[6] do you have an *MLA Manual of Style*?[7] Look here, this is your chair. How many times have you sat in it? How many times have you plopped your bottom in this chair and thought about things, looked at the things on your desk? How many words were in your thoughts? What did you look at on your desk? Did you look at the computer, at the screen, did you look at this camera sitting on the desk? Do you have film in this camera? You do. How many pictures have you taken? Do you like to take photos? What if I took a photo of you, sitting against the bed, naked and smiling at me? What if I did? What if I put this camera up to my eye and take a photo of you? Here are your clothes, now, your dirty clothes, all piled up in a hamper as well as on the floor, shirts&socks&panties&bras&jeans&skirts, you need to do your laundry, girl, these clothes smell. And here, here, here is your closet; more clothes; more clothes. Clean clothes. They all look the same. Here is your carpet. A rented carpet, actually. Like this apartment, this rug does not belong to you. Here is your bottle of wine that I drink from (and I do take a drink, a pause in my monologue, and when I am done I continue, she looks at me, sitting naked on the edge of the bed, and I say:) here is your bed, the bed you have slept many nights in; the bed, in fact, that we have made love in, that we have screwed in, balled in, banged in, fucked in. I wonder how many other men you've had on this bed? Over the years. No, don't answer. This is your room; your rented room; this room does not belong to you; and you have to ask yourself well what the hell *does* belong to me? We own very little. But your body is yours; you own your body; this here is your body; this body that I have fucked twice this evening; this body I used to make love to until you stopped wanting to see me – but now, here we are, here we are again; again, here is your body. But what *is* in a body, what's in a face? Nothing at all that death won't soon erase. For a second there, I almost believed that your body was special, and just for me.[8] But here, here, here we have two

[4] Not much; she borrowed some info from a friend.
[5] She did.
[6] She didn't.
[7] She had a tattered copy.
[8] From a Tyburn Jig song written by Jordan Faris; guitar by Mike Hemmingson.

bottles, here are two bottles of wine; one empty, one still filled with the divine. We drank all of this other, this poor, sad, stupid bottle. We also drank a lot at that bar: beer beer beer. But I think we need more – we need something else. Need something to keep us going. How I ask do you feel now?

She says a little tired, and a little tense, too.

Still?

She says yes.

I tell her lie down. She does, on her stomach. I sit on her butt, gently, and start to rub her neck and back. She goes ummmn and I ask if she likes and she says she likes and please do go on and I say that we are still-lives, time and everything else has stopped here: this moment we find ourselves in. She says that she has been thinking about her family, her mom&dad thinking about how they are all different, yet alike, I say yeah: the ingredients of a family.

She says take my sister for example; she's a good example; she's a year younger than I am. We look alike; she tends to be more feminine in nature than me. This is what I think, anyway. No one has actually come out and *said* this but I think they think – well, maybe I'm just paranoid, maybe I have an inferiority complex or something. My sister goes to a different university, one back east. Here I am going to a university on the west and she's back there with all those silly-ass New Englanders. Natch, she joined a sorority. She's probably having a great time. I know she is. She has all the good-looking, shallow-brained guys she could ever want. All she cares about is buying things: clothes&jewellery&-make-up. A new car. She's always talking about how she needs cars, new cars, all cars, *cars cars cars*. If a guy has a nice&fast car, you bet she'll go out with him, no matter what he looks like or what kind of personality he has. Is she easy? Dunno. Does she put out for these car guys? Who can say. I've never asked; I suspect she does; she does. And she'll go out and spend forty bucks on a new make-up kit she doesn't need with the money our parents give to her and all I can think of is that forty bucks could have bought groceries for the week. My sister gets this from my mom. My mom is just the same: always buying things that aren't necessary; talking about buying things; wishing she had more money so she could buy more things. The desire for the material – but I'm sure this subject is mundane. Mmmmn, you have a good way with your hands, you know. I dunno – I guess I also like material objects, but not in the same way as my sister&mother. I like computers, or TVs, VCRs, anything electronic&exciting. I have this fascination with technology. My father is the same way. I get it from him. Dad is always taking things apart and putting them back together, just to see how they work; he likes to know how things tick; tick-tock like a clock. That's how I am. Those are the differences and samenesses in my family. But we *are* very close.

I say you're lucky; I don't think much about mine; I don't like to compare and analyze. I hate it; just would rather not think of it, thank you sir. One Christmas I went hungry and I was alone and I thought – well, that's a different story for later on in this text and it is really depressing. Promise.

I keep massaging her and asking do you like this and she says you bet and I move my hands down even more, I spread the cheeks of her ass, looking at the openings of both her ass and vagina; I rub a finger over her asshole, my finger to her cunt and ask if she likes that and she says you're a nasty boy do you know that? do you know how *naughty* you are? and I tell her I do, moving mouth down, licking asshole, licking cunt lips, feeling myself getting hard, stroking my cock as I lick&suck, moving up, entering, Kathy gasping like film noir, and when we are done, when we are done fucking for the third time tonight, I see that there is no more wine; I want more to drink; so I get up, leave the bedroom. I go into the kitchen and open the fridge where I find a six-pack of beer. I open a beer, drink, turning to see Cynthia, Kathy's roommate, sitting on the living room couch. She's wearing a light lavender suit with black pumps and a white blouse, gold-rimmed glasses; she's looking at me, I'm standing naked, my cock still half-hard, cock coated with the products of fuck, and I'm drinking a beer. I smile and say hello to her and she says hello back and I return to Kathy's room.

I tell Kathy about it.

She says shit.

She says get dressed.

I put on jeans, shirt.

She slips on a long nightshirt.

We both go into the living room.

Cynthia is still on the couch, watching TV.

Kathy & I sit on the opposing loveseat.

Kathy says what are you watching?

Cynthia says nothing really; the news; something about the economy; always the economy and how it sucks. It does suck.

Kathy says sorry about Mike, he didn't know you were here. I drink beer.

Cynthia says I'm sick of all this economy bullshit. The recession. And all that bullshit.

Kathy says I said I was sorry about Mike.

Cynthia says sorry? why? I'm happy for you. You've been complaining lately about not getting any. I don't know why you dumped him in the first place. You should keep him; keep him like a pet, like a dog with a wagging moist tongue.

Kathy says I mean about him walking out like that because we didn't know you were here. I thought you were at work, I thought you had to work until nine or ten.

Cynthia says maybe I'm too quiet when I come in; I'll make more noise in the future.

Kathy says he was embarrassed and she says to me isn't that right, you?

I go yes.

Cynthia goes why?

Kathy goes *you know*.

Cynthia says you don't think I've never seen a naked guy before? I'm glad for you, Kathy. But are you? Are you glad for yourself?

Kathy says sure.

Cynthia says he's a good lover, right?

I drink beer.

Kathy says probably the best I . . . and she looks at me and adds but I don't want to inflate his ego, you know.

Cynthia says you like him a lot; you kept saying to me, these past weeks, *why did I dump him? I like him a lot. Why did I treat him like dirt?*

Kathy says I said that?

Cynthia says you sure did.

I probably did.

So how did he wind up back here?

I asked him.

Oh.

We went out for a few drinks.

Well that does it every time.

Kathy says so I said to him *why don't we go back to my apartment?*

And what did he say?

Kathy says he said *sure*.

I say that's what I said. So what's up, Cyn?

Cynthia says you want another beer there?

Sure.

Cynthia says plenty in the fridge, go help yourself.

I get up to go to the fridge and I say to Kathy do you want one? and she says no and Cynthia says she looks like she's had enough and I ask Cynthia if she wants one and she says sure so I get two beers, one for me, one for her, and sit back down with them.

I say I feel funny.

Do they know what I mean?

I ask what's on TV.

They both say:

The news.

Cynthia says the goddamn economy; the fucking economy.

Kathy says I thought you had to work until nine or ten.

Cynthia says I was at work. She says I heard you; the both of you; I could hear you in your room, Kathy; you cannot mistake those sounds; I knew.

I ask did you know it was me?

Cynthia says not until you came out buck nekkid; otherwise you were just an anonymous male sound.

I say you remembered me: my name&face.

Of course.

Kathy says why wouldn't she recall you? It's not like I have ten zillion men waltzing through here; it's not like it's been a generation since your last visit.

Cynthia leans over to the TV to change the channel, saying there must be something else on one of these stations other than news – a sitcom, cartoons, a sad love story.

I say it's almost like when you go back home. You have memories of a place, a home – of furniture and the way things are situated; the way things smell. An – an overall feeling and/or sensation. You walk in and you know the surroundings, perhaps intimately, and yet you still feel like a stranger; like you do not belong; like you're just passing through; not a traveler, but reduced to common tourist; for a moment, you actually become one of the fixtures.

Cynthia says I could hear you both and you both sounded – happy.

I say I feel at peace and I don't know why; I seldom feel at peace.

Cynthia says I tried picturing what was going on in your room. I had these images. I tried to imagine the positions you were in.

Kathy says the last time I was on my stomach. We made it three times tonight and that last time was really nasty. He was rubbing my neck&back and it felt really good; I was just relaxed and we were talking about things like normal people do; but I was more into his hands and the things those hands were doing. He had his hands on my ass. He reached down to put his mouth there; his tongue was there. I felt a chill. I wanted him. I let him take me. As he touched me, as he screwed me, I closed my eyes and thought of a film that's soft around the edges.

Cynthia says I can't stand the stress anymore; work work work; that's all I ever seem to do. People yell at me at work – everyone yells at me. CYNTHIA!!!! The customers, too. My boss. My boss's boss. No one is satisfied. All for the buck, the mighty green buck. The necessity of currency. Look at those people on the news! Scrambling on the trading room floor, the Dow-Jones Industrial Average. People on Wall Street we will never meet having nervous breakdowns as they mess up our lives in ways they may never know. I think I would be happier if I had more control over situations.

Kathy says you remember what I said the other night. Cyn? I said *now look at us: two single girls and no dates; no one asks us out anymore*.

I say but two good-looking single girls.

Cynthia says modify; I get asked out, but by creeps. Jerks. Older men, too. I should say *old men*. I bet my boss would like to do me; he hinted at it on occasion. It's sexual harassment but who cares? If I slept with my boss – if I *had* – would things be different now?

Kathy says no one really asks me out; maybe I scare men.

I say you do – you scare the shit out of me.

You better be joking.

I'm mortally terrified of you!

Hey!

Cynthia says the world is running out of men, that's all; suitable men, i.e.: desirable men, i.e.; there will always be creeps&jerks&dirty old coots. I got fired from my job, that's why I'm home early.

Kathy says what?

Cynthia says they said *you're fired* and I said *well I quit*. But I guess maybe it would've been better that I was fired, so I could collect unemployment.

Kathy says why, I thought –

Cynthia says crap biz; I just couldn't take it any longer. I said *screw you all* and they said *you're fired, bitch.*

Kathy says so you have no job?

Cynthia nods saying another thing to make me less desirable. But I do have some money in the bank, and I'll get a severance check tomorrow. I have to go out and look for another job; that's the part I hate. But where am I going to find a job? Maybe I should go back to school and get a degree finally.

Kathy says you should; you could get financial aid like I do.

Cynthia says I was never any good in school. Not in high school, not in my two years of college. I was born to work; I'll work until I die.

Cynthia stands, stretches, takes her glasses off; she says I think I'm going to take a bath; a nice, long, hot bath; that's what I'm going to do.

Cynthia goes to the bathroom, closes the door. We hear the water running.

Pause.

Pause.

Pause.

Kathy says I feel – I feel bad for her.

I say yes so do I.

She says I know what you are thinking.

What?

You – you want to go in there.

In?

There.

The bathroom?

Yes.

I say do you want me to?

She says I think I do. I want you to go in there. Will you please go in there? Make her feel better the way you have made me feel better.

I get up. I go into the bathroom.

I return to the living room an hour later. Kathy is asleep on the couch. I lift up her legs, sit, place her legs on my lap.

She wakes, sits up, yawns.

She says I fell asleep.

I say I see that.

She asks how long was I asleep?

Not long.

I was having this dream.

Umm.

I was – I dunno if I can say. I felt like a spy in this dream; felt like I was witnessing top secret images; felt like I should've been enjoined or disbarred from seeing what I was seeing.

I say enjoined? disbarred? where do you get these words?

I go to college.

Oh.

She says in this dream I was in Heaven; I was in the halls and chambers of Elysium. You knew – you could feel – that at one time there was peace, eternal accord, but it was not so everlasting anymore. No more. Peace was gone, it took a hike. The angels were fighting among themselves – they were . . . I'm, I'm not sure if I should reveal all this to you.

Why not?

I was . . . entrusted. If I told you . . . well, I don't even *remember* what happened in the dream, so I guess it doesn't matter . . . Tell me . . . *tell me* . . .

What?

What happened.

I say it was your dream; I wasn't there.

She says in the bathroom, I mean.

I say Cynthia is in bed; she's sleeping.

Kathy says I wanted to go in there; I wanted to go in there and be with you two. Instead . . . I fell asleep and went to Heaven.

I say she took a bath.

Kathy says I want all the details.

There are none.

There are always details.

I say I went in there, I went into the bathroom, and I said to her *I've come to help you.* She said *you did: well thanks.* And she said that she wanted to take a bath that was very warm and with plenty of tiny little bubbles. I thought that was a very good idea. Clean the skin, clean the body, clean one's hair. She said she didn't want the water to be too hot; just wanted it relaxing hot; very very warm.

Kathy says I know what she means.

I asked if she wanted my help; if she wanted me to assist her in bathing.

She said?

She said *help should never be refused.*

Yes, that sounds like something she would say; so she took a bath?

I say she ran the water; we both watched the tub fill; she put in bubbles and the bubbles formed quickly, like a protective layer, like some kind of nest, or armor to hide in.

Kathy murmurs thousands of tiny little bubbles . . .

I say I recall, as a child, I would take bubble baths with my toys.

Kathy says I've only taken showers all my life; I don't take bubble baths; I never have; maybe I'm deprived; maybe someday I will take one.

I say she said my name; Cynthia said *Mike* and I asked her if she wanted me to leave and she replied that she thought I was going to help her; so I offered to undress her.

Did you?

No. She turned away from me, as if shy; she, yes – demure. She took off her top first; that blouse. I only saw her naked from back, her back, a naked back. Saw her tan line. Noticed a small mole on her back – small&dark. She then removed her skirt, as well as her nylons. I could see her breasts now.

Kathy says they are bigger than mine.

I say a little bigger but not that much.

What color underwear did she have on?

Pink.

She likes pink, always has. How girlish of her, hm? Me, I dig green. Army green.

I say she looked at me for a moment; there was no expression on her face; then she took the underwear off.

Kathy says she saw you naked a while ago, so now you have seen her.

I say she doesn't have any pubic hair; she shaved it all off.

I know.

You know?

She told me.

She told you?

Kathy says she said *I hate having a hairy bush.*

Oh.

I guess the hairs bug her.

Yes; that's what she told me too.

Kathy says actually I have seen her naked too.

You have?

Yes; we're roommates; we're both girls; at least I think we're girls; we're close friends, after all.

I say yes, yes you are; you are friends.

Go on.

I say naked, she stood before me naked; the bath&bubbles were ready. She put a foot in to test the temperature, just the sort of image you'd expect. She said it was just right and I knew she'd say that, like a perfect little postcard with dialogue balloon or something; then she got in.

Kathy says all those bubbles . . .

I say she rested into the bath; this is when I approached her.

She says so you went to her.

I knelt by the tub; asked how she felt; she said she felt much better.

I guess a bubble bath can do that for you.

I said to her I want to help.

Kathy says that's what you wanted; you went in there for that; I wanted you to go in there and do that; make the connection.

I took a washcloth in my hand. First, I washed her back. Then her front. Cleansed her breasts. Her breasts were in my hands; nipples were pink took one nipple between my fingers – ever so gently – and caressed it; I wanted to make love to that single nipple.

And what did she say?

She didn't say a word.

Sometimes she can be the quiet type.

I washed her stomach; she stood up then, turned around and I washed her ass.

Kathy says you like a nice ass.

She had a nice ass, yes; she turned again and I washed her shaved pussy; her cunny; her box. Washed her thighs&legs. Even washed her feet, although I was unworthy.

And her hair?

Yes; I put shampoo in her hair, my fingers did their walking on her scalp, all that blonde hair. Then she sat back in the bubbles. She said *too bad I don't have a rubber duck*. We both laughed.

Kathy starts to softly sing rubber ducky, you're the one, you . . . you make bathtime – la la la la lahh la lots of fun . . . rubber ducky la la la la . . .

I say I just stood there, looking at her. Then I knelt again. She stared at the wall. We did not talk.

Not at all?

But then we did talk; a little bit of talk.

What did you talk about?

I say nothing much; I don't recall; I remember every other detail except what we talked of. I'm not sure how long this lasted. She stood up again and she had all these bubbles on her body. She stepped from the tub. I took a towel and dried her. Dried her from top to bottom, covering the same ground I did as I cleaned her. I helped her dress. First, the pink panties; it was nice to slip them on her, snug them around that ass. She had some PJs there that she was going to wear to bed. I put those on her. I took her in my arms, picked her up like a small wife or child. Like a child. Like an infant in my arms, I carried her to her room. I saw that you were asleep on this couch. I carried her to her bed. Drew the covers up to her neck. She looked like a turtle. I kissed her on the forehead. I came out here and found you still asleep. I sat down, putting your legs on my lap. You woke up and told me of a partial dream about war bound angels. Then I told you this story.

Kathy says maybe I should have gone into the bathroom with you.

Maybe.

Then I wouldn't have slept or dreamt.

Tell me about your dream.

I forget the details; I've forgotten the dream.

I ask were you watching TV?

I was sleeping.

Oh. Yes . . . Did you dream?

I think so. I dunno.

Cynthia comes out of her room, rubbing her eyes.

She says I couldn't sleep.

I say you seemed so peaceful in your bed.

Cynthia says I was lying there and I closed my eyes but I knew I couldn't sleep. I didn't want to sleep. I didn't want to have any dreams. I never have nice dreams so the ones I do have I'm afraid of. Why is this? I deserve something nice now&then.

I tell her to sit down, to sit next to Kathy.

Cynthia sits.

I say you two look right together sitting there like that.

Cynthia says we've been friends for a long time.

Kathy says yes, a long time.

Cynthia says to her I took a bath, Kathy.

Kathy says I know.

He helped.

He told me.

He's helpful&kind.

He can be.

Cynthia asks what's on the TV?

Kathy says I dunno; I was sleeping; I had this very strange dream.

I stand, look at them, and sit on the other couch and look more; I say she had a dream about angels.

Cynthia says really?

Kathy says I don't recollect all the details.

Cynthia says maybe if you went back to sleep you'd dream about it again.

Kathy says maybe I could go back.

Cynthia says I hate sleeping; too easy an excuse to hide and I hate excuses.

Kathy says I guess I could return to that time, I guess I could. I dunno if I'm sleepy or not. I dunno.

Kathy yawns.

Cynthia says I was in my room, in bed, in my rented room but a bed that belongs to me; I closed my eyes; I thought *I don't really want to be here*. I wanted to be somewhere else.

Kathy lies down, her legs stretched across Cynthia's legs.

Kathy asks am I asleep yet?

I say it's hard to say.

Cynthia caresses one of Kathy's legs.

Kathy asks am I dreaming again? now? tell me.

Cynthia says it's hard to put your finger on it.

Kathy goes ummmn; she says can someone tell me a story? then maybe I'll sleep.

Cynthia says I don't know any stories.

Kathy yawns again and says I dunno . . . I'm just not ready to die yet.

I have a story. I tell her, I tell both of them, this:

One Christmas, I went hungry. I lived alone, as I do now, and there was no one in my life, unlike there is now. Usually, I went home every Christmas for a family dinner. I really looked forward to those family meals because they were the rare times I ever ate *well*. Ever since I was on my own – since I was twenty – let's say I left home, well not like that, I mean to say that my parents kicked me out of the house when I was twenty, they said it was time for me to grow up and go outside into the real world, and so I lived day to day when it came to food; each day I went out to get lunch I lived on pizza, taco shop specials, submarine sandwiches for a buck-fifty, that sort of thing: this was the extent of my nutrition. None of the girls I knew (I say this with a laugh, waiting to see if Kathy might contradict me) knew how to cook. (I laugh again:) I used to say I'd marry the first girl I met who could cook; who could keep me well-balanced with all the USDA approved daily requirements, the four basics and whatnot. No, I did not eat well, except when I went home – went home on Thanksgiving&Christmases&sometimes my birthdays. Turkey&ham&mashed potatoes&vegetables&candy yams&biscuits that were warm to touch&taste, melting butter on top. Just thinking about it now, thinking about it makes me want to go home&feast, to just go home where it's safe. Safe, yes, and warm. Sometimes, at home, you just don't have to think about things. Anyway, one Christmas I didn't go home for dinner. The ritual had always been: my mother would call the day before and ask what time I'd be coming over tomorrow and I'd say well, what time do you want me over? and she'd say whatever time would be fine. Sometimes I'd go early, sometimes late, depending how I felt; but I could *taste* that dinner in my mouth, I could *feel* it in my stomach, I could perceive the wine that went along with it, and I'd know that, that night, I'd go to bed feeling okay with the night, because I'd had, yes, that rare healthy meal. But this one Christmas in question – and it wasn't long ago – she didn't call; my mother, I mean to say, did not call. I kept waiting&waiting but the phone did not ring. I had gone out to a party that Christmas Eve, and there were girls at this party, and I got drunk at this party, and I was talking to some of these girls who were also drunk, but, although I think I could have, I did not get into a situation where I may have spent the night with any of them, for at my place, my home, I was alone and always alone, it was my area of solitude, and I kept thinking that night: *my God, I might be alone for the rest of my life.* I guess Christmas-time can get to you like that. When I returned from the party, I expected a message on my answering machine, from my mother, but there was none. I went to bed. The room was spinning. I wondered why she had not called. I had a dream that night; yes, Kathy, I too can dream – I dreamt that my mother&father came to see me and they said we're really disappointed in you, son; *we know what you did and the price you had to pay and are paying even now.* They said they were saddened by the horrible things I had done, the acts committed, the crimes realized. They said you should not have abandoned Beth and left her to the wolves. I protested, I defended my innocence like a man facing the guillotine. I said I hadn't done anything, that I was merely a victim of circumstance; I was only acting on my fears&needs so how could I be held accountable for being human? I said I was fragile. That speeding car, her swiftness with a knife, that violent night on an alien lawn under a full moon of dismay, none of that was my goddamn fault! I woke up from this dream and for some reason I felt my parents were dead. But no no no, I told myself, it was a dream and everything was okay. I told myself that my mother would call; she'd call and I'd go over and I'd have a good dinner that Xmas. *I could just smell that food.* So I waited for the phone call. Maybe they did hate me for some reason, I thought; maybe there was some validity to that dream. So I phoned home; I broke down and phoned over there to find out why they had not phoned me. My mother answered; I felt relief. She was sick, she said she was sick. The flu. My father as well, she said. They were both sick, felt very bad. I asked aren't you going to make that big Xmas dinner? because I was very hungry and she said no, she said they were both too sick to eat and they couldn't even get out of bed. I did not confess that I was hungry. She said well, merry Christmas: it doesn't really feel like Christmas, does it? I said no. You see, I didn't have any money. After I got off the phone, I looked into the fridge for something to eat. I had a few hot dogs and an apple and an orange. I watched *A Christmas Carol* on the TV; bah humbug and all that usual stuff. I knew this food would not be enough but it was all I had. I never felt . . . well, I told myself that this would never happen again; I'd never allow myself to be this lonely again; to be *that* lonely. Then, I'd never have to be hungry. And I would never face the full moon with such antipathy.

Kathy mumbles, eyes closed, she mumbles Christmas . . . family . . . always the same . . . my sister . . . but I love her . . . and my father . . . no matter what.

Cynthia caresses both of Kathy's legs and says you have nice limbs.

Kathy goes ummmmn, thank you.

Cynthia says they're beautiful.

Kathy says do you like?

Cynthia says to me hey don't you think she just has the sexiest legs?

I say huh? oh yeah: sexy.

My mind is still on the story.

I say her legs have always turned me on.

Cynthia says this is one thing that has always made an impression on me about you, Kathy: these legs. *Les jambes de vous* if my French is correct. The shape; the muscles; the tan; wonderful, wonderful columns.

Kathy says that feels good, your hands there; your hands are smooth.

I say girl hands.

Cynthia says I like touching you, I like the way you feel.

Pause.

I say I see the two of you making love, it's very clear in my mind; I see you both undressed, on a bed; maybe Kathy's bed. You are touching her, Cynthia, as you are touching her now, only more so, and it is obvious that you care a great deal for each other; you could be deep in love. You are both kissing, passionately necking, and holding onto one another. You make love in this room, which is dark, the only light comes from the screen of the word processor, the words&sentences of the text flashing on you, your naked bodies. I am sitting in a corner, sitting in a chair, smoking a slow smoke, and watch; I watch your sex, lighting one cig after another. I do not join, for this is something between the two of you. In fact, I am not invited; I only watch.

Cynthia says I can see that, too; I can see it just as you describe; I can feel it; I can taste it. I want that, I want to make love . . . Kathy? Kathy . . . Kathy?

I say Kathy?

Cynthia says hey . . .

I ask is she asleep?

Cynthia says she's asleep.

I say she's dreaming now.

Cynthia says I have a story too and she looks at Kathy, still cuddling Kathy's legs and she says well maybe she'll hear in her sleep and have dreams about my story and she asks do you want to hear my story, Mike? I tell her that I do. Cynthia says I have been thinking of this story, this story of mine, and trying to figure out where it begins. Where it begins, I believe, is some years ago, three, no, four years ago, on my twenty-first birthday, I had just turned the big two one, the legal drinking age, the age I could get into bars. I didn't know Kathy then, but I would soon, I would meet her at the school. I was going to college then, before I realized that I wasn't made for academics and was doomed to the working world. But these girlfriends of mine, Nicole and Gretchen, they decided to take me out. They were already twenty-one. So they took me out to one of those places where exotic male dancers dance; you know, men with all those muscles and have all that oil on their hairless bodies and perfect tans and perfect teeth. I won't get into the details other to say that I enjoyed myself; what woman would not? We'd been drinking, my friends&I, we'd been drinking and smoking a few joints. I was pretty high, and when I came out of this bar where these good-looking men danced their dance, I was horny. I was really horny and mad that I didn't have a boyfriend. I *had* a boyfriend not too long before that, and he was good in bed I'll admit, but he was a real jerk, a creep, and this is why I dumped him, I said later days to you, boy blue. Anyway, I was mad that my desire would go, on my twenty-first birthday, unquenched. Gretchen must have seen this on my face, she suggested maybe we could go to a bar I could pick up a hunk not unlike the hunks we had seen dancing and, in fact, maybe I could've picked up one of the hunks who were hunk-dancing, and had some fun. (You see, it was announced in that club that it was my b-day and one came up and wiggled his naked ass at me and told me I could touch him, so I did, I reached into his g-string and felt his dick&balls but his dick, although warm, was limp because he was probably used to this all the time.) But I said no to Gretchen. I'm not, and never have been and nor will I ever be, the kind of girl who goes into a bar to pick up a dick. So – drunk, stoned, horny and alone, I went home. I was still living with my parents at the time. It was dark, everyone was asleep, and I went to bed. I got into my nightshirt, I went to bed and, well, masturbated. I had fantasies of those men. I fantasized (I'm almost ashamed to tell you this but I will) I fantasized that they were all in my room, a dozen or so of them, and they were all naked&hard, standing in a line, each one taking his licentious turn, a good twenty minutes or so from each, on me, in me, just the sort of naughty birthday present that only exists in your subversive head-thoughts, and so that's how I satisfied myself, finger to clit, dreaming of being gang-banged by a bunch of muscle-bound men I did not know, unknown faces&cocks in the dark. I mention this episode because where it *really* started – you could call my night out with the girls the *prologue* to this tale – was the next morning, which was Sunday morning. I woke up and looked out my bedroom window and saw, in the backyard, a beautiful boy. My bedroom window looked onto the backyard and this young boy, wearing cut-off shorts only, was mowing the lawn. I know who it was: Daniel, the boy next-door. I used to baby-sit him, when he was just a kid. But looking at him, I saw that he was a kid no longer; no, this boy was no *boy* but on the edge of being a man. Perhaps he had been lifting weights, as boys his age start to, for he had the beginnings of a fine definition on his chest, stomach, and arms; but certainly not as much, as abundant, as those exotic dancers the night prior. He had a nice tan, too, and I remembered that Daniel made his spending money by mowing&tending lawns around the neighborhood. My father's health was poor, and I don't have brothers, so we hired Daniel to mow&tend the back&front yards each week. Paid like fifteen bucks, I think. I had seen him before, many times, but why was I now seeing him in this light? – I mean, why was I checking him out like meat? He was only thirteen. Yes, thirteen. I remembered what I was like at thirteen, the sexual feelings I had. I didn't lose my virginity until I was fifteen but the first time I had given a boy head, I was twelve. He was fourteen, a freshman in high school, the brother of this girl I knew. He had long hair, listened to Led Zeppelin all the time. He introduced me to pot and oral sex. The first time scared me and I hated it when he came in my mouth. But after a while, I began to enjoy this, especially when he did it back to me and it made me shudder. Why didn't we fuck if this went on for so long? I would have let him if he wanted to, but he never wanted to. All he was interested in was oral. This lasted until I was thirteen. He got into trouble and went into juvenile hall and I never heard from him. It was a while before I had another boyfriend. Anyway, I was looking at Daniel and realized, too, he was no kid anymore, not that bratty kid I used to baby-sit. I thought this absurd, me being twenty-one now and giving the eye-ball to a fricken thirteen-year-old. I knew this must have been the remains of the night, those feelings, so, lying in bed, watching Daniel mow the yard, I masturbated again, hoping to get it out of my system. I didn't think about him again, not until I saw him – it was about a week and a half later, maybe two, and I was driving home from college, at the time thinking I should quit because it wasn't for me – and I saw him walking home from school, the junior high nearby. He was with some buddies and they all had their shirts off with slight muscles and dammit if I didn't think they all looked just *good*. I thought there was something wrong with me, I thought I was a pervert. I shocked myself even more when I stopped the car, which was my VW bug at the time, and called out to him. *Daniel!* I said, *Daniel, you want a ride home? It's me, your neighbor, Cynthia, I used to baby-sit you, we live next-door to each other, do you want a ride home?* His buddies all made sounds and punched him in the arm and I could tell they were pushing him to go, take the ride, look at that older girl! I should have driven away. I looked at myself: I was wearing a sundress with a ribbon in my hair. The dress was cut low, showed a lot of skin. Did Daniel take my offer? Yes. Slowly, embarrassed – his face was red – he came over to the car. I asked him if he wanted a ride home, or was he doing something with his friends? Daniel said well it's not that long of a walk. I said it is, it's almost a mile. Daniel looked back at his friends; they were all watching, and I knew, as he knew, that he had to, just to impress his buddies. So he got in and his buddies all said *all right! Way to go Dan!* and I acted like I didn't hear them and so did he, and we started to go and Daniel said *those guys*. I told him I was sorry if I embarrassed him and he said it was nothing. He still had his shirt off, and closer now I could admire what his body was turning into; I saw a small line of hair from the bottom of his navel disappearing into his jeans. He saw me looking, blushed, and moved to put his shirt on. I told him not to, I grabbed his arm and said no. I felt a rush of heat from him. *What was I doing?!* This poor kid. Was I crazy? I must've been, because I was feeling turned on. It'd been some months since I'd had any sex and I was . . . crazy, nuts, I guess. I asked *do you remember when I was your baby-sitter, Daniel?* He said sure. Now that I think of it, I baby-sat him when I was with my oral sex boyfriend. *This* is what gave me the dirty idea. I told Daniel not to be afraid and he said *I'm not*. I drove to a remote area, where they were building new houses. No people around. I parked the VW. I turned to him. I was rubbing my leg like I'm rubbing Kathy's, and he saw my dress go up. I noticed something in his jeans: he was getting hard in there, an erection was pleading to burst. I could tell he was nervous; he was fidgety. I told him not to be. He said *what are we going to do?* I said *what do you want to do?* He didn't know. I told him, my own face flushing. I didn't know why I was going to do what I was about to do but for him not to get the wrong idea. I didn't know what the hell I was saying but he said okay. So I got my head into his lap. He was tense to say the least. I told him to relax. He said okay but he didn't. I unbuttoned&unzipped his jeans. He was wearing white underwear, the kind boys his age wear. I pulled his jeans and underwear down and his cock sprang out. Like that – boing boing, bouncy-bounce; all red with heat coming off it. Wasn't a big cock; thin like a thin hot dog; would probably get bigger as he got older. I took him in my mouth and not *five seconds later* he came! He came so much I couldn't swallow it all. It spurt, like a bottle with pressure, a good five or six times. Come rolling down his dick and all over his little balls. I have to admit I was quite shocked; I mean, with that one boyfriend I had, and other boyfriends too, there was never so much; but they were all older, of course. He was only thirteen, you know, and he probably had so much building inside him.

Another thing that surprised me was how sweet he tasted. Come is always a little bitter for me, always salty; but his was kinda sweet, and I wanted more. I licked it off his balls. He was still hard, so I sucked him some more. This time it took a minute or two for him to come again. I sat up, wiping semen off my lips, and looked at him. He still smiled (still embarrassed) and asked what he should do. I didn't say anything. He reached to touch one of my breasts, but he didn't have any idea what to do with it. I looked out the car window, wondered if I was a dirty old lady. Me, twenty-one, corrupting this kid. But when I looked at him, I thought what a fine, handsome kid he was, and I felt turned on all the more. His dick was getting hard again, can you believe it? So back down I go; his thing still wet with saliva and come. This time he ran his hands through my hair, relaxing, getting into the flow of things. The ribbon unraveled. I didn't take him out of my mouth after his third ejaculation, kept it there, sucking my merry way to hell. His dick was limp only for a short while. I had his little thing and his balls in my mouth. I knew, since he was so excitable&young, that he could achieve a fourth hard-on soon. In no time, he did. Now, *this* time, it took him like fifteen or so minutes to come, and there was very little, but still sweet, and when he was done I told myself that's it, I'd just blown him four times and my jaw hurt. One of my tits was sticking out of the dress; I pushed it back in, sweaty. Daniel pulled his pants up, like he knew that was that, like he knew maybe he couldn't get it up again. I saw my reflection in the rear-view: my make-up was smeared, my hair was a mess, come on my chin. What must this boy be thinking? I drove us home. We didn't talk. He put his shirt on. Before he got out, he tried to kiss me; I turned my head; he pecked me on the cheek. I watched him go to his house, looking at his butt and thinking he had a nice butt and wondering what . . . I went in, no one was home, I washed my face, brushed my teeth, then took a bath, not unlike the bubble bath I just had with your help. Thought I was going to have a nervous breakdown. Who was I to do such a thing? But I thought, *I gave him something he'll never forget in his life*, thinking of the first time my first boyfriend went down on me when I was twelve, making me come several times like I had done with Daniel, eating me out for an hour, and the wonderful memory, albeit decadent, I had/have of that time. Pondering on what I had given to this boy, I became excited, and in that bath I fingered myself, pleased myself, knowing it was not, and never had been, enough, knowing that I may go even further in this new chapter of events. What did I do? you ask. I did go further. But not so soon, because there were other things going on. Well, yes, I did seduce the kid again; he came over, when he knew I was alone in the house, and I did do to him what I did in the VW, splendor in the bug, and I could see it, I could see what he wanted: he really wanted to lose his virginity. That's what he told me; he said he wanted to pop his cherry and I had to laugh, it sounded so funny coming from his mouth, that sweet mouth. So we did it. What other way is there to say it? I took him to my bed and we got undressed. He was so – eager, and didn't know what to do; I thought this was sweet. This went on for a while. Not all the time. I had college, he had school, but the closer summer came, the more we got together. He seemed to mature, sprout, with each passing day (now doesn't that sound like a cliché?). He had a slight mustache now. I was impressed with him and impressed with myself because by that time he'd become quite a good lover; he didn't come so fast, and I'd taught him how to, well, uh, *eat*. He started sending me love letters then, in the mail or leaving them at my door. He *was* in love, I guess. This is when I started to get nervous. Hey, I was just doing this for fun, okay, you know, teaching a boy how to be a lover and having some fun in the process. I didn't want this to happen but I guess I should've known it might. But that's not the worst, no, the worst is the morning I was going to my car, I was on my way to a class, some dumb-ass class I didn't want to go to but I had to, and I was a little hungover because I had been out drinking with Nicole&-Gretchen again, when I heard someone call my name, a woman calling my name, she says CYNTHIA I HAVE TO TALK TO YOU! It's Daniel's mother, a woman in her forties, she's in a robe, hair in curlers, and she has this notebook in hand. She's stomping my way, she looks furious, and she's waving the note-book like an evil wand and she says I WANT TO TALK TO YOU YOUNG LADY and I see the notebook has Daniel's writing in it, and I'm thinking oh shit and she says I'VE BEEN READING SOME OF DANIEL'S WRITINGS and I'VE BEEN READING ABOUT *YOU*! I didn't know what the hell to say so I say should you really be prying into your son's private stuff? and she goes HE'S MY SON AND I CAN DO WHAT I

DAMN WELL PLEASE and this is when she tells me that she knows what I have been doing, she says YOU'RE A DIRTY GIRL and that I should have shame. I'm just standing there, frozen; I don't deny anything, but I don't admit nothing as well. She says to me *IS IT TRUE?!?* She says OR IS HE JUST MAKING IT UP? I tell her it's none of her business but I guess I could have lied, said, *Oh, he just has boyhood fantasies*. So she says YOU BETTER STAY AWAY FROM MY SON YOU LITTLE TRAMP AND YOU'RE LUCKY I DON'T TELL YOUR PARENTS ABOUT WHAT YOU HAVE BEEN DOING I COULD EVEN HAVE YOU ARRESTED FOR MOLESTATION! I wanted to tell her he was hardly a kid anymore, but the law might say otherwise. Oh, Jesus could you see it, me arrested?!? I got into my car and left. I knew it was over and part of me felt relieved that it was. Daniel wrote me a few more letters, saying he was sorry that his mother found the notebook. I ignored him. His mother sent him away for the summer and that was probably just as well. It was. When he came back, he didn't seem to have any interest in me. Maybe he met another girl. But that isn't the end of this story. The real end is this: not too long after the encounter with his mother, while Daniel was away that summer, I had another going-out-to-my-car encounter. From out of the bushes this boy emerges, a boy Daniel's age, and he just gets into my VW with me, no asking, no words, he just does it. I recognise him as one of the boys I had seen Daniel hanging around with. He smiles and says hi, says his name although I can't remember it now. I asked him what he wanted. He says to me *I know what you've been giving Danny and I want some of it*. I act like I don't know what the heck he's talking about. He laughs and tells me Daniel has been telling them (his friends) all about it, about us, what I do, and I believed it, you know how boys are: they always have to brag about their conquests; I was the same, actually, and still am: always telling my sexy stories to girlfriends, when I have sexy stories to share. So this bold kid says to me I want some, I want what you give him. I tell him to get the fuck out. He reaches over, grabs my hair, he says *give it to me bitch my dad always says you gotta get rough when the bitches try to nigger out on what they're born to give* and my did it hurt, the way he had my hair, so I screamed and punched him in the nose. He wasn't expecting that, I tell you! His nose begins to bleed. He puts a hand to it, looks at all the blood. He starts to cry. I say *get out or I'll hit you again you brat!* and he runs out. It was after that I changed, this is when I knew I had to change: I had to readjust to a violent world.

I tell Cynthia I have a story similar to that, that I had an experience, at twenty-two, with a thirteen-year-old girl. I ask Cynthia if she wants to hear my story and she says yes, I want to hear it. We both look at Kathy, who still sleeps, legs on Cynthia's lap, Cynthia still rubbing them, and Cynthia says so what's your story? I say if I were ever to write this experience down, I would title it –

THE WATCHMEN LEAVE THEIR STATIONS

– but, as I think about it, perhaps the events of this encounter are not as dramatic as my memory would like to give credence to. The girl's name was Isabelle; a very pretty young girl, and I met her through her mother. Her mother was forty or something. When we'd met in the bar, I thought she was mid-thirties, and she looked good, but it was, you know, dark, and I was kinda drunk. What was this woman's name, anyway? You recall the daughter, but not the mother. Oh, yes: Margo. Margo the Mother. Needless to say, Margo took me back to this trailer she lived in and there we had this drunken fuck and fell asleep. I woke up before she did, saw that she was older than I was led to believe, and without her make-up . . . well, she wasn't *that* bad, but when it came to older women, I didn't pick them that old. Thirty-five at most. Oh well. I looked around the trailer. It was quite messy. Saw that Margo was waking up so I pretended I was asleep. I heard her say *Christ, I have to get to work* and she nudged me and said *hey you wake up now.* I acted like I just woke up and asked what time it was. She said it was late, she said it was nine o'clock.

I said the world isn't even alive at nine.

She said not for a vampire like y'all.

We both went oh oh oh.

She said so what do you remember of last night, sweetheart? anythin'?

I said hey sure what kind of guy do you think I am? and although I didn't want to, I moved to kiss&touch her.

She said ahhhhh, now.

I told her I liked doing it in the morn.

Do you now?

Mornings are the best.

Now, lovebird, last night wasn't so bad.

Yeah, okay.

But I ain't no mornin' love-girl.

I should tell you, Cynthia, that she talked with this southern accent, just like I say it.

She said I really have to get mosyin' to work.

You work?

I don't exist on nuthin', sweetpants. I got me a kid to feed.

Kid?

She's a kid: a youngun, I don't know where she is, she's around here somewhere. She's a good kid. You dint see her last night? She sleeps on the sleepin' bag on the floor there. But it was dark and you were drunk.

I said you talk funny.

She said you talk funny, dear, but at least you're all cute.

I said don't tell me you're from Georgia.

She said oh Gawd no. I'm from N'Awlins. Grew up there.

I told her (for the hell of it) (and maybe I wanted to) that I felt like fucking.

She said no, not here, we don't have time, and maybe my kid might come in.

I said then I just wanted to go back to sleep because I had this very bad hangover.

She got up, naked, and she was a little chunky I saw, and she went to take a shower.

She said as she went in you're a bum, you know, but you probably already know this.

I said sure.

She came back out, dried off, and put on a waitress' uniform. She said look, sorry, but I gotta rush.

I told her how awful my hangover was.

She said I do have to go but I guess you can stay and sleep awhiles, if y'all want. Kay, lover? This place is tiny, so just close the door, go when you feel better.

She left.

I lay there, then lit a cig. Wondered why I was here. Thought I should probably get up&go.

Don't know when it was, ten minutes later, a young girl in a long shirt down to her ankles came in. She had straight brown hair, soft pale skin, long legs, retainers on teeth. I could see small buds of breasts.

She looked at me, didn't seem surprised, and said (with a southern slant as well) good mornin'.

I said hey who are you? Margo's kid?

She said her name was Isabelle and she asked, real snooty like, who the hell are you?

I said she was a snot, I said you're a snot and my name is Mike.

She just stood there so I said you're not the friendly type are you?

She said I'm friendly. Thing is, most of Momma's men friends don't stick 'round long 'nuff to be friends with.

I said well I'm not going anywhere right now.

She said you will soon.

I said are you so sure of that?

She said they all leave: they come, they go.

I asked why do you say that?

She said it's the way it is.

Your mother have a lot of men friends?

Sure; she finds them in bars.

How old are you?

She found *you* in a bar, right?

Well, yeah, that's where we met last night.

I heard you two comin' in.

Did you?

I was on the floor here.

I didn't see you.

I sleep on the floor, in this here bag.

Always?

Not 'nuff room on the bed there, with a man friend always with Momma.

Oh.

I'm too old to sleep with Momma anyway.

So how old are you?

When I was smaller, I used to.

What?

They would do it while I was there next to them. They thought I was asleep but I weren't.

Oh.

Like I heard you two last night.

Oh?

She said I never knew my Daddy. You like my Momma?

I said I guessed I did.

She said do you now?

Sure.

Bet she looked diff'rent in the mornin' than she did in that bar. And you're younger than she is.

I said old story; story of my life; older women.

Isabelle asked how old I was.

I told her.

She said oh that ain't so old.

Maybe not.

She said Momma's forty-eight.

I laughed.

She asked what's so funny?

Last night she told me she was thirty-eight, she told me.

Isabella said oh, then I guess she is.

I said those women *always* lie.

She said whaddya mean *those women?!*

Oh, you know.

I dunno. But you like my Momma, right?

Sure.

I think she likes you, too. But she had to get off to work, y'know.

I know. She said I could sleep a bit. But I couldn't fall back to sleep.

Isabelle said so instead you smoke that smelly cig'rette.

I asked does it bother you?

She said yes.

I said I'd put it out, and I did.

I asked where does your mother work?

Didn't she tell you?

No.

She's a waitress.

That I know. Where?

This dumb ol' diner.

Oh.

Surprised?

No.

I didn't think so.

I asked her, again how old she was.

She asked why do you wanna know?

I said I just do.

How old do I look?

Dunno.

Guess, you silly.

Fifteen?

She smiled and said no.

Fourteen?

No.

You can't be thirteen?

Yes.

Thirteen?

Yes.

Thirteen.

Thirteen.

I said well.

Well what?

I said young.

She said so.

I said so.

She said I was gonna make breakfast. You want some break-fast?

I said that would be nice.

(CUT TO:)

We were sitting on the floor of the trailer, eating scrambled eggs&bacon.

I said this is really good.

Isabelle said oh you're just sayin' that.

I said I haven't had a nice home-cooked meal since – since I dunno. This is really good.

She said Momma taught me how to cook. Said I needed to know 'cause one day I'd be on my own and all that. Ahh, one day I'll find a man and marry him and have babies and I'll have to cook for him and the babies. Hmmmn. I wonder what that will be like.

What?

Gettin' hitched and all.

I said that's a long way for you.

She said I just know I'll be happy! I'll only marry a man that'll make me happy. I don't wanna be sad. Like Momma is sometimes. She still loves Daddy whoever he is.

I went ummmn, eating eggs.

She said I never knew him.

I said that's too bad.

She said my babies will know their daddy. We'll all be happy together. Never have to worry about a thing in the world – food or money or rapists or killers. We'll have a house. The house will be clean. We'll have cars. Credit cards. VCRs. We'll go to operas and art galleries. We'll fly to Europe.

Um-hm.

You don't believe me?

I do.

You ever been married?

Nah.

Why not?

I was engaged once, when I was twenty-one. Just not too long ago. But that's a different story; in fact, it's a different life.

What happened?

Don't remember . . .

You just don't wanna say.

I don't . . . I don't remember.

What? You senile already?

I didn't want to talk about this. Too much pain. I told her a lot of things happened . . . no one specific thing. What I recall most is an image, an image of . . . of the moon.

The moon?

Moon.

Isabelle asked did you love her?

Well . . . yes.

You think about her a lot?

Sometimes.

You have dreams about her?

No, not anymore. Used to – have these strange . . .

Seems like it was all just yesterday? Last month or what?

You ask funny questions, you know.

She said what was her name?

Who?

The intended bride.

I said Beth.

Elizabeth?

I said you're pretty smart for thirteen.

She said I've been married several times.

Yeah sure.

She pointed to her head&said I mean up here, this is where I have been married.

I asked what, none of them work out?

She said you always look for perfection in the wrong place and then she asked me hey don't you ever dream?

What's that?

Tell me about your dreams.

I said they're mostly just nightmares. Dreams, you see, are nice. What I have are not *nice*. They are bad. You don't want to hear them.

She said dreams are all that matter, Michael, it's all we ever have.

(CUT TO:)

A few hours later we were playing the board game Monopoly, still on the messy floor. She had more hotels&money than I. Margo, in her waitress uniform, came in as we were playing.

Isabelle said hey, Momma.

Margo said to me you, you're still here?

I said guess I got caught up in this game.

Isabelle said we've been playin' games all day and I've been winnin'.

Margo said oh.

I said she beats me all the time.

Margo said to me I certainly dint expect to find y'all here, sweetbuns; I just thought you'd sleep&go.

Isabelle said we had breakfast.

I said I was sorry and that I'd go if she wanted me to.

Margo said no, no, that was awright. I'm glad you're all here. I was just gonna get dressed and head back to that great li'l bar where we met, you know? But I do need an escort and well you *are* here.

I looked at Isabelle and Isabelle nodded.

I said sure sounds great I could use a drink or two.

Margo said or ten.

(CUT TO:)

Night.

I was really drunk.

I was pounding on the door to the trailer.

Isabelle answered, wearing shorts and a tank top.

Nipples of her tiny breasts hard.

I said where's that Momma of yours?

Isabelle said I thought she was with you.

I thought so too.

She left with you. Did you lose her?

I said she was making quite a scene in there, at the bar, that Momma of yours. Was talking to every man there. Ignoring me. Who does she think she is anyway? I thought I saw her leaving with this man, I'm not sure. I thought she might've brought him back here.

Isabelle said she still might, who knows.

I said do you really think she took off with another man?

She said probably; Momma often does; that's why the men don't stay 'round long.

I ranted well your Momma is a whore! a slut!

Isabelle looked at me, cold.

I said I'm sorry, Isabelle. I didn't mean to say that about your Momma.

Isabelle shrugged and said it's okay because you're right, she is a whore. But she's still my Momma and I love her, whore or not.

I said maybe I shouldn't stick around; maybe she'll bring that man here; I don't wanna cause a scene.

Isabelle said well it'd bring some excitement to all the boredom 'round here.

I asked do you think she might bring him back?

She said Momma doesn't always bring them here, not if the man ain't married and has a nice place to take her to.

I said it's cold out; I think it's going to rain.

She said I was thinkin' it might.

Where should I go?

We can play another game.

(CUT TO:)

I woke up on the floor.

In my clothes.

Feeling like shit.

Isabelle was on her Momma's bed, in the same shorts and tank top.

She was looking at me.

She said Michael.

Yeah?

Get up.

I said what the hell? and looked around.

I said I guess your Momma didn't come back.

Isabelle said she doesn't when she has two days off from work, like now. This is her *weekend* as she calls it so she doesn't come back for two days from now.

I asked what happened?

She said you don't recall?

I saw that there were a lot of beer cans around; I asked about them.

Isabelle said last night you walked down to the liquor store, in the rain, 'cause you wanted some beer. You even gave me one. I usually don't like beer; I like wine.

I said I remember the rain.

Yes.

I hate the rain.

It's almost Christmas.

I hate that too.

That's what you was tellin' me last night. We talked a lot.

Did we?

You – you don't *remember* do you?

She seemed hurt.

I said what?

She said it don't matter none.

(CUT TO:)

We were eating lunch.

Sitting on the floor.

I said I want to take you somewhere, Isabelle.

Out?

I said we can go and have fun, even in the rain.

She said I think it's stopped.

I said but it's cold out there.

She said why go out there when we can stay in here?

You like being cooped up in here?

She said we create our own world here; we don't have to play by the rules; we can make the game up in here. Out there – out there in the cold&rain – it's a different game; it's *The World*. There are no *dreams* in the world. In here, we don't have to listen to anyone; no one can control us and tell us what to do, what is right or wrong. We have books and a small TV. We have – each other.

I said, we do.

She said I just want to stay inside here, with you.

(CUT TO:)

She said I want you to make love to me, this is the night, this is the time, I want this and I told her no, I couldn't do it. I looked down at her, her small face, her lean, delicate body. I was surprised that I had been doing this, on her Momma's bed, an hour's worth of kissing, *making out* as she called it. I had grabbed one of her little breasts, the taste of her retainer's on my tongue. She had a slender leg around my waist and she said you have to make love to me, I have to know. Knowing very well the trouble this whole thing could deliver on me, I pulled off her shorts. She wore yellow panties with duck imprints. I had to laugh, just a little. When I removed her panties, I was both frightened&delighted by her virgin sex. Yes, she was a virgin, she had told me so. She said I've never made love with anyone. She had light brown pubic hair; her opening small, pink, fresh. I had never seen a vagina as so, not having had sex until I was fifteen, with girls that age, girls who had already been fucked more than once. I could not help myself: I put my mouth on her, I took her in, her smell, her taste, and with like your younger lover, Cynthia, the girl was ambrosia&impassioned. What am I doing? I thought. But I was down there well over an hour, enraptured with my licking&sucking, Isabelle buckling, quivering, crying out, sweating, coming, and coming again, juices flowing into my mouth like rivers of sugar. I wondered if she'd ever had an orgasm before. Tired, I lay my head on her stomach, listening to the rain outside. Like you, Cynthia, I felt the guilt, but I knew I had just given her something she would never forget, something that she would always recollect fondly. She whispered *you must make love to me now*. She took my face into her small, warm hands, staring at me and saying *I have to know*. She said *you have to make me a woman*. I knew there was no getting around it. I told her it might hurt. She said she knew. I positioned myself over her, placed my cock down there, and wondered if such a small opening could take me without agony. Just getting the head in was difficult. She was wincing, in that dark, with pain, I could tell. I told her I'd stop and she said no no she wanted this now. I entered her, pushing hard. Isabelle wailed, not unlike those cries of pleasure that had preceded when I gave her oral. I felt a warm rush down there, warm&wet, and knew it was blood. I almost withdrew, but she pulled me closer and told me to go all the way and she didn't mind how it hurt. So I did, slow at first, then frantic, the smell of her sweat&sex in my nostrils, her hair, tangled, her kisses on my neck, her hands on my back&ass, her grunts, soft grunts, her small ass in my hands as I lifted her butt, lifted her so I could plunge deeper, plunge fast, hard, myself breathing into her shoulder, her hair, the bed squeaking, squishy sounds at her groin as our connection made haste, her stomach against mine breathing air in&out heavily, her breath against my neck warm as I fucked, and came, came inside her, just coming&coming like it'd never end, not once thinking of the consequences should I impregnate a thirteen-year-old girl. And when I was done, I fell on her, weeping, feeling so dirty. She ran her hands through my hair and said I love you, husband: we'll be happy together. She said we'll have babies and they will know you. We will go places. To art galleries. We'll got to Europe. We'll hold hands in the sunset and be a postcard. We'll have a clean house.

I said Isabelle, I'm sorry . . .

What, dear?

Sorry, I'm . . .

What? making love to me?

You're just a kid.

She said I am *not*.

I said no, not now.

I said oh God Isabelle . . .

She said don't hurt me! You can't hurt me!

No . . .

She said (her blood on us both) I don't wanna be sad! Remember what I told you? We have to be happy at all times. What else *is* there?

Isabelle . . .

And she said make love to me again, if you want.

(CUT TO:)

She said I will crown you my prince.

I said prince?

King?

I like king.

You are King and I am Queen.

Of what country?

What country do you want?

This country.

She said you can't be King of America; you'd have to be President, and there's no nobility in *that*; it's not a life-long occupation. And I don't wanna be First Lady. Our country – it'll be far away. In Europe, y'know. It can be in any time we want – now or in the past or the future. It can be a small country, but we'll be powerful. We are powerful. We are respected.

I said you decide then. We can make up our own nation.

Okay.

She said a magical kingdom! WITH beasts&knights&elves&-maidens.

Maidens.

I was once a maiden; a damsel in distress.

Were you now?

She said you saved me. This is when you were fightin' for your family's God-given right to rule this land. Our country was in turmoil: evil was all around. Bad wizards and conspiring witches with trolls&vampyres. I was being led in a dungeon by this wicked overlord. They beat me and did bad things to me. They were not nice at all. You loved me, you did. And you and your – your merry men – came and saved me. Then you

established your rule, your right to the throne recognized. I
became your wife.

I said and you became queen.

(CUT TO:)

She said who can take this from us?
Hm?
She said who can deny us?
I said no one; we're alone.
Yes, we're alone; no one can lay a dirty finger on us.
No.
These people on the outside – they all have unclean hands.
They're all bastards.
They hate us.
They do – but why?
She said they don't understand that's why.
No, they don't.
They don't understand dreams.
They hate us.
They bite us.
They file complaints.
They snicker.
They pass judgments.
She said no one will ever comprehend our life.
No.
And do you love me?
God, yes.
We'll fly away.
Away.
To a never-never . . .

I fell asleep with her there, Cynthia, asleep on Isabelle's Momma's bed and the sheets stained with her new womanhood. I had
this dream, too. The dream had two parts. In the first, Margo
came home with some man, and seeing us in her bed, she freaked
out. The man was worse. He had plans. He had a gun and he shot
all of us. We were on the floor, bleeding with bullet wounds.
Margo dead, Isabelle crawling to me, crying. In the other part of
the dream, Margo came home, and she was alone, and Isabelle

and I had to run, run away together, with my car, the law after
me, and we drove through Amerika: fugitives.

Driving in a car:
   She said don't drive so fast.
   I said we have to.
   It scares me.
   Are you afraid of cars?
   No. Yes.
   I know cars. Don't worry.
   But do we need to drive so *fast*?
   Yes.
   I'm scared, honey.
   Don't be.
   She said we're out in the *world*.
   I won't let them take you.
   What we left behind . . .
   We're starting over.
   Will we be happy?
   We will.

In a motel room:
   She said this room makes me nervous.
   Hush.
   I just feel . . .
   I said what?
   Michael?
   Come here, hug me.
   She asked are you happy?
   I said you're with me; how could I not be happy?
   We have this: us.
   It is ours.
   No one can touch it or hurt it.
   We should go – go all over Amerika.
   She said we need to go where dreams are made; where the sun
is always out and there is no rain.

Driving in a car:
   She said all this driving is gettin' to me.
   I said we've seen a lot of Amerika.

She said we could have driven all over Europe.
We're almost there.
To our life?
Just like we dreamed.

In another motel room:
She said I hate all this runnin'.
I said we have to run. What do you think they'll do if they found us?
She said I don't want to think about that.
No.
She said how much time do we have left in this play?
Not much.

We were standing in a stagelight and she was pregnant:
She said we're here.
I said yes.
She said this is it.
I said yes.
She said we are married.
I said yes.
She said we are safe.
I said yes.
She said we're gonna have a baby.
I said a child; my child; I always wanted a child; your child; ours.
Feel her, here. Feel her.
Her?
Her.
How do you know it's a girl?
She said I just know. And she'll be happy. We'll all be happy: together. Never have to worry about a thing in the world – food or money or rapists or killers. My baby will know her daddy. All my babies will know their daddy. We'll have a house. The house will be clean. We'll have cars. Credit cards. VCRs. We'll go to operas and art galleries. We'll fly to Europe.
– *Isabelle? Isabelle, where are you? Oh Jesus . . . I had this dream, you see. I want to tell you about this dream. We were in this gulag – this prison – somewhere, and they were torturing us. They called us names we didn't like. There seemed to be no way of getting out of*

there. One night, the watchmen left their stations. They just bailed. The path was clear. We could have left, escaped, ran away. We could have been safe. We were weak but we still could move. We didn't. We stayed. We maintained to the familiar. We didn't take advantage of the situation.

– and then I was on the floor of the trailer, the killer was leaving. Margo was dead, I was dying. Isabelle crawled to me, to hug me, to bleed on me, to die with me.

I said it was all a fantasy, it was all a dream.

Isabelle said it's all we have that matters.

And she died.

I woke up then, not certain if I was awake or in the dream, or dying from gun shots, and maybe I was dying or dead, or in a motel, running with Isabelle through Amerikan landscapes of the haunted, the chimeric crux of the matrix, but I saw that I was in the trailer, in the bed, and Isabelle, peaceful, was asleep next to me. My head was clear, I saw what I had done, and knew my dreams had told me what my life may be like. I did not want any of this, I did not want this at all, this terrible mistake, this error in judgment, this second of silly lust and reverie; maybe one day I would pay for it, but I had to go! I had to run like I ran in the dreams but I had to do this one solo so I carefully, quickly, quietly got out of the bed, put on my clothes, took one last look at Isabelle and the blood that was dry, and I left, I left her, I never looked back.

We sit there, looking at one another, and Cynthia says maybe we should put her to bed. I tell her I think that's a good idea. She says will you help me? and I say I will and we both lift Kathy – she stirs but does not wake – and take her to her room, place her in bed, the bed we had been making love in not but a few hours ago, and we cover her with a blanket, and we look at each other, Cynthia&I, and we look at Kathy, and we leave the room. In the hall, we stop, immediately kiss. She says we have to go to her room. She takes my hand, she leads me there, we undress and lie on the bed. She says I am not like Isabelle, I am not a young virgin. I say I'm not like Daniel, I won't need instructions.

She says you mentioned an engagement once.

I say in the Isabelle story.

True?

What?

Were you engaged?

Yes.

Beth was her name?

I don't look at Cynthia when I say yes, her name was Beth.

What happened?

Don't remember.

She smiles, kisses me, reaches down and grabs my cock. I'm not quite hard yet. I lay back. Cynthia goes down and sucks and I think about the four times Daniel came in her mouth. I want to do a lot of things to Cynthia. I pull her PJ bottoms, I reach into them, running my finger along her asshole, thinking of Beth. She says she likes that. It could be Beth's voice. She looks at me, my cock against her cheek.

She says I want you to fuck me the way you fucked Kathy.

I say do you?

She says you can do anything to me tonight, do anything to me you did to her. Do anything to me you didn't do to her.

I tell her that I had wanted to fuck Kathy in the ass but Kathy doesn't like that, wouldn't let me.

She says I know.

Do you?

She says that's why you're playing with my asshole now.

I say you like it that way?

She says I like getting fucked any way.

She stands, opens a drawer in her dresser. First, she steps out of her PJ bottoms, leaving the top on. She takes from the drawer a small jar of Vaseline. She scoops some on her fingers, squats, applies it between her buttocks. She takes another scoop, comes to me, rubs the jelly on my cock.

I say you're not kidding.

She says I'm burning; all this tension; all this talk; all that we have done tonight. I need to be taken in a terrible way; the worst way.

I feel deviant; I feel perverse; I feel as though I am in the celluloid of one of those triple-X movies I watch now&then. I have often thought that no one truly leads such nice pornographic lives, doing all those kinky things, thinking these thoughts in solitude when I have rented&watched pornos, but recalling that, yes, in fact, I have, now&then in my life – as I am in this moment of my life – acting out, in flesh, my most vile fantasies. And when I have rescinded such, as I am now, when I have thought back, looking into my head for those nasty bedroom spectacles, I conjure the image of Beth, Elizabeth, crazy sweet Beth and her vampyre-look and anal sex carnalities; that is, to say, my former fiancée, Beth, could only get off if she was getting it up the ass; there was just no other way, she had to have it in that forbidden girth, and she would rub her clit *going to town!* she'd say *going to town!* as I fucked her in the ass, and she'd come, come hard, come unlike any other woman I have ever known, and I would just look at her, in stupefaction, asking myself where did I find such an odd femme? In fact, I could ask myself the same thing, as I hover over Cynthia, Cynthia on her stomach, with her rear hoisted in the semi-light of her bedroom, Kathy dreaming her angel dreams in the other room. Cynthia whom I am about to penetrate in the same manner as I had wanted to enter Kathy, as I had entered Beth numerous times in our past life together. I could ask myself how did I get into this situation tonight and I should feel lucky, for indeed, many men would feel fortunate, many men would have envy, some would call me a sick pig, some might raise their brows and some may deem me an anti-feminist, a user of women, a taker, as it were; but all in all, here I am: in this apartment with two women and I have, in the course of the night, had them both in the most intimate way possible, as I have fucked my memories as well. Cynthia lets out a deep sigh as I enter her, but not with the same ease I used to have when going into Beth. Cynthia is tight, resists, but finally succumbs. I push Cynthia's rear down, wanting her to be flat on the bed, and she does this, turning her head to look at me, blonde hair in eyes, asking *how does it feel?* I tell her it feels good and she says the same. She bunches the pillow, places her head on it like a delicate object of renown, looking to the wall, as I begin to fuck her. She emits small noises from mouth, closing eyes.

I reach under her, to find her cunt, her button, hoping, at first, she might do this herself, but knowing it is a job I will have to take on myself, for she isn't Beth, she could never be Beth, no one could be Beth; when I used to reach for Beth's cunt, she'd tell me she wanted to do it herself. She'd say there was a special way she did it that no one else in the world could so she'd do it and she just wanted me concentrating on fucking ass. Beth, oh, Beth, what happened? I remember the first night I met her, in that underground club, where they were playing dark gothic music from England (how I wound up in that club I don't know, I had dropped acid that night); Beth was dressed like a ghoul: with a torn black lace dress, knee-high leather boots, very pale skin, purple-dyed hair that fell past her waist, and black lipstick. In my state of mind, I thought she was the most beautiful thing I had ever seen; I had to talk to her, so I did, and we seemed to get along well. She had a soft, low, sweltering voice, almost like a child's at times, and sometimes like a grown woman's who has seen too much of the ugly orb. She said she wrote poetry; I asked what kind. She said *the kind about the nightfall of life.* I laughed. She said *what's funny?* I asked her age. *Twenty.* I asked what do you know about life's darkness&twilight? She said she did. I told her I was frying on acid. She asked if I had any more. I said I did. She held out her hand, the devil child expecting a treat. I fished from my jacket pocket a tab of LSD and she took it and said *let's go someplace.* This is what I really liked: at the time I was heavily into fry and didn't know that many girls who cared for the drug as much as I, with the pious fervor of an impassioned Baptist. Where we wound up was at her small apartment. She had a room covered in purple, draped, mantled, assuaged with that goth-favored color; on the walls were posters of The Velvet Underground, Jim Morrison, Ian Curtis, Siouxsie and the Banshees, Bauhaus and The Cure. She wouldn't stop giggling; the acid was very strong. We were drinking red wine, which she dribbled down my chest, told me was blood, the nosferatu's nectar. She had some coke on her person. We were quite fucked-up. She looked splendid without her clothes: oh-so-very-pale skin, not ravished by the sun. She said she hated the sun. Her skin was so smooth, couldn't fathom it was real. She had dyed her pubic hair purple as well. I went down on her; she had an odd taste I could not place – not bad, just peculiar. She said *come on baby fuck me.* Bauhaus was on the stereo, "Bela Lugosi's Dead" – how quaint, how perfect. She reached to take my hands in hers as we fucked, her legs spread out, breasts flat on her chest, nipples pinkish-brown. I kneeled by the side of the bed, taking her; she sat up some, nipples now erect, lips smeared in black, eyes Egyptian, purple hair tangled everywhere across her face&-

shoulders. I wanted to change positions. I turned her over. She asked if I was going to sodomize her. I said I didn't have any plans but I would if she wanted me to. She said *that's the only way I can really get off*. I spread her cheeks, looked, saw this was no virgin flower bud here, it opened so easily, the width of it, so I slipped in, using the lubricants from her cunt, and she cried OH YES and reached down to whack-off her clit, coming instantly. After fifteen minutes of this, she must have read my mind, she knew I was going to shoot soon, she said *don't come in me baby I want to suck you off*. I lay on the purple bed and she took me in her mouth, cock dirty, and I thought this girl is really kinky. After I burst in her mouth, she told me she liked all the tastes mixed together: her pussy&ass, my sperm. She put her head on my chest, said she liked me a lot. She was stroking my dick and it got hard again. She got on top, slipping me back into her ass this way. I looked up, grabbing her tits, saw the joy on her face, sex&acid, finding this all so strange. I knew I'd have to keep seeing her. When I went to the bathroom to take a piss, she followed me, knelt before the toilet, looked up with her make-up-smeared eyes. She wanted me to piss in her mouth. She opened her mouth wide to prove it, tongue pink and long. She held it open as my urine splashed off that tongue, some going down her throat, some dribbling off her chin, down her chest, onto the linoleum floor. She wiped her mouth, made an *ummmmn* sound, smiling at me. She stood, tried to kiss me. I turned away. She smiled&said they were all like that – stick all sorts of shit into her mouth to eat but they didn't want to taste it themselves. I grabbed her then, pushed her against the wall, and kissed her, tasting what she had to offer. This excited me. I threw her on the bathroom floor, hard. She told me yes, told me to be rough. I lifted her legs, found her asshole, and went in for the third time that night. I slapped her. I pulled at her hair. She scratched my body in many places. I shoved my cock, coated with her ass, down her gullet, so deep she nearly gagged and I told her to take it take it take it *coming coming coming*.

We went to sleep after that.

She made breakfast. She looked different, but still pretty: like a doll. Like something that could shatter with ease. We went to the park later. She wore all white: white skirt, white blouse, white sweater, white wide-brimmed hat&shoes. She said *do I look like a sacrifice?* We held hands like new lovers do, kissed a lot. She told me she didn't want this to be a one-night stand. I didn't either. She let me read her poetry: images of cemeteries&dead horses. Weeks became more weeks.

She said she loved me. She called me *baby* and *dear* a lot. She worked at a bookstore, selling volumes she said one day she might write herself. Somewhere along there, we got engaged. We were dropping plenty of acid, three times a week, and doing a copious-ness of coke. She also liked to drink Southern Comfort. Our sex got more and more violent. Once I banged her head against the wall so hard, blood seeped from her nose. I licked it away. We would spend hours, in a drugged haze, connected by cock&ass. I would fuck her that way all night, into the morning, coming seven, eight, nine times until I had nothing left in my balls to give. But her ass wanted more. She had a thick dildo, and I'd ass-fuck her with that as she sat on my face, allowing that stranger, her pussy, to juice itself into my mouth. We would go for drives, we would stop at certain points because she wanted to give me head. Then she wanted my piss.

I was feeling more&more – filthy, a miscreant outside the halls of Eros. Once, she was writing a poem, sitting at her desk, naked, and she turned to me and said *are we really as bad as we think we are? have we strayed from the Garden of Eden?*

I said yes, we have taken up camp far from the garden, made our home in the naughty yard. She laughed&said *I can't wait until we get married.*

Cynthia says *fuck me harder* and I think about marriage more and wonder if I ever loved Beth. I told her I did, mostly to please her. I turn Cynthia over on her back, Beth in the head, placing Cynthia's legs on my shoulders, going back into her ass which is not unlike Beth's ass after all, Beth the anal-fuck goddess of this vile state we call the land of coitus. I push Cynthia up, her feet near her ears; she looks at me with wide eyes as I drive like Mad Max deeper into her colon; she gasps, says it hurts a little; I ask if she wants me to stop and she says no and I go even harder, wanting to hurt her, I think, knowing I would not have stopped even if she said yes. *Cynthia, Cynthia,* I say her name, but I still have Beth on my brain, I can see her so clearly, alive: I can see those times when I would jack-off on her tongue; she'd lie there, mouth open to receive, the head of my cock at tongue's tip, jism slowly seeping thickly. She would draw it in, suck on it, make some of it flow out, come-bubbles on her puckered lips like a European porno. Sometimes, giving me a blow, she'd spit my seed on her palm, rub it all over my cock, making me more sticky, and give me suck again, doing the same with the second load.

Beth, Beth, my decadent nymph, what the fuck happened to you! Where have I buried you at last? Have I forgotten already, so soon? Am I this insensitive to the intricacies of life? No no – I don't want to think of Beth and our eight months in iniquitous bliss. I was a different human then, not the one I am now: here in the apartment with Kathy&Cynthia. I have to converge on Cynthia, but the more I try, the more I see Beth. I feel wanting for who I was; I feel excitement for who I was, and I know that I am with Beth now, and I come, I come into Cynthia's intestines, and she grabs onto me, acting like maybe she's have an orgasm too, and we lay like that for a bit, finally letting go, her legs on the bed now, I to her side, wishing for a cigarette or a drink, thinking of all the couplings I have had this night, the memories&history of my life with sex, in this far corner of the naughty yard.

I tell Cynthia that I can't sleep here and she says she knows. She wants a kiss. I kiss. I gather my clothes and return to Kathy's room, wondering if I'll get aroused again, wake her, have her, top off this bizarre evening. She's still quite asleep. I lay next to her. She goes mmmmmnnnnn and I wonder about her continuing dreams. I move to hold her, feeling grimy, Cynthia all over me, the haunting of Beth's revenant all over me. I fall asleep, just a little, that strange place of half-sleep, having a half-sleep half-dream where I'm in a car with Kathy&Cynthia, Cyn is driving, and then Kath is driving, she's saying *my new name is Forget-Me-Soon, I'm your little Forget-me-Soon*. They are dropping me off somewhere. They wave as they leave me in this somewhere; their car gets smaller, smaller, smaller, smaller, smaller, smaller, smaller, smaller, and then it's no more. I wake, feeling chilled, knowing it was just a half-dream and I have not been abandoned to be alone on the wrong side of the garden. Kathy has turned, her face in my chest, curled in fetal position, her breath warm, a Kathy-breath. I look at her computer, still on, the document of a marine biology paper still on the lit screen. Is daylight soon? I look out the window, see the corner of the moon, a moon that was in full view just a few hours ago. The moon. What had Isabelle

asked me? About Beth? I said the moon. The moon&Beth.
Somewhere in that relationship, the engagement was broken
off, and we were enemies, the sort of thing that happens to me
often, and there were those few months when we did not see or
speak, until that party, that night of the party, at a house in the
suburbs; how we both got there I don't know but we were, it was
a big party, and when I first looked at her I didn't think this was
Beth, this was just a girl who kind of looked like Beth, this Beth
who was not Beth but had short hair, and it was black, real short,
like a boy's, and she didn't have the primordial black lipstick so
appurtenant to the look of Beth – red lips now; and she wore a
tight tight tight dark blue dress and high heels and she moved my
way, slinked my way, smiling a little, saying *hello Mike* in a Beth
voice and I knew then it was Beth. I stared at the long gold
earrings she wore, for she'd never had earrings when I knew her,
when she almost became a wife. She was sex. She also smelled
different, but this may have been a gap in my memory. No, no: I
had not forgotten my Beth, I could see this imputation in her eyes,
despite the cordial smile; I wanted to say this; I dared not. What
could I tell her about these months I had spent away from her;
first we had been enjoying our bodies&minds in ways that would
have made the residents of Gomorrah blush; and now back to
priesthood? Indeed, I was like a monk in a citadel, for in those
months of disunion, I had not slept with anyone else, I had not
gone out to find new confreres. I stayed behind doors, reading,
watching TV; went to work, went home, and that was that. But I
wouldn't tell her this, and I wouldn't ask about her activities
since the adjournment of our connection, fearful that she might
tell me that she was having the time of her life, true or not. Even
coming to this soirée was an effort on my part, but I knew I had to
return to the interaction with other human beings sooner or later;
that, while it was going to take time, I would have to relearn
feeling at ease with the outside world, cast off those sensations
that I was being stalked by the unknown; that I was free to
venture out, show my face in the yard, without dread of apprehension, without consternation of incarceration and villainy. In
the light of the sun or glow of the moon, I often felt I was in the
lion's maw, the dragon's asylum – I was a spy in a foreign nation
and any second the secret police of this country's sovereign hand
would capture me, torture me for information and protocols.

Indeed, I had gone to this party at the last moment, telling myself it was time to move on. Why did other people seem so horrible to me? What did this have to do with Beth? Was this time of solitude – I liked to call it my *healing process* to make me feel better – necessary? It did not matter now, for here I was, and there was she: Beth; and there was no doubt about this: Beth; just a much different-looking Beth. And I considered this night, this get-together: for the moon was out&full, the night sky clear as refined plasma in an IV tube, a California night so close to Winter's breast. I did not run away from her, as I divined I might should this chance rendezvous ever occur. I could have, and by all means I should have; maybe I should have run, that first time, in the dark smoky club where we met. I hardly make the right moves, doing what I know I should not do, straying from the mantel of righteousness and God – like taking Beth into my arms that night at this party; it was a capricious move. She almost pushed me away. I saw she had a cigarette in hand. She should have burned me with it; scorching of the flesh is what I needed. Yes, she almost pushed me away but in that single moment where all truth resides, she embraced me as well, she took me like a perplexed foundling, she was the mother I had always hoped for, a matriarch that didn't allow me to go hungry when the inimical times came; for a passing moment, I thought she was going to cry – and I was certain I would break down and reveal to her what a liar I was, a coward. I thought of the intangible likeness of ecstasy when we fucked, our groveling way of fucking, and wondered if we were meant for each other, the antithesis of the first man&woman. It was a Jacques Monad sort of scenario: the chance and necessity of it all. She said my name over&over and people around us gave us inexplicable looks. Wondered if she knew anyone here, had friends here. I didn't really know anyone, maybe one or two people. I was an interloper, and I liked it as such: I was invisible, free to move untouched in the realm, through pedestrians, space&time. Beth held me, said my name over&over again; it was nice&good&clean. People kept glancing at us, frowns on faces, as if we were vagabonds; malefactors. Perhaps our crime was the scene of affection. I took her aside, took her to a far corner where we could be alone. We had to talk over the music and the laughs and the words of others. This party was not like the kind of parties she&I were used to, the baccha-

nalia no, this party had too much order&uniformity. We touched
each other like the classical lovers of Greece, antiquity in our
gaze, having been separated for what seemed like decades, those
spaces filled with discourse&adventures suitable to be sung by
blind men with bare&bleeding feet. I said *Beth* and she looked up
at me and from behind her new look, behind the average maga-
zine-type make-up, I saw the Beth I once coveted&cherished.
She said she had some coke but I stopped her, told her she should
not. I said we had to change our lives from now on, we had to be
reborn in this earth. She told me she had, citing me as a relevant
cause. I told her I was not an evil person, that I had, in fact, once
been angel (not unlike those Kathy is dreaming of now); she
laughed and said *well where are your wings, Michael?* I was
curious, now, about her life: wanting to know what she had been
doing these past months. She told me her life was like the temple
Samson had destroyed when he regained his strength. She said
but instead of potency she felt as if she had grown irresolute. It
was then that I acceded to the overwhelming inclination to
protect her, to shield her from the imps of mortality. We decided
to leave this party. She said she was renting a room in a house not
too far away, which was a mile from the local university, which
she said she had applied to for higher educational purposes. We
started to walk there. It was one of those nights; I was ready for
anything. I looked up, commented on the moon. She grabbed me,
pulled me down on someone's front lawn. It was quiet out; the
house of the lawn had no lights. She said *take me take me
here&now* and I tried to fight her away and she dug her fingernails into my face&neck and I felt the blood, the very warm
blood, run down, run out of me. Sex&violence, that's all I've ever
had in my life; this castigating I accepted fully, with all the
consequences&corruption. One moment, Beth&I were locked in
such a callous clasp that there were no misgivings that it would be
the final grasp for both of us, that we would rise to Heaven
together; that, untied, united, we would cast aside our mutual
cloaks of pain and go on to some premium glory. *I woke up in a
bed, in a cold room, and the moon was at the window, the full moon,
bright. I smiled at this moon and looked at the body next to me.
Beth's body. She was breathing slowly, her chest rose with each
intake of life. I felt good. Here we were, in this bed, alone&safe.
Nothing in this city or world could touch us here, nothing could*

extend its bitter arm and caress us with enmity. I moved against her. She was warm. I grabbed at her. She stirred. She called out to her father, in sleep. I closed my eyes and imagined myself cleansed of the dirty life we once shared. I was back on the grass, the wet grass – or was that my blood? I was caught up in a grapple for both life&fuck. Beth was tearing at my clothes; she squeezed my balls and I screamed. She relished this wretchedness. She kept telling me that I would never leave her again, we would be bound forever, we would marry and the only way the union could end would be murder, or worse. She hissed like some snake of old, going *murder murder murder*. I tore her skimpy slut's dress down the middle, pried it off her like reptilian flesh. She was naked, pale under the moon, and I said *you like this bitch, yes yes, how much you so very like it*, and pushed her down, her face into the wet blood grass, mounting her rear, a coyote's cry from her – and that wonderful full moon. I lost my edge and she bucked me off, was on top of me now, her hands around my neck. In her eyes, I could read that she apprehended we could never amount to anything, we would never have anything, and she was going to end all anguish now, terminate the memory&image she had of me like grease on a slate, *wipe wipe wipe*. I clawed at her bare breasts until they bled but this did not stop her intent. I hit her in the face; her nose broke; she fell to the ground. I kept hitting her face until her visage was raw meat, my hands bloody stumps. I prolonged this vehemence because there was no turning back now. I was driven. I was going to take this perdition to its pinnacle. *I woke up on the bed and looked at my hands. My hands were all right, my body was all right. I was back in Beth's bed. I sighed; it was a dream, that grass scene a whole dream, and there was undeniable comfort in this knowledge. But Beth was not beside me. I called her name. I could still smell her; the imprint of her body remained on the mattress. I saw that the bathroom light was on. I got up, knocked on the bathroom door. Beth, are you there? No answer. I went in. She was lying in a full tub. The water was pinkish-red. There was a sharp knife next to the tub, on the floor, blood on that tiled floor, blood smooth&clean, blood dripping from the arm that hung outside the water: the opened gash on small wrist. She had also, I noticed with interest, opened up her neck. The artery was languid as it pumped out the final quart of essence out of the temple of Beth. Her eyes were rolled up, toward the window and the full moon:*

uninhabited&aloof. I thought I'd never see a finale as exquisite as this. This was her swan song and no one could take it from her. She was – emancipated. I went to her, I went to her, I went to her, she stood up, she got up from the grass, her face a dominion of mess. She said so this is what you wanted all along? I charged, throwing her down again, my hands at her neck this time, using more force than she had on me. Die die *die I screamed as I woke up in the bed and the moon was peeking through and Beth was not there. I could still smell her and the imprint on the mattress was evident: new, so very new, so very Beth. I had been having this dream that I was following Beth's car in my car and it was late and we were going somewhere and as she went across an intersection a fast big car ran a red and hit hers, dragging it, smashing into the wall of a building, a loud sound, and I jumped out of my car and saw that she had been crushed in her car, almost chopped in two, her eyes popped from the sockets, blood everywhere, a baby growing in her womb, a reverie of two deaths, but I was glad now it was all just a dream, but she still wasn't there, so I called her name, I called her name, I called her name. I saw the bathroom light was on, the door partially opened. I was not going to get out of that bed; there was no way I was going to get up and go in there. Its interior would be a mystery. I would not look upon her body again. I only wanted to sleep. A simple desire. I didn't know what was real anymore. I grabbed Beth's pillow and hugged it to me, cried into it, cried, thinking that this will always be my prison.*

I seize Kathy, hard, waking her with strident resonance, howling into her hair like a primate in Cimmerian periodicity, thinking *the moon the moon the moon.*

LILING'S CURE

Delilah De Silva

Liling dried her soft hands and face and applied some compact powder on her skin. Still unblemished and youthful. Next, she proceeded to roll her glossy lipstick delicately over her small, round mouth. With a heavy sigh, she wheeled herself out of the bathroom and greeted him silently with her dimpled smile.

He gazed at her and she lowered her head coyly to the floor. It was his eyes; the peaceful color of the ocean-blue. Deep and shining. On his part, he admired hers, with their thin, feline slant and brown-sugarish tone. His stare made her feel like a delicacy. The sound of ancient sitar melody lulled in the dim-orange hue of the bedroom. Wisps of smoke curled warmly in the air as they rose from the burning incense of ylang-ylang. Liling inhaled the thick and sweet scent, filling her lungs with its seductive intoxication. Her limbs loosened and she peered through the translucent darkness, watching his lean, white body rest against the wall. He got up, pulled the wheelchair closer to the bed and whispered roughly into her tiny ears, "You look beautiful, darling. Absolutely stunning."

A tingle raced up her spine. Dazed, Liling's lips lingered against his high cheekbones as she waited for his strong, muscled arms to lift her cautiously from her seat and plant her gently on the waterproof sheet which laid over the purple, satin cover. Two, fluffy, wine-red pillows helped prop her head comfortably without any strain. Quickly and deftly, he peeled off her silky, pink blouse, the long, floral skirt, the lacy, black lingerie which he brought with him for every visit and finally the diaper which he respectfully placed on the bedside table. He did not mind her wetting herself. Liling stroked his milky back as his fingers traced through her sleek, black hair. "I love you," he kept murmuring, fixing his bold, blue eyes on her exotic loveliness. "I love you." Of course she believed him. Since the car crash two years ago, never once did he flinch when he touched her. Instead, it was almost a year ago when he was responsible for her very first orgasm. There was no turning back. She was greedy for more and he willingly supplied her with his mega-doses of painkillers.

"Ouch!" she yelped. He had seized her by her hair, yanking her head back and biting her slender neck hungrily. She clawed at his sweating pink skin as he travelled down to her small breasts and sucked at her right nipple while tweaking and pinching the other in a deliberately painful manner. However, she did not protest. This sort of pain was healing. This sort of pain reminded her of her aliveness. This sort of pain freed her. For so long after the operation which sliced her lower legs off, she had remained numb and corpse-like. It was he who resurrected her, with violence.

Closing her eyes, Liling smiled as his long, moist tongue flicked with feathery sweeps over the tips of her goosepimply nipples. Descending to her navel, he smothered her golden-yellowish belly with drooling kisses and cheekily resorted to parting her stumps. Unable to bear the excruciating pleasure, she moaned, arched and pressed her chopped legs close against his blonde head. With vengeance, he prised her thighs open, digging his nails into her butterish skin. She screamed as he tugged sharply at her triangular tuft of black hair. "Bitch!" he growled and she groaned approvingly. Seconds later, just as she was struggling to gulp some air, he stuffed three of his fingers into her tiny, creamy slash and churned the flow of her sticky fluids. "You Asian chicks are so tight and cute. Makes me horny, baby." The same lines. Each month. Each visit. Somehow, those words seemed to draw out the savage in him and transformed him further into an insatiable carnivore.

In one single move, he picked her up and flung her on her front, her backside, inviting to be slapped. Slap. Slap. Slap. Liling squeaked and pleaded. Tear-stricken, she begged it to end. Her buttocks parted, she trembled insanely as his tongue massaged her crack. Then, he paused, oiled his erection and spiked his way into her filthy exit. In In In. As expected, he finished halfway only and vented his frustration by cupping her rear and scraping its tender, lemony skin with his teeth. Once appeased, he slid back into kneeling position and overturned her dainty, quivering frame. Her supple arms flailed wildly in the perfumed emptiness and hit him against his broad, hairy chest. They wrestled. He laughed and slithered between her butchered limbs.

Her engorged lips throbbed as he expertly tickled her feminine hood. Up Down Up Down Up Down. Her bones rattled and she jerked, pounding her drenched self into his open, panting mouth. He drank her as she burst freely into him. Her agony, her bitterness, gushed out of her and he received and received, lapping every ounce of her pain and deep anger. His wide mouth was her temporary respite. No doctor, no drugs, relieved her as he did. She came and she came. Sparks of bluish white dots flashed in the semi-darkness as his licking quickened in its pace, circling her entire dripping inner and outer lips while simultaneously drilling two of his fingers into her rear hole. In Out In Out In Out.

It was at this point when Liling floated and drifted across the room, perfect and beautiful as she was before the tragedy. Her slim, tanned legs danced and flew above the humping, writhing bodies on the bed. She wiggled and jiggled and threw her head back, laughing at herself and her messiah, without whom she would not last the month.

Suddenly, she jolted and spirited back into the energetic motions of her flesh. Impaled by his massive, reddish-white erection, she gripped his waist as if holding on for her dear life. He rode into her, his hot spurts channelling tidal waves inside her dark, warm womb. Her phantom legs locked him around his powerful buttocks. She could feel them. They were real. They were there. No one could take her legs away from her. They were with her now. With him.

Liling twisted and wept, her face contorted into a mesh of emotions. His white largeness swallowed and wrapped itself around her golden-brown smallness and she desired to be crushed. Again and again and again.

He sponged her clean and towelled her dry. Feeling slightly limp, she allowed him to secure her diaper around her hips, dress her up and comb her hair. The waterproof sheet, the sexy lingerie and the satin cover were bagged and hidden in his car. The window was opened to let in the winter air and soon the fragrance of ylang-ylang faded into nothingness.

"Hello, Dad."

"Evening, Rob."

"Where's Liling? What did the doctor say?" Robert helped himself to a beer from the refrigerator.

"The usual. She's in good spirits. He prescribed more medication. I've left them on the dining-table."

"Thanks, Dad. I really appreciate you for taking her to her monthly appointments."

"That's what fathers are for. Liling's sleeping now. See you soon. I'll get your mum to drive over with dinner. Cheerio."

Arthur slipped on his coat and closed the door behind him.

SWEATING PROFUSELY IN MÉRIDA: A MEMOIR

Carol Queen

THE BOYFRIEND AND I met at a sex party. I was in a back room trying to help facilitate an erection for a gentleman brought to the party by a woman who would have nothing to do with him once they got there. She had charged him a pretty penny to get in, and I actually felt that I should have gotten every cent, but I suppose it was my own fault that I was playing Mother Teresa and didn't know when to let go of the man's dick. Boyfriend was hiding behind a potted palm eyeing me and this guy's uncooperative, uncut dick, and it seemed Boyfriend had a thing for pretty girls *and* uncut men, especially the latter. So he decided to help me out and replaced my hand with his mouth. That was when it got interesting. The uncut straight guy finally left and I stayed.

In the few months our relationship lasted, we shared many more straight men, most of them – Boyfriend's radar was incredible – uncircumcised and willing to do almost anything with a man as long as there was a woman in the room. I often acted as sort of a hook to hang a guy's heterosexuality on while Boyfriend sucked his dick or even fucked him. My favorite was the hitchhiker wearing pink lace panties under his grungy jeans – but that's another story. Long before we met him, Boyfriend had invited me to go to Mexico.

This was the plan. Almost all the guys in Mexico are uncut, right? And lots will play with me, too, Boyfriend assured me, especially if there's a woman there. (I guessed they resembled American men in this respect.) Besides, it would be a romantic vacation.

That was how we wound up in Room 201 of the Hotel Reforma in sleepy Mérida, capital of the Yucatán. Mérida's popularity as a tourist town had been eclipsed by the growth of Cancún, the nearest Americanized resort. That meant the boys would be hornier, Boyfriend reasoned. The Hotel Reforma had been recommended by a fellow foreskin fancier. Its chief advantages were the price – about $14 a night – and the fact that the management didn't charge extra for extra guests. I liked it because it was old, airy, and cool, with wrought-iron railings and floor tiles worn thin from all the people who'd come before. Boyfriend liked it because it had a pool, always a good place to cruise, and a disco across the street. That's where we headed as soon as we got in from the airport, showered, and changed into skimpy clothes suitable for turning tropical boys' heads.

There were hardly any tropical boys there, as it turned out, because this was where the Ft Lauderdale college students who couldn't afford spring break in Cancún went to spend their more meager allowances, and not only did it look like a Mexican restaurant-with-disco in Ft. Lauderdale, the management took care to keep all but the most dapper Méridans out lest the coeds be frightened by scruffy street boys. Scruffy street boys, of course, is just what Boyfriend had his eye out for, and at first the pickings looked slim; but we found one who had slipped past security, out to hustle nothing more spicy than a gig showing tourists around the warren of narrow streets near the town's central plaza, stumbling instead onto us. Ten minutes later Boyfriend had his mouth wrapped around a meaty little bundle, *with* foreskin. Luis stuck close to us for several days, probably eating more regularly than usual, and wondering out loud whether all the women in America were like me, and would we take him back with us? Or at least send him a Motley Crüe T-shirt when we went home?

Boyfriend had brought Bob Damron's gay travel guide, which listed for Mérida: a cruisy restaurant (it wasn't) and a cruisy park bench in the Zocalo (it was, and one night Boyfriend stayed out

most of the night looking for gay men, who, he said, would run
the other way if they saw me coming, and found one, a slender
boy who had to pull down the panty hose he wore under his jeans
so Boyfriend could get to his cock, and who expressed wonder
because he had never seen anyone with so many condoms; in fact
most people never had condoms at all. Boyfriend gave him his
night's supply and some little brochures, about *el SIDA* he'd
brought from the AIDS Foundation, *en español* so even if our
limited Spanish didn't get through to our tricks, a pamphlet
might).

Damron's also indicated that Mérida had a bathhouse.

I had always wanted to go to a bathhouse, and of course there
was not much chance it would ever happen back home. For one
thing, they were all closed before I ever moved to San Francisco.
For another, even if I dressed enough like a boy to pass, I
wouldn't look old enough to be let in. But in Mérida perhaps
things were different.

It was away from the town's center, but within walking distance of the Hotel Reforma. Through the tiny front window,
grimy from the town's blowing dust, I saw a huge papier-mâché
figure of Pan, painted brightly and hung with jewelry, phallus
high. It looked like something the Radical Faeries would carry in
the Gay Day parade. Everything else about the lobby looked
dingy, like the waiting room of a used-car dealership.

Los Baños de Vapor would open at eight that evening. They
had a central tub and rooms to rent; massage boys could be
rented, too. I would be welcome.

The papier-mâché Pan was at least seven feet tall and was
indeed the only bright thing in the lobby. Passing through the
courtyard, an overgrown jumble of vines pushing through
cracked tile, a slight smell of sulfur, a stagnant fountain, we
were shown up a flight of concrete stairs to our room by Carlos, a
solid, round-faced man in his midtwenties, wrapped in a frayed
white towel. The room was small and completely tiled, grout
black from a losing fight with the wet tropical air. At one end was
a shower and at the other a bench, a low, vinyl-covered bed, and a
massage table. There was a switch that, when flipped, filled the
room with steam. Boyfriend flipped it and we shucked our
clothes; as the pipes hissed and clanked, Carlos gestured to the
massage table and then to me.

Boyfriend answered for me, in Spanish, that I'd love to. I got on the table and Carlos set to work. Boyfriend danced around the table gleefully, sometimes stroking me, sometimes Carlos's butt. "Hey, man, I'm working!" Carlos protested, not very insistently, and Boyfriend went for his cock, stroking it hard, then urged him up onto the table, and Carlos's hands, still slick from the massage oil and warm from the friction of my skin, covered my breasts as Boyfriend rolled a condom onto Carlos's cock and rubbed it up and down my labia a few times and finally let go, letting it sink in. He rode me slow and then hard while the table rocked danger- ously and Boyfriend stood at my head, letting me tongue his cock while he played with Carlos's tits. When Boyfriend was sure that we were having a good time, he put on a towel and slipped out the door. Carlos looked surprised. I had to figure out how to say, in Spanish "He's going hunting," and get him to go back to fucking me, solid body slick from oil and steam; if he kept it up, he would make me come, clutching his slippery back, legs in the air.

That was just happening when Boyfriend came back with David. He was pulling him in the door by his already stiff penis, and I suspected Boyfriend had wasted as little time getting him by the dick as he usually did. He had found David in the tub room, he announced, and he had a beautiful, long *uncut* cock. (Boyfriend always enunciated clearly when he said "uncut".) David *did* have a beautiful cock, and he spoke English and was long and slim with startling blue eyes. It turned out he was Chicano, second generation, a senior Riverside High who spent school breaks with his grandmother in Mérida and worked at Los Baños de Vapor as a secret summer job. We found out all this about him as I was showering the sweat and oil off from my fuck with Carlos, and by the time I heard that he'd been working at the Baños since he turned sixteen, I was ready to start fucking again. David was the most quintessentially eighteen-year-old fuck I ever had, except Boyfriend's presence made it unusual; he held David's cock and balls and controlled the speed of the thrusting, until his mouth got preoccupied with Carlos's dick. David told me, ardently, that I was beautiful, though at that point I didn't care if I was beautiful or not, since I was finally in a bathhouse doing what I'd always wanted to do and I felt more like a faggot than a beautiful *gringa*. But David was saying he wished he had a girlfriend like me, even though I was thirty, shockingly old – this actually was what almost all of Boyfriend's conquests said to me, though I suspected not every man could keep up with a girlfriend who was really a faggot, or a boyfriend who was really a woman, or whatever kind of fabulous anomaly I was.

Then someone knocked on the door and we untangled for a minute to answer it, and there were José and Gaspar, laughing and saying we were the most popular room in the Baños at the moment and would we like some more company? At least that's how David translated the torrent of Spanish, for they were both speaking at once. Naturally we invited them in, and lo and behold, Gaspar was actually *gay*, and so while I lay sideways on the massage table with my head off the edge and my legs in the air so I could suck David while José fucked me, I could watch Boyfriend finally getting *his* cock sucked by Gaspar, whose black, glittering Mayan eyes closed in concentration, and I howled with not simply orgasm but the *excitement*, the splendid excitement of being in Mexico in a bathhouse with four uncut men and a maniac, a place no woman I knew had gone before. Steam swirled in the saturated air like superheated fog, beading like pearls in the web of a huge Yucatán spider in the corner; David's cock, or was it José's or Carlos's again, I didn't care, pounded my fully opened cunt rhythmically and I wished I had her view.

You know if you have ever been to a bathhouse that time stands still in the steamy, throbbing air, and so I had no idea how long it went on, only that sometimes I was on my back and sometimes on my knees, and once for a minute I was standing facing the wall, and when Boyfriend wasn't sucking them or fucking me, he was taking snapshots of us, just like a tourist. The floor of the room was completely littered with condoms, which made us all laugh hysterically. Rubber-kneed, Gasper and David held me up with Carlos and José flanking them so Boyfriend could snap one last picture. Then he divided all the rest of the condoms among them – we had more at the hotel, I think that week we went through ten dozen – and got out his brochures. He was trying to explain in Spanish the little condoms he used for giving head – how great they were to use with uncut guys 'cause they disappeared under the foreskin – and I was asking David what it was like to live a double life, Riverside High to Los Baños, and who else came there – "Oh, everybody does," he said – and did they ever want to fuck him – of course they *wanted* to – and did he ever fuck them –

well, sure – and how was that? He shrugged and said, as if there were only one possible response to my question, "It's *fucking*."

When we left, the moon was high, the Baños deserted, the warm night air almost cool after the steamy room. The place looked like a courtyard motel, the kind I used to stay in with my parents when we traveled in the early sixties, but overgrown and haunted. The Pan figure glittered in the low lobby light, and the man at the desk charged us $35 – seven for each massage boy, four each to get in, and six for the room. Hundreds of thousands of pesos – he looked anxious, as though he feared we'd think it was too much. We paid him, laughing. I wondered if this was how a Japanese businessman in Thailand felt. Was I contributing to the imperialist decline of the third world? Boyfriend didn't give a shit about things like that, so I didn't mention it. In my hand was a crumpled note from David: "Can I come visit you in your hotel room? No money."

ALMOST TRANSPARENT BLUE

Ryu Murakami

Translated by Nancy Andrew

IN THE MIDDLE of Oscar's room, nearly a fistful of hashish smoldered in an incense burner, and like it or not, the spreading smoke entered one's chest with every breath. In less than thirty seconds I was completely stoned. I felt as if my insides were oozing out through every pore, and other people's sweat and breath were flowing in.

Especially the lower half of my body felt heavy and sore, as if sunk into thick mud, and my mouth itched to hold somebody's prick and drain it. While we ate the fruit piled on plates and drank wine, the whole room was raped by heat. I wanted my skin peeled off. I wanted to take in the greased, shiny bodies of the black men and rock them inside of me. Cherry cheesecake, grapes in black hands, steaming boiled crab legs breaking with a snap, clear sweet pale purple American wine, pickles like dead men's wart-covered fingers, bacon sandwiches like the mouths of women, salad dripping pink mayonnaise.

Bob's huge cock was stuffed all the way into Kei's mouth.

Ah'm jes' gonna see who's got the biggest. She crawled around on the rug like a dog and did the same for everyone.

Discovering that the largest belonged to a half-Japanese named Saburō, she took a cosmos flower from an empty vermouth bottle and stuck it in as a trophy.

Hey, Ryū, his is twice the size of the one ya got.

Saburō raised his head and let out an Indian yell, then Kei seized the cosmos flower between her teeth and pulled it out, jumped on the table, and shook her hips, like a Spanish dancer. Flashing blue strobe lights circled the ceiling. The music was a luxuriant samba by Luiz Bon Fa. Kei shook her body violently, hot after seeing the wetness on the flower.

Somebody do it to me, do it to me quick, Kei yelled in English, and I don't know how many black arms reached out to throw her on the sofa and tear off her slip, the little pieces of black translucent cloth fluttering to the floor. Hey, just like butterflies, said Reiko, taking a piece of the cloth and spreading butter on Durham's prick. After Bob yelled and thrust his hand into Kei's crotch, the room filled with shrieks and shrill laughter.

Looking around the room, watching the twisting bodies of the three Japanese girls, I drank peppermint wine and munched crackers spread with honey.

The penises of the black men were so long they looked slender. Even fully erect, Durham's bent fairly far as Reiko twisted it. His legs trembled and he shot off suddenly, and everyone laughed at the sight of his come wetting the middle of Reiko's face. Reiko laughed too and blinked, but as she looked around for some tissue paper to wipe her face, Saburō easily picked her up. He pulled her legs open, just as if he were helping a little girl to piss, and lifted her onto his belly. His huge left hand gripping her head and his right pinning her ankles together, he held her so that all her weight hung on his cock. Reiko yelled, That hurts, and struck out with her hands, trying to pull away, but she couldn't grab on to anything.

Her face was getting pale.

Saburō, moving and spreading his legs to get more friction on his cock, leaned back against the sofa until he was lying almost flat and began to rotate Reiko's body, using her butt as a pivot.

On the first turn her entire body convulsed and she panicked. Her eyes bulging and her hands over her ears, she began to shriek like the heroine of a horror movie.

Saburō's laugh was like an African war cry, as Reiko twisted her face and clawed at her chest. Squeal some more, he said in

Japanese, and began to turn her body faster. Oscar, who'd been sucking Moko's tits, Durham, who'd placed a cold towel on his wilted prick, Jackson, who wasn't naked yet, Bob on top of Kei – all gazed at the revolving Reiko. God! Outasight! said Bob and Durham, and went over to help turn her around. Bob took her feet and Durham her head; both pressing hard on her butt, they began to spin her faster. Laughing, showing his white teeth, Saburō then put both hands behind his head and arched his body to drive his cock in even deeper. Reiko suddenly burst into loud sobs. She bit her own fingers and tore at her hair, because of the spinning her tears flew outward without reaching her cheeks. We laughed harder than ever. Kei waved a piece of bacon and drank wine, Moko buried her red fingernails in the huge butt of wiry-haired Oscar. Reiko's toes were stretched back and quivering. Her cunt, rubbed hard, gaped red and shone with mucus. Saburō took deep breaths and slowed down the spinning, moving her in time with Luiz Bonfa's singing of "Black Orpheus". I turned down the volume and sang along. Laughing all the time, Kei licked my toes while lying on her stomach on the rug. Reiko kept on crying, Durham's semen dried on her face. With bloody tooth marks on his fingers, sometimes growling like a lion from the pit of his stomach – Oh-h, I'm gonna bust, get this cunt off me, Saburō said in Japanese and thrust Reiko aside. Get away from me, pig! he yelled. Reiko grabbed at his legs as she fell forward; his come shot straight up and splattered and sprayed on her back and buttocks. Reiko's belly quivered and some urine leaked out. Kei – she'd been smearing her own tits with honey – hurriedly slid some newspaper under Reiko.

That's jes' awful, she said, slapped Reiko's butt and laughed shrilly. Moving about the room, twisting our bodies, we took into ourselves the tongues and fingers and pricks of whoever we wanted.

I wonder where I am, I kept thinking. I put some of the grapes scattered on the table in my mouth. As I skinned them with my tongue and spat the seeds into a plate, my hand felt a cunt; when I looked up, Kei was standing there with her legs apart, grinning at me. Jackson stood up dazedly and stripped off his uniform. Grinding out the slim menthol cigarette he'd been smoking, he turned toward Moko, who was rocking away on top of Oscar. Dribbling a sweet-smelling fluid from a little brown bottle on Moko's butt, Jackson called, Hey, Ryū, bring me that white tube in my shirt pocket, OK? Her hands held tightly by Oscar, her bottom smeared with the cream, Moko let out a shriek: That's cold! Jackson grasped and raised her buttocks, got his cock – also thickly coated with the cream – into position and began thrusting. Moko hunched over and screeched.

Kei looked up and came over, saying, That looks kind of fun. Moko was crying. Kei grabbed her hair and peered into her face. Ah'll put some nice mentholatum on ya afterwards, Moko. Kei tongue-kissed with Oscar and laughed loudly again. With a pocket camera, I took a close-up of Moko's distorted face. Her nose was twitching like a long-distance runner making a last spurt. Reiko finally opened her eyes. Perhaps realizing that she was all sticky, she started for the shower. Her mouth was open, her eyes vacant, she tripped again and again and fell. When I put my hands on her shoulders to lift her up, she brought her face close to mine. Oh, Ryū, save me, she said. An old smell came from her body. I dashed to the toilet and threw up. As Reiko sat on the tiles getting drenched by the shower, I couldn't tell which way her reddened eyes were looking.

Reiko, ya big dummy, ya'll jes' drown. Kei shut off the shower, thrust her hand in Reiko's crotch, then squealed with laughter to see Reiko jump up in panic. Oh, it's Kei. Reiko hugged her and kissed her on the lips. Kei beckoned to me as I sat on the toilet. Hey Ryū, that cold feels good, right? Since I was cold outside, I felt hotter inside. Hey, ya got a cute one. She took it in her mouth as Reiko pulled back my wet hair, sought out my tongue like a baby seeking the breast, and sucked hard. Kei braced her hands against the wall and thrust out her butt, then buried me in her hole, washed free of mucus by the shower and dried. Bob, his hands dripping sweat, came into the shower. There're not enough chicks, Ryū, you bastard, taking two of them.

Swatting my cheek, he roughly dragged us, dripping, just as we were, into the next room and threw us on the floor. My prick, still tight inside Kei, twisted as we fell. I groaned. Reiko was tossed like a rugby pass up on the bed and Bob leaped on top of her. She struggled, raving, but she was pinned down by Saburō and a chunk of cheesecake was crammed into her mouth, choking her. The record music changed to Osibisa. Moko wiped her butt, her face twitching. There were traces of blood on the paper. She showed them to Jackson and muttered, That's awful. Hey Reiko, that cheesecake's good, huh? Kei asked, lying on her stomach on the table. Reiko answered, Something's thrashing around in my stomach, like I'd swallowed a live fish or something. I got up on the bed to take her picture, but Bob bared his teeth and pushed me off. Rolling to the floor I bumped into Moko. Ryū, I hate that guy, I've had it, he's a fag, right? Moko was on top of Oscar, who rocked her while he gnawed a piece of chicken. She started to cry.

Moko, you're OK? It doesn't hurt? I asked. Oh, I don't know anymore, Ryū, I just don't know.

She was rocked in time with the Osibisa record. Kei sat on Jackson's knee, sipping wine, talking about something. After rubbing her body with a piece of bacon, Jackson sprinkled on vanilla extract. A hoarse voice yelled Oh baby. A lot of stuff had ended up on the red rug. Underwear and cigarette ashes, scraps of bread and lettuce and tomato, different kinds of hair, blood-smeared paper, tumblers and bottles, grape skins, matches, dusty cherries – Moko staggered to her feet. Her hand on her ass, she said, I'm famished, and walked to the table. Jackson leaned over to apply a band-aid and a kiss.

Pressing her chin on the table, breathing hard, Moko attacked a crab like a starving child. Then one of the blacks stuck his shaft in front of her, and she took that in her mouth too. Stroking it with her tongue, she pushed it aside and turned again to the crab. The red shell crunched between her teeth, she pulled out the white meat with her hands. Piling it with pink mayonnaise from a plate, she put it on her tongue, the mayonnaise dribbling onto her chest. The odor of crab flowed through the room. On the bed, Reiko was still howling. Durham pushed up into Moko from behind. Her butt jiggled, she held onto the crab, her face twisted, she tried to drink some wine but with the rocking of her body it went into her nose and she choked, tears in her eyes. Seeing that, Kei laughed loudly. James Brown began to sing. Reiko crawled to the table, drained a glass of peppermint wine and said loudly, That tastes good.

"Haven't I told you over and over not to get in too deep with that Jackson, the MP's are watching him, he's going to get caught one of these days," Lilly said as she snapped off the TV picture of a young man singing.

Oscar had said, OK, let's finish up, and opened the veranda doors. A piercing cold wind blew in, a fresh wind, which I could still feel.

But while everyone was still lying around naked, Bob's woman Tami had come in and gotten into a bad fight with Kei, who'd tried to stop her from hitting Bob. Tami's brother was a big gangster, and since she'd wanted to run and tell him, there was nothing I could do but bring her along here to Lilly's place. I'd heard Lilly was a friend of hers, she'd talk her around. Until just a few minutes ago, Tami had been sitting over there on the sofa, howling, I'll kill them! Her side had been raked by Kei's nails.

"So don't I always say you better not bring in punks who don't know anything about this Yokota territory? What would you have done without me, huh? You wouldn't have got off easy, Ryū, Tami's brother is real bad."

She drank a swallow from a glass of Coca-cola with a lemon slice floating in it, then passed it over to me. She brushed her hair and changed into a black negligée. Still seeming angry, she brushed her teeth and shot up on Philopon in the kitchen with the toothbrush still in her mouth.

"Aw, come off it, Lilly, I'm sorry."

"Oh, all right, I know you'll just go and do the same thing tomorrow . . . But listen, you know, the waiter at my place, a guy from Yokosuka, is asking if I want to buy some mesc. How about it, Ryū? You want to try it, don't you?

"How much is it, for one tab?"

"I don't know, he just said five dollars, should I buy it?"

Even Lilly's pubic hair was dyed to match. They don't sell stuff to dye the hair down here in Japan, she'd told me, I had to send away for it myself, got it from Denmark.

Through the hair over my eyes, I could see the ceiling light.

"Hey, Ryū, I had a dream about you," Lilly said, placing her hand around my neck.

"The one about me riding a horse in a park? I've heard that one before." I ran my tongue along Lilly's eyebrows, which were growing out again.

"No, another one, after the one in the park. The two of us go to the ocean, you know, a real pretty seaside. There's this big beach, wide and sandy, nobody there except you and me. We swim and play in the sand but then on the other side of the water we can see this town. Well, it's far away, so we shouldn't be able to see much, but we can even make out the faces of the people living there – that's how dreams are, right? First they're having some kind of celebration, some kind of foreign festival. But then, after a while, a war starts in that town, with artillery going boom, boom. A real war – even though it's so far away, we can see the soldiers and the tanks.

"So the two of us, you and me, Ryū, just watch from the beach, sort of dreamy like. And you say, Hey, wow, so that's war, and I say Yeah, right."

"You sure have some weird dreams, Lilly."

The bed was damp. Some feathers sticking out of the pillow pricked the back of my neck. I pulled out a little one and stroked Lilly's thighs with it.

The room was dimly gray. Some light stole in from the kitchen. Lilly was still asleep, her little hand, with the nail polish off, resting on my chest. Her cool breath brushed my armpit. The oval mirror hanging from the ceiling reflected our nakedness.

The night before, after we'd done it, Lilly had shot up again, humming deep in her white throat.

I just keep using more, no matter what, I've got to cut down pretty soon or I'll be an addict, right? she'd said, checking the amount left.

While Lilly had been rocking her body on top of mine, I'd remembered the dream she'd told me about, and also the face of a certain woman. As I'd watched the twisting of Lilly's slim hips . . .

The face of a thin woman digging a hole right next to a barbed wire entanglement around a large farm. The sun was sinking. The face of a woman bent down to thrust a shovel into the earth, beside a tub full of grapes, as a young soldier threatened her with his bayonet. The face of a woman wiping away her sweat with the back of her hand, hair hanging over her face. As I'd watched Lilly panting, the woman's face floated through my mind.

Damp air from the kitchen.

Is it raining? I wondered. The scene outside the window was smoky, milk colored. I noticed the front door was ajar. Yesterday, since we were both drunk, we must have gone to bed without closing it. A single high-heeled shoe lay on its side on the kitchen floor. The tapering heel stuck out, and the curve of firm leather over the front was as smooth as part of a woman.

Outside, in the narrow space I could see through the open door, stood Lilly's yellow Volkswagen. Raindrops stuck to it like goose bumps, and then the heavier ones slid down slowly, insects in winter.

People passing like shadows. A mailman in a blue uniform pushing a bicycle, several school children with book bags, a tall American with a Great Dane – all passing through the narrow space.

Lilly took a deep breath and half turned her body. She gave a low moan and the light blanket that had covered her fell to the floor. Her long hair stuck to her back in an S shape. The small of her back was sweaty.

Scattered on the floor was Lilly's underwear from the day before. Far away and rolled up small, the garments were just like little burn marks or dyed spots on the rug.

A Japanese woman with a black shoulder bag looked around the room from the doorway. Her cap bore some company insignia, the shoulders of her navy jacket were damp – I thought she must have come to read the gas or electric meter. When her eyes got used to the dim light, she noticed me, started to speak, seemed to think better of it, and stepped outside again. She glanced back once more at me, naked and smoking a cigarette, then went off toward the right, her head cocked to one side.

Through the space outside the door, now open a little wider, passed two grade-school girls, talking, gesturing, wearing red rubber boots. A black soldier in uniform ran by, leaping over the muddy spots just like a basketball player dodging a guard to shoot.

Beyond Lilly's car, on the other side of the street, stood a small black building. Its paint was peeling in places; "U-37" was written in orange.

Against the background of that black well, I could clearly see the fine rain falling. Over the roof were heavy clouds, looking as if someone had smeared on layer after layer of gray pigment. The sky in the narrow rectangle that was visible to me was the brightest part.

Thick clouds swollen with fever. They made the air damp, made Lilly and me sweat. That's why the crumpled sheets were clammy.

A think black line slanted across the narrow sky.

Maybe that's an electric wire, I thought, or a tree branch, but then it rained harder and soon I couldn't see it anymore.

The people walking in the street hurriedly put up umbrellas and began to run.

Puddles appeared on the muddy street even as I watched and widened out in a series of ripples. Played on by the rain, a big white car moved slowly along the street, almost filling it. Inside were two foreign women, one adjusting her hairnet in the mirror, and the other, the driver, watching the road so carefully that her nose was almost pressed against the windshield. Both were heavily made up; their dry skin appeared to be caked with powder.

A girl licking an ice cream bar passed, then came back and peered in. Her soft, blonde hair was plastered to her head, and she took Lilly's bath towel off the kitchen chair and began to wipe herself dry. She licked ice cream off her finger and sneezed. When she raised her head, she noticed me. Picking up the blanket and covering myself, I waved at her. She smiled and pointed outside. Putting my finger to my lips, I signaled her to keep quiet. Looking toward Lilly, I laid my head on my hand to show she was still sleeping. So be quiet, I gestured again, my finger to my lips, and grinned at her. The girl turned toward the outside and gestured with the hand holding the ice cream. I turned my palm upward and looked up in a pantomime of noticing the rain. The girl nodded, shaking her wet hair. Then she dashed outside and came back drenched, carrying a dripping bra that looked like one of Lilly's.

"Lilly, hey, it's raining, do you have washing hanging out? Get up, Lilly, it's raining!"

Rubbing her eyes, Lilly got up, saw the girl, hid herself behind the blanket, and said, "Hey, Sherry, what are you up to?" The girl tossed the bra she was holding, yelled in English "Rainy!" and laughed as her eyes met mind.

Even when I gently peeled the band-aid off her ass, Moko didn't open her eyes.

Reiko was rolled up in a blanket on the kitchen floor, Kei and Yoshiyama were on the bed, Kazuo was by the stereo, still holding tight to his Nikomat, Moko lay on her stomach on the carpet, hugging a pillow. There was a slight bloodstain on the band-aid I'd peeled off, the hurt place opened and closed as she breathed, reminding me of a rubber tube.

The sweat beading her back smelled just like sex juices.

When Moko opened the eye that still had false eyelashes, she grinned at me. Then she moaned when I put my hand between her buttocks and half turned her body.

You're lucky it's raining, rain's good for healing, I'll bet it doesn't hurt much because of the rain.

Moko's sticky crotch. I wiped it for her with soft paper, and when I stuck in a finger, her naked buttocks jiggled.

Kei opened her eyes and asked, Hey, so ya stayed over last night with that whore-lady?

Shut up, stupid, she's not like that, I said, swatting at the little insects flying around.

Ah mean Ah don' care, Ryū, but ya got to watch about getting a dose, like Jackson said, some of the guys around here have got it real bad, ya could rot to pieces. Kei pulled on just her panties and fixed coffee, Moko stretched out a hand and said, Hey, give me a smoke, one of those mint-flavour Sah-lem.

Moko, that's Say-lem, not Sah-lem, Kazuo told her, getting up.

Rubbing his eyes, Yoshiyama said loudly to Kei, No milk in mine, OK? Then he turned to me – my finger still in Moko's ass – and said, Last night when you guys were messing around upstairs, I got a straight flush, you know, really right on, a straight flush in hearts – Hey, Kazuo, you were there, you can back me up, right?

Without answering him, Kazuo said sleepily, My strobe's gone somewhere, somebody hiding it?

Jackson said I should wear makeup again, like I'd done before. That time, I thought maybe Faye Dunaway'd come to visit, Ryū, he said.

I put on a silver negligée Saburō said he'd got from a pro stripper.

Before everybody arrived in Oscar's room, a black man I'd never seen before came and left nearly a hundred capsules; I couldn't tell what they were. I asked Jackson if he might have been an MP or a CID man, but Jackson laughed, shaking his head, and answered, Naw, that's Green Eyes.

"You saw how his eyes are green? Nobody knows his real name, I heard he'd been a high school teacher but I don't know if it's true or not. He's crazy, really, we don't know where he lives or whether he has a family, just that he's been here a lot longer than we have, seems he's been in Japan an awful long time. Don't he look like Charlie Mingus? Maybe he came after he'd heard something about you. He say anything to you?"

That black man had looked very uptight. I'll give you just this much, he'd said, then rolled his eyes around the room and left as if he were making an escape.

His face hadn't changed even when he saw Moko was naked, and when Kei asked him, How about some fun? his lips had trembled but he didn't say anything.

"You'll get to see the black bird sometime, too, you haven't seen it yet, but you, you'll be able to see the bird, you've got them kind of eyes, same as me." Then he'd gripped my hand.

Oscar said not to take any of those capsules, because Green Eyes had once passed around laxatives. He told me to throw them out.

Jackson sterilized a battlefield syringe. I'm a medic, he said, so I'm a real pro at shots, right?

First they shot me up with heroin.

"Ryū, dance!" Jackson slapped my butt. When I stood up and looked in the mirror, I saw what looked like a different person, transformed by Moko's painstaking, expert makeup technique. Saburō passed me a cigarette and an artificial rose and asked, What music? I said make it Schubert and everyone laughed.

A sweet-smelling mist floated before my eyes and my head was heavy and numb. As I slowly moved my arms and legs, I felt that my joints had been oiled, and that slippery oil flowed around inside my body. As I breathed I forgot who I was. I thought that many things gradually flowed from my body, I became a doll. The room was full of sweetish air, smoke clawed my lungs. The feeling that I was a doll became stronger and stronger. All I had to do was just move as they wanted, I was the happiest possible slave. Bob muttered Sexy, Jackson said Shut up. Oscar put out all the lights and turned an orange spot on me. Once in a while my face twisted and I felt panicky. I opened my eyes wide and shook my body. I called out, panted low, licked jam off my finger, sipped wine, pulled my hair, grinned, rolled up my eyes, spit out the words of a spell.

I yelled some lines I remembered by Jim Morrison: "When the music is over, when the music is over, put out all the lights, my brothers live at the bottom of the sea, my sister was killed, pulled up on land like a fish, her belly torn open, my sister was killed, when the music is over, put out all the lights, put out all the lights."

Like the splendid men in Genet's novels, I rolled saliva around in my mouth and put it on my tongue – dirty white candy. I rubbed my legs and clawed my chest my hips and my toes were sticky. Gooseflesh wrapped my body like a sudden wind and all my strength was gone.

I stroked the cheek of a black woman sitting with her knees drawn up next to Oscar. She was sweating, the toenails at the end of her long legs were painted silver.

A flabby fat white woman Saburō had brought along gazed at me, her eyes moist with desire. Jackson shot heroin into the palm of Reiko's hand; maybe it hurt, her faced twitched. The black woman was already drunk on something. She put her hands under my armpits and made me stand up, then stood up herself and began to dance. Durham put hash in the incense burner again. The purple smoke rose and Kei crouched down to suck it in. At the smell of the black woman, clinging to me with her sweat, I almost fell. The smell was fierce, as if she were fermenting inside. She was taller than I, her hips jutted out, her arms and legs were very slender. Her teeth looked disturbingly white as she laughed and stripped. Lighter colored, pointed breasts didn't bounce much even when she shook her body. She seized my face between her hands and thrust her tongue into my mouth. She rubbed my hips, undid the hooks of the negligée, and ran her sweaty hands over my belly. Her rough tongue licked around my gums. Her smell completely enveloped me; I felt nauseated.

Kei came crawling over and gripped my cock, saying, Do it right, Ryū, get it up. All at once spittle gushed from one corner of my mouth down to my chin and I couldn't see anymore.

Her whole body glistening with sweat, the black woman licked my body. Gazing into my eyes, she sucked up the flesh of my thighs with her bacon-smelling tongue. Red, moist eyes. Her big mouth kept laughing and laughing.

Soon I was lying down; Moko, her hands braced on the edge of the bed, shook her butt as Saburō thrust into her. Everyone else was crawling on the floor, moving, shaking, making noises. I noticed that my heart was beating terribly slowly. As if matching its beat, the black woman squeezed my pulsing prick. It was as if only my heart and my cock were attached to each other and working, as if all my other organs had melted.

The black woman sat on top of me. At the same time her hips began to swivel at tremendous speed. She turned her face to the ceiling, let out a Tarzan yell, panted like a black javelin thrower I'd seen in an Olympic film; she braced the grayish soles of her feet on the mattress, thrust her long hands under my hips and held tight. I shouted, felt torn apart. I tried to pull away, but the black woman's body was hard and slippery as greased steel. Pain mixed with pleasure drilled through my lower body and swirled up to my head. My toes were hot enough to melt. My shoulders began to shake, maybe I was going to start yelling. The back of my throat was blocked by something like the soup Jamaicans make with blood and grease, I wanted to spit it up. The black woman took deep breaths, felt my shaft to make sure it was deep inside her, grinned, and took a puff on a very long black cigarette.

She put the perfumed cigarette in my mouth, asked me quickly something I didn't understand, and when I nodded she put her face to mine and sucked my saliva, then began to swivel her hips. Slippery juices streamed from her crotch, wetting my thighs and belly. The speed of her twisting slowly increased. I moaned, getting into it. As I screwed both eyes shut, emptied my head, and put my strength into my feet, keen sensations raced around my body along with my blood and concentrated in my temples. Once the sensations formed and clung to my body, they didn't leave. The thin flesh behind my temples sizzled like skin burned by a firecracker. As I noticed this burn and the feeling became centered there, I somehow believed I had become just one huge penis. Or was I a miniature man who could crawl up inside women and pleasure them with his writhing? I tried to grip the black woman's shoulders. Without slackening the speed of her hips, she leaned forward and bit my nipples until blood came.

Singing a song, Jackson straddled my face. Hey, baby, he said, lightly swatting my cheek. I thought his swollen asshole was like a strawberry. Sweat from his thick chest dripped onto my face, the smell strengthened the stimulus from the black woman's hips. Hey, Ryū, you're just a doll, you're just our little yellow doll, we could stop winding you up and finish you off, y'know, Jackson crooned, and the black woman laughed so loudly I wanted to cover my ears. Her loud voice might have been a broken radio. She laughed without stopping the movement of her hips, and her saliva dribbled onto my belly. She tongue-kissed Jackson. Like a dying fish, my cock jumped inside her. My body seemed powder dry from her heat. Jackson thrust his hot prick into my dry mouth, a hot stone burning my tongue. As he rubbed it around my tongue, he and the black woman chanted something like a spell. It wasn't English, I couldn't understand it. It was like a sutra with a conga rhythm. When my cock twitched and I was almost ready to come, the black woman raised her hips, thrust her hand under my buttocks, pinched me, and jabbed a finger hard into my asshole. When she noticed the tears filling my eyes, she forced her finger in even deeper and twisted it around. There was a whitish tattoo on each of her thighs, a crude picture of a grinning Christ.

She squeezed my throbbing cock, then plunged it into her mouth until her lips almost touched my belly. She licked all around, nipped, then stroked the tip with her rough pointed tongue, just like a cat's. Whenever I was on the verge of coming, she pulled her tongue away. Her buttocks, slippery, shiny with sweat, faced me. They seemed spread almost wide enough to tear apart. I stretched out a hand and dug my nails into one side as hard as I could. The black woman panted and slowly moved her butt from side to side. The fat white woman sat on my feet. Her blackish-red cunt hanging down from under sparse golden down reminded me of a cut-up pig's liver. Jackson seized her huge breasts roughly and pointed to my face. Shaking the breasts that lay on her white belly, she peered into my face, touched my lips split by Jackson's prick, and laughed Pretty in a soft voice. She took one of my legs and rubbed it against her sticky pig liver. My toes were moved around — it felt so bad I could hardly stand it — the white woman smelled just like rotten crab meat and I wanted to throw up. My throat convulsed and I nipped Jackson's prick slightly; he yelled terribly, pulled out, and struck me hard on the cheek. The white woman laughed at my bleeding nose, Gee that's awful; she rubbed her crotch even harder against my feet. The black woman licked up my blood. She smiled gently at me like a battlefield nurse and whispered in my ear Pretty soon we'll have you shoot off, we'll make you come. My right foot began to disappear into the white woman's huge cunt. Again Jackson thrust his prick into my cut mouth. I desperately fought down my nausea. Stimulated by my slippery, bloody tongue, Jackson shot his warm wad. The sticky stuff blocked my throat. I heaved pinkish fluid, mixed with blood, and yelled to the black woman, Make me come!

WHERE THE
WILD ROSES GROW

Mark Timlin

This story was inspired by a song by Nick Cave which he recorded in 1995 with Kylie Minogue. I was impressed by the tune, the lyric, and the video that accompanied it, and I felt that there could be more to the story. The title and theme of the song are used with the kind permission of the songwriter.

ON THE FIRST DAY the hot wind whipped hard across the central Australian desert and blew sand abrasively against the faded paintwork of the ancient Ford pick-up truck as it crawled across the dusty blacktop, the needle on the fuel gauge banging dangerously against the peg that showed that the petrol tank was empty.

The driver relaxed a little when he saw a signpost that told him that a town called Refuge was only a few kilometres down the highway. He lit his last cigarette and tried to remember how long it had been since he'd had human contact.

As Refuge got closer, the features of the land softened slightly and as he bumped over the narrow bridge that crossed the river that ran sluggishly beside the town he noticed red roses growing bloody and wild on its banks.

Seventeen-year-old Eliza Day was staring through the dirty, fly-blown plate glass window of the diner where she waitressed, as the truck pulled into town and stopped in front of the single pump of the small gas station that together with the diner, a general store and pub called The Moon In The Gutter made up the entire commercial area of Refuge.

God, it's so hot, she thought as she fanned herself with a menu. When will the rain come and give us a break? And she swatted half heartedly with her hand as a sand fly buzzed around her head.

The truck was the only thing that moved in the heat and she watched as the driver climbed out of the cab. He was in his twenties, tall and thin with a slight stoop in his ragged denim shirt and jeans, over brown, high-heeled boots, and his long hair was as black as a raven's wing. Eliza's heart lurched at the sight of him. She wore nothing under the short cotton uniform dress that her boss insisted she wear and she could feel sweat running down from her armpits and between her breasts and staining the material until it was almost transparent. My God, she thought as she squinted through the haze at the driver's sharply featured face. He's gorgeous. And she blushed as she rubbed her damp thighs together and felt them grow damper still at the sight of him.

She continued watching as Jo-Jo the proprietor of the garage pumped gas into the tank, replaced the cap and took a few notes from the driver's hand.

Don't go, she prayed. Please don't go.

As if he had heard her, the driver turned and surveyed the decaying township, got back into the truck, started it with a puff of smoke from the exhaust pipe and swung the vehicle across the road and parked it outside the diner.

Eliza ducked back out of sight, then went back to her place behind the counter as the driver exited the vehicle again, climbed onto the boardwalk and through the door directly in front of her.

Close up he was even more handsome than she'd thought, with a few days' dark stubble darkening his cheeks and the most penetrating blue eyes she'd ever seen.

He looked round the empty tables and seats then at Eliza before he walked across the gritty lino floor and took a seat at the counter. "Hi," he said, pulling some notes and coins from the breast pocket of his shirt. "I think I've just got the price of a burger, beer and a pack of Marlboro's."

She smiled shyly at him, ignoring the cash in his hand. "How do you want your burger done?" she asked.

"Bloody," he replied, as he watched her take the top off a bottle of beer, freezing from the chiller.

She felt his eyes still on her as she turned and called the order through the hatch to the kitchen at the back.

"What's your name?" he asked when she turned back.

"Eliza. Eliza Day." She smiled again and stared into his eyes.

He smiled back and shook his head. "No," he said. "You're the Wild Rose and you are the one."

"That's what people call me around here. The Wild Rose. How did you know?"

"I didn't. It just seemed to fit you."

"And I'm the one for what?" she asked, although she thought that she already knew.

"You'll find out," he replied, smiled again and sipped at his beer.

"What's *your* name?" she asked.

"Just someone," he said. "Someone passing through."

"But I must call you something."

"Must you?"

"Yes."

"Then call me Joe. That fits me as good as anything."

"OK, Joe. Where are you heading for?"

"Nowhere," he said. "Nowhere special, I might hang around for a bit."

Oh good, she thought. "Where will you stay?" she asked.

He shrugged.

"They have rooms at the pub," she said.

"No money," he said. "I'll camp out in the truck. I'm used to that. Where do *you* live?"

"I've got a room at the back here," she replied. "It's not much, but it goes with the job."

At that moment, Sonny, the chef, owner and proprietor of the diner, and by definition, Eliza's boss, shoved the hamburger through the hatch and she placed it in front of Joe, who took a bite, then almost delicately wiped the bloody gravy that dripped down his chin off with a napkin.

"That's good," he said, washing the mouthful down with beer. "What time do you finish?"

"Seven."

"Can I see you later?"

"Maybe."

"I'll call for you at eight," he said.

She hardly had time to think before she nodded. "OK," she said.

After he'd finished his meal he went back to the truck and drove through the tiny town back to the bridge that ran over the sluggish river. He pulled off the road to the riverbank where the breeze was slightly cooler and the wild roses grew in profusion, their petals the same scarlet as Eliza Day's lips.

He sat in the bed of the truck on top of the old mattress where he slept when no other accommodation was available, lit a cigarette and dozed in the shade of the cab until it was time to meet the young girl.

Eliza was more excited than she could ever remember as she got ready for her visitor. After work she hurried to her room, stripped off her damp uniform and stood naked for a moment in front of the mildew stained mirror in the door of the old wardrobe that made up a quarter of the furniture in the room that Sonny allowed her to stay in for nothing as part of her meagre wages. Sonny was all right. Unlike most of the other men who passed through the town he didn't undress her with his eyes, and although at first she'd feared it, he never came knocking at the dead of night to try and force his favours on her. When the diner closed at seven, he just exchanged his dirty white jacket for a leather one, and drove his ancient Holden back to Mrs Sonny, who waited on the small holding they owned with their two children.

Joe hadn't undressed her with his eyes either, although she wished that he had.

She was happy with the sight of her slim, tanned body with only two white stripes where the bikini she wore covered her breasts and sex, and she tossed the long blonde hair that fell into a tangle around her shoulders off her face and stuck out her tongue at her own reflection, before she went to the little chest next to the wardrobe and carefully chose her underwear. White lace bra and panties, very brief, and she blushed again as she caught a second look of herself in the mirror as she opened the wardrobe door to choose a dress. I wonder, she thought. He said I was the one, I wonder if *he'll* be the one.

For Eliza was a virgin. Unlike her school friends from the town and surrounding area, Eliza had refused to surrender her innocence to the first farm boy who asked for it. She was more choosy. She was waiting for the right one, and perhaps Joe would be it.

At eight precisely there was a knock on the door of her room. It opened directly onto the car park at the rear of the diner. Joe was standing there, a single red rose in his hand when she opened it. "I thought this must be right," he said. "And I bought you this." He gave her a red rose and she felt the thorns bite into the skin of her fingers as she took it from him.

"Thanks," she said. "Come in, I'm afraid it's not much."

"Better than what I've got." And he entered the room and sat on the arm of the broken backed sofa and watched as she filled a juice bottle with water and put the rose inside.

"It's beautiful," she said.

"Not as beautiful as you," he replied, and he saw her blush and he grinned. "So what do we do in a one-horse town where it looks like the horse died?" he asked.

She smiled at his words and said, "Pub or pub I'm afraid. The diner's closed."

"Pub it is then," he said, and reached out his hand as he stood up, and she took it and they left the room and walked towards The Moon In The Gutter together. And the sun was setting through the haze of the evening and the clouds that sat on the edge of the horizon were like purple ribbons on a golden bedspread.

When the pub closed he took her home and kissed her gently at the door. Eliza shuddered in his embrace and she felt tears smart in her eyes which he wiped away with his thumb before he said, "What's the matter?"

"I don't know. I'm just happy I guess."

"Good."

"Do you want to come in?"

He hesitated for a moment. "No not tonight. It's not quite right. Can I see you tomorrow?"

"Yes," she whispered. "Yes of course."

"Same time?"

"It's Saturday. We close at noon. Come in the afternoon."

"I'll do that," and with another kiss he vanished into the dark, and Eliza felt herself begin to ache with want for him.

On the second day Joe arrived not long after Sonny had left the car park in a cloud of dust. Joe carried another rose and when he handed it to her he said, "I've been picturing your face all night. My Wild Rose, I believe you are more beautiful than any woman I've ever seen."

"That's the loveliest thing anyone's ever said to me."

"It's just the truth."

"I doubt it. You're just a flatterer." But she smiled and added, "But don't stop."

"I won't."

"Where did you stay last night?" she asked.

"I slept down by the river where the wild roses grow so sweet and scarlet and free."

"It sounds beautiful," said Eliza Day.

"It was. But still not as beautiful as you."

She blushed again. "Come in," she said. "I got some beer from next door. It's cold."

"Good," he said and walked across the floor and put the second rose into the bottle next to the first which had already started to wilt and drop in the heat.

She gave him a bottle that glistened with moisture and he twisted off the cap and drank deeply. "What do you want to do?" he asked.

"You know," she replied boldly.

"Are you sure?" he asked.

"Of course."

"There'll be no turning back."

"I know."

He stood, took her hand and led her over to the bed. "Give me your loss and your sorrow," he whispered.

"I will. I've waited forever for this. You are my first man."

"I know I am. I was always going to be. Wait no longer," he said and kissed her on her lips.

He was as gentle as a man could be with her, undressing her slowly on that hot afternoon, then himself and as they lay together their sweat and juice mixed pungently together and as the rose petals fell onto the table one by one, Eliza cried out and looked through the window and saw the thunderheads gathering on the horizon, thick and black like flowers piled on a grave and illuminated by the occasional flash of sheet lightning.

They stayed together until almost dawn, making love, and for Eliza it was the best night of her life.

Then as the sun began to rise Joe left her with a kiss.

"Come visit me later," he whispered. "I'm parked down by the bridge."

"Stay," she begged.

"No. Come later. It's Sunday. I need to pray."

"What time?"

"Do you work today?"

She shook her head.

"Give me a couple of hours," he said, and slipped through the door and she was alone.

She could barely contain her impatience, but waited until almost midday before walking down towards the river. She saw the pick-up from the bridge and ran down towards it. The truck was empty and she looked around in confusion until she heard Joe's voice from the middle of the tangles of thorny wild roses. "This way," he said. "Be careful. Those thorns are sharp."

She pushed aside the ropes of bramble and found Joe sitting by the water's edge. "You came," he said.

"Of course."

"Sit beside me."

She did his bidding and they held hands.

"I'll be moving on soon," he said.

"No."

"I must."

"Let me come with you."

He shook his head sadly.

"Please."

"You wouldn't like the places I go," he said. "They're not for people like you."

She thought with the innocence of her youth that she could bind him to her with love and she kissed him on the mouth. He responded as she knew he would and soon they were naked with only the sound of the hot breeze in the rose bushes and the trickle of the river to remind them where they were. Eliza lay on her back and watched as the thick clouds that had been gathering all night and that morning finally shrouded the sun and the wind picked up and shook the rose vines so that the petals fell around them like red snow.

When they made love he knelt above her and said, "The roses are dying," and picked one from its stem and carefully put it between her teeth and a thorn pierced the skin and one perfect pearl of blood stood out on her lip, and she saw the terrible sadness in his blue eyes as he whispered the words. "As all beauty must die." And the last thing she saw was the rock that he had in his hand before he brought it down on her face and the last thing she felt was the rain that came at last and washed the blood from her eyes like the tears she'd cried all her life.

NICOLE

William T. Vollmann

THE NEXT THING Jimmy knew, he was on the street and it was dark and he was whore-hunting. He saw women dancing on the sidewalk; he was sure that they offered both acute and obtuse triangles; but they would not go to his hotel and he did not want to go to theirs because he did not like to feel trapped at the same time that he felt dizzy. – How fine the moonlight was, though! It made him retch. – He saw a whore leaning against the side of a reflective building, waggling her skinny knees although her high heels and her butt did not move and her head was cocked against her shoulder so that she could watch men out of the corner of her stupid little eyes. She said doll you want a date? and Jimmy said thank *you* for the offer but tell you the truth I'm looking for my friend Gloria you know the one with the big tits? – Oh that's just an *excuse*! sneered the whore, at which Jimmy cocked his head very wisely and said I never excuse myself except when I burp. Do you ever burp? Gloria doesn't. – Oh Christ, said the whore, who was as slender and unwholesome looking as a snake, and she stalked around the corner, heels clacking angrily. – Next he had several offers from a pimp who said he *knew* Jimmy would be satisfied, so Jimmy looked as dumb as he could and said wow pal sounds like a good one and you'll never believe this but I left all my money back at my hotel. – Don'tcha even have twenty on ya? said the pimp. – Jimmy said don't I wish but God's truth is I got one hundred two hundred dollars back home in fact I got *lots* of money in fact I think I may even be a *millionaire*, so bring her by pal I only live two hours away from here what do you say? – When the pimp heard that, he didn't even bother to answer. He crossed the street, shaking his head, and Jimmy stood leaning up against a wall and laughing inside himself with snotty little gurgles like a bottle of Scotch pouring down the toilet. Finally he found a whore who would go with him. He looked around to make sure that the pimp wasn't watching and showed her forty dollars. Her name was Nicole, and she looked rather more than young, twenty-five maybe and strung-out, but not sharp and hard like a piece of broken glass, only used up like a dirty eraser, so he figured she would be OK with her lank hair curling around her ears and her ear-rings of white plastic pearls, so he said Well come on and Nicole looked at him tiredly with her skin stretched dry and tight across her forehead and Jimmy said Nicole your blue eyeliner's smeared you should fix it if you want to stay beautiful and Nicole rubbed her forehead and said she had a headache. He said well come *on* baby come with me then you can buy yourself a painkiller.

I don't usually go to the man's place, Nicole said. You promise you won't hurt me?

I promise, Jimmy said. If I wanted to hurt you, he explained to her very logically, you couldn't get away from me anyway.

That's not true, said Nicole. I could kill you easy.

Well see, said Jimmy grandly, you have nothing to worry about. You can kill me easy, so why be nervous?

He took her up the street and she kept asking how far it was. Three more blocks, said Jimmy. The light glowed in her hair.

The first thing she asked to do was use the bathroom. He heard her shit. I suppose she must be nervous, he said to himself. Jimmy had once been a reader, so he knew how in Auschwitz or Treblinka there was a ramp leading up to the gas chambers called the Road to Heaven where all the women had to wait naked and squatting while the men were finished being gassed (they went first because they did not need to have their hair cut off for the submarine crews), and while the sheared women waited they usually emptied their bowels and the guards laughed and laughed like hooded pimps in an alley and now history repeated itself as Jimmy stood nipping on a fresh beer and waiting for Nicole to complete the preparations for her little ordeal. Well, he said to himself, *I* can't help it if she's nervous. She's got a job to do.

Silently he said Gloria, are you still there? Gloria?

When Nicole came into the kitchen she was naked except for her red shirt. – You want a half-and-half? she said.

Sure, Jimmy said.

Will you *take care of me* first? she said smiling; her face glowed, she seemed so sweet like Gloria.

Sure I will, he said, what do you want me to do? (He thought she meant for him to jerk her off or otherwise *affect* her. He sometimes liked to fool himself.)

Will you pay me first? Nicole said patiently.

Oh fine, Jimmy said. He got the forty dollars out of his wallet and gave it to her.

Then Nicole sat down on the chair in the kitchen and took his penis in her hand and he saw how her arms were discolored everywhere with abscesses and needle tracks and he leaned forward a little so that Nicole could put his penis into her mouth and she began to suck at it smoothly, rapidly and Jimmy looked down at the top of her head and wondered if her eyes were open or closed and then he looked at the wall and watched a cockroach crawling down between the gas pipe and the sink, and he listened to the noises that her lips made sucking his penis, and he listened to the loud ticking of her cheap plastic watch. Jimmy was not thinking about anything in particular, but his penis began to get hard right away. As soon as it was entirely stiff like some dead thing, she took it out of her mouth and rolled a rubber onto it with her lined and grimy hands. – Now take your shirt off, Jimmy said. – He stepped back from her and dropped his clothes to the floor. Nicole sat wearily on the chair, rubbing her forehead. When she pulled her shirt over her head he saw that she had a cast on her left wrist. Her breasts were big and sad like owls' eyes.

You want my coat for a pillow? said Jimmy.

Nicole shook her head.

All right then, he said, get down on the floor.

The kitchen floor was black with dirt. Nicole lay down on it and raised her legs to make her cunt so nice and tight for him, and Jimmy stood over her watching the groping of those legs, which were speckled with boils and lesions, until her left ankle came to rest on the chair that she had sat on, while the sole of her right

foot had to be content with bracing itself against Jimmy's refrigerator. Her breasts lay limp on her belly, as round as the faces
of polished brass pendulums of clocks. Jimmy stood enjoying her
for another moment, liking the way she looked as she lay there
between the refrigerator and the wall, brown-skinned and almost
pretty, with a white plastic cross between her tits.

Are you Catholic? he said.

Yes, Nicole said.

Jimmy strode around naked except for his socks, inspecting her
cunt like an emperor. This was the best part. Nicole gazed up at
him and pulled the lips of her slit taut and up to show him the
ragged pear of pinkness inside, and her cunt-lips glistened under
the kitchen lights with the brightness of metal foil. – Your pussy
is just like a flower,* Jimmy complimented her; all the same he
did not want to get his face too close to it. He got down on his
knees; he leaned his weight on his arms as if he were doing push-
ups (for Jimmy was always a gentleman who would not hurt a
woman with his weight); then he stuck his penis into her. She had
told him that he was her first date of the night, but her cunt
seemed to be full of something viscous like come or corn syrup.
Maybe it was just the lubricant she used. Anyhow, it stank. She
had great black spots on her thighs that might have been moles or
more probably the subcutaneous hemorrhages of Kaposi's syn-
drome as Jimmy well knew from his profoundly intellectual
studies. Every time he thrust into her she grunted. He could
not tell whether this was because he hurt her or because she did it
to excite him and so get it over with faster. He did not feel that she
hated him and her body was trying to expel him; more probably
she just endured him and trusted to the frictionlessness of the
corn syrup or whatever it was to protect her from being hurt by
his thrusts (in direct proportion as *his* sensation was diminished),
but the corn syrup did not much work anymore to soothe that red
raw-rubbed meat between her legs, so Nicole just tried not to
think about what was happening and grunted at Jimmy's every
painful thrust and bit her lips whenever he grazed an ovary. She
gripped his balls tightly all the time so that the rubber wouldn't

---

* "I still remember the effect I produced on a small group of Gala
tribesmen massed around a man in black clothes," wrote Vittorio Musso-
lini. "I dropped an aerial torpedo right in the center and the group opened
up like a flowering rose. It was most entertaining."

slip; she dug her fingernails into his balls, either by mistake or to make him come. But after thirty seconds Jimmy knew that he wasn't going to be able to come. Maybe if she'd just sucked him off he could have done it, but what with the rubber and the stuff in her cunt he couldn't feel much. Jimmy fucked and fucked until he got bored and then told her that he was done. – Call me, he said politely. – Later his prick started to itch, and he worried about disease.

THE NEW FIANCÉE

N. T. Morley

Meredith got home from work around midnight and discovered the beautiful woman sitting in the living room. It took her a moment to register her surprise, especially given the casual comfort with which the woman sat on the couch sipping a glass of red wine. The woman, a strikingly tall and quite breathtaking ivory-skinned brunette, was very dressed up – much like Meredith herself – as if she were about to spend the night at the opera, or had just finished doing so. The woman's dress, long and black, was slit on both sides almost up to her hips, revealing the full length of her shapely legs. The dress was also low-cut and showed that the woman had quite ample, perfect endowments. Perhaps in her midthirties, she was strikingly beautiful, her jet-black hair and pale skin accenting her rather Nordic features.

'Hello," Meredith said nervously.

"You must be Meredith," said the woman, without getting up. She looked Meredith over quite blatantly, not even trying to disguise the up-and-down motion of her eyes that focused first on Meredith's face, then slid down her body, then slowly stroked upward to rest on the single slit in Meredith's dress – not quite as high as that in the strange woman's dress, but more than revealing enough to show what shapely legs the girl had – then continued up to take in the slight swell of Meredith's small but perfect bust. Meredith felt her face getting hot as the woman's eyes lingered over her breasts, then slowly rose to meet Meredith's gaze, fixing her with a hungry stare.

"I've heard a lot about you," said the woman.

"Ah, Meredith," said Phillip, appearing from the kitchen with a Scotch in one hand and a bottle of wine in the other. "We've been waiting for you." He topped off the woman's drink and sat down opposite her on the big white armchair, propping his feet on the coffee table quite indelicately and taking a sip of his Scotch.

"You remember me telling you about Yvanna, my ex-wife?"

Meredith gave a shiver.

"Please, Phillip, *former* wife. Ex-wife sounds so unfriendly."

"We're anything but that, my dear," said Phillip with a lustful glance at Yvanna. He then looked at Meredith with the kind of lascivious sense of ownership he always gave her when he knew he would soon prove just how profoundly he had his new fiancée under his control.

"With our wedding date set, I figured it was time for you and Yvanna to get . . . acquainted."

Again, Meredith shivered. She saw Yvanna's eyes flickering over her once more with the immodest gaze of the heartless seducer suddenly set loose upon an ingénue, and knew immediately what was to be expected of her.

As if to assert her independence, Meredith quickly assessed Yvanna's body, attempting to display the same kind of unrepentant randiness that the self-composed woman showed toward her. She could see the older woman's sensuous curves, the firmness of her full breasts capped by hard nipples tenting the thin fabric of the black opera dress. Meredith let her eyes caress those perfect tits, knowing that within moments she would be called upon to touch them, kiss them, perhaps even suckle them, before being bidden to travel further into depravity and perform services foreign to her. She knew she would be expected to touch the woman lower down, between the slits of that dress and, without a doubt, underneath the dress itself. That, she could not even comprehend; her head spun at the very thought of it. It was all Meredith could do to look at the woman's breasts and know she would soon be touching them. But those bright green eyes of hers did not linger on Yvanna's ample tits; on the contrary, Meredith let her eyes drift upward to Yvanna's piercing, frosty blue gaze and, unable to keep up her façade of self-confidence, whimpered softly and dropped her eyes submissively.

She could feel her nipples hardening under her dress, standing out plainly through the thin satin, as if advertising to the woman the effect she was having on her.

"That's a very nice dress," said Yvanna with a smile, her eyes lingering on Meredith's chest. "I hear you're a hostess at a chi-chi restaurant. I'm surprised they let you wear a dress like that. Much less without a bra."

Meredith wanted very badly to cross her arms in front of her. Her arms even twitched involuntarily, as if seeking a chance to cover her embarrassment. But Meredith did not let herself hide her breasts from Yvanna's devouring gaze. Phillip had long since forbidden her that privilege. Instead, she stood there, her nipples hardening even more under Yvanna's stare, a quiver starting deep in her body as she nervously answered.

"Th—thank you, Ma'am. The . . . the owner says it helps bring the customers in."

"The owner? Is he the one who told you it was all right to wear that dress without a bra?"

Meredith's face grew hotter as she blushed uncontrollably.

"Yes, Ma'am, but that's not why I wear it that way," said Meredith. "My Master told me to wear it this way."

"Phillip, you dog. You're just like you always were. If anything, you're worse. Remember when you sent me to court wearing that see-through dress?"

"I remember," said Phillip.

"And no bra or panties at all," Yvanna sighed. "I thought the judge was going to charge me with contempt. Luckily, he was a man of liberal tastes. Just a few moments alone in his chambers and I was back in the court's favors."

"You never told me that," Phillip snapped.

"Mmmm, didn't I?" smiled Yvanna. "Yes, it was a striking example of judicial corruption, and quite a lot of fun. Lucky for me it's too late for you to punish me." Turning back to Meredith, Yvanna smiled and said, "Phillip used to send me all sorts of places without panties." She paused and smiled broadly at Meredith. "You *are* wearing panties, aren't you, dear?"

"Y-yes, Ma'am," said Meredith. "Just – just a thong."

"A thong. Let me see, dear."

Meredith's eyes went to her Master, whether to check if it was all right or to beg not to do it, Phillip didn't notice or care.

"My ex-wife and I are very close, darling. Show her your panties."

Meredith began to lift her dress, nervously feeling the satin bunch in her grasp. She brought the dress up to her waist, revealing her minuscule white lace thong, which barely covered her pussy and showed quite clearly that it was shaved smooth. The crotch of the garment was so small that Meredith's full pussy lips, now unaccountably swollen, squeezed around the sides, revealing the piercings Phillip had placed there.

"Come here, darling. Let me have a closer look."

Meredith nervously walked to Yvanna's side, and with a glance at Phillip, knew what was expected.

Meredith lifted her foot and placed her high-heeled shoe on the coffee table, leaving her legs spread.

"My, my," Yvanna said, reaching out to stroke the moist crotch of the thong. Meredith stifled a whimper as Yvanna touched her. "Such pretty things you buy your slaves nowadays, Phillip. And such pretty jewelry." Yvanna's long, slender fingers slid under the crotch of the thong and teased Meredith's pierced lips apart. Meredith gasped and let out a long, low moan as Yvanna slid two fingers into her. She struggled to remain standing, knowing that to fail to do so would bring punishment. Perhaps a spanking, or worse.

Meredith could not bear the thought of being punished in front of her Master's ex-wife.

"She's soaking, darling. She's positively gushing. She's your own little blonde tsunami. Phillip, is she more of an exhibitionist than I was? Does showing her tits off all night turn your little slave on *this* much?"

"I don't know," chuckled Phillip. "Ask her."

Yvanna's eyes locked with Meredith's, and the older woman's two fingers slid deeper in, her thumb teasing the swollen nub of Meredith's pierced clitoris. Meredith let out a faint whine and bit her red-painted lip as she tried to stay standing.

"Does it, Meredith? Does it turn you on to show the customers your tits?"

Yvanna's thumb pressed firmly on Meredith's ringed clit, and Meredith bit her lip so hard that for a moment she thought she might have drawn blood.

She took a deep breath and managed to speak.

"Yes, Ma'am. It does turn me on. But that's not why I'm wet."

"Then why are you wet, darling?"

Meredith had had the best intentions of confessing it, knowing that no show of coyness would get her out of the evening's expected services. But now, she found her throat closing with embarrassment. Her face turned deep red, suddenly so hot that she felt she might pass out.

Yvanna chuckled.

"I know why you're wet, dear," said Yvanna. "It's because you know I'm going to fuck you. And you've never been with a woman before."

Meredith whimpered as Yvanna's fingers slid in and out of her cunt. It was the first time she'd ever been touched like that by a woman – the first time a woman had touched her there at all.

"Y-yes, Ma'am," said Meredith breathlessly.

Yvanna's hand came out of Meredith's cunt, and the younger woman let go of her dress, feeling the satin snake its way down her legs as Yvanna reached up to touch her face. Taller than Meredith by six or eight inches, Yvanna found it easy to reach Meredith's mouth with her fingers – but Meredith, well trained, still leaned down to make it easier on her. Meredith obediently parted her lips and accepted Yvanna's slick fingers into her mouth, licking them clean. She had done it so many times – been *trained* to do it – that it was second nature to her. But the taste of her cunt had always come to her ripe and fresh via Phillip's body – his fingers, his tongue, even his cock.

Never on a woman's fingers. But Meredith licked, hungrily, the taste of her own pussy sending tingles of electricity down into her body.

Yvanna's fingers came out of Meredith's suckling mouth glistening with spittle.

"There's no point in being a flirt about it, then," said Yvanna, her voice suddenly filled with command. "Take off your dress."

Meredith began to turn toward Phillip, but stopped when Yvanna's harsh voice snapped, "Meredith!" Meredith turned back to Yvanna, shocked, and the brunette's cold eyes froze Meredith to the bone.

'You've been given to me," she said. "If Phillip wants to stop me, he will. For now, you do exactly what I tell you to do. And don't look to him for advice."

"Y-yes, Ma'am," Meredith whimpered.

"Now take off your dress before I take it off for you," said Yvanna.

Meredith felt a little quiver go through her at the harsh sound in Yvanna's voice. She had heard that same harshness many times in the voice of her Master, and it never failed to make her desperate to please him.

Meredith took her foot off the coffee table and turned more fully to face Yvanna. Her hands quivered as she reached up to the left strap of her dress and gently eased it over her shoulder. So insubstantial was the dress that one side of it immediately fell away, revealing Meredith's bare left breast with its firm, pink nipple plainly erect from arousal. Hesitating only slightly, Meredith eased the other strap off her shoulder, and the dress went sliding down to her waist, revealing both small but perfect breasts, showing by their glowing pearlescence that her Master never allowed her to sunbathe.

Meredith wriggled her hips, pushing the dress down over them. It slid down her thighs and pooled around her high-heeled shoes. Obediently, she stepped out of the dress, now naked except for her shoes and the quite-soaked thong.

"Lovely tits," said Yvanna. "Quite a nice body in general. Do you have her work out?"

"Two hours a day," said Phillip. "Mostly on her legs and abdomen."

"Yes, I see that," said Yvanna, running her hands down Meredith's slender legs. "She must be able to fuck like a demon." Meredith obediently leaned into her, allowing Yvanna to get a good, firm hold of the back of her thighs, where hours of Phillip's prescribed workout had built the perfect muscles for pushing herself onto his cock – or anything he chose.

Yvanna reached up and grabbed Meredith's bare ass with a slap, squeezing her firm buttocks tightly. Meredith could feel the pressure against her cunt, and caught her breath.

"Are you, dear?" Yvanna asked. "Are you a rollicking good lay, a fucking racehorse when there's a cock around?"

"I-I try, Ma'am," said Meredith nervously.

Yvanna polished off her red wine and leaned over to set the

empty glass on the coffee table behind Meredith. "He always does it to you from behind, right? Never face to face."

"Y-yes, Ma'am," said Meredith, blushing furiously anew as she looked into Yvanna's eyes. "Only from behind. He only takes me from behind. I —" she paused, her voice quavering. "I've actually never been taken the other way. Face to face, I mean."

"Never?" smiled Yvanna. "Never in your life?"

"Never," said Meredith, dropping her eyes.

"Show me," said Yvanna with a smile, spinning Meredith around and pulling hard on the girl so she stumbled backward onto the sofa, legs spread and straddling Yvanna's lap. "Show me how you fuck."

Meredith could feel the heat coursing through her with the rough touch of her Master's ex-wife. Much as she had been taught to do in lap-dancing for her Master's male friends, Meredith leaned forward and ground her body rhythmically against Yvanna's, working her hips back and forth. They moved effortlessly, the many hours of exercise having rendered Meredith a lithe and capable sexual athlete.

Meredith began to rock back and forth harder, pumping her hips in just the way her Master liked her to fuck herself onto him. She felt her pussy flooding uncontrollably in trained response to the motion, her copious juices soaking through and spilling over the tiny lace thong in an instant. Droplets of her juice dampened Yvanna's dress. Yvanna firmly repositioned the hapless girl to face her now, and chuckled as Meredith rubbed her breasts in the older woman's face. She reached to curve her arm around Meredith's thigh, pulling the younger woman firmly against her. Her hand found Meredith's cunt, plucked the laughable covering of the lace thong out of the way, and began to stroke it again, more firmly this time, rubbing Meredith's slit and occasionally plunging two fingers inside. Now moaning openly, Meredith fucked herself onto Yvanna's hand, pulsing eagerly toward orgasm.

"Kiss me," said Yvanna. "Let's see if he's pierced that tongue of yours yet."

Meredith felt a shiver go through her at the use of that word "yet" – her tongue had not been pierced.

"Please, dear," said Phillip from behind Meredith. "You're giving away all my tricks."

"It's all right, darling," said Yvanna. "I've got a few tricks of my own. Now kiss me, Meredith, the way a woman likes it."

She felt her nervousness growing as she leaned her elbows on the back of the sofa; how *did* a woman like to be kissed? Meredith herself mostly liked to be held down, hair tangled in her Master's fingers and her face and buttocks rosy and tingling from an hour or more of firm slaps, as her mouth was forced open and savaged by the fiercely-thrusting heat of her Master's tongue. But she suspected that most women, perhaps Yvanna included, wanted a gentler, more tender kiss, and so that was what Meredith gave her, nervously and tentatively pecking her before pressing her mouth against the older woman's hungrily. But when her tongue slid gently into Yvanna's mouth she felt an unexpected rush of excitement that both confused and aroused her, sending an uncontrollable wave of hunger through her cunt.

It took her a moment of deep kissing to recognize what was having such an effect on her.

Yvanna's mouth tasted like Phillip's cock.

The taste was overwhelming, and unmistakable; Meredith had swallowed her Master's organ enough times to know every nuance of that rich, musky taste. But not just his cock was there; Meredith could also taste, mingled with it, the taste of his come. Her Master had come in Yvanna's mouth.

Meredith almost pulled back, even as arousal ferociously took her over. But by that time, Phillip had come behind her, and his fingers snaked into her hair, holding her in place as Meredith's mouth was eagerly taken by Yvanna's thrusting tongue. Phillip held her there as his hand traveled up her thighs; hungrily, without even knowing she was doing it, Meredith pushed herself onto his hand when he touched her cunt. Two fingers slid into her easily, and Meredith began to work her hips again, this time even more eagerly than before.

She was wet. Unaccountably wet. Juice dripped down onto her Master's fingers and rivulets of it baptized her thighs. Meredith fucked herself desperately onto her Master's hand, even as the hot flame of jealousy exploded in her. *She sucked his cock*, she thought as Yvanna kissed her. *She sucked my lover's cock.*

But Meredith knew she had long since abandoned any claim she might have had on Phillip's sexual pleasures. She had given him unquestioning obedience – and he had chosen to dally with this woman. Meredith, then, would dally with her too, as she was being ordered to do.

She would make love with Yvanna, with the woman who had just been taken by her Master. She would service the woman, for her Master's pleasure.

"Mmmmm," cooed Yvanna when Phillip let Meredith go. "She tastes almost as good as you do. And quite an eager little kisser. I wonder if she'll like the taste of me on your cock as much as she likes the taste of you in my mouth."

Again, Meredith's stomach churned as jealousy flashed through her, but she let the fear and envy drain away as she felt Yvanna's hands touching her breasts, pinching the hard nipples, and Phillip began to finger-fuck her. Meredith's hips worked fervently, pushing her cunt onto first two, then three of her Master's fingers as Yvanna pulled her upper body forward and began to suckle Meredith's tiny tits.

"She's got me wet as a schoolgirl," gasped Yvanna. "Do something about that, will you, Phillip? You know what a girl likes. You've seen to it so many times yourself; I'm sure Meredith will get the hang of it quickly."

Meredith's head swam as Phillip gently eased her off the couch, pushing her head between his ex-wife's thighs as Yvanna swept the insubstantial fabric of her dress out of the way. There, fully revealed, was a smooth-shaved and unpierced pussy, glistening with juice. Clearly, Yvanna *still* didn't wear panties.

Phillip's hand, firmly holding Meredith's hair, pushed her face between the older woman's thighs as Yvanna slid her ass forward to the edge of the white sofa. Before Meredith even had a chance to think about it, she was licking.

She almost expected the taste that greeted her – the taste of Phillip's pleasure, the sticky aromatic juice that told Meredith her Master had not only made love with this woman, but had done it *twice* – at least – and had been brought to completion by the shaved pussy that Meredith was now expected to service. And yet, when she did feel the thick jizz leaking onto her tongue, she felt another surge of jealousy – but by then, her Master's hand was so firmly in her hair that she could not have pulled back if she had wanted to.

And she didn't want to. Blessed with the taste of her Master's come, even leaking out of this hussy's cunt, Meredith eagerly began to worship, suckling at Yvanna's clit and licking down to her tight opening. Yvanna moaned softly; when it became quite clear that Meredith was going to not grudgingly, not just willingly but *enthusiastically* service the older woman, Phillip released his grip on Meredith's hair and firmly grasped her thighs. Meredith moved to open her legs, obediently, as she had been taught to do whenever her Master touched her there. But before she could even do that, Phillip had forced them open and tugged the crotch of her thong well to the side.

The distant rattle of her Master's belt buckle sent a sudden thrill through Meredith; it made her dizzy with excitement to know that even after pleasuring himself with this woman twice, he could still get it up for her. There was only an instant for her to think about that before the thick head of her Master's cock violated her, big enough to stretch her open painfully in the first instant of penetration even *after* she had been opened up first by two of Yvanna's slender fingers and then by three of Phillip's thick ones. But the flood of juice that met the Master's cock as he sank into her slicked the way so amply that by the time Meredith was thrusting herself violently onto Phillip's cock, only cascading waves of pleasure were exploding through her near-naked body. She devoured Yvanna's cunt with newfound fervor as the older woman moaned and cried out, seizing Meredith's head with both hands to force the girl's eagerly suckling mouth more firmly against her shaved cunt. The feel of that possessive gesture was what finally drove Meredith over the edge into an intense orgasm, and her tongue only worked faster as ecstasy flooded through her. Her hips, too, picked up force, pounding her cunt so hard onto Phillip's cock that he grabbed her hips and forced her to hold still while he ravaged her – ten thrusts, twenty, thirty, while Meredith continued to come, soaring high on her orgasm even as her swift tongue brought Yvanna off – and then Phillip let himself go deep inside her, inundating Meredith's cunt with the same blessed issue that had so flavored Yvanna's.

Whimpering hungrily, Meredith continued to lick even as Yvanna reclined on the sofa, practically hanging off of it. The older woman thrashed back and forth, moaning loudly as Meredith serviced her too-sensitive pussy. Finally, Yvanna pushed Meredith off, and the young blonde looked up panting, her mouth and chin running with the thick juices of Yvanna's cunt and the pungent savor of Phillip's come.

"Not bad," said Yvanna breathlessly. "She's taken to it quickly. Phillip, I think she'll learn to become quite a little cunt-licker before the wedding, don't you?"

Behind Meredith, Phillip chuckled. He leaned over his slave, pressing her into the sofa as he kissed his ex-wife tenderly.

"She'd better," said Phillip when his lips left Yvanna's. "You remember which wife Yvanna is, don't you, Meredith?"

Her face cradled in Yvanna's lap, Meredith said softly:

"Yes, Sir. She's your fourth wife."

"I thought we'd work backward," said Phillip cheerfully. "Antonia's flying in next week."

"Mmmm," cooed Yvanna. "She's the one with those fantastic tits, isn't she?"

"That's right," said Phillip.

Yvanna laughed lightly. "I don't have to be back in Paris until the fifteenth. I think I'll stay for that. Unless it's an imposition, Phillip?"

"Not at all, my dear," said Phillip. "Meredith, you'll be happy to keep our guest entertained while she's here, won't you?"

Meredith affectionately kissed Yvanna's ivory thigh, her blood quickening at the scent of her Master's pleasure still wafting from deep inside.

"Yes, Sir," she said breathlessly.

Yvanna caressed Meredith's face and stroked her hair with her long, thin fingers.

"It's so sweet of you to let me try out your fiancée, darling," said Yvanna to Phillip. "She definitely passes the test."

THE PLEASURE CHATEAU

Jeremy Reed

WHEN BETTY CAME to she was lying on leather. The black surface mouled itself to her body. Someone had sprayed her hands with gold body paint, for they became instantly visible to her as two fluorescent toads squatting on either side of her. She was lying face down, and the positional arrangement of her hands and feet was such that she couldn't move. But there was no crudity of handcuffs or shackles. Some sort of invisible adhesive tape secured her immobility. Betty rested her head on the point of her chin. She was lying facing a blank maxi-screen. The room was lit by two flaming torches, one protruding from the mouth of a white statue, the other socketed into a kneeling marble form. The pervasive stillness was like being at the bottom of a lake. Betty imagined panthers, jaguars, pumas, slumped down beside her. Black on black.

What she recalled was the bizarre dinner table, the conspiratorial stretches of conversation that had been issued wide of her, the unnerving silence that pervaded the château – and green – the man's lenses that had fixated her, as though she had confronted an alien with emerald VR contact lenses instead of eyes. Her mind was busy reassembling fragments of the narrative. The woman talking to her from behind the limo's partly open window, and the other one in the moulded leather skirt, the sexual liturgies delivered by the midget and the two oriental pashas, the hints at a menagerie contained within the house. Visuals flashed across consciousness. She had found herself in this position often in the past, but always voluntarily. Dungeon bondage was one of her specialities, an elegant cigarette drooping from her cherry gloss lips as she hung suspended from a chain, a man kneeling in front of her, blowing her engorged erection. It was so close to death, and the mutual stimulus came from this recognition. Betty regarded each S&M trip as a pre-death initiation. She often hoped to die in an act that was as flagrantly anti-social as it was self-debasing. Violating convention by bringing its administrative bureaucrats down to their gold-plated knees for her whiphand was part of Betty's attraction to being a prostitute. It allowed her to undermine those proponents of political correctness – politicians, bankers, accountants, lawyers – the whole glitterati of moral pretence had opened wide for enemas, or shouted obscene imprecations as the whip had established slats like a blue venetian blind across delicate flesh.

Betty blamed herself for having ended up captive at the château. She should have considered the possible dangers in being transported out of town. She usually dictated her own reference points, and only rarely and to her detriment allowed a client this prerogative. Her neck was free, and she hadn't been blindfolded. She could assess the sizeable dimensions of the room in which she was bound. The torches assisted her in this. They gave proportion to the dark. Betty anticipated anything. She was doubtless being watched on a closed circuit screen, and she knew at some stage the four people would impose their needs on her vulnerability. She remembered on another occasion having been whipped with pink roses – the man had gone on and on striking her oiled bottom with the generous heads, and when they snapped on their stems, he would place the flower to his lips and then float it in a large terracotta bowl of red wine. Betty wondered if they were discussing among themselves what they would do to her. It should be the preferences entertained by the implacably cool men and the aesthetically perverse women. Tyrannical pleasures of every kind had been carried out on Betty's submissive body. She had acquiesced to bondage because she trusted in the master's ability to modify his threats. Here the terms were potentially unconditional, as no demands had been raised. Her subjective fears were of orgiastic violation, at least of

the kind that appeared to exploit her nature as a woman who
possessed a penis. Betty liked the contradiction. To receive an
orgasm as a diva and to impart that received pleasure to a woman,
was to her a complementary unity.

Without warning the screen became animated. Betty was
looking at an intimate love scene between Leanda and Nicole.
She knew she would be punished for being made a voyeur to their
amatory games. Leanda was down on all fours, her bottom filmed
by a transparent pink triangle. Nicole's tongue was working like a
hummingbird's across her slit. Occasionally she would pause, and
apply a lipsticked pout to Leanda's bottom. She would leave the
outline of a red carnation on her cheeks, and then return to
stimulating Leanda's pussy. Nicole's bottom was framed in
identical panties. There was now someone behind Nicole, only
the buttocks were male, despite the extreme delicacy of the
cunnilingus being delivered. And Nicole was instantly excited.
She began transmitting to Leanda something of the pleasure
being imparted to her. Her bottom was rotating to the man's
tongue. He had instantly found the exact location of her excitement. The three of them continued in this chain of oral stimulus,
only after a time Nicole offered Leanda's haunches to the man,
and she by lying on the floor in the opposite direction to the
couple, and by inserting her head between the man's parted legs,
was able to suck his genitals in concourse with the rhythm he had
struck up with Leanda. Nicole teased his balls like sweets. She
pecked them tentatively, lipping them as a fish might the surface
of a lake. The man had now slipped down Leanda's pink panties,
and had worked himself fully into her back passage. Leanda was
impaled on his deep, slowly articulated strokes. He was enjoying
it, and intent on making her wait. Nicole kept on nibbling, her
legs spread wide, while a fourth androgynous partner entered the
scene, and squatting in front of Nicole lifted her on to his
engorged cock, establishing by that a complete quadruple geometry. This rhythm continued with each partner building towards climax. Nicole's legs were hooked right over the kneeling
man's shoulders. As she moved convulsively towards orgasm, so
her tongue manipulated the other man to thrust conclusively into
Leanda. There was a slackening of the tension that had sustained
the four.

The film cut dead, and the screen reverted to a blue rectangle.

Betty imagined that this was a taster of things to come. The first in a series of films that would culminate in live action. She lay there staring at the blue meditative blank. It was like a bit of sky got into a dungeon. Betty imagined treating the space as a swimming pool, and diving into a blue membrane that parted fluently round her body.

Images jumped out at her again. This time the camera followed. Nicole from behind as she walked the length of one of the château's corridors. She was dressed in a seam-splitting emerald sequined miniskirt. The thin indigo seams of her silk stockings pronounced the curve of her legs. She was walking with deliberate provocation in the direction of a recessed window guarded by a stone lion. And without warning, the two oriental girls who Betty had seen at dinner appeared, one in front and one to the rear of Nicole. They too were dressed in costumes that hinted at fetishistic ritual. Their manner was less challenging than oneiric. They looked like dream figures jumped out of Nicole's head.

Nicole froze. Her hands dropped to her hips, and her bottom continued to rotate in full circles despite her immobility. The oriental girl positioned behind Nicole, began walking slowly towards her affecting the same stylized manner of walk. She looked like she had been stitched into royal blue silk, her red heels matching her scarlet wig. And simultaneously, the girl who had materialized by the recessed window began to move in from the opposite direction, her movements exactly synchronizing with her partner's. They appeared to be moonwalking, their progress indefinitely delayed. There were rooms to left and right of the corridor, but Nicole made no attempt to consider the options of escape. Rather she seemed excited by the prospect of danger. The two women closed in on her, all three of them dressed as though they were models in a Herb Ritts shoot. Betty found herself triggering with anticipation. The oriental woman behind Nicole, at the risk of splitting her seamless dress, knelt down and brought her head to the height of Nicole's bottom, and with unexpected ferocity slashed open the zip on her emerald skirt. The upper part of Nicole's body looked like a flower escaped from its sheath. The skirt hung open in a V, and the two hands busy caressing her buttocks began slowly to manipulate the sequined fabric, looking to have it give, but finding an extreme flexibility in its tightness. The erotic thrill was in the difficulty of stripping Nicole. Mean-

while the other woman was kneeling in front of Nicole, and her
hands slipping around the waist attempted to assist her partner in
taking off the moulded skirt. Nicole was growing visibly more
excited by the delay. She wanted to be free and unrestrained, but
instead was confined to this glittering second skin. The constricted skirt would only give fraction by fraction, and Nicole
made no attempt to assist her captors. But by degrees the crack of
her naked bottom appeared. She was wearing nothing but a black
silk suspender belt under the skirt. The combined efforts of the
two women succeeded in finally forcing the skirt to the back of
Nicole's thighs, and from there to her shoes. The green scales
sparkled like a tropical fish on the stone floor. The three women,
with Nicole in the centre, walked hand in hand down the corridor
towards the stone lion. Betty thought the place resembled a
chapel. The tenebrous atmospherics were gothic. When they
reached the lion, Nicole was transformed into an assertive dis-
ciplinarian. The creature held a riding crop in its stone jaws. The
two women were made to strip, and bent over the lion's body.
Nicole began flicking the whip over their round bottoms. The
decorations made by her work were like painting. Red stripes
began to appear alternately on their buttocks. A series of horizontal cuts that followed the curve of the flesh. Nicole appeared
excited by the correction she was administering. She would stand
back admiringly, her left hand straying across her own bottom as
though empathizing with the severity of her discipline. Neither of
the girls was bound, and neither made any attempt to elude their
voluntary punishment. Rather one, or both of them appeared to
be ascending the scale towards orgasm. Their breathing grew
heavier, there was a spasmic thrust from the pelvis which commented on pleasure. And as climax was anticipated, so Nicole
increased the ferocity of the whipping. A throaty howl, pitched to
a note of ultimate pleasure was wrung out of the throat of first one
girl, and then the other. And pleasure attained, they crumpled,
subsided to their knees, backs still facing the camera. Nicole
stood over them, the perfect locket-shaped proportions of her
bottom accented by her green spike heels. She returned the whip
to the lion's jaws, knelt down, and began kissing the buttocks she
had ravaged.

At this point, the heavy reverberation of a door being open and
shut announced Leanda's entry into the film. She too was seen

from behind. She was carrying a large black wooden heart in her arms. She was dressed in nothing but minimal see-through blue panties. She walked on high matching heels. The corridor was now strewn with big yellow chrysanthemums. Leanda was seen walking through that yellow ruckus. She held the black heart out in front of her, and there were diamante sprays in her hair. She walked towards the recessed window, a leopard padding behind her, the big cat evidently trained to obey her instructions. Betty froze. Her heart turned over at the prospect of a leopard inhabiting the château's corridors, and perhaps being admitted to the dungeon. The rehearsed elegance of the film surrogatized the pointers towards implicit danger.

Betty was fixated as the leopard switched sides. It went over to Leanda's left as though informed by some subliminal message. Leanda's journey from one end of the corridor to the other seemed to occupy a lifetime. It was a passage through the underworld. Betty watched as the leopard waited obediently for Leanda's instructions. Leanda stood off at a short distance from Nicole, whose tongue had shifted to one of the woman's toes. With her bottom resting on her heels, the sensitive underside to her feet had become charged as erogenous zones. Nicole was finding those places where the nerve impulses came alive. She did this by following the other woman's finger, for she outlined on her right foot the map that should be pursued by Nicole's tongue. Leanda stood there imperiously surveying the kneeling triptych. The leopard remained sitting upright at her side. At a sudden command from Leanda, the big cat stepped forward and ran its tongue the length of Nicole's spine. The latter evinced no disquiet at the proceedings and continued to excite the oriental girl through pressure on her foot. At another command from Leanda, the big cat altered its strategy, and began caressing Nicole's bottom with its tongue. The film cut at this image, and Betty was left to reflect on the surreal juxtaposition of Nicole receiving oral stimulus from a leopard.

The screen returned to a blue rectangle. Silence packed the leather dungeon. Betty kept killing the impulse to panic. The atmospherics works into her until she felt her mind had interiorized the place in which she was captive. She was trapped in a cell within a cell. She hallucinated orgiastic excesses. There were penises in every orifice. Her lips, her ears, her bottom. She was lying on a red velvet cloth thrown over a grave sunk into the flagstones. Her masochistic convulsions were too much for her perpetrators. She objected to nothing. Debasement couldn't touch her. She defused sexual frenzy by her inability to be shocked. And in between fantasies, she was preparing herself for her captors. She knew a door would open at some stage, and the staccato tap of spike heels articulate a direct line towards her. Would she be blindfolded and handcuffed, her neck placed in a collar? Her mind backtracked to events in the past when she had been exploited. It happened rarely, as Betty's job was about attaining the upper hand, and when it did, the resulting imbalance had her reassess her psychology. She had never quite locked the door on the man who lived in a rented room in her psyche. He was recalled in the codification of her sexual pleasure. Her universe was still phallocentric, although in every other aspect of her life, she chose to live as a woman. On the occasions when she was exploited, the man appeared. He came out of a green painted door, and stood there a long time blinking into a light to which he had grown unaccustomed. He seemed to want to remind her that he too had a part to play in her nervous impulses. He seemed to be saying, "Don't lock me in here for ever. The door is open even if the windows are boarded up, and besides, I need to speak. I'm left too solitary. All I have is a place in your unconscious."

And he was here again now, as she lay there waiting for release or punishment. He was dressed as she used to be, in blue jeans with a dark tailored jacket and a white button-down shirt underneath. He was holding a pair of dark glasses in one hand. He was tentative at first, and clearly suspicious of being hurt. He stared at her as though implanting his image as a reality. He wanted to be really sure she took him into account. Betty thought how it was like seeing someone standing at the end of an alley, someone you thought you knew, but nevertheless surprised by his being there. He seemed casual but assertive, bored, but wired to immediate action. Betty felt a sense of irreconcilable guilt at having neglected the person she had once been. But there was no way in which roles could be reversed. She couldn't any longer have him assert dominance, and herself go into the dark room and live there on periodic recall. Too much had happened to allow for this regression. But he was there to give her strength. He was called

Mike. She had answered to that name for her entire childhood and youth. Mike. He had run for a red ball in a park circled by cypress trees. He had built imposing sand castles, lit bonfires in October woods, run with a dog through village streets at nightfall. But at some stage his development had been terminated. He was no longer needed in the mirror. His plain clothes couldn't compete with the girl's skirts and tops that Betty had adopted. But at first he had been phased out slowly. He was wanted during the day – he was Mike at school – even if Betty resented it, and his place was assured at family meals. But upstairs he wasn't required. Foundation, lipstick and eyeliner disguised his features. Male clothes were discarded for silk panties and a short skirt. Betty had luxuriated in the feminine. Mike had grown to be a satellite on occasional recall. But he was wanted whenever Betty dressed as a girl, picked up girls, and laid them with a man's authoritative sex. His role was increasingly confined to a testosterone level.

He was standing there sad-eyed, asking Betty to listen to his psychological advice. Mike didn't want to be violated. She could tell that. He was holding out for respect. He was saying, "Don't let them rape us. Think of me. I don't want to be had like a woman. Oppose these people. They have no right to invade our body. I shall come between you and them. I shall be the reproachful image which will interpose between you and pleasure."

Betty steadied her focus on the man she had forgotten. His awkwardness and sense of rejection were becoming less pronounced now that she gave him the space to claim a partial identity. He kept coming at her from a past given autonomy by the present. This time he was reading by the seawall in the white room. The book was opened and partly screened his face. A girl in a minimal red bikini bottom was sunning three towels away. She was listening to a Walkman. It was a beach scene from Betty's youth. That day, that hot moment, were freeze-framed into her mind as she waited in agonized suspense for her captors. Mike wasn't reproachful of having been denied a life. He was just there offering her his psychological support.

Without warning the screen came to life. Betty found herself facing the dungeon in which she lay, only the film had been shot with more accentuated light. A teenage girl, dressed in a black beret, a black micro-skirt and sheer tights was sitting legs arched on the leather floor. The master of ceremonies was sitting opposite her, silently reading a large book. Betty recognized the man as the one at dinner who Nicole had called John, his steel-blue hair and aesthetically delineated cheekbones drawing attention to the idiosyncratic manner in which he buried his smile behind pursed lips. This man was closed to every form of overt emotional expression. Some intrinsic editing process cancelled out all spontaneous responses. He was deeply absorbed in reading. The schoolgirl placed her thumb in her lipsticked mouth, extracted it, and began tickling herself under her skirt. Her eyes bumped up big and black. When the voice track cut in, the man was heard instructing her in the erotic arts. "The width of a woman's shoe should be directly proportionate to that of a man's penis. The one should fit the other like a glove. Place it." Betty watched as the young girl slipped off a precocious stiletto, lifted the man's erection from the folds of a silk tunic, and neatly inserted it into a pointed red shoe. With considerable dexterity she also accommodated the scrotum to the heel part. "Now blow on it, nothing more," his voice commanded. The young girl lifted his genitals in the red stiletto and began to blow rhythmically on the sensitive glans. Disdaining to show any sense of pleasure, the man continued to read. Clearly thinking in stereo, and restraining sensory impulse for mental concentration, he continued to read. "In the course of giving head, a woman should reapply her lipstick three times, the tone dramatically reddening as climax is neared. The rhythm should be slow and investigative. The culinary etiquette of eating asparagus being one example, rolling a soft chocolate on the tongue being another, practising on Japanese toes being recommended, so too the application of lips to a red carnation. The student should begin by applying a thin coat of honey to the frenulum, and using tension points as mouth-stops. Proceed."

Betty found herself transfixed as the young girl produced a lip brush and a pot of honey, and extracting the man's erect penis from the shoes began to coat the skin with a fine lacquering of amber honey. She applied herself with the meticulous diligence of a make-up artist. She pulled her head back and examined her work. For good measure she tinctured honey into the slit, took out a scarlet lipstick and satisfied that it was exactly the right tone, began delicately to apply her mouth to the engorged cock. Savouring the honey, her tongue flicked between her lips like a snake's. The man registered no appreciation of her oral expertise. The girl began assiduously to work up from the base to the head in dabbing flicks, and then increasing her tempo proceeded to flatten her tongue more firmly into the skin. She applied the pressure necessary to give a love bite to the triggering head. The man continued to consult the book while the girl experimented with various rhythms. There was no least sense of synchronicity in their actions. The girl stopped at this point, checked her lipstick and applied another layer of scarlet gloss. She now took the penis into her lips, resting the shaft on her nether lip and working at it with the upper. Little by little she took it into her mouth, demonstrating the tongue rolling a soft chocolate method, her green eyes looking up at the man's expressionless ones. He showed no vestige of pleasure at the girl's alacritous versatility. He continued to read impassively. The girl now began to feed on his cock. She took it in like a rigid mauve banana. Her movements were vigorous, she was going down on it and taking it deep into her throat. It was like she had discovered a favourite flavour and was anxious to know it to the full. After a time of working at this committed speed, she stopped for a pause and touched up her lipstick. It was the third part of the prescribed ritual. Once again the man demonstrated no premonition of pleasure at her making up a last time to bring him to orgasm. The girl seemed instinctively to know a strategy best calculated to please. With her painted red fingernails she began tickling his balls, while her mouth was strained to an expansive oral accommodating his taut sex. There could be little doubt that the man was nearing an orgasm, despite the emotional repression he showed. And the girl sensed it too, for she took all of his cock into her mouth and increased the tantalizing motion of her fingertips. The man jolted three or four times in spasmic thrusts, and the girl held him tight inside. They remained like that for a long time, she unwilling to release him and he declining to make any comment on the climactic experience. He continued to read with the same unimpassioned note of boredom. Eventually the girl let his penis go, and the film cut out as she returned to her sitting position opposite the master of ceremonies.

Betty was left wondering what action had ensued. Did the girl masturbate to the man's instructions? Did she ride him later on, their two bodies floating like somnambulists on a bed removed from time? Did she discover that although she was connected to his penis he was untouchably far away in another dimension? Perhaps they were living in parallel ones. Betty had known men who were never able to come. They experienced pleasure, but were unable to ejaculate. They could make love for hours but to no conclusion. She usually avoided these, for they tired her with their unappeasable frustration. She had read how Marcel Proust, when he was unable to relieve himself at the sight of a naked boy, had a cage of rats brought into the room. His thrill came from seeing the rats attack and kill each other, a perversion that Betty surmised would be sympathetically viewed at the château. Proust had a dread of direct sexual contact, and half of Betty's clients were the same, preferring to act out elaborate fantasies than to engage in one to one sex. Microphobia. Autophobia. She just wanted to get out of this dungeon, and go back to a familiar bar by the port. But she could hear footsteps now, and the grating of hinges as a heavy door was ceremonially unlocked.

The leather floor cushioned acoustics, but Betty heard the jab of two pairs of spiked heels cross the intervening divide, and stop at the level of her feet. She couldn't look round to see who was standing behind her, and she tensed in the uncertainty. Someone or something was licking her toes, and adrenalin shot through her circuit as she realized it might be the leopard. And if it was, the leopard might be instructed to work its way upwards to her thighs. She was still staring at a blue screen. She believed that if she projected hard enough she could travel through it. Her astral propulsion would power her like a jet. Her captors would find nothing but a hole burnt in the blue.

The asperity of a hot tongue interrogating her toes, ceased. No one came forward. Betty lay there every nerve alert, as the silence was punctuated by the rapid breathing of an animal. Then it appeared. The leopard walked along her right side on an extended lead, and sat down in front of her head. Betty was able to observe how the cat's feet had been fitted into four high heels, the five-inch stilettos that Nicole wore with her constrictive leather skirt. The consequences were those of creating a surreal monster. It also meant that although the animal was deprived of claws, the leather heels would be equally effective instruments should the

creature lash out with its paws. Betty thought she was connected
with a nightmare. At any moment she would wake up and consign
the incident to a dream. The leopard settled down and lay on the
floor, eyes lazy with potential menace. Betty felt nothing. Fear
had displaced her. She wasn't here or anywhere. And quite
suddenly there were two figures standing with their backs to
her, right and left of the leopard. They were dressed in identical
black leather. The curve of their figures told Betty that they were
women. She imagined it was Leanda and Nicole, features disguised by masks that left holes for the eyes and mouth. Neither of
the two paid any attention to her. Rather, they acknowledged the
torches, and stared direct at the flame. When she looked again she
could see that one of the women was performing a rite with a
black dildo. She was intoning a chant, and offering the mamba to
the statue. She held it to the marble lips, and Betty heard the
voice engaged in a liturgical imprecation. The leopard yawned,
and flexed its stiletto paws. Betty had the apprehension that the
dildo was being offered up prior to its entering her. She had a
vision of the two women strapping it on respectively, and violating her with the fierce pretence of being men. And where were
the two men? She could hardly believe they had left the château
after dinner, their long wavering headlights pushing white feelers
through the country dark. Were they in a relationship, the two of
them hiring a penthouse overlooking the harbours, the red and
green shipping lights winking on the night waters? And did the
man with emerald lenses change them to violet or orange? Betty's
suppositions were conjectural. She had lived for so long amongst
people who were of indeterminate or exchangeable gender, that
she took no-one's sex at face value. She knew only the odd and the
extreme. Men who dressed up as women for sex, were to her the
norm. And she had been had in the past by women who strapped
on dildos with the intention of entering her as men. She knew a
client who kept a cupboard full of interesting shapes, colours and
sizes. Some of them were personally made for her. There were
green, blue, mauve, silver and gold artificial phalli which for her
extended the vocabulary of sexual possibilities. How many women or men had been made love to by a gold penis on which was
drawn the eye of Horus? And for purposes of pure decoration, the
woman had dildos encrusted with jewels, metallic or velvet phalli
which instead of flowers she placed in a vase beside her bed. That

room came back to her now. The woman pleased that she wasn't a real man, for the ritual surrounding the wearing of a dildo thrilled her. So too did the making out of instructions for the craftsman who delivered her specifications in a series of satin shoeboxes.

Having offered the mamba up as part of a weird ritual, the leather figure kissed it, and returned to her standing position facing the statue. Betty kept blanking out by closing her eyes, in order to avoid the leopard. The creature remained slack, but tensely alert. It was like a tuned guitar, waiting to be played. The two figures continued to stand with their backs to her and then one of them, without warning, spoke. "You will be released at dawn, and driven back to the city tomorrow tonight. You will never know this place again, nor will you remember where it is situated. You are a paid captive. You are expected to obey. You have been given a drug which will subliminally alter your conception of time and space for a week. Your memory of what has happened here will be erased. So too the knowledge that you have eaten flesh from the sacrificial penis. For it was penis we ate at dinner, that most subtle of homeopathic aphrodisiacs. Your priapic virtues will increase enormously as a consequence."

Betty listened as the female voice she took to be Leanda's continued. Not even her inurement to the most bizarre fetishes had prepared her for the idea of ingesting penis, and then being confronted by a leopard in a dungeon. The voice was informing her that she would be their unconditional slave for the night. She would be led from the dungeon to an attic. As the voice ceased, so the two oriental girls came into the dungeon, released Betty from the adhesive tabs, and placed her in soft leather handcuffs. They had changed their costumes to medieval ones cut in scarlet and black velvet. They served as officials, and Betty was led out of the dungeon into a long bluely lit corridor. There were recessed windows and heavy wooden doors concealing entry into other rooms. To Betty it was like walking into the second of the three films she had observed on the blue screen. At a certain point in the corridor, two figures appeared in front of them. It was the midget, easily identifiable by his rhinestone-encrusted coat, walking ahead of the monkey. They were carrying what looked like a black coffin, open and uninhabited, and the monkey's red jacket made a bold statement in the lugubrious shadows. The march had become a procession to the château's interior. Betty had been put in a red and black robe, and she walked silently between her guardians. The corridor seemed endless, but cut off at a right angle, and they proceeded through the open doors of a vast hall, the black and white marble floor reminding her of the lozenged tiles a client had in her swimming pool. The hall was furnished with baroque mirrors, their tranquillizing and dead faces suggesting traps into which the observer would disappear. Opulent cobalt and dark green rugs formed a mosaic around an open hearth. The logs must have been recently lit, for orange tigers leapt up the chimney. The detailed compartmentalization of walls and ceilings suggested an attenuated accuracy towards gothic. There was a glass case in a recess, presenting what to Betty looked like human skulls. A complex vocabulary of dissolute nerves had ordered the design. Gothic mingled with a clinically minimal modernity. Glass tabletops contained books splashed across their surfaces, nothing was random, everything to the last displacement was stylised, and written into the owner's nerves. Heavy red roses, involuted and inviting the eye to meet the fold of a turban, flopped from a dark blue vase. There were mummies stood up vertical in glass cases, positioned on either side of a door that admitted the procession into another corridor. The coffin bearers continued at an undifferentiated pace, the monkey squealing at intervals in querulous chatter. Betty followed, taking in everything as a series of film stills. It was like being involved in a shoot for a perverse rock video. She was the S&M victim being forcibly marched towards sexual retribution. And the corridor continued with the same monotony as its predecessor, only the subdued ceiling lighting was set at a lower volume, making the journey one carried out in semi-darkness.

At the end of the corridor they began mounting a broad wooden staircase. There were statues placed on the landing, one of them representing a black hermaphrodite, and the other a neo-classical bacchante with an erect phallus protruding through decorative leaves. Their footsteps resounded in the passage, before they ascended a flight of spiral stairs. Betty could see from the tilted-back coffin, that it was empty. The midget and the monkey maintained a practised equibalance in climbing the stairs. The ascent was at a slower pace and the four women removed their heels to climb the steeper gradient. They were going up towards the attic, and despite the pathologically maintained decorum of the company, Betty found it hard to take the proceedings literally. She was a specialized hooker, and not a passive victim to be exploited by orgiastic rites. There was still a way out if she didn't panic, but her recall of how she had got here, and where she had come from, was diminishing. She grabbed at the idea the subliminal drug must have entered her chemistry. Did she know her name? What was her address and telephone number? Was there a past and a future? Was she really back in her room dreaming that she was being conducted through a labyrinth of mazes to the château's secret rooms? Betty was feeling progressively disorientated. The sadistic metaphors and politicized suggestions directed at her were permeating her unconscious. She imagined that she was being led to her execution. They would dress her in a black cocktail dress after her death and place her in the coffin. They would bury her in the château's vaults, and like Madeleine Usher she would rise and walk through the corridors at night. There would be flame issuing from her mouth, her hands, and her feet. She would be a vampirical simulacrum, eating up people's desire with fire. Ashes would be found in the sheets in the morning. And in time the château would auto-combust from her inimical charge. Betty plotted these things as they mounted a final flight of stairs. The top floor was brightly lit in contradistinction to the subdued light of the lower floors. Betty was shocked to see a menagerie of creatures in cages staring out at her from their various locations. There were cockatoos, a yellow-eyed wolf, diamondback snakes, an albino monkey with blue eyes, an armadillo, and what she took to be a mongoose. The landing had been made into a surreal zoo, the exhibits juxtaposed to cause maximum discord.

Betty kept wondering if she wasn't on a hallucinogenic drug cocktail. An acid compound spiked with morphine. She was led into a bedroom that had been prepared in advance. A four-poster bed draped with black silks stood central to the room. A mirrored ceiling reflected a mirrored floor. There were three nooses suspended from different planes of the ceiling. A metaphysic existed between the elaborately decorative and the incorporation of brothel fetish. Betty was led to the coffin which had been placed open on the bed, and told to lie face down inside it. She obeyed with a compliancy that shocked her only into an awareness of how little control she had over her actions. The red and black tunic removed, she lay naked on the silk lining. It hardly surprised her that the black coffin should be lined with indigo silk. She had no conception of how many people were in the room, nor if the midget and his red-coated monkey assistant had retired back to the château's ground floor. The drug was causing her to relax and accept her vulnerability. She was left alone, but she could hear the regular cut of a whip laying into soft buttocks. It was a dull monotonous sound that lacked human punctuation. By averting her head slightly she could see that it was the monkey who was mechanically bullwhipping what looked like the man who had worn emerald lenses at table. He was wearing leather trousers with the back cut out, and the monkey indifferently lacerated the area of flesh presented by this exposure. The punishment was too disconnected from the monkey's own sense of sexual stimulus to indicate any mutual arousal. The severity of the blows were neither modified nor increased.

Betty heard rituals being conducted in Latin, a liturgical incantation delivered antiphonally by male and female voices. She understood that some rite of sexual magic was taking place. An offering was being presented to a phallic altar by a man whose skin was coloured by bright red make-up, an impasto foundation which was toned to resemble a Matisse red. His eyebrows were two black brushstrokes. Betty thought she heard the resonating vibration of gongs operating at a frequency just recognizable to normal audible receptivity. She went in and out of consciousness. Betty could hear the terminals macrocosmic and microcosmic being invoked, and the words *power-zone* and *scarlet woman*. Offerings were being made on a psychosexual plane. A sacrifice was being prepared.

At some stage Betty was commanded to stand. She stood up in the coffin and felt hands on her shoulders turning her round. It was a masked stranger she faced, two eye-slits and a gash of red lipstick showing through the mask. The woman manoeuvred her so that she followed her into the coffin, her legs going up over Betty's shoulders, and there really wasn't space, and she was awkward with her hands constricted, backing off so as to bring a division between their bodies, and then sensing the woman's urgency, bringing her tongue into contact with her clit, stepping up its sensitivity as though she was entering the door of a cave to an interior forest. There was a woman inside the entrance with violet hair and leopard spot skin. She was setting fire to trees and the animals were running. They were bolting for shelter, or swimming across great lakes. The woman inside was distraught with frustration. She wanted to be forced back by the intrusive thrusts of a giant phallus. She was hoping for stars to explode in her veins. Betty felt herself being entered from behind. She knew she was being taken by a woman wearing a dildo, for the insertion was cold, and the rigidity of the object inflexible. Betty settled to the pain of tight entry, and the liturgical imprecations grew in their intensity as the lights dropped and were replaced by black torches. From the rhythmic pressure asserted, Betty could tell that the woman mechanically pumping her was herself being possessed from behind. An orgiastic chain was giving physical expression to the ceremonial chant. But the drug was again in evidence and Betty found herself taken on intricate biochemical journeys. In her mind she was swimming underwater, her body brushing against dolphins, the blue panes of water opening fluently as she accompanied the fish to a submerged ruin. Betty was open to the sound-waves transmitted by the dolphin's nasal passages, and her correspondingly alerted sense perceptions had her body glow. She had followed the school to a coral-encrusted hulk. There were ten dolphins that formed an exact circle round two drowned bodies that continued to copulate despite their being dead. And once, when the man temporarily withdrew his penis from the woman, she could see that it was gold. Then he swung his head back and stared at her, and his eyes were gold. She wanted to ask the couple why none of them needed to breathe, but the dolphins created an impenetrable vibrational wall, and she had to remain a detached spectator to events. It was when she realized she wasn't breathing, that the scene changed, and she spiralled back direct to the surface.

Betty wasn't being spared by her partner, and while she drifted a man had thrust himself into her lips. His penis tasted of lipstick. But she was hurrying away again, running naked with her arms full of dresses down a high street she partly recognized, only the shops and houses had changed order, and when the rain came down it blotched her skin with blue splashes. It was an inky rain that ran cobalt in the gutters. She didn't know where she was running, only that she'd recognize the place instantly when she saw it. There were eagles in the sky, and one of them dropped a red flag at her feet. She draped herself in it, and ran on with the dresses loading her arms. The traffic had its lights on, and the rain flashed up in white dipped arcs. Betty was aware of the urgency of the man's thrusts, he was gagging her with his deep placement, it felt like her mouth was being expanded to three or four times life size. But mentally she had found the place. She went in through a wide open door. The shop was dark. There was a white cat sitting on the counter. The silence was loaded. It was a mannequin came out of the dark, wearing a white wedding veil spotted with blood. She knew without questioning it that the thing could speak. "You will wait in this shop a thousand years," it said. "When the wind comes in, rusty eyed and dragging its dead tail, and when the rain arrives in the form of a sequined fish, expiring, deoxygenated, and the sun bounces in as a red ball no larger than your compact fist, then . . ." The man was starting to come, for she could feel the hot salinity decanted into her throat, his agonized pleasure exploding from a volcanic core. And no sooner had he withdrawn, than another penis entered her mouth, and the chant continued, a ritual incantation gradually receding to a sustained whisper. Betty didn't know how long she had been here, or after a time even what had happened or was happening. She moved between inner consciousness and jabs at reality. But she was aware at some stage that she was being marched back through the confused maze of corridors, and this time she was dressed in a violet tunic, and someone had placed flowers in her hair. The midget continued to walk ahead, and the monkey kept an exact pace. They were going back through halls, complexes, and she was finally shown into a bedroom. It was almost dawn. She had completed her journey to the end of the night.

JOU PU TUAN

Li-Yü

After leaving the hermit, the young man went his way mumbling and grumbling:

"A fine saint indeed! Here I am, just twenty, barely at the threshold of manhood, and he expects me to take the tonsure, to renounce the world, and to suffer the bitterness of a monkish existence. Has such heartlessness its like in all the world? I only went to pay him my respects because formerly, before becoming a hermit, he was regarded as one of the leading lights of Confucian scholarship. I fancied he would dig up heaven knows what magic spells and bits of occult wisdom to help me on my way. But instead, he has the gall to treat me as a stupid child, and his only gift to me is this absurd and utterly uninspired epigram, which is like thunder without lightning. The whole thing is preposterous. As a future official and dignitary, I shall some day govern a whole district with a population numbering tens of thousands, and he fancies that I won't be able to govern my own wife. Is it unreasonable of me to desire a little practice in the wind-and-moon game a little experience before marrying? That's what he was trying to forbid. But otherwise I should be going into marriage with my eyes closed and might even choose the wrong woman. And to top it all, he tells me that someone might requite me for past transgressions by violating the securely guarded honor of my house. As though the woman who gets a paragon of manly qualities like me for a husband had any need to be seduced by another man! My own wife unfaithful! – Why, it's out of the question.

"I should really tear up this incompetent epigram and stamp on it. But no, I'd better not. I can use it as evidence later on, to stuff down his venomous throat. If I ever meet him again, I'll show him his epigram and put him to the test, to see whether he admits his mistake."

After thus deliberating, he folded the epigram and put it into his belt pocket.

Returning home, he bade his servants seek out all the marriage brokers they could find and commission them to search the city and countryside for the most beautiful of marriageable girls. She must be of respectable and distinguished family; and he insisted that she must be not only beautiful, but intelligent and well educated as well. There was no lack of offers. What paterfamilias would not have been glad to have him for a son-in-law, what daughter would not have taken him for a husband? Each day a number of marriage brokers came to him with their suggestions. Where the candidate was not too high in the social scale, the matchmaker would bring her along to be introduced and inspected at first hand. But in the case of a distinguished family which insisted on its forms and observances, she arranged to have the young man, as though by chance, cross the young lady's path in the courtyard of one of the temples, or while she was taking the air out-side the city walls.

All these meetings and tours of inspection proved to be quite useless. A certain number of worthy young persons were unnecessarily jolted out of their peaceful routines and sent home again with vain pangs in their tender little hearts. For of all the candidates who were brought forward, not a one met with the exacting suitor's approval.

But one of the marriage brokers said to the young man:

"Now it is clear to me that among all the young candidates there is only one who is worth considering: Miss Noble Scent; her father is a private scholar, known throughout the city by the surname T"ieh-fei tao-jen, Iron Door Follower of the Tao. She alone can meet your stringent requirements. But in her case there is a difficulty: her father is an old crank who adheres rigidly to the ancient customs. He would certainly not permit you to inspect his daughter before marriage. Consequently I fear that even this last hope must be abandoned."

"Iron Door Follower of the Tao? How did he come by such a strange surname? Why does he not wish his daughter to be seen? And if he keeps her hidden from all eyes, how do you know she is beautiful?"

"As I have told you, the old gentleman is rather crochety; he cares only for his books and avoids all society. He doesn't see a living soul. He lives in a splendid country house outside the city, with fields and meadows round it, and it makes no difference who knocks on his door, he refuses to open. One day an unknown admirer came to see him, a respected gentleman from another part of the country, who wished to pay his respects. He knocked at the door for some time and when no one answered, he cried out, but in vain. Before going away he wrote an epigram on the door:

> For a wise man ivy and vines
> Are protection enough, he needs no door.
> Yet this noble lord – who would have thought it –
> Hides behind an iron door.

When the master of the house found the epigram, he decided that the two ideograms, *t'ieh*, iron and *fei*, door, summed up his character perfectly, and he chose them as a surname. From then on he called himself T'ieh-fei tao-jen: Iron Door Follower of the Tao. He is a wealthy widower and his daughter is his only child. As for her beauty, it is no exaggeration to liken her to a lovely flower, a precious jewel. In addition, her father has given her an excellent education and her little head is full of learning. Poems, essays in poetic prose, songs, stanzas – she is familiar with them all and can compose in any form. Her upbringing, as you may easily surmise, has been extremely strict, and she has hardly ever set foot outside her maidenly quarters. She never goes out, not even to the traditional services on temple holidays, and there is simply no question of visits to relatives and friends. She is sixteen years old and has never been seen in public. Even we three go-betweens and six marriage brokers have no wings, we can't fly into her living quarters. It was only by the purest accident that I myself caught a glimpse of her not long ago.

"Yesterday I chanced to pass the house while the old gentle-man was standing outside the door. He stopped me and asked if I were not Mother Liu, whose trade it was to arrange marriages. When I answered in the affirmative, he invited me in and presented his daughter. 'This is the young lady, my only child,' he said, and continued: 'Now I should like you to look around and bring me a suitable son-in-law who is worthy of her and has the qualities he would need to be a son to me and the prop of my old age.' At once I suggested that the young gentleman would be an appropriate match. He said: 'I have already heard of him, he is said to possess high intellectual gifts as well as external advan-tages. But what of his character and his virtue?' To this I replied: 'The young gentleman is distinguished by a spiritual and ethical maturity far in advance of his years. His character is without the slightest blemish or weak point. There is only one thing: he absolutely insists on seeing his future bride with his own eyes before the betrothal.' At once the benevolent look vanished from the old gentleman's face, and he became very angry: 'Nonsense. He wants to see her first – that may be permissible in the case of a venal powder-puff, a rutting mare from Yangchow. But since when is it the custom to expose the honorable daughter of a good family to the eyes of a strange man? A fine thing that would be. An impudent demand, which makes it clear to me that the young man is not the right husband for my daughter. Not another word!' With this he broke off the interview and sent me on my way. So you see, young man, there is nothing more to be done."

The young man thought the matter over carefully.

"If I were to marry this beautiful young girl and take her into my own house, there would be no one but me – for I am without parents or brothers – to keep an eye on her. I should have to stay home all day guarding her, there would be no chance whatever to go out. But if I went to live in her house, there would be no such difficulty, for this ancient guardian of virtue, my father-in-law, would keep a good watch over her in my absence. I should be able to go out with an easy heart. The only point that bothers me is not to see her first. What confidence can I have in a matchmaker's prattle? Why, there's no limit to what her kind will say in praise of a possible match." Such were his thoughts. To Mama Liu he said:

"If I am to believe you, she would be an excellent wife, yes, just the right wife for me. I should just like to ask you this one thing: to find some way of my getting the merest glimpse of her and hearing the sound of her voice. Then if the general impression is favorable, the match is made."

"See her first? It's out of the question. But if you don't trust me, why not go to a soothsayer and consult the little straws of fate?"

"There you have given me a very good idea. I have a friend who is an expert at conjuring spirits and telling fortunes, and his predictions have always been confirmed. I shall ask his advice. Let us wait to see what fate decides. Then I shall send for you and tell you what has happened."

So it was agreed and Mama Liu departed.

Next day the young man fasted and bathed and asked his friend the diviner to his house for a consultation. In the house-temple lit by candles and filled with incense, he solemnly explained the business in hand, humbly bowing his head and speaking in a muffled voice as though praying to a higher being:

"The younger brother has heard of the unsurpassed beauty of Miss Noble Scent, daughter of Iron Door Follower of the Tao, and would like to take her for his wife. But only his ears have heard of her charms, his eyes have not seen them. Therefore he begs leave to ask the exalted spirit whether she is indeed so beautiful and whether the exalted spirit recommends a marriage with her. If there should be even the slightest blemish in her, he would prefer to abandon the idea of marrying her. He fervently implores the exalted spirit to give him some gracious hint, for he does not wish to forfeit all happiness by trusting in idle prattle."

After stating his request, he made the fourfold sign on his forehead in reverence to the unknown spirit. Rising once more to his feet, he took from his friend's hand a piece of wood from the magic *luan* tree, symbolizing the spirit, held it chest high, and waited with bated breath to see what would happen next. Then he heard a sound, as of a brush passing softly over paper. A pluck at his sleeve awakened him from his trance. His friend was holding out a sheet of paper. On it was written a quatrain:

Number 1:

No need to doubt this message of the spirits:
She is first in the grove of red flowers.

Yet there is cause for alarm. So much beauty attracts suitors.
Whether the marriage is happy or not – is a question of
morality.

The young man reflected: "It is clear then that she is a first
class beauty. That is the main thing. As for the second part of the
communication, it does not mince words about the danger such
beauty involves. Can it be that the melon has already been cut
open? – No that is very unlikely. Let us wait and see what the
second communication says. There must be another since the
first one is headed Number 1."

Again he held out the magic wood, then again he heard rustling
and received the second communication, which ran:

It would be presumptuous to bank on your wife's fidelity;
Accordingly, if the husband values domestic harmony,
He will lock the gates and not admit a fly.
The tiniest fly-dropping will spoil a jewel.

> Written by Hui-tao-jen the
> returned follower of the Tao.

The three ideograms Hui-tao-jen were familiar to our young
man; as he knew, they spelled the surname behind which the
Taoist patriarch Lü Shun-yang (Lü Yen, also known as Lü
Tung-pin, b. 750 A.D.) had hidden; he was also acquainted with
the patriarch's life and personality; in his time, the young man
recalled to his satisfaction, he had been a great devotee and
connoisseur of wine and women. So, it was *his* spirit that had
entered into his friend during the séance and guided the brush.
Well, yes, he had thrown a little cold water on his projects by
warning him of women's infidelity and bidding him to be on his
guard. But there was no need to worry on that score. He would
have his father-in-law, that old-fashioned guardian of morality,
in the house to watch over his wife's virtue. What else was Iron
Door good for? Moreover, lines three and four of the second
communication were a clear allusion to him. There could be no
doubt that the spirit approved of his choice.

He made a bow of thanks toward the empty air, intended for
the spirit of the patriarch Lü Shun-yang. Then he sent for Mama
Liu, the marriage broker.

"The spirit has spoken in favor of my marriage with Miss Noble Scent. A personal inspection is not necessary. Go quickly and settle the details." Thus dismissed, Mama Liu made all haste to the house of Dr Iron Door, and informed him that her client no longer insisted on previous inspection of his bride-to-be.

"But he did at first," Dr Iron Door grumbled, "and by so doing showed himself to be deplorably superficial, the kind of man who attaches more importance to externals than to superior character. He is not the son-in-law for me. I must have a man of the utmost moral rigor, who takes a thoroughly serious view of life."

Intent on her fee, Mama Liu summoned up all her ingenuity to overcome his resistance:

"If he wished at first to see the young lady, his only motive was one of kindness and tact. He was afraid that she might be too frail and delicate for married life. Once I was able to set his mind at rest on that score, he was overjoyed to hear how strictly and carefully she had been raised, and how, thanks to your guidance, she had become a veritable epitome of maidenly virtue. That decided him, and he bade me intercede with you to honor him by taking him into your worthy house."

Flattered at these remarks, Dr Iron Door nodded his approval. Then it was a sense of delicacy that made him wish to see her first? And it was her sound upbringing that decided him? That sounded sensible and argued very much in the young man's favor. And he gave his paternal consent.

And so on a lucky calendar day the young man was received in Dr Iron Door's home, and with Noble Scent on the carpet beside him, made the traditional bows to heaven and earth, ancestors and father-in-law. At nightfall when he was at last alone with her in the bridal chamber and she lifted her veil, he fixed his eyes upon his bride in feverish expectation. For to the last moment a doubt had lurked in a corner of his heart; to the last moment he had thought that Mama Liu's assurance must be slightly exaggerated, a product as it were of poetic license. But now that he was able to view her close at hand, in the full light of the lamps and candles, his heart leapt with delight. Her beauty exceeded his wildest expectations. Perhaps the best way to give an idea of her charms will be to quote a passage from a recent essay "in memory of the glorious lady of Tsin":

"Over her person hovers a cloud of dark mystery, a veil of unyielding reticence. Her face and every part of her body are bathed in purest beauty. When she smiles, one would like to take her charming face in both hands. But her charm becomes truly irresistible only when she pouts and knits her brows.

"To be sure, her tender waist and the nine sensitive zones of her body seem almost unequal to the battle of wedlock. Her body seems as soft as if it were devoid of bone structure; even a soft chair offends it."

How shall we describe the joy of union between bridegroom and bride? Once again we leave the task to a recent essay, this one entitled "Springtime in the Tower of Jasper":

"From beneath half-closed lids the stars that are her eyes flash an angry message: no! Awakened from deep slumber, the peach blossom declines to open its slender calyx. But eager for the fray, the tongue forces a narrow passage between the lips of the fragrant mouth. A blissful moan—and long pent-up feelings pour forth unrestrained. The dew of desire forms into tiny beads on the silken skin of her breasts. Two pairs of eyes open slowly and gaze plunges deep into gaze. Two hearts flare up into red fire."

Unquestionably Noble Scent was a peerless beauty, but to her partner's grief she was an utter failure at the "wind-and-moon game" and the hopes with which he had looked forward to his wedding night remained at least seven-tenths unfulfilled. Small wonder. Thanks to the traditional upbringing she had received from her strict, ultra-conservative parents, she wore an armor of virginal modesty and reserve, against which his tender assaults bounded off without the slightest effect. He was quite dismayed at her lack of response to his advances. If he allowed his language to become even mildly daring or frivolous, she blushed and took flight. He liked to play the "wind-and-moon game" not only at night but also in broad daylight, for it seemed to him that his pleasure was very much increased by the possibility of looking at certain secret parts of the body. On several occasions he attempted, in the morning or afternoon, to insert a bold hand beneath her clothing and to strip off her undermost coverings. The reception was not what he had bargained for. She resisted vigorously and screamed as though threatened with rape. At night, to be sure, she permitted his embraces, but quite apathetically as though merely doing her duty. He had to stick to the stodgy ancestral method, and any attempt at more modern, more refined variations met with fierce opposition. When he attempted the "fetching fire behind the hill" position, she said it was perfectly disgusting and contrary to all the rules of husbandly behavior. When he tried the "making candles by dipping the wick in tallow" position, she protested that such goings-on were utterly nasty and vulgar. It took all his powers of persuasion even to make her prop up her thighs on his shoulders. When their pleasure approached a climax, not the tiniest little cry, not the slightest moan of happiness was to be heard from her. Even when he smothered her in tender little cries of "My heart, my liver," or "My life, my everything," she took no more interest than if she had been deaf and dumb. It was enough to drive him to despair. He began to make fun of her and to call her his "little saint."

"Things can't go on like this. I must find some way of educating her and ridding her of those awful moral inhibition – the best idea would be some stimulating reading matter." So saying, he repaired to the booksellers' quarter. There after a long search he procured a marvelously illustrated volume entitled *Ch'un-t'ang*, "The Vernal Palace." It was a celebrated book on the art of love, written by no less a man than the Grand Secretary, Chao Tzu-ang. It included thirty-six pictures, clearly and artfully illustrating the thirty-six different "positions" of vernal dalliance, of which the poets of the T'ang period had sung. He brought the book home with him and handed it to the "little saint." As they leafed through page after page, he whispered to her:

"You see that I haven't been asking you to join in any monkey business of my own invention. These are all accepted forms of married love, practiced by our venerable ancestors. The text and pictures prove it."

Unsuspectingly, Noble Scent took the volume and opened it. When she turned to the second page and read the big bold heading: *Han-kung yi-chao*, "traditional portraits from the imperial palace of the Han dynasty" (second century B.C. to second century A.D.), she thought to herself:

"There were many noble and virtuous beauties at the court of the ancient Han rulers – the book must contain portraits of them. Very well, let us see what the venerable ladies looked like." And eagerly she turned another page. But now came a picture that made her start back in consternation: in the midst of an artificial rock garden a man and woman in rosy nakedness, most intimately intertwined. Blushing crimson for shame and indignation, she cried out:

"Foo! How disgusting! Where did you ever get such a thing? Why, it sullies and befouls the atmosphere of my chaste bed-chamber."

Whereupon she called her maid and ordered her to burn the horrid thing on the spot. But he restrained her.

"You can't do that. The book is an ancient treasure, worth at least a hundred silver pieces. I borrowed it from a friend. If you wish to pay him a hundred silver pieces in damages, very well, burn it. If not, do me the favor of letting me keep it for two days until I have finished reading it; then I'll return it to my friend."

"But why do you have to read such a thing, that offends against all human morality and order?"

"I beg your pardon, if it were as offensive and immoral as all that, a famous painter would hardly have lent himself to illustrating it, and a publisher would hardly have been willing to defray the production costs and distribute the book. You are quite mistaken. Since the world was created, there has been nothing more natural and reasonable than the activities described in this book. That is why a master of the word joined forces with a master of color to fashion the material into a true work of art; that is why the publisher spared no costs and as you see brought the book out in a de luxe edition on expensive silk, and that is why the plates are preserved along with other literary treasures in the archives of the Han-lin Academy, in the Forest of Brush and Ink, so that future generations may draw knowledge and profit from it. Without such books love between the sexes would gradually lose all charm and ardor; husband and wife would bore one another to tears. Gone would be the pleasure of begetting children, dull indifference would take root. It is not only for my own edification that I borrowed the book, but wittingly and I think wisely for yours as well, in the hope that it would prepare you for motherhood, that your womb would be blessed and you would soon present me with a little boy or a little girl. Or do you really think that a young couple like us should espouse the ascetic ways of your *ling-tsun*, your 'venerable lord,' and condemn our youthful marriage to barrenness? Are you aware of my good intentions now? Was there anything to be indignant about?"

Noble Scent was not entirely convinced.

"I cannot quite believe that what the book represents is really compatible with morality and reason. If that were so, why did our forebears who created our social order not teach us to carry on openly, in broad daylight, before the eyes of strangers? Why do people do it like thieves in the night, shut away in their bed-chambers? Doesn't that prove that the whole thing must be wrong and forbidden?"

The Before Midnight Scholar replied with a hearty laugh.

"What a comical way of looking at things! But far be it from me to find fault with my *niang-tzu*, my dear little woman, on that account. It's all the fault of the preposterous way your honorable father raised you, shutting you up in the house and cutting you off from the outside world, forbidding you to associate with young girls like yourself who could have enlightened you. Why, you've grown up like a hermit without the slightest knowledge of the world. Of course married couples conduct their business by day as well as night; everyone does. Just think for a moment; if it had never been done in the daylight with others looking on, how would an artist have found out about all the different positions shown in this book? How could he have depicted all these forms and variations of loving union so vividly that one look at his pictures is enough to put us into a fine state of excitement?"

"Yes, but what about my parents? Why didn't they do it in the daytime?"

"I beg your pardon. How do you know they didn't?"

"Why, I would surely have caught them at it. I am sixteen, after all, and all these years I never noticed a thing. Why, I never even heard a sound to suggest that . . ."

Again the Before Midnight Scholar had to laugh aloud:

"Ah, what a dear little silly you are! Such parental occupations are not intended for the eyes and ears of a child! But one of the maids is sure to have heard or seen a little something from time to time. Of course your parents would never have done anything within your sight or hearing; very wisely they did it behind closed doors, for fear that if a little girl like you were to notice anything, her mental health might be upset by all sorts of premature thoughts and daydreams."

After a moment of silent reflection, Noble Scent said as though to herself:

"That's true. I remember that they occasionally withdrew to their bedchamber in the daytime and bolted the door after them – can that be what they were doing? It's possible. But in broad daylight! To see each other stark naked! How can it be? They must have felt so ashamed."

"I beg your pardon. For lovers to see each other naked in broad daylight, why, that's the whole charm of it; it gives ten times more pleasure than doing it in the dark. And that is true of all lovers – with two exceptions."

"What are the two exceptions?"

"Either he is ugly and she is beautiful, or she is ugly and he is handsome: in those two cases dealings by daylight are not advisable."

"Why?"

"Dealings between the sexes give full enjoyment only when both parties feel drawn to one another body and soul, as though by a primordial force, and long for physical union with every fiber of their being. Let us suppose that she is beautiful, that with her full, soft forms and her delicate, luminous, smooth skin she resembles a well-polished jewel. Drawing her close to him, her lover will strip off layer after layer of her garments, and the more he sees of her, the more his desire will increase; his member will stiffen of its own free will and stand up big and hard and strong. But then suppose that she looks toward her partner and discovers ugly features, misshapen limbs, coarse, hairy skin, in short a veritable goblin. He may have been almost acceptable as long as he had clothes on, but now he lies there before her in all his ugliness. And the greater the contrast between his fiendish aspect and the soft radiant beauty of her own body, the more horrified and repelled will she be. Even if she was fully prepared for physical union, must her desire not turn instantly to nothing?. And he in turn, must not his javelin, which only a moment before was standing up so proud and big and strong, shrink to the most dwarfish size at the sight of her obvious revulsion and distaste? In short, there can be no joyous battle of love between a pair so unequally matched. If they should attempt it just the same, the end is sure to be a lamentable fiasco. Better let them do battle at night when they cannot see each other plainly. That is the one exception.

"The other is the reverse: he is handsome, she is ugly. The situation is exactly the same, no reason to waste words on it.

"And now we come to our own case: here it is equal to equal, radiant skin to radiant skin, well-formed youth to well-formed youth. And now I ask you: Have we any need to take refuge in night and darkness, to crawl under the covers and hide from one another? Should we not do better to show ourselves to one another in broad daylight and delight in the sight of our bodies in all their natural beauty? If you don't believe me, let us make a try. Let us just try it once in the daytime."

By now Noble Scent was half convinced. Despite the modest "no" of her lips, she was almost willing. A slight flush came to her cheeks, revealing her mounting excitement and anticipation of things to come. This did not escape him, and in secret he thought: "She is gradually becoming interested. No doubt about it, she would like to play. But her senses have barely begun to awaken. Her hunger and thirst for love are very new to her. If I start in too brusquely, she is very likely to suffer the fate of the glutton who gobbles up everything in sight without taking time to bite or chew. She would get little enjoyment from such indigestible fare. I'd better bide my time and let her dangle a while."

He moved up a comfortable armchair and sat down. Drawing her to him by the sleeve, he made her sit on his lap. Then he took the picture book and leafed through it page by page and picture by picture.

Unlike other books of a similar kind, the book was so arranged that the front of each leaf bore a picture and the back the text that went with it. The text was in two sections. The first briefly explained the position represented; the second gave a critical estimate of the picture from the standpoint of its artistic value.

Before starting, the Before Midnight Scholar advised his pupil to examine each picture carefully for its spirit and meaning, for then it would provide an excellent model and example for future use. Then he read to her, sentence for sentence.

"Picture No. 1. The butterfly flutters about, searching for flowery scents."

Accompanying text: "She sits waiting with parted legs on a rock by the shore of a garden pond. He, first carefully feeling out the terrain, takes pains to insert his nephrite proboscis into the depths of her calyx. Because the battle has only begun and the region of bliss is still far off, both still show a relatively normal expression, their eyes are wide open."

"Picture No. 2 shows the queen bee making honey."

Accompanying text: "She lies on her back, cushioned in pillows, her parted legs raised as though hanging in midair, her hands pressed against 'the fruit,' guiding his nephrite proboscis to the entrance of her calyx, helping it to find the right path and not to stray. At this moment her face shows an expression of hunger and thirst, while his features reveal the most intense excitement, with which the viewer becomes infected. All this is brought out by the artist with remarkable subtlety."

"Picture No. 3. The little bird that had gone astray finds its way back to its nest in the thicket."

Accompanying text: "She lies slightly to one side, dug into the thicket of cushions, one leg stretched high, and clutches his thigh with both hands as though his obedient vassal had finally found its way to the right place, to her most sensitive spot, and she feared it might go off and get lost again. This accounts for the shadow of anxiety on her otherwise happy face. Both parties are in full swing, quite preoccupied by the spasmodic thrill of the 'flying brush' and the 'dancing ink.'"

"Picture No. 4. The hungry steed gallops to the feed crib."

Accompanying text: "She, flat on her back, presses his body to her breast with both hands. Her feet propped up on his shoulders, he has sunk his yak whisk into her calyx to the shaft. Both of them are approaching ecstasy. The way in which the artist pictures their physical and mental state at this moment, their eyes veiled beneath half-closed lids, their tongues enlaced, reveals the master of the brush."

"Picture No. 5. The dragons are weary of battle."

Accompanying text: "Her head rests sideways on the pillow; she has let her arms droop; her limbs feel numb as though stuffed with cotton. Resting his head sideways against her cheek he presses his body to hers. He too feels as numb as cotton. The ecstasy is gone. The 'aromatic soul' has fled, the beautiful dream has passed the peak and evaporated into nothingness. The barest thread of life is discernible. Without it one might think the two of them were dead, two lovers in one coffin and one grave. The picture brings home to us the sublimity of bliss savored to the very end."

Up to this point Noble Scent had obediently studied the pictures and patiently listened to the commentary. But as he turned another page and began to show her Picture No. 6, she pushed the book away in visible agitation and stood up.

"Enough!" she cried. "What's the good of all these pictures? They are just upsetting. You look at them by yourself. I'm going to bed."

"Just a little patience, we'll run through the rest quickly. The best is still to come. Then we'll both go to bed."

"As if there weren't time enough tomorrow for looking at books. For my part, I've had quite enough."

He embraced her and closed her mouth with a kiss. And as he kissed her, he noticed something new. They had been married for a whole month. In all that time, she had held the gates of her teeth closed tight when he kissed her. His tongue had never succeeded in forcing or wriggling its way through the solid fence. Until today he had never made contact with her tongue; he hadn't so much as an idea what it was like. But now when he pressed his lips to hers – what a wonderful surprise – the tip of his tongue encountered the tip of her tongue. For the first time she had opened up the gate.

"My heart, my liver!" he sighed with delight. "At last! And now – why bother moving to the bed? This chair will do the trick, it will take the place of the rock by the pond, and we shall imitate the lovers in Picture No. 1. What do you say?"

Noble Scent with affected indignation:

"Impossible. It's not a fit occupation for human beings. . . ."

"There you are perfectly right. It is an occupation and pastime more fit for the gods. Come, let us play at being gods." So saying, he stretched out his hand and began to fiddle with the knot of her sash. And despite her grimace of disapproval, she cooperated, letting him draw her close and permitting him to strip off her undermost covering. As he did so, he made a discovery that fanned his excitement into a bright flame. Aha, he thought, just looking at those pictures has sprinkled her little meadow with the dew of desire. He undid himself and set her down in the chair in such a way that her legs hung over his shoulders. Cautiously he guided his bellwether through the gates of her pleasure house, and then began to remove the rest of her clothes.

Why only now?, you will ask. Why did he begin at the bottom?

Let me explain: This Before Midnight Scholar was an experienced old hand. He said to himself that if he tried to remove her upper garments first, she would feel ashamed and intimidated, her resistance would make things unnecessarily difficult. That is why he daringly aimed his first offensive at her most sensitive spot, figuring that once she surrendered there she would easily surrender on all other fronts. Herein his strategy was that of the commander who defeats an enemy army by taking its general prisoner. And the truth is that she now quite willingly let him undress her from head to foot – no, not quite – with the exception of a single article of apparel which he himself tactfully spared: her little silk stockings.

After their three-inch long (or short) "golden lilies" have been bound up, our women customarily draw stockings over the bandages. Only then do their toes and ankles feel at ease. Otherwise their feet, like flowers without leaves, are unlovely to behold.

Now he too cast off his last coverings and flung himself into the fray with uplifted spear. Already his bellwether was in her pleasure house. Groping its way to left and right, slipping and sliding, it sought a passage to the secret chamber where the "flower heart," the privy seal, lies hidden. She helped him in his search by propping up her hands on the arms of the chair and, in tune with his movements, lithely twisting and bending her middle parts toward him. Thus they carried on for a time, exactly in accordance with Figure 2 of their textbook

Suddenly, way down deep, she had a strange feeling of a kind that was utterly new to her; it did not hurt, no, it was more like a sensation of itching or tickling, almost unendurable and yet very very pleasant.

"Stop," she cried, bewildered by the strangeness of the thing. "That's enough for today. You are hurting me." And she tried to wrest herself free.

Thoroughly experienced in these matters, he realized that he had touched her most intimate spot, her flower-heart. Considerately acceding to her wishes, he moved away from the ticklish spot and contented himself with moving his bellwether slowly back and forth several dozen times through her pleasure house with its narrow passages and spacious halls. The intruder made himself thoroughly at home on her property, and she was over-

come by an irresistible desire to punish him for his insolence.
Choking would be a fair punishment she thought.

Removing her hands from the arms of the chair, she let his back
slip down and dug her hands into his buttocks. This enabled her
to press closer to him, an operation in which he helped by
clasping her slender waist in his hands and holding her as tightly
as he could. Thanks to the intimate conjunction thus achieved –
they were now exactly in the position illustrated in Figure 3 – she
held his stiff thick bellwether firmly enough to start slowly
strangling it. While sparing no effort and answering pressure
with pressure, he saw that her eyes were clouding over and the
stately edifice of her hair was becoming undone.

"*Hsin-kan*, my heart, my liver," he panted. "You seem to be on
the verge – but it is very uncomfortable in this chair; shall we not
continue on the bed?"

This suggestion did not appeal to her. She had the rascally
intruder just where she wanted him; just a little longer, and she
would choke the life out of him. At this late stage, she was quite
unwilling to be cheated of her pleasure. If they were to move to
the bed now, he would slip away from her. No, this was no time
for interruptions! She shook her head resolutely. Then closing
her eyes as though she were already half asleep, she said – this was
her pretext – that she was much too tired to move.

He decided on a compromise: leaving her position unchanged,
he placed his hands beneath her seat in such a way that she could
not slip down, bade her throw her arms round his neck. Pressing
his mouth to hers, he lifted her up carefully and thus enlaced
carried her into the bedroom where they went on with the game.

Suddenly she let out a scream: "Dearest, ah! ah! . . ."

She pressed closer and closer to him and the sounds that issued
from her mouth were like the moans and groans of one dying. It
was clear to him that she was on the threshold. And he too at the
same time! With his last strength he pressed his nephrite proboscis into the sanctum of her flower-temple. Then for a time
they lay enlaced as though in a deathlike sleep. She was first to
stir; she heaved a deep sigh and said:

"Did you notice? I was dead just now."

"Of course I noticed. But we don't call it 'death.' We call it
'giving off an extract.'"

"What do you mean by 'giving off an extract'?"

"Both in man and woman a subtle essence of all the bodily humors is at all times secreted. At the peak of amorous pleasure one of the body's vessels overflows and gives off some of this extract. Just before the flow, the whole body, skin and flesh and bones, falls into a deep, unconscious sleep. Our physical state before, during, and after the flow is called *tiu* 'a giving off of extract.' It is depicted in Figure 5."

"Then I was not dead?"

"Of course not. You gave off an extract."

"If that is so, I hope I may do it day after day and night after night."

He burst into a resounding laugh.

"Well, was I not right to recommend the picture book as an adviser? Is it not priceless?"

"Yes, indeed. A priceless treasure. We must consult it over and over again. A pity that the friend you borrowed it from will want it back again."

"Don't you worry about that. It was I myself who bought it. The whole story about the friend was just made up."

"Oh, that is good news."

From then on the two of them were one heart and one soul. Noble Scent became an assiduous reader of *The Vernal Palace* and from that day on she could not praise it too highly. Like a diligent pupil, she made every effort to put her learning into practice, and never grew weary of experimenting with the new forms and variations of the wind-and-moon game. The prim "little saint" grew to be a past mistress at the arts of love. Determined to keep her vernal fires supplied with fuel, the Before Midnight Scholar ran untiringly from bookshop to bookshop, buying more books of the same kind, such as the *Hsiu-t'a yeh-shih*, "The Fantastic Tale of the Silk-Embroidered Pillows," or the *Ju-yi-ch'ün chuan*, "The Tale of the Perfect Gallant," or the *Ch'i p'o-tzu chuan*, "The Tale of the Love-Maddened Women," and so on. In all he bought some twenty such books and piled them up on his desk.

Together they devoured each of the new acquisitions and then put it away in the bookcase to make place for new reading matter. Both of them were so insatiable in their thirst for discovery that three hundred and sixty pictures of vernal positions could not have stilled their appetite. They were like the lovers we encounter in novels: an orchestra of lutes and guitars, a whole concert of bells and drums would not have sufficed to express the harmony and happiness of their hearts.

So far all was for the best between them. And yet something was amiss; something that injected a discordant note into the harmony of their young marriage.

The relations between father-in-law and son-in-law left much to be desired. As the reader already knows, Dr Iron Door was a crotchety, old-fashioned gentleman, an eccentric if ever there was one. He looked back fondly on the good old times, cherished the honesty and simplicity of our forebears, and abhorred the empty affectations of the profane crowd. Licentious talk was strictly taboo in his presence. What he liked best was earnest discussion on themes drawn from the teachings of Confucius.

The very first evening after the Before Midnight Scholar came to live under his roof, Dr Iron Door looked askance at his fashionable clothing and his smooth, ingratiating ways which the old man judged to be quite superficial. From the very first moment, he took a dislike to this smooth, excessively handsome young man.

"Plenty of fine leaves," he grumbled in secret, "but no fruit, no solid kernel; from his kind my daughter will get little support in her old age and affliction. However," he continued with a sigh of resignation, "the forms of this marriage have been observed; he has punctiliously provided his betrothal and wedding presents, and we have draped our house in the traditional red; the mistake has been made and cannot be unmade. Let us wait until the wedding is over; then I will take him under my strict paternal discipline and teach him to be an honest and in every respect scrupulous man." Such was his plan.

And he put it into execution. From morning to night he brooked no misconduct. The least mistake, whether of commission or omission, brought the young man a sound paternal scolding. Even the slightest incorrectness in walking, standing, sitting, or reclining called forth severe criticism and long-drawn-out commentaries.

But as the only son and heir of parents who had died while he was still a boy, our Before Midnight Scholar had long been accustomed to a good deal of independence. He could hardly have put up for long with all this tedious discipline and pedantic backbiting.

Several times he was on the point of giving his father-in-law a piece of his mind, of telling him in no uncertain terms that he had had enough of his schoolmasterly ways. But then he thought of Noble Scent. A serious dispute with the old gentleman might upset her and introduce an unwelcome dissonance into the hitherto so admirable harmony of their conjugal lyres. Accordingly he controlled himself and swallowed his indignation. But when there seemed to be no end to his swallowing, the effort became too much for him and one day, after long deliberation, his mind was made up.

"From the very first," he said to himself, "it was his daughter I was interested in. But because he was so attached to her and the thought of her leaving home was so distasteful to him, I did him a favor and moved in with him. His only thanks was to subject me to the crushing weight of his *T'ai-shan* authority, to tyrannize me in every way he could. By what right? What entitles a worm-eaten old pedant and doctrinaire like him to lord it over me? Do I have to stand for it? He should be grateful to me for putting up with his nonsense and not telling him what I think of his antiquated ways. But instead of that, he goes on scolding and bickering and trying to make me over in his image. Let him practice his pedagogic arts on someone else, not on a dashing young genius like me. And besides, who says that his daughter is the only pebble on the beach? I was planning all along to go out into the world sooner or later, to 'steal perfumes' and 'fish for pearls' and do some writing on the side. Who says that I have to be chained to a single woman all my life?

"I'm good and sick of being nagged at all day, of being taken to task every time I say a word. Well, it's a good thing I haven't stirred up any scandals outside the house; why, the old tyrant would be quite capable of condemning me to death. What is to be done in such a situation? Would an open quarrel help? Nonsense, it wouldn't change him a bit. Should I be patient and keep swallowing my grievances? No, enough is enough. There is only one possibility: to go away and leave Noble Scent to his care. I shall simply tell him that I must withdraw somewhere to continue my studies undisturbed and prepare for the next examination. That sounds innocent enough, the idea will surely appeal to him. If in the course of my travels chance should favor me and cause another beauty, a love predestined me from another existence, to cross my path, so much the better, Of course I shall not be able to marry her, but to pass a few pleasant hours with a 'cloud sprite on the magic mountain' will be very nice too."

His decision was made.

His original idea was to speak first with Noble Scent and then to take leave of her father. But then he told himself that she would no doubt be dismayed at the thought of foregoing her accustomed bedtime pleasures, that she would stir up a tearful scene and possibly talk him out of his plan. To forestall this eventuality, he modified his tactics and unbeknownst to her spoke first to his father-in-law:

"Your submissive son-in-law is beginning to feel rather lonely and cut off from the world in this remote mountain town. He feels the need of the inspiration that comes of association with eminent professors and with students of his own age. He is wasting his time and making no real progress in his studies. In view of all this he begs leave of his revered father-in-law to set out on a journey; he wishes to visit the big cities in the plains, to look around him and extend his horizons. His aim is to seek out a worthy citadel of cultural life, where he will meet inspired teachers and form valuable friendships among fellow students. There he will pitch his tent. Then when it comes time for the great autumn examinations, he aspires to betake himself to the provincial capital and show his mettle on the intellectual battlefield. He will do his best to carry off first or at least second place, so proving that he was worthy to be received into so honored a family.

"What is your treasured opinion? Are you inclined to grant your permission?"

The stern father-in-law was obviously surprised and pleased.

"At last a sensible word. In the six months since my esteemed son-in-law came to dwell beneath my roof, these are the first words worthy to strike my eardrums. I can only commend your wish to depart with a view to continuing your studies. Excellent, excellent! What possible objection could I have to your plan?"

The Before Midnight Scholar continued:

"You have given me your paternal consent, but there is still a difficulty: I am very much afraid that your *ling-ai*, your 'commanding darling,' will accuse me of heartlessness if I leave her now, so soon after our marriage. In my modest opinion, it might be best to put it to her as though the decision had originated with you, my estimable father-in-law, and not with me, your insignificant son-in-law. Then she is unlikely to create difficulties, and I shall be able to go my way with a clear conscience."

"Very true! I am entirely of your opinion," said Dr Iron Door. Soon afterward, within hearing of his daughter, he suggested to his son-in-law that it was high time for him to bestir himself into the world and prepare to win a meritorious place in the second state examination. At first the Before Midnight Scholar showed little enthusiasm for the idea; now the old man adopted a tone of severity and repeated his suggestion in the form of a command, to which his son-in-law could only incline.

Poor Noble Scent was at the very height of her newly discovered conjugal transports. When she heard of the impending departure and separation, she felt like a baby torn suddenly from its mother's breast. At first she was quite inconsolable. But at length, since it was her father's will, she inclined like a good, obedient daughter. As compensation, to be sure, she demanded, during the last days and nights, as much advance payment as was humanly possible, on the love debts that would accrue during his absence. He for his part was well aware of the lonely nights ahead of him on his long journey, and did his very best to fortify himself against the impending period of continence. Thus the couple's last nights built up to a veritable orgy; the young people clung together like glue and lacquer, drinking their fill of the delights which are ordinarily kept secret and of which lovers are reluctant to speak in the presence of outsiders. Then at last the time had come. After taking leave of his father-in-law and wife, the Before Midnight Scholar set out, accompanied by his two personal servants.

My esteemed readers will learn in the next chapter of the extraordinary adventures he was to meet with on his way.

WATCHING

J. P. Kansas

I Brian

I'D ALWAYS WONDERED if my wife ever masturbated when she was alone. Since Lois worked at home, she had plenty of opportunity, but we had never discussed it.

I was almost certain she knew that I did. I subscribed to the most respectable of the so-called men's magazines. My collection of erotic videotapes, begun during my bachelor days, now residing on the top shelf in the den, was an open secret. And she sometimes made half-joking allusions to the practice of masturbation, when she wasn't in the mood for sex and declined my advances.

She played with herself sometimes when we made love, and I found that extremely exciting, but that was different, because I was there, because she knew that I was watching, because I was inside her as she did it.

But did she do it when she was alone? I had no idea.

That day at lunch I started to feel like I was coming down with something. Although by the time I got back from lunch, I felt all right again, I decided to go home early. It was a Friday in July and things were slow. I put a few things in my brief case and told my secretary that I was taking some work home.

Thinking it would be fun to surprise her, I unlocked the door and came into the apartment as quietly as I could. We're lucky enough to have one of those apartments that go on forever in a pre-War building facing Prospect Park. The room she uses as her office is separated from the rest of the apartment, in what was once the maid's quarters. When I went down the hall to her room, I found that she wasn't there. She hadn't mentioned that she was going out when I'd spoken to her just before lunch. Puzzled, I returned to the entrance foyer and saw that her keys were sitting on the side table, so I knew that she was home.

I realized that I was hearing the television, so I began to walk toward the den. I had only taken a step or two when I noticed that the voices seemed familiar. I stopped walking as I tried to place them. It took me a moment to recognize it as the soundtrack of one of the adult videotapes in my collection, and when I did I felt a sudden lurch in my stomach, of embarrassment and surprise and fear and anger and confusion and excitement – most of all excitement. I was very, very aroused.

The fact is, I was consumed with the desire to see what she was doing – to watch her watching that video without her knowing that I was watching her.

My heart pounding, I held my breath and looked down the hallway. From where I was standing, it appeared that the door to the den was open. The way the furniture in the room was arranged, if she was on the couch facing the television, I would be able to see her without her seeing me.

Ashamed of myself, but knowing I intended to ignore that feeling, I slipped out of my shoes and walked down the hall in my socks as quietly as I could.

I stopped just at the door to the den, as soon as I could see in. She was, as I had supposed, sitting on the couch with her back to me. I could see most of her body, but only the back and one side of her head. She would not be able to see me, even in her peripheral vision. She was wearing a loose skirt and a sleeveless blouse that buttoned up the front.

As I had thought, she was watching a videotape from my collection. The cardboard box I kept them in was on the floor next to the television. The cover of the one she was watching lay on the top of the box. She had selected one that had three or four relatively short episodes, unconnected by narrative or plot, all of one man and two women – as it happened, my favorite situation to watch. I looked at the screen, the performers were still dressed. I wasn't sure, but I thought that it was the first episode on the tape. They – and apparently she – had just begun.

I realized that I was holding my breath, and let it out as silently as I could. I gripped the doorframe with my left hand.

Lois was watching without moving. Her left hand held the remote control for the video player. Her right hand lay on the couch beside her.

On the television, the man and the two women – one blonde, one redhead – were standing in a bedroom, embracing and kissing. The redhead, in front of the man, had unbuttoned his shirt. The blonde, standing behind him, helped him take it off, as he helped the redhead off with her blouse, her large breasts tumbling out as she unfastened her brassiere. She rubbed her breasts against his muscular chest while, behind him, the blonde took off her blouse and pressed her breasts – much smaller than the redhead's but still very beautiful – against his back.

I ached with arousal and I longed to touch myself, but I did nothing. Lois still sat unmoving, apparently unaffected by what she was seeing.

The man was stepping out of his shoes as the redhead knelt in front of him. She unfastened his belt and loosened his pants. I thought I heard Lois sigh as the man's penis was briefly visible, just before it largely disappeared again into the redhead's mouth. Considering how long it was, it was amazing that she could accommodate it as well as she could. Behind the man, the blonde went onto her knees and licked the man's buttocks. There was a close-up of the woman's tongue running up and down the cleavage.

I heard a sigh that did not come from the television, and now, finally, I saw movement on the couch. Lois had brought her right hand under her skirt between her legs. Her left hand abandoned the remote control and was cupping her right breast through her blouse. Inside my underwear, my penis was agonizingly erect. I could not remember ever being so aroused. Still, I did not touch myself.

On the video, the man had reluctantly pulled the redhead to her feet, and was now himself kneeling in front of her. He and the blonde removed her skirt, under which she was wearing stockings and a garterbelt but no panties. Her pubic hair was trimmed into a neat line, only about an inch wide. The man and the blonde both licked her at the same time, their tongues meeting between the redhead's labia, which she held open with both hands.

Lois shifted position on the couch and stood up. She unfastened her skirt and let it drop onto the rug in front of the couch. She sat down again and put her fingers into her panties. The sight of my wife playing with herself as she watched the same erotic video I had so often enjoyed was unbearably exciting. The skin of my face felt hot and taut.

On the screen, the blonde had taken off her skirt, and now all three performers were completely naked. They climbed onto the bed and arranged themselves into one of the many familiar configurations of such a grouping: the man was on his back; facing toward his head, the blonde straddled his mouth, and the redhead crouched between his legs with his penis in her mouth.

Ordinarily, the activity on screen would have held all my interest, but now I was even more fascinated by what my wife was doing than by the activities on the video. Lois was unbuttoning her blouse. Although I'd seen her breasts countless times, I now waited with almost maniacal anticipation. With one hand, she unfastened the front clasp of her brassiere and pushed the cups aside. I sighed silently to see her milky breasts, the nipples puffy and dark. She pinched them, one at a time, and made them hard. I exhaled silently and squeezed the doorframe harder.

On the video the trio had rearranged themselves. Now the blonde had turned around and straddled the man in the opposite direction. Curled over him, she joined the redhead in licking and mouthing his penis.

Lifting her hips, Lois used both hands to slip her panties off. I caught a brief glimpse of her beautiful bottom before she sat down again. Now I could see her finger move up and down along one side of her clitoris, as she sometimes did while I was inside her.

I was paralyzed with arousal and indecision. I wanted to continue watching, and I was ashamed of my voyeurism. I wanted to reach for myself, timing my orgasm to coincide with hers, and I wanted to end the agony of desire and make love with her. And what would happen if she noticed my presence? Would she be angry? Embarrassed? Ashamed? Excited? Amused? What would happen, especially, if I announced my presence by reaching orgasm, as might happen now at any moment?

Of course, I could try to steal away as quietly as I had come, and then return to the apartment at my normal time. I glanced down at the crotch of my pants, comically distorted by my erection, and decided that that was not a sensible idea. I could, perhaps, retreat to another part of the apartment, wait until I heard her turn off the television and put everything away, and then pretend to arrive home.

I was kidding myself: I wasn't going anywhere. As to what would happen when she realized I'd been watching her, I'd take my chances.

Between her legs, her fingers were moving faster. She lifted her feet to the edge of the couch and let her knees fall apart. It looked like she had inserted her fingers into her vagina and was using her thumb on her clitoris. I had never seen her do anything like that, and my groin tightened, my testicles feeling charged and ready to burst.

On the screen, the performers had changed positions again. Now, the two women were side by side on the bed, both on their knees and shoulders. Awkwardly, they kissed and caressed each other as the man, behind them, moved back and forth, stroking his long penis a few times in the one before quickly moving to the other. The soundtrack was filled with women's sighs.

Lois was sighing along with them. I ducked back into the hallway as she changed position again, and then cautiously peeked in to see that she was now standing on her knees on the couch, her left hand reaching between her legs from behind, her right from in front, both moving frenziedly.

I could no longer resist, and almost without thought I took a step forward into the room. At that moment, the sighs and the groans from the television reached their peak. There was a close-up of the man withdrawing his penis and ejaculating, moving his penis back and forth so that his semen would fall on both women's buttocks. The two women, each with one hand in the other's labia, reached or pretended to reach their climaxes, too.

As I walked toward her, Lois' hands stopped for a moment, and then moved even more quickly, and her entire body shuddered powerfully. Her orgasm was a beautiful sight, familiar yet suddenly completely new, and more arousing than ever.

Suddenly I was coming, too, and I was sorry I wasn't inside her. I reached her just as the last spasm coursed through me. I took her in my arms as I felt the thick wetness spreading against my groin. I kissed her deeply, running my hands over her wonderful naked body.

If she was surprised or embarrassed, she didn't indicate it. Still kissing her, I struggled out of my pants. We lay down on the couch without speaking and I entered her, still hard, more aroused than ever, my fluids mixing with her fluids. We let the videotape continue to play, now on the next episode, as we made love.

II   Lois

For all the usual reasons that seem to come up after five years of marriage, Brian and I hadn't had sex in a few days, and after he'd left for work, I went back to bed and quickly made myself come. It left me feeling unsatisfied, and I was thinking about Brian all morning.

Brian called me just before lunch, as he usually did, and we had a brief, routine conversation. I wanted to ask him if he still loved me, but I didn't. Did he know that I made myself come when I was home alone? Did he wonder? Would it make him upset to know that I did, or would it excite him? I wished we could talk about things like that.

I called him in the early afternoon, telling myself I wanted his opinion about some work that I was doing, but really just because I wanted to hear his voice again. I was surprised when his secretary told me that he'd just left for home. He hadn't said anything about leaving early when I'd spoken to him in the morning. I asked his secretary if he was feeling sick, and she told me he'd seemed fine. I wondered if he was having an affair.

I doubted it, but the idea had made me angry and afraid and excited at the same time. I'd really done no work at all in the hour since I'd hung up the phone. I wanted to make myself come again. I thought about Brian discovering me in the middle of making myself come, and the thought only made me hotter.

If he'd really left from home when he'd told his secretary he was leaving, he'd be home at any minute. If not – if not, it didn't matter.

I wandered through our ridiculously large apartment, on my way back to our bedroom.

Of course, I knew Brian jerked off regularly. Ninety per cent of men admit it, another nine per cent lie about it, and there's something wrong with the other one per cent. Brian was a reluctant member of the ninety per cent. Whenever I teased him about it, he seemed embarrassed. Sometimes when I walked in on him in the bathroom without knocking, I found him suddenly careful to keep the towel around his waist, which he normally never was. He subscribed to a high-class girlie magazine, although he claimed to be interested in the articles. But he had never gotten rid of the collection of porno videos he'd accumulated before I met him, and from time to time I'd notice that the carton he kept them in had changed position on the shelf in the closet in the den. Sometimes I'd wake up in the middle of the night to find his side of the bed empty and the sound of the television coming from the den. I might have assumed that he was just watching late-night TV or a real movie, but you don't watch a real movie going back and forth between fast forward and normal speed.

I had reached the doorway to the den. I suddenly realized that I wanted to let him find me watching one of his porno tapes – that is, if he was really coming home. If he was off having an affair, then the hell with him. I'd just watch without him.

As I went to the closet, I felt frightened and excited. It reminded me of once when I was a child and I entered a toystore to shoplift a doll my mother wouldn't get for me. I'd been too afraid to do it, and I rushed out to the street sure that everyone in the store knew what I'd been planning to do.

Now I had the courage to carry my plans through, at least as far as taking the cardboard carton down from the shelf and opening it up. There seemed to be a lot more tapes than when I'd first seen it, two years before we got married. Was I misremembering? I picked up the one on top and looked for the copyright notice. The tape was from the previous year: he'd gotten it recently. *So he's still buying these things*, I thought, unsure what to feel. At least, I supposed, it was better than him having an affair. As if, I contradicted myself, he couldn't do both.

I looked at the pictures on the box. There were two pictures each of four different threesomes, each consisting of a man and two women. Almost every man's favorite fantasy, for reasons I've never really understood, and apparently Brian was no exception.

The setting was the same in each of the pictures: a bedroom. The decor was modern American motel.

The men all looked more or less alike: in their late twenties or early thirties; reasonably slim and fit; not particularly handsome; and endowed with a large cock. I wondered why the men in porno videos always had enormous cocks. I'd thought men were always worried about the size of their cocks. Wouldn't the sight of such large ones make them worry more? I realized that the men watching were supposed to identify with the performers in the videos, rather than compare themselves with them, but it seemed unlikely. Whenever I saw a beautiful woman in a movie, it sure didn't make *me* feel more beautiful. How, I wondered, did Brian feel about seeing such large cocks? And how would he feel if he saw me making myself come as I watched these men with cocks so much larger than his own?

The women were a lot more varied: the first threesome included a redhead with enormous breasts and a blonde with breasts I considered normal – no larger than my own; the second threesome, two brunettes, one large-breasted, one small-breasted; the third, two blondes, one large-breasted, one with average breasts, both without hair on their pussies; and the fourth, a blonde and a brunette, both large-breasted.

The pictures showed the threesomes having sex, and they were completely explicit. I had never found pictures like that exciting. I'd rather look at a photograph of a beautifully prepared meal than a close-up of someone's open mouth while they're chewing. Like most women, I suppose, I don't usually find pictures of cocks and pussies very exciting. But the thought that Brian watched these things made the pictures enticing.

Still feeling somewhat like the child who'd resolved to shoplift a doll, I turned on the TV and the VCR and put the cassette in the machine. Taking the VCR remote control with me, I sat down on the couch and started the tape rolling.

After I fast-forwarded through the credits, the first episode began. It starred the threesome featuring the redhead and the blonde.

As the sequence began, the three of them were still dressed, and I used the remote control to pause the tape. I felt a little ridiculous. Why did I want to make myself come watching Brian's porno video? What if he *did* walk in on me while I was doing it? I sat and wondered whether I really wanted to go through with this, or whether I should just put everything away and wait to see if Brian was coming home or not.

I stared at the threesome on the screen, caught in the middle of an uncomfortable-looking embrace, and could not decide what to do.

Just then, I heard a faint sound from the front of the apartment. It was Brian unlocking the door. I sighed in relief, realizing that my fears of his having an affair had been ridiculous.

He closed the door. It seemed he was being unusually quiet, as if he was trying to surprise me. I smiled to myself. One way or another, *he* was the one who was going to be surprised.

The situation I'd put myself in was even more ridiculous. I had no time to put everything away. I listened to Brian's footsteps grow softer as he seemed to walk down the hall to my office, and then grow louder again as, I guessed, he returned to the front hall. Not finding me in my office, he'd explore the rest of the apartment. Without question, he'd find me within a few seconds.

I looked at the screen again. The performers were still frozen, and so was I.

But I'd be damned if I'd be caught in the middle of putting the tapes away – it would look like I'd just *finished* watching, rather than just *begun*, and if I was to be found guilty of the crime, so to speak – and what else would he possibly think? – I might as well enjoy the fruit of it.

So I pressed the play button. The performers continued their insipid conversation. It seemed that they were improvising the dialogue. They were terrible actors, but I wasn't paying too much attention to them because I was trying to figure out what Brian was doing.

His footsteps grew a little louder. He seemed to have reached the main hallway, which leads toward the bedroom and the room we use as our den. His footsteps stopped, and then, after a moment, resumed, but much more quietly. *He had taken off his shoes! He really was trying to sneak up on me*!

I felt indignant, although this situation was what had made me so hot to imagine. I still didn't know what to do. I had the dangerous sense that I was no longer in control. I was watching myself as if watching someone else, and I had no idea what I would do next.

The tape played on. The three performers had, mercifully, stopped talking, and bad music was playing as they kissed and fondled each other with all their clothes still on.

Keeping as still as I could, I listened to Brian sneak up the hall in his stockinged feet. It made me furious, and it made me hot.

I could no longer hear any movement from the hall. In the television screen, I could see a small reflection of part of the doorway. I could only see a little of one leg. I couldn't see his face, but I knew that he was watching me. He wasn't trying to subtly let me know he was there, and he wasn't boldly walking into the room, either. He wanted to watch me. He wanted to watch me watch his porno tape. He wanted to see what would happen. He wanted to watch me make myself come.

In an instant, the entire scene unfolded in my mind. I saw myself already naked on the couch, using both hands on my pussy, watching the porno, as Brian stood in the doorway, his pants at his knees, his fist around his hard cock. Imagining all that, I think I was unable to suppress a sigh.

If that's what he wants, I thought, *that's what he'll get*. But I was still frozen, unable to move.

I had always thought of making myself come as something very private and special, my little secret. When, at the age of thirteen, playing in the bathtub with one of the shower sprayers on the end of a flexible hose, I had first discovered how to do it, I had actually thought I had invented it, and that I was the only one in the entire world who did it. When I learned that it was completely normal, at first I just didn't believe it, and then I was disappointed. I still liked to pretend I was a young teenager discovering how to do it for the first time. I liked to tease myself, as if I didn't know exactly how to make myself come.

Sometimes when I needed the extra stimulation, I'd touch myself a little while Brian and I were having sex, but I didn't like to do that – I was afraid he'd feel that he wasn't adequate to satisfy me. And somehow that didn't count – it didn't have anything to do with the private act I kept for myself.

Now I wanted to show that act to him, but hot as I was, I was still doing nothing. Why couldn't I take even the first step? What was I afraid of?

The performers in the video were making a lot more progress than I was. I had never seen anything like what was happening on the screen. Both women were naked to the waist. The redhead, her large breasts waving to and fro, knelt in front of the man and took his cock out of his pants. It looked even larger on the television than in the pictures on the box. Incredibly, the redhead put most of it in her mouth. Even more incredibly, rather than gagging and choking, she seemed to be enjoying it.

The blonde was kneeling behind the man and kissing and licking his butt. In case anyone might have missed the point, the camera cut to a close shot of the woman's tongue moving up and down between his cheeks.

Where do they come up with these ideas? I asked myself. In seven years with Brian, I had never thought of doing something like that – and I had never gotten the idea that he was hoping I would. But maybe he was. Maybe he was secretly longing for me to stick my tongue up his butt. I thought I should be outraged at the very idea, but I wasn't. In fact, I couldn't believe how hot I was.

Almost without being aware of it, I reached under my skirt. My panties, soaking wet, had ridden up into my pussy, and they were tickling me. *I just need*, I told myself, *to adjust them.*

But as soon as my hand was at my pussy, I realized I was fooling myself. *I'm really going to go through with this*, I admitted to myself with a sigh. In fact, I was afraid it would all be over too quickly: I was already ready to come. Through my panties, my pussy felt hot and soft and full, like your eyes just before you start to cry. My breasts ached, and with my other hand I began to touch them.

I was so hot that I didn't know what I wanted. I wanted to close my eyes and I wanted to keep watching the porno tape. I wanted to make myself come as fast as I could, and I wanted to make it last forever. I wanted Brian to come into the room and make love to me, and I wanted him to stand there and watch me as I drove him completely crazy.

Was Brian as hot as I was? How could he just stand there? I wanted to turn and look at him, but I just kept staring at the television, where the man and the blonde were both kneeling in front of the redhead and licking her pussy.

Was Brian looking at the television, or looking at me? The thought that he might be watching the tape instead of me got me angry again. *I'll give him something to watch*! I thought.

Careful not to look in Brian's direction, I stood up and unfastened my skirt. It dropped to the floor, and I sat down again. Imagining Brian's face as he watched me, I slipped my fingers under the elastic of my panties and onto my pussy. It was all I could do not to come.

In the porno tape, the threesome were busy arranging and rearranging themselves, like skaters going through their required figures. I couldn't believe all the positions they found. I couldn't believe that people actually allowed themselves to be filmed doing what they were doing. The screen was filled with mouths and hands and breasts and pussies and cocks and butts.

I couldn't believe how hot it was making me. I got out of my top and opened my bra. It felt good finally to have my hands on my bare breasts. *Watch this*! I thought, and pinched the nipples, rolling them between my thumb and let my forefinger, as I'd just seen the redhead do on the tape. Each time I did it, a jolt of electricity ran down my body into my pussy.

Suddenly I didn't care that much about what Brian was seeing or feeling or doing. I just knew that I had to come. I stood up and took off my panties. My juices were all over my pussy lips. I couldn't believe how wet I was. I sat down again and rubbed myself in just the right place.

Usually, I didn't put my fingers inside myself. But on the screen, the two women were up on their knees, kissing each other and playing with each other. Behind them, the man was taking turns, going back and forth between them. There were close-ups of his big cock going from one pussy to the other. It made me feel empty inside, and I brought my feet up and let my legs fall apart and stuck two fingers inside and put my thumb on my clit.

It felt great, and I was almost there, but I wanted to feel it from behind, like the women. I got up onto my knees and reached behind myself and used both hands at once.

On the tape, everybody was coming. The man pulled out of the redhead and his cock began to spurt. He used his hand to make his come land all over the women's butts. The women were groaning and shaking and heaving.

Just at that moment, I heard a footstep, and suddenly I was

filled with embarrassment, as if it was my mother who'd caught me, rather than my husband. Ridiculously, my hands stopped moving, as if I could deny what I was doing.

But it was too late. I was already starting to come. If I didn't keep stroking myself right then, it would be a fizzle instead of an explosion, but I would still come. After all that, I had to save it. I moved both hands as quickly as I could. I came so hard I think I passed out for a moment. The next thing I knew, Brian had his arms around me, kissing me, running his hands over me. I couldn't remember the last time he'd been so passionate. He lay me down on the couch, and he got out of his clothes like a magician. I glanced down at his cock and saw the semen smeared all over its head: he'd come in his pants, just from watching me. The thought made me hot all over again. And he was already hard again, or he'd never gotten soft. Either way, he entered me easily. He felt huge, as big as the man in the video. We didn't even bother to turn off the porno tape.

HER FIRST BRA

(excerpt from *A Body Chemical*)

Cris Mazza

1981

There was one more card from Millard in November, a Thanksgiving card that said *hope to see you again . . . someday . . . somewhere*. Dale picked it up from the floor under the kitchen card table and said, "Who's this from, your mother?"

"Yuckity yuk." Leala was slicing hotdogs to go into canned beans. Dale ate lunch at about 10 a.m. when he got home from delivering tortillas to restaurants.

"Well, who is it?"

"It's a photographer I did a session for. I guess he liked me. Whose mother should we visit for Thanksgiving?"

"A *session*? What's that mean? You're working as a model? Since when?"

"About six months."

"Why didn't you tell me?"

"I thought I did." She put a plate of tepid franks-n-beans in front of him then started sorting through the mail, putting the utility and credit card bills in one pile for Dale to pay from his checking account, the rent and food came from hers. She had a session that afternoon. The guy on the phone yesterday asked how old she was and she'd answered *I'm very bold, why'd you ask?* then the guy digressed to something else, the color of her hair and eyes, how tall she was, her measurements. She'd changed her ad again. It said, *young, versatile female model for private photo sessions with imaginative photographers, you won't believe what your camera can do.*

"How much have you made?" Dale asked.

"Not much. The rent went up, remember?"

"Well let's make out a budget or something, maybe we don't have to sell anything to buy grass. Or Christmas presents for that matter."

"Sessions aren't predictable, Dale. We can't *budget* for them. I thought you were *off* grass, anyway."

"Well they use it for cancer patients, don't they? Maybe it'll help."

"Help *what*? God, what a hypochondriac, it really gets old."

"I'm getting this shortness of breath all the fucking time, dammit, I'm hot then cold, then I start sweating my fucking ass off. What would *you* call it?"

"Maybe it's menopause."

"Har-de-fucking-har." He put three huge spoonfuls into his mouth in rapid succession before chewing and swallowing. "So you wanna go away for Christmas vacation this year?"

"No, not now."

"Then when?"

She picked up his empty plate and put it with the dirty pan beside the sink. "Dale, I tried to tell you once what'll probably happen, what I'm saving for, but you wouldn't believe me. That's fine, you can pretend. Sure, everything's *normal*, right?" She boosted herself to the counter and swung her feet into the sink to shave her legs. "Luckily I don't even think you'll miss me."

The photographer handed her two fifties before she came through the door. The session was at his house – he had his living room furniture pushed to one side and a corner converted into a set resembling a dressing room in a fancy department store. A three-sided mirror and stool, clothes with tags draped over accordion partitions, big umbrella lamps preventing anything from showing a shadow anywhere.

"Okay, listen to this," the guy said. He had long hair parted in the middle, the kind that either looks dirty or if it's clean, is so fine it's like baby hair that was never cut. He also had one of those halfway mustaches that usually only sixteen-year-old boys can grow, more baby hair. "Okay, listen," he repeated, "it's like, you're shopping, it's a big day because . . . you've come to the store without your mother –"

"My *mother*?"

"Yeah, listen, you've come shopping, you took a bus or rode your bike, but you came to this upscale store where you get one of those personal shoppers. You see, you're here to get your first . . . training bra." Suddenly he ducked his head and looked through a camera on a tripod. She wasn't even on the set yet.

"Does anyone even *use* training bras anymore?"

"Sure they do, and listen, you're all excited, this is a big day for you, milestone, know what I mean? Today you become a woman . . . and all that." He stood up but continued to look at the set, not at Leala.

"And I suppose my dressing room has a hidden camera or two-way mirror. And then what, my personal shopper is a man?"

"Maybe," he said slowly. "We'll see. The important thing is, this is such a big day for a girl. It makes her feel like anything can happen. Um, hang your old clothes on the hook there, like you would in a dressing room. And here you go, try these on." He pulled a plastic Sears shopping bag from behind one of the partitions.

"I doubt Sears has personal shoppers," she said, looking inside. There were three or four practically cupless bras and matching underwear, one set white with purple flowers, one baby blue, one with pink polkadots, and one set basic white with lace. The bras were just stretchy material with elastic straps and hook in back.

"You can have them when we're finished," he said. "Do you have any that nice?"

"No I can't say that I have any like these. In fact, I don't have a bra."

"You don't?" His face and sad brown eyes and repulsive mustache seemed to leap at her, but he hadn't moved closer, just was looking at her. "Oh, good, that's great. Perfect. Like . . . this's *real*, isn't it? Your first bra."

"Yeah, whatever. Where should I change?"

"Well . . . the dressing room, of course."

She looked back at him for a moment while he touched his limp hair then touched his mustache then put three fingers over his lips and dropped his eyes.

"Of course, silly me."

He dragged another stool over so he was sitting behind the

camera. After her jeans and t-shirt were hung on the hook and her socks stuffed into her shoes (he said leave them under the stool, and let one sock come trailing out of the shoe a little), she glanced at the camera while putting on the flowered bra and underwear with her back to him, but of course she showed in the mirror, tits and trimmed bush. "Your first bra," he murmured, the camera clicking, zipping to the next frame and clicking again. "How does it feel?"

She turned to hide a laugh as a small burp. The bra actually fit her but the underwear was not bikini style. She could see in the mirror that the high-waisted underwear made her tits look even smaller, the bra like an elastic headband put around her chest.

"Oh god," he moaned, "god-in-heaven." The camera clicking and clicking. Her adrenal gland released, the chemical shot through, leaving behind a vibrating hot jello-y place in her middle. She turned slowly back and forth in front of the mirror, stretching to check her ass over each shoulder which also stretched the bra.

"*Oops!*" One tit popped out when the bra rode up. "Where's my personal shopper, I need to know if this one fits."

The guy was huddled on his stool, his face almost to his lap, no longer clicking, sort of whimpering.

"Come on, please, mister? It's my big day, help me pick one that fits."

He slid off the stool onto his knees and shuffled towards her. His head came up to her stomach. His eyes were murky and glistening, sweat on his upper lip had dampened the disgusting little mustache. He held her around her waist with one hand, pulling the flowered underwear tight against his chest, bending her knees slightly and throwing her off balance so she had to hold onto his shoulders and lean backwards slightly. With two fingers he eased the bra back over her exposed tit.

"There, it fits like that," he breathed.

"Are you sure?"

He moved his hands slowly up her body until he was holding her around the ribcage, a thumb on each nipple. He moved the thumbs back and forth, hardening the nipples under the stretchy purple-flowered material. His face tilted up. His two watery eyes right behind each thumb. "Yes, this is how it goes. Like this. Like this."

"I know sixteen is a little too late for my first bra, but my mother said I wasn't old enough," she said, making her voice airy and higher. The flowered underwear were wet between her legs.

She tried to grind her twat against his chest a little but the zingers of adrenalin were zapping her almost continuously and she was in danger of falling over backwards.

"No," he whispered, "sixteen isn't too old. Not too old at all. You had to be ready. You knew when you were ready."

"I'm ready."

"Today you were ready. Today was the day. Oh, but if only your little titties wouldn't grow any more," he sobbed, "so impatient for this day, but now they'll be ruined." He slid his hands to her back and pulled her stomach against his face, blubbering against her skin below the bra.

"Hey, mister," she breathed softly. "Today's not over yet." She touched a bald spot on his crown with a single finger. "Remember, today's my big day. And there's still a half hour of it left."

He lurched to his feet with her in his arms. "Like a baby," he smiled through his tears down into her face. He bent and kissed her gently, touching her lips with the awful mustache, while carrying her out of the set and down a hall. The room they went into was dim, but after placing her on the bed, he turned on the night stand lamp and she could see the white lace canopy, the matching white lace lampshade and bedspread and curtains, antique-looking dolls in white or peach or baby-blue satin dresses lined up on a shelf, plus little troll dolls and glass princesses, horses and china puppies, a brush and comb set on the dresser, a life-sized white teddy bear sitting in a corner.

"This isn't *your* room is it?" Leala asked, propping herself up on her elbows. He was kneeling again, beside the bed.

"No . . . it's yours."

"Huh? *Oh* . . ..," she lay back slowly. "It's the room my mother doesn't know I left to go buy my first bra, right?"

"That's right." He took off his shirt. He was as skinny as Dale but not a single hair on him, except his armpits. "Just touch them against mine while they're still little, while it's still the big day." He got on top of her, still wearing baggy green army-surplus pants. She couldn't feel any hard-on, but his hips were far below hers, on the mattress between her knees, so she wouldn't've anyway. He pressed his gaunt chest against hers, his head down against her neck, then without raising his body eased the bra up so her bare breasts were against his chest. He rocked slightly so their nipples brushed back and forth. And he started to tremble.

She could feel his heart like a fist on a windowpane, banging to get out. His swaying continued for five or ten minutes.

Leala's adrenalin buzz was long gone. She checked her watch by raising one arm in the air behind his shoulders.

Then he was easing the bra back over her, with his chest still pressed to hers. "Okay," he whispered in her ear. "I didn't hurt you." He backed up off her and stood beside the bed. "I'll leave you in your pretty room, with your bears and dolls." He clicked off the light and retreated toward the door.

"Hey!" Leala sat up. "I *would* like a doll like one of them. Where could I get one?"

"A doll shop." He was a shadowy form by the door, putting his shirt on.

"How much would it cost for me to get one?"

"Some of them are as much as $200."

"I could just get a $50 one, though, couldn't I?"

He didn't answer, buttoning his shirt, then he looked up, but she couldn't really see his eyes. It was too dark.

"A girl should have a doll like that before she gets too old . . . don't you think?"

He slowly reached for the door knob. "Too old?"

"Yeah, like . . . before she's . . . say, *eighteen* . . . don't you think?"

He opened the door and a crack of light lay on the floor between him and the bed. "I . . . guess so." Then he went out and closed the door.

She lay back on the bed with a suddenly thudding pulse, but not the same thing as the earlier neon lightning bolt of adrenalin. The wave of almost nauseous weakness passed, and she thought about the symptoms Dale described, then she got off the bed. Her clothes were folded on the sofa in the living room with exactly $100 in cash placed on top, a fifty, two twenties, a five and five ones. Maybe he'd forgotten about the two fifties he'd already given her at the start of the session.

December was a slow time for both student photographers and sickos. Leala got her hair cut into a pixie style and used some of her savings for white jeans, a white jean jacket, and several new tank tops. She had her ears pierced and wore just the two pearl studs which came with the piercing. She let Dale pay for the piercing and call it her Christmas present, but he also bought her a corduroy skirt and jacket set that was one size too big, so she exchanged it for a denim mini and peasant-style top with sequins, both from the girls department. Dale said she looked like a baby pop star in *Teen Beat* magazine.

"That'll work," she answered. "Maybe I'll get some cheap jewelry from a teeny-bopper accessory store."

"Whadda you mean?"

"Oh . . . I don't know . . . If I want to start a real modeling career, I hafta have an angle, you know? My own shtick."

"You can't start a real modeling career just because you get a few new clothes and *say* you want to be a model."

"You don't know anything about it, Dale. I've had some gigs. How many gigs have *you* had lately?"

Dale stared fixedly at the TV screen. It wasn't even on. He still had hair down to his collar, except where he didn't have hair at all, and it looked wet even when it wasn't. The flattened cushions in the chair that had come with the furnished apartment had stains now where his head rested. Sometimes he still tapped a drumstick on the coffee table while he sat there. It seemed the drumstick appeared and disappeared by magic, but she'd found it once, by accident, stashed under the seat cushion.

Leala loaded some celery sticks with peanut butter, wrapped them in a paper towel and placed them on Dale's lap on her way to the sofa. "Listen, Dale, this is really important."

"What, that I'm a failure?"

"No, but *we* are. You know? It's only been, what, three and a half years. We could just call it one of those things. We're both young, we could . . . you know, still be like our ages."

"Instead of old married farts?"

"Speak for yourself, but I guess that's the general idea."

The drumstick appeared, but he didn't start tapping. He held it up and placed the tip against his lips like a long finger saying *Shhhh.* "No."

"No? That's it, just *no*?"

He took a bite of celery then replaced the tip of the drumstick against his mouth while he chewed. It sounded like a horse chewing corn. It sounded kind of nice.

"Dale, it wouldn't be like we hate each other's guts and go to court to fight over the car and stereo. And it doesn't have to be *now*, we could do it when we're both ready, when we can both afford it, you know?"

"We can barely afford this shit *together*."

"I know, but I'm working on a plan."

"You mean becoming a famous cover girl by next week?"

"There's lots of types of modelling, Dale, and I may've found my niche, and I can even capitalize on it, expand the potential."

"Now you sound like a yuppie businessman." He swallowed what looked like a hard lump.

"I'm just saying I've discovered a way to make what I do more lucrative, and when I make enough of a stash, how about I share it with you and we, you know, go our separate ways?"

"What if I want to stay with you?"

He was just sitting there looking down into his lap like an imbecile who watches himself pee, holding a celery stick with globs of peanut butter in one hand and the drumstick in the other.

Leala stayed on the sofa for only a few seconds longer, then went into the bathroom, shook her short hair and watched it all fall into place. For the first time in her life she was glad for the strip of freckles across her nose. She wondered how much colored contact lenses would cost, because some pure green eyes would really complete the package.

Three more jobs popped up right away in January. The first just wanted her feet – feet walking, feet splashing puddles, feet showing over the side of a pick-up truck, feet on gas pedals, feet kicking a ball, feet in high heels. He said he'd done sessions with guys and older people and little kids, and some animals. When he took her out for lunch after the session, she touched his leg with her bare toes under the table, but nothing happened, so the *Feet!* exhibit he said he was working on must've been real. The second wanted her to hang laundry on a line – just white sheets and towels – on a very windy day, wearing a light cotton dress and bare feet, but the photographer was a woman and, as a matter of fact, almost didn't want Leala at all when she saw her short hair. The third worked out a little better because he said from the start he wanted a nude, but he also made her sign a form promising she was over eighteen. Still, he liked her newly shaved pussy and fucked her afterwards, but only gave her $20 for cab fare when she asked, although she was parked around the corner from his house.

EMILIA COMES IN MY DREAMS

Jindrich Styrsky

Translated by Iris Irwin

EMILIA IS FADING from my days, my evenings and my dreams. Even her white dress has darkened in my memory. I no longer blush as I recall the mysterious marks of teeth I glimpsed one night below her little belly. The last traces of dissimulation impeding the emotion I was ready to feel have disappeared. That troupe of girls is lost forever, smiling uncertainly and with indifference as they remember how their hearts were torn by passion and by half-treacherous humility. Even her face has been exorcised at last, the face I modelled in snow as a child, the face of a woman whose compliant cunt had consumed her utterly.

I think of Emilia as a bronze statue. Marble bodies, too, are not bothered by fleas. Her heart-shaped upper lip recalls an old-world coronation; the lower lip demanding to be sucked arouses visions of harlotry. I was moving slowly beneath her, my head in the hem of her skirt. I had a close-up view of the hairs on her calves, flattened in all directions under her lace stockings, and I tried to imagine what kind of a comb would be needed to smooth them back into place. I fell in love with the fragrance of her crotch, a wash-house smell mingled with that of a nest of mice, a pine-needle lying forgotten in a bed of lilies-of-the-valley.

I began to suffer from optical illusions; when I looked at Clara her body merged into the outline of Emilia's with the tiny heel. When Emilia felt like sinning, her cunt gave off the aroma of spice in a hayrick. Clara's fragrance was herbal. My hands are wandering under her skirt, touching the top of a stocking, suspender knobs, her inner thigh – hot, damp and beguiling. Emilia brings me a cup of tea, wearing blue mules. I can never again be completely happy, tormented as I am by women's sighs, by their eyes rolling in the convulsions of orgasm.

Emilia never tried to penetrate the world of my poetry. She looked at my garden from over the fence, so that everyday fruit and ordinary berries seemed the awesome apples of some pre-historic paradise, while I moved foolishly along the paths, like a half-wit, like a useless dog with its nose in the grass tracking down death and fleeing its own destiny. I was crazy, seeking to find again that moment when shadows fell across a paved square somewhere in the south. Leaning on the fence, Emilia sped on through life. I can see her so clearly: getting up in the morning with her long hair loose, going to the lavatory to piss, sometimes to shit, and then washing with tar soap. Her crotch made fragrant, she hurried to mingle with the living, to rid herself of the feeling that she was at a fork in the road.

Emilia's smile was a wonderful thing to watch. Her mouth seemed a dried-out hollow, but as you drew near to this upper lode of pleasure you could hear something trembling down inside her, and as she parted her lips for you, a knob of red flesh burst from between her teeth. Age fondles time lovingly. Morality is only safe at home in the arms of abandonment. Her eyes that never closed at the height of her pleasure would take on a gleam of heavenly delight, and looked ashamed of what her lips were doing.

In the corners where I seek my lost youth I come upon golden curls carefully laid away. Life is one long waste of time. Every day death nibbles away at what we call life, and life constantly consumes our longing for trivialities. The idea of the kiss dies before ever the lips meet, and every portrait pales before we can look at it. In the end worms will eat through this woman's heart, too, and grin in her entrails. Who could swear, then, that you had ever existed? I saw you with a lovely naked girl of astonishing whiteness. She lifted her hands and the palms were black with soot. She pressed one hand between your breasts and placed the other over my eyes so that I was looking at you as through torn lace. You were naked under an unbuttoned coat. That single moment revealed your life to me in its entirety: you were a plant, swelling and budding. Two stems rising from the ground grew together and from that juncture you began to wilt, but your body was already taking shape, with a belly, two breasts and a head where two entrancing pink weals swelled up. At that moment, though, the lower part of your body began to wither, and collapsed. And I grovelled before you, grunting with love such as I had never known. I do not know whose shadow it was. I called it Emilia. We are bound together for ever, irrevocably, but we are back to back.

This woman is my coffin, and as she walks I am hidden in her image. And so as I curse her I damn myself and yet love her, falling asleep with a cast of her hand on my cock.

On the first of May you'll go to the cemetery and there in Section Ten you will find a woman sitting on a gravestone. She will be waiting for you, to tell your fortune from the cards. You will leave her and look for explanations on the walls of boarding establishments for young ladies, but the girls' faces in the windows will turn into budding buttocks and tulip arses, and will quiver as a lorry drives past. You will be crazed with fear they're going to fall down into the street, fear that is close to the pleasure you felt at your first boyish erection and close to the terror you felt when your sister taught you to masturbate with a hand of alabaster.

Who do you think can console you now? Emilia is fragmented, torn scraps of her likeness have been borne away by the wind to places beyond your knowledge, and that is why you cannot call on her to be the medium of your calming, and anyway you have long ago learned not to mourn moments of farewell.

The sky slumbers and somewhere behind the bushes a woman moulded of raw flesh is waiting for you. Will you feed her on ice?

Clara always sat on the couch, wearing little, and expecting to be undressed. One day she took my revolver from a drawer, took aim, and fired at a picture. The cardinal's hand went to his chest and he fell to the ground. I felt sorry for him and later on whenever I visited brothels on the outskirts of the city, and paid the whores for their skills, I was always aware that I was purchasing a moment of eternity. Any man who once tasted the salt of Cecilia's cunt would sell his rings, his friends, his morals and all the rest, just to feed the insatiable monster hidden beneath her pink skirt. Oh, why do we never distinguish the first moments when women treat us as playthings, from the time when we drive them to despair? I woke up one night in the early hours, at the time flowers drop their petals and birds begin to sing. Martha was lying by my side, a treasure-house of all ways of making love, a hyena of Corinth, lying with her cunt spread open to the dawn. She caught the disgust in my eyes and surely wanted nothing better than to see me nauseated by the filth of her. I watched her sex swelling and pouring out of her cunt, over the bed and on to the floor, filling the room like a stream of lava. I got out of bed and fled madly from the house, not stopping till I reached the middle of the deserted town square. As I looked back I saw Martha's sex squeezing out of the window like a monstrous tear of unnatural colour. A bird flew down to peck at my seed and I threw a stone to drive it away. "You will be lucky, you will repeat yourself over and over again," a passer-by spoke to me and added: "your wife is just giving birth to a son."

Two little sparrows kept rendez-vous every noon behind the pale blue corsage of Our Lady of Lourdes: I was innocent when I entered the catacombs. The row of square boxes naturally aroused my curiosity. There were a few boys hanging by their bound feet from the tops of the olive trees, flames roasting their curly young heads. In the next room I found a bunch of lovely naked girls entwined in a single monstrous living creature like something from the Apocalypse. Their cunts were opening and closing mechanically, some empty, some swallowing their own slime. One in particular caught my eye, the lips moving as though trying to speak, or like a man whose tongue has turned to stone trying to crow like a cock. Another was a smiling rosebud that I'd recognize among a hundred specimens, to this day. It was my dead Clara's cunt, dead and buried, with nobody to wash her body with the mint-scented lotion she loved. Sadly I brought out my cock and stuck it aimlessly into the writhing mass, uncaring and indifferent, telling myself death always brings debauchery and misfortune together.

Then I put an aquarium on my window-sill. I had a golden-haired vulva, in it, a magnificent specimen of a penis with a blue eye and delicate veins on its temples. As time went on I threw everything I had ever loved into it: broken cups, hairpins, Barbara's slippers, burnt-out bulbs, shadows, cigarette ends, sardine tins, all my letters and used condoms. Many strange creatures were born in that world. I felt myself to be a Creator, and I had every right to think so. When I had the aquarium sealed up I gazed contentedly at my mouldering dreams, until there was no seeing through the mildew on the glass. Yet I was sure that everything I loved in the world was there, inside.

I still need fodder for my eyes. They gulp down all they get greedily and roughly. At night, asleep, they digest it. Emilia scattered her shocked scorn generously, arousing desire in all she met, provoking visions of that hairy maw.

I still remember something that happened when I was a boy. I'd just been expelled from high school and nobody would have anything to do with me. Except my sister. I would go to her secretly, in the night. Lying in each other's arms, legs entwined, we slowly dreamed ourselves into the dulled state of all those who lie on the knife-edge of shame. One night we heard soft footsteps and my sister nudged me to hide behind the armchair. Our father came into the room, shutting the door quietly behind him, and climbed into her bed without a word. That was when, at last, I saw how one makes love.

Emilia's beauty was not meant to fade, but to rot.

A MAP OF THE PAIN

Maxim Jakubowski

IT ALL BEGINS in Blackheath, in South East London. They are in the kitchen, chatting aimlessly while preparing the evening meal. He drones on about the cutbacks at the BBC and his fears for his job. She isn't really listening to him. Her mind is miles away, in a bed with another man who touches her in all the right places, in all the right ways, another man who has betrayed her so badly.

He moves over to the fridge. Opens it, searches inside.

The heat is oppressive. London has not seen the likes of it for years. And he still wears his tie.

"I don't think we have enough tomatoes for the salad," he says.

Her husband the vegetarian.

She fails to answer.

"I said we're low on tomatoes."

The information registers through a haze of mental confusion.

"I'll pop over to the 7-Eleven on the High Street," she volunteers. "They're still open. I should have bought more stuff over lunch at the Goodge Street Tesco. It won't take me long," she says.

"I'll come along," her husband says. "Keep you company."

"No, it's all right," she answers. "You can prepare the dressing."

He's always been good that way, willing to cook and do things in the kitchen. She picks up her shoulder bag, with her purse and the manuscript she's working on and walks out onto the mews.

The night air is stale and sticky. She is wearing her white jeans and an old promotional tee-shirt.

She walks at her usual jaunty pace past the Common. Toward the shops. And breezes past the convenience store where a few spotty youths are squabbling by the ice-cream counter, and a couple of drab, middle-aged men are leafing through the top shelf girlie magazines. She heads on to the railway station. Network South East. The next train to Charing Cross is in five minutes. She uses her monthly Travelcard.

At the London station, she calmly collects her thoughts. Smiles impishly at the imagined face of her husband, waiting all this time for the final ingredients for the salad, back at their house. She catches the tube to Victoria and connects with the last train departure to Brighton.

Once, with her lover, she had gone there for a weekend, yeah a dirty week-end, she supposes. It was on the eve of a political party conference and the seaside resort had been full of grim-faced politicians and swarms of television journalists. She'd spent most of her time outside the hotel room where they had fucked more times than she had thought possible in the space of thirty-six hours, absolutely terrified of venturing across her spouse, or some colleagues of his who might be familiar with her, even though he worked on the business and economics side and she well knew he could not be in Brighton right then.

Katherine spent the night ambling up and down the seafront, enjoying the coolness of the marine breeze and sea air after the Turkish bath of her London suburbs and the publisher's offices where she worked. It was wonderfully quiet; no drunks to accost her, just alone with her thoughts, the memories, the scars of lust, the mess that her life now was.

Her lover had betrayed her. And she, in turn, had betrayed both men.

She wanted to wipe her mind clean of everything, to erase the wrong-doing and the pain she had inflicted on them. To start anew, like a baby arriving into the world, free of fault, innocent, like a blank tape ready for a new set of experiences, a new life almost.

In the morning, she booked herself into a small bed and breakfast on a square facing the old pier. She shopped for new clothes, which she paid for by credit card. She ate fish and chips, like a tourist and even found the Haagen-Dazs ice-cream parlour she remembered from a previous visit to one of the backstreets. Maraschino cherry delight. The weather was warm but nowhere near as bad as London. On the promenade, she bought a floppy straw hat to protect her pale skin from the fierce sun. She took a nap in the afternoon in the cramped room of the small hotel. Before dozing off, she had switched the TV on and seen her husband on screen looking all jolly and smug on the business lunch programme, reporting from the car park of an automotive parts factory. It had been recorded two days earlier. She awoke later from a dream-free sleep, enjoyed a leisurely bath during which she depilated her legs and cut her toe nails, and, clean and refreshed, slipped on the new lightweight dress she had purchased earlier, low-cut, dark blue with white polka dots, billowing away down over her long legs from a high waist.

"First night away," she remarked to herself, as she walked out into the dusk.

She meets this guy in a pseudo-Texan Cantina. He says he's from one of the unions. She's had a couple of beers, and he offers her a glass of tequila. It burns her throat and stomach.

"I canvass for Labour locally, where I live," she tells him, to indicate that at least they share the same political affiliation. She's always suspected, despite his indifferent denials, that that bastard of a lover she'd been involved with had actually voted Tory. How in hell could she have slept with him?

He smiles at her, well, more of a leer really.

So what? she thinks.

She follows him, his name is Adam Smith, back to the bar of the Old Ship where he is staying for the conference. It's already pretty late, and there are only a handful of people left in the penumbra of the bar. She has a couple of vodka and oranges. Her head feels light. Better this than the heavy burden of all the memories and the guilt, she reckons.

"Is that a wedding ring?" the guy enquires, pointing at her finger.

"Yes," she answers. "Does it bother you?"

It all floods back. How her lover would delicately slip both the wedding and the thin engagement rings off her fingers before ceremoniously undressing her from top to bottom, before they would make love in the basement to the sound of the whirring fan and the light of the long-life candle she herself had bought near the Reject Shop on Tottenham Court Road.

"No, I was just wondering, that's all," he remarks.

"If it bothers you, I can take them off," Katherine says.

"No, no," he says, annoyed by this turn of events. But while he is still saying this, she has already wet her finger and slipped both the rings off, deliberately dropping them at the bottom of her glass.

"Satisfied?" she asks.

Is she drunk, he wonders? "They'll be closing the bar any minute, I reckon," he says, ignoring her earlier remark. "Can I entice you up to my room for a final nightcap?"

She isn't drunk. Just a bit lost, she guesses. She looks at this man called Smith of all things. His tie isn't straight, his shirt has a few drink stains, scattered across its front. She can read him like a map. But what the hell?

"Yeah, why not?" she answers, grabbing her bag still loaded with the manuscript from her old life, and stands up, abandoning the rings in the half-empty glass of booze.

As he inserts the electronic card into the door, he leers at her again. Why must he be so obvious, Katherine thinks?

The door swings open.

He stands aside and Katherine walks in.

The room is medium-sized, dominated by a large king-size bed. A door on the right leads to a bathroom. On the walls, anonymous prints of naval victories from the Napoleonic wars. She smiles; it might have been worse: it could have been the classic print of the Eurasian woman with the blue face. If it had been, she thinks she might have walked straight out again.

He follows her in and the door slams quietly.

He walks to the bedside table where a large bottle of scotch stands, no, bourbon. Four Roses.

He takes his jacket off. His shirt is straining at the waist, his girth stretching the button holes.

"Drink?" Adam suggests.

She hates the stuff but answers "Why not?" That's how it's supposed to go, isn't it?

"So," he sits down on the edge of the orange-brown bedspread, loosens his tie. "How much?"

"How much what?" She hesitantly sips the harsh booze from the glass.

"How much do you charge? All that married woman crap doesn't cut much ice, you know. I don't care, I'll pay the going rate." He takes a thick black leather wallet from the inside pocket of his jacket. Opens it and pulls out two fifty pound notes. Katherine notices there are quite a lot more where they came from.

He hands her the cash. "Okay," she says, taking it.

She stands to begin undressing.

He smiles.

She unzips the dress where it cinches her waist and pulls it up above her head. And off. All she is wearing is her underwear. The black bustier and knickers set and the matching suspender belt and dark stockings. What she always wore for the assignments with her lover. Her skin is pale, her tummy flat like a marble table, her thighs full, the tight suspender belt biting in to the skin above her hips.

She moves to unhook the bustier but Adam interjects: "No, keep your top on. You haven't got much up there. I'd rather you didn't."

She stands there, legs apart, wondering what to do next. Thinking, why am I so passive? I know what I'm doing. Fleetingly, she remembers how, one night, in the thrall of rapture, he had whispered in her ear: "One day, Kate, you will walk all the sexual stations of the Cross, you see." At the time, she hadn't quite understood, but had found it sexy, him saying things like that, it fired her lust up even more. Now, she was beginning to understand.

He gulps down the contents of his glass. She obliges, doing the same. He pours more bourbon.

"Well?" she asks.

"Take your pants off," the union representative demands.

Katherine unhooks a stocking, but the guy interrupts:

"No, keep your stockings on."

She bends and pulls the knickers down, slipping the thin fabric across the nylon and over her flat shoes. She leaves the garment on the hotel room floor and straightens up again.

Her pubic curls lie flattened against her damp skin. He gazes at her lower stomach, all traces of his smile now disappearing as he drinks in the sight of her nudity.

"Come here," he says. She moves closer to him, her cunt facing his eyes, as he remains in the chair.

His fingers invade her thatch, spreading the dark curls. He slips a finger into her gash. Probes.

"You're not very wet, are you?"

Katherine stays silent.

He withdraws his finger from her sex. Brings it up to his nose, sniffs. Grunts.

"Suck my cock."

He unzips his fly.

Katherine kneels by the chair. He pulls his penis out. It's semi-erect, pinker than others she has come across. Not that she's encountered that many. A handful of clumsy groping sessions and fucking in the darkness at University, following alcoholic parties, and then her husband, uncircumcized and reliably sturdy, and five years later the damn lover, circumcized, thicker, darker, pulsating, veined like a tender tree. Life as an uninterrupted parade of male members!

She takes the man's cock between her fingers, pulls on the foreskin and the glans emerges, reddish, the colour of fever. She lowers her head, opens her lips and takes the member into her moist insides. He's not too big. She hates it when it makes her choke. Her tongue slowly makes contact with the swelling penis, circles its extremity; he tastes different, a slightly acrid, sweaty odour, musk and urine. Suddenly, she feels his hand on her head, fingers burrowing into her thick curls, pressuring her mouth to go deeper and swallow his cock up to its hairy hilt. The tip of her tongue dallies over the cock's small hole. When she touches him there, there's a trembling, a nervous shudder that courses through his whole body. She senses he is about to come and sucks harder on his now fully-grown member. He tries to hold back but she stimulates the base of his cock with her fingers while her tongue relentlessly keeps on teasing his opening.

"You bitch," he sighs, aware that she is trying to finish him off. Expediting the job.

But the surge can't be halted, and within a few seconds his whole body spasms. As this happens, Katherine opens her mouth wide to disengage herself from his throbbing cock, but he viciously holds her head down even harder and comes inside her mouth. She gags on the hot stream of come and has no other choice than to swallow the stuff. Bastard, she mutters under her breath. It sticks in her throat. She feels like being sick. Finally, he releases his hold on her head and she is allowed to pull her mouth back. She wipes her lips with the back of her hand, to eliminate the lingering taste of his seed.

His quickly shrivelling penis still dangling like a marionette from his open trousers, he gets out of the chair before she has time to stand up again and signals her to the bed. She sits on the edge, and he forces her down so that her long legs dangle over the side. He lowers himself down to the carpet, and sticks two fingers into her cunt.

"Still dry, hey?" he says, forcing his way past her labia.

She looks down at him, his face cunt-level, thinning hair bobbing up and down between her thighs. She distractedly notices there's a ladder near the knee of her left stocking. How did that happen, she wonders?

His fingers slip in and out of her sex. She has no feeling of excitement. This is what being an object is, she reckons.

"Your cunt hair is too long," he tells her, parting the curls around her opening.

"I don't go to the barbers very often," she attempts a feeble joke.

"Wait there. Don't move," he says, rising and moving over to the settee where a battered attaché-case lies. He opens it and pulls out a nail kit and a small pair of scissors.

He pulls on her pubic curls, untangling the longer ones and trims the extremities along a straight line. It feels funny. She looks down after he has completed the work. Her bush is now distinctly thinner, and the lips of her sex are plainly visible behind the growth.

"There, that's nicer, isn't it?" he remarks. "Now you can see the merchandise."

She doesn't answer.

"I want to see inside," he says. "Use your own fingers. Open up."

She obeys.

He peers inside her, his eyes piercing her innards.

Her lover used to say that her insides were the colour of coral. She closes her eyes.

"I'm going to fuck you now," Adam says. "Where do you keep your condoms? In your handbag?"

"I don't have any," Katherine replies. "I've already told you, I'm not a whore."

"Bloody hell," the man says. "Shit. You don't think I'm gonna put my cock inside there; I don't know where you've been before."

"You didn't mind my mouth," she says, a tad angrily. "That was good enough for you, wasn't it?"

Only five cocks before, she thinks. A bloody woman of experience . . . No, not even, the first two she never gave head to.

She looks at this man, and finds him ridiculous. Overweight, standing there with his small cock peering out between the curtains of his half-open trousers.

She giggles.

He reacts badly and slaps her across the cheek.

"Don't . . ."

"I've paid. I'll do exactly what I want to do, woman."

"Bastard."

He slides his belt out of the trouser top, and she's totally unprepared for this, as he grabs both her wrists and binds them together. Tight. She's too slow to react. Vulnerable, obscenely undressed in front of this stranger with her cunt wide open, her black stockings in disarray, her small breasts feeling heavy inside the cups of her bustier, her cheek still on fire from the blow. Adam pulls her by her bound wrists towards the bathroom, pushes the door open with his foot.

Katherine is frightened. What now? She has read too many serial killer novels. For Christ's sake, she edits them. In her bag over at the bed and breakfast, there's even a manuscript for one that takes place in Arizona. *Fiction editor found slaughtered in Brighton hotel.* Will he slit my throat and arrange my mutilated body in a pornographic vision that goes beyond obscenity? Will he carve off the tips of my breasts, insert the carving knife in my cunt and slit me all the way up like a chicken? Will he cut my labia off and display them partly chewed inside my open mouth?

She shudders.

He pushes her down on the toilet.

"There," he says.

"Yes?" she enquires.

"I want you to pee, and I want to watch. Come on, open those legs wide, wider, now. Come on. Show me that piss squirting out of you."

"No," she says.

"Yes."

"Undo my hands, then maybe. If I can manage it."

He does. She tries.

Katherine has never peed in front of a man, of any one. She blushes intensely. Closes her eyes and concentrates. He fills a toothbrush mug with water and forces her to swallow. And again. She can feel the warmth inside her stomach, the muscles tensing. He keeps on standing there, silent now, watching entranced the quivering, moist entrance to her cunt.

Finally, the flow is unleashed. The odorous liquid flows.

It feels both painful, like a particularly strong period bursting from her and rupturing some remote part of her body, but also pleasurable, like a fourth division orgasm, a satisfying but unremarkable feeding of the lust inside, not unlike the routine lovemaking she had been having for ages with her husband.

Adam watches as the thin stream of pee first dribbles out, then streams arc-like into the bowl, emerging from the thin opening between her cunt lips. As she tightens her throat, he approaches a finger, allows the liquid to pearl over it like a cascade, and inserts it suddenly into her pouring aperture. Then another finger, yet another and savagely stretching the muscles inserts his whole fist into her. Katherine screams in agony. But the windows of the hotel room are closed and Brighton doesn't hear.

Finally, the flow stops and he withdraws his hand. It still hurts and she is about to cry, as he slaps her face again and cries out:

"You bitch, you enjoyed that, didn't you."

She nods.

"Stick a finger up your arse."

She makes a gesture of protest but he swings the belt close to her cheek.

He pulls her off from the toilet bowl, pushes her onto her knees, on all fours. Manipulates her so that her rump points upward and guides her right hand (how could he know she was left-handed?) toward the dark cranny of her anus.

"Now," he said.

To urge her on, he places his foot above her other hand, as if to tread on it.

She slowly inserts her middle finger into the puckered aperture. The ring of muscles rebels against the intrusion and she barely manages half a nail.

"More," Adam says, and steps harder onto her free hand.

She pushes the finger harder. The ring of flesh relaxes. She feels another need to pee, but holds back. Finally, the finger plants itself deep inside her arsehole, spearing herself up to its first joint. The feeling is not unpleasant.

"Dirty girl, hey? Slut."

She looks up at him.

"Take it out."

She does. "Lick it clean."

She does.

Then, despite her tired protests, he binds her hands together again with the leather belt and pulls her back toward the bedroom. She stumbles and he allows her to fall over the settee. He stands back and says:

"Yeah, that's it. Keep your legs wide open. I'm still going to fuck your brains out, you know. I can get condoms on room service, if I want. Whenever I want. Bitch."

He takes a swig from the bottle of bourbon and sits back on the bed, smugly watching her spread-eagled across the settee, her genitals in technicolour display like a centrefold in a skin magazine.

"Whenever I want," drinking from the bottle again.

Half an hour later, he has fallen asleep and Katherine manages to untie the belt and liberate her hands. She dresses hurriedly, abandoning the black knickers she's had to wipe her moist crotch with. She feels soiled, violated like never before. The man's jacket is draped over the chair by the door. She pulls out his wallet and takes all the cash. At least six hundred pounds.

Softly, softly into the Brighton night.

It's now New York.

Autumn has come, or rather Fall as they call it over there.

Katherine has travelled to Manhattan and found a drab, cheap room in an equally cheapo rundown hotel a few blocks off Times Square, where she often has to jostle with local prostitutes in the somewhat seedy reception area, she picking up her keys – there are never any messages, they booking in their furtive johns. Soon, the working girls begin to recognize her and become friendly. The sultry weather is fading fast. She spends mornings in the Park, reading older books, Dickens, Thomas Hardy, all the novels she should have studied better when she was at Cambridge, where she'd got her 2.2 because of a silly indulgence where she had written mock haikus for one of her assigned essays. She'd deserved a 2.1 at least, she knew, her tutor had said so, but she'd also wasted too much time at pointless parties and playing ingénues badly in college plays. Sitting calmly in the sparse grass, the rumour of the traffic distant, the top edge of the surrounding skyscrapers just about visible from her vantage point, she thinks of the past. Over and over. How she first betrayed her trusting if rather dull husband with a dangerous lover, who soon became too possessive, too disturbing, until she felt she had to break things off and he went berserk. He'd always wanted to bring her to New York, she remembered. How frightening the day he had told her he had already purchased tickets for them, two or three months ahead in time, and served her with this ultimatum to come to America with him and not return to her husband. She'd panicked.

For her lover to exact a desperate vengeance in the way of men who have projected their deepest fantasies upon a muse only to feel betrayed by their ordinary, selfish and fallible humanity. Yes, he was one for muses. What did he see in her? Why her? She knew she wasn't worth it. She didn't have his sense of romance, she had a cold heart, she had prosaic aspirations but then what else could she have desired with a husband who wore a suit and tie as if it were a lifetime achievement and though a couple of years younger than her, looked and acted as if he were already in his forties?

She closed her copy of *A Tale of Two Cities* and sighed.

Soon, she'd finish the book and would need something new to read. This afternoon, she could walk down Fifth Avenue to the Village, past the Flatiron Building and onto Broadway, to Tower Books on Lafayette. Soon, she also knew she would be running out of money. The Brighton cash was already dangerously low and the hotel's weekly bill would exhaust it in a few days. By now, she supposed, her credit card must be invalid. And even if it weren't, she did not wish either of the two absent men to find out where she might be.

She gathered her few belongings, putting the now empty diet Coke can into the brown paper bag together with the well-fingered paperback, strapped on the shoulder bag in which she kept her passport, diary and the remaining cash and headed for Central Park South. She wore a white and red tee-shirt advertising a London mystery bookstore and a wrap-around skirt of many colours, both of which she'd found in a Goodwill thrift store near 22nd Street, shortly after her arrival here.

A detour on the walk back to the hotel and she moved down 46th Street, past all the jewellery stores towards the Gotham Book Mart, where the second-hand stock was often reasonably priced. None of the books, however, caught her fancy today and she crossed the Avenue of the Americas and continued toward the bustle of Times Square. Tourists queued impatiently at the reduced-price theatre ticket kiosk. She ignored all the British accents among the Babel-like cacophony of the conversations.

The yellow taxis roared down Broadway as she crossed the main road under the shadow of the gigantic neon displays. Katherine looked up. There, that's where the black girl at the hotel had said it would be. A fading sign: *Girls Wanted For Burlesque Show*. On both sides of the small theatre's entrance were large emporiums selling all the latest video and electronic junk.

She ignored the Israeli salesmen aggressively pitching their wares to any tourist lingering long enough outside and walked through the side entrance into the building.

"My friend Lisa sent me," Katherine says.

The little guy smoking an evil-smelling cigar lounges back in his chair and looks her over. At the front of his cluttered desk is a board with his name: *Guy N Bloom*. The office smells of damp and old newsprint. On the wall, old kitsch posters of past vaudeville shows coexist with full-colour spreads of more recent, and explicit beefcake, tanned women flashing obscenely gaping pink split beavers, many of them signed *To Guy, my favorite guy* and other such witticisms.

"Your top," he indicates.

Katherine pulls the white tee-shirt over her head, her breasts fall free, she hasn't been wearing a bra. She's never really needed to wear one.

The response is predictable.

"Not much up there, hey?" the older man says.

"I know I'm not very voluptuous, but . . ." she begins to say.

"I like your accent, though. Limey, hmm?" He smiles. A mask of kindness almost invades his lined features. "Tell you what, you look a bit Irish to me. Pull your hair back, all those curls, there's too many of them."

She follows his instructions and bunches her myriad curls together and pulls the thick clump back to reveal her forehead. She doesn't like herself like this, her forehead is too large.

"Interesting," says Bloom. "You're not really that beautiful, but you've got something, you know. You're different; I think the guys might well like you. Pity about the tits, though. Turn round and give me a looksie."

She does.

"No need to take it all off, just pull the skirt up. Let me see your butt. Yeah, thought so, great legs, honey, ass is a bit big, very white, not seen much tanning. Definitely, they'll like you."

He explains the terms of employment.

"How much money you make is up to you. The better you are, the more they like you, the more tips you'll get. It's all tips. We don't pay any insurance, so you look after yourself. You supply your costume, or lack of costume should I say . . ." he sniggers.

"No funny business inside the theatre. What you arrange outside is your own business, and I don't want to know anything about it. Understood?"

"Yes, I understand," Katherine says. "When can I start? I really need some money. Bills to pay, you know."

"First shift starts tomorrow at two, honey. I might actually come and have a look myself, you're different, should be interesting. Sometimes I regret I'm no longer a young man. Maybe your bump and grind routine will be more intelligent than the other gals. Show some imagination."

Of course, Katherine thinks, I have a degree in English from Cambridge, what do you expect?

And thinks one brief moment of her erstwhile lover, who made such a song and melodramatic fuss after she had rejected him of the fact he had never seen her dance. Well now, honey, you'd have to pay, she says under her breath.

The other girls explain how to string the whole thing together. Katherine has bought herself a spectacular bikini, spandex or something like it, shiny, leather-like, and another dancer, a girl with a pronounced Tennessee drawl lends her a feather boa and some silk scarves and shows her how best to drape them around her body. In the cramped dressing-room, she slaps on her best scarlet lipstick and loses one of her soft contact lenses, the last one from the old British prescription. The floor is filthy and she can't find it again. She takes the other out. Things are blurry now. At least, she won't see all the bloody men in the audience too close. A saving grace.

"Have you chosen your tunes?" another dancer asks Katherine.

"What tunes?"

"You know, kiddo, the music you want to dance to."

Kiddo. The girl under all her flaky make-up is barely out of her teens. Worn before her years. Katherine will soon turn thirty. She reckons she might well be the oldest here. Never mind.

"I hadn't thought of it, really. I'll dance to anything they play."

"Here, use this," the girl says, handing her a CD. "It's great, but the rhythm is not really me. You have it, you use it."

Katherine peers at the label. *Shake* by the Vulgar Boatmen.

She waits in the wings, watches the first three girls do their numbers. She can't believe it. They are lewd, provocative, dirty, wonderfully indecent. She can't do any of this. Really, she can't. What am I doing here? In Times Square, cesspool of the western world, where a few doors away a derelict cinema is still screening *Deep Throat* and black pimps sashay down the street like living clichés, and there's Bruce Springsteen's *Candy's Room* booming in the air as the black girl gyrates on stage and bends and stretches her body to an impossible degree and the time comes and Katherine holds her breath back and makes her way to the illuminated stage.

"Go, blondie, go," shout the other dancers as she reaches the centre of the proscenium. They sense it's her first time and show solidarity.

But the music doesn't start, and she stands there, paralysed, crucified under the dual assault of two glaring, hot spotlights, her medusa curls held aloft by the conditioning mousse, her shiny underwear glittering, her legs long and white, all the bruises from back in London now faded away. She wets her lips. Tries to see the audience and can only distinguish a few trouser legs emerging from the outlying darkness. Not even a dirty mac in sight.

A guitar chord and the song begins.

She swings her hips to the beat, pulls the green silk scarf draped over her shoulder across to her throat, caresses the material as it lingers there, a fragile noose of fabric, her knees bend to the rhythm, her bare feet drag slowly across the stage floor, she closes her eyes one moment, pulls with her free hand on the other scarf circling her wrist and waves it in the air where it floats slowly, suspended like a slow-motion kite during the festival at Blackheath, the scarf swims down and lands on the gentle rise of her breasts. She dances in one spot, her body circling the area in a steady motion, every breath in her soul singing parallel to the melodic waves of the rock and roll tune. Her fingers linger over the silk square now protecting her pale chest, she slides them down the narrow slope, from the brown mole at the onset of her cleavage to the tip of her left breast, where she rubs the still concealed aureola through the recalcitrant plastic-like thickness of the bikini bra. Katherine remembers the bump and grind tradition and, when the beat accelerates, with an artificial smile piercing her scarlet lips she pushes her bum out, and then her crotch. Dance, girl, dance. She takes hold of the silk scarf still draped over her chest, slips it between the thin strap and pulls it across the valley separating her two slight promontories, and out again, throws the piece of fabric in the air and allows it to drift down to the stage floor where she kicks it away just a few inches with her toe, as her hips keep gyrating mechanically to the music which seems to be growing louder and louder. She unclips the bra and loosens her breasts, soon to cover them chastely with the other silk piece until now adorning her throat like a thin choker. She feels her nipples growing erect under the thin gauze. Her body undulates steadily as she lowers both her hands and begins to gently massage her nipples through the fabric, like she saw the other women do before and when the chorus of the song jumps in, she pulls the silk piece away to reveal her front unencumbered. A few claps in the sparse crowd. She dances on, Salome of only two veils. She can feel sweat rising through the pores of her unveiled skin. A clammy feeling under her armpits where she had shaved only yesterday afternoon. Her upper lip, which she'd bleached at the same time, itches. The beat goes on. Come on, baby, give us more skin. She dances on, trying somehow to lose herself inside the relentless music. Bump and grind. Push your bum out; shove that crotch forward, show them how the mound of your cunt stretches the fabric of the bikini bottom. Bump. Grind. Push. Shove. The song ends. Another begins without a pause for breath or reflection. Every stage number is divided into three ritual parts, three songs or pieces of music. The new tune is an old big band blast. Brassy. She

quickens the movement of her wavering shoulders and the geometrical patterns her arms are tracing in the glare of the harsh spotlights. She moves two steps forward, closer to the edge of the stage
where small coloured bulbs imprint rectangular patterns of gaudy
colours over the white skin of her legs. As her hands keep on
caressing her breasts, she feels a tremor in the pit of her stomach.
She recognizes it, the onset of lust. Like when they were in his
office, clandestine adulterers and she knew he was about to pull his
underwear down and release his thick, dark, tasty cock. She opens
her eyes to chase away the dream of the past and for the first time
sees, albeit in a myopic blur, the eyes of some of the men in the
audience. Hungry. Malevolent. Get on with it, they say. Katherine
slips her fingers under the elastic of the bikini bottom. Pulls the
garment an inch away from the flesh of her stomach. Tease them a
bit, she thinks. A cavalcade of pianos attack the chorus and she
swiftly pulls the knickers down. She now stands fully nude, her hips
and shoulders still adhering to the syncopated whirlpool of the big
band sound. Isn't the song over yet? she doesn't feel sexy at all. She
feels very much alone.

She has never stood nude before in front of more than a single
man; never even skinny-dipped or gone to a nude beach. How
many are there in the audience? She peers sideways into the stage
wings. The other girls are no longer watching. But Bloom is, the
damn cigar still hanging from his lips. She can't read the expression
on his face from where she stands. She twirls around, remembers
the wooden pole over there on the far side of the stage. Waltzes
toward it. Shove. Bump. Thrust. Grind. Her body feels wet, the
sweat must be pouring down her back, there's no air, the spotlights
are so fucking hot, Jesus, the sweat must be sliding down between
the crack of her arse. She reaches the pole and grabs it; her hands
are moist as she circles the pole and sketches a few new improvised
dance moves like a medieval virgin courting a maypole. The
apparatus is in fact metallic. She grinds against it. The hard, round
circumference mashes against her pubes, she places her breasts
against it and it fills her valley. The song never ends. She throws
her head back, the delicate orbs of her breasts stand free, firm,
shiny under the film of sweat, she bends at the waist and blushes
instantly as she senses her vagina gape open as she does this. But the
audience can't see, she's too far from the front rows. She stands
again. Dance. Dance until the end of time, Kate. She wriggles her

backside, keeps on massaging her breasts, if only to keep her hands busy, the movement is quite mechanical as if she were spreading soap or foam over her chest. Yes, yes, he did do that when they had shared their first bath tub. The song ends. One more to go. A familiar riff splits the brief silence. The Rolling Stones. *Satisfaction*. Much too fast, what is she going to do now? For encores? She has to continue, do more. Needs the tips. Show them more. She moves back to the edge of the stage, dances with exaggerated languor as she mentally rakes up the good times, the bad times, the wedding in the chapel of their old college in Cambridge. Her left hand moves from breast to navel, and she pushes it deep with a corkscrew motion into the narrow pit of her belly button. A guy in the audience whoops and hollers. The other hand also abandons the tender nipple it had been tending and hovers over her sex. She swivels her hips like a belly dancer. The finger parts the hair, the darker curls, tip-toes like a scalpel across the now moist aperture. The other hand joins it soon and holds the lips open. She's so wet, it must be dripping onto the stage floor. She squats on her haunches and deliberately inserts one finger deep inside her cunt, as the guys in the front row open their eyes wider than they ever thought they could. She can no longer hear the music. Keith Richards must still be playing. She moves the finger deep inside, impales herself on it while a finger from her other hand squeezes her protruding clitoris. A hand emerges from the audience, holding a green bill. Closer, girl, closer. She inches her cunt forward until she's in a precarious equilibrium on the very edge of the stage. The man, whose face remains in the shadows, slides the money into her gaping cunt. She inches her way back. Stands up, the bank note sticking out from her innards. Dances. Bumps. Grinds. Thrusts. The audience whistles, applauds loudly. The music has now ended. Lisa, the black girl who'd sent her here, is waiting over there by the side of the stage to do her turn. Katherine bows to the invisible men in the darkness. Her audience. She pulls the note out from her vagina, half of it is soaking wet with her juices. She waves it. The men shout all sorts of things at her. She sticks two fingers back inside, twists them round to further loud yelps and brings them to her mouth where she licks them clean. Prisoners of lust, he had once described their fatal liaison. The stage lights dim and she can make out more of the meagre audience. There's only a dozen of them, but the noise they're making is enough to fill a soccer stadium. She recalls

Brighton and Adam Smith, turns round and gets down on all fours and, sobbing gently, thrusting her rump out toward the anonymous men, she cruelly pushes her still lubricated finger into her arsehole. She's about to pull it out and show them how she can also lick shit like the best of sinners when Bloom and two of the other burlesque dancers hurriedly pull her off stage to the loud protest of the screaming guys.

"Are you crazy?" Bloom screeches at her. "You fucking slut, you want to get us closed down?"

The girls all look at her as if she were insane.

"Goddam limey. She's deranged, a freak, you must be sick to get your rocks off this way."

"Get her outta here. I don't want to see this woman again. She's downright crazy. Out."

They bundle her into her day clothes.

Back on Times Square, a thin rain falling, likely to mess up her perm, Katherine unclenches her fist and extracts the bank note. It's a hundred.

Certainly worth a few more miles on the clock, on the road to nowhere.

In Miami, she discovered some men had long, thin cocks and all-over tans.

On alternate days, Katherine cruised the clubs and discos in the art deco district of Miami Beach, window shopping like any other tourist, quenching the ambient heat with a steady diet of cold sodas and ice-creams, while on others she worked a few continuous shifts in a shady strip joint – here, they no longer called them burlesques – all the way up the less fashionable area in the Northern reaches of Collins Avenue, beyond the Adventura Mall, where the highway to the Everglades began. Now, she'd perfected her act. Kept it simple, cleanly sexy, beyond the temporary madness, the excesses of Times Square. She grew accustomed to shaking her gangly body, grinding her crotch with a grimace feigning ecstasy against the metal of the central pole, thrusting her white, square butt toward the punters, teasing the vociferous crowd, keeping her legs together, letting her hands do the roving, a mechanical spectacle tailored to the unsatisfactory pop songs she had thread together to punctuate her movements.

The nights were long and empty in her room at the beachside

inn. The paint on the wall flaked in places creating ever-changing Rorschach tests in the humid penumbra. Six in the morning was always the worst time, and time and again she had to control herself and not pick up the pink telephone and call London. But which one? Which past man? And then always remembered the time difference. And anyway what would she say? Sorry? I'm really sorry, but I don't want to come back. She read a lot. At Bookstar they deep discounted and the other day, even though she couldn't really afford a hardcover – she's not getting very good tips – she had indulged and bought the new Anne Tyler novel, which she read in small doses, to stretch the pleasure.

Sunday is her day off and like a good working girl she goes to the beach, with a basket of fruit and a cold box full of drink cans. She's got this new rather daring outfit, with a thong cutting deep into her crotch, separating the two globes of her backside like a piece of meat. But she always keeps her top on. Her husband would approve. Her skin burns easily, so she has to shield carefully under a parasol. The sand gets everywhere, as she ritually turns onto her stomach, then her back and again her stomach, and tried to concentrate on her reading. She knows that later she would have to use the shower nozzle against her cavities to excavate the millions of small grains stuck to her perspiring skin, nestled between her bum cheeks and even inside her vagina.

This rugged-looking man walked by her parasol, briefly obscuring the sun. Out of the corner of her eyes, she saw his feet in the sand just a few inches away from her town.

"*Guapa muchacha*," he said with a strong Hispanic accent.

Katherine looked up.

"Hi," she said.

"You're not from here," he remarked.

"No, I'm not."

He sat himself down next to her; he wore a silk shirt with exotic rainbow patterns and baggy trousers cinched at the waist.

"Let me have a guess," he smiled.

Katherine smiled back.

"I know, you're Australian. I saw that movie, you know."

She burst out laughing, her hand flying up, lost her page as the book fell into the sand and closed.

"You look like Nicole Kidman, the chick who married Tom Cruise."

"So I'm told. It's all the curls, you see. But no, I'm not from down under. I'm English, you see," she explained.

"No kidding," the man said. "I'd never have guessed. You look more Swedish, or Dutch, you know."

"Actually Irish a generation or two back," she said.

"Very beautiful," he flashed ivory white teeth that must have cost a small fortune in dental care.

"Thank you."

He took her hand in his, shook it and introduced himself:

"My name is Steve Gregory," he revealed.

"That's a very American name," she pointed out.

"Well, not really, it's Gregorio. Esteban Gregorio. But I changed it. Came over from Cuba. What about you?" he asked her.

"Eddie," she said.

English Eddie was her stage name. Her damn mother had insisted on making her second name Edwina.

"That's wonderful," he exclaimed and offered her a cigarette.

A hundred meters away, the sea murmured and the waves of the Caribbean lapped the warm shore.

Katherine sighed.

Steve had brown eyes. Dangerous eyes. The sort she'd seen before, the type of eyes that could make her do things she shouldn't. The top buttons of his shirt were open to reveal an abundant growth on his brown chest. She surprised herself by looking down at his trousers and the strong bulge there, and thinking what sort of shape his cock must be.

Later, he took her for a light but spicy salad lunch to this hut further down the beach. It was delicious but she drank too much wine. He seemed genuinely surprised when he found out where she worked, but he kept his hands to himself. He told her about Cuba, spoke of politics and food and, gazing at her, of things of beauty. And fast sports cars.

And was dumbfounded when he learned that she did not drive.

"You mean you haven't got a car?" he asked her.

"No, I've never even taken driving lessons."

"Amazing," he said.

"Well, I'm just an old-fashioned girl, I suppose," she answered.

When they parted in late afternoon, he had a business appointment he just couldn't put off any longer, he gently kissed her on

the cheek. Gallant to a tee. She had expected more. He promised
to come and see her at the club very soon.

"You must be a fantastic dancer," he said. "I can't wait."

In fact, Katherine wasn't very good at the dancing thing, really.
The other girls working at the joint were all so much better, they
had more natural rhythm, the blacks and the Latinas. So, to
capture the attention of the men in the audience, she knows she
has to offer something different. Not just her amazon build and fair
skin and heavy hips. She has shaved her sex, banned the dark curls
from between her strong thighs and only kept a thin line of pubic
thatch rising straight above the gash, like a small arrow pointing
toward her navel. Maria, who helped her do it one evening, had
suggested she trim it in the shape of a heart, but Katherine felt that
would be quite vulgar and inappropriate. Before every shift, she
carefully places a cube of ice over her nipples to render them erect,
hard, more prominent, then dries the aroused tips and rouges them
with shocking red lipstick. Then, she dips the stick toward her
outer labia and colours them beautiful, a fine line on either side
delineating the lips, gently separating the geometric poles of her
nether opening. She has to remember during her act not to smudge
the war paint too much. The other dancers don't like her too much.
They think she's a snob, can't really gossip or indulge in silly small
talk like they do between sets. She's the first stripper they've come
across who spends her time in the dressing room when not on duty
actually reading books. By people they've never even heard of. Not
your usual Stephen Kings or John Grishams. Thinks she's clever
and better than us, does English Eddie, they grumble between
themselves.

It's the little extras, Katherine knows, that keep the tips coming.
She pouts like other dancers, smiles hypocritically as she sheds the
thin items of exotic clothing, sticks out her tongue in pre-orgasmic
languor, licks her fingers as she would a penis, bumps and grinds
like the best of all sluts, teases the invisible males out there
carelessly, quickly opening her thighs wide and obscuring the
forbidden vista with the palm of her hand, bends over unchastely
to reveal the darker band of skin dividing her arse, dances the night
and day away, while her mind remains on cruise control, empty of
thoughts. She senses the clients in the outlying audience, the smell
of man, a quick thrust of her lower stomach forward and there must
be one there, no, there, who's jerking off to the sight of her, his hand

buried deep inside the trouser pocket, holding his cock in a tight noose as he moves the envelope of his palm and fingers up and down the trunk and comes all over his underwear. She rubs her damp crotch against the small Afghan carpet she now dances on, to avoid splinters in her feet, grinds her lower stomach against the hard floor and a few artificial moans escape as the music quietens momentarily, and somewhere in the back row must be a guy with his dick actually out, rubbing away furiously under a newspaper or a magazine while he drinks in the sheer erotic vision of her and imagines her spread-eagled on some filthy bed while he fucks her like there was no tomorrow. Likely story. Yes, they masturbate, they dream, they drool, and this way, she rationalizes, she has power over them.

Control.

Of men.

Like the two left far behind.

The house lights come on, the stage lights dim and the dancers stream out and tour the front rows. They are fully nude. Some of the guys in the audience leave then, while others hurriedly move to the edge of the stage if there is still free space. With their back to the men, the women move from seat to seat, up to a couple of minutes next to each respective guy, words are exchanged, greenbacks change hand and the transaction completed, the stripper either sits on the guy's lap while he paws her breasts until his time is up or alternately stands in close proximity to the punter and allows his hands to wander all over her body. The first two customers say nothing and Katherine moves on to the next seat. The man remains silent, but nods positively. He slips her a couple of crumpled notes. He's old. He rises, he's short, but then most men are compared to her. She moves closer to him, her bust rising gently. He peers at her eyes. His own are watery and vacant. He lowers his hand to her cunt, and swiftly inserts a finger inside her, stretching her dryness.

"Hey!" she exclaims. "Off limits."

But the elderly customer fails to respond. They can mangle the dancers' breasts, guessing which are real or silicone-assisted, they can slime over their skin to their heart's content, they can touch, caress, tiptoe like piano-players over the soft bodies, but not down there. His finger moves deeper and Katherine is obliged to open her thighs more to facilitate his intrusion. His nails are scratching her insides. His breath stinks to high heaven. She's about to seize his errant hand to pull it away when the next dancer in line jostles up to her for her turn and the man withdraws and sits down again. Katherine moves on down the flesh parade. It only took a minute or so, or was it more? None of the other men want her, they've had their fill of skin elsewhere already.

It itches like hell inside. She just hopes it's not bleeding from his nails, that he has not infected her. She's an illegal alien, enjoys no medical protection.

Back in the communal dressing room, she grabs a small pocket mirror from her bag and rushes to the toilets. Spreads her thighs open and examines the inside of her vagina. Yes, there's a bad scratch there, but it's not bleeding. She forces herself to pee, to evacuate any foreign elements. She washes herself out thoroughly. When she returns to the backstage area, all the women from her shift have already gone. A couple of dancers from the six p.m. batch have arrived and are already undressing. Katherine sits herself by one of the make-up mirrors and cleans the lipstick away from her body and slips on a cotton shirt and a pair of loose, baggy shorts. She replaces the mirror in her bag and pulls out her purse to safely put away the meagre notes from the parade. Jesus. Her heart misses a beat. There's no money at all in there. She swears mightily under her breath. A Latina dancer she's never seen here before gives her a strange look. One of the girls must have taken it. Could have been any of the women. None of them really liked her. Shit. She had all her cash in there. She can't open a bank account because of her status. Nearly two hundred and twenty dollars, she remembers. How the fuck is she going to settle her bill at the inn tomorrow? Buy groceries. She'd never raise that much in tips in such a short time. Even if she were sheer sex on a stick. Complaining to the elusive club gaffer would be quite useless, she knows.

At the stage door stands Steve. He's now wearing a sharp pale grey suit and she's never seen shoes so shiny. The Miami dusk feels sultry. He smiles at her as she walks out of the joint.

"Hey, you were incredible, Eddie. Are all English girls like you, tell me?"

She answers with a feeble smile and explains what happened.

"Ah, pretty woman, don't worry, it's only money," he says.

He leads her to his car, parked just outside, a big convertible with shiny metal hubs and metallic green paintwork. He opens a door for her, and she gets in.

"Yeah, but I needed that money, you just don't understand."

As he settles into the black leather driver's seat and switches on the ignition and the air conditioning starts up with a vengeance, Steve says:

"I know how you can earn a lot of money."

"When?" Katherine asks.

"Right now, if you wish," he answers and picks up a cellular phone. The car glides away from the kerb as he begins a long conversation in Spanish. She can't understand a word of course. She'd taken French as her foreign language at the Epsom grammar school. Wasn't even very good at it.

A mile or two down the road, he completes his transaction on the phone.

"All set, honey. For a girl like you, no problem. You see, you're exotic. Good money. Indeed," he flashes her a broad grin, slips a cassette into the car's system and a raucous beat fills the car, drums and all sorts of wondrous percussion punctuating a joyful Latin tune.

She says nothing but looks at him enquiringly.

"Relax, Eddie, relax, it'll be good. Really good," he says.

She doesn't like the "honey", the "exotic" or the "relax". But what are the choices?

A penthouse suite at the Fontainebleau Hotel. A valet has taken the car to be parked. Katherine feels out of place in her shabby casual wear, but Steve reassures her. "It's not important, Eddie, don't worry." The lift alone, shiny mirrors and gold-plated knobs everywhere must have cost a million. A long corridor with expensive prints all the way down the walls like a museum or an art gallery. They reach the door. Steve knocks three times. They open.

"This is Eddie," he introduces her.

There are half a dozen dusky middle-aged businessmen in expensive silk suits that put Steve's garb to shame. This is real money, she recognizes. Further back, there is another man, sipping a glass at the huge bar overlooking the balcony. He's black, a giant, must be all of seven feet.

"Meet Orlando. You're from England, aren't you? You won't know him, of course, he's with the 'Gators. One of our local heroes."

The black guy mumbles something as he weakly shakes her hand.

"A drink, Eddie?" one of the businessmen offers unctuously. "Absolutely anything you want. A bit of food, we can call room service, if you feel like a snack." All the guys are watching her attentively. Katherine feels uncomfortable. Never liked hotel rooms since that first time, that Tuesday at the Heathrow hotel when she had for the first time gone over the edge and jettisoned part of her life.

She declines the offer of food, has an ice-cold beer. Dos Equis.

The black guy still stands silently at the bar, looking her over. Most of the businessmen have settled onto chairs and a couple of massive couches. Waiting.

Steve sets his own glass down and comes over to her.

"See, it's like this, Eddie. One thousand dollars. Yes, a whole thousand bucks. My commission is twenty per cent. Fair? No?"

She feels her stomach sinking. What's worth all that cash?

"What do I have to do?" she asks.

"A live show. These gentlemen are important business contacts of mine, all the way from South America and down there, they don't have the entertainment we have here in America, so they want to enjoy a real special show."

A private show. Katherine breathes a sigh of relief. It could have been worse, much worse, she supposes.

"But I left my stage gear at the club," she points out. "You should have told me; it's not really sexy with these things I'm wearing now."

A frown crosses Steve's face.

"Oh, come on, don't be coy, we're not paying this sort of money for just a strip turn. A live show. Sex. Real sex. Fucking. Here on the bloody carpet, girl, where they can all see it all up close."

"What . . .?" she protests.

"With Orlando here," Steve adds, pointing at the towering sportsman. Absurdly, in her utter confusion, she vainly tries to guess which sport: basket ball, football, baseball? He continues: "Orlando is a legend. They call him the black stud and my friends wish to see him in action, with a blonde, with very white skin. You. *Comprende*?"

She looks at the black athlete. He is impassive.

"I can't."

"Yes, you can, bitch, and you will. You're not going to disappoint my friends, are you? Or you'll damn well feel my mighty wrath, woman. Don't disappoint me," he threatens her. She swallows hard, gulps down the end of her beer. Steve takes her right arm and leads her to the geographical centre of the room, all the businessmen sitting in a circle of sorts around the spot, none of them more than ten or at most twelve feet away. Yes, they would have a good view. Full cinerama widescreen gynaecology in close-up. Better than IMAX.

"Okay, come on, now," Steve says brusqely.

She keeps on standing there, hesitant.

He is becoming increasingly irritated.

"Eddie, I'm losing patience."

He suddenly takes hold of her shirt and pulls it open. Reluctantly, she takes it off.

The men all smile.

"Orlando, she's all yours. Let's see that famous big black dick at work," Steve says excitedly. "Ride the white bitch. Ride her."

She unbuttons the shorts and slides them down her hips and legs. Her black knickers haven't been washed for a few days. There's a small hole on one side. She blushes, bends and with her back to the ring of businessmen, takes them off. She looks up. Orlando is already down to his underpants. His chest is quite hairless, the colour of ebony. He wets his lips as his gaze explores her exposed body. The bulge in his crotch rises slightly as he catches sight of her shaven sex. She places her hands needlessly in front.

He extricates his cock from the pants.

It dangles out against his taut thigh.

"Jesus Christ," she says.

His penis, still soft and unaroused, is enormous. Like a donkey, she thinks. I can never take that inside. It'll rip me apart. He faces her, a few inches away from her. She shivers. His thing down there is like a stick of wood, heavily veined, delicately textured. She smells the man, his odour is strong, fierce. She accumulates saliva at the back of her mouth and swallows it down.

"Suck him, make him grow," a voice says in the background, outside of the circle of light in which she feels imprisoned.

She kneels down, touches Orlando's cock. Lifts the shaft to her dry lips. Underneath she sees the heavy sack of his balls, the lined thin skin holding the heavy testicles, the bulging scrotum. She approaches her mouth. She can feel his member throbbing as she holds it. It's growing already. Her tongue emerges and reaches the tip of his glans. He has no foreskin. She closes her eyes and moves her head, her mouth forward. The cock slides between her lips, brushes against her teeth and, pulsing all the time, lodges itself against the back of her throat. She almost chokes and has to adjust her position, raising her head slightly, still the sportsman's penis grows until she feels her whole mouth full, invaded. Her tongue moves around the thick shaft, licking, caressing, tasting the man.

"See, it fits," she hears Steve, commenting. "I told you she was a big girl. Look at that ass, the butt of a queen, truly."

She sucks and sucks to little emotional reaction from the black giant. She's afraid he will come in her mouth, literally drown her throat with his semen, choke her to death. Right then, he places a hand on her freckled shoulder and says: "I'm ready, girl, now." And pulls his cock out of her aching mouth.

The massive member stands tall, an inch away from her face. She finally opens her eyes. She's never seen a cock so big, so thick, so long. No, she mentally protests, it'll kill me. It'll never go in. It's physically impossible. It stands at attention, rigid and hard, like a lethal weapon.

She turns around. Steve and half the men have got their cocks out or trousers down. They all seem incredibly thin and long.

"He's got to wear a condom," she protests.

"No," says one of the men.

Katherine stands firm.

"Then I can't go along with it, I just can't," she says. It's possibly her out.

"For a thousand bucks, you'll do what we say," Steve screams at her. "This ain't no government health education advertorial."

He walks over to her and suddenly punches her in the stomach. She bends forward, not so much in pain, but out of breath.

"There, that's a gentle warning." He pushes her head down to the floor, "Okay, black stud, poke her. First, turn her over so we've a good view."

Orlando moves her body round, spits into his palm, wets his cock and positions his raised dick right by her opening. Katherine is on all fours, rump raised to his level, he pulls her hips up and she almost loses balance. She feels the tip of the cock brushing hard against her outer lips. The black man thrusts hard and the glans enters and jams, only, partly embedded inside her. Her muscles already feel so stretched, she squirms. Her involuntary movement loosens the inner labia and the main shaft moves an inch forward. It hurts. Bad. His large hands seize her rump as he pushes again.

Two of the men are betting.

'It'll never go in."

"Yes, it will. She can take him. Hey, Steve, the stud needs some lubrication, help him out."

She hears him move close and feels a cold liquid pouring down over her ass and into the vaginal gash, pearling over the black cock. Champagne. Orlando grunts, thrusts hard, his hips dictating the sharp movement, the shaft moves further up her cunt. How much more? She moans. Tears are coming to her eyes. One final shove and he is finally all in, she is tearing, she is being cut in two. The black man begins to move inside her, the top of his cock feels as if it's moved so far it's inside her stomach, scraping manically against her inside walls. The movement increases and she blanks out her mind, the pain down there now feels like an anaesthetic, remote, someone else's. Eternity and over.

"Great ass, hey. Love that mole under the left butt, or is it a beauty spot?" Steve remarks from his vantage point.

White on black.

Black cock inside white cunt.

"Turn over," one of the men says. "Missionary, now."

Orlando disengages. It feels like a hole inside her. He pulls her over and down, settles her shoulders and the back of her head on the carpet. She looks down on her body. She is gaping open. She gasps, it'll never close up again. The outer lips are redder than they were with all the lipstick. The black sportsman, with his cock still at full mast kneels down and with one hand moves the cock back into her. He bobs up and down over her, as the dick slides in and out until it reaches port and impales her totally. Then he pulls her legs up and places them over his own shoulders, still thrusting savagely inside her all the time. For the first time, she feels an early wave of pleasure run through her. Her nipples are so sensitive. Why doesn't Orlando touch them? Please. Her lover did. The black man's breath grows shorter. She senses his climax approaching as his eyes open and close in quick succession as he pistons on inside her, his big balls slamming like a metronome against her bum.

"Hey," Steve shouts out. "Orlando, my man, don't come inside her. Let's see your spunk on her face."

The stud digs ever deeper into her. Vaginal farts punctuate his movements as the air left inside her is displaced by his sheer bulk. Finally, he pulls out hurriedly and his come spurts out like a geyser, white, creamy, burning hot over her shaven mons and her thighs.

"He missed the target," one of the jokers says.

The black guy, spent, looks Katherine in the eyes. "Sorry," he whispers. "I needed the money too. Gambling debts."

He walks away, standing tall, to fetch his clothes.

Quarter of an hour later. Orlando has left and all the business-men have had another round of drinks. Katherine is still spread out on the thick carpet of the hotel suite, aching madly, her legs still obscenely apart, the lips of her sex still unnaturally dilated, it still hurts too much to close her thighs and steal her live porno movie away from the men.

"So, gentlemen," Steve says. "Good show, hey? Nothing beats a big, strong blonde. Any of you want a sample now? Please yourselves. No extra cost."

How can he, Katherine mutters?

The South Americans confer between themselves. Finally, one of them says: "Thanks, but no thanks, compadre. That pussy's been used up for today. I'd float in there. I don't care about the black guy, they're all bloody animals, but I don't know where that pussy's been before. I've a family, you know. Get rid of her."

Steve pulls her up. She staggers across the room. He slips her an envelope, together with her crumpled clothes.

"It's all there. Now you can nicely bugger off, Eddie. And don't even think of ever mentioning this to anyone or I'll cut you up so badly your mother wouldn't recognize you. Understood?"

He opens the door and pushes her out into the corridor.

She's quite naked, she knows she looks a real mess, the black stud's spunk is still seeping out somehow between her lower lips, or is it some sort of personal secretion? There's a bad bruise on the inside of her thigh.

As he closes the door:

"I'd slip something on pronto, girl, if I were you. There might be a hotel detective on the prowl," he laughs.

She hurriedly dresses and makes her way to the lifts. Yes, her lover had once said, I will celebrate you like no man has ever done, Kate. Yes, all the things he would say as his fingers kept lingering in the small of her back after the act of love.

She's travelled to Las Vegas. Another stage of her American kaleidoscope. She'd remembered someone once saying how cheap the food and hotels happened to be, subsidized as they were by all the gambling. One of her directors had been there for a bookselling convention, and mentioned the fact. Like a modern Jack Kerouac heroine she'd made the journey on Greyhound buses, crisscrossing the vast plains and their surrounding roadside galleries of decrepit motels and gas stations. And then, one morning at dawn, racing out of the desert into the garish canyons of light of Vegas, she had come across her new, temporary home.

She found a small residential hotel at an unfashionable end of the Strip, where the gamblers never went and working-class families with kids, mostly from New Jersey, stayed. She even managed to bargain down the weekly rate. She avoided the big casinos and the glittering joints. Not again. She tried to get waitressing jobs, but they all said she was too old. Did they mean unattractive, she wondered? Here, most of the women were icily perfect. Surgically designed to appeal to the average American male. Frosty lipstick, eye shadow galore, tight skirts, no visible panty line. Not quite her.

After costing her room and the steak breakfast specials ever on offer all around, Katherine estimated she could last a whole month before she would run out of cash. I need a holiday, anyway, she thought.

She often walked out to the desert when night fell, to breathe in the pure, dry air. She grew to recognize all the amazing species of cacti growing in the wilderness that surrounded the town. The night sky was so amazingly clear. If only she could remember which constellations were which from her wasted school days. The heavens were a subtle tapestry of lights, delicately enhanced by the reddish glow of the electric city illuminating the surrounding mountains.

Less than a year ago when she and her husband had moved into their new mews house, before all hell broke loose over her affair, she had intended to fulfil an earlier ambition and begin writing stories in earnest. She'd finally have a study, a space of her own. Nothing had come of it. Life had conspired to thwart her again.

Now was the time, Katherine decided, buying a yellow legal pad.

The story begins.

"My husband is a good man. My husband is a gentle man. Even though the passing of the years has hardened him and he is no longer the young man with whom I shared my early student poverty, he is still the man I sleep with. I smell his stale breath when he awakes in the morning and it does not offend me. I see the faint stains in his underwear before I load up the washing machine and it doesn't shock or disgust me. My marriage is the most important thing in my life. I treasure it. I protect it from the storms. I shield myself behind it. I've messed up so many other things, but my marriage will survive against the odds and divorce statistics. It will work. It must work.

"My husband and I argue a lot. He cries when we go to sentimental films, while my eyes remain dry. I have a cold heart, you see. I'm not romantic. I don't know why. The way I was brought up, I suppose. We've lived together seven years, married for five of them. Two flats. One house. No children. My husband wants us to have babies, and he is becoming more insistent. Soon I shall turn thirty; I mustn't leave it too late, he says. I don't want kids right now, I tell him but what I mean is that I don't want kids at all. I don't like the way adults go all soft and mushy in the presence of babies; children get on my nerves, they cry, they show off, they are loud. I would be a bad mother.

"Once I could have justified my actions by invoking my career, my brilliant career. Now I can no longer do so. People think I have a prestigious job, but it's not what I thought it would be. There are too many frustrations. So, I am left with much emptiness.

"The lovemaking is not what it used to be. We're growing older together. Too familiar with each other. All too often, at night, he is tired and falls asleep without even finishing reading the financial papers. He is ambitious, has lofty aspirations for his own career. Works hard. Some times, in the morning he feels randy and arranges his body against mine, presses himself against my back, rubs his cock against my arse, lazily fingers my breasts. I wet my fingers and lubricate my opening and manually insert him. On most occasions he's only half-erect. He screws me in utter silence. I like being taken from behind. It makes me feel more sensitive. Our morning fucks barely scratch the itch in my guts. Oh, there's nothing bad about it. I'm sure most other couples are no more animated or passionate than we are. Once or twice a year, he whizzes me off to a small country hotel for a long week-end. The lovemaking is better. I even orgasm sometimes. But in the mornings, it's always over too fast. He comes inside me and my thighs are all damp as he pulls out and rushes to the bathroom. He only has a half hour left to shave, wash, dress, eat before he leaves for the studio or the outside broadcast he's been assigned to. But, all in all, he is a good, kind man, my husband. He forgives my trespasses. Tolerates my wild, irrational tempers. The tall man I married for better or for worse."

She put her pen down. Enough for today.

She takes a coach and visits the Hoover Dam, one hour's drive out of Vegas.

The view is majestic. The vast expanse of water in the lake is utterly surreal in this desert environment. She journeys down with visiting crowds to the bottom of the dam, to the heart of the concrete monster and feels quite dwarfed by the sheer power of the construction. At the end of the tour, she goes to the cafeteria with its huge bay windows at water level and sits herself down with a coffee and a sticky cake. A man accosts her. Identifying his accent is easy. He's Welsh. Works in local government or education, it doesn't quite register with her. But it's nice not to have to communicate with yet another Yank. He's here with a group of friends. Fellow professionals, he insists. Enjoying a spot of gambling. They're having a small party and card game in their room at the Mirage tonight. Yes, the Casino with the live volcano outside. Would she like to join them? She must be homesick, surely. It would be nice to hear more normal accents. Two of the boys are from Bristol, he tells her.

Once in the room, she first notices the other woman. Auburn hair, round face, dark glasses, black halter top and tight white jeans. The other men, the Brits, seem unappealing. More like lager louts on a sun, booze and sex holiday to Ibiza. Her host, his name is Maurice, effects the introductions. She quickly forgets the men's names. Two of them are junior doctors and the third one a sales executive, a rep for a pharmaceutical company who's probably picking up the bill. The woman's name is Vicky.

It is not my real name, she tells Katherine when she joins her in the bathroom where they powder their nose and cheeks. "It was Liliana, but it was wrong. I just don't feel like a Lily or a Liliana, really. So I changed it."

She is American, from Phoenix, Arizona, has been in Vegas six months now, some waitressing, some hosting, a personal escort agency had found her tonight's gig. "Very respectable, classy, you know, they actually advertise in the local papers. So you're English too? Who do you work for?" she asks.

"I don't," Katherine answers. "Freelance," she explains. Why complicate matters? She knows all too well why she has been invited here tonight. Fresh meat. Orifices.

There are dark shadows under Vicky's eyes. Her face is heavily freckled and the freckles continue all the way down her front and disappear inside her cleavage. Her neck is intensely pale. She wears her hair up in a delicately sculpted bun. She is quite small and delicate and once must have been ever so pretty, baby-faced until time finally caught up with her. Her eyes, once the sunglasses come off, are revealed to be dark green. Hypnotic. Under the halter top, she has medium-sized breasts, Katherine sees, as Vicky lifts the material to powder her tits. A reflection catches her eye in the mirror. Katherine can't stop herself staring at the other woman's breasts. They are so round. Almost perfect. Pierced. She's even a touch envious of both these impeccably rounded orbs and the striking adornments. She'd never have the guts. She used to faint at the dentist's.

"You're very pretty," she tells the other woman.

"Thanks, dear." She readjusts her top, wriggles her bum inside the tight jeans. "Shall we? Your English buddies are waiting for their entertainment."

The men ply the girls with drinks. The ensuing conversation is rowdy, suggestive but innocent enough to begin with. Maurice, who seems in charge of orchestrating the proceedings, is particularly boisterous, and his jokes are actually on occasion witty. They order snacks from room service, and the obligatory champagne. Katherine relaxes. Gazes at the men. Tries to imagine what they would all look like in their birthday suits. That one must have a hairy chest, what about the beer belly on the other one, another must surely have a big cock, don't like the last one though, looks a bit evil.

"Well, boys, this is Vegas. Time to gamble. What's your poison?" Maurice asks.

"Poker."

"Strip poker."

They all giggle and look toward the two women sipping their drinks on the mustard couch.

The pharmaceutical rep devises an infinitely complex set of rules for the game, to ensure they all shed clothing fast enough, including Katherine and Vicky, who are assigned to respective card players.

They play.

Vicky is the first to end up unclothed. Katherine still has her underwear on. And garter belt and stockings. She knows from experience how much men like her when she wears them. The carousing Brits are soon all shirtless, one is down to his jockey shorts.

The American woman has a small, compact body, her legs are not that great, and sports two thick gold rings on her nipples. Adorned à la modern primitive. The rings glisten inside the pierced puckered, dark red skin of the nipples. Katherine can't disguise her intense fascination. Neither can the guys; their tongues almost sticking out when they catch sight of Vicky's extraordinary boobs and their unnatural metal extensions. One of the medics deliberately loses his next hand to carry Vicky to the next stage where forfeits begin.

"She has to play with her tits," one of them orders.

Vicky does.

She twists the darker skin between her nimble fingers, pulls the tips of her round breasts through the hoops of the rings, distends the flesh to impossible proportions. Asks the man nearest to her to lick her fingers and then smears the moist secretion over her abnormally erect nipples. They are all entranced. Katherine included.

Vicky tires of manipulating herself. "Next round," she says.

Inevitably, all the clothing is shed. The men sit there around the table, self-conscious, exchanging nervous glances at each other, a couple of them are semi-erect, another handles himself but fails to harden his stem; too much drink.

"Isn't this great?" Maurice exclaims to break the silence. "More champagne, ladies and gentlemen." He stands up to get the last bottle from the room service trolley. He has a fat, floppy arse.

He brushes past Katherine as he pours the drink for her and, with his free hand, roughly fondles her left breast. She finds it, and him, deeply unpleasant and shivers. He ignores her reaction.

The women are now excluded from the card game and the men play between themselves for forfeits. Katherine looks over at Vicky. The auburn-haired woman has settled back on the couch, her legs wide open in a truly indecent posture. She joins her, thighs together, more demure. She can't stop herself looking down at Vicky's bush where she notices a thin line of secretions separating her cunt lips. Vicky notices her gaze. The inner juice seeps into the thick rust-coloured vegetation.

"I'm a bit excited," she confesses. She's a bit drunk. "I hope they ask us to do it together first," she says.

Katherine bites her tongue. She's never had any kind of sexual contact with a woman before. Well, there was this girl, Diane, back at grammar school. When they showered after hockey one day, Katherine had once blushed to her roots when she had been caught daydreaming and staring at the other girl's budding breasts and the first growth of thin hair on her pubis. She looks into Vicky's green eyes. She has an uncomfortable feeling in the pit of her stomach. On the other hand, she's getting wet, inside. Anticipation?

Inevitably, British males have so little imagination, that's what the guys ask for.

Vicky takes Katherine's hand and leads her to the carpet. The men settle in their chairs, pulling them away from the card table, idly fingering their cocks.

She gently pushes Katherine down, her back against the floor. She slides back, parts Katherine's thighs, opens her legs wide and moves her head towards the beckoning crotch. She licks the shaven lips, and a jolt of raw electricity runs through Katherine's body. Jesus. Vicky gnaws at the entrance and soon inserts her tongue inside the now dripping vagina. The men have grown totally silent. The agile, experienced tongue moves in as deep as she can manage it. Katherine closes her eyes. The warm, velvety, darting tongue then moves upwards and envelops her clitoris. Katherine can feel the bud swelling. She can no longer control her body and a spasm races across her stomach. The tongue deftly extracts the expanding clitoris from its thin hood and Vicky moves her head forward slightly so that her teeth are now chewing Katherine's button. Jesus. Jesus. She sighs. He used to do it exactly the same way. But the American woman quickly tires and now uses two fingers to bring Katherine off. As she does so distractedly, she whispers:

'You taste really nice."

Katherine looks down at the auburn bun bobbing up and down between her thighs and the jerky movement of the hand ending up inside her, stimulating her inner parts with knowing cunning and talent. The pleasure moves up and up through her.

"69?" Vicky suggests.

She circles Katherine's body and lowers her own, hairy dark cunt over Katherine's face as she lies down on her, stomach to stomach, breasts almost joined, slightly out of alignment. She licks away at her cunt again in the new position and Katherine timidly extends her tongue upward where it loses itself in the woman's thick, curly bush. She has to use her fingers to find a way through the pubic hair, separates Vicky's cunt leaves and slips her tongue inside the other woman.

She tastes so strong. Katherine almost gags initially, but overcomes her reluctance and begins licking the inner walls opening up above her. Vicky is a prolific secreter and soon her juices are flooding Katherine's mouth, settling in a ring around her mouth, pungent, an abundant gluey deposit.

"Wow," says one of the men.

Soon, Katherine finds a rhythm and her tongue patterns its in-and-out intrusions against the movement of Vicky's head and mouth lower down. It even settles into a routine. She feels the heat increasing in her throat and lungs. She must be so wet down there too. It's both repugnant and perversely pleasing. She wonders if men really enjoy it.

A hand strokes her damp forehead. She opens her eyes again. It's one of the men.

"Oh, it's a waste of talent," another says. "Now for the real stuff."

Yet another walks over as Vicky disengages herself and Katherine is left sprawled, open, spread-eagled on the carpet as the men surround the two women.

Passively, Katherine and Vicky allow the men to position them, next to each other, on all fours as two move to the front and insert their cocks into the women's mouths and the remaining two fuck them doggie-style from behind. The cock in Katherine's mouth is flaccid, and all her best efforts fail to raise it from the dead. In her rear, Maurice pistons away, punctuating his thrusts with hard slaps on her rump. He withdraws, and exchanges positions with the medic who'd been screwing Vicky. The new cock plunges into her still dilated opening, and the guy quickly comes. In her mouth, the useless cock is just another piece of meat. The third man removes himself from Vicky's mouth as Maurice, still hard, keeps on screwing the American woman relentlessly and positions himself behind her. The plump man's labouring instrument is very thick and painfully stretches her cunt muscles. However, he ejaculates quickly, and Katherine feels her innards drowning in the mixed come of the two men. The man in her mouth still labours on, to no avail.

"Hey, not there," Vicky screams, next to her. Katherine turns her head but cannot see what Vicky is complaining about to Maurice, or the other man. She's no longer sure who is doing what to whom.

After all the fun and games are over, the two women wash themselves out in the adjoining bathroom. Katherine watches the men's seed mingle in the tub with the soapy water, as it seeps, on and on from her body as she squats over the bathtub.

"Well, that was quite fun," Vicky remarks, adjusting her make-up in front of the bathroom mirror.

They leave the Mirage together and become friends. But they never have sex together again. "I prefer men," Vicky tells her one morning when Katherine, curious, questions her. "Anyway, your heart wasn't in it. You're not truly bi."

When the cash runs out, Vicky helps her get a job in a peep show on the wrong side of town, where she herself does the occasional shift when funds are short. The money's good and the security guys see to it that there's no funny business. Six hours a day, Katherine sits in a cubicle in diaphanous lingerie, while men open the door to enter the other side of the closet, a glass window separating them. There is a telephone to communicate between the two areas. For five dollars, the men get three minutes during which she strips and follows their utterly predictable instructions. They are without surprises. They ask her to touch herself. Breasts. Pussy. Sometimes even feet. For an extra ten dollars, which they can insert through a hand-sized aperture in the glass partition, she will spread her legs wide and open her vulva to their gaze, for an extra twenty, she will even insert a flesh-coloured dildo inside her cunt and pretend to masturbate. Invariably, they all lower their trousers to jerk off. An attendant has to wipe the come off the glass partition and sweep the floor with disinfectant every fifteen minutes or so. When rent day approaches, Vicky teaches her a new trick, which is strictly speaking not allowed, but where the management operate a blind eye policy. For another fifty dollars, she will also allow the guy to thread his hand through the opening and paw her. One day, one man goes too far and scratches her badly. Katherine gives up the job and packs her meagre belongings. There are too many books, all used, read a few times each already, too much to carry. Vicky says she'll join her. They leave Las Vegas and head for the Coast.

Katherine is waitressing at the bar of a big hotel near LAX. Randy businessmen make half-hearted passes, but don't seem too disappointed when she politely turns them down. She's not the Angeleno type. The tips aren't too good and the hours are long and awkward. She still lives with Vicky; they share a small apartment in a block near Pacific Palisades. Vicky sometimes disappears for days on end. Katherine never asks where she has been. There are often marks on her body. One morning as she surprises her in the shower, Katherine sees that the small American woman now sports a snake tattoo weaving its way down from her navel to her bush. Christ, that must have been fucking painful, she thinks. Another time, she sees a bad scar on Vicky's rump. Deliberate. Burnt into the flesh. They are seldom together at the apartment any more. Waitressing and sex work hours seldom coincide.

It's Katherine's day off. Big plans for today; she's going to lounge by the communal pool and finally start Proust. She's been putting it off for years. And next, she's planning on Dostoevsky. She's always been meaning to fill these gaps in her literary culture.

She lies in bed, vaguely daydreaming as always of the men she has left behind. Does she still love, miss, think of them? She just doesn't know any longer. Vicky walks in. She looks rough.

"Hi, Kate? Got the day off, hey?"

"Yes."

"Listen. I badly need a favour," she says. "I'm feeling damn rotten. My period has started and I'm in pain all over. But I've been paid in advance for a job today. Can you go there instead?"

"What sort?" Katherine enquires.

"A film."

"Nudity?" Katherine asks.

"Yeah, of course. But if you ask, they won't show your face. There are lotsa other girls involved, so they won't mind."

Vicky runs to the bathroom where she is promptly sick. She returns, awfully pale and tense. She nervously insists. "Please, I just can't face it today. Be a pal. Please."

Katherine acquiesces. She's stripped before. Never before a camera, though. And she likes Vicky in a quiet, affectionate way.

Vicky books a cab for the afternoon. It's a villa in the Hollywood Hills. She bargains with the producers.

"It's all fixed. He even said that if you're real glamorous, you could get a bonus. I told him you're incredibly tall and have wild hair. He was very excited. You'll have to doll yourself up a bit. Here," she extracts a note from her handbag. "Fifty bucks, buy yourself something special at the mall, something nice. You English gals have so much taste."

Katherine spends it all, and more, at Victoria's Secret, where the lingerie is supposed to be English but comes from somewhere in Ohio or thereabouts, she read in a magazine. The underwear is slinky, the silk glistens, she knows how easily she could become a serious silk fetishist with stuff like this. She could spend a fortune on underwear alone. A black slip that adheres to her body through the sheer force of gravity, a pair of knickers, more like a thong, the sheer fabric dissecting her bum cheeks and enhancing the drop of her wide hips. A brassiere that hooks up at the back like a corset. Stockings as soft as flesh. In the cubicle, she looks at her body in the mirror. She feels the onset of wetness between her thighs. God, I'm such a slut.

The villa has white walls, most of the furniture has been moved out the main room, and its windows open up on a large pool outside. They're already filming there when she arrives. A brassy, artificial blonde stands inside, the water lapping around her waist, her breasts are large and unnatural. A silicone job, no doubt. A tubby guy sits on the edge and she is sucking his cock with a distinct lack of enthusiasm, while the camera peers into the action in close-up. The cameraman is incredibly hairy and wears only Bermuda shorts. Out of camera range, two other couples lounge around, some nude, others with towels around their waist. She recognizes one of the men. It's Steve; Esteban, from Miami.

He sees and waves.

"Hey, if it isn't English Eddie?"

She acknowledges his presence with a silent gesture.

The peroxide blonde in the pool changes position with the man and he starts sucking on her genitals, once the cameraman has changed his film. Her pubes are also peroxide blonde. The straw yellow patch seems so damn wrong. A young guy, who looks more like a student, but is actually the director, shouts out:

"Come on, give it some more life. You're supposed to be enjoying it."

The porno actor ignores him and chews away impassively.

Finally, "Cut. Let's move on to another scene. Everybody's here. The whole cast. Orgy time, kids."

She's asked to strip. They won't even let her wear the new lingerie. A female assistant powders her thigh to hide a small bruise, then moves on to another one of the women who spreads her thighs open and instructs the gofer to powder over the pimples spreading like a rash around her cunt.

The director orders them to spread out in a daisy chain by the pool side. She's asked to fellate the guy in front of her as he lies on his back and Steve rams her from behind and the peroxide blonde from the previous sequence licks out his arsehole and fingers his balls while he moves in and out of Katherine.

One fleeting moment, she imagines her husband out on the town with a group of other journalists and friends, maybe tomorrow his brother the architect is getting married; they have a meal in China-town, cruise the pubs getting increasingly drunker and land in some Soho film club to watch dirty movies. He recognizes her cunt, and is sick as he is forced to watch the alien penis invade her private sanctum in larger than life dimensions. Which is how he must have felt when he had learned of her cheating. The hurt.

Steve pumps away, whispers:

"Fancy meeting like this again, lady. Destiny, I'm sure."

The director has them change positions.

Now a small redhead is asked to eat her out while Steve's long, thin member invests her mouth and forces its way almost down her throat. Another's hand roughly manipulates her nipples, twisting, pulling, squeezing between sharp nails. She can't see anything. The strong lights blind her and all she can hear is the monotonous whirr of the nearby camera's motor as it captures the scene and her infamy forever. The redhead isn't very good. She has a small bald patch and a birthmark on her back, like a map of Italy. Her aroma is distinctive. Do all redheads smell this way?

Behind her, she hears one of the guys cry out that he's coming, and the cameraman rushes off to catch the moment; the man's momentary partner fakes aural orgasm. Katherine tastes the pre-ejaculate filtering from the tip of the Cuban's cock shortly before he withdraws. The sparky assistant brings them all cool drinks and they move inside the villa.

The women don't speak to each other as they troop in. The men follow. The tubby one has lost his erection. As the next camera set-up is prepared, he strokes himself to regain his rigidity. It doesn't work. The director asks the girls to help him out.

"I don't do that," the redhead says.

The peroxide blonde says:

"He smells. At the pool was enough."

Katherine lowers her eyes when the young director looks in her direction.

"Okay, okay already," he calls the young assistant over. "Hey, Markie, this is what they taught you at film school, no? Help the poor guy out."

"You bastard," the all-purpose assistant answers, but moves over to the temporarily impotent actor and takes hold of his cock as she lowers her mouth toward it. "Better not film any of this."

Soon, the actor is functional again.

He's instructed to mount Katherine in the missionary position while the others adopt a variety of lovemaking positions around them. He squeezes himself inside her and quickly loses his hardness. They're filming the others. He moves ever so slightly inside her so as not to slip out. He winks at her. She's quite happy to keep on pretending. This goes on forever, and no one notices their lack of ardour as the other couples make up in noise and movement for the faking couple.

"Cut. You can all rest a bit now. Steve," the director calls over to him. "You seem fresh. In better shape than the other guys. Okay, you and curly hair here, let's do the anal."

The others walk away to the pool.

Katherine suddenly realizes what comes next.

"No, no, I can't do that," she says, pleadingly, to the men, the young whey-faced director, the aggressively erect Steve and the sweating cameraman.

"Love," the director says. "It's part of the deal. Every hard-core movie has anals now. That's what the guys want. Don't tell me you've never done one. Everyone in the business has to. It's the money shot."

"I won't come inside you," Steve adds. "When the time comes, I'll pull out and do a facial, okay?"

The cameraman signifies his assent.

"No," Katherine timidly pleads one last time.

Steve takes hold of her wrist and twists it hard.

"Eddie," he says, "you're a bit of a tease, aren't you. I remember the last time, you like to play hard to get, hey; you always have cold feet, don't you?"

Markie the assistant comes over as they set Katherine down on her stomach and help her raise her rump so that the camera can catch it all. They adjust the lights. Shine the warm spots on her utterly exposed rear. Markie carefully sponges Katherine's genitals and between her cheeks, to clean the perspiration away and then gently pours some oil around her anal aperture as well as Steve's penis still standing at attention.

Katherine closes her eyes. She's never been entered there. Penetrated. Fucked. Sodomized. But, she remembers all those nights lying in silence next to her sleeping, cuckolded husband, her whole body consumed by the thoughts of transgression. Her lover had soon discovered how sensitive she was down there and they had often speculated about it. Sometime after they had split up and he was writing her these desperate letters to get her back, change her mind, he had revealed that for weeks he had kept some butter in the fridge in his office for that very purpose.

The cameraman adjusts his focus.

"Filming."

Steve inserts one finger inside her to spread the oil around. With his other hand, he parts her arse cheeks as wide as he can and places his hard cock against the puckered opening. Initial pressure, the sphincter muscles resist and he makes no headway. He grabs his stem and holding it in a tight vice manually begins to spear her anus. The head moves an inch or so past the outer ring. It feels like constipation backwards. She clenches her teeth. The lubrication takes effect and with one swift move the head inserts itself. Katherine holds her breath.

"Yeah, nice and slow," the cameraman, or is it the director, says.

She's tearing, she knows it. Her opening is being sundered.

Literally split apart. She's often fingered herself there, but this is like a knife, a pole, a gun.

Steve thrusts his hips and breaks through. The cock savagely tears in and impales her to the hilt.

Katherine screams.

This is worse than anything ever. She wants to faint, die, make it all go away. Her whole soul seems focused on the opening to her arse where the long, thin cock is planted. Steve ceases all movement. She senses the cock still growing inside her, her inner walls being forcibly pushed further and further back.

"Focus closer. Now. Now."

The man initiates a steady movement, a quick coming and going inside her guts. To her utter shame, Katherine feels an odious sort of pleasure, excitement radiating out from her forced aperture down to her cunt, up through her stomach. Her heart falters. The movements increase. Every reverse movement of the cock a few inches out of her hole pulls the inner flesh out, the tight, textured pink private flesh sticking like glue to the dark thrusting cock, and then back in again. Secretions accelerate, coat the moving penis trunk in a ring of white thin cream.

"Hey, she looks good," another male voice explains. The others have come in from the pool to watch the action.

"Yes," says Steve, between regular thrusts. "She has the perfect butt for anal. Great fit, man."

The other man is in front of the kneeling Katherine. She looks up. He's growing erect, his pole rising steadily as he keeps on watching the Cuban digging into her depths in a metronomic movement, and her head shaking forward with every thrust.

"What about a DP, man?" the voyeur asks the director.

"Good idea," he says.

Katherine's mouth is so dry. She gasps for breath.

"Look, she's all flushed," the other man says.

Katherine's face and chest have gone a deep shade of pink. Like a stain racing across her body, as the orgasm approaches, stronger than anything before. The cock in her arse still keeps on moving deeper, seemingly labouring her intestines, she wills it further, her inner muscles gripping the hard tool, sucking it in a vampiric embrace.

Steve slows down, pulls her back slightly, still carefully lodged in her rectum and the other porno actor slides down on his back and moves under her raised upper body. She can feel her sweat raining down over him. He slithers into position and positions his cock under her sex lips. She feels the wetness shamefully dripping from her cunt onto his glans and he inserts himself.

"Jesus, Jesus, Jeezus . . ."

Both men are now fucking her.

They move in unison. As one thrusts, another retreats to the edge of his respective opening. Fire races through her. Her mind is on fever. They now coordinate their movements and thrust inside her together. The cocks rub against her inner walls, teasing each other through the thin layer of skin separating them. She imagines the vision of her double penetration on the cinema screen: the two inhumanly large cocks tearing her pale, white skin in two, digging ever deeper holes, the inhumanly dilated ringed anus as one pulls back, the gaping vaginal gash open like a flower of desire as the foreign object buries itself inside her ever-accommodating cunt. Her husband and her lover watching, both masturbating away. This is me, this is me, she says.

"I'm running out of film," the cameraman says. "We need the come shot."

The two men withdraw violently, wrenching her guts, take hold of their cocks and pump away manually at speed and come. Over her. Her face. Her rump.

"Lick it," the director says.

Her tongue moves across her lips, tastes the salty emissions, it sticks in the back of her throat when she tries to swallow.

"Good show, Eddie," Steve says, smearing his come all over her smooth back side. "We should do it again, in private, you know. I can teach you some more tricks."

The other women quickly expedite another sequence where they gluttonously eat each other out for the length of another roll of film. Katherine rests. Sips several cans of beer. It grows dark outside. All the actors are growing tired.

"I've got another few minutes of film left," the cameraman points out. "Waste not, want not. Anything we haven't got in the can yet?"

Steve says to the director: "Do you want to try and do something different? I've only seen it done once, you know, by Cameo, a double cuntal."

"That would be good," the young man says. "Who?"

"I'll do it," Katherine says.

The positioning is awkward. It's not painful; since the black guy in Vegas, she knows she can take any size. And by now, neither of them can stay fully hard. They clumsily do the act. One of the cocks keeps slipping out. Neither man feels the friction of the two pricks against each other inside her very stimulating. Ten minutes is all it takes. They might salvage two minutes in the edit.

Cut.

That night, she writes again in the yellow legal pad.

"My lover is a pornographer. My lover writes vile stories in which he degrades me. I am always amazed by how white his eyes are, peering into mine as he moves inside my body. He has dark curls on his chest and whispers dirty words in my ear when we are engaged in the act of love, making wild promises he will never keep of all the cities and places he will one day take me to. My wild lover whose hair never stands still says he no longer wants to share me. He betrays our original agreement and scares me deeply. He is unpredictable. I never know what he will say or do next. To me. To my ignorant husband.

"When my lover loves me he positions me on the bed or, more often because of the unfortunate nature of our clandestine encounters, on the floor. He cups his hands under my bum, and raises it slightly while his mouth approaches me. He parts my lower lips with gentle, loving care, brushing my moist curls back and kisses the outer folds of my sex. He takes his time. He does not hurry. He teases my senses like an expert. He knows every inch of my body and trips the light fandango all over. He divides my sex into dozens of distinct areas and knows the right word and touch for each. Mons. Outer labia. Inner labia. Folds. Bud. Hood. Walls. Vagina. Cervix. Spots all the way from A to G. Where did he learn all this? Watching porno movies, he says. His tongue moves inside me and he takes my clitoris, the small bud, in between his lips. He chews, he licks, he sucks and bites it and the inside of my cunt. He tastes my moist intimate secretions and never protests. I know I smell down there. He sniffs me and smiles. He perspires and I drink in his sharp scent. Until I cry enough, I want you inside me now. And his thick, dark cock plunges in to me. Chews my ear lobe. Licks the acrid perspiration from my arm pits. He has no shame.

"As he fucks me, my lover inserts a slow finger up my arse, beyond the tiny ridge of flesh that just hangs there like a superfluous growth. We copulate, his finger pushes, slides, swivels, rotates inside me and a warm feeling invades my stomach and I almost pee all over him as we move together convulsively and my head bangs against the bed rest or the office wall.

"After love, we talk. And he frightens me again. We share saté sticks and Tesco dips in the darkness. Once he brings sushi pieces.

"We fuck again. Like animals. Over and again. He never tires. We are sore. I never want to go home.

"The last time I saw my lover, it was pouring and my hair was flat and he held an oversize umbrella to protect himself. I shouted at him, swore. He didn't say much, just handed me this letter he had written and walked away through the drizzle. Peace, is all he asked. How can you, I thought? But my erstwhile lover sometimes has no decency. He is a wild, dark-haired man. My late lover who angers me so much I once almost tried to hire some thug to go and break his legs. I suppose I read too many crime books."

Her insides ache. She goes to sleep.

A few days later, Katherine almost collapsed with pain while serving behind the hotel bar. The head barman sent her home and she went to see a doctor. She had a bad infection. No doubt someone on that crazy film shoot. At least it wasn't Aids. All the money she had saved had to pay for the necessary antibiotics.

Vicky has gone. One morning, her clothes and belongings were no longer there. On her own, Katherine could not afford the rent.

She looked at her face in the bathroom mirror. Her brown eyes seem dull. She has spots. She took a long bath, soaking in the warmth. The hairs above her crotch are growing back, hard, wiry, the shaving had irritated the skin and she squeezed some yellow pus from a small pimple there.

She packed her clothes in a canvas tote bag, leaving the legal pad on the dresser. She had only managed to write a few pages. E for effort.

Once on the highway, she hitched North to Seattle. Not one driver made a pass at her during the course of her journeys up the coastline.

*   *   *

They seek her here, they seek her there, they seek her everywhere, but Katherine hides her shame among the deep forests of
the Pacific Northwest, reaches the Seattle hills and the vast
expanses of blue water that surround the city. She takes up
smoking. It rains a lot. On clear days, she gazes at Mount Rainier
looming over the horizon of the Seattle skyline. On the way here,
she has lost most of her clothes, and barely has enough to keep her
warm as winter approaches. But she still holds on to the sheer silk
lingerie from Victoria's Secret, even though she has no occasion
to wear it any longer, living as she does in tight, soiled tee-shirts,
an old brown leather waistcoat, a birthday present from her lost
husband, and patched-up jeans.

She moves like a white ghost through and beyond the sexual pale.

There's an advertisement in the local free paper. An agency is
looking for entertainers. Good pay. Open mind required. The
first job she is given is to jump out of a massive cake at a party for
a group of Microsoft localizing editors celebrating the completion
of another software development project. She is given a skimpy
outfit, all glitter and vulgarity. She emerges from the hollow cake.
They're all so young. Boys really. She steps out and dances on the
table top. They holler and cheer like frat boys. She shakes her
butt, tweaks her nipples inside the thin fabric of the oversize bra,
and then pulls her small tits out to another triumphant roar from
the boys. Later, she smears the remnants of the rich cream from
the cake all over her body and allows the drunken technicians to
lick it off her. Very few actually take advantage of her, barely a
tongue or a hand ventures lower down. After she has cleaned up,
she joins some of the guys for a friendly drink. They're rather
boring. Even here, most can only discuss computer lore. One of
the young men stares at her behind thick round glasses. She goes
home with him. He's clumsy but gentle and she stays with him
for a fortnight. He buys her small cute presents, a teddy bear, a
bracelet. Katherine doesn't like cute. He's besotted with her.
Gets a small ring, some special alloy that means a lot in computer
land, proposes marriage. He doesn't care about her past. Loves
her. Will make her happy. It's never an option for Katherine,
Martin is kind but he just has no poetry. She leaves his condo
without even writing him an explanatory note. That's what I do
to men who worship me. You should have known.

She is used and abused.

In a vacant car lot next to the Egyptian Theatre, she gives blow jobs for just a few bucks. The men come in all shapes and sizes. When they lower their pants or open their flies, she smells the evil in them. They come unwashed, young and old alike. She retracts the foreskins and licks away the smegma, swallows them with her eyes wide open. Soon, she has a regular clientèle, all modestly content to be fellated by the tall English chick, who will eat cock to their heart's content, but no she won't fuck. She doesn't do that, dear. She could open an art gallery with portraits of men's appendages. Soon they all taste the same and she grows used to the salty streams coursing down her throat. They like it when she swallows and some pay her more.

Some local prostitutes object to this outsider taking business away from them. They ambush her one night and kick her badly in the ribs and the face. Cut large chunks of her hair off, but she has wild curls to spare. She hurts for weeks and accepts the needle from some biker on Capitol Hill. It helps. Blanks out the hours. The memories. The guilt. The biker shares her with some friends. She needs the dope and indifferently becomes their plaything for a while. Deke, the leader, brands her, an inverted swastika on the inside of one thigh, she's property. She sleeps with three bikers in one filthy bed, they take turns with her. The session lasts three days as they move from orifice to orifice like a sexual tag-team, violating her without feeling, playing with her like a raggedy doll, inserting objects, bottle tops, Swiss army knives, fruit. To keep her submissive they feed her the heroin. Needle marks, punctures on her arms would scare away the punters, oh yes they have plans for her, so they teach her to inject the dope into her cunt lips. The high is phenomenal.

My adventures as a whore, she reflects in a rare moment of lucidity. Might even be a book in it, she thinks. Kate in the land of cunt.

A businessman picks her up one evening while she is cruising Mercer Street. He's good to her. Convinces her not to return to the bikers. Even accepts to provide her with the now necessary junk for her habit. He sets her up in a small apartment. He's married of course. He visits her three times a week. Gives her some spare cash. She starts buying books again. But she's too passive and he soon tires of her. Takes her to a leather club and offers her in exchange for some form of life membership. She is trussed up, whipped, fucked in the darkness by one man after another until she is sore and her lower lips actually blister, she can't see any of them as a latex mask covers her face. She is roughly handled, fisted by men as well as women, tied to a rack, pissed on, slapped. In the cold morning they let her go. The businessman has taken back the keys to the flat. He's out of her life. She wanders the wet streets.

There's a reading and signing at the Elliott Bay Bookstore. It's a British mystery writer. She once met him at a party at some conference she'd had to attend in Nottingham. He doesn't actually recognize her but takes her back to his hotel afterward. She's pleased to follow, having nowhere to go. He's very full of himself, actually reads her a new story he's working on once they're in bed together. The story's okay, but the editor in her does feel it still needs some more work. He's obsessed by her arse, fondles it with genuine awe and affection, but draws back when she presents her damaged sex, and refuses to make love to her. Scared of catching something. He leaves her sleeping in the hotel room when he departs very early in the morning for his next gig in Vancouver. She has a mighty breakfast on the room. His publishers are probably picking up the tab, anyway. She smiles, the industry at least owes her this; she was bloody underpaid . . .

Her cunt heals. It's a resilient body part.

She finds a job in a peep show cum strip joint on the corner of First and Pike, facing Pike Place Market where they sell English papers, only a few days old. She does a girl-girl show, anonymously Frenches these other chicks while the thin audience sip their microbrews against the roar of the rock music on the sound system. One of her co-workers takes a shine to her, but Katherine easily convinces her that on stage it's fine, a job, but she has no further interest in women. The woman, her name is Judy, dolefully accepts this and they become friendly. Judy keeps on raving about the sheer beauty of Katherine's body. It's unusual, not common, she points out, you've got style, girl. She convinces Katherine to go in for a piercing. Judy sports a ring in her navel. The guys love it, you know, you'll get much better tips. Body jewellery turns them on. In the basement of a record shop that specializes in vinyl, she slips her knickers off while Judy smiles at her. The heavily tattooed owner guides her to an operating table, lowers it and places Katherine's ankles into stirrups. He rubs ice over her cunt. Says it's better than an injection. His fingers part her and he presses against the thin hood of her clitoris, the membrane swells. Nice, he remarks. Nice and plump. As Judy, whose idea it all is explains, you'll see Katherine it's even more spectacular than the navel, hands him the sterilized needle and walks across to hold Katherine's hand. The universe explodes inside her head when he threads the needle into and straight through her clit hood. Hold on, one of them says. The pain doesn't last long. Fucking Jesus. Her lower stomach is on fire. She clenches all her vaginal muscles, breathes deep, relaxes one moment, breathes deep again, expels the air, her sphincter lets go and she feels a thin stream of shit extruding out of her back orifice. She blushes deeply. Don't worry kid, the guy says, I'm used to it. But already the localized pain is less intense. She feels all wet around her thighs. God, has she also peed over herself? The guy wipes the black plastic table. He threads a small pearl onto the needle and it slides down to lodge itself between the fleshy hood and her bud. It's beautiful, Judy exclaims. Suits you fine says the man with the tattoos. More ice to dull the sensation. Katherine finally manages to relax. Don't touch yourself down there for a few days, the guy says as he later releases her from the table, the pearl now fixed in place, this foreign object peering out all shiny and precious from between the lips of her sex, this adornment, this jewel inside her jewel.

Judy is right. Men do like it.

A Japanese executive takes her to his suite on the top floor of the Madison-Stouffer. All Puget Sound and the islands beyond are spread out, a Cinemascope vision, beyond the bay windows. Apart from the Sky Needle, there is no way you could be any higher in all of Seattle. He strips her, places her against the tall windows, flattens her against the glass, spreads her legs, an offering to the sky outside, she has to close her eyes for fear of vertigo, only the plate glass separates her nudity from the void outside and the ground fifty or so floors down. He licks her rear, caresses the thin pale hair at the small of her back, her breasts are squashed against the glass, he slides his head in between her parted thighs, advances his tongue and inserts it from behind into her gaping cunt. He licks the pearl, chews her bud until the orgasm races through all five foot ten of her from top curls to toes. Later, he offers her an expensive jade necklace after inserting it one piece at a time into her vagina, then pulling it out with deliberate slowness, every piece bathed in her juices which he proceeds to clean with his tongue.

Her daily existence becomes a Sadeian procession of humiliation and pleasure.

One man asks her to pummel his body, harder, harder, I want it to hurt, before he can get hard. She concentrates on all those in the past, the betrayers, the abandoned, to focus her anger and strikes him with repeated fury. When the blood begins to flow from his nose and lips, she panics and flees, without payment.

She signs on for a porno loop. Three black men fuck her in the arse in quick succession while she stands bent over a wooden table. The filmmaker only has a super-8 video camera and never turns to film her face. For days afterwards, the pain endures and she hurts when walking. They've actually torn her. To think she once shuddered at the thought of Caesarians. She heals. For another pervert, she accepts to be tied up in a cave where she is administered an enema by a pocked, butch dyke, while he noisily jerks off. She wallows in the expelled liquid, rubs her skin, bathes in the shit-infested waters surrounding her on the black rubber sheet. She allows a one-legged grizzled and bitter Vietnam veteran to fuck her with his stump. While he moves the bone inside her bowels, he loudly sings *Born In The USA* off-key. And then actually cries when she leaves his motel room.

The cycle of inevitable degradation continues.

Like a penance.

One night, in dire need of junk, she's at the bar of this swank hotel, looking for passing custom when Steve Gregory walks in. Silk suit and all attitude.

"Christ, baby, you've let yourself go," he says. "But, you see, it's destiny, we meet again."

She smiles feebly.

"I need cash, Steve," Katherine says.

"You need a fix, more like. If you stay here, you're not even going to get spare change, Eddie."

He ponders one moment.

Her brown eyes beg.

"Come to the car," he says. She follows.

He drives out of town. Parks in the darkness, near the Boeing fields. Slips his hand under her blouse. Feels her up.

"Still nice and firm," Steve says. "That's the nice thing about smallish tits, they seldom go flabby. That's an asset you've got there, honey."

He opens the glove compartment and hands her the junk. She shoots up. It's good quality stuff. She listens to the stars out there, allows the river of ice to invade her whole body. It's too strong, like a whack to the heart, she's obliged to put her head on his shoulder.

"I'll take care of you, Eddie," Steve says.

He doesn't even want to fuck her anymore. She's beyond it.

"See, I know this very private club down in New Orleans," he tells her, caressing her cheeks with genuine care and concern as she dozes on. "I think we're going to make a great team, you and me, Eddie. A great team. You'll like it there, the food is just too much and it's never cold. You've never told me if you like sea food? Do you?"

She assents with a shake of her head, his fingers move through her hair, playing with the tired curls. "Goodbye Seattle," she whispers. She likes it when men play with her hair. Yes, she does.

Katherine dreams.

Of New Orleans. A city she has repeatedly been told is wonderful. Fragrant. And deliciously evil.

Yet another place her lover insisted he would take her to and no, he hadn't. They had not embraced in an assortment of fancy New Orleans hotel rooms which had once been slave quarters and where cockroaches roamed free. And never would. A city of cemeteries, storms and bewitching music.

Her pale skin shivers as a last ferry leaves the harbour for the journey across Puget Sound to the scattered isles.

New Orleans.

Katherine finally sleeps. The pain goes away.

GINCH

Michael Perkins

YEARS AGO YOU probably would have recognized Parker Coleman's name. Parker Coleman – wasn't he one of the movers and shakers who put together the Woodstock Festival? A record producer? One of four guys Bob Dylan slugged in 1968?

Parker popped up everywhere in the sixties; it was a decade he always claimed he invented. Certainly he exploited it better than almost anyone else I've heard of under thirty. Parker was a Zen hustler with a beard before the words "hippie" and "business-man" were joined together by *Time* magazine. While the rest of us floated lazily downstream on what we had been told was the current of history, smoking good weed and blithely awaiting the news that the revolution of consciousness had swept the board room of General Motors and the Pentagon, Parker made a few grand by swimming upstream – hawking psychedelic buttons, T-shirts, records, rock magazines and concerts, and once even a child guru from Ceylon named Bubba Sammy.

You might say that Parker saw us coming, because he was always paddling the other way. So he made money in the sixties, and he got a lot of ginch – his word for fuckable women.

Ginch. Think about it, because it will tell you everything you need to know about Parker's attitude toward women. His Kansas accent, overlaid with the street black's drawl he'd picked up, stretched the middle of the word like a rubber band.

Since his reputation as a cocksman was nearly as great as his reputation as a hustler, Parker had ample opportunity to select candidates for his private stable of ginch from among the finest examples of concupiscent American womanhood. There always seemed to be two or three twenty-two-year-old deep-breasted, deep-fried long-legged blondes dressed in eye-popping T-shirts trailing him as he moved from appointment to appointment, usually in a limousine. It was boom time.

Then one morning Parker woke up in a rented house in Topanga Canyon, and the sixties were over. National Guardsmen at Kent State shot the shit out of them. The seventies dawned gray and cold, and Parker's tired Aquarian customers – a generation of big-eyed Keane children – went home to catch some Zs. When they woke up, they began looking around for jobs.

Parker had overextended himself financially. When his customers disappeared back into the middle class from whence they'd come, he was wiped out. An overnight has-been.

Decline is somehow more uncomfortable to bear in California than in colder places where people work for a living, so Parker returned to his native city of New York and took a loft on Varick Street in Soho where he could meditate and try to figure out his next move. It didn't take him long to come up with the idea of making pornographic movies: low investment, high return, and ginch to boot.

In short order he had established himself as the boy wonder of porno films. Small distinction, perhaps, but his own. He cranked them out in his loft like home movies, which is what the loops you see in porno theatres basically are – good old American home movies full of fucking, sucking, golden showers, S/M, and come facials for the apple-cheeked girls Parker recruited from his stock of ginch.

The first time I talked with him on the telephone, he was getting ready to shoot his first feature film, a rip-off of *Charlie's Angels* that – naturally – he called *Parker's Angels*. He woke me out of a sound Tequila-induced sleep into one of the worst hangovers that ever sank its claws into man's cerebellum.

"Yeah?"

"Nick, this is Parker Coleman. Grinning Bare Productions, you know."

He sounded like Ralph Williams selling used cars on television. I moved the receiver a few inches from my ear and picked dirt from between my toenails while I listened. I used to meet him a lot at parties, but we'd never spent more than five minutes together. What he wanted was for me to write a script for him. He'd seen stuff I'd done in the underground papers and I guess he figured I was good enough to do the job for him, and poor enough to accept the postage stamps he wanted to pay me with.

He was right, of course. I was two months behind on the rent, and Con Edison had already turned off my electric typewriter, freeing me to spend more time in the air-conditioned comfort of my favorite saloon, a small establishment on Sheridan Square where I was running up a tab as long as my arm.

"I'm not talking peanuts, Nick. This is big time. *Parker's Angels* is going to revolutionize the business. I know how to publicize a film, if you don't know my reputation. Gerry Damiano is small potatoes, if you know what I mean."

"I've heard of you," I allowed. Grudgingly, because tiny golfers were using my brain for a driving range.

"Isn't that title great? *Parker's Angels*. Tell me it isn't great. And we're going to have the greatest collection of ginch – prime California stuff – you ever saw."

I put the phone closer to my ear, perking up at the thought of Marilyn Chambers doing her number while I looked on, script in one hand, my rod in the other. I'd never written a porno film before, but even through a hangover, the perquisites were tantalizing. I get horny when I'm hung over, and all I could see was a vision of Marilyn rehearsing song and dance numbers on my stiff prick. I agreed to visit Parker in his loft that afternoon.

Three hours later I was panting up the steep wooden stairs to Parker's loft. On his metal door in gold lettering were the words:

Parker Coleman's
Grinning Bare Productions

I pushed open the heavy door and walked in, hoping to find Parker in the middle of shooting a scene for a film. I was disappointed. All was quiet. No naked ladies running about with semen on their thighs. I picked my way through a maze of boxes, stacked film cans and movie equipment and saw, at the end of a long hallway plastered with posters for porno films, a man and a woman sitting on a couch watching an old movie on color television.

Up close, Parker looked like a disheveled teddy bear. So this was the cocksman, I thought: he wore a full black beard, a dirty T-shirt featuring Paul Newman's baby blues studded with rhinestones and a pair of wool pants – it was a hot day in July when I saw him – over which a belly the size of a watermelon loomed. He was a teddy bear whose stuffings were coming out, but he sat on that ratty couch like a goddamned emperor, while the blonde sitting next to him rubbed his bare feet.

He started talking – Parker talked more than any man I've ever known, in the same obsessive way other people chain smoke – but I wasn't listening. I was staring at the blonde, and trying my best not to look like I was staring.

So this was ginch: clear California features you see a lot of in porno films, a tan so deep it looked built in, lush red mouth and sparkling whiter-than-white teeth genetically engineered to fit around the head of a cock, and a body that relegated Raquel Welch to the pin-ups-of-the-past department. It was all big and firm and fresh and caramel and it made me want to shake my fist at the destiny that hadn't dropped one just like it on my doorstep. I nodded at her in the direction of the nipples I saw poking through the thin material of her halter top, and she smiled back so quickly I almost missed the glory of it, the corners of her mouth turned up like wings.

The only thing that bothered me about the blonde were her eyes. There was no one home behind her eyelids, which drooped like paper blinds over the windows of an empty furnished room.

Parker was talking, but I interrupted him. Much as I needed the small fee he was offering me, I had to find out about her.

"Can she talk?"

"I don't encourage it, Nick. Let a woman talk, and pretty soon you're in trouble. She sure can move her lips, though. I'm trying to teach her how to suck cock and sing 'Yankee Doodle' at the same time, but she's a slow learner. College dropout. About the film, do you think you could get right on it? I gotta have something on paper, man. This film is going to be a biggie. I've got backers begging me to take their money."

Parker must have noticed that he wasn't getting my undivided attention, because all of a sudden he started talking about the blonde, with the possessive pride of a homeowner talking about a new lawnmower.

"Bliss is going to be in the film, you know, Nick. But the real star – now there's prime ginch, nothing cut-rate. A ringer for Farrah Fawcett-Majors. Great idea, huh? Every guy in the country crazy about that dizzy ginch, and we're going to cash in on it."

I looked at Bliss. She was off in a world of her own, a dreamy look in her eyes that I couldn't identify. Watching her was like having a wet dream while awake. If she was high on something, I hoped it was the smell of semen. She reminded me of a robot, one of those rubber sex dolls you buy for $19.95 from an ad in a men's magazine and blow up like a balloon. Bliss was an appropriate name for her: she was blissed-out.

Like most American men of my age and background (32, midwest, Berkeley, divorced, blah, blah, blah), I'd paid lip-service all my life to the idea of female equality simply because I wanted to fuck, and the ladies available for fucking were feminists, at least in the living room. But I was weary of having to deal with women as if they had brains; I was ready for some unradical, unpretentious sex doll who would perform whenever and however I wanted. I was ready for ginch, in other words.

Or was I? I think the truth is that I was torn like any Catholic schoolboy between the brainlessly pornographic vision of ginch before me and a life-time's indoctrination – by women, of course, from my mother to my unlamented ex-wife – in the notion that women have souls as well as cunts, feelings as well as nice tits.

Fortunately for me, Parker's mother back in Kansas had not raised any such dummies. When he wanted something, he was absolutely tuned in on the price he would have to pay. Seeing that I was so hypnotized by Bliss that no business was going to get done until my attention was distracted, he put his hand on her shoulder and gave her a gentle push in my direction. It was as if he'd pushed a button located somewhere between her shoulder blades.

Bliss drifted toward me like Linda Lovelace stepping from the screen, red tongue moistening her wet lips. Her hand went straight to my crotch and lightly brushed the painful erection that beat like a trapped Gooney bird behind my zipper. I reached out a tentative hand to stroke her golden hair, looking up briefly to see Parker smiling like a man who's just made a deal that's not going to cost him anything.

Bliss fell gently to her knees and tugged my tool from a pair of blue French briefs I was particularly proud of, stared until she was almost cross-eyed at my humble staff, and darted out her tongue to lick the tip. Both of her hands encircled the shaft as she introduced the throbbing head into her mouth, her tongue swirling around the length as if she were eating a double-dip Baskin-Robbins cone.

"Jesus Christ!" I shuddered, bent double over the heated pleasure at my groin. I couldn't help myself. I had not exchanged one word with Bliss, and in one or two minutes I was going to erupt like a geyser into her throat. I saw Parker smiling impatiently from the couch, as if to say, *Come on, get it over with,* and the next thing I knew I was coming, while Bliss's head bobbed back and forth in a receptive rhythm as steady as a sewing machine's.

Her mouth came off my cock with a sweet *pop,* and she stood up, a vague, satisfied smile on her face.

"Thank you . . ." I blurted, but she went back to sit on the couch next to Parker without answering me.

I was zippering my fly, feeling considerably shaken up by the blowjob, when Parker started talking again.

"Okay, Nick, now that we've got that out of the way, maybe we can get down to business, huh? You think you can put together something on paper I can show the money guys? I got a lot of notes."

"How soon do you need it?"

"Yesterday, man. Everything in this business is yesterday."

"How about by Monday?" It was Friday afternoon, fading into evening. I thought I'd give myself the weekend, and sit at the typewriter until the damned thing was finished. Considering the money he was offering, it was a lousy deal, but I knew I had to see Bliss again. If I did the script, I could invent a thousand reasons why I had to drop by the loft. So we talked money, I accepted a very small check as advance payment, and Parker explained what he wanted me to write. He was an idea man, he said; it was up to me to fill in the details. While he talked, I watched Bliss. She listened to him like she was hearing her Master's voice.

Like most survivors of the sixties, I'm wary of sentiment, but even if I didn't know that what was happening to me when I looked at Bliss used to be called love by movie heroes in the forties, I knew something unusual was going on in my head: I felt protective toward her. Parker obviously didn't give a shit for her – why else would he have let her blow me? – but my motives were pure. They would allow me to take her away from Parker without a second thought.

It didn't occur to me that she might not want to leave Parker. The Lone Ranger, savior of beautiful ginch, had made up his mind, and to hell with reality.

I went to work on the script for *Parker's Angels* that evening, after borrowing the air-conditioned apartment of a friend who was off to the country for the weekend and hauling my electric typewriter to his living-room outlet. I cashed Parker's check at the bar, paid off part of the tab, bought two six-packs of beer, and hallucinated about Bliss while I filled in the salacious details of the script outline Parker had given me.

I worked late and slept till noon the next day. Sunday in New York in the summer: when I left the borrowed air conditioning and stepped onto the sidewalk, two scenes under my arm and a desire to see Bliss so strong I only paused for coffee and a donut on my way to Parker's loft, the city seemed as hot and dry as the Sahara.

I had to see her alone – to find out what made her tick, I told myself – when all along I knew that what I really wanted was to find the button in her back that made her Parker's possession. I lusted after that button.

Luck was with me; I found Bliss washing her hair when I entered the loft. She was wearing blue nylon panties and her long blonde hair was full of soap. She told me that Parker had gone out with some friends to get an egg cream and the Sunday papers, seeming neither surprised nor interested that I was standing six feet away from her, my eyes glued to her amazingly firm breasts. Shampoo ran in a thin trickle of liquid gold across one erect roseate nipple.

"I brought part of the script," I explained while she wrapped a red towel around her wet hair and cleaned out the big double sink. "I made your part a little bigger than Parker asked for."

In order to appreciate her response, you have to consider that I had never heard her talk. As Parker said, he didn't encourage it. Her tones were warm and chocolaty, but the words she spoke were delivered with all the sincerity of a long distance operator placing a call.

"I just love the men Parker finds for his films. They're so friendly. You know what I mean?"

You can see why I wondered if she was for real. Why, I threw down the manuscript I'd brought and reached for her tits, mashing my mouth down on hers while my hands moved down her body to her ass, pushing the panties down her thighs. She put her arms around me automatically, but otherwise she didn't respond, even when I dug one finger into her small, tight cunt, even when I cupped her ass with one hand and stroked her clitoris with the other. I was like a kid set loose in a goddamned candy store, reaching for the gum and the Tootsie Rolls, the licorice, and the chocolate kisses at the same time, with extra arms and dozens of hands.

It didn't matter what I did; she wouldn't respond. My hands moved over her body desperately searching for the magic button that would turn her on. Apparently only Parker knew where it was.

Not that she resisted. I pushed her across the room to the couch and plunged between her legs, groaning when my cock pushed itself into her warm juices, into that wet groove that the Parker Colemans and Johnny Holmeses of the porno world took for granted. Her long legs wrapped themselves around my hips with all the intimacy of a seat belt, and she settled in for the ride. Her eyes were closed when I looked at her, but small pleading sounds were issuing from the corners of her mouth. (Or so I thought; maybe that was my imagination getting overheated.)

I held onto her ass and her tits like some crazed rapist frustratedly trying to cram all the experience of once-in-a-lifetime sex with a desirable blonde into three minutes, but even then I was experiencing that guilt so special to mine and Parker's generation, the guilt which said, *You shall not treat a woman like a sexual plaything*.

These thoughts didn't prevent me from having one of the most memorable orgasms in a wasted life spent paying lip service to feminism while my cock twitched unheeded by the Gloria Steinem clones of my acquaintance. I mean, I came like a flood bursting through the Grand Coolee Dam. I even screamed a little bit at the end.

When I returned to my senses it was still a hot Sunday afternoon in New York, and Bliss was regarding me like a mannequin in a store window who's just noticed a fly crawling on her expensive clothes.

My guilt returned, a homing pigeon with a fine regard to post-ejaculation blues.

"That was nice," Bliss volunteered.

"Nice?"

"It was okay."

"Don't you feel used doing this?"

"What do you mean?"

"Well, Parker calls you ginch. You do anything he tells you to do. Anything anybody tells you to do."

"Didn't you enjoy it?"

"Sure I enjoyed it. You bet your ass I enjoyed it."

"Then . . ."

"But women just don't act like you. None of them."

"I'm happy. I like to screw. It makes me feel good."

I lifted my weight from her and she slid to a corner of the couch, a wide-eyed look of carnal innocence on her face that I'd last seen on the screen in a Times Square porno house. I was in the throes of the usual neurotic male reaction to a woman who likes to fuck: I felt threatened. Having come in so glorious a fashion, I could afford to nitpick. I couldn't have stopped myself if I'd wanted to: I still couldn't figure her out.

She was so vague, so blissed-out, I wanted to shake her.

"Don't you care who you fuck?"

"Sure. I like men who know how to take care of me."

"Does Parker?"

"Let's do a joint, okay? I have a hard time with questions. I think they suck."

She shook her wet hair as if my questions were taxing her brain.

She dug into a fringed leather bag on the floor and produced a joint wrapped in red, white and blue. We smoked in silence while I tried to decide on the best ploy to use to get her away from Parker. Hoping that the grass would make her more suggestible, I let her smoke most of the joint.

"What kind of hold does Parker have on you?"

"I like the dude. He understands me."

"Do you think I could understand you?"

"*You?*" She was inhaling when she answered; the rest of it was lost in a sudden coughing fit.

Being laughed at by a woman – even when she tried to cover it up, as Bliss was doing behind her coughing – is calculated to make even the best of men wonder if somehow he hasn't failed at life's ultimate test: getting laid with a certain pleasant regularity. Since I am painfully aware that I am more of an average guy than the best of men, I exploded.

"What the hell's wrong with me? I'll treat you a lot better than Parker does. You won't be ginch to me. You *cunt*."

I stopped myself before I really landed into her because it sounded just like arguments I'd had with my ex-wife, not seduction at all. "Come away with me," was all I was really trying to say, but come away to what? To a lousy tenement apartment without electricity? Parker was a celebrity, the cocksman, the Name. I was a nobody. I had no bargaining position. I suddenly realized that ginch like Bliss was not for me, just like shooting pheasant was not up my alley. Ginch and pheasant were reserved for the aristocrats of life, the hustlers, cocksmen, and celebrities. My timing was off, and theirs was always perfect.

As if to prove the truth of my perception about timing, Parker walked into the loft at just that moment, when Bliss was looking at me with stoned, empty eyes, as if I were a frog who was never going to make it to prince status. He had a guy with him who looked like he sold ties in a fag boutique, or dressed hair in Queens. He wore a Hawaiian shirt over tight pre-shrunk jeans and a silver beard that looked like he kept it trimmed with toenail clippers.

"You got a script, man?" Parker said to me, dumping the *Daily News* in Bliss's lap. (A lap, I should add, that when spread dripped my semen – my precious 100,000 sperm – onto the couch. I don't think Parker even noticed. Bliss plunged right into the Sunday funnies.)

I pointed toward the manuscript I'd brought while Parker introduced me to his friend.

"Nick, this is Terry Chiffon. He's gonna direct *Parker's Angels* for me. The best talent in the business."

We shook hands suspiciously. Terry parked himself on the couch next to Bliss and immediately began stroking her thigh. I watched his hand like a gunfighter watching his enemy's hand as it moves closer to the .45 strapped to his leg, feeling that something was going to happen that I wouldn't like at all.

"Has Bliss been taking care of you?" Parker asked, while rummaging through the pages of my script.

"I fucked her."

"Good for you. You looked like you needed it."

"Don't you give a shit?"

"What about?" he asked distractedly. Maybe he was trying to figure out my typing.

"About me fucking her."

"She's ginch, man. Ginch is made to be fucked. Don't you know that yet? There's millions of hungry pussies where she came from. She knows it. It keeps her toed to the mark."

I was about to argue with him – full of theories I'd learned from women – when I saw Terry's hand insert itself into Bliss's cunt.

She didn't drop the funny papers. I watched as he stuck five fingers into the slit I'd just oiled for him. With the other hand he unzipped himself and pulled out a long thin cock. Then he looked at Parker.

"Is it cool, baby?"

Parker's response was immediate: "You know it's cool. You're the director."

While we watched, Terry spread Bliss's legs and entered her. She looked at him over the top of the paper she was reading and then went back to it, while Terry jumped away. She was a sphinx; I realized then what I hadn't seen before: she was every man's woman, and no man's. We all fed her emptiness.

"That's some woman you've got there," I said to Parker.

"The sixties brought them all out, man. Chicks suddenly discovered they had cunts. Bliss is a dime-a-dozen chick. They're hanging from every tree. All you have to do is reach up and pick one."

Parker looked at me like I wasn't in possession of all my marbles. Rejection must have been written on my face like the words on a billboard. He was reassuring.

"She's just a ginch, man. Just a ginch."

I looked at Terry fucking Bliss and winced, remembering how her tongue had felt on my cock, thinking miserably of all the avenues of life that were closed to me.

"She's like a fucking machine. A doll," I said.

"Ginch," Parker repeated.

BLACK LILY

Thomas S. Roche

(For Paul Bowles)

THE SUN CAME up.

She might be asleep. It certainly seemed likely. If she wasn't then perhaps she had been, recently. She had stopped walking. Whether she was sitting or standing, it was impossible to be sure. She was conscious only of the newborn sun and of the infinite world of sand dunes stretching all about her. Even the hunger and thirst were immaterial. There existed only the sky and the sand.

"Amelia," she said, not knowing why she said it. It was a while later that she understood that it was her own name.

Her clothes hung destroyed on her body.

Things began to come back to her, in vague impressions, as if they were unimportant and without immediacy.

She could recall the shouts of the men at the fortress as she ran. There had been a few scattered shots. Half-heartedly, she wondered why no one had chased her, but it seemed that didn't matter. They had taken Jean; he had been the one they wanted, anyway. She was just along for the ride, and she didn't seem to make much difference in this world, where there was only the sky and the sand.

It seemed that the memories of the fortress dissolved into

nothing and she was left without a past or a future. She supposed there were worse things.

Late in the morning, a caravan happened by. It took her a long time to become aware of it. By the time she noticed, the caravan was almost gone. There were many camels led by four or five men dressed in black. She leapt up and ran to the caravan, without knowing why she was doing it. The man was tall, swathed in garments of black, his face shrouded. He regarded her calmly.

"Is there room for me?" she asked in French, instinctively assuming the man would understand. She wasn't sure where she had learned the language. It came to her as out of a dream. Perhaps, then, she was French.

He made a gesture to indicate he didn't understand. She motioned at the caravan, trying to indicate movement. The man looked at her for a long time. Finally he shrugged and motioned toward one of the camels. She let him help her onto the animal. The foul smell of dung and animal sweat was somehow comforting. She felt the thick bundles behind her, covered by blankets. She was suddenly incredibly hungry. She reached beneath one of the blankets and found a bundled mass of twigs and flowers. A crumpled blossom came off in her hand. She brought it to her face to smell it.

The man was upon her, taking the flower away from her. He slapped her wrist and replaced the thing under the blanket. He shouted at her in a language she did not understand.

The woman looked down at him blankly. Perhaps the flower was valuable. The man seemed to be cursing at her again, and the woman looked down, sheepish.

"Amelia," she said, looking up, still not sure why she said it.

The man gestured dismissively at her and began to lead the camel forward. The woman closed her eyes.

A great weight came over her. Slowly, she drifted into a trance, until she slumped in the saddle. There under the sun she fell into nothing.

When she awoke, the sun slanted across her from a high window. She had no idea how long she had slept, nor did she care. She looked around, dazed. She was in a small room, stretched on a thin mat on a clean floor. The walls were hung with rich cloth, and a houkah as high as her waist sat in the corner. She had been placed in black clothing identical to that the people in the caravan had worn. Slipping her hand under the robe, she felt that she was still wearing her clothes, the cotton slacks and shirt from Bloomingdales. Outside the shirt, she had a cloth tied around her breasts, cinched tight. It was uncomfortable, and puzzled her. But she was wearing her Western clothes. Thank God. Then even her concern dissolved and she wondered to herself what would have happened if the man from the caravan had disrobed her. It all seemed so immaterial. Possession of her body seemed such a nebulous concept. She relaxed into the mat and faded in and out of consciousness.

After a time, there was a knock on the door. Disinterested, she lay there without answering for a long time while the knocking continued. She stared blankly at the door. Finally there was nothing.

She was achingly hungry. Her needs were such that she could hardly feel anything outside of her hunger. But she could not bring herself to move, and even the pain of her hunger seemed irrelevant.

Amelia. She was called Amelia, she suddenly remembered. Her father called her "Amy", sometimes "A", pronounced like "Ay". For everyone else it was "Amelia". That was all she remembered clearly. Occasionally things would surface, and then drop out of sight into her mind, deeper than ever. The taste of birthday cake. The smell of leather inside a new car. The sound of President Truman's voice on the radio. Newsreels of the Bomb at Hiroshima. A harsh voice cursing her in French, foul breath in her face, sudden pain. Then it was all gone, and there was nothing that existed, except the sleep and the body she seemed to inhabit.

Once, when she reached under the black hood-and-mask to scratch the side of her head, something struck her as strange. Her hair had been cut. She felt sure it had been short before, but not this short. After the surge of panic, lasting half a second, she felt a vague curiosity. Why had she been shorn?

The knocking came again, and went. More time passed. Finally the door opened without a knock, and a girl came in bearing a tray of food. The girl was veiled, her eyes dark and intriguing. Amelia wondered if this was what the travel guides meant by "exotic". The woman looked down submissively as she knelt beside the cloth mat. She waited there while Amelia struggled to sit up, then reached for the food. The hunger, long unnoticed or denied, came upon her like an avalanche.

She had to yank the mask down to eat, which pulled it across her eyes. So great was her sudden hunger that she didn't care or take time to readjust it. She ate blindly, stuffing her mouth full of the thick, heavy bread and then taking great handfuls of the smoky-tasting grey paste, and eating that with her fingers. She felt dizzy, sick. But she kept eating, and gulping down water from the metal cup. The water was foul and barely drinkable. There was also some tea, but she was unconcerned with that for now.

The girl knelt, watching her through the whole thing. Amelia remembered suddenly that in her past life she had always been terrified to let people see her eat. That was one of the many reasons she was so skinny. The memory made no sense to her, as if it had happened to someone else, or she had seen it in a movie.

She finally lapsed, slipping back onto the mat, the mask still pulled down over her eyes. She lay, blinded, breathing hard from exhaustion. Her orgy of consumption had left her spent. The girl immediately took a cloth and wet it from the carafe of water. She took hold of Amelia's hands and started wiping them, cleaning away the thick paste and the crumbs of bread. When Amelia's hands were clean, the woman moved to her face. She began to wipe Amelia's mouth, meticulously cleaning away the smears of food.

Amelia's mask was still down low, her mouth exposed, her eyes covered. Amelia didn't have the energy to pull the mask away so that she could see better. She could just barely see the woman's mouth and chin, lips slightly parted, as the woman cleaned Amelia's face. After a time the mask was tugged up a little and the woman looked into Amelia's eyes, just for a moment. Amelia felt a rush of stimulation and a sudden terror of seeing, which the woman seemed to sense. The woman pulled the mask down across Amelia's eyes again and moved back to cleaning her mouth and chin. She started on her upper throat.

Amelia felt a curious sort of comfort, her face being stroked with the cool water while she recalled the brief moment of looking into the mysterious eyes of the beautiful woman. Amelia felt a curious desire, all of a sudden. She felt quite sure it had been months. Except for that French soldier at the outpost. . . .

Her mind refused to remember, and Amelia's need blotted out

everything else. She found herself fascinated by the woman, seduced by her image. She remembered a moment a long time ago, before her last lover . . . but that woman had been a school-teacher, and Amelia had been uninterested in pursuing an affair. She could not recall the woman's name.

Amelia wasn't sure what she was doing. She leaned forward and kissed the woman, through the veil, feeling the warmth of her lips and the softness of her tongue through the gauzy fabric. The woman responded, kissing Amelia back. The woman set down the cloth and pulled away her veil. Amelia still could not see, but that only heightened the taste of the woman's lips and the slick feel of her tongue sliding into Amelia's mouth. With her first demanding motion in days, Amelia squirmed against her, pulling the woman close. The woman melted into her arms.

Slowly, without passion, the woman began to open the laces of her garment. She took Amelia's hand and placed it on her breast. Amelia felt a curious sort of terror, but could not imagine what she could possibly be afraid of. She didn't remember there being anything dangerous about this behavior. She took the woman's breast into her hand and caressed it, feeling acutely the hardness of the nipple against her palm. She lay in darkness as she touched the breast, drifting into confusion, as if she weren't quite sure what the breast was. Amelia felt the woman's slender fingers across the back of her head, felt herself being pulled forward as the woman leaned against her. The woman guided Amelia to her breast and Amelia's lips closed around the nipple.

She suckled there for a time, her lust having flared and subsided. She still desired the woman, wanted to touch her, devour her. But the intense need had settled into a faint ache deep inside her body, and it was enough to suckle on the woman's breast while the woman stroked Amelia's head.

After a time, the woman laid Amelia down again and began to kiss her, draping her breasts against Amelia's lips and then chest. The woman began to reach under Amelia's robe.

Amelia felt a wave of panic, not knowing why. She took the woman's wrist and started to shake her head, vehemently, saying "No. No. I don't want to." But she knew that wasn't true.

The woman didn't understand. She kept trying to get under Amelia's robe, to unfasten it. The woman made a gesture with her mouth, as if trying to convince her. Amelia felt her stomach go weak, churning uncontrollably, her body aching for the woman to repeat the gesture against her. She remembered another person making that same gesture. . . . Amelia shook her head vigorously and motioned the woman away.

Impassively, the woman adjusted her garments. She took the tray and left the room while Amelia lay there, unmoving. Tears had formed in her eyes.

She could not remember the mores, the social fabric of upper-crust New York society which had prevented her from making love to the girl. All she knew was that she could not do it.

Amelia drifted for ever. She had begun to forget the experience with the woman, but it came back in lush, sensuous morsels, making her squirm on the mat. She was fed and washed several times. She was much neater after the first time, requiring less cleaning afterwards. Amelia was vaguely aware, the third time she was served, that this was a different woman, as it had been the time before – three women, equally beautiful and equally different than Amelia. Each time, after she had been cleaned, Amelia would find herself kissing the woman, hungrily devouring her tongue, reaching out for her body. But she refused each woman in turn, prevented by some unknown force from making love with her, however much she wanted it.

After the third meal, Amelia slept for a time. She awoke to the scent of sandalwood and musk incense. It was dark outside, and there were no lights in the room.

She felt the mask being removed. Someone was kissing her – it was a man. She tasted his tongue and felt the surge of her need. With a curious enthusiasm, Amelia realized that she was going to be taken. She felt an aching hunger. While she suddenly knew that she could not remember the color of her mother's eyes, or the address of her childhood home in Long Island, or the name of the man with whom she had travelled to this country, and that she should be able to remember these things, she knew, deeply, instinctively, that her giving herself to this man, or more accurately, being taken, did not spell decadence the way it would have to give herself to the women. That is why, she knew, she must succumb, dissolve, submit. That is why, she knew, she must be devoured by him.

That is why she became his.

Amelia's back arched, and she presented her lips for his consumption. She felt his rough hands on her robe, unfastening it, opening it up. He did not remove the mask yet. Amelia's head whirled in conscious surrender.

The robe came open, and he removed it from Amelia's body. He unfastened the sash around her breasts. She felt an explosive freedom. He had considerable trouble with her cotton slacks and shirt, as if he had never seen such garments before. But Amelia did not assist him. She lay passive, allowing him to take rather than giving herself to him, not wanting to break the spell of freedom that her inaction offered.

The pants and shirt joined the robe on the floor. Then her undergarments.

The smell of sandalwood filled her nostrils.

She moaned softly as she felt the man's hands on her breasts. His caress was strong, insistent, but there was an underlying gentleness, as if she were a profoundly important person, but belonged wholly to him. Amelia was still blind, but her mouth was exposed and he kissed her briefly before disrobing himself. Then he lay upon her, his naked form against her, as she presented herself for him. With his hands and his mouth and his body, he took her. He possessed each part of her body with sensuous fervor, starting with her breasts, continuing to her mouth, slowly working over her belly and back, then gently entering her with his fingers. Amelia remained passive, delighting in the sensation as his fingers slid smoothly into her. It was after that that he pulled her body against his. He guided her mouth to his shaft and, giving herself fully, her eyes still shrouded, enveloped by darkness, Amelia began to feed.

This was a transgression against her social code, but somehow its context was different than her other desired transgressions. Inexplicably, she pictured herself smoking in a bathroom somewhere; then the momentary image faded. The man guided Amelia onto her back, coaxing her legs open. She knew that the time had come. He laid himself fully on her, and she felt a sharp pain as he penetrated her. It had indeed been a very long time; she suddenly remembered the last time she had made love – it was in a hotel in Algiers with a man named Jean; then that memory dissolved and she only knew that she was making love now. A curious wave of fear went through her as she felt him settle down on top of her. Then her fear dissolved like the memory.

His lovemaking was gradual, as if he sensed that she had been slightly afraid. But Amelia's passivity gave way as his slow thrusting grew more deliberate. She pressed her thighs together around his body, feeling an astonishing sense of well-being. Perhaps it was that sense of well-being that caused the curious shaking in her belly and thighs. She began to moan, and it felt like she was having some sort of attack. But it felt curiously good. The curious feeling grew stronger and stronger, the pleasure blotting out all else. Her buttocks pressed against the mat as he made love to her, thrusting deep inside; then she lost all control of her body and it seemed that she passed into a world of sensation, her skin tingling. She felt a sudden shock of guilt and shame, which then dissolved to an oddly satisfied feeling. It was not unlike being extraordinarily drunk, as she could just barely remember having been once or twice, but the newness of the sensation fascinated her. After a time, she lost the feeling – it slipped away through her fingers like grains of sand scattering about her. When she did, she was aware that the man had finished inside her and was kissing her neck hungrily. He seemed very pleased.

The sensation had been unpredictable – like nothing she had ever heard about. As if she had passed into a new realm of the spirit. Perhaps she was dead, and this was Heaven. Or Hell?

Definitely Hell, she thought, caressing his back as he kissed her, hard, nipping her lip so that she tasted blood with a frightened thrill.

The sensation returned to her, briefly, in a gentle spasm inside her. It was most certainly a horrible transgression against the laws of her tribe. But she no longer remembered what those laws were, or who had made them.

Abdelsaid was unwilling to let them do it, at first. He had told his three wives that they were to provide the French visitor, Monsieur Breton, with food, to ensure that he was properly taken care of, and see to his physical needs if he would allow them to do so. They had offered, but each time the Frenchman had refused.

"You see," Abdelsaid told them. "As I told you. They have many of them in France. They fill the streets there, I heard it from the man who tends the camels. It is no surprise. Why not let me have my peace with him?" Abdelsaid smiled mischievously.

The three wives were like snakes, though, always possessive. Always acquisitive. The Frenchman had seemed so eager at first, they said. All three reported the same experience. He desperately sought their lips, their breasts, their bodies, wanting to touch them. But he had refused when they offered to provide for him.

"Monsieur Breton wants *me* to provide," said Abdelsaid angrily. "That is their way. Why else would there be such a thriving French market in the Black Lily, that would allow us to live with such finery?"

But his wives were insistent. "The Frenchman expressed such interest! Allow one of us to be present, in case such needs arise!"

"No! I forbid it!"

The voices of his three wives rose in cacophony, like a terrifying anti-song, something from Europe played on one of those portable boxes. Something horrible. Abdelsaid finally gave in, having known from the start that it was hopeless.

Abdelsaid was a stern man. But he could not stop the wind, nor hold the sun at one place in the sky.

Amelia continued to drift in and out of consciousness, floating in the curious pleasure of a life without memories. There was nothing before the man. Nothing before the harem. Nothing but the sensations of the sun streaming through the high window, the taste of the food the women brought, the sensations of Abdelsaid taking her. She knew only surrender.

Abdelsaid. He had wanted so much to know her name. She had known that from the way he had spoken to her, in Arabic, caressing her ear with his tongue. The way he had pointed to himself and said firmly, "Abdelsaid".

She had wanted very much to tell him her name, as well. She felt for a moment that something was there, that there was a place where she had had a name, that she had once been named. Perhaps she had known her name just yesterday, or only a minute ago. But it slipped away like it was nothing, and she just looked sheepishly up at Abdelsaid, wishing he would kiss her and caress her and enter her and make love to her once again. Abdelsaid waited patiently for the woman to tell him her name. But she did not. It was as if she did not know. He pointed at her and said over and over again, "French?" Amelia looked at him blankly, feeling that she did not know what the word meant. Finally she nodded and said "French," pointing to herself. Abdelsaid shrugged and seemed to accept that.

He spoke for a time to her in the language she did not understand. The language was soothing, seductive, and she found that it was not important that she understand him. Her head came to rest in his lap and he stroked her hair gently while he spoke to her, his voice a rhythmic caress as if he were reciting poetry. She fell asleep with her head in Abdelsaid's lap, and soon he left her.

"Amelia," she said after he left; at first she wasn't sure why she said it, and then she understood that it was her name. Why couldn't she remember it before? She would have to tell Abdelsaid.

When Abdelsaid returned, he brought the women with him. All three. Identical, lush, beautiful. Their bodies rounded and full beneath the flowing clothes. So unlike Amelia, with her scrawny, underfed body. Amelia looked around blankly, not understanding. The three women set out a second mat in the middle of the room.

Abdelsaid knelt beside the mat and began to kiss Amelia.

The women disrobed silently, setting their clothes just out of reach. They reclined on the mat, their bodies entwining, casually, their arms around each other. Amelia watched, overwhelmed. Abdelsaid was also watching them. But soon he was watching Amelia. Then his hands were upon her as he kissed her and gently coaxed her against him.

Amelia leaned on Abdelsaid and took him into her mouth. The three women caressed each other, their bodies seething, flowing together, becoming one. Amelia's lips slid deftly over Abdelsaid's shaft, as they had done before. Absent-mindedly, she rubbed her thighs together as she suckled on Abdelsaid's cock. She felt the curious sensation rising inside her again, though not quite coming to fruition.

After a time, the naked women filled and lit the houkah and Abdelsaid smoked. He gave the houkah to Amelia, who sucked the smoke into her lungs. It was harsh, bringing back vague memories of school gymnasiums and the back seats of cars, but those memories faded as quickly as they flared, and disappeared in the smoke.

After a time, Amelia felt very strange, as if she had fallen asleep but were still moving. Her body was enveloped with pleasant sensations. She watched Abdelsaid's three wives with hunger and curiosity. Their bodies were so different than hers, though very, very beautiful.

Then Abdelsaid bent down to kiss her, and she knew it was time. Amelia no longer wore the strange, impractical clothes under the robe, the ones she'd been wearing when Abdelsaid first came to her. Not even her underwear. Just the sash, holding her slight breasts flat against her body. Amelia went to take the robe off, but Abdelsaid motioned her not to do so.

He did not undress her this time. Instead, he simply lifted the robe, bunching it around her upper thighs and buttocks. Amelia felt him pulling the robe tight through her crotch. She felt Abdelsaid pouring oil between her buttocks, some spilling on the robe. Amelia watched the three women, who had begun to kiss each other, their limbs twined in a lush ménage.

Then Amelia felt a rush of fear and surrender as Abdelsaid mounted her from behind, but not in the fashion he had done before. The sensations were very different this time – stronger, perhaps because her need was so great. It was then that she became aware of the woman's smell. The third wife was against her, placing herself on the mat. Her thighs spread around Amelia, and Amelia, without thinking, began to work her tongue between the woman's legs, tasting something unfamiliar and oddly delicious.

The third wife moaned softly.

Abdelsaid was continuing to thrust gently inside her, silently moving in and out between her buttocks. The sensations were curious indeed, but not at all unpleasant. Amelia's whole body began to shake. And then suddenly Abdelsaid was finished. Amelia slumped, spent, against the mat.

Abdelsaid motioned toward the three women, speaking to them sternly. Amelia watched, without understanding. She heard the French word "Monsieur," perhaps it was the name "Monsieur Breton". She had known a Monsieur Breton briefly, in Nice. He had been a drifter, living nowhere, floating. But was a happy man. Amelia felt sure that she and Monsieur Breton had been lovers; fleetingly, she remembered a pleasant afternoon of sex in her hotel room. The three wives seemed to be arguing violently with

Abdelsaid. The third wife was trying to open Amelia's robe. Abdelsaid grabbed Amelia, shouting, and held her against his body.

Sheepishly, the three women moved away from Amelia. They dressed in silence while Abdelsaid watched. Then the three women left the room. Abdelsaid followed them, and did not pause to kiss Amelia good-bye.

Abdelsaid cursed the women for trying to engage Monsieur Breton against his wishes. "He was plainly enjoying himself with me," said Abdelsaid cruelly. "He didn't need a trio of women devouring him. I already told you about the French!"

"You saw that thing the Frenchman did to Aouicha! He was enjoying it!"

Abdelsaid was losing his temper. "No! That's a French custom! It is not something they enjoy. It's considered a duty." He tried to change the subject.

The women argued with him late into the night. Finally Abdelsaid threw up his arms and forbade any of them to lay with Monsieur Breton. They were to satisfy his hunger, and that was it. But Abdelsaid knew that it would be impossible, that his secret would soon be discovered.

These moments with the French woman, then, were like succulent morsels for him to savor. Like the dried petals of the Black Lily. Their time together was to be brief. It made Abdelsaid very sad.

He made his way back to the French woman's room, his heart filled with longing.

Abdelsaid came to her again before the next mealtime, without his wives. His passion was incredible, his thrusting almost violent. Amelia was sure that he would break her in half as he possessed her, though there was a delicious thrill to his desire and at no point was she afraid. But she was left hungry and wanting, the aching need inside her. She wondered if it was possible to satisfy it some other way, to bring on that pleasurable sensation. Perhaps to cause it herself? She tried, but found it impossible. She grew lonely and afraid and began to weep in the darkness.

She had never had an identity, never known her name. It did not seem right that it should upset her. For she existed only in the present, only as a part of this elaborate ritual in the Sahara. She was nothing. Amelia had ceased to exist. Perhaps she never had existed. So why did nonexistence torment this nameless woman?

She wept for a time. But when the weeping passed, it seemed that, too, was gone for ever and had never been. Perhaps as a dream.

What happened seemed natural, when the third wife came once again to feed. Once the meal was over, the wife undressed herself and began to kiss the Frenchman. The Frenchman's lips found the woman's breasts and he suckled for a long time while the woman stroked her hair. Then, eagerly, the third wife lay back on the mat, spreading her legs, presenting herself for the Frenchman's skilled kiss.

Amelia found that as she made love to the woman, her very being was subsumed into the woman's body. When the woman cried out, Amelia discovered that she had long ago forgotten who she was, or what she was doing.

She lay, in a curious, pleasant warmth, as the woman rolled her over and began to slip her hands under the robe. Amelia tasted the woman's tongue, and they kissed deeply as the woman's fingertips traced a path up her thigh.

The woman's fingers slipped between Amelia's legs, searching, seeking. The woman's eyes grew wide.

Flushing red, the woman drew back. It sounded as if she were cursing. She quickly gathered up her clothes, bursting into tears as she carried them away. Sadly, Amelia watched after her, confused, the ache of her desire unsatisfied. She wondered again if it was possible to bring the sensation upon herself, but it seemed as hopeless as before.

This was unacceptable. Abdelsaid knew it would be so. He had been flirting with disaster by bringing the woman here, even disguised as she was. He had become wealthy, by local standards, from the trade and export of the Black Lily. He could certainly afford a fourth wife. But the three existing would not stand for it.

"She will take away your affection!" they shrieked. "She will devour all of your love! They are like hungry beasts – especially their women! It is unfair – we cannot have a French girl here! It is improper! You must send her away!'

The three wives spoke in unison, overwhelming Abdelsaid. He would have fought with them, but he knew it was a fight he could not win. On the rare occasions where the women agreed on something, their collective will was unbreakable. Abdelsaid knew, sadly, that it was hopeless.

But he could not send the woman away. He had lost all sense of reality. He felt that he must make her his, for ever. Abdelsaid had fallen in love with the strange French woman without a name. With Monsieur Breton.

There was only one way that the French woman might be allowed to stay in Abdelsaid's house. Abdelsaid argued with his three wives for what seemed like hours. Finally, they agreed. Upon this condition, the French whore could live with them indefinitely. But Abdelsaid had to provide the Black Lily from his private stock. He assured his wives that there was more than enough Black Lily to accomplish the task.

The third wife returned to Amelia, bringing food. Amelia's memories of the incident were vague at best, but she felt an overwhelming sense of worry and of emotional need, and a desire to make love to the woman, to make everything all right. Amelia reached out, but the woman resisted. Finally, she gave in and allowed Amelia to kiss her, but her lips were stern and unmoving.

Amelia finally let the woman go, accepting the food. After the long hours of unknowing worry, she was famished. She ate greedily. In addition to the usual food, there were several large, dark flowers. The third wife plucked off the petals and encouraged Amelia to eat them. Amelia sniffed at them, unsure, but finally let the woman put the petals in her mouth. The taste was thick and sweet. It was some sort of dessert. But not a terribly exciting one. Amelia swallowed each of the petals, and the wife looked satisfied.

Amelia tried to kiss the woman again. But the woman pulled away and Amelia was left in the darkness, lonely and filled with a terrifying desire.

She slept more deeply that night than ever before.

In the morning, the first wife came to her with food and the black flowers. Amelia ate first the food and then the flower petals, wondering. It seemed more savory to her this time. Again the woman refused to kiss Amelia after the flowers had been eaten. Amelia lapsed back into sleep. She did not know how many times she awakened and ate and drank. The taste and smell of the flower seemed to fill her consciousness.

When Abdelsaid came to her, many meals later, her need was intense. Abdelsaid kissed her, deeply, for a long time before he unfastened her robe and helped her out of it. He touched her chest, feeling the thin hair growing there between her breasts, toying with each of her nipples. Slowly he drew his other hand over Amelia's thigh. His hand came to rest in the hollow between her legs, seeking, more clinical than erotic. Amelia felt a curious absence of sensation, though her desire was still overwhelming, perhaps more than before. Abdelsaid seemed satisfied, and left Amelia with no more than a kiss.

Amelia was not disappointed, only curious. Why had he not wanted to make love this time?

The hair of her loins had begun to fall out, scattering across the mat like leaves in Autumn.

He was aware of the woman, upon him. He could not recall how he came to be there, or what his name was, or even whether he had ever existed. Encompassed in her caresses, the insistent mouth and breasts of the woman, guided by her demanding movements, he came to want her. A curious sensation came over him as the woman sank down upon his body, pressing his cock deep inside her. Had he been here before, thrusting up into the woman's naked body while she whispered soothing luxuries to him? He found, after a time, that he could understand her words. When the sensations exploded inside him, he felt an intense pain, as if his body were being torn in half.

Later, much later, he became aware of another woman. But the first was still there. There was a warm touch upon his cock, the taste of her tongue, the texture of female flesh under his hands. There was the warmth, the muscled figure of the man behind him, penetrating him while the three women took their turns using their mouths and hands upon his shaft, their bodies sprawled underneath his kneeling form, pressed as it was against the man. He knew, somehow, that he belonged to these four people, the man and the women. They were as one being with five bodies.

He tried, shortly after the moment of his orgasm, to remember his name. It was only then that he understood. He did not have a name, and never had.

★   ★   ★

Abdelsaid was optimistic. The trade in Black Lily was increasing. The decadent palaces of the French, it seemed, couldn't get enough of the flower. And it was indeed rare. It grew only in the mirage oases in the southern part of the country, and the plants would not take root anywhere else. And Abdelsaid was one of the few traffickers who could find the flowers in the wild, and lead the caravans out again.

While the colonial government had declared an official crackdown on sale of the substance, and promised brutal retribution against all traffickers, the soldiers and policemen preferred to line their pockets rather than interfere with the rights of free trade.

The locals mostly smoked the drug. The Europeans indulged alternately. It was only those who ate the drug who experienced its most extreme effects. Regardless, once the substance was taken out of the desert, it lost some of its secondary properties, and served primarily as a hallucinogenic. Certain of Abdelsaid's business partners were discussing the possibility of establishing an export trade through European shipping companies, of smuggling the substance to a country where it could be sold legally.

Now that he had Breton to lead the caravan, Abdelsaid was able to devote his attention to these more complex matters of business. Breton had learned the trade, had learned to speak and understand Arabic. He had proved an excellent guide. Breton's knowledge of French had suffered, however, as he learned Arabic. Abdelsaid supposed it had to be a heretofore unknown side effect of the Black Lily. There was nothing to be done about it.

And it was such a small price to pay. Any price was small, for Abdelsaid had kept the Frenchwoman he desired, albeit in a somewhat different form. But the love of the Black Lily knows no boundaries. Abdelsaid told himself this whenever he looked with pride at the Frenchman. Whenever he shared him with his wives.

It was enough, to have this small bit of luxury in this cruel world, thought Abdelsaid. For any amount of luxury is preferred to none, and some is preferred to very little. And no one can stop the wind, nor make the sun stand motionless in the sky.

Breton guided the caravan endlessly, from Abdelsaid's town to the oasis many miles across the phantom sand. He was one with the desert.

Breton knew he was from another place. But he also knew that place no longer existed.

Breton knew that he had been sent here, to guide the caravan through the endless desert. Perhaps he had been sent by the gods of his tribe, cast out. Perhaps to bring a blessing to Abdelsaid and his family, for Abdelsaid was infertile. Breton would be the father of Abdelsaid's children. Already Aouicha was with child, and Mimouna suspected also she might be pregnant. Breton imagined these children, in a sense, were a gift from a merciful deity, perhaps a gift from the Black Lily. Breton thought of the sons or daughters as a gift from the universe to Abdelsaid.

Perhaps these gifts were like the visions Breton saw as he slept or daydreamed. The sensations that flowed over him in his dreams. The intimate knowledge of a woman quite unlike Aouicha or Mimouna or Outka. She was more like a boy than a girl, and a mournful boy at that. She was English, he thought, or possibly French. He wondered if perhaps he had loved this woman at some point. He felt sure that he had not, that his union with her had been a matter of convenience.

Breton released his thoughts of the strange woman as he guided the camel train into the oasis, knowing he must turn his thoughts to practical matters of trade and the highest possible price for the blossoms of the Black Lily. He let his memories of the strange woman fly away on the wind, scattering like grains of sand through his fingers. He knew the woman was gone now. It was over.

LEONE or the
buffet of the Gare de Lyon

Régine Deforges

Translated by Maxim Jakubowski

IT ALL BEGAN in the Train Bleu, the restaurant of the Gare de
Lyon.

The Christmas holidays had just begun. The railway station was
surrounded by busy crowds, rushing, laden with cases, bags and
skis. Leone, having delivered her mother and children, was
settling up with the grumpy cab driver moaning about the traffic
jams he'd just driven through.

"And they still complain about the price of petrol, even at ten
francs per litre, shouldn't be allowed to drive damn cars . . .
Christ, retirement won't ever come too early."

Leone gave him a good tip, to calm him down and watched a
faint smile transform his weary face.

"That's very kind of you, madam. Have a nice journey."

Her mother had managed to find a porter, the two kids were
waiting quietly, pacified by the promise of dinner in the restaurant before they boarded the sleeping car. Their behaviour was
particularly impressive seeing they were so excited by the coming
disruption to their everyday life.

They followed the porter to the lift that went up to the restaurant. Passing under the great clock, her son remembered an episode from Tardi's *ADELE BLANSEC* that had greatly impressed him. The children were agog at the baroque decor of the place. The abundance of gold, the walls and ceilings so full of colourful paintings, the warm nudes, the heavy silver trolleys laden with roasts, and in particular those bearing an impressive stack of patisseries which made their mouths water.

The maitre d' found them a comfortable corner and brought the menus. Sophie, full of the assurance of her lone five years, declared peremptorily that she would not have soup but snails.

"That's very heavy for an evening meal," the grandmother said.

"It doesn't matter, mother," Leone said. "It's the holidays."

A grateful Sophie winked at her mum. Jacques, older, chose sausage and andouillette "with really a lot of chips" he added. Leone and her mother, less ambitiously, selected a consommé and grilled meat with a decent Bordeaux wine.

Once they had ordered, and the wine was promptly delivered to the table as requested, Leone chose to relax and lit up a cigarette while slowly sipping a glass of wine.

Two young men, in their early thirties, looking merry, both rather handsome and weighed down by luggage, came to sit across from them, picked up their menu and ordered. Then, like Leone, they each lit up a cigarette and looked around them. They noticed her simultaneously and smiled pleasingly, impressed by the spectacle of the unknown woman. Leone demurely smiled back. She knew she was pretty, draped in the soft, black wool outfit that showed off her pale complexion and her ash blonde hair. She looked away but still felt the men's gaze on her. Her son also noticed their interest and, with a distinct sense of ownership, remarked:

"Why are those two guys looking at you like that?"

"It's because they think mummy is very pretty," said Sophie, cuddling up to her mother, to demonstrate that Leone was hers and hers alone. Which provoked Jacques to stand up and come over to kiss his mother. She held them both tight against her, laughing, pleased with the proximity of their warm young bodies.

"Those are indeed very lucky kids," one of the men whispered rather loudly.

It was trite, but the sound of his voice was pleasing to Leone.

The waiters brought the dishes. Jacques sat down again and laid siege to his sausage with gluttony, while Sophie struggled with the snail tongs. For a few moments, they ate in silence.

From time to time, Leone would look up and across to the nearby table. On each occasion, she would catch the eyes of one or the other of the friends. Soon, she felt herself become increasingly uneasy. "What a pity I'm not alone . . . they're both rather handsome. I'd find it difficult to choose between them . . . but, why choose? . . . Oh, what a fool I am, anyway, they'll soon be leaving . . . I'd like to leave, too . . . How it would be nice to be alone in Paris for a few days . . . Strange how these men attract me . . . It's reciprocal, they both like me too . . . what should I do? . . . I'd like to see them again . . . know where they live . . . I just can't speak to them, not in front of mother and the children . . . Oh, how life can be awkward!"

She pulled out a cigarette from the pack. A flame was struck. One of the men was offering it to her. She lit up her cigarette and thanked him with a nod.

The plates were cleared away and the meat was brought on. Increasingly disturbed, she was rather tersely answering the children's questions. Sophie pulled her by the sleeve.

"You're not even listening to me. What are you thinking of?"

Leone kissed the child.

"I was thinking how bored I will be without you around."

She tried to feign interest in her own mother's discourse: she was worried how her daughter would spend the holidays. Heard Jacques asking whether he would be having the same instructor as the previous year, and if he could still go to the movies in the afternoon.

Once again, her eyes met the gaze of the two men. This time, she didn't break the contact. She could read their desire, it was the same as hers, brutal and transparent. She felt her face go all red and looked away. There was something obsessive about their presence, her heartbeat quickened, her hands were becoming clammy, the bottom half of her body turning to lead. Shards of lucidity kept on telling her she was mad, ill, a sexual pervert. She took another cigarette and broke three matches in a row in a futile attempt to light it. The man who had offered her the flame earlier stood up, his light shivering slightly as he approached it. Leone took hold of the young man's hand to bring it to the level of her cigarette. This brief contact caused her turmoil. The lighter's flame went out under her breath.

"I'm sorry," she said, looking up.

Her emotion reached its pinnacle as she witnessed the pale and stirring face of the man. He switched the lighter back on. Leone breathed the smoke in deeply with great relief.

"Thank you."

He returned to his seat, said a few words to his friend who was smiling back at him. The arrival of the dessert trolley was a welcome diversion. The children wanted a taste of each single one: the chocolate mousse, the rum baba, the egg cream, the raspberry pie, the blackcurrant sorbet, the chocolate cake, the iced meringues, the tarte tatin, their eyes were all over the place. The two men chose their desserts under the admiring gaze of the kids. Leone took only a coffee, which provoked some witty remarks among the men about how women knew to protect their waistline. Even though it was all rather banal, Leone laughed along with them, pleased by this fortuitous contact which would very soon come to an end on the station platform.

The time was nearing, Leone requested the bill and a porter. They offered to carry her luggage, but gave up smiling when they saw how many she had.

"Where are you going?" one of them asked.

"Morzine," Sophie said.

"What a coincidence, so are we," they said together in such harmony that all three burst out laughing.

Her mother watched Leone with disapproval while the children looked jealous. They reached their sleeping car. The ticket controller opened the door connecting the children and the grandmother's cabin. They moved and jumped between the compartments with noisy glee. Leone walked out into the corridor, and noticed the two men coming towards her from the other end of the car. The same emotion that had overcome her in the restaurant returned, only more violent now. She had to admit to herself that she wanted both of them together, that their joint desire was inflaming hers. "I'm a complete freak," she thought. A good thing matters would go no further: them to Morzine or wherever, she in Paris. Sadness suddenly swirled over her at the thought of being alone in Paris, in the grey, cold and muddy

December Paris, while others left for the snow and holidays, maybe even some sun.

"We were looking for you . . . You will come and have a glass of champagne with us?"

"No, thank you. It's not possible, the train is about to leave."

"But until Morzine we have all the time in the world."

"I'm not taking the train, I'm only seeing the children off."

"Oh, no . . ."

The harmony of how they expressed their disappointment and the sad look on their faces touched Leone so much she couldn't stop herself from chuckling gently.

"Don't pull such faces, you both look as if you've just lost your best friend."

"Yeah, I suppose it's a bit like that," whispered the darker-haired one.

"Come with us," said the other. "It's stupid to stay in Paris at Christmas."

"Yes, yes, why don't you come along?"

"But I can't, my job . . ."

"You can phone in tomorrow and say you're sick."

All the while, Sophie had been quietly listening to the conversation and watching her mother and the two young men in turn. She took her mother by the hand.

"They're right, it would be nice if you came along with us."

"You know it's not possible, my darling. Go and see your grandmother."

"Come, we'd so much like to know you better. Even if you can't stay for the whole holiday, come for two or three days."

"No, I tell you, it's not possible. Anyway, I'd have nothing to wear. I can't go to the mountains and the snow dressed like this."

She pointed at herself, showing them how her black shoes couldn't adequately replace decent après-ski and her thin grey stockings substitute for warm leggings; and her delicate kid gloves, they would fall apart in the snow.

"It doesn't matter, everything you need we can buy there."

She did not answer. All three of them kept on watching each other, twisted up in their desire to huddle together, to caress one another, to love. Leone felt a pang of anger: "They're right, what's so important in Paris? I was only staying behind because I didn't feel like going with mother and the children . . . But . . ."

Can one go like this, with people you don't even know? . . . The only thing I know of them, is that they want to screw me . . . It's getting on my nerves, after all . . . and then, what would mother think, if I stayed here, like that . . . she's not stupid . . . and the children? . . . oh, to hell with the kids . . . if I did go? . . . It's not possible, I haven't got my toothbrush . . . or any make-up . . . I'd be such a sorry sight tomorrow morning . . . but they are so handsome . . . why not give in to their lust . . . and mine . . . so?"

"Madam, time to get off, the train is about to depart."

The ticket controller stole her away from her thoughts. She waved farewell to the two men and walked into the compartment to kiss her mother and the children. Like on the occasion of every departure, Sophie cried, her tears soon dried by Leone's kisses. Jacques wanted to open the window onto the platform; his mother convinced him not to, because of the cold. She kissed her mob one last time and got off the train. The controller closed the door behind her.

Like most people, she hated farewells on station platforms, it made her cry. Without even waiting for the train's departure, the final kisses blown from her lips, she began moving towards the exit. She passed the wagon where the two men were standing on the running board.

"Come, you can go back tomorrow if you want."

She stopped, her whole body braced towards them, torn between the desire to jump aboard and conventional morality.

"I'd really like to, but . . ."

The train gave a jump and slowly set itself in motion. She moved as if to climb on. She mechanically walked alongside, like someone trying to postpone the moment of separation from a loved one embarking on a long journey.

"Come . . ."

She felt herself lifted up, torn off the ground by two strong sets of hands and found herself in the now accelerating train, between the two men now looking at her with both satisfaction and worry.

"But it's a kidnapping . . . you're mad!"

But the sound of her voice, her bright, cheerful eyes, her moist, half-open mouth, contradicted her words.

If looks could eat, they were already devouring each other, truly amazed by the formidable aura of desire now surrounding them.

The spell wasn't broken by the appearance of the ticket controller who did not appear surprised to have an extra passenger. There was a spare seat. Leone wanted to pay for her fare, they would not allow her. They ordered another bottle of champagne.

"To celebrate our journey."

They introduced themselves: Gérard, Dominique. She only remembered their first names.

"I'm Leone."

"Let us drink to Leone's health."

They raised their three glasses. The champagne was lukewarm, but it wasn't important; it was only a symbol of their understanding.

Leaning on their elbows in front of the corridor window, they silently watched the procession outside of dark buildings, broken here and there by some light from a window, as they travelled through the sad Paris suburbs. Gérard put his arm around Leone's waist, while Dominique took hold of her shoulder. Without shame or false modesty, Leone gave in to the reassuring sense of well-being running through her as well as the heat of the two men. They stayed that way for some time, savouring the certainty of pleasures to come. Soon, the lights outside were few and far between and there was only the black hole of the countryside.

They moved into one of the compartments and helped Leone take her coat off. She remained standing, arms on her side, confident, calm. Only her breath quickened. Dominique pulled her towards him, gently kissing her face, her neck. She felt her body harden against his, thrust her lips forward and this first kiss was so voluptuous she almost fainted out of joy. Gérard turned her round and also kissed her with voracious brutality. She moaned. While Gérard prolonged his kiss, she felt Dominique pulling the zip of her dress. Without interrupting their kiss, he helped the young woman's arms out of the garment and let it fall softly to the ground. She stepped out of it and now only wore a short grey silk slip, lined with ochre lace. The hands of the two men moved across the smooth surface of the slip. They rubbed each other against her and she felt their hard cocks against her stomach and buttocks. She moved slightly, to feel them better. She thought they were getting even harder. Gérard abandoned her mouth and, sitting on the bunk, pulled down the shoulder straps of Leone's slip and brassiere. Her breasts burst out, heavy and voluptuous. Gérard buried his face in them, his mouth squashed against her musky mounds. He took a step back to admire them better. The train's movements echoed through them, bringing the breasts alive, their raised nipples begging for kisses and bites.

"How beautiful you are!"

She pulled Gérard's head against her chest. He greedily nibbled one tip. Leone let out a small cry.

"Oh, I'm sorry. Did I hurt you?"

"No, no, go on."

Gérard resumed his caress while Leone abandoned herself, a glutton for more.

Dominique was watching the spectacle of Gérard's mouth moving from one breast to another while his hands roamed freely over her splendid chest. He slipped off the already crumpled slip and the already wet knickers. He brought them up to his nose. Leone was naked between the two still-clothed men, she now only wore her suspender belt, her stockings and her shoes. Dominique could no longer hold back. He pulled his penis out and, arching Leone back towards him, holding her by the hips, drove into her. She struggled a bit, but the young man strengthened his hold on her and thrust himself in even deeper. His sex must be quite large, for she had never felt herself as mightily invaded as this. He moved slowly inside her, whispering:

"I love you, you are so good."

Gérard's mouth and hands kept on bruising her breasts, Dominique's cock surged on ever harder, a deep, savage lust rose inside Leone who came with a scream as Dominique spurted inside her. He briefly stayed within her, holding her up, kissing and pecking her back. Gérard pulled her away from his friend's body and laid her down on the cot. He hurriedly tore off all his clothes, scattering them around the compartment and threw himself into Leone. He took her without consideration. She barely had enough time to register the surprise of her intense arousal before they climaxed together, in total silence.

Leone felt as if time was standing still. Her body, blissful, floated. The swinging movements of the train completed the illusion.

"I'm thirsty," she whispered.

Dominique poured her some of the tepid champagne, she
swallowed it in one gulp. He ran a wet towel over her body,
which she was grateful for, and assisted her in rolling down her
stockings and suspender belt. He then undressed.

Gérard grumbled. He was beginning to doze, and looking at
him, Leone and Dominique began laughing.

"Here, some champagne will do you good."

He took the bottle from Dominique's hands and drank straight
from it. The foam slipped out of his mouth, down his neck and
lost itself in the hairs on his chest. He burped and apologized, lit a
cigarette that he handed over to Leone and offered Dominique
another. They were sitting on the cot, their legs hanging over the
edge, curled up together, smoking in silence.

It was Dominique who interrupted their daydreaming, sliding
down to the floor between Leone's legs. His warm and skilful
tongue soon awakened her senses again. She moaned as she held
the young man's head against her stomach. With her free hand,
she searched for Gérard's penis; aroused by his fingers, it rose.
Kneeling on the bunk, he brought his cock to the level of Leone's
mouth; she lapped at it gently like a cat drinking milk. Dominique
helped her slide down on the cot, and pulling her up, lowered her
down on his member. Gérard, disappointed, stroked himself
gently. They all three climaxed together.

Leone fell asleep in the middle of a sentence. But her sleep
didn't last long. She was woken by a cock moving inside her.
Later, one of the young men sodomized her. She barely had time
to register the pain before she came again, at excruciating length.

Early in the morning, when the ticket controller knocked at the
door to announce their arrival in Morzine station, she thought she
wouldn't even be able to stand up again, her whole body ached so
much. Aching, but satisfied. She shrieked in horror when she saw
herself in the mirror. The circles around her eyes spread all the
way down to her cheeks, her lips were swollen from too many
kisses and bites, her tangled hair gave her the look of a wild,
wanton woman.

"I can't go out like this. It looks as if I've . . ."

"Yes, you did," the men answered, laughing.

She shrugged and tried to make herself presentable. Her night
companions weren't much of an improvement on her. Once she
had dressed, they pulled her towards them.

"You don't regret it? You know, it's the first time we've made love to the same woman, together."

"For me too, it was the first time," she said, still a bit red-faced.

Dominique cupped her chin.

"You musn't be ashamed. We fell for you at first sight and you for us and it was wonderful."

She gave them each a big fat kiss on the cheeks, like you give to good friends, or children.

"Yes, it was wonderful."

"So, are you staying on?" asked Gérard.

"No, it's not possible. I'll hire a cab to Geneva and will then catch the first plane back to Paris."

They insisted but understood that she had made her mind up. "Keep an eye on my mother and my children disembarking, I don't want them to see me like this."

Gérard was the look-out while Dominique and Leone stayed back, huddled together, holding each other's hand. Leone knew she could grow attached to this tender, handsome, blue-eyed boy who made love so well. But her own life was already so full, there was no place left for further adventures. She regretted it.

Gérard returned, he'd found a cab and seen the family leave in another.

"Are you sure you don't want us to come with you to Geneva?"

"No, thanks, I don't enjoy farewells."

She got into the taxi, turned back to wave at them. Dominique was running behind the car. She guessed what he was asking: "Your name, your address." She looked away, smiled and settled down in the comfort of the seat. It was warm in the car, the snow-covered landscape was pretty in the morning light, the driver ignored her and remained silent. Images from the previous night floated back to the surface of her memory, raising exquisite feelings of pleasure. It felt like the dawn of time: before the creation of sin. She slept all the way to Geneva, a smile of ecstasy on her lips.

THE GIFT

Stella Duffy

HE HAD GONE to work. Finally gone to work after the morning ritual – pulling, dragging, wrenching him from sleep, I had parcelled him off, pressed him into his work clothes, packaging him into Anyman for another day. I stayed in the small weatherboard house, stuck in the small thin house, close and hot in early morning humidity.

Summer lingers into late damp March.

The kids – breakfasted, shouted at, washed, cried, dressed, tears dried, lunch packed, cuddled, kissed – finally at school. And outside grey drizzle fell steaming on a morning of screaming children and red angry women hidden in identical versions of the same day. All rubber gloved. All staring out of kitchen windows. Through dusty glass there never was time to wash, out on to the same grey green back gardens as the same thick rain beat on the same rusting tricycle.

But for me there is a knock at the door.

I opened the door. It was a woman. Six foot, covered in leather. Skin-tight worn leather legs, rising from heavy black boots buckles gleaming, muscled calves and smooth thighs – sinews marking the line of touch to her waist. A silver belt, two inches wide and detailed, symbols circling her torso. Cropped jacket, topped with black helmet and shiny mirror glasses. I see myself in the covers of her eyes.

I stare at the vision, the mouth the only exposure, big soft lips parted, saying something unclear, and then –

"So I wondered if I could come in? Until it stops raining . . . it's not really safe out here, slipping . . . and sliding."

She is Maori and takes off her boots, leaving them at the door and walks barefoot into the hall, padding into the hall. It seemed larger, as if growing to accommodate this woman. This Woman. She went through the kitchen door, removed her gloves and, with the light behind her lifted off her helmet, shaking out an elbow's length of hair.

The Woman sat. Brown eyes deep and heavy lashed grinning at me, wide set above a broad soft nose. Her lips maroon red and wide and full like a welcome stain. There is a faint moko on her chin. Like it is just growing in. Like it comes from inside out.

I ask where from. I ask why. The Woman begins to answer me, her voice coming low and soft as a half smile.

". . . and Sarah, is there coffee? It wasn't far, but I am wet . . ."

I made coffee.

(She knows me. She named me.)

The kettle on, I watched as the Woman lifted off her jacket – muscled arms hanging the heavy article on the back of the chair – and straightened her dark red shirt.

She stretches forward, flings back her hair like an unwanted bedsheet.

She, swinging on her chair so I can't help but follow my thoughts to her breasts, smiles at me. Smiles, rising and falling in thin silk.

We drank coffee in silence.

The coffee cups drained, sat side by side on the kitchen table. I picked them up, added more hot water and watched the cups sink beneath a blanket of soap suds and scattered sodden cornflakes.

Yellow gloved I slid my hands beneath the water.

The Woman slid her hand along my arm.

The water through the glove is warm. Its pressure holds the glove against my hand.

The Woman's hand is warm. The pressure of her lips on my neck holds my breath inside my lungs.

The Woman is warm outside. I am warm inside.

But my skin shivered in expectation and surprise and unsurprise, in awareness and willing ignorance.

The cups sit side by side on the draining board.

A fingernail-full of soap bubbles slides down the side of the cup.

The Woman slides down the side of me.

My leg is smooth. So is the Woman's touch.

So is her mouth.

I fumbled with my gloved hands, stripped myself of kitchen yellow.

Ungloved, my hands were naked.

I will be soon.

One glove falls, thumb filling with water.

Turns. Sinks.

As does She.

As do I.

And now hands which have been soft become sharp and lithe and everywhere, all over me, strong hands writhing and seething, and pulling at my hair, pinching my nipples, in my eyes, my ears, mouth, cunt, deep for me. Softest-in-the-world lips to breasts, mean teeth clawing their way through my thin skin. I am hip bone impaled. Ten long fingers everyplace at once, entangling my hair, toes clawing, not caressing but harassing hard and sharp and constant and overwhelming and she is touching me she is making me and she is wanting me and I am wanting too until wanting becomes hard and solid, wanting is made woman, is made flesh in our joining and into the exquisite agony of persistent touch I am teased taunted bullied goaded, into orgasm, into bloody bitter piercing coming and I cry out and I arch and I am the same shudder and am those long hands on which my body centres itself pivoting and am those dark eyes and am and am no more and I am.

In bed, I studied the Woman. Long and wide and full. Colour glancing off her body like shaded sunlight. Heavy as warm oil. The Woman had brought food – avocados from the Philippines and melon from Fiji, strawberries and fat grapes. Summer fruits and autumn night closing outside.

Sated, we turned to the window as the first sky rocket touched its zenith.

Someone else was putting on a firework show, unwittingly and intentionally for the sole pleasure of the Woman and me. A single silver light climbed, disappeared for a second and became seven white stars. Points of green exploded into solid, starred orbs. It went on.

It goes on. She and I sit spellbound. There is no "as if". The display is for us. The last rocket falls.

The Woman falls to me. Falls in my lap. Lapping. Lapped. I stretch my hand through the Woman's hair and find they are not tresses or curls, but locks. I am locked in. Single strands of long black hair twist and bind me to the Woman. Lock me to the Woman.

I don't want to look for the key.

The room is bigger and the bed softer than it was before.

Before the Woman.

I lie in the Woman's arms.

The Woman lies in my arms.

But this is the Truth.

We sleep with the Southern Cross carved into our eyelids and in the morning are rainlight wakened.

And he never came back.

And they never came back.

And the Woman stayed forever.

And it was real.

It is real.

Because I say it is.

She and I are the word made flesh. Make the word flesh.

Because I say so.

MOBIUS STRIPPER

Bana Witt

1 Hot Nazis

I was riding on the 7 Haight bus to my massage job downtown when I sat down next to a thin friendly blonde girl. She was on her way to the clap clinic. She said she had clap of the throat. She might have gotten it from a girl she had worked with on a porno film. I had never met anyone who'd done porn before, or even seen any for that matter. She said she was working for these really nice guys called the Mitchell Brothers and told me just to call their theater if I wanted to work.

I was very excited by the idea. I had just started to get into S&M: having boyfriends who liked to tie me up or spank me, biting hard, doing things that left marks and looking at my own marks after a long night. I thought I was about as kinky and decadent as anyone. I called after thinking about it for a few days. I went to an interview at the O'Farrell Theater and was confused by the incredible similarity between the two brothers. They were fine-boned, relatively small men, with a way of making the bizarre seem totally routine. The older brother was Jim, the younger, Artie. They asked me if I'd ever done this sort of work before and I said no, but that I was a masochist and loved to be beaten and they could really do it if they wanted. There was a list of other things they asked if I would do. I said yes to them all.

They told me they were going to do a series of short, very hardcore films called *Ultra Core*.

A few days later I went to a large brick building in the Tenderloin. It's across from Hyde Street Studios now. I was overweight and not nearly as flashy as the other women, but much more enthusiastic. They had this outrageously beautiful makeup woman who was also from Fresno. Years later she would fall in love with my friend Patty at my wedding.

The title of the film was *Hot Nazis* and I was to play a lesbian Jew. I was very impressed when I heard Michael Bloomfield was writing the music. There were no scripts.

One room was a reproduction of a bleak concrete bunker. At one end was a large radio. On the wall to the left was a barbed wire cage filled with straw and bones, fresh bones from cattle legs. There was a large wiry German shepherd gnawing on one of the bones. Myself and a girl named Virginia were to be in the cage. I took her aside to find out if she really liked women. She did. She had done a lot of this work before. We were given torn thermal underwear to wear and smudged up a little. The first scene to be shot was of us getting it on in the straw. I had no idea having an audience would get me off so much. Virgina knew the ropes and nothing was faked. I was pretty submissive. She gave ferocious head and finger fucked me until I screamed.

The crew applauded our first scene. Then Artie (in retrospect I know it was Artie) asked me if I would fuck the dog. It boggled my mind. I wanted to be a trooper, but the dog! I declined and Virgina attempted to get the dog aroused. The dog growled. They left him alone.

The rest of the action focused around a tall gaunt man named Vernon, who played head Nazi and his girlfriend Enjil, a beautiful Nordic woman. There were several men playing Gestapo guards and a woman with dark hair named Monique. They did some scenes of the guards fucking one another and the girls, and then it was my turn again. I was to be held down on a table and screwed by Vernon. Everyone was doing hits off a full bottle of liquid amyl nitrate. I was lying on my back and he started out by running a riding crop across my body. Slowly he began tapping it on the insides of my thighs. He hit harder and harder, at which point my girlfriend was supposed to pull him off and he was to continue by screwing me. Only he wouldn't stop whipping me.

Every time he lifted the crop there would be a bright new red
stripe on my body. She tried to pull him off and he pushed her
into the barbed wire that was wrapped around the cage. He
returned to continue beating me now for real. He was laying the
whip into my very white skin as hard as he could. Finally Virginia
yelled "CUT!" to the cameramen. They realized we weren't just
acting and subdued Vernon. In the film the welts were unbelievable. Virginia's leg bled real blood from the barbed wire.

They wanted just one final insertion shot on the table. I lay
down, face up. I asked Monique for a hit of the amyl nitrate. She
tilted the bottle and poured the whole thing up my nose and into
my eyes. The burning was unbelievable. I jumped up screaming,
and then I started rushing. It was like I'd shot speed and jumped
off a cliff at the same time. Everything was buzzing and my ears
were ringing and I couldn't get my breath. Jim had gotten water
and was flushing my face with it. I knew I was going to have a
seizure. I knew I was going to be blind. I knew I should go to the
hospital. It was the most total, complete panic I've ever had.

In the space adjacent to the *Hot Nazis* set was a room with an
elaborate bed. It had been used in a scene from the brothers' film,
Sodom and Gomorrah. I lay there for a long time while they
continued to shoot the movie. I finally realized I wasn't going to
die, that I was a lesbian Jew in a storage building in the
Tenderloin of San Francisco. Artie came in to see how I was.
We had sex for the first time and I finally felt the cord being cut
from the tule fog and tract houses that had been my home.

2 Dabbling in S&M

I never have liked going nude. I have rarely been thin enough to
be proud of my body. I'm thick through the waist. I have almost
no tits. I have great confidence in my face and legs, but as far as
my torso is concerned, I would just as soon leave it covered up.
I've had a few boyfriends who were very comfortable nude.

I also get cold very easily, but I just don't like people to look at
my naked body. It's not shyness. It is simply that I feel I cannot
pass muster. I've been with and around so many beautiful sexy
women, it has left me humble in that regard. A lot of men like to
look at your body, like when you're walking across the room.

That bothers me. I never felt confident unless I was actually making body contact. I knew I was better at the tactile than the visual.

I think my hating to be nude in front of people is why I got off so much on the movies. I got off from proving how hot I was, if not pretty, and because of the adrenaline from being terrified. I was lucky they didn't require any acting. I was way too scared to think clearly, but it made the sex great. The best part came afterwards, rehashing the films in my mind. I would be in retrospective bliss for weeks after a shoot.

When I was twenty-two I made up a list of everyone I could recall having had sex with. It was nearly two hundred people in length. Apparently I was active before the AIDS epidemic. I was unbelievably lucky on that one. Only two of them were real tricks, everything else was in films or for recreation.

Late in 1975 I answered an ad in one of the sex magazines that said they were looking for nude bondage models. It sounded like good, non-boring work. I called and talked to a man who seemed pretty lucid and straightforward. His name was Ron Reynolds or something close to that. Anyway, his initials were R.R. He had a little S&M Victorian in Oakland. I remember I'd never ridden BART, the local subway system, and I rode BART over from San Francisco. He picked me up in a stationwagon that smelled like a dog. He dressed like he sold cars, and seemed very gentle and polite. He wore very thick glasses with black frames that made his eyes look intense and maybe a little psychotic, but not enough to make me uncomfortable.

We drove to his house and I could still smell the dog. The place was divided into different torture rooms, with women attending them who dressed in leather, looked cold and unforgiving, and did domination scenes with men. There was never any standard sex. And this Ron guy was that way with me. Everyone I had done nude modeling for at that point had tried to fuck me, but he didn't try. It seems when sadists and masochists really become purist, The Scene is the whole thing, and the pain or the mood or the concept replaces orgasm and generic sexual activity.

We went to a room where he did photography. There was a large Irish setter sleeping in a shipping kennel. The door was open and she was very friendly, but she was the source of the omnipresent smell of dog. I was getting around fifty dollars an hour. The twisted pros of the industry really liked me even though I wasn't the standard tits-and-hair nude model. I was trusting, good natured, liberal, and incredibly submissive.

He had me model a number of weird leather arrangements. One was a leather hood with no holes in it, except one to breathe through. It pulled over your head like a falcon's hood. My hands were handcuffed behind me. I posed in a number of positions for about an hour: on my knees with my head bowed, or lying on my side on the floor under a floodlight, or sitting backwards in a chair. I never felt fear. It took me a long time to learn fear.

After the shoot he told me he really liked me. He had several live-in slaves and wanted me to join the crew. I thought it could be fun. It seemed like the beginning of an interesting cult.

On my second visit they began my initiation. He gave me a name with his initials in it: Morrow. All of his slaves had his initials in their name. Two pretty young girls came in, one was a young blonde with a gold ring through one lip of her pussy. I thought it looked great. I was told not to make eye contact with anyone and to always respond to Ron as Sir. That was hard to do with a straight face.

I was told to kneel in front of a bad painting of a woman with her head bowed. While I recited lines of devotion and submission, they whipped me. It was tremendously exciting and it hurt just enough. They had the line between pleasure and pain memorized.

They had a cool set-up for doing pain scenes. Beforehand they would give you a key word. If things ever got too heavy you could just say the word and things would stop.

I bellied up on living there. My main objection was that the place was tacky. If Ron had money or taste, I think I could have bought into it. But the furniture was ugly and old, the house smelled like that damn dog, and Ron was no prize. When I left that day, I thought, if I'm going to be a slave, I'm going to be a rich slave. *The Story of O* became my bible.

After seeing the blonde girl at Ron's and reading *The Story of O*, I decided to pierce my labia. I'd been working on films with a lot of other girls who had various piercings: labia, nipples, noses. I thought a gold ring looked pretty sexy. It was also like a badge showing how hardcore you really were. I didn't know any of the technicalities of correct piercing. I took a couple of pain killers and got out a large upholstery needle. I did clean it with alcohol. I'd gotten a small gold self-piercing hoop to put in after I'd made the hole. My friend Patty came over to watch. She was intrigued. She and I had watched each other do some pretty bizarre things.

It was hard to get the needle to go through because the skin was very thick and rubbery. I had to really push and ended up having to put a cork behind it and then pushed it through. Bled like mad, got the earring in. Swelled so much in a day I wasn't able to walk. It was shiny and swollen and felt like red ants had nested there. I couldn't even think of wearing pants. By the third day I gave up, I pulled it out. It started healing within twelve hours and was completely healed in two days. It was miraculous.

I found out how to do proper piercing much later on. What you do is start on antibiotics a week before you do it and continue to take them for a week after. It cuts down on the grief I went through. I've met a lot of people over the years into ritualist piercing. They all used antibiotics.

3 Lower Haight

The most depressing place I've ever lived was at the bottom of Haight Street near Market. My apartment was in a three-story building that had originally been three flats, but they had been divided in half lengthwise to make six apartments. I lived in one of the back three where you had to use the outside stairs. I was living on SSI for being crazy, writing a lot of tortured poetry, taking drugs and screwing my brains out, like some people do on SSI.

I met Joanne while living on Lower Haight. She was the hottest woman I've ever known. When I met her we were both doing live all-girl sex shows at the O'Farrell Theater. My friend Artie took me to the dressing room on my first day and introduced us.

She was sitting on a table in front of a make-up mirror smoking a cigarette and wearing only a beat-up motorcycle jacket. With her laconic expression, her long naked legs, her short brown pubic hair, and her tiny nipples against the heavy gold zipper of the jacket, she looked like one of Warhol's women: jaded, bored and beautiful. She had gigantic cool and the prettiness of an East

Coast socialite gone bad. She looked me up and down and
sounding like Nico on valium, she said, "I can't wait to get to
work."

It turned me on completely. From then on it was a competition
to see who could be the most hardcore and the coolest. Doing
shows with her was more fun than I'd ever had.

Our first time together was in the Ultra Room when it first
opened. The Mitchell Brothers had come back from a visit to
New York with the idea. The entire room was upholstered in
black leather and measured about ten by fifteen feet in length.
There were ropes and pulleys hanging from the ceiling with
square mirrors set into the wall at eye level. All the girls could see
their own reflection, but from outside the customers could see in.
Two or three women would work the room at the same time,
giving head to each other, using dildos, or just masturbating for
the audience.

We started the show with three women in the room. We would
flirt and kiss and hump each other, rapidly getting more and more
bold until we were screaming and carrying on like mad women. I
was on my period and Joanne gave me head. It wasn't pretty.

Here's what made it even more memorable: Herb Caen, a local
newspaper columnist, had come to the O'Farrell that night. He
brought a member of the Rockefeller clan, who had to go outside
to throw-up after watching us. I'm sure it was better to do than
see. The next day Caen said in his column that the show was the
most disgusting thing he'd ever seen. Business tripled.

Joanne had a son who was six years old. He'd grown up around
drag queens in the Castro District. He knew more about sexual
aberrations than most adults, and would do gut-wrenching im-
personations of drag queens trying to pick up tricks. Joanne got
into angel dust, which I couldn't handle. But there was a lot of
this other drug called MDMA around (now they call it Ecstasy). I
would score it at Toad Hall on Castro Street. We shot it up a
number of times and made love. It made you incredibly sensitive
and horny. We thought we'd achieved sexual enlightenment.

We went to gay bars sometimes after work and would see how
outrageous we could be, like I would give her head on the dance
floor while she danced and held a martini in her hand. She loved
being passionate in public, and so did I. Rumor had it Joanne had
even fist fucked a gay guy on the bar at the Stud on Folsom

Street. She made me feel like Pollyanna. I was in awe. I get total recall when I think of Joanne.

Also while living on Lower Haight, I befriended a strange photographer who called one night and asked me if I'd like to go meet his coke connection in the wine country and be like a present to him. I'd never been a present before and agreed.

The coke dealer was a big, gentle man who collected guitars and antiques, and had lots of dogs. The photographer also brought a beautiful girl who was about nineteen. She had thick chestnut hair and a Playboy Bunny body. Her name was Arrega. The two guys wanted to see us make love but she refused, and later asked me if she could come to my house the next day.

She moved in for a month and the photographer was crushed. It gave me great pleasure to watch men go nuts over her and then find out she was with me. She turned tricks on Polk Street occasionally while I was taking Isadora Duncan dance lessons at California Hill. We slept together but I was very jealous because she was still seeing men and ultimately threw her out.

After Arrega, I had an affair with a gangster and his wife. I first met them at a couples party in Oakland. We did three ways for a while, but as usual in those situations, I fell heavily for the woman. She was a tall, svelte submissive blonde he had rescued from the streets. I saw her alone for about six months while he was doing a short stretch of time in jail.

She disappeared and after he got out, while he was searching for her, I slept with him alone. He always had great drugs. He slept with a .357 Magnum under the pillow, which seemed kind of exciting to me for a while, then some remnant of common sense burst through when I heard at the bathhouse that the Hell's Angels had a contract out on him. Then Sonny Barger, the Oakland Hell's Angels leader, called my house to threaten him. I went back to my mother's house in Oroville for a while to chill out. I saw him on the Bay Area tv news, talking about his wife's disappearance through a voice processor with a mask on.

That was followed by a relationship with a fastidious hippie guy who worked for the Post Office, had been to Afghanistan (and never recovered), and could fuck like a man possessed. He was hunky but a little too chubby, with flawless auburn hair to his shoulders and a full beard. He decided to rescue me.

We'd been having polite dinners and good sex. He didn't

shoot-up and had a nice apartment in the Avenues. I never cooked at my house and there were always dirty dishes in the sink. We'd had pizza one night and had slept at my place. For breakfast I'd decided to heat the pizza and blithely turned on the oven to heat, going into the other room for a few minutes. When I returned the entire top of the stove was covered with cockroaches. Big ones, baby ones. They were jumping around on the hot stove, and were so thick you couldn't see the top. I guess they'd been breeding in the oven.

I realized my life was grimmer than I really wanted, that maybe I had suffered enough for art, and moved into his apartment in the Avenues.

4 Tahoe

The first porno people I worked with besides the Brothers were from Los Angeles. The word around was that they were Mafia-backed. A lot of LA people came to shoot porn in San Francisco at that time because it was a lot less likely they would get busted here.

The people who "acted" in these films had a tremendous network going. I found I could call anyone who I'd worked with or even heard of and ask them about a potential employer. If someone didn't pay at the end of the shoot, or was horrible to work with, the word spread like lightning. I had about four pages of notes listing producers' names, and the opinions of other actors and their past experiences with them.

The first duo I worked with from LA were really sleazy. They wanted to make a ski-oriented film and were going to take the entire cast to Tahoe for a week. They also brought along a skiing coach, some camera men and the director's dad. We got a huge house at Northstar.

The director's dad liked to tell stories. He had been a hobo for a time and would tell about hopping freight trains and drinking sterno. I had never heard of such a thing. They would drain the fluid out of sterno cans used to heat food and mix it with Tokay grape wine. They called it Tokay and Squeezins. I couldn't believe he was still alive.

They had asked me to shave my crotch for the shoot, which I

did but the second day I had broken out with razor burn. It was hideous. It looked like prime teenage acne all over my pubic area.

When we went skiing, it was a disaster. I had not skied since I was seven years old, and had very poor balance and muscle control. My dance teachers had always called it "your neurological problem", but it was a little more vague than that. My first time down the bunny hill I broke through the surface of a frozen-over creek and was totally drenched in ice water. The woman who played my favorite girlfriend in the film sprained her ankle and it became grossly swollen.

Our first scene together in the shower was shot the next morning around my razor burn and her ankle. Mostly I gave her head. The level of sexual excitement was so intense that everyone said they'd have to re-shoot the rest of the film to bring it up to our level. We could make each other come just by looking at each other.

We hung out together at the house when everyone else went out to the casinos at night. She had brought some heroin with her and we would smoke it and make love. It was like camp for decadent San Franciscans. I had never gotten to go to real camp because of my asthma.

On the third night there I had returned to my own bed to sleep and had a grand mal seizure. It was generally controlled by a drug called Dilantin, but I think the heroin cut right through. I woke up on the floor with a number of people I did not recognize staring down at me. I had wet my pants. I did not know where I was. It was several hours before my memory came back. The girl I had been with held me and stayed with me until I got reoriented. I had never had a seizure in front of strangers before but everyone handled it well.

I think the film was called *Snowballing* or something like that. I made a couple of hundred dollars a day and it was nice to get out of the city. I never saw the finished product.

Here's how I ended up with epilepsy:

I was a tremendously emotional, spoiled, asthmatic child who loved horses. I was stick thin and pale, and the floor of my room was stained from the ever-present vaporizer. My parents bought me a horse when I was ten to encourage me to be active, and to shut me up.

We found a totally wild, part-Morgan pinto mare up north in a town near Oroville called Bangor. We managed to tame her to some extent but she was always pretty crazy. She was even going over fences after about a year. I had a British ex-cavalry riding instructor who wasn't there the day of the accident, but my father was and some visitors from LA. I was jumping a course of fences about four feet high and wearing a helmet that was not appropriate for jumping. The real "brain-bucket" style has a wide leather chin strap. This had elastic. My horse took a bad fence, caught the pole above her knees, crashed on the far side and did a somersault. I was under her at the time.

They say the saddle held her weight off me and that I was probably hit in the head by a stirrup iron. When they took me to the Children's Hospital I was walking and talking but remembering nothing. The doctors sent me home. My mother was there and being a nurse, saw that my pupils were radically different from one another, a sure sign of a serious head injury. She took me to another hospital where it was determined I had a fractured skull. I didn't remember anything for three or four days. I returned home after a week in the hospital and this part I remember like a photograph. I was walking to the refrigerator for orange juice when I felt a big pressure on my forehead, then I felt tremendously drunk. I woke up with my face under the water heater, staring at thick dust motes and the pilot light, my legs wet with piss, and my mother saying, "You've had a seizure, just relax."

My body ached for days, as if I'd been bucked off a horse.

5 Highway 1

I came down the stairs with my little dog to answer the door at six in the morning, wearing only a long black and orange bathrobe. I was excited about seeing the man who was waiting there because I didn't get to see him very often, and then only at his whim.

He had called at 5.30, drug-crazed, belligerent and exciting, demanding that I throw out whoever was in my bed, which I did. His name was Artie Mitchell and I had met him when I worked on my first porno film. He had continued to call after the work was through. Being addicted to bizarre sex, he was the only person I'd ever met who had no fear of the physical or chemical edge.

There was an air of chaos and sleazy glamor that permeated his life, now confirmed by the silver limo at the curb driven by his hunky blonde cousin who smiled as I was pulled without resisting into the back seat littered with children's toys. I'd heard his wife was fertile.

I complained to him that I hadn't locked my apartment door and he told me with drunken gallantry that he would replace whatever was stolen. There wasn't much there anyway.

He had an uncommon ability for calling when I was on my period, but it wasn't really that hard because I was bleeding more often than not. We did some cocaine and soon were humping like mink on the approach to the Golden Gate Bridge. Being concerned about the nice gray velour seats I told him I was bleeding heavily. He told me he didn't care. We had hot, wet, mad menstrual sex on the bridge at sunrise, filling the back seat with orgasms while my little dog slept peacefully on the floor.

We took a break on the road to Mount Tam, where he pulled out a wad of money and wiped the blood off me and himself. He threw the bloody money on the floor with the dog and lit a joint.

Heading north on Highway 1, we picked up a suntanned girl hitchhiker with tangled blonde hair like the morning after. She was happy to be picked up by a limousine but after we'd started up again she saw the puppy and the blood money and got nervous. He teased her for being squeamish, and asked me to recite some poems. After she heard them, she asked to get out. We pulled over and left her by the roadside. We accelerated our intake of drugs.

We drove another hour up the perfect California coastline, then turned off on a dirt road that led to a little trailer with a small group of people standing around and sitting in lawn chairs drinking beer. We got out of the car and he told me they were his relatives. There was a sweet comfortable woman in her fifties who he said was his aunt. I was in my bathrobe with no shoes on. She was nice to me anyway.

The men had just been abalone diving. They were telling extravagant stories with their hands. I was astounded that my friend would ask anyone to meet relatives in my condition, but they took it well. They joked that they thought someone had died when they saw the limo in the driveway.

We stayed too long and he renewed his drunkenness with beer and hot sun well into the afternoon. When we finally left, we stood up in the open sunroof and made bird noises, calling to the crows.

We resumed our passionate fucking as we returned to the city. The tinted windows amplified the darkness, smudging the edges of things. It was late when we arrived and he wanted to eat, so we went to Japantown where they didn't care that I had no shoes. I ate sushi for the first time, and being so high it seemed to slither down my throat.

A week later I got a card from him: the ace of spades folded in a dollar bill covered with dried blood. I framed it and hung it on the wall.

A CASTLE IN MILTON KEYNES

Sonia Florens

HE HAD PURSUED me relentlessly. I gave up and surrendered. Out of guilt, out of lust, and sheer lassitude.

I had betrayed him a few years before and I felt I had no other choice now but to insist he punish me as he saw fit. Repentance must come, I reckoned. To purge the evil of my cold heart. To wash the past away in one quick swoop.

"The first hint of your infidelity," he had explained to me, "was when you came to me smelling of cigarette smoke, of dead ash. You put your lips against mine and the damn tobacco was all over your breath. I was breathing in another man as I kissed you."

I lowered my eyes, fluttered my lashes.

He knew.

We parted ways.

There were other men. Minor, unfulfilling adventures. But none could erase his spell over me, the look of sheer danger in his eyes that kept me feeling ever wet on the inside.

I suppose that in the time we spent apart, he also came to know other women. The female form is his major weakness. But I can forgive that. Because all the while he kept shadowing me, writing, threatening, phoning. Loving me in that crazy way of his.

So, one morning in March, a few days before that damn Trade

Fair I just couldn't face attending once again – year after year of
pointless negotiations with Eastern European entrepreneurs who
just had no clue and had no subtlety whatsoever trying to get their
paws into my underwear and thought taking meaningless options
and inviting me for drinks at their hotel bar was the epitome of
sophistication and seduction – I walked over to his building early.
Half an hour or so before I knew he usually arrived. Stood by the
door and waited. Wondering all the time whether I was doing the
right thing.

He arrived. Didn't even blink when he saw me there (later,
though, he confessed that his heart just dropped twenty fathoms
when he realized it actually was me).

"I'm back," I said.

"You haven't changed," he said quietly.

"Yes, I'm the same," I answered.

His hand stayed in his coat pocket, fingering his keys.

"Back for good?" he asked.

"Forever and again," I promised.

"Good."

We went inside and he fucked me unceremoniously on his
office floor. We didn't talk. Just did it. It was good. As it always
had been. Time and time again, he got hard. And harder.
Ploughed me. The phone rang on and off throughout and we
blissfully ignored it. Every time, he plunged deeper into me,
extending my legs over his shoulders to ensure further penetration and I knew only too well that with each successive thrust he
was trying to hurt me, but I bit my tongue and let him take his
revenge. I was the guilty party. The betrayer. His fingers in my
rear stretched me, tore me, impaled me, but it was all right. It was
fine. He had to get over his anger. And the pain he was causing
also excited me like I never thought it could.

Later, I told him:

"I have done you wrong, I know."

"Yes, oh yes, you have, my love," he said, pensively. "Two
bloody years of longing, of constant ache inside, of sleepless
nights that went on and on with no end in sight. Christ, you did
make me suffer. But, you see, there was also hope against hope.
That one day I would get you back . . . That somehow the
impossible would happen. I never really gave up totally, even
when things were at their darkest."

"I'm sorry. I'm sorry. Truly, I am," I babbled.

"You hurt me so," he said, now with tears in his eyes.

"So punish me," I told him.

"No. Now is surely the time to bury the past, forget the whole damn mess, start things anew."

"I insist, you must punish me," I heard myself saying. "I deserve it all. Do to me what you will, my dark-haired lover. Anything."

He looked at me strangely. Smiled gently.

"Are you sure?" he questioned me.

"Absolutely," I answered.

"Fine," he said.

So my lover took me to the castle in Milton Keynes. One hour or so up the M1, travelling with no rush in the middle lane. I couldn't see anything. He had carefully placed a black silk scarf around my head, fastened it tight, covering my eyes. He said it was Milton Keynes. I believed him. We'd spent the right amount of time driving up the motorway. But I suppose it could as well have been Blackheath, Finchley, Hendon or even Scarborough for all I knew or cared. It didn't matter. Castles all smell the same, I reckon.

As I stepped out of the car, I sort of thought this was all very silly, was I really ready to star in the Milton Keynes version of "The Story of O"? Why had he allowed me to retain my underwear? In the book, that hadn't been the case. Was the feel of the leather car seat caressing my bare buttocks an experience I had ever fantasized about? Would it initially have been cold against my flesh, then gradually warmer; would the fabric stick to my skin, would I sweat, squirm? And now I wouldn't even experience that.

I wore my grey tailored power suit, the one with the stripes, made of quality wool. A white opaque cotton blouse completed the demure display, black sheer nylon stockings, my best, and matching bra, knickers and suspender belt set, black also. But right then those particular details were my secret. My lover didn't know; he hadn't watched me dress. I knew how he loved it when I wore stockings the old-fashioned way. Made my long legs look even longer, he would always say.

So the castle door opened. Well-oiled, it didn't even creak in the slightest. Just a normal English spring day, a light breeze fluttering around my ankles and neck, not even a gothic day.

He guided me in, one hand on my waist, our steps echoing around the hall.

Then, I stopped feeling his faint touch against me. Was he still there, harbouring in the silence, or had he departed the premises altogether? This was already the first sign of emotional torture: I wasn't to know whether he was ever present while all sort of terrible things would be done to me, to my body. Something inside me wanted him around, for my mental comfort, I suppose, but on the other hand, what would he think of me, react to the spectacle of my body being defiled, would I ever be the same for him ever again, thereafter?

Not knowing, that was the worst sort of punishment.

A voice – not his – said:

"Stay where you are and spread your legs apart."

I obeyed.

Still the faint trace of an echo, bouncing between stone floor and high ceiling.

Standing in silence, trying to guess how many pairs of eyes might be watching me, male and/or female.

Something, a cane? a whip handle? brushed against my left cheek, tracing the faint line of my scar. Cold. I shivered briefly.

Then a hand took hold of my jacket, pulled on the sleeves and manoeuvred my arms out of it. Another brief moment of silence and inaction, while I tried to listen to all the minute sounds, murmurs of nearby voices, distant chirping of birds outside, almost inaudible scraping of material against material, against flesh? Was there another woman nearby, also wearing stockings?

"Stand still," the male voice reiterated. I was sure I hadn't moved.

I opened my lips, ready to say so.

"Jeezus . . . " A sharp, sudden smack on my rear, before any sound could even escape.

"You may not speak," the unknown man said, severely.

It didn't hurt, but I had been completely taken by surprise.

"Spread your legs wider apart," another deep male voice instructed, almost angrily.

The material of the grey skirt was tight against my thighs. It was awkward to assume the desired position without moving the rest of my body, which I knew they would disapprove of.

I felt the thin object against my knees, then it moved up my right leg, grazing the fabric of the stocking, slowly, lazily upwards, reaching mid-thigh when it moved into the empty triangle below my crotch. I shivered again, expecting its next movement. It made contact with my knickers, right where my sex was. I imagined a surge of electricity bolting through my body and felt the first wetness inside my cunt, and my sex lips engorging and opening slightly, pressed as they were against the silk of my underwear.

"Good," one of the men said. "Stay like that."

Then, nothing happened for some time. I stood uncomfortably listening to muffled noises all around. There were some more people arriving, chairs being arranged, seemingly in a circle around me. I was about to become the main attraction. Right there, in the hall. Looked as if I didn't even get to graduate to a traditional gothic dungeon. Like in the books. Like in the movies. I must have smiled.

Another violent whack on my buttocks. This time it hurt.

"What's so funny, bitch?"

"Nothing," I summarily replied.

This time it was a whip and it struck suddenly twice, once on my shoulders and then immediately again on my breasts.

"This is your last reminder, woman. You may not talk."

I bit my lips as the pain and the adrenaline subsided quickly. Took a deep breath.

Some were talking in low voices, but it was too indistinct for me to really hear anything. But some of the voices were definitely female. And one was certainly my lover's.

Behind the dark piece of cloth that obscured my vision, I closed my eyes. Tried to picture him with another. Was she sitting on his lap? Where was his hand? Was she also blonde? Was his cock hard, was she holding it as she laughed at me, standing there helpless, ready and willing to be ravaged by their combined obscenities?

Warm breath against my cheek. An intriguing smell, sweetish, a complex fragrance half human, half artificial, a remote smell of lemongrass. Male, I knew, as he moved closer, examining me, brushing against my back. Hands touching my breasts through the blouse, feeling them, cupping them, weighing them. Then his hands moved to my chin, to my lips, a finger slipped inside my mouth, a nail grazing my tongue, withdrew, out again the humid finger passed over my cheeks.

I could hear the sound of the unknown man's breathing and the warmth radiating out from his body.

Goosebumps.

The hand retreated from my cheeks, neglecting my eyes and forehead. To be quickly replaced by the cold feel of metal against my throat. A blade.

I knew this was a test and was careful neither to move or utter a single sound.

The sharp metal edge drew a slow line down from my neck, over my white blouse between the valley of my breasts, then further along past my stomach, over my crotch and disappeared into the open triangle of my stretched grey skirt. It reached the lower edge of the garment and I felt the zip being pulled, either by the person wielding the knife or another protagonist. The skirt came loose and fell to the ground. The tip of the knife moved up and was inserted behind the taut elastic band of my black knickers and swiftly cut through the material like butter. The underpants were pulled from my body to facilitate the journey of the knife through them from front to back. The bisected knickers were then swiftly pulled away from the suspender belt, leaving me bottomless.

The cold air moved against my bare genitals and posterior.

A long, thin finger, certainly a woman's, journeyed through my pubic curls and brutally pushed past my lips and entered my vagina.

I swallowed hard and held my breath as the finger explored my innards, drawing moisture as my body reacted uncontrollably, lasciviously, to the intrusion by releasing its natural secretions. She moved her finger around inside, enjoying the warmth and the growing humidity, her nail brushing slowly against my clitoris. My whole body trembled and I knew my cheeks must have turned red for all to see.

"Thirsty?" the woman's kindly voice enquired.

I nodded, careful not to say anything.

"Good," she replied.

Almost simultaneously, a man's voice, hard and authoritative: "Hold your arms up," it ordered.

I stretched my arms toward the invisible ceiling, my face still hot and red because of my embarrassing posture, standing there as if crucified, my bare bottom thrust outwards at the unknown spectators, the woman's digit still burrowing inside my cunt, my juices accumulating inside, ready to pour out shamefully over my thighs once she pulled her finger out, no doubt.

Both my hands were seized and manacled to pulleys which had been lowered down from on high in the hall. At first, the traction on my wrists was slack, but someone quickly reduced the slack in the ropes and I was forcibly pulled up and my feet barely adhered to the ground in my high heels.

The mockery of being crucified.

The woman's finger retreated out, soaking with my juices. My lower lips remained wide open, dilated, sticky.

"Drink."

A plastic bottle was placed against my lips and up-ended. It was only lightly carbonated mineral water. Couldn't quite place the taste. Not Perrier; another brand.

Initially, it was welcome and refreshing, cooling down my dry mouth before gurgling down my throat. Then it was enough, but the bottle wasn't moved away and I had to swallow the liquid faster to avoid choking as the water swam rapidly through my lips and straight down my throat. As soon as the bottle was empty, it was replaced by another. And yet another. The third bottle was Badoit; I could recognize the chalky background of its taste. They allowed me a minute or so's break before emptying the fourth bottle inside me. I felt ill, now. My belly was bloated. I must have looked as if I was a few months pregnant, held there on display, the ropes imposing such an undignified stretched-out position, open, vulnerable.

What's all this water in aid of, I wondered, as the final drops from the fourth bottle travelled past my tongue in a direct trajectory to my stomach?

I expected another bottle to be placed against my lips, but this was it. No more.

The silence returned.

I was forced to move my body slightly as cramp was reaching my left foot, and the water inside me sloshed from side to side.

Christ! I realized what they were up to. And the moment I did, there was nothing I could do to stop it. Or slow it down.

With my legs wide apart and my cunt still splayed open, there was no holding back the urine and it roared out of me like a jet, splashing loudly all over the stone floor. My face must have been redder than beetroot at that moment, as I suffered this impossible humiliation. Would it ever end? My pee kept on coming and coming, its stream still gushing out like a geyser, splashing my thighs and my stockings, cascading over my shoes. On and on and on. Finally, my bladder exhausted itself and the stream came to a spluttering end.

I felt bad, used, dirty. What would they do next? I already imagined the most diabolical perversions. And something in me, deep inside, was already looking forward to it, while the more sensible – civilized? – part of me was damn angry, eager for revenge. I had never been able to control my anger well. It had always done me much disservice.

"Isn't she just beautiful?" I heard my lover say.

"Yes," replied another man. "Great arse. Just love that dark mole right on the bottom curve of those cheeks. I'd love to bite it off."

I shuddered.

Another: "That cunt seems nice and tight."

"But it's quite accommodating," my lover said. "She'll take a lot."

"And at the rear," a woman asked, "has she any experience?"

"Not with me," my lover said. "She never wanted to. But when she betrayed me with the other, I know they tried it."

"And that is why you want her punished, is it?" an older man's voice asked.

"Yes," my dark lover said. "And don't even tell me it's petty, I know that already."

"So be it," the older man said.

I heard steps, and a door close. They wanted me to believe my lover had left, but I knew he would stay and watch. I could still feel his silent presence and his eyes feasting on the indecent spectacle of my bare flesh. Brightly conscious of the pornography of the fact that my upper body was still fully clothed, while my lower half wantonly displayed itself, wet stockings stuck to my legs, the strong smell of urine and fear surrounding me, held apart like a sacrificial offering, like a piece of meat, devoid of all will . . .

"Ready her."

A regiment of hands trooped over my body. The soiled stockings were peeled off, and the high-heeled shoes. The ropes were lengthened somewhat so that shoeless, I was still forced to stand on the tip of my toes to support myself. Scissors cut through the garter belt and the blouse and the brassiere strap, and the remaining flaps of shredded material were pulled away from me.

I was totally nude.

They tightened the band across my eyes. There was no hint of light.

The whip came first.

I'd read the books, seen the films, I know. This I somehow expected. But the pain was still hard to bear and I knew that my rear by the end must be a garish spectacle of crisscrossed red Mondrian patterns. I counted the blows. Thirty in all. Then a few gentler ones against my breasts, making my tips now impossibly erect. I think I even managed to pee a bit more when the last few lashes of the whip caught the outer edge of my crotch.

"She can take the pain," someone said.

Then my ankles, still wide apart, were seized and fastened to the floor where they must have fitted metal loops.

Hands reached for my cunt and held my lips apart, while an acolyte began brushing me with some sort of sticky liquid over my whole genital area. And forcibly poured further quantities of the gooey stuff into me, using at least two or three fingers and stretching my opening even more. What was it?

They relaxed the ropes holding my arms and a gentle pressure on my shoulders indicated I should lay down. I did. Thoughtfully, a rug had been laid out on the stone floor and I spread out on it keeping my limbs apart. The contact of my raw behind against the rough surface was a trifle painful at first.

As soon as I was in position, they opened me up even wider, increasing the angle of revelation spreading from my crotch and my breasts, before tethering my ankles to the metal rings, as well as my hands high up behind me. The way I was now, all and sundry could look all the way into me, into the sheer pinkness he always enthused about. The bastard. This wasn't a joke any longer.

"Bring in the dog."

I struggled fiercely, but they had me tied down very efficiently and I couldn't move even the centre of my body. My paltry attempts only served to increase the painful scraping of my well-whipped buttocks against the rug's coarse material.

"No, not a dog," I screamed. "You can't, you just can't, it's not
. . . allowed, it's illegal. It's, no . . . Please," I begged, tears
welling up inside my eyes. Which they of course couldn't see, did
not wish to see.

Horrified at the prospect ahead – even in pornographic stories
this wasn't allowed, it overstepped the mark – I had forgotten the
earlier ban on my speaking.

"Quiet, bitch." The man who said this slapped my cheeks
several times until I felt blood inside my mouth.

The liquid they had inserted inside my cunt was burning me a
bit, felt dreadfully sticky.

I heard muffled steps, movement approaching my outstretched
body. Expecting the worse. I knew there was no way I could take
this. I'd be sick, surely. Jesus, Jesus, not a dog. It'd tear me apart,
injure me. They couldn't do this to me. Surely? How could my
lover allow this? Maybe he was no longer here.

I thought I heard a whirring sound somewhere in the dark
background. A camera. They were filming the whole thing. The
swine, the bloody fucking bastards.

"Woof, woof," a woman's voice, giggling almost uncontrollably. The others all around me all went "Woof, woof" in unison.
A choir of animals.

A wet, floppy flannel, like a tongue, began slobbering all over
my cunt.

Behind it, a real tongue. A woman's. You recognize those
things. Licking me.

The flexible appendage burying itself in my curls, tickling my
engorged outer lips. Her lips grazing the skin of my mound as she
delved deeper.

"Woof, woof," the choir continued. The woman's tongue was
licking me clean, with the application of a docile pet, a dog. Must
have been honey they had spread inside me. I heaved a huge sigh
of relief. Relaxed a touch, as the woman went about her cleaning
business. Blushed deeply when her tongue almost corkscrewed
through between my lips and began sucking out the goo from
inside. Unavoidable excitement steadily rising through me. The
woman imitating an animal was oh so thorough as she patiently
licked, sucked, nibbled at me to extract every ounce of goodness.
And every move of her cunning tongue sent fierce arrows coursing through me; I felt a deep flush spread from my cheeks down

to my neck, shoulders and breasts. I was a thousand times madly alive. Ignorant of my mounting fervour, she slaved away, unemotional, systematic, hungry for my taste. My limbs pulled frantically at the restraints; to no avail. My insides were turning to jelly. I even thought for one brief moment that my bowels would let go. The sensations inside me increased exponentially as the woman's tongue caressed my dilated cunt. My throat tightened. The pressure of her roving tongue switched up to my clitoris and I literally exploded. I came.

Loudly.

Screaming like an animal myself. Too far gone now to remember the previous instructions of silence.

I sighed, following the uncontrollable release.

I wasn't punished for my shameful outburst.

They had what they wanted: I had been brought to orgasm, not by an animal, but like an animal. Wanton. In full view of their obscene assembly. And not any old orgasm; the best I could remember in ages. Where had the woman learned her skills?

"Interesting," the voice of the older man was heard again.

The woman's mouth moved away from my genitals, dropping spittle over my cunt.

"Impressive," he said. "Would a real animal have given her so much pleasure? Could be an interesting experiment . . ."

"No, please. You can't be serious," I pleaded. "I draw the line somewhere, and bestiality is definitely out. Leave it to the pages of the under-the-counter-books. It's too damn scary. I'd do anything else. You can do anything to me, but not that."

"Anything?"

"Yes," I whispered.

So, anything it became.

I sucked men's cocks. Strange how every single one not only tastes but feels different. You know, the texture of the skin, the geography of foreskins, absent or stretched, the topography of bulging veins against the tongue. After an hour or so, my jaw ached and the bulging members all became a blur. For all I know, they could even have slipped the dog in between the parade of men and I might not have noticed. Smell of skin, talcum, cologne, sweat, urine, they all merged as I sucked away like an automaton. They all came in my mouth, different flavours ranging from acrid to sickening, sweetish to bitter. I've never liked the taste of men's come and every time forced myself to swallow it without allowing my tongue to linger on the taste, for fear of gagging. Some were thick, others were long. They filled my mouth and swelled unconscionably until there was nowhere for them to expand further and I had to control my breathing lest I choke. Hard as steel, soft as gristle, pliant, rough, bent, odorous, I can tell you stories of cocks, evoke their gaudy geography in all shades of disgust.

Finally, they tired of my mouth and I knew that none of the penises I had milked had been my lover's.

They sat me in a chair, legs apart as always and lathered my groin, before shaving my wonderful curls away, leaving me absolutely bare, my open gash like a red wound between my thighs. Every one present lined up to lick me clean, men and women, few of them were as good as the dog. I became very wet but didn't come. Had no energy left for it, I thought.

I was then unshackled and made to bend over, hands and knees to the rough floor, while alien objects were inserted inside me, forced through my openings, twisted relentlessly inside me until it became painful and I had to beg them to stop.

They took the cloth away from my eyes at long last, and I saw the hall in all its faded grey glory and my lover sitting in front of me in the same chair I had been summarily shaved on. I was instructed to keep my head high as he lowered his trousers and began slowly masturbating while every man present took his turn fucking me from behind under the attentive gaze of my lover. He never lowered his eyes once; neither did I as they all pounded into me, tearing at my increasingly bruised opening, alternatively releasing their hot spend inside my vagina or quickly disengaging themselves from me before spurting over my back, like in a bad porno movie.

I never saw what any of them looked like.

My lover controlled his jerking off to the rhythm of the men penetrating me, never allowing himself to orgasm. At last, they had all taken their turn, I was still on my knees, come streaking down the back of my thighs and drying all over my back and buttocks, my lover signalled someone standing behind me. This beautiful tall woman with flowing dark auburn hair walked across to him, pulled up the scarlet silk evening gown she was wearing, turned round so she was facing me and lowered herself onto his cock. I wanted to look away, but I knew they wouldn't let me and anyway I was fascinated. His thick cock parted her plump lips. I briefly noticed she sported a small golden ring in one of her labia, her pubic hair was dyed dark red and she sported a tattoo of a penis between her navel and cunt. He entered her and she took him into her up to the hilt, the spectacle of her cunt fading into his thick bush assaulting my senses as she began heaving herself up and down on him. I became transfixed by the spectacle of their lovemaking, hypnotized by the junction of their sexes and the white juice that appeared to emanate from her and accumulated in a thin layer at the base of his cock. As I watched the two of them, someone behind me brutally inserted a finger in my anus, then another, forcing the sphincter muscles apart.

"She's not quite ready," a man remarked.

I was pulled up from the floor and made to squat. In this position, my sex gaped wide open.

In front of me, my lover and the tall woman disengaged. His seed was spilling out of her cunt. She ordered him to clean her and he lowered himself to the ground and began licking his own come out of her body. As he obediently did this, she fixed me in the eyes and said:

"Empty yourself."

I didn't get it.

I looked puzzled.

One of the men who had fucked me earlier brought a chamber pot around and placed it under my squatting buttocks.

"There," she said. "You'll have to make some space in there, whore. Empty yourself."

I lowered myself onto the chamber pot, but the man next to me pulled me up and indicated I was not allowed to sit and had to do the deed while only supported by my heels. Again, he took my hands and bound them behind my back, which made equilibrium even more problematic.

"Hurry up, bitch. We haven't got all day," the woman shouted at me.

I was beyond humiliation. I tightened my stomach muscles, applied all the pressure I could muster on my bowels, pushed, held my breath, and managed to force some meagre faecal matter out of my arse. It dropped the requisite two feet into the bowl. I pushed again with all my might and two further mini-parcels of shit extruded themselves out. They pulled me away. For one moment,

I feared they might want me to eat it. I had said I would do anything. I was made to bend over with my bum high in the air and my lover, my gentle lover, my dark lover licked my cleft clean.

Gently he then applied some cold cream to my anal aperture and slipped a finger in to test the elasticity.

"This is going to hurt, my love," he whispered in my ear as he spread the cream around the rim of my arsehole and forced some inside.

I knew what was coming.

Again they covered my eyes and my hands were tied to the pulleys and raised upwards. Another man shackled my feet to another set of ropes and these were gradually pulled up so that I was now suspended in the air, a few feet from the ground, quite horizontal, my whole body outstretched to all poles. A nude spread-eagled magician's assistant, with both supports and all my varied private apertures fully visible to the congregated audience.

I heard furtive movements underneath me. Preparations for the next ordeal.

Both my wrists and ankles were beginning to hurt, bearing the weight of my whole body. Then, they allowed the ropes holding me up to slack and I was slowly lowered to the floor. Not quite all the way. Once I was a foot or so from the ground, my buttocks made contact with the rigidly erect penis of a man. My horizontal descent was halted and I felt a woman's fingers – I knew because of her long, sharp nails digging into my flesh – pull my cheeks apart and test the lowering resistance of my anal opening now smothered with lubricating cream. The cock digging against me was manoeuvred towards my hole, directed toward its entrance like an arrow and the ropes loosened again and I was instantly impaled on the expectant penis. It hurt like hell. Felt as if my whole body was being torn apart from its very centre, excruciating agony spreading out in concentric circles, radiating outward like the sheer fires of hell. I'm sure I screamed. I can't remember. And then the man began moving inside me, up and down and up and down again and again and every outward movement felt as if my very bowels were being pulled all the way out of my body with pincers. Inside my arse, I could feel his member growing, expanding with the relentless inevitability of an exploding galaxy, pounding against the inner walls, sliding remorselessly deeper towards my heart, abetted by the lubricating cream. I could feel the lips of my sex, just a few inches above the unholy junction of my arsehole and the cock, gape wide open with every successive thrust of the guy inside me. Then, another man positioned himself, straddled me, I could faintly detect the musky odour of his sweat, more hot, warm flesh pressed against my cunt opening and swiftly moved in, brushing the still tender lips apart, which stretched as they were could offer no resistance. I had two men inside me. They found their rhythm and through the pain, I listened to my lust rising. Further hands began manipulating my nipples, twisting, pinching, pulling at them. Fingers and unknown objects roamed my exposed body. My mouth was pulled open and another cock inserted. And then a second one.

Truly fucked.

All my cavities explored.

It was some crazy scenario: the woman who services four men simultaneously.

I gave up all resistance, allowing my muscles to go slack and welcomed the shuddering invasions, disconnected my brain from the rest of my body and welcomed the mighty sensations of pleasure course through my veins, travel at the speed of light over the whole surface of my bare skin. I closed my eyes. Incandescent blackness overcame me. I beckoned it. I was just a body. An instrument of pleasure. Desire made incarnate.

The men thrust.

The men pushed against my physical limits.

The men all dug their cocks deeper than anatomy allowed.

My juices flowed. Out of control, seeping from every extremity past the attacking poles of flesh.

My lover watched.

One man came. I balanced his ejaculation on my tongue and rubbed it against the soft surface of the other man's cock still pounding my cheeks.

The second man came, and his warm jet splashed against the walls of my vagina, drowned its flow over my swollen cervix and he withdrew instantly, sucking our now mixed fluids out of my cunt onto my stomach.

The third man came in my mouth but maintained his thick cock at full stretch, forcing its way almost down my throat, and the bitter goo slithered down into my digestive system.

The fourth man still kept on pounding into me. Savagely

drilling his impossibly long cock ever deeper into my rear. Jesus, it would never be the same again, would never close up, I thought, as my bowels felt all liquid, melting under his blows and I briefly imagined the purple mushroom-like tip of his penis swimming in the inner sea of my boiling shit.

Finally, he came. He roared loudly, exhaling his pleasure in a wholesome burst. The pulleys were brought into operation again and I was levered upwards off his rigid stem. It exited my gaping rear hole with an obscene plopping noise, dripping with an unholy compound of our mingled secretions.

All of a sudden, I was thirsty again.

They left me suspended for, I reckon, another ten minutes. Then the black silk scarf that obscured my vision was pulled away and my sight restored. The men were all dressed now and ritually left the room in a single file, leaving just my lover and the tall woman.

In silence, they cleaned me with a warm wet flannel.

Liberated me from the embrace of the ropes.

Then the woman left, after a gentle peck on my cheek.

"You were wonderful," my lover said.

Should I weep or should I cry?

"Am I forgiven?" I asked him.

"For now," he answered.

He had new clothes for me. I liked them, he had chosen well but then he's always been a man of good taste. Knows my fondness for waistcoats and white tops.

As we exited the castle in Milton Keynes and walked towards our red car, he looked at me with godamn so much affection in his eyes:

"So?" he enquired.

"Yes," I confirmed. "Even with the pain, I did enjoy it."

He smiled.

"What about you?" I asked my lover.

He said nothing and kept on smiling.

As we passed the Watford motorway services half an hour later, he said to me:

"This is only the beginning, my love. I know this dungeon in Epsom."

I looked ahead at the road. Night was beginning to fall. Soon, we would be back in London. My hand was shaking a bit. Fear? Expectation? And inside my body the tides of lust were already rising.

THE SEX LIVES OF CHAMELEONS

Cristiana Formetta

translated by Maxim Jakubowski

for Danila who has never seen the snow

Force of will is just a question of practice.

You need a bit of training, but you learn to struggle, and you can become whatever you want to be.

When I look at myself in the mirror, my image does not correspond with the image I have of myself. So, I change it. I adopt multiple personalities. They merge and alternate.

It's a dance with the cosmos which can last whole days and nights. Night is my baptism. I close my eyes and when I wake up I have a brand new skin.

1

"What's happening to you?"

Mauro's voice made me jump; it's so typical of him to always arrive on the scene silently. "Hurry up. We've lost too much time already," he continues. And throws a stack of photographs onto the table. I pick them up, look at one, then another, and then all of them.

"They look fine," I say. But the truth is I know all too well how bad they happen to be.

"Of course. To anyone who's not an expert, the photos will look good," Mauro continued. "But both you and I know this is not your real face," he concluded, pointing a finger towards one of the photographs as the light of the sun shining violently through the curtains obliged me to look away.

"At any rate, you're done with your anger for now, I trust? Where is all the wickedness? Not in this photograph, my dear. Nor here . . ."

"I have several other projects to finish before I can focus on the book . . ." That was how Maxim advised me that the publication of the book had slipped to November.

He reiterated that I had to be patient and enjoy the wait.

For him, it's easy. He talks about writing, he thinks like a writer. In his books, Maxim tells stories of things that appear to belong to a whole different world, a world so different from mine, a bigger and more dangerous world. Maybe that's what brings us together, so intimately.

Maxim says I have talent, as if talent was just the act of writing a simple story in a minor mode. My stories pleased him and now his American publisher will be publishing one of them.

My stories in America, it's hard to believe.

I just can't believe that Mauro has refused to give me the photos.

At home, I look at myself yet again in the mirror and concur that Mauro is right. This is not my true face, just a passable imitation. If my friend Danila was here, she would realise it too. Danila isn't easily fooled, she would soon notice that I have lost my metallic eyes.

Danila says I have metallic eyes, grey eyes that sometimes turn green, and sometimes dark blue. It's fairly uncommon, not that many others had noticed. He, however, quickly acknowledged the fact and transformed my eyes into heavy metal. He said I had the eyes of an owl, because I am always checking who is around me, memorizing their gestures, their voice, their expression, until

I think I know them intimately, even to the extent of unveiling their weak spots.

A particularity common to all predators, I think.

Photographs. I have a house full of them, pinned to the wall, stuck with adhesive tape to the mirrors. Everywhere it's my face, on my own or with friends. Here we are, Danila and me, at the Carnival a few years back. She is dressed as a witch, and I am wearing a clown's three-pointed hat. It must be quite late in the day, because in the photo Danila's eyes are red. Whereas my eyes seem fixed on a distant point, my lips frozen by what looks more like a grimace than a smile.

Who knows if owls, of all feathered creatures, conceal their wrinkles beneath their deep stare?

I can't stand in the same place for more than half an hour. It's always been this way, ever since I was a small child I've had this urge to burn off energy any way I could.

Is that what consumes me inside?

Year after year, my waist narrows, my cheekbones get sharper, the dark zones beneath my eyes go hyperactive, pale brown shade changing to pale violet. The brains sucks energy from the body, and slowly it will begin to disappear.

I'm becoming transparent, Maxim. Now you can look inside of me and use all the small details I have provided you with to bring your imagination to life. Even when I ask you for a way out, because I can't join you in London, or in New Orleans, this city you like so much. I keep on asking you because we are wasting so much time, and I don't know what to answer, I don't know what to say. This is also the truth, even if I talk to you of Toronto, although it is a lie, another dead end.

You dislike Canada, Maxim. It's too cold there.

I walk alone through the city for almost an hour. It's raining and my boots trace deep patterns in the mud. I quicken my pace, flinging my legs ahead as if I were participating in a military parade, if only to warm myself. It's strange, I've never felt cold before at this time of year. To tell the truth, I'm seldom cold and am always wearing the same sweatshirt under my leather jacket, even in the midst of winter. Yet, today I can't help shivering, and it's already March.

I reach the area of older buildings in the historic part of town and ring the bell several times. The door finally opens. Trevor looks at me without saying a word. I am soaked to the bone and just can't stop myself from trembling. Trevor does not invite me in, and neither does he order me to stay put. He just keeps on looking at me with a self-satisfied smirk on his face, his upper lip frozen in a sneer. I know that expression, that face well. It's my face superimposed over Trevor's features. The face of someone with definitive goals in life, and the sheer ambition to reach them.

"Come inside," he says. Trevor speaks good Italian, although he has a distinct foreign accent.

Trevor's apartment is always untidy. His television sets are stacked up in all four corners of the room like sacred stones in an Indian ritual. Rising above it all is a smell of paint and solvents, tobacco and perspiration, which doesn't seem to bother him. His attention is fully focused on my hands now beginning to unbutton my faded shirt. A piece of clothing that has seen better days, as has Trevor. He has talent, he could be a great painter, but he just isn't. The pictures he paints have no inner strength, no meaning. Trevor is no longer able to make art talk, ever since the day he recycled himself as an illustrator of children's books. This compromise has greatly helped his finances, but it destroyed him as an artist. He could have been a wonderful painter, and now he will never be one. Yet, Trevor keeps on dreaming, believing that a trip to Italy, an exhibition and a hovel rented out on the cheap will help revive his spirit. Trevor thinks I can be his muse, and this dream sustains him. Basically if you are thirty-eight years old in 2003 and the critics haven't had a kind word for you since 1996, you have a desperate need to dream. Trevor is finished, and he is not aware of it. Trevor is a dead man walking.

His shoulders surprise me. I would never have thought Trevor had such large shoulders. Now I understand why his jackets fit him so badly, either too large or sleeves too short. I haven't yet seen him naked, or tasted his mouth for the first time. He probably tastes of whisky which he drinks regularly, too often and too strong. Trevor takes me into his arms and pulls me towards him, allowing his hand to caress my breast, my hip, and he does all this so silently, not even allowing himself a sigh. He is cold, detached. He knows me well and and doesn't trust me. He is aware of the fact that I seldom do anything without a reason and is probably wondering why I am here ever since I arrived.

He pulls my shirt away, then my bra, caresses the curve of my back with his fingers, which makes me shiver. Never before have I been touched with such tenderness.

His eyes are wide open and gazing at me. They are pale green and it almost looks as if he is about to start crying.

Because it's now happening.

But Trevor hasn't the time to consider things long enough as my own hands are already exploring him, moving up and down his thighs until I reach his groin. I can't help myself from touching him, kissing him, losing myself inside his smell, letting my tongue draw a thousand arabesques across his body. I watch Trevor's eyes soften, the green become more intense, and I feel him swallow.

Everything is in the right place. Trevor's trousers are on the floor, my legs straddle his body. I feel him lifting me by the waist and furiously entering me. His hands grip mine and pin me back, allowing me no movement that could disrupt our precarious equilibrium. Trevor brushes some strands of hair away from my face. He wants to look at my face, and he will keep on doing so all the while as he moves inside me. Our bodies are perfectly embedded in each other. Trevor plunges deeper into me, and I do my best not to scream out aloud. But I must, as he watches me. Trevor wants it all, the white skin of my breasts reddening beneath his bites, the taut muscles of my stomach as he drills into me. Every spasm, every emotion betrays me. This is truly the only way to know another: carnally.

Trevor seeks total control. Good, because so do I.

I want to capture all of him, how he moves, how he walks, how many times he brushes his teeth before he goes to bed. I want to steal his most intimate thoughts. I want to experience his sadness and make it mine, binding myself to that ironic smile of disenchantment that crosses his lips.

I want his English accent.

I want to know the reasons for his divorce, the true reasons, not the ones he tells everyone else.

I want his ash-blond hair between my thighs.

I want to devour him. Digest him.

This desire is so strong, so obvious, that it can be read all over my face. Trevor is not surprised, because he has no reason to doubt me.

My face is his face, my will is his will.

I should maybe have warned him, prepared him for this. Too late, now. Too late to hold all this at bay. Trevor is so overwhelmed by the love I have in store for him that he attempts to struggle free; he is upset and ready to lie to save himself. But the equilibrium is now broken. My hands are free, finally able to touch Trevor's hair, while my tongue chases him, hunting him, hungry for his saliva. Our sweat mingles, cancelling out all forms of friction, we are so totally dishevelled, a total mess. To let oneself go in such a way is a benediction. Our hands wander all over, clumsily, awkwardly. To each of my caresses, Trevor answers with a moan. He's not quite ready for this, not yet, but he knows that my madness is rising. But I am in control of him. Of his breath. It's a death rattle. Long, unending.

Morning catches us in the throes of an embrace and confused.

Trevor moves his face closer to my breast, and his unshaven skin brushes against me. Under the bed covers I feel his legs solidly fastened to mine, a position made even more uncomfortable by the white streamlets of sperm still leaking from my cunt.

Have we slept like this all night?

Chaotically clutching one another, with our legs squeezed together higgledy-piggledy. I smile. Our bodies, in such ridiculous embrace, are an insult to the art of perspective.

"What are you thinking of?" Trevor asks, lighting a cigarette.

"I'm thinking of the book I want to write," I answer.

"Is it that important?"

"Yes."

"More important than me?"

I remain silent and kiss him. His mouth is both small and fleshy, like the mouth of a child. As a matter of fact, Trevor is no longer Trevor. He's just a fifteen-year-old who does not understand the meaning of words like failure and frustration. He's a shy high school boy with cauliflower ears who will never get used to wearing spectacles.

Trevor is no longer the man whose face is so close to mine. He is another who looks like me, but is so much weaker.

"I'd better go, now."

"Stay a little."

"I can't, Trevor. I have things to do."

I quickly slip on my sweatshirt and my jeans. I walk towards the window and note with satisfaction that it isn't raining any more. My hair is dank with sweat, and brushing my fingers through the strands fails to revive them.

I miss my things, my house. I want to listen to my phone messages and check on my electronic mail. But Trevor takes me into his arms, holds me against those broad shoulders that make me feel both small and gracious in comparison. I have taken a decision, now is the right time.

"I will not be going to Toronto with you," I say to him.

Trevor's embrace tightens, becomes more insistent.

"You know all too well that my son lives there. I can't abandon him. He's only two years old; he needs me. You just can't ask me to stay here forever . . ."

"Actually, I wasn't asking you to."

"What do you mean?"

"That you must return to Canada, Trevor. There's nothing here for you, neither fame nor fortune."

I move away. Trevor is attractive, but I no longer want him.

"So, what about this night? Why did you come here and stay the night?" he keeps on asking me.

"To fully understand that this was the right thing to do. To take control again, Trevor."

I concentrated and stared straight at the door.

"And if you do manage to leave, it will mean once and for all that I control you, Trevor," I said in one breath.

Trevor's only reaction was a feeble laugh, but there was no joy in it. Right now his shoulders were so much less imposing. Hate is such a sterile emotion, so empty and impractical. Unless you have the means to avenge yourself.

"So, you'll be going to New Orleans with Maxim, will you?"

"Yes."

Trevor's voice is already full of resignation.

"Will you sleep with him?"

I remain motionless and silent.

"Will you go to bed?"

★   ★   ★

On my way out, I am cheered by the fact that the rain hasn't broadened the streets, that the night wind hasn't blown the manhole covers away. The mild air brushes against me harmlessly. I've stopped shivering. I hurry along, and should be home in an hour or so. Of course, one day I should learn to drive, but for now I have no need for it. My independence will not be threatened by a spring storm. And of course there are so many advantages to travelling by foot, small occasions when you can meet people along the road. I see a photographer's sign and walk into the shop. I speak to the owner, a quiet, pleasant man in his fifties.

Photographs. I have a house full of them, but always want more. I just can't resist the temptation of a midday snap. Four flashes in quick succession, four small stamp format images and it's done. Now I wait for the film to dry, thinking back to what Danila said, all the chatter about my metallic eyes, owls, birds of prey, predators of all ilk.

Danila is mistaken when she confuses me with an owl. Owls are creatures of habit, and their rhythms always remain the same, sleeping by day, hunting at night, or so it goes. I'm a cold-blooded animal. I assess the dangers ahead, analyse them. I pretend to be dead, defenceless, and all the time I am observing. I evaluate the adversary, extrapolate his movements, determine what his weak points are. Then I devour him. Assimilate him.

I take over everything I can from him and can then imitate him. It's a natural talent of mine. Like being ambidextrous or owning iridescent eyes of an indeterminate colour, capable of changing according to the light or the darkness.

I take the photograph and look at myself.

My face is no longer my face. There is no longer any trace of youthful fury, or unrestrained and improductive ambition.

There is no longer any evidence of passion.

All excesses have been polished away.

My eyes are not the colour of grey metal. Now, they are gems, limpid green emeralds, sharp and defined.

I meet Maxim at the Hotel Diplomatic. I have brought with me a copy of the Chet Baker biography, the present I had bought for him. It will keep him company when he takes the plane that will return

*him to London. Maxim always talks of London. He's both in love
with and a prisoner of that city. In his books, he writes with infinite
subtlety and in excessive detail, chapter after chapter, of places,
because he has been everywhere, and knows that nothing compares to
home.*

*Maxim will travel again, I know. But he will always return home.
He does this time after time because his dance with the cosmos is
complete. Mine has barely begun.*

"You have nothing to lose," he says.

*It's true. I can pack my cases at any time, without leaving
anything behind, neither a true friend, nor an unforgettable lover.
My life is so pitiful, barely a speck in the sky. But today the sky is
greyer than usual. The sky is a dark cloak that hides important
things from view.*

2

The young woman's fingers were caressing his chest. The sort of
caress that awakens you.

"You're very pretty for your age," he said.

Her name was Lisa.

In the darkness of the room, Trevor admired her white skin
and the small, firm breasts peeping out of her lacy bra. Lisa
allowed herself to be examined, displaying no embarrassment.
She continued to brush his skin with a light touch. She seemed at
ease, much more so than Trevor. She now began licking his chest
and his stomach with the expertise of a professional. Trevor
closed his eyes. Lisa's face buried itself between his legs. The
heat from her tongue penetrated his veins, warming his body and
senses. Clinging to her, Trevor began moaning. He took hold of
her head, pulling her sharply against his stomach. Trevor was
excited, but also annoyed by the assurance Lisa displayed beneath the sheets.

Love. Sex. Lust.

What do you call a blow job on a first date?

"I'll call you a cab."

Trevor moved to the bathroom and began running the water.
Once it was hot enough, he stirred it firmly with his extended

fingers. Small bubbles of air remained stuck to the hair on his arms. Blame it on the chlorine, he thought.

"The taxi has arrived," Lisa shouted out from where she was standing at the door.

"Do you want me to see you off?"

"It ain't necessary. See you tomorrow."

Trevor has hung a copy of the poster from his exhibition on the bathroom wall. A successful show, although it might be his last. With these paintings he has finally confronted the heart of his carnal, lascivious work. A landscape of imaginary bodies, men and women obscenely linked by love and death. Arms and legs, loose and akimbo, initially together and then parcelled off like pieces of meat in a mad and murderous sequence. Not bad for someone who for years has only displayed children's book illustrations in public. With painting after painting, Trevor has given life to a snuff movie of his very own, a defiant answer to all those who had accused him of no longer being alternative and cool.

For the time being, Trevor is satisfied. Tomorrow, he will have to decide what to do about his art and his own life. Right now, all he wants is a coffee and a cold shower. But first he must shave.

That beard was definitely not a good idea, even from a purely aesthetic point of view.

Trevor takes the razor and applies an abundant quantity of foam to his cheeks. With the beard on, he betrays his forty-odd years and how much he has grown older.

Trevor hates growing older. Or wiser.

In Toronto, Trevor works for a large publishing house, and enjoys a good professional reputation. But he no longer wishes to be involved in children's books. Designing book covers is just a job, and it doesn't make him feel much like an artist. On the contrary, the money has changed him; it makes him feel cheap, like a character in a B movie. He no longer wears the rough woollen sweaters he once liked so much, but a suit and tie, as they fit so much better into his new life. A life full of weaknesses and compromises. And it is all those compromises that he has made that now make him feel so old inside. The young kid who pretended to be Superman, has turned into an adult like Clark Kent, a tired Clark Kent. But if Clark Kent is none other than Superman with a pair of glasses, Trevor simply remains Trevor.

With or without a beard. Which is why, today, with the help of a
cheap disposable plastic razor bought at the nearest supermarket,
he begins to shave with fast, steady strokes. And his old face
emerges through the thick white foam, just like in that short film
he recalls watching some years back*. In which a man kept on
shaving his face and never stopping until his whole features
became a mask of blood. Trevor slides the blade up and down,
covering every square inch of his skin, but by the time he has
finished, there is not even a scratch. Just his smooth, shiny face.
How banal!

*I want Los Angeles. A city I have only ever seen in films, a city
whose images are bathed in an incredible array of colours. Art and
spectacle. Beaches and indolence. Rum and cocaine.*

   *I don't know that face of America, but I know I could learn to love
it. Maxim, on the other hand, only loves New Orleans.*

   We both agree to meet in New York.

   *America is a territory that both dilates and shrinks at the same
time. Maybe New York is the capital of the republic of dreams.
Maybe New York is the territory and I am the map. Maxim is late.
Maybe even he has managed to lose himself within the stretch marks
of this country.*

   *I wait, and the waiting appeases me. I kill the time, creating
Chinese shadows with the light shining through the windows of the
forty fourth floor of the skyscraper. Like in a novel where all the
characters are beautiful, rich, famous and fly away into the sky.*

   Without ever falling back down to earth.

3

No one apologised to Mauro for the fire. Not his roommate who
accidentally started it, or the British authorities who because of a
series of legal mix-ups failed to initiate a proper enquiry.

   As a matter of fact, Mauro reflected, the British bureaucracy
turned out in the end to be no more efficient than the Italian one.
A lot of talk, but there always appeared to be some obstacle when
it came to move into action.

* "The Big Shave" by Martin Scorsese

He'd gone to London in the hope of making it as a photo-grapher and setting up his own studio, one with black and white walls, a magical space he could share with just his cat. But that pipe dream was now defunct.

"It's because of the fire. It's all because of that damn fire," he kept on repeating between his clenched teeth.

At first, in London, Mauro had acted like a proper tourist: he'd visited the City, taken walks by the Thames and gotten drunk in almost every Covent Garden bar, effortlessly wasting his money. He had then decided to pack his bags and move outside the centre of town.

The area was nowhere as fascinating and cosmopolitan as the West End, but because of this, accommodation there was so much cheaper. In Holloway, Mauro rented a small flat which he shared with two other dreamers, a young man and young woman he had met during the course of his wanderings through Chelsea and Kensington. Solveig was Danish and very pretty. She was de-termined to become a model because someone in Denmark had once told her she was tall and thin enough to make a success of it. Solveig was 1 m 83, almost ten centimetres taller than Mauro and barely filled a B cup. Her skin was the colour of milk and the hair falling down across her shoulders was a stream of golden curls. A splendid porno amazon queen. Sadly, outside of the bedroom, Solveig didn't make the grade. It was painful to watch the gawkiness of her movements. The lessons in deportment had come to nothing. Solveig was a perfect sack of potatoes made in Denmark.

Paul, on the other hand, was Irish and played guitar. Half Irish, to be precise. His father was in fact Scottish, but despite this cocktail of genes his hair was not red but jet black.

Paul was convinced he would become a rock star and, although his celebrity was all in his mind, he already adopted some of the lifestyle of the rich and famous, moving steadily from pot to cocaine and, whenever funds from his mother back home per-mitted, the cheapest heroin available.

Mauro loved his new companions in crime. They somehow made him feel wiser, a most rewarding feeling to have.

However, since he'd been in London he'd only sold a few photographs to a minor magazine, but he was still convinced he was on the right road. It was just a question of time; sooner or later everything would click. But now, following the fire, time had slowed down. And things seemed to be coming to an end.

It had been an accident. The police had no doubt about it. That evening, Mauro had been at a nearby pub with Solveig and another friend of hers, a rather attractive brunette, also a would be model. Paul had remained at the flat. He often stayed back, thinking of having a bath and relaxing a bit. He'd filled the tub with lukewarm water and fragrant foam, and as a final touch he'd lit some candles.

"They give the atmosphere such a pleasant feeling," he'd told the police.

Damn candles, the fool had dozens of them, in all shapes and colours, not only around the bathroom but all across the flat. In the kitchen, his bedroom, even in the airing cupboard.

Why in hell should he have a peppermint green candle in the narrow airing cupboard? In the days following the fire, Mauro asked himself that over and over again, but could never fathom an answer. What then happened was so obvious. What occurred was bound to happen. Paul had lit the candles on the window sill. Maybe in his imagination they were like a lighthouse, a bright light that would lead his friends home. What a wonderful idea!

"The damn prick didn't even think of pulling the curtains back," Mauro cried out, talking aloud. And the old woman sitting next to him opened her eyes in response. Several of the passengers on the coach turned round to look at him, but Mauro didn't take notice. He was still thinking of that evening. Of the polyester curtains catching fire. Of the smoke spreading across the rooms. He was thinking of the flames slowly moving like fiery snakes towards the dark room. Of the explosion that destroyed everything: furniture, clothes, all his photographic equipment.

In his mind, he could picture Paul naked and dripping with water, running out to the street below. The crowd surrounding him screaming in terror.

"It's your stop," the old woman said.

Mauro stared at her, still dazed.

"Via Alessandrini," the elderly woman repeated, with a strong Bologna regional accent.

The coach braked suddenly. A fat, sweating man was holding on for dear life to the metal bar above his head. Mauro picked up his backpack and made his way towards the exit.

*   *   *

"You're scared of living. You can't write if you're scared of living."
There is kindness in his smile, but I recognise a hint of reproach in his
voice. I try to change the conversation.

"I don't like this restaurant. It's like a huge barn full of strangers.
I'm disorientated."

This time Maxim openly laughs. I call for the waiter and order a
steak, all the time keeping my thoughts to myself. There are so many
people scattered across the room but I don't know any of them.
Maxim has been here before . . . He points out a well-known actor to
me, a regular here who appears to have the bad habit of eating with
his elbows on the table.

"We're not so different, you know, you and me," he says.
The waiter arrives with the steak.
"You're right, Maxim. You're quite right."
I place my elbows on the table and begin to eat.

4

Trevor was woken up by the noise of a bus braking suddenly on
the street outside. He tried to go back to sleep but couldn't. His
eyes focused on the Florentine-styled wallpaper covering the
apartment's walls. He found the design distasteful. It made
him want to wake up somewhere else, or at any rate far from here.

He made an effort and got up. There was no way he could sleep
again, he had too many things to do, too many appointments he
could not afford to miss out on. He took a striped cotton shirt and
a pair of jeans from the cupboard. No jacket.

Trevor was already inside the taxi when he realised he had
forgotten something. He asked the cab driver to wait and ran up
the stairs. He took the packet he had left on the armchair and
returned to the car. He looked at his watch. It was a quarter to
nine and he was already late. Patience: she would wait for him.

The taxi dropped Trevor off on Via Alessandrini, just by the art
gallery. Lisa came towards him and invited him in. There was no
one else around, not one customer. He always felt strangely
uncomfortable with her around.

"Something wrong?" Trevor asked, feeling sweaty under his
collar.

"Yes, the air conditioning is not working."

"So I see."

Ignoring the Canadian's discomfort, Lisa led him down the art gallery's main aisle. Where Trevor's paintings had originally been, there were now just empty spaces on the walls.

"It went rather well," Lisa said. "The public was curious about your work. The brutally tortured bodies of beautiful women . . . I'm still unsure myself whether you love women or hate them." As if she was demanding an answer, Lisa's hand took hold of Trevor's and guided it towards her breast.

"Don't be silly. Federico could arrive at any moment."

"Would that worry you?" She smiled and led him into a side room. "Federico wouldn't find us here," she assured him.

Trevor tried to remember where the light switch was and recalled when he had been here before. He did know this room, had been here on the opening evening of the exhibition when one of his paintings had been hanging on the wall there. He'd sold that particular one for a sizeable amount, and there now was just an empty space on the wall. An emptiness that gave Trevor confidence, almost urging him to act on what was happening. He moved closer to Lisa. Today she wore a flower print dress and high heels, highlighting the lean curves of her youthful body. Trevor ran his hand across the thin material of the dress and felt the gentle rustle of the undergarment she must be wearing. She moved back slightly, rolled her stockings down to her ankles and expertly slipped them off. She held her legs wide apart and offered herself to Trevor's gaze.

"Do you want me?" she asked.

Yes, he wanted her. He wanted to tear her clothes away and explore every inch of her body. He wanted to touch that soft skin toned from all the hours spent swimming. He wanted to move his lips hard against hers and listen to her voice speaking to him from within, hoarse, dirty. He wanted it all and he wanted it now.

It appeared as if Lisa could read his thoughts as she lowered herself down and unfastened his trousers. Trevor pulled her dress off, took hold of her waist and pulled her towards him, not that Lisa was unaware of his desires. He kissed her. And took her, like that, still standing, her back pushed hard against the naked wall. Trevor ached to bite her lips, her neck, her breasts, but she stopped him just in time.

"Not that way. It would leave marks.'

So Trevor increased the rhythm of his thrusting. System-atically ploughing into her until Lisa began to pant harder and harder, and her voice turned into a silent scream.

Some time later, Lisa's clothes crumpled like tissue on the floor. She picked them up and dressed again. She adjusted her hair and her make-up until she was satisfied with her restored appearance.

"How are you?"

Trevor looked at her in amazement. There was no longer a single trace in her of the unstoppable, violent lust that had earlier transformed her childlike face.

"I'm fine," he answered.

"Very good. I think I heard Federico's voice. He must be outside."

"Better join him, then."

Lisa walked out of the room into the gallery and threw herself into Federico's arms, passionately embracing him, with convin-cing enthusiasm. Trevor observed them from a distance. No, there was nothing to worry about. Federico only had eyes for Lisa, and was unaware of anything else. Trevor came forward.

"Hi, Federico."

"Hello, there. I was about to ask Lisa where she'd hidden you."

"Nowhere. I was just waiting for you."

Federico put his hand forward. His handshake was warm and honest, which made Trevor uneasy. He liked Federico; he was a good man. He'd built the art gallery from nothing into a genuine international attraction, and it hadn't gone to his head. He'd stayed the same, just a few more wrinkles, and a much younger fiancée.

"Trevor has a present for you," Lisa announced triumphantly. And quickly turned back towards the Canadian man. "Come on, don't be shy."

Trevor just then remembered the small parcel he was holding in his hands. He had wrapped it clumsily, and with some reluctance he handed it over to Federico.

"He did it for you. It was my idea," Lisa said. Excited by the young woman's revelation, Federico moved forward and took hold of the present, examined it closely. It was a small acrylic on paper sketch, drawn quickly but with much precision. Maybe a portrait of Lisa, or at any rate of a woman much like her. No, it was actually her in the picture, lying fully naked between two men, two faceless bodies mounting her, blending with her in a flurry of colours.

Federico looked at the picture and went pale. He turned to his friend.

"Is it a fantasy of yours?" he asked.

Trevor made a face, almost repressing a smile, not that he had any reason to be cheerful. He looked at Lisa and felt the sudden urge to slap her around, and was sorry he had not done so earlier.

"No, it's *her* fantasy," he said, and walked away.

I've been in London one week. Maxim has found me a place to stay and a job so that I can pay the rent.

I try and believe that London is just another stage on the road, another step in my waltz with the cosmos and not the ideal place to drop my anchor. Because there is something about this city that fascinates me, but at the same time also mines my spirit and slows my concentration.

Maybe London happens to be the capital of the Republic of Dreams. Here, every street is like a trick of the mind behind which hides a blind alley.

This city is a wonderful mess; first he leads me to seek the impossible and then it hurts me because I cannot grasp it.

I'm in London to learn the writer's trade. But for now, I work as a waitress.

I keep on telling myself I must be patient, that things will be better tomorrow, but once again it's all a terrible mess.

The worst thing of all is that I had never dreamed of becoming a writer, even when I was a child. Then, all I wanted to be was an astronaut.

4

A woman's body can be drawn or framed, but it always retains its own standards of individual beauty. The beauty Mauro sought to explore had first crossed his path just after his twelfth birthday when his mother had bought him his first camera, a Kodak Instamatic. The Kodak had quickly become his favourite toy, a toy which had gradually become a hobby and later a genuine vocation. He was self-taught, learning all he could through his own means, and was proud of the fact. He worked hard and was always on the move, as travel was at the root of his photographic education. He'd met Trevor in Toronto and managed to convince him to follow him back to Italy to set up a photographic and art studio where they could both confront the beauty of women against the beauty of Rome's ancient ruins.

But the project never saw the light of day.

Caught between the thousand or so problems of his divorce and a dangerous attraction to alcohol, the Canadian man had just proved unable to get his act together. Mauro had never forgiven him. He'd abandoned him there in Italy, surrounded by his paranoia, and had flown to London, a city he thought would be ideal to bring his own dreams to life

And then the whole world had collapsed around him, as fate had intervened, and he was now in a mess, with the devil on his tail and desperately in need of money.

Mauro had initially thought of packing up and leaving. It was a strong temptation to go home, see his parents again.

He instinctively knew this was a time for reflection. What he basically needed was some sort of order in his life, to sort things out. Maybe some place where he could eat whenever he wished, sleep eight hours a night without others making a fuss, without squatters in all corners.

He wanted to stay warm beneath the old flannel bed cover. He wanted to smell espresso coffee and see a breakfast table all made up and ready.

Mauro also desired many other things. Harmony. Equilibrium. And a form of serenity he had sought for a long time now and could somehow not seize. And assuredly not here in the bleakness of Holloway. Nor between these four old walls.

Returning home was an alluring thought, but going back as a loser was another kettle of fish altogether. For Mauro it would mean once again having to face the stern gaze of his father, the envious disapproval, the criticism.

He knew that his old man expected this. He knew the bastard would laugh out aloud about his travails and dreams.

*   *   *

Mauro's father was a simple man. He wasn't an artist, had never worked in Switzerland, nor was he a sculptor.

Mauro had once invented those lies in order to be noticed, to carve himself an aura of some sort. But Mauro's father understood nothing about art.

He was a butcher. He spent his whole days between dead cows and pigs, and was satisfied with his lot, because it was real work, honest and reliable. A job his son had total contempt for.

Many years before, the old man had once brought Mauro to the back of the shop in a vain attempt to teach him about his trade. Under Mauro's firm gaze, he had begun skilfully cleaning up a lamb for the slaughter, even though the animal was struggling wildly.

"It's not enough to wear a set of overalls. You must also cover your face and your neck in case they bite you, which would be very painful," he explained.

Mauro nodded and pretended to understand. But he just couldn't fathom the reason for such dedication, and watched the whole scene with disgust, until the time came for him to try.

"Be brave, there's nothing to afraid about. Hunger is frightening. But once you've learned a trade you'll never be hungry again."

His father was right. Maybe he should have listened to him better. And now, he had drifted off that straight and narrow road and was sorry for himself like a sobbing woman. And without even being aware of it, he was fleeing from one part of the world to another. Always further from home. Always further from a way of life he could neither understand or love.

London, Manchester, Glasgow: Mauro was acquainted with a lot of people and was ready to take on any job to widen the distance between the life he had chosen and the one his father would have wanted for him. So when a little-known stroke magazine asked him to work in the hardcore field, Mauro set his pride aside and accepted.

Porno shoot.

Group sex full of thrusting and violence.

Porno shoot.

Four whores being mounted by a black stud.

"It's not a problem," Mauro had said.

The next day as he reported for the job, his liver hurt.

The premises had been furnished in superficial luxury. The furniture and varied knick knacks were in ersatz hi-tech style long overtaken by the whims of fashion.

Such unnecessary details, he thought as they all knew the only place they would be focusing on would be the bed. The bed was to be the main protagonist in this comedy, not all the shoddy details.

Mauro had slowly set out all his equipment, although he was aware that the others were impatient to get on with things. It was almost as if all they wanted was to have it all done with quickly so they could all go home.

Mauro no longer had a place of his own and was in no hurry. The four heavily made-up young women were already sprawled across the bed. Mauro ordered them to undress and spread their legs across the bed cover for some test shots. In reality he had no genuine need for these, but it was the first time he had been involved in a job like this and he needed more time to get the hang of things.

To find the right light? No. Maybe to get used to their shaven and open cunts, and be able to take these damn photos without being physically affected himself.

Mauro was nervous. Both nervous and also excited by what he could see. His erection was pressing against the tight zip of his leather trousers, as he suggested the black man strip, hoping that the sight of a naked man would temper his spirits.

Off came the shirt and tie, and then trousers and underpants. Yes, he could keep his gold chains on. A black naked stallion, with gold chains, quite a sight! Above all, his cock was huge. And the black guy's penis was thick and hard, as if an instant confirmation of the urban legend about black men's sexual superiority. This, together with the minimalist environment of the set and the pale skin of his future preys on the bed, brought the whole scene to life, in Mauro's mind.

And the fucking was like a cocktail of movement and choreography. So much more different and arousing than the spineless groping and vulgarity he had first seen in the second-rate Italian porn films of his youth, featuring Moana, Luana and company.

The black man had no need to pretend; he knew he was the one in charge. And the way he held open the women's gaping cunts just as he was about to impale them with his monstrous cock was all the evidence needed. He didn't penetrate them, he broke them open, and as ever with a wide smile and gleaming white teeth.

Mauro's hands were sweaty. Hypnotized by the spectacle he had stopped taking photographs and, right now, just watched the action, and the black guy's radiant smile, the game of submission and power that was unfolding in front of his eyes. And the black man looked back at him. With a sneer across his face, he muttered something to Mauro, it sounded like, "Just do your damn job, the Italian . . .", and his smile broke out again. His perfectly aligned teeth lit up his dark face. Mauro on the other hand was growing even paler. He thought he was a professional and now he was just some poor guy from the provinces doing a shitty job to earn enough to buy himself a flight back to Italy.

Return to Italy. Why not?

Mauro still had some contacts there. Friendships which could still prove useful.

Trevor's exhibition could well be the right occasion. The Canadian was a generous man; he would surely lend him some money, and could maybe offer him some sort of decent job like preparing the catalogue for his next show.

Mauro felt it would be worth trying. It was just that he wasn't quite ready to confront his father in sack cloth and ashes and having to apologize.

In London, I have no regular boyfriend.

From time to time I go with a younger man, probably the poorest of all those I serve at the restaurant. It's not a complicated relationship, free of future commitments which might tie me down. I don't even know what he does for a living, it's of no matter to me. All I do is watch his taut muscles, his sculpted arms when he undresses. Naked, he is splendid. Next to him I know I look so plain.

5

Trevor had agreed to meet Mauro in a small café not far from the art gallery. The decor was all green marble, from ceiling to floor, absorbing the heat of the sun outside and muffling the sound of steps.

"New shoes?" Mauro asked.

"How did you guess?"

The two sat down at a table facing the street. The sound of the traffic outside reached them, noisy but also familiar.

"You look good," Trevor said.

"So so. I could be worse. To be honest, I've lost everything, my house, my clothes, all my prints and the photographic equipment which had cost me a small fortune. But I'm not about to call it a day."

"That's a healthy attitude."

Mauro tried to smile, but he had to force himself. Trevor's reassuring words didn't help him feel any better. Starting all over again was too painful a thought, and he just couldn't do so on his own.

"I need your help, Trevor. I'm not asking for money, just help."

"Is that why you asked to see me?"

"Yes," Mauro confessed.

Trevor remained silent, sipping his coffee and listening to the sound of the cars hooting away outside as they stewed in a traffic jam.

"I'm not sure I can be of assistance," Trevor finally said. "The exhibition has just come to an end and in a few days I am leaving for Canada."

"Exactly. That's what I wanted to talk about," Mauro interrupted him. There was a hopeful ray of light inside his eyes.

"Let me go with you," he continued. "In Canada we could do great things together."

"Are you serious about this?"

"Definitely," Mauro continued. "You and I together, like in the old days."

Trevor closed his eyes, as if reflecting about what his friend had just said. But when he opened his eyes again, his gaze was hard, almost full of bitterness, and Mauro had to hold his breath. Before he even realized what was happening, the other's fist flew into his face, throwing him to the ground.

A young woman at a nearby table screamed. Quickly various other customers came to Mauro's rescue, helping him back onto his feet. He indicated to the others not to worry, that what had happened was unimportant, just as Trevor walked out of the bar.

He now stood alone just outside the door, waiting for Mauro to join him. He had a black eye but it wasn't too painful.

"*What the fuck was that all about?*" he screamed. "They say I should call the police."

But Trevor had no wish to talk. He knew it was better to surrender to all this noise outside. Noise is an abstract concept, it has a thousand faces but weighs nothing. Words were like stones and Mauro kept on questioning him. What a hypocrite.

"I know you fucked my wife," Trevor said. And the quietness of his voice could not conceal his anger. Some words are heavier than others.

A second punch caught Mauro on the nose.

I don't like love stories. And I don't like poetry. Poets are stupid creatures who insist in ordering life into rhymes and embellishing it. But life is nowhere as beautiful as they want to make you think it is.

Life is like prose: it does not bother itself with nobility. It feeds on your fragility, it takes all your mistakes into account and throws them back in your face when you least expect it.

My own life is no exception. It's both foul and wild, as my comfort grows and feeds me, until I am full. Life has the face of a cannibal.

6

Trevor pulled a cigarette out of the packet.

This is the last one and then I'm giving up, he thought to himself. And then changed his mind. He had never been particularly concerned about his health, so why do so now? He knew the risks as his mother had died of cancer. But he was not afraid of death. It was like an old friend, and when the time came he would be ready to face it. The thought of dying did not disturb him. The thought of arriving at whatever gates with his clothes and hair reeking of tobacco smoke had a definite sense of irony.

But his soul already reeked of memories and things past, to the point of pain.

*   *   *

It was almost summer but Trevor missed the snow. White snow surrounding houses and filling the roads. Snow covering Kate's face and concealing her features.

Kate, his wife. A woman who had once betrayed him and that he could not yet find in himself to forgive.

Trevor felt angry that he had not seen any snow for over a year now. Which was also the last occasion he had seen Kate and the child.

He really had to stop thinking about her, and all the days they had once spent together. As he still did every damn hour of the day!

Trevor had met Kate in a small art gallery. She was there to acquire a painting and Trevor could not help himself observing her, wondering why she had chosen that particular image. Even more so here, in an area the tourist guides to Toronto seldom listed. But she didn't look like a tourist, more like a regular from Trevor's circle of friends. Trevor's acquaintances were mostly painters too, the sort of artists who had to take on two and sometimes three jobs just to afford the canvas and brushes.

Kate, on the other hand, did not appear to have any financial problems. In fact, she had acquired a painting. One of his. But why that one? It was a picture of two lovers in embrace, a strong, sensual image.

Sexual.

She didn't seem to be that sort of woman. There was a severe, almost aristocratic demeanour about her, and an arrogant and determined look in her eyes which fascinated Trevor.

It was as if Kate could read his mind.

"I like it because I enjoy love stories," she said. "And all love stories have a strong erotic charge."

"And this one does?" Trevor teased her.

Kate blushed imperceptibly.

"I just love this," she explained. And there was a smoothness in her voice, enough to have Trevor fantasising about the two of them in a bed, naked and clutching each other, like the lovers in the painting.

Trevor craved to hear those words of hers again, but in private, whispered to him as he caressed her breasts and stomach.

Kate had somehow recognised his lust.

She accepted Trevor's invitation and followed him to his flat.

She slowly took her clothes off and went to lie on the bed. He watched her. He touched her with his fingers, finding exquisite pleasure in this initial contact. He delicately slid his hand between her thighs. She was wet, but it was a few more minutes before Trevor was free to slip his fingers inside her, extracting a soft moan out of her.

"*I love it. I love it. Do it. Do it.*"

Trevor moved on top of her. He pulled her up by the waist and entered her, taking no precautions. This was no longer the 80s, when nights had been wild and daring, but Trevor was still usually careful. With Kate he had no compunction mounting her raw.

He wanted to feel her. He wanted to fill her to the brim, and own her body and soul.

Kate was never more beautiful, so much his, than in that moment. She had now forsaken her pride and had given herself to him fully.

Trevor knew he now owned Kate and he finally complied with her wish. "*Faster and harder,*" she begged him.

Trevor fulfilled her request with animal rage. He took her face between his hands and kissed her. Swallowing her cries, as if he were afraid to let them escape through the apartment's windows.

"I did not want it to happen . . . Not this way," Kate said, rising from the bed. But Trevor thought differently. This was surely the way it should happen, both matter of fact and lustfully.

"Don't go. Stay."

Trevor's request surprised Kate.

But that's how love ambushes you. It creeps up to your shoulders, and stabs you in the back, leaving you wounded and bleeding on the ground.

To have punched that bastard Mauro in the face wasn't enough to heal the wound. It was no more than the foolish reaction of a child who's had his toy stolen by another. But that toy had been *his* and Trevor could not accept having lost it. Even though he had been the one to push Kate into the arms of his friend, he was now the one seeking a divorce.

What did he expect? That he should always be ready to forgive her fragility, her angers and her silences without reacting? Without a word of protest?

Trevor had just signed the documents, and he was convinced he was doing the right thing.

He wanted to bid goodbye to this spiritless life, and its troubles that sapped his strength over and over. He wanted to break up this failing marriage into a thousand pieces. But the thought right now of that small white band on Kate's finger where the wedding band had been had a strange effect on him. No way did it provide him with that sense of power or freedom it should have done.

All Trevor now felt was so much more empty than before and the knowledge of this scared him to death.

I'm walking down Charing Cross Road. It's already getting dark when a drunkard stops me. He takes hold of my arm and asks me for small change. His nails are filthy and there is alcohol on his breath. I pull away from him and mutter a few words in Italian, pretending not to understand his language. As I walk away, the drunkard shouts after me. Something about my being a "stuck up Italian cunt who should go back to her own country". I'm not sure whether this is a threat or just a suggestion.

7

Ever since I was small, I have believed my father was a hero. Like in a Marvel comic. For me he was the brave protagonist of a thousand adventures. He was my father, the invulnerable.

I admired him for his strength of will, for his habit of undervaluing danger which I thought was an extraordinary gift, almost as good as walking on water. My father was never scared, even when we experienced an earthquake. It was the earthquake we went through in the 1980s which shook all Italy and when whole buildings collapsed. I remember that day well and am unlikely to ever forget it. I was just a small girl, staying in her little room. when the first major tremor happened. The light went out and the glass in the windows shattered as if hit by a missile. I slumped to the ground, closed my eyes and began to pray.

That was the moment my father walked in. He took me in his

arms, and carried me down five flights of stairs, dodging the fallen masonry and broken glass.

I still had my eyes closed. I only opened them again once we were all gathered together in the street outside. With eyes now open wide and full of tears we saw how badly the whole area had been struck. Whole families just standing there and discovering the rubble of a palazzo which had just lost its whole front.

The walls of my house had cracked open like chalk and we all shed tears. All of us with the exception of my father who was attempting to maintain the morale of the people by saying, "Nothing to worry about, a bit of plaster and it'll look even better than before."

It feels incredible, but he was right, as we found out in time.

My father was a courageous man. He did not tolerate obstacles or limits to one's achievements, particularly so when it came to his own family.

He'd already suffered one heart attack, but still, every morning, I'd see him sitting at the table having his coffee, with a lit cigarette hanging from his lips, even though the doctors had expressly forbidden him to smoke. At first, I'd pretended to ignore him, but one day I'd finally lost my patience and asked him why he was being so obstinate. He replied that it was all because of the heart attack.

So he then explained to me why it was the heart attack's fault. It had taken him to the very gates of death, but not far enough to reach his destination. That knowledge that he had escaped death's clutches had made him stronger, and now he believed he was immortal, like God.

I'm sure that if God's heart had been as damaged as my father's he would have resisted the temptation to smoke a cigarette every ten minutes or so. But Dad was too enamoured with his dreams of power to think of that, and the second heart attack took him by surprise. One sad December day, his heart stopped and he died. Just like that. He died and was buried like any old wretch.

I inherited very little from my father, heredity wise. Just moral standards I could pass on to posterity.

All I borrowed from him was a taste for smoking. I light a cigarette and I feel invincible, as if I were smoking a piece of God himself, having compressed and rolled the tobacco inside the thin paper, and indulging without a filter. It's a feeling of omnipotence which gets even stronger, depending on the circumstances; for example, every time I find myself at Marconi airport, returning from a long trip.

I set my feet down on the ground and I feel like a goddess. Strong and powerful. Full of courage and good sentiments, because yet again the plane hasn't crashed and I am still alive. So I light myself a cigarette and it's the best one of the day.

"You're not allowed to smoke here," a hostess shouts at me. She gestures at me with her arm. "You must go over to the bar."

"Thanks a lot," I respond. And turn back towards Mauro who's come to pick me up from the airport. "What a cow . . ."

Mauro half smiles as we make our way to the bar. He'd likely smile more but his face is still bruised and painful.

"So, are you going to tell me what happened? Who did this to you?" I ask him.

"Trevor . . ." he whispers.

"Trevor?"

"Yes, him." Mauro shrugs his shoulders and looks sad. "I was sure he hadn't found out."

"Oh, come on . . ."

"I'm serious. I didn't want to hurt him."

"You should have thought of that before. Why in hell did you go to bed with his wife?"

"His ex-wife," Mauro corrected me.

"Ex-wife," I repeated after him, incredulous. "Correct. So that was OK with your conscience."

Mauro was silent for a few seconds.

"It never occurred to me."

"What do you mean?" I asked him.

"Trevor. I was always trying to understand his side of the argument, but he's the one who gave up on Kate. He didn't make the slightest effort to hold on to his marriage. He was too busy acting the part of the doomed artist . . ."

"*Shut the fuck up,*" I said angrily. "He has more talent than the two of us put together. It's just that Trevor hasn't broken through yet. Just a question of luck." My words caused Mauro to fall silent. He looked at me with his wide, nutmeg-coloured eyes, took my hand firmly into his to calm me down.

"Fine, you know better. Trevor is a genius and I'm a piece of shit. But for now let's make peace and have some coffee."

We sat down at the airport bar and ordered a couple of coffees and a plate of snacks. I was starving and ate almost all of them, but it wasn't enough. With hungry eyes I began staring at the warm pastries behind the counter. Mauro couldn't help smiling at me.

"You haven't changed at least," he said. "You still have the appetite of a wolf."

"You're wrong. I have changed," I replied.

"Is that why you've returned to Bologna?"

"I was missing spaghetti and tomato sauce."

"Be serious."

"I am. You try eating fish and chips seven days a week and tell me if I'm wrong. It's better here. Even the airport coffee is delicious." All the while sipping a tar-coloured espresso and pretending to be ecstatic.

"You can tell me," Mauro insisted. "Did you come back for Trevor? I know he rang you . . ."

"We just exchanged gossip. Nothing more."

Mauro's gaze was fixed on me. I knew he was studying me.

"In England, things were not as I expected," I confessed to him. "I managed to publish a couple of short stories in a anthology, then nothing more." As I was talking, I spilt some coffee on my sleeve. Impassive, I wiped the stain dry with a tissue.

"I've been offered a job as an editor in Turin. Correcting and improving manuscripts. It's well paid and I've said yes," I said resolutely.

But Mauro did not approve of my decision.

"It sounds dubious to me. You went to England to write a book and now you're content to read other people's books. It's a pity. After everything you've achieved . . ."

"Actually, I haven't done that much," I replied.

"Does that apply to Trevor too?"

Mauro was beginning to get on my nerves. This was becoming more of an interrogation than a conversation.

"Why bring Trevor into it? He's a closed chapter," I said.

"I don't believe you. You go all pale every time I mention his name."

Sunk. Mauro has caught me out and now my appetite has gone. I can barely breathe in and that's a damn effort.

"Did he tell you that he's returning to Canada?"

Go fuck yourself, Mauro. Just shut up.

I've tried everything not to have to think about of him and have no intention of doing so now. All I want to look at is the fluorescent light hanging from the ceiling and burning my eyes. I want to stop the tears from running on my face. I want a cigarette but no one here is smoking and I'm losing my mind.

Trevor. Every time Mauro says his name, an invisible hand takes a grip of my shoulder and drags me down a well of memories.

"*I want to get out of this bloody place.*"

I'm losing my balance. I'm screaming out in pain.

Trevor's name steals my lucidity and my concentration.

I'm hurting like a dog. And, like a dog, I still feed on the scraps of that night.

"*What are you thinking of?*" *Trevor asks, lighting a cigarette.*

"*I'm thinking of the book I wish to write,*" *I tell him.*

"*Is it that important?*"

"*It is.*"

"*More important than me?*"

His question hung in the air and stayed there. Like a hook which I could hang myself on if only my hands could reach it. But I didn't. I knew that hook could not support my weight and I would fall heavily to the ground.

Trevor was asking me how important he was to me. He asked with his eyes lowered and this angered me. I hated it when he did that. I hated Trevor and I hated his eyes when they negligently shifted downwards and avoided me. It made me feel like taking a hold of his face and yelling at him to stop. But on this occasion I controlled myself, but it was to be the last time. It's his fault, it's all his fault.

I know that expression, that face. It's my face superimposed over Trevor's face. The face of someone with a definite goal and enough ambition to achieve it. But ambition on its own is not enough. Trevor's eyes betray his insecurity. It will not help him to keep his eyes lowered and hidden behind his eyelids. I know those eyes, because I know Trevor and the doubts that assail him. He is like me. I know that for him too every day starts the same way. I imagine him looking at himself in the mirror and wondering, looking for something inside, a reason to forge ahead with the day or not. I see him, as he blames himself for being so stubborn, reaching wildly for something he should have taken hold of firmly when he was twenty years old, and that now appears like a mirage in the distance.

Because I see Trevor every time he surrenders.

I see him and I see my own face, like a reflection in the mirror. Everything he feels, I feel too.

I recognize myself in his weakness, in the daily temptation to give up, to fuck once and for all with art and this journey that exhausts me. Like him I am scared, and just want to be normal again, and at peace with myself. To return to the days when everything was so much more spontaneous, and there were no goal posts to reach, and to manage to say "I love you" and to be able to live with that.

Yes, Trevor. I must confess I want to say I love you.

Such a simple thing, isn't it?

To say I love you, and that I love you so much that I will not be able to write another word for the rest of my life, because this love is so strong and so intense that it drains all my energy.

Yes, Trevor. This love makes me weak. And it makes you weak. Maybe you didn't know, but that's the way things are.

If I now say I love you, I won't save your life. All I will provide you with is a pretext to accept it, to become content with what you have, even though that's still not enough to be happy. For folks like us, happiness is inappropriate. For folks like us, happiness is a state of unthinkable boredom. Surely we are not ready to set our pride aside and give up the fight. We lack the courage to accept our fate and to love each other for what we truly are.

We're two losers, Trevor. Two beautiful losers who were lucky enough to meet each other and recognize ourselves, as if our reflections were seeking one another. But you are you and I am me, and we will know how to benefit from the occasion.

It's better to pretend not to notice, to cover our faces with masks, to start wearing another character.

It's easier to smash the mirror.

8

My eyes are red and clouded with tears. I can barely see, but on the other hand all my other senses feel stronger, more acute, and sharpen my perception of reality.

The memory of that night now feels less painful, now that the din of the airport has brought me back to the present.

The nauseating smell of this place, a blend of sweat and disinfectant, invades my nostrils and almost makes me sick. I try to get a hold of myself and wipe my face with my sleeve. Now it's no longer stained by the coffee but also my make-up.

"I didn't go to bed with Maxim," I tell Mauro. "I lied to Trevor."

"I'd assumed that."

"I wanted to," I continued. "I wanted to move away from myself in order to be free and live my dream life. But life is not as beautiful as I thought it was."

Mauro and I walk towards the exit. I finally manage to light a cigarette and the first mouthful of smoke is wonderful. Even Mauro gives in and indulges in a Marlboro.

"You still love him," he tells me. "That's why you've come back. To stop him catching that plane that will take him home."

I listen to Mauro's words in silence. He looks as if he's waiting for me to say something. An apology, maybe a clever fairy tale I could just there and then pull out of my head, just like a magician pulls the traditional rabbit out of his hat. But this time, there's no way out, I've exhausted my stock of lies and self justification. There are no more white rabbits or thunderous applause ahead of me, just weariness.

Here we are, I thought. My dance with the cosmos ends here. I've reached the finishing line, cut the ribbon, but I've only won the consolation prize: a job as an editor and a failed photographer who thinks he can act as my confessor. Was it worth sacrificing everything, even Trevor, for such a meagre bounty?

"And what if he doesn't want to stay?" I ask Mauro, my voice a thin fillet of sound. "As a matter of fact there's little to keep him here, not even me."

Mauro shrugs.

"Trevor is alone, as you are. And when you're on your own, one place is as good as another."

"How would you know that?" I tease him. But his response is quite serious.

"There is no place where happiness is automatically guaranteed." He looked around, watched all the people wandering around between the announcements of arrivals and departures. "Some of them still believe, but soon enough they will realize they've made a mistake," he said.

I nodded. All this fascinating crowd of nomads, all anxious to explore other worlds, just like a swarm of flies.

Mauro had won. I no longer wished to escape.

"Shall I take you straight home or to Trevor's?" he asked.

"I don't know yet. Give me just a minute."

I walked away from him and went back inside. The airport crowds made me dizzy as I watched the people rushing from one end to the other. Some were worried they were running late, others furious because their flight had been cancelled. Another was complaining because his luggage had been lost and it reminded me of Trevor's first day here in Bologna when he had created such an uproar over his suitcase going missing. I recalled his reddening face, the nasal voice hurling insults at the airline clerk, and how much Mauro had been laughing as he explained to me that this unlikeable quarrelsome person was a friend of his.

And this is how love catches you by surprise. With a rude gesture. It runs into you, without even asking whether it's right to cross your path. With no reason. Without even thinking of what it will do to you.

MEMORIES THAT LINGER ON

Carlos Benito Camacho

Translated by the author

Although I was born and grew up in the city, I spent fragments of my life in the country. Once, when I was a very young boy, my mother became ill and could not look after the six of us kids. While my brothers and sisters were taken care of by relatives who lived in the city, I was sent to the country to stay at an uncle's.

Uncle Miguel lived on a small farm, which was about 75 miles from the city. He was a tenant farmer who worked a 50-acre rectangular piece of fertile land. Like my mother he was born and grew up in the country and was a devoted Catholic who attended church every Sunday. He was married to Aunt Jane, a woman who was half his age. Since they were a childless couple, it was deemed convenient that I stayed there for a whole year. I did not like the idea of having to spend such a long time away from my brothers and sisters, in some remote place where I had never been before. But they said I had to go when my uncle's old pick-up truck stopped out in front.

My arrival in that exotic place was an unnerving experience. I was scared to death by those scrawny, rural dogs, which welcomed the urban alien with growls and barks. The first days were awful. I was homesick all the time. Hidden in some nook of that house, I would cry silently in sobs. My uncle's solemn and distant presence was no solace to me, but Aunt Jane was a warm lady who cheered me up, talking to me as she smiled, giving me cosy hugs which fed my childish heart with sprinklings of mirth.

As my uncle was away all day long, working in the field, I spent most of the time with my dearest Aunt Jane. She worked hard, too, doing the household chores, but she always found time to fit me in, taking me for a walk to the river or giving me a ride on one of the horses. She got up at dawn everyday, milked the cows, made the fire with wood in the out-kitchen, and then she made breakfast. When Uncle Miguel left for work, she would go over to wake me up. Although I was already wide awake, because of the cocks' crows and her hustling around the house, I always shammed sleep and let her walk over and sit on the edge of my bed; and the magic moment came when she kissed my forehead as she gently rumpled my hair for a while, whispering nice things in my ear. And I woke up, letting myself be caught in her intense blue-eyed look which warmly seeped into my soul on those beautiful country mornings when the golden beams of sunlight slantingly streamed in through the window panes. Then I smiled at her, smelling the smoked hair which flowed down over my face. Being touched by that motherly woman's warmth made me feel safe at home.

Of course she knew I was pretending, but, since she was very fond of me, too, she acted as if she did not know about it. Affection was something my stern mother could not express. So it became a petty yet important game I loved to play. But the time came when I had to leave. I did not want to go back, but they said I had to, otherwise I would lose my first year at school. Besides, my mother had recovered by then.

My mother was a pious woman who hammered into us Biblical stories and prayers.

To go to church was compulsory, as we had to live by her strict moral codes. Even though there were times when she was in a good mood, she would get so worked up when she found one of us at fault, venting her wrath on all of us. She would also quarrel with my father when he came back late. Perhaps it was that strained atmosphere which had made of me a withdrawn, shy boy who did not speak enough to assert himself and who had trouble relating to his classmates.

But I was sensitive and had an intense inner world. I had

learned to love the open, green spaces where life sprouted lavishly and quietly everywhere. That is why every year, when the school began, I escaped the cold, strident urban world and ran to shelter under my aunt's affectionate care for more than two months. I did not feel lonely by her side, since she was the only one who really understood me. My mother never objected to my going away every year, but she would always say to my uncle, "make him pray," before we left.

Although Aunt Jane was born in Argentina, her parents were from Durham, a small city in northern England. My aunt's father was an experienced foreman who came to work for the railways, which were run by the British at that time. They arrived in Argentina in the late twenties, spending five months in Buenos Aires and two years in Rosario. Then her father was transferred to Cordoba where they lived five years, moving again at the end of that period to finally settle in the Northwest. It was here where my aunt was born. Athough Mr Cavendish had bought a farm by then, he still worked for the railways, but as the manager for the local station this time.

Thinking that it would be a matter of months before the strife came to end, Mr Cavendish left South America to serve England at the outbreak of World War II. But once he had left they never heard of him again. Deprived of her husband, my aunt's mother became feeble at the end of the war and eventually fell victim to a chronic disease. When she died, away from her mother country, her eldest son, George, took charge of the farm.

Five years later, under Peron's regime and in a country which held meager prospects, George and his younger brother decided to go to England. The three of them agreed to sell the farm, house, and furniture, sharing the money among themselves in equal lots. But my aunt, who was twenty now, decided to stay in Argentina. After her brothers' departure she found herself alone and married a man who was forty-two.

My uncle was a tall, slender man with handsome features, but, like my mother, he seemed to be unable to express much affection. He was a God-fearing believer who, like most of the Argentinians, was narrow-minded and followed the fetishistic ritual of lighting candles to a motley collection of plaster saints, virgins, and faded, black and white pictures of Evita. He was a man who slid along his cultural groove.

In sharp contrast with him, my aunt never went to church, nor did she talk about religion. Although she had attended only primary school, she was a broad-minded woman to whom one could talk about any subject. She could speak, read, and write both Spanish and English.

But it was the latter which she had more knowledge of, since her mother had taught her to read and write it properly. She kept an old trunk full of books which her parents had brought from England. She read them every evening in the amber light of an oil lamp.

As summer went by, I came back to the country bigger and taller as I developed into my teens. Although I had lost interest in fishing at the river and roaming about in the forest looking for nests or shooting birds with my slingshot, it was the need to be myself by my aunt's side, in that quiet spot, which brought me back. I was now at secondary school and had begun studying English. So, spending time with my aunt was a big help. She was the best teacher I had ever had. She was so poised and collected when she taught me. I would always sit close to her to listen to the English words which she carefully pronounced for me as she read one of her books. It was very nice to feel her warm breath when she spoke looking into my eyes. She made me feel as if I still were her little child.

But I was a teenager now. I was more than sixteen and had already started to strongly feel the sex drive inside. Once when I was seventeen, I was staying at my uncle's for a weekend. On Saturday, he had left early to the city to attend the Lady of Mercy celebrations and was expected back in the evening. I had checked if the hired man had harrowed the patch of land in which corn was going to be sown and then helped my aunt do her daily chores when we were having lunch in the shade on the verandah.

It was hot and quiet; there was no noise, except for the steady chirp of cicadas and the occasional whinnies of a horse in the pen. From where I was sitting at the table I could see the heat waves rise from the ploughshares lying in the parching midday sun, at the side of the thatch-roofed shed.

We had not said anything yet. We just ate, looking into each other's eyes from time to time, communicating in a language known only to us, as a warm breeze played gently with her loose, red hair. Something subtle and tender lay in those eyes which made me feel at ease and complete.

"Have you asked her out yet?" she said.

"Yes, I did, but she turned me down. I'd thought of taking her to the student day party, but at first the words wouldn't come out, and when I finally had the courage to ask her to come to the party with me, she said that she was going out with somebody else. I felt like a clumsy idiot," I said.

"Don't you ever feel like that. Wherever and whoever you are with you will always be a gorgeous boy and a wonderful human being," she said, as she put her hand on mine to reassure me.

"How do you like the meal?" she asked.

"You always cook wonderfully, Jane," I said.

"How about going to the river for a swim? It's quite hot today. It would be nice to splash about for a while in the cool water. They say after the last rain the river rose, leaving some deep pools where you can swim," she said.

"It sounds like a good idea," I said.

Walking a path that ran along the middle of the farm, we set off for the river at around three. Reaching the property limit, we crossed a barbed wire fence and began threading our way through the lush vegetation. Here and there flocks of birds, perched in trees, would suddenly soar up with a whirr, startled at the sight of two human beings.

A sense of anxious expectation, which I could not account for, quivered inside me as she held my hand leading the way. The warbling of birds and the constant chirping of cicadas reverberated in my ears, as the fresh scent of bracken and aromatic herbs filled my nose and lungs. I heard the sound of running water as the path began winding through willow trees. The sun-flecked ground became sandy; then the trail tilted, ending up at the river shore.

We took off our shoes and padded along, feeling the wet sand under our feet by the clear water that rippled over stones. We stopped at a place shaded by willow trees standing above on the river bank. Taking our hats off, we sat down for a while and then my aunt said, "You go in first."

"No, let's go in together," I said.

My aunt got her pants off, but left her flowered blouse on. Down below she was wearing black, cotton shorts which fit her tightly. I had always thought that her skin was beautiful, and when I saw her white plump legs, a nice tickling feeling shuddered throughout my body.

When I was a little boy my aunt not only saw me in underwear, but also saw me naked when she washed me in the bath, scrubbing me with a sponge, and when she so daintily rubbed me dry with a towel afterwards; and although it had been a long time ago since I began having my bath myself, I had grown used to her seeing me in underwear. So I took off my shirt and pants and walked with her into the cool water, which flowed slowly at this point where the stone-strewn, sandy riverbed was deep and almost level.

We swam for a while, playing and splashing water at each other as we laughed. But amid the frolic, Jane suddenly choked with water and started to cough as she hung onto a boulder standing out in the pool. Worried, I came up close to help her. "I'm all right," she said, with bleary eyes, gasping for breath as she leaned backward against the boulder.

I was standing in front of her in waist-deep water when the current gently pushed me up against her. I instantly felt her warm legs touch mine. I looked intently at her, and for a moment I thought that the freckles on her red face might just as well be bits of grated chocolate on strawberry cream. A shiver stirred my groin as I looked into her eyes, raking her dripping hair off her forehead. Then I realized what I felt for her that day was something I had not felt before. It was something magic which had grown out of our special relationship.

I was on the verge of kissing her mouth, but I hugged her tightly instead, feeling her bulging bosom against my chest. Then she put her hands on my face and said, "I think we should go back," and waded out of the water. When I came out to get dressed, she was looking at me as she stood on the shore.

Her stare slowly crept down my body and stopped at the middle, where my hot stiffness was straining against my white cotton briefs. But I did not feel embarrassed. It felt all right being watched by her.

Although I still felt that special son's love for her, sexual desire for my aunt had awoken inside me. And I am quite sure that she felt something new and different, too, aside from the sweet, motherly love which she always felt for me, by the way she watched me as I came out of the water that day. But she was my aunt, so I wrote it off.

Next Monday when I went back to school, I felt unusually at

ease in the crowd of students, as I noticed that the girl that I used to like did not appeal to me as much as she had done the week before. I studied hard and sailed through all the last term school subjects. When school finally finished, I was elated about the prospect of studying at the state university next year, just as my aunt had told me to do, and about the fact that I was going to see her again, taking another break from the hectic city life.

I had planned to be there sometime in the first week of January, after. I had spent Christmas day and New Year Eve with my parents and siblings. But about three weeks before the year ended, we got a letter from a relative in Buenos Aires, informing us that my grandmother, who was eighty-eight, was in hospital and that she was expected to die at any moment. As my mother was not feeling well, it was agreed that Uncle Miguel would travel to the capital city and stay there as long as necessary. But before he left he asked me to help Aunt Jane look after the farm.

Despite the sad event, I was happy to leave earlier than I had expected. So I packed up right away, throwing a couple of books and a few magazines for us to read in the evening and also enough batteries for the radio and the torches. My uncle could never get the inefficient state-owned company to supply the farm with electricity as it was in a far-flung corner of the province, about 35 miles off the main road, at the end of a winding, dirt lane. Except for the tractor and truck in the shed, the old, colonial style house, with its oil lamps at night, was really a 19th-century enclave.

When I arrived that evening, we stayed up, talking about my grandmother's serious condition, and catching up on our lives. The first week we toiled all day long and by the time we sat down for supper, we were exhausted. Then work slowed down and we could afford to read or play games after supper. On the 24th I did not even work in the field, and as we had already done the shopping, we had enough supply to tide us over a week. So after I had fed the horses and cows in the morning, I could wind down for the remainder of the day.

To ward off the heat of the day, I sat in the shade of the big tree at the side of the house. I had just started poring over Sigmund Freud's *Theory of Dreams* when Aunt Jane's image at the brook three months before suddenly arose in my mind. Then to no avail I tried to concentrate on my reading. So I closed my book and, looking up at some point in the tree, I sank into a libidinous reverie. The sudden clatter of a bucket on the well coping broke in on my train of thoughts. Aunt Jane was drawing water. I felt terribly attracted to her, as I watched her for a long moment. At forty-five, the household chores kept her buxom body in good shape. She turned her head, looked at me and smiled, squeezing down the pump lever.

Just before noon I had temporarily succeeded in putting out of my mind the erotic thoughts about Aunt Jane. I had never made love to a woman yet and my sex drive was extremely powerful, and that day the hidden hunger for her, which had unfurled from some nook in my self, came over in waves down my groin until I felt a tightened, hard package in my pants. At lunch we were discussing Nietzsche's *Beyond Good and Evil* when I found myself ogling at my aunt's clothed breasts. "Hey, wake up! I'm talking to you", she said. Then I steadily looked at her face. She blushed and looked away.

I wanted her so much, yet at the same time I wished this craving for her had not started. I had to do something to engage my attention. Accordingly, I saddled up the sorrel mare, took the shotgun, and rode ten miles to the moors where I had set three days earlier some bird traps to catch partridges. But when I got there I was not myself; mysterious, conflicting forces seemed to have overwhelmed me. I got off and tethered the mare to a shrub. It had rained the night before. The afternoon sun sucked out the moisture from the wet earth and I could feel the hot waves of vapour rising up as I walked. Two partridges had been caught, but I set them free and I did not feel like going shooting. I was thinking of her. I went back to the mare, slid the shotgun in the scabbard, got on and cantered back home.

The sun slipped down in the west behind the mountains, plunging the heavens in diaphanous saffron and aquamarine. Below, nature's colours had been subdued by murk, which crept out from the forest, the sugar cane field, and out of the well. Dim light streamed out from the out-kitchen. Aunt Jane was making dinner. I picked up the torch and went inside. I lit the lamp in the bathroom, took off my clothes, and got into the tub. The water was lukewarm and nice on my nakedness.

As I soaped my body, my mind slunk back to the thoughts about Aunt Jane. I imagined her naked coming out of the river with water dripping down her body. Rivulets ran across her belly down her pubic region, her wet skin shining in the sun. I reached out to pick up the sponge from the window sill and I noticed her underwear next to it. I slowly rubbed my body with her wet briefs. Then I got up and wrapped them around my glossy tight stick. I pretended I was deep inside her as I rubbed my self back and forth. Out of the corner of my eye, I saw Aunt Jane watching me through the door which I had left ajar. I turned to look but she was gone. Or perhaps I had just imagined that I saw her watching me. I became even stiffer at the thought that she was watching me. I derived great pleasure being watched by her. Then her voice calling me to dinner from somewhere in the house interrupted my train of thoughts.

At supper we were quiet; we did not even mention the fact that it was Christmas Eve. She seemed restless and avoided my eyes as though she felt embarrassed about something.

"You are not eating," I said, "Are you all right?"

"I'm fine," she said.

After dinner we unsuccessfully tried to entertain ourselves with a word game. Then she said she was tired and that she was going to sleep. I lingered there for a while thinking. Then I went to bed myself, too. But once in bed I was not able to sleep, so I sat up. I tried reading, but it did not work. I was extremely anxious. If I could find a way to tell her the only thing I had held back – how much I needed her.

It was about midnight when I got up for a glass of water. As I came out of my bedroom, I looked across the hall. To my surprise, a chink of light faintly spilt out from under the door. Driven by burning curiosity, I stealthily moved closer to take a peek. Fixing one eye on the keyhole, I could see only her head which rested on a pillow. In that dim light she seemed to have a troubled expression as she looked up at the ceiling.

I drank the water then I came out onto the verandah. The world outside was blinded by a moonless, pitch-black night. Only the stars above twinklingly witnessed my behaviour as I skulked around to the other side of the house. Slouching down, I approached her bedroom window. The warm summer breeze played with the white, lace curtains, which were partially open. The sheet on her bed was pulled back. I could make out her whole body. She squirmed restlessly on the bed for a while, then pulled up her white gown, exposing her plump legs. My heart pounded with excitement as I swallowed. Her hand slid down her body and underneath her black briefs as she slightly opened up her legs. Watching her fingers move under the cotton fabric, I began shaking. I came back into the hall and stopped in front of her bedroom door, hesitating. Not being able to bridle my over-flowing lust any longer, I went in.

She quickly pulled down her gown as I went in. But once I closed the door behind, she stared at me intently. "I love you, Jane, and I need you and want you," I finally said, as I stood there. I took off my underwear and I showed off an inflamed club which protruded long and red. She took off her gown and said; "Come to your mum." Then she got off her briefs, and I lay down at her side. My lips crushed against her big mouth in a long deep kiss. Then my tongue slid down her white skin and began suckling at her strawberry-like nipple. It felt so nice, so sweet as she took my hand and put it down in between her legs and guided me to rub her where she liked most. She moaned. Then I kissed her plump leg as I slid my warm tongue up her thigh. She opened wide her legs and I pushed my tongue deep into her wet slippery cave. I licked, and licked, and licked, as if I were her little cub. And I licked a hardened tiny toggle of flesh I had found in her blonde bush. And she shivered and shook with delight. Her happiness made me immensely hard. And my thick burning rod with a red, throbbing bulb on top wanted her so desperately as I snugly shoved into her cosy wet sheath. She sighed, moaned and screamed as I moved, and rocked, and rammed in hard back and forth, slowly, relentlessly, for a very long time, as if forever; and then we began losing ourselves to become one in the silence of the night.

THE CASTLE OF COMMUNION

Bernard Noël

Translated by Paul Buck and Glenda George

WHO HAD BROUGHT me back? I felt I had rolled against sky before
the final splash of light carried me through my door. Not so, I was
lying on my bed. The new moon was smiling down at me. As our
eyes met, she turned aside, picked up a goblet and held it out to
me – and night immediately flowed back, recaptured me.

I went. The wave was strong, its crest carried me. I went
towards an island that looked like a high table set on the sea. The
wave set me down at its foot. I saw the cliff, then again the sky,
unless it was the steep of the cliff like a vertical sky. I remember. I
stretched out my arms and opened my hands. Something very
soft trickled, drop by drop, along each finger. These are the
remains, I thought, but, "the remains of what?" was the question
that shook me awake.

"What's your name?" I asked.

"Emma," replied the young moon.

She turned away again, this time to look for something. I closed
my eyes. When I reopened them, Emma had quietly returned to
my side and her hand was already rubbing my shoulder with oil.
Then I realized I was still naked. She too.

"Why are you naked?"

"I don't know," she said.

I drew her to me. She let it happen naturally. But the tenderness that touched me was less rousing than my sudden desire to speak to her.

"The difficulty," I said. "The difficulty is in having no recollection, being ahead of one's memory. I don't know whether I'm coming or going . . ."

"Yes," she nodded. "It's the white shadow."

"Why did you say that?"

"I don't know."

She looked at me closely, but there was nothing but abandonment in her eyes. Her warmth was slowly transferred to me. But I still wanted to speak, maybe to make up for all the time I had remained speechless. Yet as my lips half-opened, she cut me short.

"Sometimes," she said, "I see words . . . then I say them."

I was content just to watch her, before persevering with:

"The difficulty is to have done something, say, opened a door, then to realize that there was no door, and yet you've opened it . . ."

"You're almost healed," she said. "I love you."

Slowly she withdrew from my arms, the tip of her breast brushing my shoulder as it passed. She straightened up on the bed, positioned herself facing me, sat back on her heels and looked at me. Suddenly she fell backwards, her two hands forming a crown for her sex, offering it to me. The pressure of her hands made her slit gape slightly.

"Come to me," she said.

I obeyed, feeling the words I had not said return to my throat.

But Emma's forthrightness was already rousing my flesh, the pleasure all at once driving me mad. She watched me with an upside-down smile that gave her appearance a dark side. I remember. I am on her and I lean forward. Slowly, I lean over further to butt against the tips of her breasts. She slides under me. Her skin, which is extremely smooth, feels good to my skin and hands. We are between two waters. I let her slide more quickly so as to seize her belly as it passes and bring my mouth to it. She swims desperately, but her every movement only increases the undulation of her sex against my lips. For a long time, a long time, this dance continues, before I climb back up along Emma and lie body to body. Then the night from within us escapes, scraping our teeth as it goes.

One morning, I feel renewed. I step outside and the whole village is at my door. They fête me, but silently – it is in the light on their faces. The leader steps forward to shake my hand. The others, nodding their heads, approve this gesture. I am no longer an outsider. Before long, each leaves for his work, but not before setting at my door an egg, a cheese or maybe some firewood. Emma and I tinker with these riches, and then we walk down towards the sea.

From then on I lived only for Emma. I loved her, in different ways – spread out in the water, spread out on the land and upright in the air. It seems we had no other activity than pleasure – or awaiting pleasure.

During that time I forgot the desert and the hereafter of a memory that I had intended to run through in my own. I was here, nowhere but here. That is to say, I was completely involved in Emma's body. Now I search for words which might give me an illusion of that body, of her spontaneous alternation of sweetness and wildness. What else do I know? Simply that pleasure cannot be a memory. Yet, I remember. Sometimes my tongue slides out of my mouth to lick Emma's absence. I remember: Emma seizes my sex and pushes it into her. Later, day has dawned. I watch. Emma has fallen on her back near the bottom of the bed. She sleeps, one leg thrown across me. Her fleece is tainted and wiry. Some sperm seeps from her slit, and the insides of her thighs are marked with large white patches. I sit up and slide my hand across the sticky flesh. The mucus covers my fingers and I notice a fine thread of blood. I push: it throbs, broadens, becomes deep and red. There is a sort of hiccup, and an overflow of spunk runs over the back of my hand. I observe it moving slowly down my wrist, and while it does so, something strange happens to me – something I would not know how to explain, for there is only the trickling and a voice in my head which says: life is transparent . . . life is transparent . . .

After that I know nothing more about the place, nor Emma, nor above all about myself. I fall. I feel happy. But naturally, before long, I want knowledge afresh, or rather, to recapture my knowledge. I row through time and secrete words.

Words? Always the same of course, but sex and its movement are always the same and yet always different. Speech too has its saliva. Words which speak, which do not speak, which are finally something other than memory, because before long they produce an image which is not recollection but the beginning of *repetition*. I remember. You are speaking to me. You are sitting on your heels like all the women out there. You have that haze of light on your face that I remember even more than your face. No, it is to my sex, erect before you, that, sitting naked, you are speaking, the sound of your expiration making each word edge dyingly through your teeth.

"My vainglory my gem my finger my felon my sharp-pointed my snub my walnut my planting my balk my burrower my gourmand my gowk my stopple my dart my pillar my filthiness my stealer my stake my regiment my thief my wretch my stock my kingling my pointel my postel my orphan my imp my hungered my lance my jewel my settle my spur my celerity my pile my tunneller my dotard my mole my falchion my cockrow my skinful my pipe my diviner my glaive my stiff my cockle my ravisher my spear my weathercock my sparkling my jack my arrowhead . . ."

I remember. Like a heartbeat in my ear. But perhaps it is only my tongue beating hard against my teeth's cage. Sometimes I am so hollow that you come inside and the shadow cries out for mercy. Then I stretch out my hand and there is a little reddened gold because night is drawing in. The room is a hole in the stone: an open tomb. You are no longer speaking to me. Your halo has also reddened. If I lift my hand slightly I do not know whether I am seeing the sky or the sea.

I remember. We are naked, stretched out on the white sheet, both motionless, waiting for night's arrival to erase the $=$ sign we form with our bodies. I closed my eyes a long time ago. I see bygone days falling like leaves. The breeze from that falling turns my seven skins one by one. I see the cells shit into my blood, the air carry that filth up to my throat and throw it out. Then night falls.

"Sweet," I say. "Sweet."

You do not reply. You are dark. My hand moves, moves slowly towards you. It runs a little way down your side and then suddenly accelerates and scales your thigh. It marks time there,

as if to be forgotten, before it slides towards your abdomen and
knots its fingers in your fleece. Another halt. You breathe against
my fingertips. You wait and I wait. One of your hands has moved
towards me, secretly. I feel it coming. I avoid it by arching my
back. "Be good," you murmur. Your hand touches me, climbs
calmly onto my belly, runs to my thigh, drops down and slips
under the fold of my buttock. You are there like a shadow that I
cannot see in the shadow but know is there lying in wait for me.
Suddenly I think: I love you. Your hand starts to caress while
mine crosses the curly bush, lets itself slide along the outer labia,
then slowly extends each finger to cover your whole sex. Listen.
Don't move. Wait. I see a millipede at the base of my abdomen
and its feet become the lashes of a huge red eye. Your hand is
under my balls. Your hand holds the reins. Not yet. Don't get
hard yet. A bubble of silence swells around us. You explore my
buttocks and I imagine that I too have a large mouth there.
Beneath my hand, you tremble, and a pulse blooms at my
fingertips in reply to your palpitations. "Emma, Emma, Emma,"
I say very quickly, feeling a liquid oozing from your labia. Your
index finger pierces me: I am a ring of flesh that I squeeze and
ease to play on your finger. You arch against my hand pushing
harder. Its pressure is enough to open you. You have a moist slit.
I love you. I touch your clit, you moan, roll against me and our
deranged hands lose themselves on all the flesh that comes their
way. Passing near my face, mine brings me your odour and I want
to take hold of the nape of your neck. I want to. But you bite my
shoulder, then my throat. I search for your sex with all my
fingers. You brush them aside, straighten up. I open my eyes
to surprise you on the move, but see only the air in the room has
turned milky and you are swimming backwards towards me. You
float above me. You place your knees in the hollow of my armpits.
You lean forward. You run your lips over my sex, then your
tongue, then your half-open mouth. I have eyes in my crotch –
eyes that would like to roll between your teeth. But when your
lips gently encircle me, there is a great surging back through my
whole body, as if the fact that my cock was stiffening was
returning my sight back to its proper place. Your knees squeeze
tightly and I part my eyelids only to see the mound, where the
sweet valley gapes, coming down towards my face. And there is
your odour. I open my mouth straightaway to drink up that

odour. My tongue is stuck out. Yours slides along the huge vein. I swell. I knock against the roof of your mouth. It is me down there who fills your mouth. But more of me is here in my extended tongue which now pushes between your other lips. I am a bow and you the string. Now you suck the whole shaft and me, I lick, I nibble. You become earthy, humid and deep. I plough your entire furrow. I remember. Emma lets rip. Her mouth goes down, draws up – a loving bracelet that my member fills. At each movement to the base her nose batters between my balls and her breasts bang against my belly. I love. I love. The dear tongue of my mistress clings to the head of my cock and its sweet saliva oils my weapon. My nose, meanwhile, has pushed to the most hollow part of the furrow while my tongue dances around the stiff little clit. The anus contracts level with my eyes, then purses its lips and allows a glimpse of a fillet of pink flesh beyond the brown rim. I love. You love. We love. Emma pitches her hips, discharges a slightly bitter juice on my nose, rubs her cunt against my swollen lips in a swirling motion which corresponds exactly to the dancing of my mouth. The swirling increases. Hairs caress my entire face. I knock against the back of her throat at each slide of the bracelet to the base of the shaft. Her breasts beat my belly like two little heels. Each jerk by Emma deposits a moistness which spreads across my chest. I bathe my index finger in the hollow of her mound, smear it with the fragrant mixture of saliva and juice, then, while my tongue travels up the entire furrow, I suddenly thrust it into the pink whose corolla winks. There is a groan. Emma's hands slide beneath my buttocks, part them, and her finger does the same to me. Her crotch is resting on my chest. We turn together. We write our love. Gravity accelerates in the empty sky. Down below the moment draws near. A ball of whiteness descends the inside of my marrow. My balls burn. A sudden surge of will impels me to unstick my mouth, withdraw my cock. Emma groans, complains. "Come! Come!" she cries. I throw her across the bed, sit astride her, cover her, stab her to the hilt. Silence. The light is on her face. We look at each other. We no longer have any skin between us. Same warmth, my sweet, same dance of flesh on our bones, same trembling among the branches. Life is so alive in my head that my eyes bulge. Silence . . . I love. You love. We love. Our breathing deepens, forms a rhythmic pattern, installs in our bellies the certainty of being together. Calm, calm. Light on the down of your cheek. You smile. You invite me. You spread your heartbeats through your entire belly so that the wall's pulsations set my tool awry. I smile at you. I raise myself up. I draw my cock slowly out of you. I watch it emerge. Then, with a movement we would like to be inexorable, I thrust it into your consciousness, withdraw it, thrust it farther. You vibrate. You sweat. You sheathe me with long, long palpitations. I swell again. Contemplating it once more between our legs, I admire you for making this arm blossom at my base. This arm, this bone at whose root swings a double orange. You raise your sex to meet this machine. You gobble it up, you swallow it. I watch it being gulped down, exaltedly. You take hold of it, pumping with all your strength, squeezing, beating, but I manoeuvre away and with the same exaltation see my penis emerge inch by inch and uncover its head. But you refuse to let go of the engine and you push up your mound to pursue it. I remember. The hair roots were full of slaver. It was a flooded meadow beneath the water, and my penis pointing towards the source's mouth was sticky and steaming. Then, I had the mad desire to plant myself in that greasy ground, to be plastered with it, to have its residue all over my body. I took Emma's hands, plunged them one after the other into the source and used them as brushes to paint myself with its colours. I remember. I am your savage. I have just pinned you down. I dance. You cunt about before me and I pin you down again. "Go on, go on," you say. "Fill my hole to the brim. Leave nothing there but the room you fill and the longing for you, my longing to be fucked by you." I get stuck in. I plunge. I drive into you till I make your shoulders tremble. The bumping of my balls against your arse excites me further. I love you. I catch hold of your breasts. You thrust your pubis so hard against me that it hurts. You claw my back, my neck. You knot your legs around my waist. You contract your vagina till it becomes the jaw it dreams of being. You cling to my neck. Positioned on my hands and knees, I sway so you can mark time with our passion. I love you. Your jaw encircles me, and I do not know whether it is her or me beating in the flow of sweet saliva. You love me. You stream down. I say: "Suck me till your thirst is quenched." And I say, or I think: "Odour of pleasure, I love you; fountain of time, I love you; source of the imaginary, I love you; hole of surpassment, I love you; crown of penises, I love you." Your heels pommel my buttocks. You are the pendulum of a crazy clock. Your mouth enters my mouth so that our tongues fight between our teeth. I now support our career with only one hand. With the other I gather liquid flowing from your hole, then use it to smear our lips. Then I strike you with it, lash you with it. Enraged, you squeeze me harder and the pendulum swings even more wildly, and I cry: "Eat me!" And you: "Again. Further. Further." I am only that red bone in your mouth. Above there is the long trail of a scream between your teeth. Below, your soft mouth contracts. Here you are tied my beauty, tied to my tree and ready for the great explosion. But the knot remains immobile and central while shooting along our limbs, and rolling to the depths of our communal memory we share the same cry.

The July night covered us again with its gentleness, and so as not to disturb it, the ocean's surface barely rippled. Nothing was more urgent than youth and happiness, as far as life can go, for happiness renders youth tireless. Before long our bodies were feeling their way again. We knew that, contrary to the order of rhetoric, it is not a matter of exhausting *the subject* but of making it exhaustible.

One day, having climbed the cliff, we came across the place of our first meeting, and I asked Emma what significance the ceremony, in which I had been held worthy of her, held for the village people.

"It seems the festivity used to be held at the new moon preceding each solstice and each equinox. The custom only recommenced a few years back. But I had never heard of it till the old man came to ask my parents to prepare me for the ceremony. He said: the Lady has chosen her. The Lady wants her. I believe my parents were afraid. They agreed without a murmur. And you, well you do not displease them now. My father said: he could have eaten our hearts, but he's a man."

As I knew nothing of the ceremony's end, I should have liked Emma to describe it to me.

"I don't know," she said. "Virgins only come here if they have been chosen as new moon. The old people say we must deflower the new moon."

"But who chose you?"

"The Lady. I told you."

"What lady?"

"The one from the island."

I had never heard of this other island. I wanted to know where it was.

"Over there," Emma motioned, pointing out to me a spot on the horizon just opposite the terrace. It looked two or three hours away by boat. A very tiny island.

"Have you ever been there?"

"No one has ever been there. It's forbidden and people are afraid."

"Afraid of what?"

"The Lady."

"But who is this lady?"

"The one who arrived naked."

In a flash I saw her again. The Beauty. The hair. The triangle. The walk.

"Why are people afraid?"

"The island is well-guarded. There are dogs, arabs, armed black men. Mariners say that anyone who lands there never returns."

"Are you sure?"

"That's what they say."

"And the village accepts that? There are many men here."

"The Lady's rich. She buys everything the men catch in the sea. She brings us everything that comes from elsewhere. It's enough not to meddle in her affairs. That is the order."

"And what does she do?"

"She has a large castle in the middle of the island."

"And before?"

"Before what?"

"Before the Lady ruled here?"

"I do not know. The Lady's older than me. The village has always depended on the island."

There was a shadow behind my eyes. I had not known it to begin with, but suddenly I realized I was not seeing Emma anymore. Like a blind man I stretched my hand towards her face, then my tongue towards her tongue. The shadow persisted. At that time, towards her, I was no more than the fool of my own folly.

That night I left our stone house and the white bed to go down to the inn and talk to the fishermen. They greeted me, teasing:

"Emma is beautiful, isn't she?"

"And what a pleasure, young man, by the look of you!"

I bought drinks and their friendliness expanded with every bottle they emptied of the dark wine. At last, when I thought the moment was right, I asked:

"What's that island you can see from the top of the cliff?"

The lightheartedness disappeared abruptly. The mariners looked at me then at each other, before one of the oldest finally decided to answer:

"It's Countess Mona's island. You pleased her, since she picked you out the other night."

"Is it always she who chooses?"

"Yes. She presides over our festivals. She started them again, after all. Old Bastien, the one in charge, defended the tradition well but without the countess it was probable that our virgins would keep their holes stoppered till marriage."

"And Mona? Is she from here?"

"The island belonged to her father, and her father's father. But the old man did not care much about us. Mona looks after us better, though we must not go near the island."

"You have never been there?"

"No. It is forbidden. There are dogs and black men. Sometimes when the wind is strong you hear those beasts from hell howling . . . After all it's her home!"

"Does no one ever go there?"

"Friends of hers who arrive in their yachts from the other side of the sea."

"And what if I went there, to her island?"

"She said it is better not to go."

"She has spoken of me?"

"She said it's better not to go."

"At any rate, your countess would not eat me!"

"Who knows?" shrugged the old man.

While calling for drink to put an end to my interrogation, he gave me the half-condescending, half-pitying smile that old people sometimes have.

From then on I had but one idea – to see Mona again, to visit her island, her castle. Although I took great care not to show this desire, my assiduity with Emma abated. I kept silent in order to imagine and thus envisage, but who has faith in his own visions?

Frequently, in the afternoon, I escaped to the terrace. I had been able to obtain a telescope easily, but though it drew the island nearer, it did not show me anything. I succeeded in spotting a large white yacht, the castle not at all. The island was hilly enough to conceal it. In any case, did they not call anything the least bit bigger than the poky village houses a castle?

The map told me nothing either. No doubt the island was off the main route, or else so tiny that reduction to scale made it invisible.

I secretly prepared for my expedition, making a habit of borrowing Emma's father's boat. It had a shallow draught and I quickly familiarized myself with its handling. The weather was calm, my hopes high: what have I to fear from Beauty?

LILLY'S LOULOU

Michèle Larue

Translated by Noël Burch

My mistress abandoned me over a Chinese restaurant. There are at least twelve on *la calle Cuchillo*, a busy street in Havana's *barrio chino*. The Cuban Chinese chefs threw thick Mexican spaghetti in their soups instead of rice noodles, which always riled my Lilly. When I heard that eight chefs were due in from Canton to teach the locals how to make genuine sharks' fin soup, I was frightened: I myself am pink – the color of flesh, in fact – and I look a bit like a sausage. When my mistress said melted condoms had been known to replace the mozzarella on Cuban pizzas, I thought to myself that the contents of a condom, i.e. yours truly, might make tasty meatballs in their soup.

I'm ten inches long and an inch and a half in diameter. I'm veined and flexible like a *paupiette de veau*. Two alkaline batteries set me to twitching, with a choice of three speeds. For years I was Lilly's favorite dildo. Nestled in a red velvet zip-bag next to a round-tipped candle, I toured the world in her trunk. She always flew during the off-season so that she could negotiate a whole row just for the two of us. She took me out of my case when the movie began. In the darkness, she slipped me under her panties where I started buzzing in low gear like a fly caught in a lace curtain. Lilly began to pant as she slid me sidewise under her panties and pressed me to her flesh. My hum became muffled as I drilled into the zones she chose around her clitoris, then over the little bridge of flesh to the anus. There, I skated around in circles. . . . After a while, my mistress would heave a little sigh and drop me under the seat. She rarely reached climax in the air. When the plane landed, she would pick me up with a fistful of crumpled newspapers.

On the infrequent evenings when Lily was at home alone, I played stand-in, alternating with a black, cone-shaped competitor called Plug. I never knew much about Plug's capabilities, but they must have been far inferior to mine. One morning, as I emerged from the bag where Lilly had forsaken me all night long, I noticed him lying on the bed. Whenever she chose me for her evening bodyguard, she told all her boyfriends she would be getting her beauty sleep at home that night. I was delighted to count among the treatments meant to make her even more desirable. As she stepped out of her bath and slipped into a slinky Chinese negligée and mules trimmed with black swan feathers, my mistress would already be planning an orgasm. Pulling back the blankets, she would stretch out on the cool percale sheets. I could feel her finger applying a male-scented gel, then the touch of her clitoris as I swung into action. She would put me down and caress herself with her fingers. Pick me up again. Arch her back to see me standing between her thighs. Her pleasure came in moans that made me feel proud. The next morning her hand would come looking for me under the sheets. She'd give me a few licks with her tongue, spit on my tip, and back to work!

When Lilly had a man in her bed, she would let me watch the lovemaking that I had, in a way, initiated. She would bring the man into the bedroom and take me out of my case. I heard the usual "it sure is big" or "just like the real thing." Wearing the string she never removed with any partner, and for which she was known as "Lilly-string," she rubbed me against her pink lips to make them moist. When the man tired of my collaboration, she would throw me on the carpet. But sometimes she quietly picked me up again while the man was in the shower. To finish herself off. To drench me with her juices. The mechanism would stop just in time for me to feel her spasms, and it would be my turn to feel the throbbing of my mistress's body. Her little squeals were more audible and attractive without the sound of my motor. When the man came out of the shower, kissed her cheek, and asked, "Was it good for you, too?" it was as if he were talking to me.

My role was usually restricted to surface-work. Except for that one time in Africa, when we ran out of batteries. I had a whale of a time! My mistress took me firmly in her hand and slowly drove me nearly halfway inside of her. Never before had she thrust me thus into the sheath of her flesh. It was in Zimbabwe that I realized what Plug was for. Actually, Lilly's cavity wasn't my size. Her eyes had been bigger than her stomach when she picked me out in her favorite sex-shop on the Rue de la Gaîté in Paris. Was she trying to talk the price down when she told the salesmen I was too big to be of use to anyone? It was under a tent in the African bush that I first experienced confinement inside my mistress, and every night I wanted more. It was soft and maternal in there . . . I still have fond memories of that expedition, although, without my vibratory powers, never once during the long safari did I manage to bring her off.

And so now I don't belong to Lilly any more. She sold me – traded me, rather – for two boxes of Robusto cigars scarcely thicker than a little finger. How's she going to manage with those, unless she ties them in a bunch?

The tall black man who bought me puts on a silk fuchsia vest every evening. He claims that anyone who lives for any length of time in Chinatown (where he was born forty years ago) will inevitably turn tradesman. Orestes – for such is his name – has ignored this year's big craze in Havana: going in for a barman's job on a Caribbean cruise ship. He devotes himself solely to managing my activities, an occupation well suited to his tropical indolence. Any effort to entrust him with something other than coaching my depraved little body – keeping an eye on the workers painting the family *terrassa*, for example, or having sex with a woman – makes him terribly nervous. He's often so stressed that his body ceases to function and he has to lie down. If it were in my power, I'd rebel against this boss of mine, who thinks the exhalations of an expensive scent should fill the street where he walks. Fortunately, I have little contact with the man. I change condoms several times a day and pass from hand to hand: I'm a dildo for hire. When I'm squeezed into a Chinese rubber, it reminds me of Lilly's tender sex. Her tight vagina. Between jobs, my manager takes me back and washes me clean. When I'm dry, he pours white rum all over me. "She" never washed me at all. I've never seen so many black men and women at close range before. The rum has so blurred my memories of Lilly that I can scarcely recall her scent. Some days, I feel homesick.

ALL EYES ON HER

M. Christian

THE CITY SAT around her. From where she was standing, nothing but the silver squares of windows seemed to be watching. But she knew better; she could feel them sitting behind their desks, in their living rooms, in the bedrooms, in their beds, watching her.

The gravel and tar paper of the roof was hot underfoot, but she enjoyed it. It was the totality of it, the completeness of the act, that made her nipples into hard knots, and stoked the fire of her cunt. Wearing slippers, shoes, or anything else would've made it incomplete, would've ruined the statement: standing naked on the rooftop, letting the city watch her.

At first Cindy didn't think she could do it. It was a private thing, a crazy thing, something to lay back in a warm, soapy tub and think about – rubbing herself into a rolling orgasm. In the real world the roof was hot, the gravel hurt the bottoms of her feet, and a hard, chill wind cut over the concrete edge of the roof and blasted through her.

Despite the pains in her feet, the chill air, and the hot tar, she stood naked on the roof of her little five-story apartment building, a fire roaring in her cunt.

– there, that little square: formed out of an un-athletic dough, he watched her. His cock was small, and barely hard. He pulled it, tugged at it, the warm roll of his stomach brushing his hand as he masturbated. Slowly, he got harder and harder till all of his few inches was strong and hard in his hand. The fat man watched, smiling, happy and excited. When he came, he selflessly groaned, and got his window messy.

Cindy watched the city watching her. Looking at one silvery window in particular she lifted her right hand to her left breast and stroked the soft skin and pinched the hard nipple.

– they watched her. Taken with her brazenness, the attitude of this obvious species of urban nymph, who could say who started it? Maybe it was Mike who first dropped his shorts and started the kiss, his rock-hard cock fitting so perfectly, so nicely between them. But then it couldn't been Steve who started it, who put his hand between them to feel his own straining erection. Was it Mike who dropped to his knees and started a grand suck? Or was it Steve? Who came first? Did Steve fill Mike's mouth with bittersweet come? Or did Mike explode all over Steve's face? Or did it really matter? The end certainly justified the means . . .

Cindy looked up at the sun. It bathed her, baked her; her skin vibrated with the heat of it, the fire it coated her with. Right still on left, she felt her breast, playing with the texture of it, the underlying muscle, the strong tip of her nipple. Sun on her, she moved left to right, massaging her breasts under the gaze of the warm sun.

– sitting on their bed, she watched the woman on the rooftop across the street. The sun was almost too bright, too hot, and for a moment she thought about what she had to do: shower, get dressed, go to work. But the woman, the daringness of her, the casualness of her, kept her glued to the window. She didn't seem crazy, but that's what she had to be. To stand up there in the sight of God and everyone else, and rub herself like that. It turned her on something fierce. It made her horny, that's what it did. She savored the word as she pulled herself up from sitting to all fours. Her breasts pulled away from her body in this position – they strained against her body and rolled in her house dress. Without thinking, she put a hand down the front of her dress and cradled one of her breasts. The nipple was so hard, it ached, it was so hard. Cautiously, she squeezed and pulled gently at it. Fire raced through her. Her legs felt like they were going to collapse. The woman across the street, touching herself, it was like she was crazy, touching herself and thinking about her nipples and between her legs she could feel herself grow wet –

Her legs were tired, so Cindy lowered herself down till she squatted over the hot gravel roof. Her breasts were heavy and tight, her nipples ached to be touched and sucked. No thought. Not a one. Watching the city watching her, Cindy put a hot hand between her hot legs. Her thighs were wet, her cunt was a damp forest of blond curls. Her lips were wet and hot. She ran a single finger from her clit to her cunt to her ass, and shivered in delight.

– bent over the chair, her ass in the air, her arms down the chair back, her knees on the seat, she could feel Bob's tongue playing with her cunt. He loved to eat her, and, God, he was good at it. She pushed herself back towards his face, trying to get his hard, strong, tongue deeper into her soaking cunt. Then he found her pucker asshole, and started to tongue around it. Christ! She felt like screaming. She needed cock now, right now in her soaking pussy, she needed to be filled, fucked, she wanted to come and come and come! Then Bob was at her clit, and the world seemed to boil down to the points of her nipples, the glow of her ass, the wetness of her cunt, her lover's tongue, and the joy of her clit. She was so lost, so incredibly lost getting ready to come, that she almost forgot to look up, to look across the way to see what the chick on the roof was doing next –

Cindy's cunt juice ran between her fingers. She was so wet. Her cunt was soaking, her clit was a hard bead between her legs, tucked between her lips. She'd worked out a system, and it was working real good: first she'd plunge her hands deep within herself, up and deep till she could swear THERE was her cervix, THERE her G-spot. Then she'd pull out, slow and hard, pushing aside her hot, soaking lips till her fingers glided past her clit. Then she'd work it, rubbing around and around the little bead of her clit. Then back – back to her cunt, the depths of her, her hot lips, her clit, over and over again.

Sometimes she'd use both hands, pushing all fingers into herself like some huge cock. Sometimes she'd use just one, saving the other, wet and smelling of her cunt, on the knots of her nipples, her aching breasts.

Then she came, fast and oh-so-hard, with the whole world watching.

KISMET

Michael Crawley

STUART MET HER in Toronto, which is ironic. He was from Vancouver, sometimes known as LaLaLand North. The rest of Canada knows that Vancouver is a haven for drop-outs, druggies and weirdos. Toronto, by contrast, is still often called "Toronto-the-Good".

It was February, in a McDonald's on Yonge Street, at three in the morning. They were both sitting at the counter. Stuart noticed her eyes first. They were big, the colour of hot chocolate, and sad beneath creamy lids. Her face was thin, feral. The hair that tumbled from beneath a plain navy beret was violently red. She cradled her styrofoam cup in both thin-fingered hands. When she bent her head to sip, enormous hoop earrings swung against her cheeks.

Despite the time and the place, Stuart didn't think she was a professional. A pro wouldn't have worn a thin shapeless turquoise topcoat. It concealed without protecting, which is the opposite to what a whore would choose. In any case, she was too old. She had to be about his own age, forty. Yonge Street whores range from prepubescent to old hands of twenty.

Stuart should have drunk up and left. There was a bed waiting at his hotel and it'd been a tiring night. Waiting hours for a mainframe to come up so you can keyboard your last seven entries is more fatiguing than pounding the keys all night.

He *should* have left, but he crooked a finger for another coffee instead. The woman looked so incredibly vulnerable. It's hard to walk away from that. There are so many possibilities. A woman's weakness can give a man the opportunity to be chivalrous. Or it can be exploited.

Stuart had been in Toronto for ten days, with no real human contact. He'd been sleeping through most of the mornings, watching TV in the afternoon, and starting work when the rest of the office left. His friends and family were all back in "Van". He was hungry for some sort of emotional interaction.

A dozen gilt bangles jingled as the woman heaved a macramé bag onto the counter, fumbled out a cigarette to slot between lips that were far too red, and started fumbling again. She found a bookmatch with just one match left and struck it. It spluttered out.

That gave Stuart his chance to perform a tiny courtesy. He slid off his stool, walked the length of the counter, and flicked his lighter. She bent to the flame without looking at him and nodded her "thanks".

Stuart went back to his stool, vaguely disappointed, vaguely resentful.

Her cup had to be empty. The kid behind the counter said something to her. She shook her head and lifted styrofoam to her lips, but Stuart was sure she was faking that there was coffee left. Her throat – her long slender throat – didn't make any swallowing motions.

Nowhere to go? No money? Could she be a battered wife who'd finally walked out? That'd make her even more vulnerable, more in need of his chivalry, more . . . Stuart didn't complete the thought. Everyone has a dark side. Most of us just don't look into those shadows, right? Best not to know what lurks there.

She stubbed half her cigarette into a foil ashtray, faked another sip at her empty cup and groped for another smoke. Stuart decided to have a second stab at being nice.

She swivelled on her stool to meet him, took the cigarette from her mouth between two fingers, touched the back of his flame-bearing hand with her nail-tips, looked up at him, and asked, "Should I?"

"Should you?"

"Smoke another cigarette."

The sensible answer would have been, "That's up to you."

Stuart told her, "Yes," in a firm voice.

"If you say so, I will."

She had a rusty contralto. Stuart moved his neck inside the collar of his topcoat. Her voice had been like velvet stroking his nape. The sharp points of her fingernails had left tingles in his skin.

"Would you like another coffee?"

"Should I?"

Stuart snapped his fingers and pointed to her cup instead of answering.

The kid looked at him. Stuart said, "Two".

The woman said, "Virginia."

Stuart said, "Stuart, with a 'u'."

They sipped coffee in awkward silence. When Stuart was done he cleared his throat. "It's late."

"Should I go home?"

"I would." She had a home to go to? Was he glad for her, or disappointed?

"How should I get there?"

Stuart shrugged. "Is it far? Do you have a car? Do you need a cab?"

She spilled coins onto the counter. Her finger counted a dollar eighty-five.

"Do you need cab fare?"

"Should I?" again.

"I'm working at the TD Centre. Hawkins and Bradley – if you wanted to repay me sometime." He pulled out his wallet, half-extracted a twenty, and paused. "A better idea. I'll call a taxi and drop you off on the way to my hotel, okay?"

She huddled in the far corner of the cab and looked out of the window, silent. So – he'd been wrong. It wasn't a pick-up. At least he'd had a few words of conversation with an attractive woman. As lonely as he was, those moments were worth the extra cab-fare and the price of a coffee.

As she got out she looked back at him, lips almost parting, but she didn't smile and she didn't even say goodnight. Stuart decided not to think about her again. He'd been ready to sin, so the memory would be a guilty one, but he hadn't followed through, so there'd be no secret pleasure to savour.

The night-line on his desk rang at six-forty the next evening. "Should I go for a walk or is it too cold?"

Something icy flopped over inside Stuart's chest. He collected himself and said, "Do you have another coat?"

"No."

"It's too cold out for that one. Stay home."

"And?"

"And what?"

"What should I do at home?"

He almost snapped, "Read a book, watch tv, whatever!" but he said, "Think about tomorrow and get an early night."

"Tomorrow?"

"Meet me for breakfast. Nine-thirty. Get a cab to the Sheraton. I'll pick up the tab."

"What should I wear?"

"Hold on." Stuart laid the phone down. He needed to think. She was the most frustrating . . . But it was exciting too, wasn't it? "Should I this, should I do that?" Did she have *no* mind of her own? And if she *didn't*? What would that be like? A puppet woman, doing absolutely nothing without his permission, and perhaps doing *anything* that he suggested?

But that couldn't be, could it? No one was that pliant – that *blank*. Then again, what if she was? How could he resist putting her to the test? What would he be missing if he just walked away? If he didn't find out he'd never forgive himself.

He picked the phone up. "Something attractive."

"Attractive."

"Sexy."

"Very well. What do you like?"

This wasn't happening. It couldn't be. The bubble would burst. He'd tell her to do something, and she'd refuse, just like any normal woman. Best to pop the illusion right then.

"Do you mean to tell me that if I told you to meet me stark naked under your coat, you would?"

"Is that what you'd like?"

"Of course not. Do you have a short skirt?"

"Yes."

"A see-through blouse?"

"Yes."

"That'll do then."

"Stockings, pantihose or bare legs?"

Stuart felt an erection starting to grow. "Stockings."

"Heels?"

"High. The highest you have."

"Nine-thirty. Thank you Stuart."

He stared at his screen, blind to the glowing numbers. He couldn't go through with this. She obviously had a problem, a mental problem. It'd be wrong, evil, to take advantage of her. He just wouldn't show.

And then she'd be there, with a cab waiting for fare, and her with a dollar eighty-five in small change. He had to show. Anyway – she was likely playing a game with him, right? She would be the one who didn't show. She'd be home, with a manfriend, laughing at the poor sap who was going to get up early to meet some fantasy woman for breakfast. That was fine. *He'd* show, and it'd be worth the small humiliation of being stood up to have a clean conscience and it all over with.

But she did show, her coat flapping, tottering on five-inch heels, thighs almost skinny beneath a tiny skirt. He had to endure the embarrassment of eating breakfast in a public place with a woman who was wearing a transparent blouse with nothing beneath it. Stuart supposed it was his own fault. He hadn't *told* her to wear a bra, had he?

She ordered what he ordered and he sat there staring at her breasts while trying to look as if he wasn't. They were worth looking at, much too full and heavy for her slender frame and with dark brown nipples the size of demi-tasse coffee cups.

She owed him, didn't she? Two cab fares and a breakfast he'd sweated through? He'd collect, say goodbye, and forget her. Perhaps he'd pay her off with a hundred and put her in her place. She might not be a prostitute but she was certainly a slut, of sorts. She was there to be used, so he'd use her, just the once.

Stuart signed their bill and said, "Follow me."

She was two paces behind him, except in the elevator, all the way to his suite. "Humble" demands humiliation. That's what he'd give her. For once in his life he was going to screw a woman with absolutely no concern for her pleasure, unless she balked, of course. A part of him wanted her to balk, to refuse, to say, "No!"

He'd *make* her say, "No".

"Hang your coat up and take your clothes off."

She didn't say, "No."

"Kneel in front of me."

She didn't say "No".

Stuart mauled and kneaded her breasts. She stared at his belt buckle, expressionless. He pinched the rubbery tips of her nipples. He took them between his fingers and his thumbs and shook her breasts. She didn't complain. She didn't react. He tugged, pulling her breasts into obscene shapes. Her expression didn't change. His thumbnails dug in. She took a sharp breath.

"Did that hurt?" he asked.

"Some."

"Do you want me to stop?"

"Only if you want to."

"Do you like it when I hurt your nipples?"

"Should I?"

Christ she was frustrating! "Open my fly."

She pulled his zipper down and dropped her hand back to her side.

"Take it out! Take my cock out and suck it!"

Cool fingers groped inside his pants, found him and tugged him out. She held him delicately with a thumb and two fingers, like an aficionado with a fine cigar. Her mouth formed an "O". She leaned closer and took the head of his cock between her lips. Her cheeks hollowed.

"Deeper!"

Her lips slithered down his stem. Stuart felt the head of his cock glide across the flat of her tongue to nudge at the back of her throat.

"You like it, don't you?" he demanded.

She nodded.

"You're a horny slut! A whore!"

She nodded again.

"I'm going to fuck your face! What do you think of that?"

She withdrew, slowly, smearing his stem with brilliant red lipstick. "If that's what you want, Stuart."

It was lust and it was anger, so mixed together that he didn't know where one ended and the other began. He locked his fingers in her riotous hair and thrust deep into her waiting mouth. He'd take his pleasure of her mouth. He'd choke her with his cock. He'd make her gag. He'd . . .

She took his pounding, her tongue pushing up under his cock to press it hard against the roof of her mouth. She'd done it before, often. She was nothing but a . . .

He came.

She showed initiative for the first time, sucking hard and long, drawing his come out through the eye of his cock like an infinite length of knotted silk. She sucked and gulped and gulped and sucked until his guilty pleasure became a shameful ache.

"Enough!"

She gave one last hard draw before releasing him.

Stuart didn't tuck himself in. Leaving his cock dangling from his fly would show her how little he thought of her. He dropped a fifty at her knees and told her, "There's cab fare. I have to get a nap now. I work late hours."

She dressed and left without a word.

When the phone on his desk rang at six-forty he knew who it was.

"Do you want to see me for breakfast?"

Did he? Of course he didn't. This whole thing was sick, kinky. The sooner it was over the better.

Did he? Of course he did. Being married didn't equal "all fantasies fulfilled". His Janice was a reasonably sexy woman. They made love twice a week, most weeks, which wasn't bad after twelve years of marriage. He respected his wife, and that was the problem. She was worthy of his respect, which meant there were things she wouldn't do, and that he wouldn't dare suggest she did. You don't risk a marriage for the sake of a few extra thrills, do you?

That meant that there were sex acts he'd never tried, and had half resigned himself he never would. Now – now the opportunity had leapt into his lap, as it were. How could a man turn his back on that? Anyway, the chances were that those things weren't that great, once you'd tried them. Get them out of his system, that was it. He was far enough from home that what he did wouldn't be real, anyway. Work out those dark desires and then he'd be much more content with what he had at home. In a way, he'd be doing Janice a favour, not that she'd ever know, of course.

A voice cleared its throat on the line. She – Virginia – was waiting patiently for his answer.

"No – I won't meet you in the lobby. Come straight up to my suite. I'll order room service."

"Nine-thirty?"

"Yes."

"What should I wear?"

Damn the woman! How was *he* supposed to know what was in her closet? Still . . .

"Hose and heels again."

"Yes Stuart."

"Do you have a button-through dress?"

"Yes Stuart."

Yes, yes, yes! Didn't she know any other word? He'd push. There had to be some point that she'd say, "No".

"No underwear."

"Very well, Stuart."

"Do you have some lubricant? Baby oil or something?"

"Yes Stuart."

Hell! She didn't even ask what for. Perhaps she knew. Perhaps that's what she wanted.

"And some rope? Cord? Soft cord?"

"How long, Stuart?"

"Six feet should do."

"Yes Stuart."

He hung up before his perversity made him tell her to bring a whip or something. If he had, would she have? He wouldn't know, would he, unless . . .

Stuart touched his screen-saver off and concentrated on nice safe numbers.

Her dress was a faded blue floral print, mid-thigh long and straining across the swaying masses of her breasts. She might have had it since she'd been a teen and less developed. It reminded him that once she'd been young and innocent, so he had her take it off before they sat down to eat.

It was very different, eating alone with her, him in robe and pyjama pants, her in just heels, hose, bangles and earrings, which is more naked than total nudity. He could look at her breasts all he liked, with no pretence. They had a very slight sag. He was glad of that tiny imperfection. It made her more vulnerable.

They were freckled as well. Did that mean she was a true redhead? It was strange, he'd used her mouth – used it in a way that he'd never have dreamed of using Janice's, but he still hadn't seen her pubes, not really. She'd turned away as she'd laid her dress aside and then she'd slipped into her chair at the table. He'd been watching the sway of her breasts, so he'd missed even a glimpse at her mound, her *mons veneris*. Still, he would see it. He could see it right then, if he wished. All he'd have to do was tell her to stand, come closer, and let him inspect her. He'd be able to look close, and long, in broad daylight.

He'd never done that to Janice. He'd *seen* her sex, of course, as she dressed or undressed, or in the dim light from the bedside lamp, but he'd never actually *inspected* her, like meat.

That's what Virginia was – meat. Pliant, pliable, warm human meat, to be prepared to his own recipe and consumed quickly or at leisure, whatever his mood might dictate.

"Play with your nipples," he said, just as calmly as "more coffee please".

She laid her knife and fork aside. "How would you like me to do it?"

"To please yourself. Show me how you'd do it if you were alone."

"Yes Stuart." She cupped her breasts on her palms and wobbled them, staring down at her own jiggling flesh as if he wasn't there. Well, that's what he'd told her to do, wasn't it? Her fingers squeezed and kneaded, milking herself in towards her nipples. She leaned backwards, tilting her face towards the ceiling. The stroking became more urgent, coaxing blood into those dark staring centres. They engorged, grew larger and harder. Her hands smoothed higher. Fingers made rings about each puffy halo and compressed, pouting them. She released her right breast and strummed the fingers of her right hand across the tip of her left nipple. Was her mouth slackening with desire? It was hard to tell, with her head tipped so far back.

Her fingertips caressed up the sides of her nipple, soft as petals, stroking from base to tip and base to tip, again and again. Her nipple responded, and there was a pulse under her pale skin. Her nipples weren't pointed cones, like Janice's, but rigid flat-topped turrets, almost the same circumference from base to tip.

She took that blunt tip between thumb and finger and pinched it flat. A sigh escaped her mouth. The bitch was getting off on her own caresses! She hadn't reacted to *him*, but she did to herself.

"Suck it!" he said.

"Yes Stuart." Two hands squeezed and lifted. Her head bent

forward and down. Her lips parted. A kitten-tongue lapped out, point tickling the flat peak.

"I said, 'Suck!'"

"Sorry Stuart." She drew her entire nipple into her mouth. Her cheeks worked. Her lips and teeth mumbled more flesh, drawing more soft white breast into her mouth, creasing its skin, drawing it into an elongated pear.

She might have made a little growling sound deep in her throat as her head shook, but he wasn't sure.

"Bite on it! Chew on your own nipple!"

Her mouth worked and her face looked as if she felt some pain, but how could he be sure she was really obeying?

"Come here and show me!"

She was wobbly on her heels. Her fingers trailed the table. When she stood by him her left nipple was a few inches above his eyes so that he looked up at it. It was wet with her spit, and she *had* obeyed. There were teeth marks, deep and almost blue. Stuart touched. He rolled the cylinder of hot flesh between his fingers, working the teeth dents out.

She sucked air. Her eyes were glazed. All he'd done was touch her nipple.

He trailed a finger down her cleavage, across her midriff, past her navel.

She shivered.

Her pubic hair was ginger and frizzy, trimmed short and shaped to end exactly at the fine crease where the curves of her belly and her mound met.

His fingers twirled a tuft and tugged. "Who did you trim this for?"

"For you, Stuart."

The ridge of her clitoris was thick. Was it always like that, or was it because of him? He stroked the wrinkled skin and thought he felt a stirring beneath his finger.

The lips of her sex were swollen and slightly pendulous, protruding through the ginger fuzz. He poked. The lip yielded, soft, limp. His prod had pushed it back, indenting it. He watched as the flaccid flesh slowly recovered its shape.

This was fun! Her pussy wasn't a part of a living woman. It was a toy. Stuart eased the hood of her clitoris back, exposing a tender arrowhead. When he released her sheath it crept forward again, but not quite so far. Just a hint of the raw pink still showed.

When he shucked it again and blew across it, Virginia's belly tensed, winking her navel. When he slid a finger inside her, just far enough to get a grip on her sex's lip, and pinched, she shuddered. Pleasure? Pain? Did it matter?

Stuart folded three fingers together and thrust them up into her, where she was slick corrugated heat, all delicate membranes and very *internal*.

She groaned and swayed – towards him.

He pulled his fingers out. They were sticky. When he parted them strands of translucent stuff stretched between them. It smelled like canned pineapples, with a vaguely metallic tang.

Stuart held his tacky fingers up to her face. "Suck them clean!"

She made a meal of it, gobbling up her own juices, slithering her tongue between his fingers and licking at their webs.

Stuart said, "Masturbate," and added, "as if you were alone," before she could ask for detailed instructions.

She spread her too-slim thighs, making shadowy hollows behind her tendons. Two fingers of one hand took her clitoral shaft in a scissors-grip. Two of her other hand hooked up inside her pussy. The fingers held still as her hips moved, slowly at first, then faster and faster. The head of her clitoris flashed in and out of view. She got wetter. Soft slurping noises became sharp wet splashing sounds.

Stuart looked up at her face. It was blank, eyes hidden behind heavy lids, but she was biting her lower lip.

She froze. Stuart thought for a moment that she had reached her climax, but then her fingers were jerking on her clit and she plucked the two fingers from her wet insides, flattened that hand and slapped it up at her engorged lips, short sharp fast slaps, wet slaps, wet enough to splash tiny drops of her oozings onto his face.

The sinews inside her thighs quivered.

Stuart grabbed both of her wrists. They fought him for a second then relaxed, but her belly was vibrating with urgency.

"I didn't say you could come," he said.

"Sorry, Stuart."

"Go to the stool and bend over it."

He lashed her ankles to two legs of the stool, low down, and her wrists to the other two legs, just below the padded seat, leaving her enough slack to flatten her palms on the green velvet. With her body leaning like that, at forty-five degrees, her breasts hung. There were tiny silvery creases radiating from where they were rooted, beneath her armpits, another delicious imperfection.

Dangling like that, her breasts seemed almost detached from her body, separate entities. Stuart prodded one. It swung, slapped the other, and sent trembling ripples through it.

"Sway," he said.

She did. He watched, directly and in the dressing table's mirror. He stood behind her and reached around her body, taking a breast in each hand. His fingers milked at her. He stared into the mirror, watching disembodied hands manipulate Plasticine breasts, pluck pretend nipples.

His erection grew, tenting the silk of his pyjama pants out between the flaps of his robe. The wet spot on the silk nudged between the cheeks of her bum.

"You brought baby oil?"

"In my bag."

He parted her buttocks and dripped oil onto the base of her spine. It trickled. It ran the valley to the little brown crater and soaked into it for a dozen drops before overflowing and dribbling to coat the backwards pout of her sex. Stuart's finger traced the glistening, pausing at her anus, rimming before probing.

She inhaled sharply, but the ring of muscle was totally relaxed.

"I'm going to bugger you," he said.

"Yes, Stuart."

"Have you been sodomized before?"

She paused before saying, "Would you like me to have been?"

"I want the truth, damn you, not what you think I want to hear!"

"Then – yes, Stuart."

"Did you like it?"

She didn't answer. He slapped her bottom. "Did you like it?"

"I think I'll like it when you do it, Stuart, if that's what you want."

He wasn't going to get the truth out of her. There was no truth *in* her. It didn't matter. She was going to have something else in her, something more powerful than truth – his cock deep in her rectum. A universal truth?

Stuart parted his fly and let his cock lance out. He slopped oil into his palm. It splashed in his haste, saturating the front of his pyjama pants. It didn't matter what the hotel's laundry service would think. Nothing mattered except the constricted tunnel of flesh that was waiting for his cock.

Two fingers wriggled into her anus, preparing the way, ignoring whatever *she* felt, pleasure or pain. The head of his cock was screaming at him, "In! In!"

Thumbs prying her open, sliding insecurely on a sheen of oil. Nuzzle up tight, an impossible invasion. The entrance was so small, and he was so bursting big, bigger than he'd ever been. Push. Push. An elastic giving sensation. Push again. A rubber collar, spreading. A – a – a . . .

A plop. My God, he was in! The head of his cock was past the ring. Muscles closed around his cock's neck, but he was in and there was nothing that was going to stop him going the rest of the way. The eye of his cock was staring up a long dark tight passage, assessing the cruel glee it was about to feel.

Stuart took Virginia by the bones of her hips, fingers hooked into delicate hollows, and he pulled . . .

There was a long divine dragging slithery sensation, and he'd done it! Even if he stopped right then, he'd done it. He'd buggered a woman!

But he didn't stop. His cock took insane control, making him thrust and pull back and thrust and pull back and thrust and thrust . . . and he came. He came a glorious come, pumping thick and hot, shuddering and groaning aloud.

Stuart left her there, tied to the stool, and went for a shower. She was in the same position when he returned. It was as if he hadn't done it, except for the snail-trail down the inside of her thigh and the glistening of her still-parted sphincter.

He untied her and retied her, hands behind her back. He had her give him a blow-job like that, with no help from him. It should have taken an age, but she was good at what she did. Her mouth started soft and loose and slow and noisy, gobbling and wobbling on him. Once he was urgent-stiff again, she clamped firmly and accelerated, nodding fast, faster, fastest. His cock's head rippled across the roof of her mouth, and he came again.

It wasn't even noon yet.

There was compassion and affection in him. That was bad. He had to absolve himself, a little.

"Get dressed. I'm going to buy you a coat."

"You don't have to."

"I want to. I don't like the way you look in that one. I want you to look sexy – for *me*."

The shopping concourse below the Sheraton links with another, and another. You can wander for miles beneath Toronto. In February, you're grateful.

He bought her a short black plastic coat, lined with fake fur, and a pair of boots to match. *She* didn't choose them. What *he* liked, *she* liked. It wasn't until they passed a jeweller's that she showed any interest in anything.

Stuart asked her, "What are you looking at?"

"Those earrings. They're lovely."

"They look like the ones you're wearing, but smaller."

"Yes."

"You really like them?"

"Yes."

"Then they're yours."

She didn't even tell him he didn't have to.

He told her he'd take her home in a cab again, but she said she had something to do downtown. She asked him, "Tomorrow?"

He nodded and turned on his heel before sanity made him change his mind.

She arrived in his suite wearing her glossy new coat.

"I have a surprise for you."

"You have?"

She posed, one leg turned in front of the other, a shoulder drooping, and opened her coat. Her being naked under it didn't surprise him at all. He'd half expected that. What shocked him was the earrings he'd bought her. She was wearing them – one through each freshly pierced nipple.

Stuart felt a twinge of nausea that was instantly washed away in a flood of lust. He took her on her back, on the scratchy carpet, thrusting into her frantic as a teen, arched up from his waist, his eyes feasting on the mutilations that she'd endured for *his* sake.

"How on earth did you get that done?" he asked, once he was calm and drained.

"There's a place in a side street, between King and Queen. They do piercing and tattooing. Should I get a tattoo?"

He thought of her mound, shaved bald and reading, "Stuart's".

"No," he said. "Let's go buy you a dress."

When her nipples had healed enough that he dared touch them he used those rings a lot. He steered her by them, and used them to tug on, and once held fistfuls of ice on them, to claw the chill *inside* her flesh. Stuart took her in every position he could dream up, tied and free, orally, anally, between her breasts and vaginally.

When he told her that the next day would be his last in Toronto for a while, she didn't cry. She simply told him that she really needed to borrow five hundred dollars.

That was a relief. Five hundred was cheap, and it would constitute a "pay-off". It transformed their relationship from "emotional" to "commercial". He counted out ten fifties and waited for her to tell him she couldn't make it for the next day, but she didn't. She just confirmed, "Nine-thirty?"

She arrived with the vee of her coat showing a thick woollen sweater. It was the first substantial garment that he hadn't bought her that he'd seen her wearing.

When she took off her coat the sweater was very short – covering half her midriff, and she was naked from it to her boots. She posed again, but not like a model. She put her fists on her bare hips, spread her thighs and thrust her pubes at him.

"Does this look nice? This is what I needed the money for."

His bile rose again. She'd had another piercing – the lips of her sex. A row of tiny golden rings glittered at him, four to each side. There was a thin gold chain threaded through them, sealing her. A tiny gold padlock dangled between her thighs.

"Here's the key. There's just one. It's yours."

Stuart had to force himself to come in her mouth.

That night he had no work. He walked the frigid streets, head down into ice-particles that travelled horizontally, until he found her home. There was no answer. He took note of her address, returned to his hotel, made a tiny parcel of the silver key and three one-hundred dollar bills, and mailed it.

It was two months before they called him back to Toronto. The parcel was waiting at the Sheraton's reception, "Return to sender. Addressee moved. No forwarding address."

There was no message waiting at the office. The phone didn't ring at six-forty.

The next morning he scoured the streets between King and Queen, looking for a "place that did piercing, and tattooing".

He found one just after noon, with dusty windows and curly cardboard displays of digital watches.

"I'm looking for a woman, a customer of yours."

The gnome with tobacco stains on his moustache said, "Yes?"

"Her name is Virginia. I don't know her last name. You did some – work."

"Tattoos or piercing?"

"Piercing."

"Ears, nose, nips, navel or pussy-lips?"

"Er – nipples, and er – lips."

"Skinny woman? Big boobs? Red hair?"

"That's her. Do you have an address? She moved you see, and . . ."

"Against policy, I don't have it, anyway."

Stuart pulled out a fifty.

"I really don't got it, but I tell you what – she's coming in for some more work, today, three o'clock. You want to come back?"

"Could I wait?"

"Sure. Come in back. There's magazines, and I'll get you some coffee."

The magazines were all "trade". The little man brought bitter coffee in a mug with a Canadian Pacific Railways logo. Customers came and were ushered by an enormous fat man into tiny curtained booths. Sometimes needles buzzed, sometimes there was the sharp smell of alcohol and the occasional, "ouch".

There was more coffee at one and two. It was hot in that room. That – and the antiseptic – and the thought of what was going on in the booths, made Stuart start to feel nauseous. It was a struggle to check his watch. At three the little man came back again and took a seat opposite Stuart.

"She's late," Stuart said, mumbling on a thick tongue. "You ain't been so nice to Miss Virginia, 'ave you?"

"Huh?"

"Miss Virginia. She made a commitment to you. You dumped her."

Stuart tried to stand but his knees were jelly. "What do you – you mean?"

"You should get back with her. She'd like that."

"I – I brought the key."

"That's nice. Tell her yourself then."

"Wha? She's . . .?"

The fat man jerked the curtains to a booth open. Virginia was there, standing naked . . . No, sagging naked. She was hanging from . . . Stuart's gorge rose. Virginia had been pierced again, a lot. There were rings through the flesh at the backs of her wrists, and behind her neck, and her ankles and . . . and they were all on cords – cords that hung down from a framework high against the ceiling.

The fat man pulled on a dangling cord. Virginia's head lifted. She smiled at Stuart. "Hello Stuart. You've come back to me?"

The fat man grunted, "Yes, he's come back to you, Virginia."

Stuart toppled off his chair. The gnome produced a pair of tailor's shears and started to cut up the legs of Stuart's pants. The fat man jingled a palmful of golden rings. His other hand held a pair of peculiarly shaped pliers.

TAROT

Florence Dugas

translated by Maxim Jakubowski

Noon was gently moving towards two o'clock. As it was already summer time, no one could tell: somewhere in the world it's always noon.

It was as if the sun had given her a sign and she hadn't returned to work.

The sound of her heels against the stone of the road and the side pavement is like a clamour of victory. She supplies a rhythm to the city, and her thin, long legs move, map and order its topography, like a defiant army marching ahead under the new found sun, celebrating the coming of spring. It is good to feel the heat spread across her skin, caressing her knees like two warm hands, even moving up between her thighs now no longer under the protection of nylon. The sun almost draws a crown of gold around her head, as if she is a chosen one. From time to time she even swings her head either way to the side, like a racehorse in heat. Saying "yes" and "no" to her invisible mount while her heavy stream of hair undulates across her back. She straightens her back, holding her stomach in and the flow of her hair swims gloriously in motion.

She walks as if leading a victory parade.

"Parade." The very word echoes studiously across her brain, to the rhythm of her heels, and it amuses her to invent more meanings for it. To parade is more than just walking at random, no mere promenade where you never know where the next step leads. "To parade is to move like God across his garden," Brisset used to say. It even makes her look a little drunk, dizzy from her newly found freedom. Walking along, parading, as if she were about to become the heroine of some medieval ballad sung by a troubadour below the window of a captive king. All this sun is so unusual. Walking as she does, head high, she can no longer hear Paris surrounding her, just the sound of her heels clicking along; nor can she see the cars and passers-by, just the winged Genie of the Bastille, flying high up there close to Icarus. She is on parade: she's come out of her shell, the whole world is on offer to her, her steps are conquering space, taking her into a whole new dimension.

The clock on the Gare de Lyon betrays an impossible hour, that even the sun denies.

"The next train to leave? Well, you've got the Paris-Vintimille, in ten minutes. Seats? Oh, as many as you want. Non smoking? Isn't the weather lovely? The sky is so blue. Yes, I understand."

The railways guy sitting behind the immediate departures window is actually not bad-looking at all.

It's true, there are few people on the train. In her compartment, just five men: four of them are playing cards while the fifth further down appears to be sleeping already, with just his neck and short greying hair visible from her vantage point.

With all those empty seats available, she chooses to sit on the right hand side, so she can enjoy the sun for the rest of the afternoon.

She feels blandly happy, sunny, watching all the stationary cows outside pass by.

The train does not stop before Valence.

She walks out onto the platform to get some movement into her legs. A two-minute stop. Up there, the sun hasn't moved at all but the heat is now more oppressive, a sign they are further south, in the Midi. She can feel the sun rising ever so stealthily up her thighs, so much more aggressively than in Paris, and this metaphor first makes her smile, then causes her to feel dreamy.

She shakes her head. "I'm becoming delirious," she thinks.

But on the other hand she feels ever so free.

She returns to the compartment from the other end, and walks down the rows of seats, as the train begins speeding up again, swaying dizzily between the wooden seats.

The man with grey hair is not sleeping. He is watching her navigate her passage, struggling against the train's increasing motion, as if he were looking through her and not even seeing her. The possibility that somehow between Paris and Valence, on this stolen afternoon, she has physically dematerialized amuses her when she thinks of it. Is the man not really looking at her? He is quite handsome, in a prematurely greying way. His eyes are the same colour as his hair, pale grey veined with black – a man of marble. As she passes him, she gazes at his hands, laid out flat on the table. Quite beautiful hands which in her imagination she is already placing within her intimate theatre, the hands of a pianist, or there again a surgeon's hands ready to sew someone's wound up, or even a pair of warm and dry hands alighting on her knees, sliding up her skirt, moving into her underwear and grabbing her bum cheeks, hands capable of measuring her arse so much more than the sun outside.

She shakes her head, both amused and annoyed by her own clichéd fantasy.

The four men are still busy with their card game. As she passes them, she sees it is a tarot deck, the same high numbers and cards, but something catches her attention: the images on the cards aren't the ones she knows, the end-of-century scenes so familiar to the tarot. She imperceptibly slows down, still moving ahead though and turns back to look again, not quite brave enough to stand still. She's right: the characters on the cards are mostly undressed, unlike the images she's familiar with. The man nearest to her, an ebony-coloured African man, still holds four cards in his hand – two small squares as well as an eleven and a twelve: on the first one, the characters are sitting around a picnic scene imitating Le Déjeuner sur l'Herbe, the woman sitting is naked, but the man lying down also is, as another who is leaning towards her as if to bite her breasts is getting undressed. She has

difficulty seeing the other card, obscured as it is by the man's
thick black thumb, but again the woman in the boat is nude. On
the twelve, she can only see the upper half of the card: a ball
somewhere in the background, but on the right hand side the
image of a man seemingly offering his cock deferentially to two
sitting women whose clothes have been partly pulled open, one of
the women is thrusting her peach-coloured glove-covered hand
towards the imposing virile member. The man whose cock it is
has grey hair, and it makes her think straight away of the silent
passenger in the seat a few rows back.

The negro throws the twelve down, and another of the men
adds the twenty. She just has the time to glimpse the image of
four men sitting at a table playing cards, all in the buff, while a
woman under the table is seemingly sucking off the player on the
left. The illustrator has frozen the scene just as her mouth is
about to devour his mushroom head and her cheeks are delicately
deformed by the intrusion.

She shrugs her shoulders. Scenes from a brothel, she reckons,
no doubt a Belle Époque set of cards.

She walks back to her seat, and distractedly watches the landscape roll by, sky moving between white and blue. The Rhône river
flows heavily by, moving between nuclear power stations. At any
rate, the stations do not affect the area's luminosity.

She feels movement to her left and turns. The man with grey hair
is already there, looking over her shoulder. And like earlier, he
has the same distant and detached look, as if his eyes are fixed on a
point some ten centimetres behind her.

"May I?" he says, sitting next to her.

He definitely has a vague English accent.

He calmly pulls up the arm separating their two seats, deliberately abolishing all distance between them, or any form of
misunderstanding.

"May I . . ." These are the only words he says, and her quiet
agreement, as she does not object, is all he needs as approval, as if
those two words and the unspoken answer will justify all that will
follow.

The man's right hand skims by her neck while his left hand
takes hold of her knee. His skin is just as she expected: warm and
dry.

He allows her just a few seconds more just so she might imagine what is about to happen. His fingers tread ever so lightly across her skin, just as if he were caressing water without creating a stir across its surface.

His fragrance is both pleasant and discreet. She doesn't know why, but his smell reminds her of Louis XV furniture, burnished wood tables and pieces.

For a short while he doesn't move, his face just inches from hers, his hand almost motionless on her knee, his fingers delicately skimming her neck.

The dark clouds inside his grey eyes make him look like a phantom.

And he finally slowly bends over towards her and kisses her.

She holds on to him, slides her own hands under the fashionable grey jacket he is wearing, takes hold of his shirt, disturbs his tie . . .

The hand on her knee begins a slow and deliberate journey upwards along her thigh and cups her cunt, forcing itself against the already wet silk. The man pulls the thin knickers to one side of her gash, his fingers lingering against the soft and delicate lips with assurance. "With a sense of contained violence," she thinks aloud. And the mental image of her cunt in his grasp makes her smile and hold herself even more open. She allows her hand to slip under the man's belt, and through the thin material of his trousers grabs hold of his hardening virility, an initial contact that surprises her in its brazenness. She pulls on the zip of his flies and extricates the jutting cock now pulsing against her fingers, just as she leans her own body slightly backwards so that the man's hands might have easier access to her stomach and, she hopes, her arse.

They caress each other for several minutes. He inserts two fingers deep into the swamp of her cunt, two very long fingers with short, invisible nails deep into the pit of her stomach, exploring her with even more avidity than his cock could, seeking what she desires with almost feminine science.

He has no need to change the pressure of his fingers against her neck. She leans over of her own accord towards the cock now surging through the folds of grey material and takes it into her mouth. It feels fresh, almost cold. First the thick, split apricot which she surrounds with her tongue, bathes in her spit, then the rest of his mast as far as she can take it. Three quarters of it almost, her mouth spread-eagled by this meat of desire, to the point of gagging against this dangerous weapon heading straight for her innards. She retreats to catch her breath and impales her mouth anew against the blood-engorged tip of his cock, torn between the need to suck him forever and forever, to fill herself with his wooden citrus flavour, and the sheer craving to feel him flow wildly inside her mouth, waves breaking against the back of her throat, and the freedom to drink all of him.

The man then pulls his fingers out of her heaving cunt and, taking advantage of her leaning back position, moves them, still coated with her vaginal secretions, towards her arse and digs them both into her sphincter. She buckles, rears against the fingers now stretching her wide and, doing so, opens herself even more to his rough caress, and when the man's thumb at the front now starts applying pressure to her clitoris, she comes violently, feels her arsehole spasm against the fingers now burrowing deep inside her, and only the cock now embedded in her mouth prevents her from screaming.

He allows her to enjoy the moment. His fingers are still digging deep into the very fundament of her arse. His thumb is held hard, unmoving, against her inflamed clitoris. He gently pulls her by her hair and allows her face to rest against his chest, while she gasps for air.

Once the contractions slow down, he slides his fingers out of her and pulls her up against him as he moves onto the seat in front of her, between her splayed legs, and forcefully pulls her down onto him. Initially she fears she won't be able to accommodate him, that she's not open enough – he's so much more larger than anything she's had inside her before. His cock is still growing as he breaches her, his head brushing her labia aside as his shaft sinks deeply into her. Inside the hot furnace of her cunt, the man's cock feels as cold as ice. She bites her lips to avoid screaming when she feels the cock assault her back wall and she takes hold of the top of the seat facing her and, seizing it desperately, allows herself to sway wildly, allowing his cock to plough every inch of her insides as she holds back her pain. The man, his hands gripping the sides of her rear, helps her rise and then again and again brings her down onto him, every single time deeper and deeper, as if she were a cave with no ending.

A few metres away from her, she can only glimpse the heads of the other four men every time she rises above the seat: they are still playing cards, oblivious to what is happening to her.

For a brief moment she realises she would like to feel him flow inside her stomach, mingling his sperm with all that is floating within her, then the thought is violently abolished because she comes again, ferociously, wantonly, literally screwed on to this cock that is splitting her apart, piercing her very heart.

She is gasping for breath when the man's hands let go of her bum and move under her shirt, partly freeing her breasts from the push-up bra, lengthily caressing her hard, sensitive nipples, enjoying himself, then pinching her breasts hard to bring her back to reality from her swoon. Through the waves of ecstasy she is also confusedly angry at him for having discovered she enjoys the combination of pain and pleasure.

The man withdraws from her, settles to her left and folds his still-bulging cock so wet from the very secretions of her stomach into his trousers. Will she ever know the taste of his sperm, or just this lingering smell of wet rosewood?

His smile is muted, almost affectionate but distant again as he moves back to his seat, and the last thing she sees of him is his straight neck and his short grey hair.

She frees herself from the wet knickers now cutting into her crotch, and shudders, face against the window pane. She watches the Rhône outside. An old piece of poetry by Victor Hugo comes into her mind: "The noisy river flows, a fast and yellow flow . . ."

The heat of the sun, the coolness of the glass against her cheeks, and the dying vibrations inside her stomach now peaceful, moving away, drying up . . .

She doesn't wake up in Avignon, nor in Marseilles. When she opens her eyes again, she can still hear the subconscious echo in the air of the voice which has just announced their arrival in Saint Raphael. It is now evening, and only the sporadic lights of the approaching station puncture the darkness.

She had thought of going to Nice, but why not Saint Raphael; she's never been before.

She is now alone in the compartment. She rises, still unsteady on her legs – she'd fallen asleep in an awkward position and her left foot has fallen asleep – and moves forward with a slight limp, lacking grace, towards the exit and almost topples over as she walks down the train's steps. Blood flows back into her brain, the vertigo fades . . . She takes a few steps forward on solid ground and the dizziness returns.

"I must be hungry," she thinks. And the act of saying so makes her hungry. She walks towards the station's exit, reckoning that like with all stations there must be a bar, a bistro nearby, some Arab grocery.

But all there is nearby is a Rolls Royce parked close to the pavement, a very old model with the driver's seat open to the air and the back shrouded by dark opaque windows. The chauffeur, holding his cap in hand, turns towards her.

"Mademoiselle," he says, "we were waiting for you. Would you please . . ."

She is so surprised she allows herself to be led, just two metres of pavement between freedom and the green English leather seats of the luxury car, and the door closes silently behind her. Immediately, it's night behind the dark windows, banishing even the glow of the street lights, allowing barely pale haloes to survive, just like the mad stars in Van Gogh's skies.

The car is driven in total silence; it could well be stationary, just a hint of vibration betraying its motion. They travel for a long time, and the young woman who is hungry and thirsty and badly needs to pee, is now in a bad mood. They stop for a red light and she tries to get out but the doors are locked from the outside. She raps her knuckles on the glass separating her from the driver. The man's neck doesn't budge.

The Rolls-Royce leaves Saint Raphael and takes a small, winding road that rises above sea level and leads deep into the hinterlands. A long time. Hunger. Thirst . . .

At last, the car slows down as it runs parallel to a high wall that leads them to an intricate metal gate headed by a mess of white metal arrows. The door opens by itself, no doubt electrically controlled, unless there is an invisible caretaker in attendance . . .

Screeching across a gravel path, the car drives up to a small castle, one of the many Modern Style monstrosities that the Côte d'Azur has given birth to over the past century, and comes to a halt in front of its steps. The stylish chauffeur gets out and ceremoniously opens the door.

In a rush, the sound of the early cicadas of spring invades the Rolls Royce.

She alights, intrigued, worried, still angry. A man stands there, on the second step and, astonished, she recognizes the grey-haired stranger from the train. How in hell could he have reached this place before her?

"Please accept our apologies," he says. "You must be quite tired?"

He ceremoniously takes her hand. He is now wearing a smoky-grey lounge suit, the same colour as his eyes.

"Come," he says. "We've prepared some food for you."

She agrees to enter the castle, although she also knows this might prove a mistake, that maybe she shouldn't, now that the falling sun has retreated with all its elementary seduction, and the menace of night is ready to take over.

Once inside, she looks back, intuition or ultimate temptation. The moon is full, and shines over a freshly mowed lawn at the heart of which stands a white marble statue, maybe of Venus, or even Diana the Huntress without her slings and arrows, the languorous shape of the Goddess bathing in the moonlight.

The young woman turns back and, with quiet determination, enters the house.

"If you wish to freshen up," the man says, pointing to a door.

"Yes, I'd like to spray my war paint on again," she jokes, repressing the anxiety quickly rising inside her throat.

As she washes her hands, she gazes at the reassuring image in the mirror: she is still pretty, still looks fresh despite all those hours on the train; some would even say the darker shade below her eyes was an added bonus.

"What a face," she says though, almost out of habit.

A snack? On a small table at the centre of the Art Deco salon with its delicate furniture, she can see all the things she likes: patisseries, fruit, finger-sized delicacies, lemonade – she is still at an age where you are allowed to enjoy sweet, sugary things. In the meantime, the stranger is busy starting a fire inside the big chimney breast, kneeling in front of the initial orange flames longer than he would normally do, exposing his slim neck to her gaze, no doubt aware she is full of questions and that he is in no hurry to supply answers.

★   ★   ★

He finally rises from his prone position, while she finishes biting into a thin slice of exquisite tarte.

"I will take you to your room," he says. "You'll find something you can wear for dinner. Take your time. If you want to take a bath, just tell Nora, and she will arrange it."

With his hand, he points to a corner of the room where a young mulatto woman in a domestic's uniform is standing, straight and silent. She has pale grey eyes, shining in the light of the nearby flames like the eyes of a cat.

She hadn't even heard her enter the room.

"We dine at eleven," he adds.

They walk up a wide pink marbled set of stairs, a bit too ostentatious for her liking. Then, after passing through a red vestibule, down a long corridor punctuated by doors numbered One to Nine. At the other end, there is another set of stairs probably leading up. They stop at number Seven. The maid opens, and moves back to let her go in.

The room is spacious, with tasteful furniture. Not one piece of furniture is contemporary, but every single one, from the straight geometry of the dresser, to the make up table with its crystalline mirror and the bed shrouded with delicate millinery, appears to be brand-new, although they visibly were created in the 1920s.

On the wall, a Millet-styled print: three farm labourers resting in a field, enjoying a drink, while a woman awaits them, sitting against a haystack; it's unclear what she might be waiting for as, unlike any character in a picture by the Barbizon artist, she is fully naked and when you take a closer look, her hands though held against her knees are tied together with a thin piece of string.

This sets her thinking again of the four men who were playing cards on the train, the same sense of discontinuity between the image you would expect and the more disturbing one . . .

"Do you wish to take a bath?" the maid asks.

There is no trace of the Caribbean in her voice.

"Yes, please . . ."

The bathroom that connects to the room is huge, all green marble, all three walls covered by mirrors, as is, curiously enough, the ceiling. Exotic plants, suspended from shelves and metal stands, spread a delicate perfume of wet earth and heavy flowers throughout the the room. The bath tub, carved out of a single piece of dark marble, and held up by sphynx-like feet, is positively enormous.

The girl runs the water, pouring in perfumed oil that rises in bubbles, the strong fragrance of which blends easily with that of the green plants across the room. The perfume rising through the steam now obscuring the mirrors transports her back to that sense of dizziness she had experienced on the train, like feeling slightly drunk on an empty stomach.

The maid comes towards her, unbuttons her shirt, unhooks her bra and then the skirt. She does not remark on the fact she is wearing no knickers. The young woman allows her to do so, suddenly assaulted by tiredness, or at any rate using the tiredness as an excuse to surrender to whatever is about to happen to her.

In the water, it feels to her as if she is swimming in the immensity of the tub. Above her, she sees the shrouded reflection of a young blonde woman in the misted-up mirror, her skin ever so pale, like a white mummy floating inside a green, marble coffin, the blue grey of her eyes lost in the distance. But the steam rises and finally wipes out this lazy landscape of curves.

The maid allows her for a long period to soak in all the fragrances that the heat is now breaking up. Finally, she comes back and hands her a Japanese robe, pale green, embroidered with birds of paradise.

"Do you want me to give you a massage?" she asks. "The bath will wash the journey away, and the massage will wash the bath away. After, I shall apply your make-up. The Commander has given me very precise instructions."

She lets herself go, agile fingers skimming across her skin with exquisite softness, slowly untwisting her nerves, polishing her muscles, effectively providing her with strength again after her energy has been sapped by the bath. The maid has her lie down over a folding table once she has slipped out of the robe. First, on her stomach, she is massaged from her neck down to her heels unavoidably feeling something stirring inside her when the long, brown fingers knead her arse and thighs. But she'd rather believe it's just a feeling of comfort. She almost falls asleep anyway, listening to the gurgling sounds of the emptying bath.

She is then turned round. Above her, the mirror is clearing up. The young Creole girl is working her shoulders, the birth of her neck, grazing her breasts whose tips are hardening, not that she notices as her hands lower themselves towards her midriff, before moving back to polish her nipples from time to time. Her brown hands make the extreme winter pallor of her blonde skin appear almost indecent.

The young woman looks at herself in the ceiling mirror, and from her perspective, the mulatto girl massaging her appears closer to her than she in fact is, as if it were her mouth, her lips massaging her and not her fingers. But very soon, it is actually her darker lips that are now attaching themselves to her taut nipples, licking then sucking on her hard tips, racing across her tremulous skin, her pretty *café au lait* face soon ensconced between her thighs. All she can see is the back of her head, a mass of short, dense curls when the maid's mouth alights on her cunt, and the masseuse's tongue separates the delicate lips of her opening, skims across her dilated clit. She feels as if she wants to come that very moment if only to release all the tension building up inside her since she walked into the house. With her hands, she grasps the short dark curls and pulls the girl's face hard against her stomach – black against white – her lithe tongue butterflying over her clit now feeling more forceful, more incisive.

The young maid pulls her body down towards the edge of the table, both her legs now winging over the sides, the indefatigable tongue squirming around her red-hot button, plunging down into her wet vagina, tip-toeing across her anus and delicately forcing it open – she has never had the courage to tell any of her previous lovers how much she likes to be sodomised by a hard, burning tongue, all this while her long bronzed fingers keep on playing with her breasts. Finally she comes, no longer able to restrain her voice, flooding the mulatto girl's face with her juices. The maid rises, wiping her mouth, her chin, her nose with a towel and, curiously enough, smiles not at her but towards the mirror on the ceiling. The thought that someone has just witnessed the whole scene through a one-way mirror dawns on her with absolute certainty. What other traps are to follow? She slides off the massage table, pulls the young maid by her hair as she was doing earlier, and forces her to kneel before her and presses her face against her cunt, the heavy-lipped and violent mouth against her small blonde bush.

"Drink," she says.

And she slowly pees into the open, willing mouth that doesn't miss a single drop, still watching the ceiling as she does so, now smiling at the mirror, pleased to be conveying in such a way to the master of the house that by defiling his slave, she is resisting his will.

She is then made up, slowly, a bit too gaudily to her taste. She is then given a long evening dress, a glossy couture piece with classical lines that Madame Grey would have much appreciated. Once inside the formal dress, she feels like a marble statue sandwiched inside a skin of blackness, the exquisite pallor of her skin enhanced by the night black of the material.

No underwear or lingerie underneath the dramatic dress. The silk adheres to her breasts, her arse and her stomach; the sudden crispness of the wrap awakens her nipples.

"You are beautiful," says the young mulatto girl. "I'm happy the Commander has brought you here."

Once again the stairs. The maid guides her from one door to another. She hears a rumour of conversation; she knows that very soon she will be told where she is. She is both curious and worried and slows her steps.

The mulatto girl swings the door open and invites her in.

First, it's the intense light. There are four or five men in dinner jackets and six or seven elegantly attired women; they all briefly fall silent and watch her walk towards them. Meanwhile the grey-haired stranger moves in her direction, takes her by the hand and smiles, putting her at ease.

"You are quite ravishing," he says. And truly looks as if he believes it.

She smiles back, still cautiously, but holds on to him, surrounded as she is by all these unknown faces.

"Friends," he says, with a semi-circular gesture of his hand. "All charming people, as you will see."

Why does he not introduce her to anyone? Why isn't she even provided with a name, a surname?

Right then a servant attired in quite incongruous Louis XV style calls out loudly that food is served and they all march on into the immense dining room, where a very long rectangular-shaped table dominates the proceedings.

The plates are exquisitely sober, the silver knives and forks and crystal glasses shine wildly beneath the glow of the candelabras.

The man is at the top of the table and indicates she should sit to his left. Facing her is a very beautiful woman whose splendour has seen better days, a thousand wrinkles smiling, a thousand small pains betraying her long and cruel past history.

On her left is the the youngest man in the room; he is younger than her, his face and skin barely out of teenagehood, radiant, almost effeminate. He is all smiles and his conversation artfully banal.

The meal offers all that Provence can supply, from the most refined to the most colourful dish. Her taste buds sing along. Stylish servants see that their glasses are never empty and provide the right wine for each course: a sublime Cassis white followed by a racy Gigondas from the Aix vineyards, and soon champagne, small bubbles adhering under her gaze to the shape of the cut glasses. Very soon, she experiences a new kind of drunkenness, like an aggravated echo of her dizziness on the train. The feeling surrounds her like a scarf; she feels she is burning, her legs are like cotton wool, her breath short. Her breasts rub anxiously against the silk of the dress, her tips harden again under the black material, becoming quite visible. She has the impression that all present are watching her, evaluating her, judging her, as if the woman facing her, eating her strawberries and drinking her champagne is already promising her a whole set of caresses and indulgences. She feels as if her stomach is incandescent, a combination of fire and water, and the wide smile of the woman in front of her indicates she is aware of it, that she recognizes the torment inside her body, that behind the combined fragrance of the wines and the food spread across the now crumpled table-cloth, she has caught an early whiff of the purple taste of her inner juices. Right then, a foot deliberately brushes against hers, caressing her ankle, gliding across her leg and the silk sheathing her. She isn't sure if it is the smiling woman or her attentive host or maybe the gauche young man on her left. The champagne bubbles float upwards to the surface of the crystal glasses, and her eyes are transfixed by the thin rising columns, as if she were the one drowning inside the glass and her oxygen was running out . . .

When they all rise to make their way to the salon, she stumbles.

"Come," says the woman, holding her arm, "Are you feeling unwell? You must lie down for a quarter of an hour, allow all that alcohol to settle . . ."

Together, they climb the monumental stairs.

"I'm in number Seven," she stammers.

"No need to go that far," the woman says. "I'm in One."

The room is predominantly green, with an array of scattered heavy brown curtains; the bed is covered with a dark green satin quilt, which feels so wonderfully cool when she settles her cheek against it and allows herself to relax. The woman helps her lie down, pulling her shoes off, caressing her thin ankles, taking them into her hands as if she were about to handcuff them.

But the young girl is still overcome by that dizzy feeling and knows she would allow anything to happen.

She tries to overcome the feeling, she turns her head around, sees a painting on the wall, attempts to focus on its image, to capture some sense of reality from the shimmering fog in which the painting floats.

It's a small canvas, like the country scene in the picture in room Seven, in which a court jester is offering a rose to a comedic maid – the very image of card One in the Tarot – but the woman here has pulled her skirt up and is displaying a regal, sculptured arse to him. On closer inspection, it appears that the jester is not about to offer the rose to the young woman but is readying to pin the thorny flower straight into her satin globes. It even looks as if he has begun punishing her: a long, pink cut already crisscrosses her right arse cheek, and petals lie on the ground following the first blow, and the girl's face reflects pain and submission.

This is when she realizes that the older woman has folded her dress back up all the way to her thighs, and is now twirling the blonde curls of her pubis with her fingers, even briefly inserting a finger into her gash, then smelling it with half a smile before licking the wet finger clean, and returning her hand below to stroke her swollen cunt.

The woman suddenly stands and walks over to the wall where she rings a call bell. Then leans back over the prostrate young girl, lips grazing her mouth, skimming the breasts barely concealed by the crumpled silk of the dress, lingering over the uncovered stomach and the thighs that part automatically under her caress.

There is a discreet knock at the door,

"Come in," she says, without even looking up.

It's one of the servants who had served at the dinner table; he has a peasant's wide and tawny features, which she had earlier found almost comical beneath the powdered wig he is no longer wearing. But he is still attired in the Louis XV outfit meant to emphasize his thin waist, but which on him has the contrary effect, highlighting his thick muscles, the incredibly wide shoulders and the lack of neck. He is a heavy-set man; his ferocious eyes remind her of a dog.

"Come here," she says. "Take your uniform off. That's good. Show us your cock, now. So, what do you think, my dear?"

The object emerging from the salmon-coloured silk pants is just like the man himself: short and massive. Sitting on the edge of the bed, the woman takes hold of the purple glans between two fingers, just as earlier she had been handling the strawberries. With her nail she gently pulls on the cock's crumpled surplus skin and the shaft begins to grow. Short but very thick, no more than fifteen centimetres long but so thick she has to use both hands to circle it. The prone young girl sees it all as if in a cloud, only the painting on the wall the focus of her attention, but another part of her is also aware that she is about to be breached by this almost unreal object. The mushroom head is dark purple, the blue black veins bulge, the hard brown shaft pointing towards her emerging from dirty pink boxers shorts, the whole thing seems more animal than human.

"Fuck her now," the older woman cursorily orders.

The domestic positions himself between the young girl's thighs, spreads them wide and places her feet high up on his shoulders, his thick shiny cock lurking at her entrance and gradually forces himself in. Slowly, his cock plunges in, her diameter expanding obscenely as if it were literally sucking in this monstrous cock, and she finally feels it head butting her inner walls as the silk of his trousers and the rough touch of his pubic hair rub against her thighs. She comes immediately – the tension was too strong, the expectation too demanding.

Now the domestic methodically ploughs inside her with brute force and she cries out repeatedly, the inebriation of her orgasm blending with the alcohol vapours, thrusting her ever higher on the scales of sheer pleasure. She can't help crying, throwing her body forward, impaling herself even deeper, opening herself wider. At the same time, she feels ashamed to be enjoying this weird cock so much, and the shames doubles her pleasure, as if her being whored in this improvised way gives her latitude to scream like no other man has made her scream before, to give herself like she has never given herself before.

Prompted by the woman still sitting close to her, the domestic withdraws from her and with two sharp movements of his wrist he jerks himself off, long creamy jets streaming across the now forever soiled black dress, thick snail trails of sperm jetting from his bursting cock and landing all the way up to her neck.

The woman dismisses him with a single gesture.

Once again, she leans over towards the still breathless young girl, who is on the brink of tears as her orphaned cunt still gapes open, mumbling under her breath like a fish out of water, begging for the return of the cock that stretched her so and she kisses her. The taste of her tongue is sharp, warm and clever.

She then guides the young girl to the nearby bathroom and undresses her. "Arms up," as if to a child. Helping her out of the long soiled sheath of the dress, pulling it above her head, and then the blissful feel of water unendingly running down her neck, her back, her breasts.

Then she brings her back to the large bed of crumpled satin, her body so deathly pale against the green surface, and dries her, methodically mapping every contour of her body, behind her ears even or between her splayed toes . . .

The woman indicates the silk dress, now all crumpled up at the foot of the bed.

"Won't be much use again," she says.

From a dresser, she pulls out a maid's outfit, almost the same as . . . What was her name? Nora? – was wearing earlier. A black, straight lined skirt, a black shirt and a white apron with an embroidered pocket at the front. Before she is allowed to slip the uniform on, the older woman helps her roll on a pair of hold-up opaque black stockings and, finally, hands her a pair of dainty, zippered small boots.

The woman quickly separates her hair into thick plaits and arranges a faultless chignon, with just three or four hairpins, almost a work of art.

Inside the apron's pocket, there is a key.

"It's a pass," the ageless woman explains. "It allows you access to every room on this floor or the next. Come, girl. It's all up to you now. You must prove to us we can trust you."

And with a gentle slap on her bum, she dismisses her from the room.

In the corridor, the young girl hesitates a short while. Walk down again?

With the pass, she opens the next door, number Three.

It is empty.

On the wall a painting depicting a city scene with three young women wearing fancy hats, all holding each other by the arm, but totally naked. Somewhere behind them, another woman seen from the back is walking away, same hat, same nudity. She appears to be following a soldier whose silhouette can be glimpsed in the distance.

The three women are aligned by height, from left to right. Curiously, the shortest one sports the heavier breasts, the next one's are pear shaped, well proportioned and the tallest woman's are barely the size of two small apples, high on her chest, tiny.

"The tarots," she says to herself.

She leaves the room just as another identically dressed maid comes running.

"Ah, there you are, hurry. Number Twenty has called again."

Off they go; she follows instinctively, entranced by the madness of the place, down the corridor, up a spiral staircase, then through another passageway where they come across two other maids, one of whom is Nora, the only one whose name she actually knows, standing outside the door marked Twenty.

"What took you so long?" Nora said.

She knocks on the door and turns the handle while doing so, just as a loud "Come in!" reaches their ears. Inside are four men playing cards, with a fifth man watching them – the grey-haired man from the train, the Commander.

The young girl barely has time to register the fact that these are the same four men, one of whom is an ebony-skinned negro, the tarot players from the Paris-Nice TGV train – was it just this past afternoon? – when the grey-eyed man calls to her:

"Come, girls, come!"

Flabbergasted, she watches as her three companions kneel

before three of the men and, without even being asked, burrow inside their respective trousers and quickly gobble up the still soft cocks they discover there.

"Come here, young one," the man insists.

And now she finds herself on her knees by the black man, but the cock surging through his flies is already hard. It's like a long ebony stick, shining like polished wood under the light of the room's lamps, its skin taut like bark, an endless mast whose girth is fortunately moderate so she doesn't have to dislocate her jaw to take it all into her mouth. However, the cock soon reaches the very back of her mouth and brings tears to her eyes, a sudden burst of nausea she represses as she moves her lips back down to the cock's head. But soon she finds the right rhythm, the adequate depth.

"Keep at it," says a voice.

The man exudes an animal smell, strong, tenacious. It occurs to her that she could well be sucking a horse or a wild beast. With the hand not holding on to his cards, as none of the men has stopped playing, he occasionally applies pressure to her neck, precisely communicating the changes in rhythm he wants her to follow. He holds her by the chignon, forcing her to first slow down and savour every one of the centimetres she swallows and then relinquishes, then making her speed up and suck faster and faster, as if he were about to ejaculate in under ten seconds, each time assaulting the very back of her throat, fiercer every single time.

All of a sudden, there is a clap of hands. The black man pulls her away and fully slides his cock out of her mouth. Fascinated, she looks at the glazed, obsidian member. He pulls her up, flips her round and throws her down on the table, pulling her skirt up at the same time. She is face down on the table, as are her three companions, heads aligned next to each other; her cheek touches Nora's. The black guy bends over her and with no word of notice forces himself inside her. His saliva-coated cock plunges deep into her arsehole, quickly reaching the bottom, and never before has she felt so deeply impaled. Like an iron bar reaching for her heart, then retreating before digging into her again. Never has she been fucked in the arse so hard, so deep than by this harder than hard ebony-coloured cock, this iron cock, this cock from hell.

On the table, right beneath her eyes, is the last hand of cards, and the courtly smile of the Excuse, and his mandolin.

Nora turns her head in her direction and kisses her, digging her tongue as far as she can into the young girl's mouth, holding on to her tongue, both women grasping each other with the energy of despair as the continuous thrusts burrow through their arses, kissing and crying as the table shakes beneath them. There is a scream, a deep guttural roar and the black man stops, still planted deep inside her arse and she feels his come pouring out, burning her. She distractedly visualizes the powerful white jets irrigating her guts, like an unholy, boiling enema. Nora pulls herself away from her mouth and screams in turn, a shout of triumph as her flesh welcomes both pain and joy. But instead of withdrawing, the Negro inside her arse comes and goes a few more times and she climaxes yet again, maybe because of the angle of the table pressing hard against her clit or the influence of the many orgasms occurring all around her. She swims in a sea of lust.

There is a pause. Then she hears hands clapping, slowly, in the background, ironic, the Commander smiling, complimenting them all.

"Excellent, ladies. Thank you. Now you may go."

And specifically to the young girl:

"You're awaited in Room Four," he says.

She knocks on the door, there is no answer but she enters anyway.

There are two men in dressing gowns sitting either side of a table, talking. But the first thing she notices is that they are identical twins, although one already sports white hair, as if he has aged prematurely. She wonders what sudden emotion one day caused his hair to turn so white. He can't be much older than forty. She recognizes the two men, they were at dinner earlier but they were seated at the other end of the table and she hadn't really noticed them.

The man with the white hair is handing a piece of paper to the other. The heavy dressing gown's belt is loose and uncovers his right thigh, a heavy-set leg which she didn't expect from his cultured facial features.

The other man, not even acknowledging the presence of the visitor, is reading aloud: "They caress each other for a few minutes. He squeezes two fingers into the swamp of her sex, two very long fingers, nails cut short, into the deep of her stomach, exploring her so much better than a penis could, his

almost feminine scientific intuition aware of her innermost
desires . . ."

He stopped.

"Not bad. But why 'sex'? Or 'penis'?"

"Why indeed? What would you have written?"

"I don't know . . . Pussy and dick? A sex, it's so anonymous."

"What would a woman say when referring to her sex? 'Vagina'
is too scientific, 'uterus' is too medical. In this present context,
maybe 'pussy' is too vulgar. Or it might depend on the woman.
Anyway, I'd definitely cut out the 'swamp'. Reminds me too
much of the worst of Henry Miller. In "Quiet Days in Clichy",
doesn't he write of 'a drooling pussy that fitted me like a glove'?
No, 'pussy' just won't do. So. we're left with 'sex'."

"And 'penis'?"

"Still too generic. Its so-called exploration is no more than a
continuous series of thrusts into the pit of her stomach. Too
prosaic for what the male member is capable of."

"Why not use a metaphor?"

"Which? A split apricot? A dick-shaped mussel? A mousta-
chioed wallet? As it is I'm uneasy with the 'swamp', although I do
enjoy its muddy, soaked-earth quality, a combination of liquid
and hard matter."

"And her cunt? Just call it a cunt? Do women really think of
their parts in such a way?"

"There's just a surfeit of metaphors. You can't just string too
many of them along. 'Her cunt's swamp': it just feels wrong, too
strong an image."

"The truth is you are not enamoured with metaphors."

"That's true. So, what would you suggest?"

" 'He slides two fingers into her divine gash, all the way down
her magic walls, exploring her so much better than . . .'!"

"You're getting funnier all the time. But not very practical.
Laughter and fucking, you know . . . Many years ago, when I was
still fumbling amongst the amatory arts, at the beginning of my
literary career. I was writing erotic stories with a friend; we were
trying to use every expressive resource we could, seeking to avoid
all vulgarity, to retain a dash of poetry about it all. We tried
everything: the subjective point of view, long sentences and little
punctuation, like James Joyce in the midst of tits ands arse if you
see what I mean, then more subtle metaphors – 'under his fingers

the flower of her love garden blossomed . . . at the end of the path the labyrinth of Cythera . . . exploring her so much better than all the previous arrows of desire had punctured her . . .' all rubbish of that kind, a compost heap of mythologies. But all it proves to us is that metaphors, however deceptive and clever they might be to the intellect, just pour cold water over any hard-on; a man who thinks too much just disconnects, if I can put it that way . . . But why don't we ask this young girl . . ."

He turns towards her. She'd been standing there silently, surprised that they hadn't even acknowledged her presence until now, seeing they had initially summoned her here.

"My dear, what do you think? How do you refer to your sexual organ?"

She is somewhat taken aback, but replies: "Actually I seldom refer to it by any sort of name."

"But if you had to?"

" 'Hole' or 'pussy', most often. No, not really. It sort of depends."

"On what?"

"On the situation. Sometimes I will enjoy shocking myself by using dirty words. Especially at the rear. I seldom use 'sodomy', too Biblical in essence. 'Buggered', that's what I say, when it's about me. But that's mostly when referring to the act, not its actual happening."

"What do you mean?"

"Well, 'I'm being buggered' occurs so often figuratively speaking, that I can't really use the expression properly, if I think about it . . . But 'I want to be buggered' presents no ambiguity."

"And right now?"

"I've just been buggered," she says. "By a very well-endowed black man. His come is still inside my arse. See how useful the right words can be . . ."

She emphasizes this as the two robes both open like a theatre's curtains and two honourably sized cocks are standing to attention, like twins, ever so slightly curved, thick-veined, helmets shining between the folds of the material.

She moves towards the men, gets on her knees and caresses them both, although neither of her hands can grasp the full girth of the respective cocks. Slowly, delicately, she wanks them off; then, moving her head from side to side, she alternately sucks them both. They taste the same, smell the same . . .

But their reactions are different. Very soon, the man with the white hair lies down on the bed and pulls her on to him and quickly positions himself deep inside her. As this happens, she feels the other man's hands spreading her arse cheeks and a cock, identical to the one fucking her, forces its way into her anal opening. She screams as he tears her apart, and realises she has never been filled this way. Just a moment later, all three are motionless, she is impaled on their twin cocks, and feels they are surely about to breach the thin membrane that separates them and merge into one single hammer. One of the men is gently biting her breasts; the other scratches her shoulder. She flexes her whole body, offering her crotch even more fully, tightens her sphincter muscles and feels the cock's swollen ridge move deeper inside her, while the one in her cunt almost slips out. The invading cocks are burning her alive, but still manage to penetrate deeper within her, and as the one in her arse settles for a second, her cunt fully gapes open.

They all come almost together. The ever so slight time delay allows her to experience the stream flooding her arse, and then the waves breaking inside her stomach. Then the cocks lose some of their hardness, dilate and soften and pleasure now takes a firm grip of her own body, she whimpers and squirms while still breached by the hot twin cocks and, in a moment of panic, she seeks the mouth of the man with the white hair.

They had not even undressed and, as soon as she leaves the bed, she is once again the immediate image of a perfect, if somewhat crumpled, maid.

A telephone rings all of a sudden.

One of the brothers – they are both flat out on the bed, side by side, breathless – rises and picks up the antique set from the bedside table.

"Yes?" he says.

She looks around her. Inevitably, on the wall, there is a painting featuring two men sitting, discussing literature, on either side of a small table, the man on the right hand side holding a sheet of paper. Close to them, a naked woman, kneeling, only visible from the back, her long blonde hair reaching down to her waist, seemingly sucking off the man on the left, he one with the white hair.

"You've been summoned," the brown-haired man says. "Room Six."

As she leaves the room, they are already deep in conversation on either side of the table, with the sheet of paper held by one of them. She only hears the final words, read out by the white-haired man:

"'She flexes her whole body, offering her crotch even more fully, tightens her sphincter muscles and feels the cock's swollen ridge move deeper inside her . . .'"

The other protests:

"'Sphincter muscles' What about Sybil's Hole?"

"The Artists's Entrance?"

"The Purple Flower?"

"St Luc's Grotto?"

The door closes and she can no longer hear them.

Room Six?

The sperm poured into her is running down her thighs.

The scene in the new room is almost symmetrical to the previous one. Room Six and two women, both naked, are sitting on either side of a table, their position, their dark red hair held up in a chignon, not unlike a creature by Rossetti, the heaviness of their breasts, the exaggerated length of their nipples, the pale complexion of their pink skin and a haughty, almost disdainful, facial expression, all striking features including, as she moves closer to them, the colour of their eyes, grey changing into green.

However, this time around, they are not identical.

"Come, my dear," One says. "Come."

They ask her to stand still, between the two of them, and four hands quickly undress her, throwing the maid's outfit aside. They only allow her to retain the stockings emphasizing the pallor of her thighs. The pale hands roam across her even paler skin.

"Look, she's just been fucked . . ."

"In front and behind," says the Other, "there's a small stream of come emerging from her arse . . ."

"She's been well fucked," One says. "She is still very dilated."

"So it seems," the Other calmly declares. "I could push my finger into her arse without even touching her edges."

The young girl is momentarily shocked by the contrast between their poised appearance and the filth of their language, and particularly the clinical way in which they are describing her, as if they were conducting an autopsy.

She stands between them and, suddenly, the two women get down on their knees and with no word of warning begin sucking her cunt and her arse, licking up the drops of come drying on her skin, biting the delicate flesh, digging their tongues into the still bruised openings.

The young girl feels dizzy. The two women are so artful, even their violence has a touch of elegance, teeth assaulting her lips, fingers sliding deep inside her . . .

No man has ever sucked or penetrated her thus. One then the Other, thrusting two then three fingers inside her cunt and her arse, withdrawing them then occupying her again but this time with four digits, as if their hands were becoming slimmer, thinner, and soon she has a whole hand inside each of her openings. She moans when the hand forces her doors, but now her cunt and arse tighten around the invading wrists and she feels delirious.

Inside her stomach, two hands are searching her, carving her innards apart, parallel hands as if in prayer, as if she were the object of a terribly ancient cult, being honoured and consumed by the members of her sect . . .

She has never experienced a vaginal orgasm this strong. Her sphincters are seizing up so hard they could cut the hands off at the wrists, to hold them captive inside her forever.

"She's really enjoying this, the bitch," One says.

"You're right," says the Other. "It feels as if her arse is breathless."

"She'll never want to come any other way," says One.

They gently pull their hands out and the pain is atrocious, not just the initial one in reverse, but the very thought of losing them, to be confronted once again with the terrible void inside her stomach, the emptiness of her life . . .

"Don't worry, my dear," says One. "We have many ideas where you're concerned."

"Do you want to take her to Fifteen?" the Other asks.

"You were thinking of that too, weren't you?"

Both women slip on an almost transparent negligée, one of those spider-like clouds a star of the silent cinema would wear, and move forward with the grace of goddesses. But as for her, they leave her naked, just slipping a dog collar around her neck and leading her thus all the way down the corridor and up to the next floor on a leash. She is herself surprised at how obedient she has become, so unlike her. Or maybe they had recognized this docile streak within her, the desire to submit to a Master's orders, the repressed craving for slavery and the whip.

Had she known her Tarot better, she would have realized that in Room Fifteen she would find a Photographer, and one of those old-fashioned devices standing on a single leg and under the black cloth of which the operator must dive to ensure he is focused correctly on his subject.

The Photographer is visibly waiting for them. He is dressed in Second Empire attire, a short blouse and crumpled trousers, with a thin moustache and small Napoleon 3rd-type beard. Next to him is the young man she had met at dinner: now undressed, she can see he can be no more than sixteen years old at most. He sports the thin and curvy shape of a classical catamite, a lazy if gracious body spread over the bed, distractedly playing with his half erect cock as they enter the room.

"Hello, darlings," says the tired adolescent.

"Hello, arsehole," says the Other. "How are you?"

"So, so," says the young man. "he's only fucked me twice since night fell. Do you think he no longer likes me?"

"Don't you like him any longer?" the One asks the Photographer.

"He bores me," says the Photographer. "So what are you bringing me here?"

"Don't you think she's pretty?"

"Very," the Photographer says. "I so enjoy such pale milk-like skin."

He examines the young girl all over. She blushes at being so exposed.

"Her eyes are so shiny," the Photographer says. "Have you just made her come?"

"Insanely," says the Other.

"Sit down on the bed," the Photographer tells the young girl. Take your stockings off, please. And you, little fag, come here."

She sits herself down on a short square of black silk, in the same pose as Rembrandt's Bethsabea. It all feels like a dream. The

Photographer moves his heavy apparatus and disappears under its black cloth. She hears the muted sound of his voice, commanding her:

"No, thighs apart. Good, yes, like that. Lean backwards, steady your arms, breasts to the fore, perfect."

He reappears briefly:

"You," he says to the young boy who is pretending to be terribly bored, "come and suck me off while I'm working, it'll keep you busy."

"Yes, uncle," says the young man with a touch of irony in his voice. "Right away, uncle."

The Photographer again disappears under his cloth, and on his knees facing him, the boy with obvious dexterity pulls out a remarkable cock, disproportionate in places, whose fat and swollen helmet emerges triumphantly from a dry, nervous stem. The boy licks it quite methodically and witnesses the bulging fruit thicken even more under his ministrations.

"Swallow," says the voice under the black cloth.

Obediently, the young boy opens his mouth wide and jaws set wide apart devours the strange and monstrous fruit.

All the while, the Photographer is taking picture after picture, only making appearances to change the plates and sprinkle more magnesium into his flash, just his voice emerging from below the black sheet.

"Yes . . . Now each of you suck one of her breasts . . . Like that . . . Ah, a hand on her thigh . . . Open wider, my pretty one . . . Against that black silk background, you are just sublime. Throw her backwards, now. One kissing her, the other licking her . . . Yes . . . More profile, please, I can't see your tongue . . . No, don't look at the camera . . . Very good, head thrown back . . . and you, there, suck a bit better than that or I'll have you whipped right in front of these ladies . . ."

"Oh, yes," says the catamite, interrupting his labours.

Together with her two new friends, he has her adopt the most lubricious poses, ever on the look out for the moment she comes. Under their tongues and fingers, she experiences a whole series of orgasms, until she totally forgets where she is. Only the bright explosion of the flash, from time to time, reminds her that a man is taking photographs of her while . . .

Is it the caresses that are generating her pleasure or the fact she is being photographed? The orgasms, the flashes of light, one or the other or both are levitating her out of her body. Every time her mouth opens on a silent scream, the flash of the magnesium betrays the fact that the Photographer has captured her moment of selflessness, stolen yet a further parcel of her soul, her life . . . as if she was being emptied from the inside, as if her very substance was now flowing down her thighs, captured by the photograph, disfigured, transformed . . .

The sound of the door opening . . .

A bit later, a cock thrusting up her arse, another forcing its way down her throat, the room is now full of men and women, all the guests from dinner, each and every one fucking her in every way, and from orgasm to orgasm she feels herself grow wider, dilate until she is just a set of openings, of holes, deep abysses where cocks are ejaculating before being replaced by larger cocks or more numerous ones. Now they are penetrating her two at a time, in her cunt, in her arse, they come in twos to tease her mouth, and innumerable pairs of hands roam across her body, pinch her, sometimes spank her, and above it all the voice of the Photographer encouraging them on and on, and the brightness of the flash, and that anxious feeling that she is now no more than an empty space being furrowed, a nothingness full of come, devoured, eaten from the inside by a horde of vampires. Soon there will be nothing left of her, just some long blonde hair matted with sweat, a white expanse of flesh torn apart by caresses, a set of pale eyes she holds tightly closed while all of her is being impaled and only the violent flashes of light make their way through to her dead eyes.

Suddenly, they abandon her. From one moment to the next, it seems to her, there is no one left. She runs her hands in front of her eyes, as if she were blind and finally opens her eyes. The Commander stands in front of her and is watching her: the same cold marble eyes, the same early taste of the tomb. He gently applauds her, like earlier, but there is no sign of irony on his face.

"Very good, my dear, very good indeed. I knew we could rely on you."

He comes towards her, takes her hands, invites her to rise from the deeply soiled bed of black satin.

"Come," he says. "There is one final thing for you to do."

Together they walk down the stairs. There are so many rooms, so many passages she will know nothing about, whose anonymous numbers will not be revealed. What masked ball or orgy in Room Twelve, what improvised concert in Room Eight? They find themselves on the steps of the castle. The cicadas are now silent, the night is still far from morning, but she hesitates. The moon has moved across the roof and a wide geometrical shadow now covers a whole section of the lawn. All that emerges, on the frontier of darkness, is the statue of the goddess, even whiter in the light of the moon.

The Commander leads her to the statue. The grass is mown short and feels hard against her bare feet. She shivers, not because she is cold, as spring down here already has an early touch of summer, but because of the anxiety that always strikes towards the end of a night's party, when all is done and loneliness is about to knock on the door again and all you are left with are memories . . .

"Get up on the pedestal," he says. "Yes, like that, with your eyes facing the eyes of the goddess. Take her into your arms – very good, now your hands on her rear, yes. Now, don't move."

Methodically, he ties her to the statue with thin string. He ties her tightly, the rope biting into her flesh, her breasts crushed against the stone breasts of Venus – or is it Diana – then her legs are pulled up against the legs of marble, ankle against ankle, until she can barely move an eyelash, her face pressed against the stone head.

"They're the same colour," says a female voice.

"That's true," says another man. "Maybe it's the statue that's actually tied to her."

"Predator and prey," jokes yet another.

Are they all present?

"Let's begin," someone says. "It's time to end all of this."

The sharp whisper of the first lash precedes by a micro-second the blow that lands on her rump. She screams, or is it her tortured flesh that screams under the assault of the whip? But she is not surprised; she is already resigned, abandoned, being punished because she is innocent. Innocent of what?

She screams, tries to wriggle out, but she is tied so tightly that the marble bites into her. She cries out as the whip keeps on finding her, with every new blow her skin opens up, like paper under a knife. Soon, her arse, her back, her shoulders have become the mad canvas of a mad artist, blood spurting in lines and blotches, spreading, merging. The blood now turning her flesh dark, woman of bronze tied to woman of stone. Pain begins to anaesthetise pain, she is an open wound, furrowed, overtaken by heat, by fire irradiating from the very centre of her belly and she is aware this unbearable heat rising towards her heart will soon kill her as assuredly as the cold poison killed Socrates. She no longer screams, just feels the heat rising, the whip opening up new valleys, Venus watching her in silence, and when the time comes a ray of moonlight reaches out to seize her in its grasp, and she dies of unbelievable pleasure, part and parcel of the immense fire of the whip.

The moon finally moves behind the house, the darkness drowns the statue and its victim. They leave her tied there and walk back to the house in silence, satisfied.

There is but a bare sketch of dawn. A gentle breeze weaves across the parc, though the wind is not strong enough to lift the bloodied strands of blonde hair now slowly drying.

In an hour or two, the cicadas will begin interrupting the silence again.

Noon, Gare de Lyon. The young woman with brown hair, captivated by the sun, has walked on to the first train to depart. She will pay for her ticket on board, too bad about the likely supplement.

There is almost no one in the compartment. Further down the aisle sits a man with steel grey hair but she can only see his straight neck. Closer to her are four men playing cards, already well into their game. One is black, very black. When she walked past them, she noticed they were playing with tarot cards, the black man was about to throw down a Fifteen: a Photographer, head buried under the cloth of an old-fashioned camera, is shooting an undressed model, a pale-skinned, long blonde haired woman. At his feet, an effeminate young boy is sucking him off with studious application.

FROM *CRASH*

J. G. Ballard

I

The harsh blue lights of police cars revolved within my mind during the next three weeks as I lay in an empty ward of the casualty hospital near London Airport. In this quiet terrain of used-car marts, water reservoirs and remand centres, surrounded by the motorway systems that served London Airport, I began my recovery from the accident. Two wards of twenty-four beds – the maximum number of survivors anticipated – were permanently reserved for the possible victims of an air-crash. One of these was temporarily occupied by car-crash injuries.

Not all the blood which covered me had belonged to the man I killed. The Asian doctors in the emergency theatre found that both my knee-caps had been fractured against the instrument panel. Long spurs of pain reached along the inner surface of my thighs into my groin, as if fine steel catheters were being drawn through the veins of my legs.

Three days after the first surgery on my knees I caught some minor hospital infection. I lay in the empty ward, taking up a bed that belonged by rights to an air-crash victim, and thinking in a disordered way about the wounds and pains he would feel. Around me, the empty beds contained a hundred histories of collision and bereavement, the translation of wounds through the

violence of aircraft and automobile crashes. Two nurses moved
through the ward, tidying the beds and radio headphones. These
amiable young women ministered within a cathedral of invisible
wounds, their burgeoning sexualities presiding over the most
terrifying facial and genital injuries.

As they adjusted the harness around my legs, I listened to the
aircraft rising from London Airport. The geometry of this complex
torture device seemed in some way related to the slopes and
contours of these young women's bodies. Who would be the next
tenant of this bed – some middle-aged bank cashier en route to the
Balearics, her head full of gin, pubis moistening towards the bored
widower seated beside her? After a runway accident at London
Airport her body would be marked for years by the bruising of her
abdomen against the seat belt stanchion. Each time she slipped
away to the lavatory of her provincial restaurant, weakened bladder
biting at a worn urethra, during each sex act with her prostatic
husband she would think of the few seconds before her crash. Her
injuries fixed for ever this imagined infidelity.

Did my wife, when she visited the ward each evening, ever
wonder what sexual errand had brought me to the Western
Avenue flyover? As she sat beside me, her shrewd eyes itemizing
whatever vital parts of her husband's anatomy were left to her, I
was certain that she read the answer to her unspoken questions in
the scars on my legs and chest.

The nurses hovered around me, carrying out their painful chores.
When they replaced the drainage tubes in my knees I tried not to
vomit back my sedative, strong enough to keep me quiet but not to
relieve the pain. Only their sharp tempers rallied me.

A young, blond-haired doctor with a callous face examined the
wounds on my chest. The skin was broken around the lower edge
of the sternum, where the horn boss had been driven upwards by
the collapsing engine compartment. A semi-circular bruise
marked my chest, a marbled rainbow running from one nipple
to the other. During the next week this rainbow moved through a
sequence of tone changes like the colour spectrum of automobile
varnishes. As I looked down at myself I realized that the precise
make and model-year of my car could have been reconstructed by
an automobile engineer from the pattern of my wounds. The
layout of the instrument panel, like the profile of the steering
wheel bruised into my chest, was inset on my knees and shin-

bones. The impact of the second collision between my body and the interior compartment of the car was defined in these wounds, like the contours of a woman's body remembered in the responding pressure of one's own skin for a few hours after a sexual act.

On the fourth day, for no evident reason, the anaesthetics were withdrawn. All morning I vomited into the enamel pail which a nurse held under my face. She stared at me with good-humoured but unmoved eyes. The cold rim of the kidney pail pressed against my cheek. Its porcelain surface was marked by a small thread of blood from some nameless previous user.

I leaned my forehead against the nurse's strong thigh as I vomited. Beside my bruised mouth her worn fingers contrasted strangely with her youthful skin. I found myself thinking of her natal cleft. When had she last washed this moist gulley? During my recovery, questions like this one obsessed me as I talked to the doctors and nurses. When had they last bathed their genitalia, did small grains of faecal matter still cling to their anuses as they prescribed some antibiotic for a streptococcal throat, did the odour of illicit sex acts infest their underwear as they drove home from the hospital, the traces of smegma and vaginal mucus on their hands marrying with the splashed engine coolant of unexpected car-crashes? I let a few threads of green bile leak into the pail, aware of the warm contours of the young woman's thighs. A seam of her gingham frock had been repaired with a few loops of black cotton. I stared at the loosening coils lying against the round surface of her left buttock. Their curvatures seemed as arbitrary and as meaningful as the wounds on my chest and legs.

This obsession with the sexual possibilities of everything around me had been jerked loose from my mind by the crash. I imagined the ward filled with convalescing air-disaster victims, each of their minds a brothel of images. The crash between our two cars was a model of some ultimate and yet undreamt sexual union. The injuries of still-to-be-admitted patients beckoned to me, an immense encyclopaedia of accessible dreams.

Catherine seemed well aware of these fantasies. During her first visits I had been in shock and she had made herself familiar with the layout and atmosphere of the hospital, exchanging good-humoured banter with the doctors. As a nurse carried away my vomit Catherine expertly pulled the metal table from the foot of the bed and unloaded on to it a clutch of magazines. She sat down beside me, casting a brisk eye over my unshaven face and fretting hands.

I tried to smile at her. The stitches in the laceration across my scalp, a second hairline an inch to the left of the original, made it difficult for me to change my expression. In the shaving mirror the nurses held up to my face I resembled an alarmed contortionist, startled by his own deviant anatomy.

"I'm sorry." I took her hand. "I must look rather sunk in myself."

"You're fine," she said. "Absolutely. You're like someone's victim in Madame Tussaud's."

"Try to come tomorrow."

"I will." She touched my forehead, gingerly peering at the scalp wound. "I'll bring some make-up for you. I imagine the only cosmetic attention given to the patients here is at Ashford Mortuary."

I looked up at her more clearly. Her show of warmth and wifely concern pleasantly surprised me. The mental distance between my work at the television commercial studios in Shepperton and her own burgeoning career in the overseas tours section of Pan American had separated us more and more during the past years. Catherine was now taking flying lessons, and with one of her boyfriends had started a small air-tourist charter firm. All these activities she pursued with a single mind, deliberately marking out her independence and self-reliance as if staking her claim to a terrain that would later soar in value. I had reacted to all this like most husbands, quickly developing an extensive repertory of resigned attitudes. The small but determined drone of her light aircraft crossed the sky over our apartment house each weekend, a tocsin that sounded the note of our relationship.

The blond-haired doctor walked through the ward, nodding to Catherine. She turned away from me, her bare legs revealing her thighs as far as her plump pubis, shrewdly summing up the sexual potential of this young man. I noticed that she was dressed more for a smart lunch with an airline executive than to visit her husband in hospital. Later I learned that she had been badgered at the airport by police officers investigating the road-death. Clearly the accident and any possible manslaughter charges against me had made her something of a celebrity.

"This ward is reserved for air-crash victims," I told Catherine. "The beds are kept waiting."

"If I groundloop on Saturday you might wake up and find me next to you." Catherine peered at the deserted beds, presumably visualizing each imaginary injury. "You're getting out of bed tomorrow. They want you to walk." She looked down at me solicitously. "Poor man. Have you antagonized them in any way?"

I let this pass, but Catherine added, "The other man's wife is a doctor – Dr Helen Remington."

Crossing her legs, she began the business of lighting a cigarette, fumbling with an unfamiliar lighter. From which new lover had she borrowed this ugly machine, all too clearly a man's? Tooled from an aircraft cannon shell, it was more like a weapon. For years I had been able to spot Catherine's affairs within almost a few hours of her first sex act simply by glancing over any new physical or mental furniture – a sudden interest in some third-rate wine or film-maker, a different tack across the waters of aviation politics. Often I could guess the name of her latest lover long before she released it at the climax of our sexual acts. This teasing game she and I needed to play. As we lay together we would describe a complete amatory encounter, from the first chit-chat at an airline cocktail party to the sexual act itself. The climax of these games was the name of the illicit partner. Held back until the last moment, it would always produce the most exquisite orgasms for both of us. There were times when I felt that these affairs took place merely to provide the raw material for our sexual games.

Watching her cigarette smoke move away across the empty ward, I wondered with whom she spent the past few days. No doubt the thought that her husband had killed another man lent an unexpected dimension to their sex acts, presumably conducted on our bed in sight of the chromium telephone which had brought Catherine the first news of my accident. The elements of new technologies linked our affections.

Irritated by the aircraft noise, I sat up on one elbow. The bruises across my chest wall made it painful for me to breathe. Catherine peered down at me with a worried gaze, obviously concerned that I might die on the spot. She put the cigarette between my lips. I drew uncertainly on the geranium-flavoured smoke. The warm tip of the cigarette, stained with pink lipstick, carried with it the unique taste of Catherine's body, a flavour I had forgotten in the phenol-saturated odour of the hospital. Catherine reached for the cigarette, but I held on to it like a child. The grease-smeared tip reminded me of her nipples, liberally painted with lipstick, which I would press against my face, arms and chest, secretly imagining the imprints to be wounds. In a nightmare I had once seen her giving birth to a devil's child, her swollen breasts spurting liquid faeces.

A dark-haired student nurse came into the ward. Smiling at my wife, she pulled back the bedclothes and dug the urine bottle from between my legs. Inspecting its level, she flipped back the sheets. Immediately my penis began to dribble; with an effort I controlled the sphincter, numbed by the long succession of anaesthetics. Lying there with a weak bladder, I wondered why, after this tragic accident involving the death of an unknown young man – his identity, despite the questions I asked Catherine, remained an enigma to me, like an anonymous opponent killed in a pointless duel – all these women around me seemed to attend only to my most infantile zones. The nurses who emptied my urinal and worked my bowels with their enema contraption, who steered my penis through the vent of my pyjama shorts and adjusted the drainage tubes in my knees, who cleansed the pus from the dressings on my scalp and wiped my mouth with their hard hands – these starched women in all their roles reminded me of those who attended my childhood, commissionaires guarding my orifices.

A student nurse moved around my bed, sly thighs under her gingham, eyes fixed on Catherine's glamorous figure. Was she calculating how many lovers Catherine had taken since the accident, excited by the strange posture of her husband in his bed, or – more banal – the cost of her expensive suit and jewellery? By contrast, Catherine gazed frankly at this young girl's body. Her assessment of the contours of thigh and buttock, breast and armpit, and their relationship with the chromium bars of my leg harness, an abstract sculpture designed to show off her slim figure, was open and interested. An interesting lesbian streak ran through Catherine's mind. Often as we made love she asked me to visualize her in intercourse with another woman – usually her secretary Karen, an unsmiling girl with silver lipstick who spent the entire office party before Christmas staring motionlessly at my wife like a pointer in rut. Catherine often asked me

how she could allow herself to be seduced by Karen. She soon
came up with the suggestion that they visit a department store
together, where she would ask Karen's help in choosing various
kinds of underwear. I waited for them among the racks of
nightdresses outside their cubicle. Now and then I glanced
through the curtains and watched them together, their bodies
and fingers involved in the soft technology of Catherine's breasts
and the brassières designed to show them off to this or that
advantage. Karen was touching my wife with peculiar caresses,
tapping her lightly with the tips of her fingers, first upon the
shoulders along the pink grooves left by her underwear, then
across her back, where the metal clasps of her brassière had left a
medallion of impressed skin, and finally to the elastic-patterned
grooves beneath Catherine's breasts themselves. My wife stood
through this in a trance-like state, gabbling to herself in a low
voice, as the tip of Karen's right forefinger touched her nipple.

I thought of the bored glance which the assistant, a middle-
aged woman with the small face of a corrupt doll, had given me as
the two young women had left, flicking back the curtain as if some
little sexual playlet had ended. In her expression was the clear
assumption that not only did I know what had been going on, and
that these booths were often used for these purposes, but that
Catherine and I would later exploit the experience for our own
complex pleasures. As I sat in the car beside my wife, my fingers
moved across the control panel, switching on the ignition, the
direction indicator, selecting the drive lever. I realized that I was
almost exactly modelling my responses to the car on the way in
which Karen had touched Catherine's body. Her sullen eroti-
cism, the elegant distance she placed between her fingertips and
my wife's nipples, were recapitulated in the distance between
myself and the car.

Catherine's continuing erotic interest in her secretary seemed
an interest as much in the idea of making love to her as in the
physical pleasures of the sex act itself. Nonetheless, these pur-
suits had begun to make all our relationships, both between
ourselves and with other people, more and more abstract. She
soon became unable to reach an orgasm without an elaborate
fantasy of a lesbian sex-act with Karen, of her clitoris being
tongued, nipples erected, anus caressed. These descriptions
seemed to be a language in search of objects, or even, perhaps,

the beginnings of a new sexuality divorced from any possible physical expression.

I assumed that she had at least once made love to Karen, but we had now reached the point where it no longer mattered, or had any reference to anything but a few square inches of vaginal mucosa, fingernails and bruised lips and nipples. Lying in my hospital ward, I watched Catherine summing up the student nurse's slim legs and strong buttocks, the deep-blue belt that outlined her waist and broad hips. I half expected Catherine to reach out and put her hand on this young woman's breast, or slip it under her short skirt, the edge of her palm sliding between the natal cleft into the sticky perineum. Far from giving a squeal of outrage, or even pleasure, the nurse would probably continue folding her hospital corner, unmoved by this sexual gesture, no more significant than the most commonplace spoken remark.

Catherine pulled a manila folder from her bag. I recognized the treatment of a television commercial I had prepared. For this high-budget film, a thirty-second commercial advertising Ford's entire new sports car range, we hoped to use one of a number of well-known actresses. On the afternoon of my accident I had attended a conference with Aida James, a freelance director we had brought in. By chance, one of the actresses, Elizabeth Taylor, was about to start work on a new feature film at Shepperton.

"Aida telephoned to say how sorry she was. Can you look at the treatment again? She's made a number of changes."

I waved the folder away, gazing at the reflection of myself in Catherine's hand-mirror. The severed nerve in my scalp had fractionally lowered my right eyebrow, a built-in eye-patch that seemed to conceal my new character from myself. This marked tilt was evident in everything around me. I stared at my pale, mannequin-like face, trying to read its lines. The smooth skin almost belonged to someone in a science-fiction film, stepping out of his capsule after an immense inward journey on to the overlit soil of an unfamiliar planet. At any moment the skies might slide . . .

On an impulse I asked, "Where's the car?"

"Outside – in the consultants' car-park."

"What?" I sat up on one elbow, trying to see through the window behind my bed. "*My* car, not yours." I had visualized it mounted as some kind of cautionary exhibit outside the operating theatres.

"It's a complete wreck. The police dragged it to the pound behind the station."

"Have you seen it?"

"The sergeant asked me to identify it. He didn't believe you'd got out alive." She crushed her cigarette. "I'm sorry for the other man – Dr Hamilton's husband."

I stared pointedly at the clock over the door, hoping that she would soon leave. This bogus commiseration over the dead man irritated me, merely an excuse for an exercise in moral gymnastics. The brusqueness of the young nurses was part of the same pantomime of regret. I had thought for hours about the dead man, visualizing the effects of his death on his wife and family. I had thought of his last moments alive, frantic milliseconds of pain and violence in which he had been catapulated from a pleasant domestic interlude into a concertina of metallized death. These feelings existed within my relationship with the dead man, within the reality of the wounds on my chest and legs, and within the unforgettable collision between my own body and the interior of my car. By comparison, Catherine's mock-grief was a mere stylization of a gesture – I waited for her to break into song, tap her forehead, touch every second temperature chart around the ward, switch on every fourth set of radio headphones.

At the same time, I knew that my feelings towards the dead man and his doctor wife were already overlaid by certain undefined hostilities, half-formed dreams of revenge.

Catherine watched me trying to catch my breath. I took her left hand and pressed it to my sternum. In her sophisticated eyes I was already becoming a kind of emotional cassette, taking my place with all those scenes of pain and violence that illuminated the margins of our lives – television newsreels of wars and student riots, natural disasters and police brutality which we vaguely watched on the colour TV set in our bedroom as we masturbated each other. This violence experienced at so many removes had become intimately associated with our sex acts. The beatings and burnings married in our minds with the delicious tremors of our erectile tissues, the spilt blood of students with the genital fluids that irrigated our fingers and mouths. Even my own pain as I lay in the hospital bed, while Catherine steered the glass urinal between my legs, painted fingernails pricking my penis, even the vagal flushes that seized at my chest seemed extensions of that real world of violence calmed and tamed within our television programmes and the pages of news magazines.

Catherine left me to rest, taking with her half the flowers she had brought. As the elder of the Asian doctors watched her from the doorway she hesitated at the foot of my bed, smiling at me with sudden warmth as if unsure whether she would ever see me again.

A nurse came into the ward with a bowl in one hand. She was a new recruit to the casualty section, a refined-looking woman in her late thirties. After a pleasant greeting, she drew back the bedclothes and began a careful examination of my dressings, her serious eyes following the bruised contours. I caught her attention once, but she stared back at me evenly, and went on with her work, steering her sponge around the central bandage that ran from the waistband between my legs. What was she thinking about – her husband's evening meal, her children's latest minor infection? Was she aware of the automobile components sha-dowed like contact prints in my skin and musculature? Perhaps she was wondering which model of the car I drove, guessing at the weight of the saloon, estimating the rake of the steering column.

"Which side do you want it?"

I looked down. She was holding my limp penis between thumb and forefinger, waiting for me to decide whether I wanted it to lie to right or left of the central bandage.

As I thought about this strange decision, the brief glimmer of my first erection since the accident stirred through the cavernosa of my penis, reflected in a slight release of tension in her neat fingers.

II

The traffic multiplied, concrete lanes moving laterally across the landscape. As Catherine and I drove from the coroner's inquest the flyovers overlaid one another like copulating giants, immense legs straddling each other's backs. A verdict of accidental death had been returned, without any show of interest or ceremony; no charges of manslaughter or negligent driving were brought against me by the police. After the inquest I let Catherine drive me to the airport. For half an hour I sat by the window in her office, looking down at the hundreds of cars in the parking lot. Their roofs formed a lake of metal. Catherine's secretary stood behind her shoulder, waiting for me to leave. As she handed Catherine's glasses to her I saw that she was wearing a white lipstick, presumably an ironic concession to this day of death.

Catherine walked me to the lobby. "James, you must go to the office – believe me, love, I'm trying to be helpful." She touched my right shoulder with a curious hand, as if searching for some new wound which had flowered there. During the inquest she had held my arm in a peculiar grip, frightened that I might be swept sideways out of the window.

Unwilling to haggle with the surly and baronial taxi-drivers only interested in taking London fares, I walked through the car-park opposite the air-freight building. Overhead, across the metallized air, a jet-liner screamed. When the aircraft had passed I raised my head and saw Dr Helen Remington moving among the cars a hundred yards to my right.

At the inquest I had been unable to take my eyes away from the scar on her face. I watched her walk calmly through the lines of cars towards the entrance of the immigration department. Her strong jaw was held at a jaunty angle, her face turned away from me as if she were ostentatiously blotting out all traces of my existence. At the same time I had the strong impression that she was completely lost.

A week after the inquest she was waiting at the taxi rank of the Oceanic Terminal as I drove away from Catherine's office. I called to her and stopped behind an airline bus, beckoning her into the passenger seat. Swinging her handbag from a strong wrist, she came across to my car, recognizing me with a grimace.

As we headed towards Western Avenue she surveyed the traffic with frank interest. She had brushed her hair back from her face, openly wearing the fading scar-line.

"Where can I take you?"

"Can we drive a little?" she asked. "There's all this traffic – I like to look at it."

Was she trying to taunt me? I guessed that in her matter-of-fact way she was already assessing the possibilities I had revealed to her. From the concrete aprons of the parking lots and the roofs of the multi-storey car-parks she was now inspecting with a clear and unsentimental eye the technology which had brought about the death of her husband.

She began to chatter with contrived animation. "Yesterday I hired a taxi-driver to drive me around for an hour. 'Anywhere,' I said. We sat in a massive traffic jam near the underpass. I don't think we moved more than fifty yards. He wasn't in the least put out."

We drove along Western Avenue, the service buildings and perimeter fence of the airport on our left. I kept the car in the slow lane as the high deck of the flyover receded in the rear-view mirror. Helen talked about the second life she was already planning for herself.

"The Road Research Laboratory need a medical officer – the salary is larger, something I've got to think about now. There's a certain moral virtue in being materialistic."

"The Road Research Laboratory . . ." I repeated. The news-reels of simulated car-crashes were often shown in television documentaries; these mutilated machines were haunted by a strange pathos. "Isn't that rather too close . . .?"

"That's the point. Besides, I know I can give something now that I wasn't remotely aware of before. It's not a matter of duty so much as of commitment."

Fifteen minutes later, as we moved back towards the flyover, she came and sat beside me, watching my hands on the controls as we once again entered the collision course.

The same calm but curious gaze, as if she were still undecided how to make use of me, was fixed on my face shortly afterwards as I stopped the car on a deserted service road among the reservoirs to the west of the airport. When I put my arm around her shoulders she smiled briefly to herself, a nervous rictus of the upper lip which exposed her gold-tipped right incisor. I touched her mouth with my own, denting the waxy carapace of pastel lipcoat, watching her hand reach out to the chromium pillar of the quarter window. I pressed my lips against the bared and un-marked dentine of her upper teeth, fascinated by the movement of her fingers across the smooth chrome of the window pillar. Its surface was marked along its forward edge by a smear of blue paint left by some disaffected production-line worker. The nail of her forefinger scratched at this fretline, which rose diagonally from the window-sill at the same angle as the concrete ledge of the irrigation ditch ten feet from the car. In my eyes this parallax fused with the image of an abandoned car lying in the rust-stained grass on the lower slopes of the reservoir embankment. The brief avalanche of dissolving talc that fell across her eyes as I moved my lips across their lids contained all the melancholy of this derelict vehicle, its leaking engine oil and radiator coolant.

Six hundred yards behind us the traffic waited on the raised deck of the motorway, the afternoon sunlight crossing the windows of the airline buses and cars. My hand moved around the outer curvature of Helen's thighs, feeling the open zip of her dress. As these razor-like links cut my knuckles I felt her teeth across my ear. The sharpness of these pains reminded me of the bite of the windshield glass during my crash. She opened her legs and I began to stroke the nylon mesh that covered her pubis, a glamorous veil for the loins of this serious-minded woman doctor. Looking into her face, with its urgent mouth gasping as if trying to devour itself, I moved her hand around her breasts. She was now talking to herself, rambling away like some demented accident casualty. She lifted her right breast from her brassière, pressing my fingers against the hot nipple. I kissed each breast in turn, running my teeth across the erect nipples.

Seizing me with her body in this arbour of glass, metal and vinyl, Helen moved her hand inside my shirt, feeling for my nipples. I took her fingers and placed them around my penis. Through the rear-view mirror I saw a water-board maintenance truck approaching. It moved past in a roar of dust and diesel exhaust that drummed against the doors of my car. This surge of excitement drew the first semen to my penis. Ten minutes later, when the truck returned, the vibrating windows brought on my orgasm. Helen knelt across me, elbows pressed into the seat on either side of my head. I lay back, feeling the hot, scented vinyl. My hands pushed her skirt around her waist so that I could see the curve of her hips. I moved her slowly against me, pressing the shaft of my penis against her clitoris. Elements of her body, her square kneecaps below my elbows, her right breast jacked out of its brassière cup, the small ulcer that marked the lower arc of her nipple, were framed within the cabin of the car. As I pressed the head of my penis against the neck of her uterus, in which I could feel a dead machine, her cap, I looked at the cabin around me. This small space was crowded with angular control surfaces and rounded sections of human bodies interacting in unfamiliar junctions, like the first act of homosexual intercourse inside an Apollo capsule. The volumes of Helen's thighs pressing against my hips, her left fist buried in my shoulder, her mouth grasping at my own, the shape and moisture of her anus as I stroked it with my ring finger, were each overlaid by the inventories of a benevolent technology – the moulded binnacle of the instrument dials, the jutting carapace of the steering column shroud, the extravagant pistol grip of the handbrake. I felt the warm vinyl of the seat beside me, and then stroked the damp aisle of Helen's perineum. Her hand pressed against my right testicle. The plastic laminates around me, the colour of washed anthracite, were the same tones as her pubic hairs parted at the vestibule of her vulva. The passenger compartment enclosed us like a machine generating from our sexual act an homunculus of blood, semen and engine coolant. My finger moved into Helen's rectum, feeling the shaft of my penis within her vagina. These slender membranes, like the mucous septum of her nose which I touched with my tongue, were reflected in the glass dials of the instrument panel, the unbroken curve of the windshield.

Her mouth bit my left shoulder, blood marking my shirt like the imprint of a mouth. Without thinking, I struck the side of her head with the palm of my hand.

"I'm sorry!" she gasped into my face. "Please, don't move!" She steered my penis back into her vagina. Holding her buttocks with both hands, I moved rapidly towards my orgasm. Above me, Helen Remington's serious faced gazed down at me as if she were re-suscitating a patient. The sheen of moisture on the skin around her mouth was like the bloom on a morning windshield. She pumped her buttocks rapidly, forcing her pubic bone against mine, then leaned back against the dashboard as a Land-Rover thudded past along the track, sending a cloud of dust against the windows.

She lifted herself off my penis when it had gone, letting the semen fall on to my crotch. She sat herself behind the steering wheel, holding the wet glans in her hand. She looked around the compartment of the car, as if speculating on any other uses to which she could put our sexual act. Lit by the afternoon sun, the fading scar on her face marked off these concealed motives like the secret frontier of an annexed territory. Thinking that I might reassure her in some way, I took her left breast from the brassière and began to stroke it, I gazed at the jewelled grotto of the instrument panel, at the jutting shroud of the steering assembly and the chromium heads of the control switches.

A police car appeared on the service road behind us, its white hull rolling heavily through the dips and ruts. Helen sat up and put away her breast with a deft hand. She dressed quickly, and began to remake her face in the mirror of her compact. As abrubtly as we has begun, she was now distanced from her own eager sexuality.

However, Helen Remington clearly felt no concern herself at these out-of-character actions, these sexual acts in the cramped compartment of my motor-car parked in various deserted service roads, culs-de-sac and midnight parkways. When I collected her during the following weeks from the house she had rented in Northolt, or waited for her in the reception lounge outside the airport immigration offices, it seemed incredible to me that I had any kind of sexual involvement with this sensitive woman doctor in her white coat, listening indulgently to the self-defeating arguments of some tubercular Pakistani.

Strangely, our sexual acts took place only within my automobile. In the large bedroom of her rented house I was unable even to mount an erection, and Helen herself would become argumentative and remote, talking endlessly about the more boring aspects of her work. Once together in my car, with the crowded traffic lanes through which we had moved forming an unseen and unseeing audience, we were able to arouse each other. Each time she revealed a growing tenderness towards myself and my body, even trying to allay my concern for her. In each sexual act together we recapitulated her husband's death, re-seeding the image of his body in her vagina in terms of the hundred perspectives of our mouth and thighs, nipples and tongues within the metal and vinyl compartment of the car.

I waited for Catherine to discover my frequent meetings with this lonely woman doctor, but to my surprise she showed only a cursory interest in Helen Remington. Catherine had rededicated herself to her marriage. Before my accident our sexual relationship was almost totally abstracted, maintained by a series of imaginary games and perversities. When she stepped out of bed in the mornings she seemed like some efficient mechanic servicing herself: a perfunctory shower; the night's urine discharged into the lavatory pan; her cap extracted, regreased and once again inserted (how and where did she make love during her lunch-hour, and with which of the pilots and airline executives?); the news programme played while she percolated the coffee . . .

All this had now passed, replaced by a small but growing repertory of tenderness and affections. As she lay beside me, willingly late for her office, I could bring myself to orgasm simply by thinking of the car in which Dr Helen Remington and I performed our sexual acts.

III

Were there any limits to Vaughan's irony? When I returned from the bar he was leaning against the window-sill of the Lincoln, rolling the last of four cigarettes with the hash kit kept in a tobacco bag in the dashboard locker. Two sharp-faced airport whores, barely older than schoolchildren, were arguing with him through the window.

"Where the hell do you think you were going?" Vaughan took from me the two wine bottles I had bought. He rolled the cigarettes on to the instrument binnacle, then resumed his discussion with the young women. They were arguing in an abstract way about time and price. Trying to ignore their voices, and the massed traffic moving below the supermarket, I watched the aircraft taking off from London Airport across the western perimeter fence, constellations of green and red lights that seemed to be shifting about large pieces of the sky.

The two women peered into the car, sizing me up in a one-second glance. The taller of the two, whom Vaughan had already assigned to me, was a passive blonde with unintelligent eyes focused three inches above my head. She pointed to me with her plastic handbag.

"Can he drive?"

"Of course – a few drinks always make a car go better."

*   *   *

Vaughan twirled the wine bottles like dumb-bells, herding the women into the car. As the second girl, with short black hair and a boy's narrow-hipped body, opened the passenger door, Vaughan handed a bottle to her. Lifting her chin, he put his fingers in her mouth. He plucked out the knot of gum and flicked it away into the darkness. "Let's get rid of that – I don't want you blowing it up my urethra."

Adjusting myself to the unfamiliar controls, I started the engine and crossed the forecourt to the slip road. Above us, along Western Avenue, the traffic stream edged its way towards London Airport. Vaughan opened a wine bottle and passed it to the blonde sitting beside me in the front seat. He lit the first of the four cigarettes he had rolled. Already one elbow was between the dark-haired girl's thighs, raising her skirt to reveal her black crotch. He drew the cork from the second bottle and pressed the wet end against her white teeth. In the rear-view mirror I could see her avoiding Vaughan's mouth. She inhaled the cigarette smoke, her hand resting on Vaughan's groin. Vaughan lay back, inspecting her small features with a detached gaze, looking her body up and down like an acrobat calculating the traverses and impacts of a gymnastic feat involving a large amount of complex equipment. With his right hand he opened the zip of his trousers, then arched his hips forward to free his penis. The girl held it in one hand, the other steadying the wine bottle as I let the car surge away from the traffic lights. Vaughan unbuttoned her shirt with his scarred fingers and brought out her small breast. Examining the breast, Vaughan gripped the nipple between thumb and forefinger, extruding it forward in a peculiar manual hold, as if fitting together a piece of unusual laboratory equipment.

Brake-lights flared twenty yards ahead of me. Horns sounded from the line of cars in the rear. As their headlamps pulsed I moved the shift lever into drive and pressed the accelerator, jerking the car forward. Vaughan and the girl rolled back against the rear seat. The cabin was lit only by the instrument dials, and by the headlamps and tail-lights in the crowded traffic lanes around us. Vaughan had freed both the girl's breasts, nursing them with his palm. His scarred lips sucked at the thick smoke from the crumbling butt of the cigarette. He took the wine bottle and raised it to her mouth. As she drank he lifted her legs so that

her heels rested on the seat, and began to move his penis against
the skin of her thighs, drawing it first across the black vinyl and
then pressing the glans against her heel and ankle bone, as if
testing the possible continuity of these two materials before
taking part in a sexual act involving both the car and this young
woman. He lay against the rear seat, left arm stretched above the
girl's head, embracing this slab of over-sprung black vinyl. His
hand was raised at right-angles to his forearm, measuring out the
geometry of the chromium roof sill, while his right hand moved
down the girl's thighs and cupped her buttocks. Squatting there
with her heels under her buttocks, the girl opened her thighs to
expose her small pubic triangle, the labia open and protruded.
Through the smoke lifting from the ashtray Vaughan studied the
girl's body in a good-humoured way.

Beside him, the girl's small, serious face was lit by the headlamps of the cars creeping forwards in the traffic files. The damp,
inhaled smoke of burnt resin filled the interior of the car. My
head seemed to float on these fumes. Somewhere ahead, beyond
these immense lines of nearly stationary vehicles, was the illuminated plateau of the airport, but I felt barely able to do more
than point the large car along the centre lane. The blonde woman
in the front seat offered me a drink from the wine bottle. When I
declined she leaned her head against my shoulder, giving a
playful touch to the steering wheel. I put my arm around her
shoulder, aware of her hand on my thigh.

I waited until we stopped again, and adjusted the driving
mirror so that I could see into the rear seat. Vaughan had moved
his thumb into the girl's vagina, forefinger into her rectum, as she
sat back with her knees against her shoulders, drawing mechanically at the second of the cigarettes.

His left hand took the girl's breast, his ring- and fore-fingers
propping up the nipple like a miniature crutch. Holding these
elements of the girl's body in his formalized pose, he began to
rock his hips back and forth, driving his penis into the girl's hand.
When she tried to move his fingers from her vulva Vaughan
knocked her hand away with his elbow, holding the fingers
securely in her body. He straightened his legs, rotating himself
around the passenger compartment so that his hips rested on the
edge of the seat. Braced on his left elbow, he continued to work
himself against the girl's hand, as if taking part in a dance of

severely stylized postures that celebrated the design and electronics, speed and direction of an advanced kind of automobile.

This marriage of sex and technology reached its climax as the traffic divided at the airport overpass and we began to move forwards in the northbound lane. As the car travelled for the first time at twenty miles an hour Vaughan drew his fingers from the girl's vulva and anus, rotated his hips and inserted his penis in her vagina. Headlamps flared above us as the stream of cars moved up the slope of the overpass. In the rear-view mirror I could still see Vaughan and the girl, their bodies lit by the car behind, reflected in the black trunk of the Lincoln and a hundred points of the interior trim. In the chromium ashtray I saw the girl's left breast and erect nipple. In the vinyl window gutter I saw deformed sections of Vaughan's thighs and her abdomen forming a bizarre anatomical junction. Vaughan lifted the young woman astride him, his penis entering her vagina again. In a triptych of images reflected in the speedometer, the clock and revolution counter, the sexual act between Vaughan and this young woman took place in the hooded grottoes of these luminescent dials, moderated by the surging needle of the speedometer. The jutting carapace of the instrument panel and the stylized sculpture of the steering column shroud reflected a dozen images of her rising and falling buttocks. As I propelled the car at fifty miles an hour along the open deck of the overpass Vaughan arched his back and lifted the young woman into the full glare of the headlamps behind us. Her sharp breasts flashed within the chromium and glass cage of the speeding car. Vaughan's strong pelvic spasms coincided with the thudding passage of the lamp standards anchored in the overpass at hundred-yard intervals. As each one approached his hips kicked into the girl, driving his penis into her vagina, his hands splaying her buttocks to reveal her anus as the yellow light filled the car. We reached the end of the overpass. The red glow of brake-lights burned the night air, touching the images of Vaughan and the young woman with a roseate light.

Controlling the car, I drove down the ramp towards the traffic junction. Vaughan changed the tempo of his pelvic motion, drawing the young woman on top of himself and extending her legs along his own. They lay diagonally across the rear seat, Vaughan taking first her left nipple in his mouth, then the right, his finger in her anus, stroking her rectum to the rhythm of the passing cars, matching his own movements to the play of light sweeping transversely across the roof of the car. I pushed away the blonde girl lying against my shoulder. I realized that I could almost control the sexual act behind me by the way in which I drove the car. Playfully, Vaughan responded to different types of street furniture and roadside trim. As we left London Airport, heading inwards towards the city on the fast access roads, his rhythm became faster, his hands under the girl's buttocks forcing her up and down as if some scanning device in his brain was increasingly agitated by the high office blocks. At the end of the orgasm he was almost standing behind me in the car, legs out-stretched, head against the rear seat, hands propping up his own buttocks as he carried the girl on his hips.

Half an hour later I had turned back to the airport and stopped the car in the shadows of the multi-storey car-park facing the Oceanic Terminal. The girl at last managed to pull herself from Vaughan, who lay exhausted against the rear seat. Clumsily, she reassembled herself, remonstrating with Vaughan and the drowsy blonde in the front seat. Vaughan's semen ran down her left thigh on to the black vinyl of the seat. The ivory globes searched for the steepest gradient to the central sulcus of the seat.

I stepped from the car and paid the two women. When they had gone, carrying their hard loins back to the neonlit concourses, I waited beside the car. Vaughan was staring at the terraced cliff of the car-park, his eyes following the canted floors, as if trying to recognize everything that had passed between himself and the dark-haired girl.

Later, Vaughan explored the possibilities of the car-crash in the same calm and affectionate way that he had explored the limits of that young prostitute's body. Often I watched him lingering over the photographs of crash fatalities, gazing at their burnt faces with a terrifying concern, as he calculated the most elegant parameters of their injuries, the junctions of their wounded bodies with the fractured windshield and instrument assemblies. He would mimic these injuries in his own driving postures, turning the same dispassionate eyes on the young women he picked up near the airport. Using their bodies, he recapitulated the deformed ana-tomies of vehicle crash victims, gently bending the arms of these girls against their shoulders, pressing their knees against his own chest, always curious to see their reactions.

PRENUPTIALS

Lucy Taylor

IN HER DREAM, the witches bend over her cradle singing a lullaby. The words change, but the meaning is always the same: men are evil and lust-crazed. Fantasies of brute power lurk behind their avuncular smiles. Women exist to be demeaned and defiled and destroyed – the phallus is the sword that a woman falls on when she decides to kill herself.

We tell you about these terrible things only to protect you, coo the witches. *Only because we love you and wish you to come to no harm.*

In another land, the witches might have spread her legs and carved away her clitoris and labia. These hags do their mischief with loving lies and lewd caresses.

But you must never want these men, they croon as they gaze at her – so young and promising, her whole life spread out before her – with eyes made dead by jealousy. *You must never want to be the object of their lust.*

> *No good girl ever wants this.*
> And so is laid the curse.

There are good men in the city where she grows up, goes to school, and studies painting. Kind and generous, nurturing men. She meets them/likes them/goes to movies and to dinner with them, but she cannot recognize them as potential mates. For it is not these men that make her moist and swollen as she flies toward them like a heat-seeking missile. These men don't give her nightmares from which she wakes up wet. They don't make her heart brake to a skidding stop and cause her blood to whip and flutter like it's full of tiny electric eels.

It's the men the witches told her she must never want that make her feel like that.

She doesn't realize this is what she's looking for until she finds him.

She meets him at a meeting for people like herself who suffer from addiction problems. She never expected to find *this* kind of man at such a meeting. For aren't these men in recovery? Isn't theirs an enlightened masculinity, strong yet sensitive to women's needs? The kind of men that make good friends, but never lovers? She doesn't even permit herself to think of sex when she sits in the meeting rooms – she thinks that would be wrong. She crosses her legs and neuters herself and assumes everyone else does the same.

But from the first words they exchange, there is an uncanny link between them, the kind of instant empathy that, if they were into New Age beliefs, might lead them to conclude they'd shared a previous lifetime. Their eyes lock with a click like handcuffs closing. No bombsquad could defuse such incendiary chemistry. Right away they guess each other's secret song. For a band of witches presided at his cribside, too, only their lullaby was different and their curse was for not only him, but for his future mate: *women want only one thing – to be defiled, debased, destroyed. A woman's submissiveness is the yardstick by which a man measures his phallus.*

But you must never want to do such things, they sang as they caressed his baby penis. *Good boys don't.*

And you must never want this.

And so it is lust at first glance, rivetting and irrevocable and, after a few exchanges, he follows her out to her car.

Eyes her up and down as if she's something shiny in a gemstore window and he's about to smash the glass to get to her.

"Do you have any clothes you wouldn't mind having destroyed?"

She meets his black ice gaze. "Why?"

"Because I want to rip them off you."

She smiles and shivers, slides into her car.

But the game's begun. The distant noise she hears is the sound of witches howling.

A day or two later, their enactment of the curse is well under way. She sprawls in his bed, limbs akimbo, her brain on hold as she gazes at this source of her enchantment. He is hirsute and sinewy, virile and veined. she can barely get all of him down her throat. When she thinks of having him inside her, her pussy grips and pulses like the mouth of a child that hasn't been fed.

"This doesn't feel like a fling," he says. "I've never wanted anyone so much. I think I'm falling in love with you."

She nods and murmurs that she feels the same, although since meeting him, the night terrors from her childhood have come back. She's seen him dip his cock in poison before he puts it in her mouth.

He pulls her to him, folds her flesh against him like a silky garment. He closes his fist in her hair.

"I'm not letting you go. Understand? I'm never letting you go."

Her body's reaction to this mix of menace and endearment is so intense that it temporarily obliterates the power of thought. Her inner muscles start to clench and unclench; the motion travels to the muscles in her belly, which start to undulate. It's like giving birth in reverse – she wants to pull him in, possess him as utterly, as wantonly as he now possesses her.

He hovers at her entrance, then plunges in and halts. Like one well-studied in the tantric arts, he stays inside her, hard and motionless.

"Do you line your pussy with silk?"

She does a rippling belly dance upon her back. It's getting hard to know where his skin ends and hers begins. Her brain cooks with heat and pheromones.

"Did you mean it? About never letting me go?"

He doesn't answer, but starts to thrust. What begins as a languid glide accelerates into the stomping/pounding/piledriving frenzy of a mosh pit. Her mind glazes over, but her body was never so alive as she arches up to meet the blows delivered by his hips.

She has her answer.

*   *   *

If their nights are dedicated to sensuality, their mornings are monotonously mundane. She has coffee with him in the living room while the morning news is on. He turns pages of the paper and reads snippets of current events to her. She dips her bagel in her coffee. It smells moist and sweet as his sweat. She puts on a tasteful business suit, picks up the alligator briefcase that he suggested she buy.

He kisses her. "Good-bye, gorgeous."

When she looks back, he is standing naked in the doorway with a hard-on. The jut of it snags at her heart. She wants to go back, fall to her knees, pay homage with her mouth. At the same time, she want to leap out into traffic and let something fast and huge and hard smash her to rubble and get it over with.

"Good-bye sweetie, see you tonight."

Since childhood, she has believed that she will never marry or have children. The legal contract, the binding ties, it smacks, she's always thought, of bondage. And as for children, there's this secret fear in her – she can't say why, but has the deep suspicion that something in her might some day wish to do her children harm.

No, she will be an artist, will work only to support her art – wait tables in Aspen or Redstone or Carbondale – cultivate the friend-ship of free women like herself, maybe enjoy a lesbian love affair or two and pity the humdrum lives of the tourists, couples always, snotty kids in tow, who surely must be envying *her* unfettered artist's life. Her recurrent dreams of rape and domination will be transformed into brilliant canvases of wind-whipped mares and earth goddesses with swollen breasts and thighs as thick as tree trunks.

She will let no man contain her.

But she has forgotten her own Bewitchment and the lush allure of her cradle song.

And she hasn't counted on *him* and how they both get high on escalating the erotic games, making more real and harrowing the fantasy of possessor and possessed.

In the course of a few days, they play with ropes and knives and, most dangerous of all, they play that they're in love, that she will be his wife, and that this will last Forever.

They craft bondage scripts that they act out with her spread-eagled on the bed, bent over the balcony railing, posed bitch-style on all fours before the mirrored wall, and without an ounce of alcohol, she gets drunker and drunker until the room starts spinning, and open is the only posture that she knows.

"After we get married," she says, toying with her words as her fingers massage and cup and stroke, "what if we go to a party, and I flirt with another man?"

"Then we'll have to leave," he says coldly.

"That what?"

"We'll get in the car and drive away. As soon as we're out of sight of the house where we've been visiting, I'll reach over and tear your blouse open and rip open your bra. I'll call you a whore, and I'll drive very fast and you'll be afraid – with good reason."

"I know," she says, shivering closer to his heat, "I'll be very afraid. I'm afraid now."

"Good," he says. He is very hard now. His erection presses against her thigh.

"After we get home," he says, "I'll throw you down across the bed. I'll fuck you till you can't remember that you've ever been with any man but me. I'll make you plead for my forgiveness. I'll make you love me."

She can feel her flesh melting into his, merging with his body, at these images. Her clitoris is pulsing as if it will erupt into flame.

"I already love you," she says. Her sigh sounds like blood seeping out of a wound. "I love you, and I want to marry you."

"Oh, you will." He says it like a death threat, and it is. He kisses her, turn her around and mounts her from behind. He yanks her head back by her hair and puts the other hand across her mouth, riding her wildly and brutally, transforming her into something as bright and beautiful and lifeless as the paintings she no longer paints, suffocating her will down to embers and ash.

She has never been sure what he does with his days. For a while, she fancied that he had a secret life, perhaps some enterprise outside the law, perhaps another lover. She almost hoped he did. Now she believes he simply stays at home and naps and watches rented videos, does a 12-Step meeting now and then, meets friends for tennis. Idleness becomes him. He's like a great, sleek lounging Tom who stirs himself only to yowl and feed and copulate. He's like a force of nature. He need only *be*.

As for her own ambitions, she gave up the idea of Art in Aspen long ago. She lacks the time, the drive, the will. Making art requires energy and freedom, both of which are forfeit to her obsession. So she works at an office job and congratulates herself on her practicality and how well she manages to support them both.

At work, she is a model employee, concise and punctual, dependable. Only now and then, distracted, seeming almost dazed, she makes careless mistakes, receives a reprimand. She always takes it well. She is so prompt, so malleable, so docile.

A few of her co-workers have tried to be friends. She smiles and offers a facsimile of friendship, but in truth she is too ashamed to let them know her as she is, a one-time artist, now merely a part of *him* that goes out into the world, that plays a part. She cannot let them know she is addicted to his flesh, that she is a suicide in progress.

"When we get married," she whispers, "I want the ceremony to include the words love, honor, and obey."

"Oh they will," he assures her. He stops fucking her and grinds his cock inside her, grips her wrists. Impaled and pinned, she can feel her mind entering that red trance of sex-bliss, that small death from which she knows that she may not emerge. "You will always obey me. You *must*."

"I want you to own me," she says, hating herself as she says the words. Hating the words. Not knowing where they come from, but hating the self-loathing that inspires them.

Hating *him*.

"I already own you," he says. His dark face hovers above her. He is handsome, almost beautiful, a terrifying angel with black brows and the subdued snarl of the gentleman rapist in his voice.

She feels herself become more willing, more daring as she teeters on the edge of the void. Surely no aerialist ever practiced so thrilling a maneuver on the high wire. She is drunk with danger, half swooning from her sense of self-destruction, her seeming inability to save herself.

"I want to marry you," she says, knowing what she really

wants is not to want him. But he is the one that the witches sang about. He is her destiny.

He knows very well what she wants. He is inhumanly hard now.

"You are already wed to me," he says. "You are already owned."

She arches against him. She wants to feel the tip of his cock draw blood from her heart. She feels like she is ageing in reverse. She is that little girl again that the witches loved as their own and hated as their rival, and every kiss upon her face is poison and every touch re-opens unseen scars. In her folly, she thinks that her lover is healing the wounds, that he is filling her with him.

God, she loves Him.

One night they watch a movie where a woman kills a man to avenge her lover's death. He seems to relish this. Rewinds the tape to watch the scene again.

"Would you kill for me?" he asks.

No.

"Yes, I'd kill for you," she says in that whispery, on-the-edge-of-orgasm voice.

"I don't believe you."

"I *would.*"

When she falls asleep with her face pressed to the black pelt on his chest, she is a child again and she is loved – she has only to please him always, do whatever he says – and she will be loved forever.

Earning his love is a full-time job. A career choice. A commitment.

She hones her acting skills. She knows he senses the slightest rebellion in her heart, the smallest cache of secrets. He has nothing to do with his days but focus on her, meditate upon each nuance of her speech and body language. Is her love diminishing? Does she talk too much on the phone, take extra minutes getting home? Is she being subtly neglectful of his vast and mounting needs? Is she such a fool that she might plot to leave him?

When he grows bored, he amuses himself by finding fault with her. At other times, he gazes at her with the pride of one who's just retouched a museum masterpiece, brought it back to its former splendor, improved it, and when she questions the intensity of that look, he says, "Just thinking of all the plans I have for the rest of your life."

She had plans, too – once. If she could just remember what they were . . .

He finds her sketchbook one day, and his derision of her drawings if so surgically adroit that she feels naked as a peeled persimmon. Later, when he sees her tears, he soothes her with his skillful tongue and nurtures her with semen.

Sometimes she contemplates his Smith and Wesson as one would study a map of some exotic land. She parts herself with the cool, hard barrel and thinks that she should let the gun become her lover, that this must be the ultimate fuck. Even hotter and harder than him.

Nonsense, she tells herself. She can walk away from him when she gets ready. She can quit at any time. She gave up alcohol, didn't she? Almost five years without a buzz. No counting the high she gets from sucking cocktails from their original container. She knows he isn't good for her – she devours self-help books like bonbons. She'll quit this, too, and get on with her *real* life – it's just that she's not ready.

Yet.

She knows the game is aging her. Grey half-moons smudge her eyes. Her face has a haggard, refugee quality, but her body still throbs in sync with his. The athletic and aesthetic quality of her erotic performance is undulled. She can mimic dying with a hot, uncanny sensuality, as though she's done it many times. In the quiet of the night, she fancies she can hear her soul unraveling.

"I want to marry you."

Sometimes she says the words alone, to herself, marveling at how they sound, at the unnaturalness of them. What started as a game, a tease, is becoming real.

Love, honor, and obey.

She loves him not at all and honors him only when she must, but obey she will. She must. For doesn't she deserve to die? She's a bad girl, isn't she? For craving his flesh in her mouth, in her cunt, for aching to eat him like some ripe and rotting fruit, the sweet center spewing into her mouth and seeping down her throat as she bites and sucks and hungers more for having sucked his poison.

"I'd kill for you," she whispers.

She almost means it now. The ledge on which she walks is getting narrower. The abyss at the bottom of her lover's eyes croons to her and bids her jump.

One night he ties her with soft sashes and runs a knife across he flesh. He parts her lips. Tells her, in snuff flick detail, what he could do to her.

He could. He *might*. She's wet just thinking of it.

For doesn't love mean being fed upon, consumed, annihilated in the arms of the beloved? She learned that somewhere long ago. It feels like it's imprinted on her soul, encoded into her very DNA. Carried on her X chromosomes like a gene-linked disease.

He puts his hard-on to her lips, then the knife, then his cock. "Which one?" he says. For a moment, she can't choose.

The only thing she fears more than him is the thought that she might lose him.

On the day that she will marry him (an elaborate ceremony on the East Coast City where his parents live), she looks into the mirror as if into a crystal ball and sees the future like an evil spell spread out before her. She cannot leave him; she's too far gone. She no longer believes she can exist without him. But as her dependence on him has increased, so has her hatred; she longs to pay him back for what she's let him do to her.

Soon after their wedding, she comes into their bedroom, thinking that she'll let him fuck her one more time, give him a final opportunity to end it before she does.

She finds him fallen asleep with the tv on, hair like black fur against the pillow, thighs parted just enough that she can be tempted by his beauty one more time.

But good girls never want this.

She puts the pistol against his temple, admiring the aristocratic plane of his jaw, the thick black lashes, wondering what it would be like to fuck him with a bullet.

But she wasn't raised like that. She isn't meant to kill this way. No, her killing must be done in increments and secret.

She puts the gun away and comes to bed. The old nightmares threaten her, but she takes solace in his skin.

$$\star \quad \star \quad \star$$

When she gets pregnant, he says he doesn't want the child. A baby will take time away from him – he tells her they'll be happier without one.

For the first time since she's known him, she stands up to him. Her wrath shocks her and frightens him. The power of mother love seems to give her resolve she's never known. A child, she thinks, will be something to belong to her – to take the place of the life that she will never have. For the first time since she's known him, her life soothes down into a sluggish calm, a kind of tranquil torpor. Finally there is something of her own he cannot take away.

The baby is healthy and beautiful. She names it for her mother, and she loves it with a fierce and cannibal cunning.

But the father is the one seduced and charmed. The child becomes his little sweetheart. He dotes on her and plans for her a future full of independence and achievement.

When the baby is a few months old, she sits beside the crib one night, admiring the beauty of her daughter's face, her laughing eyes and guileless zest. Surely this child will have a charmed life – unlike her cursed one.

The baby frets as she bends over the crib. She has her father's mouth. The mother feels a rush of loss and loathing. How dare *his* daughter look forward to the kind of life that she has forfeited. Black envy seethes inside her.

She searches her mind for a gift appropriate for the daughter of the man that she despises.

And it comes back to her – bitter and seductive, the words like licorice laced with strychnine, dark and sweet and sickening.

The words change, but the meaning is always the same: men are evil and lust-crazed and dangerous . . . women exist to be debased and defiled . . .

. . . *but good girls never want this.*

You must never want this.

And so the curse is passed.

That night, when she lies down next to her husband, her sleep is deep and dreamless.